BRUCE NICOLAYSEN

THE NOVEL OF NEW YORK 1776-1783

BEEKMAN PLACE

AVON
PUBLISHERS OF BARD, CAMELOT, DISCUS AND FLARE BOOKS

BEEKMAN PLACE is an original publication of Avon Books. This work has never before appeared in book form.

Maps by Cynthia McFarland

AVON BOOKS
A division of
The Hearst Corporation
959 Eighth Avenue
New York, New York 10019

Copyright © 1982 by Bruce Nicolaysen
Published by arrangement with the author
Library of Congress Catalog Card Number: 81-52391
ISBN: 0-380-79673-2

All rights reserved, which includes the right to
reproduce this book or portions thereof in any form
whatsoever except as provided by the U. S. Copyright Law.
For information address Avon Books

First Avon Printing, June, 1982

AVON TRADEMARK REG. U. S. PAT. OFF. AND IN
OTHER COUNTRIES, MARCA REGISTRADA, HECHO EN
U. S. A.

Printed in the U. S. A.

WFH 10 9 8 7 6 5 4 3 2 1

For
Joan Nicolaysen Taubner

who brings to life
more than she takes from it

ACKNOWLEDGMENTS

Robert B. Wyatt, Julie Garriott, Elaine Keeve, Cynthia McFarland, Kathe Lewis, Bart Hackley Jr., Deirdre Hanssen, and the Reverend Eugene J. O'Brien, S.J.—all, in one way or another, have helped in the preparation of this book.

AUTHOR'S NOTE

This is book three of *The Novel of New York*. It recreates the life of the city during one of its most exciting and memorable times—the American Revolution.

New Yorkers were reminded every day of the epic struggle for the American continent. The city was occupied by enemy forces. The British anchored lethally overcrowded prison ships off the Brooklyn shoreline. At every tavern, smugglers, spies, thieves, and traitors mingled with patriots, prostitutes, and men with prices on their heads. Fires burned down half the city, and hundreds died of plague.

This is a work of fiction, but the setting is real. George Washington appears as flesh and blood—a man with an eye for the ladies, and a temper that causes him to rip off his hat and stamp it into the dirt. Lord Howe, who "liked his glass, his lass, and his game of cards," *did* delay his conquest of Manhattan while he dallied with a beautiful woman. Ben Franklin *did* propose arming the Continental army with bows and arrows because they could be shot and reloaded more quickly than rifles or muskets. France *did* give so much money to the Americans that she went broke and opened the door for the French Revolution.

Mary Delafield is a character in this romance, but, like her, many American women became pregnant during the war years because of liaisons with British soldiers. Franz von Lossow is a creature of my imagination, but in reality too, hundreds of Hessians deserted to the American side and remained as citizens—men like Henry Ashdour, who anglicized his name to Astor and encouraged his younger brother, John Jacob, to join him in this land of opportunity.

Celine de Kuyper is a fictional character, and so is her affair with Nathan Hale. But Hale was a young, handsome, robust officer—hardly the type to be ignored by the lusty women of the eighteenth century.

Life could be trying indeed in these years, especially during the winter. The trees on Wall Street were cut down for fuel and never replaced; one February it was so cold the bay froze and men used sleds to bring trees over from Jersey. Hungry people ate the pigs that normally functioned as the city's garbage disposal department—and anyone who's lived through a New York garbage strike can tell you what *that* meant. Despite it all, people fell in love, had babies, and tried to function as families.

Perhaps New York's greatest moment of glory in this tumultuous period came at the end of the Revolution, when it functioned as the seat of the fledgling federal government. Even in those days, the city was becoming a cosmopolitan meeting place. Then, as now, New York belonged not to one country, but to the world.

CONTENTS

1 The City Invaded • 1776 — 1
2 The City in Flames • 1776 — 80
3 A Terrible Winter • 1776–1777 — 148
4 The Year of the Asp • 1777 — 221
5 The Tides of Change • 1778–1779 — 308
6 The World Turned Upside Down • 1780–1781 — 406
7 Patriots, Heroes, and Lovers • 1783 — 505

OUR STORY TO 1783

MAYORS OF THE CITY

(All appointed, with the exception of Delanoy—elected 1689)

Thomas Willett	1665
Thomas Delavall	1666
Thomas Willett	1667
Cornelius Steenwyck	1668
Thomas Delavall	1671
Mathias Nicolls	1672
John Lawrence	1673
William Dervall	1675
Nicholas de Meyer	1676
Stephen Van Cortlandt (first American-born mayor)	1677
Thomas Delavall	1678
Francis Rambouts	1679
William Dyer	1680
Cornelius Steenwyck	1682
Gabriel Minvielle	1684
Nicolas Bayard	1685
Stephen Van Cortlandt	1686
Peter Delanoy	1689
John Lawrence	1691
Abraham de Peyster	1692
Charles Lodwick	1694
William Merritt	1695

Johannes de Peyster	1698
David Provost	1699
Isaac de Reimer	1700
Thomas Noell	1701
Philip French	1702
William Peartree	1703
Ebenezer Wilson	1707
Jacobus Van Cortlandt	1710
Caleb Heathcote	1711
John Johnson	1714
Jacobus Van Cortlandt	1719
Robert Walters	1720
Johannes Jansen	1725
Robert Lurting	1726
Paul Richard	1735
John Cruger Sr.	1738
Stephan Bayard	1744
Edward Holland	1747
John Cruger Jr.	1757
Whitehead Hicks	1766
David Matthews	1776

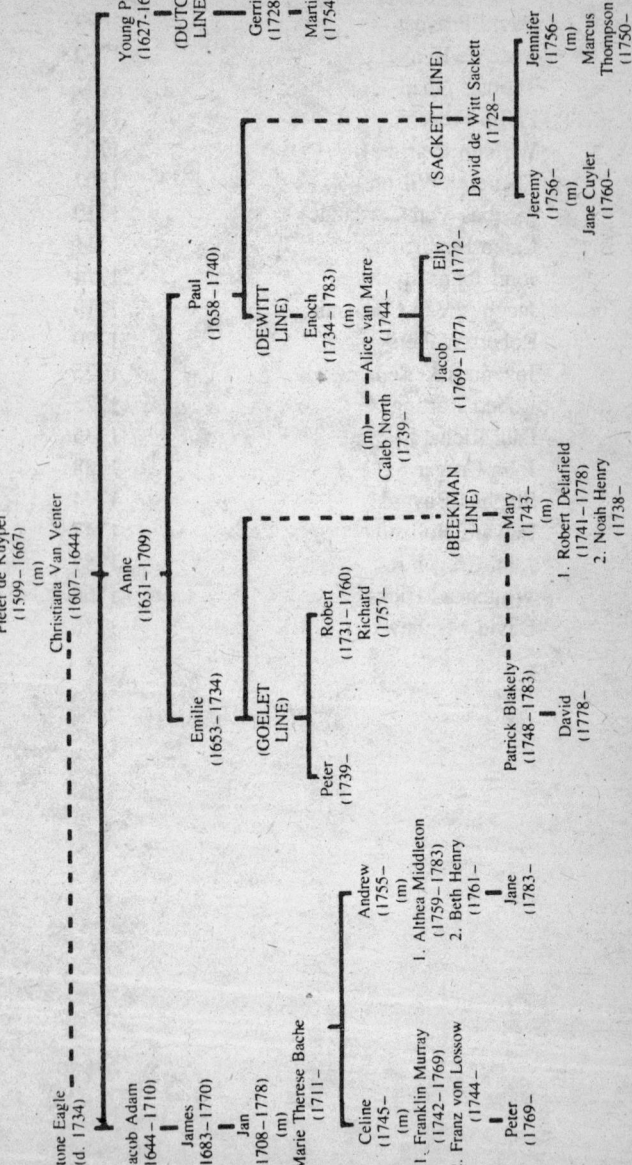

The extended de Kuyper family (selected) to 1783

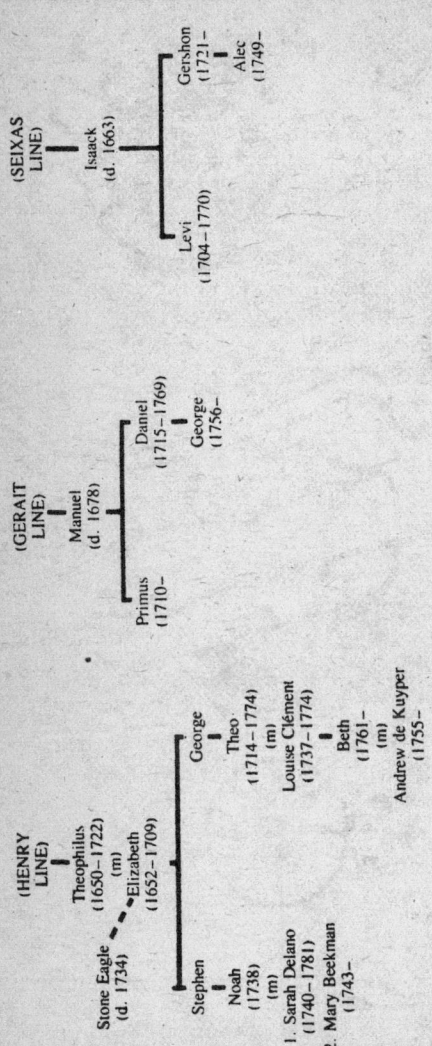

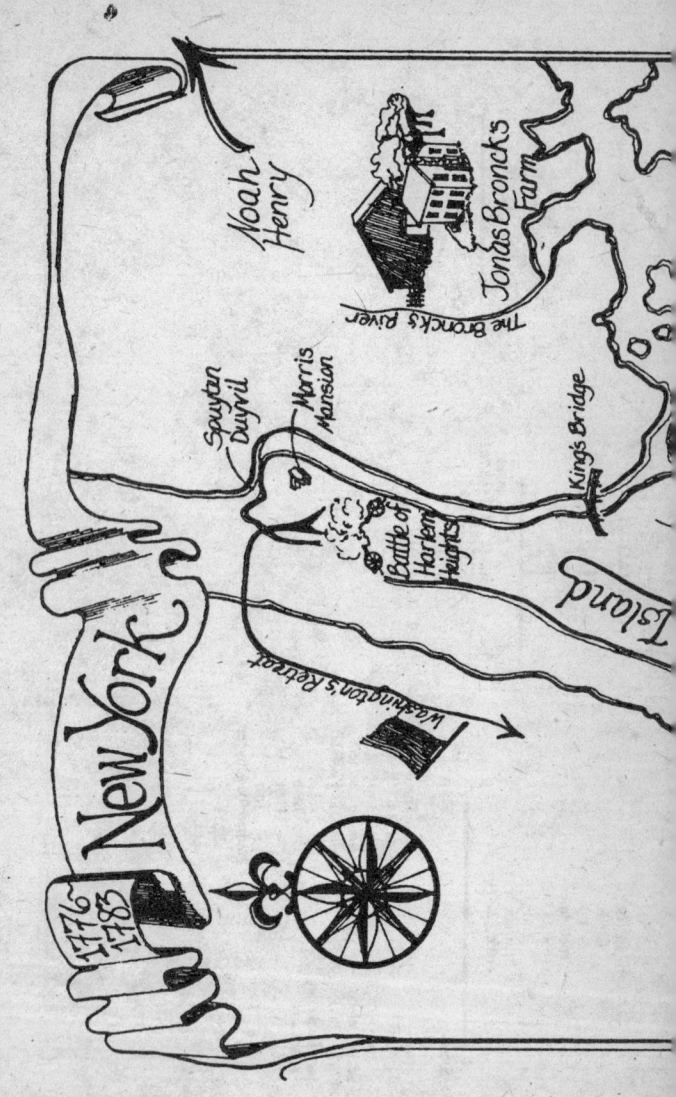

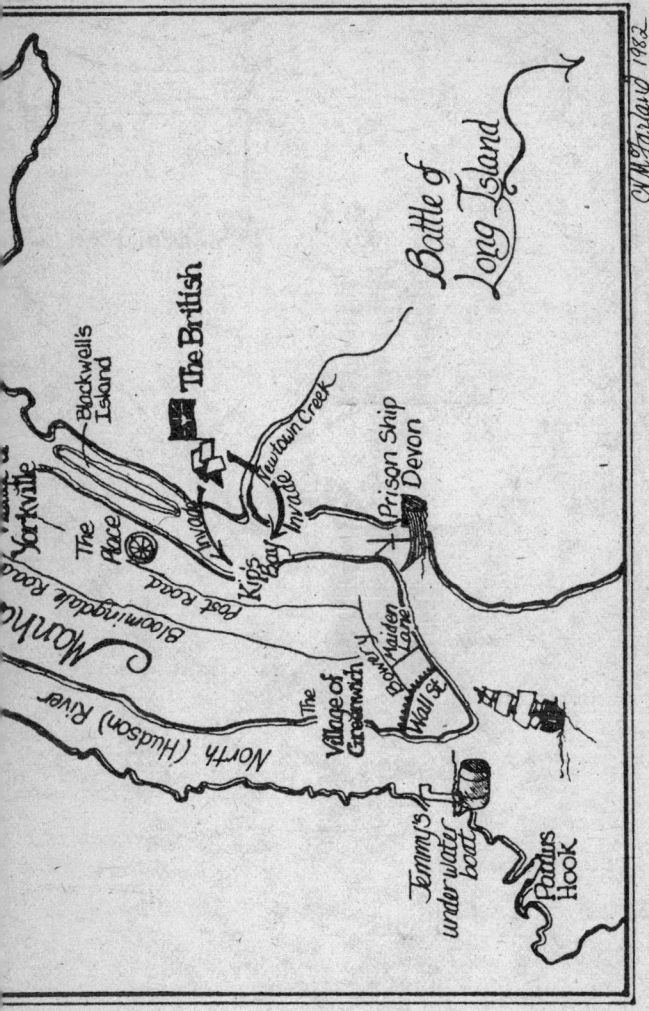

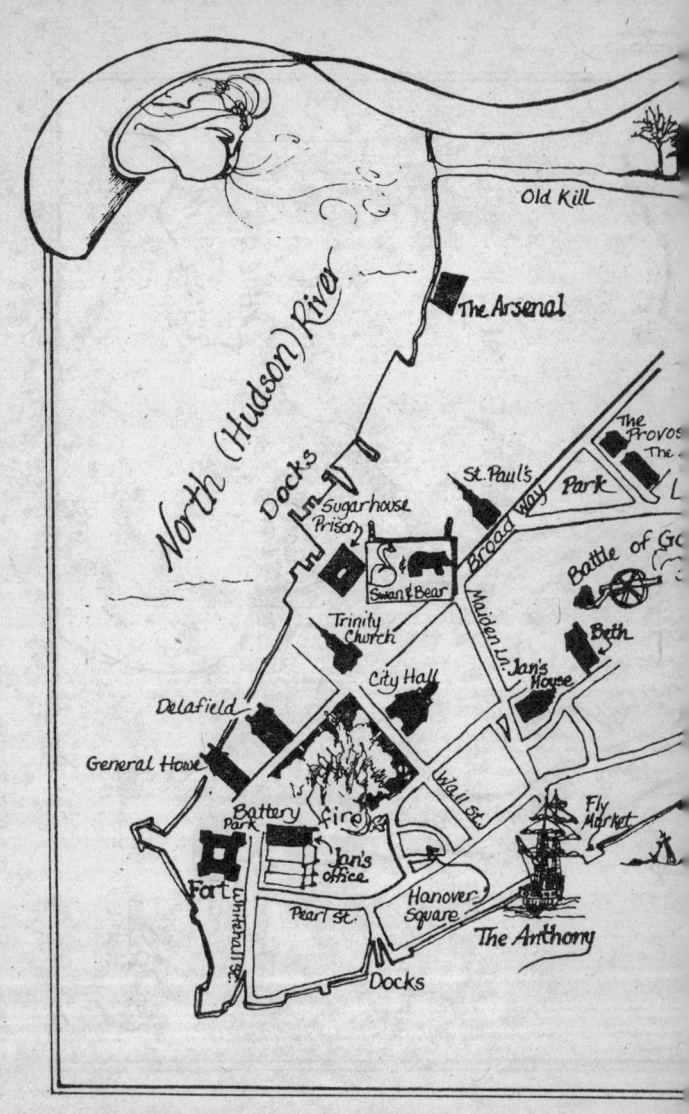

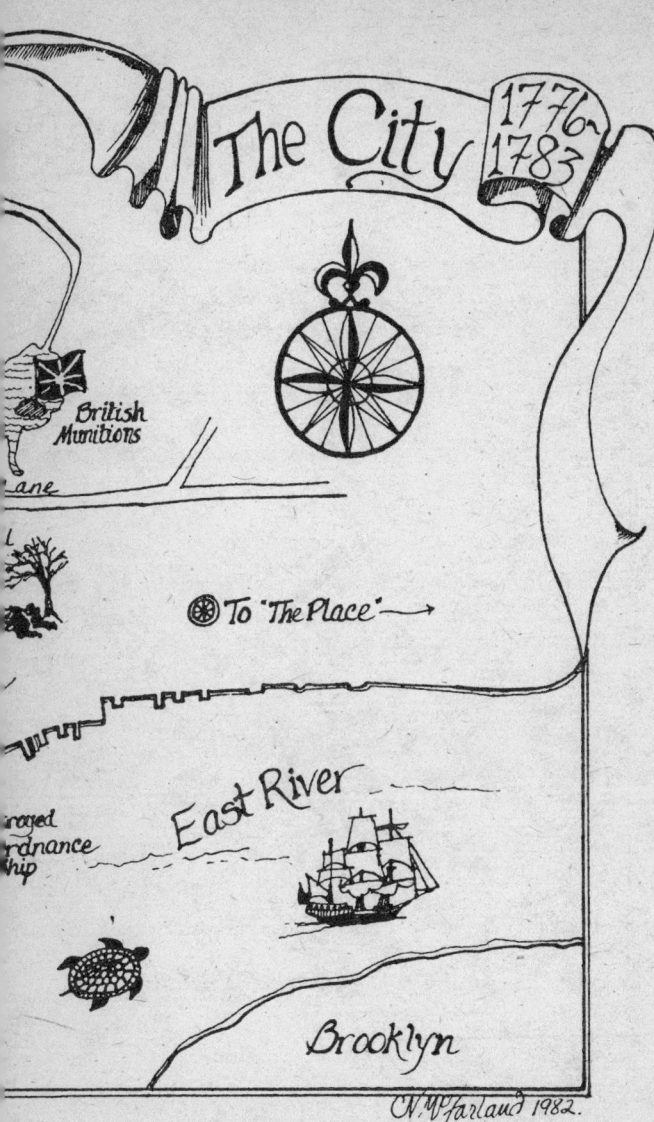

1

The City Invaded

1776

THE FIRST WISP OF DAWN WAS TINTING THE HORIzon when Celine de Kuyper Murray woke from a peaceful sleep. With her eyes still closed, she yawned and stretched her arms. She jumped as her hand brushed against the naked shoulder of the man who lay on the other side of the bed on this September morning.

Good Lord! She'd completely forgotten *him*. She waited until his heavy, measured breathing assured her he was still asleep; then she slipped out from under the light summer blanket, picked a silk robe off the end of the bed, and made her way noiselessly to the door. As she left the room, she looked back at the sleeping form and smiled.

Captain Nathan Hale was young, only twenty-one years old, but after a night like the previous one, he needed a good, long rest. The trouble with most younger men, she decided, was that they hadn't learned to pace themselves; this was something that came only with years of experience.

As Celine made her way down the broad, curving staircase, she looked the part of those New York beauties whose fame was spreading from the northern wilds of Maine to the steaming swamps of southern Georgia. Some people had proclaimed her *the* legendary beauty of the city. She was tall and slender, with a narrow waist and an ample, but not too generous, bosom. Her eyes were almond-shaped and set far apart. She had high cheekbones, a narrow, aristocratic nose, and a mane of silky blond hair. At the age of thirty-one, Celine stood at the summit of the social order of New York. Here her family—the de

Kuypers—had been increasing their fortune and prestige for one hundred and fifty years. They were, in both senses, one of the city's first families. Celine and her younger brother, Andrew, represented the fifth generation of their line to live in New York. In a country where almost everything was new and untried, the de Kuypers were old aristocracy, tested and proven.

Celine had been married for three years to Franklin Murray, one of several wealthy brothers who owned a great deal of land in the middle of the island of Manhattan. It had been an acceptable, if hardly profoundly satisfying, marriage. They had one child, born with a great deal of maternal suffering, and the doctor announced that Celine could never bear other children. Not long afterward Franklin Murray broke his neck in a fall from a horse, leaving a young and desirable widow. That had been five years ago, and since then Celine had received a dozen proposals of marriage, but had turned them all down to go her own way—much to the dismay of her father.

"Why should I marry again?" she would ask whenever he raised the subject, which was often. "I have everything I want, and anyway, if my marriage to Franklin was typical, I don't need to repeat the experience."

"It isn't natural," Jan would protest. "You should have a husband." The argument would go on and on, and finally the father would become exasperated and stomp out of his daughter's house, climb into his trap-and-horse, and make his way back to his own house on Maiden Lane, some two and a half miles south in the city proper.

That his daughter chose to remain living out in the country was another thing that bothered Jan. Why was she so pigheaded about staying out here in the house north of Kip's Bay, just across the road from the Beekman farm? Dammit! So what if it had a splendid view of the East River? Why, it was almost wilderness. The thing had made sense when her husband was alive, but now that he was gone, why couldn't she make her home in a more civilized place? There were some lovely new houses on William Street; and if they weren't to her liking, she could take her pick of several de Kuyper properties on Wall Street, Golden Hill, or Broad Way.

"Children!" he would gripe aloud as his trap wended its way down the Post Road to the city.

Celine came into the kitchen and saw that a fire had already been started in the iron cookstove. There were a half dozen servants in the house, but it was always the old black houseman, Primus, who was the first to rise. He looked up as she entered the room and pointed to the water kettle. "Be ready for your tea in a minute, Missy."

"Good morning, Primus," she said as she placed a piece of sliced bread in the toasting fork. "Heat this up for me, will you?"

The gray-haired man nodded and took the fork over to the stove. For the past few years Primus Gerait had been having "bone problems," and he walked with a slight stoop. He opened the door of the stove and held the bread in front of the flames. "Lots of soldiers on the road a little while ago," he said. "You think there's going to be trouble today?"

Celine shrugged. "The British have been building their forces on the other side of the river for two weeks. One of these days they're going to come over."

"Today?"

"Why not?"

"You don't seem too worried about it, Missy."

"What good does worrying do? Anyway, there are thousands of redcoats over there, and if they want to cross the river, who's going to stop them?"

"Why, the Continental Army, that's who," Primus said, affecting a shocked tone of voice.

"Just like they stopped the British in Brooklyn? Don't make me laugh."

Primus chuckled, and turned the bread to toast the other side. Everyone else in New York seemed scared to death over the threatened British invasion. Thousands of people had fled the city, leaving their homes and shops unattended; some men had even abandoned their wives and children. But nothing was going to scare Missy Celine. Let the British come, she'd fix *them*.

"Is the young gen'l'mans coming down for breakfast soon?" Primus asked as he brought the toasted bread to the table and set it before her.

"How should I know?" Celine replied in an innocent voice. "I suppose he's still asleep in his room."

Primus didn't bother to hide his smile as he went to the cutting board and began carving eighth-inch slices from a large slab of smoked bacon. "Young gen'l'mans like that most likely been about getting himself a big appetite, yes, yes."

"I wish you'd mind your own business," she said, trying

to look haughty and stern, but failing in the attempt. Nothing that went on in the household could be hidden from Primus— especially her own activities. The old man had worked for her family for years. Indeed, no one living could remember when the Geraits *hadn't* worked for the de Kuypers. When Celine had married Franklin Murray, Primus had come along with her. Not that the allegiance had been forced on him; Primus had been a freeman all his life. From the time Celine was a little girl it had been obvious she was his pet, and it seemed only natural that he go with her when she became the mistress of her own household. In some ways it wouldn't seem like home to her without his presence.

"Yes, yes. Young gen'l'mans like that, they use up a lot of energy," he persisted as he transferred a dozen slices of bacon to a pewter plate.

"Oh, shut up!" she said, but was unable to suppress a laugh. "What are you trying to do? Ruin my reputation? Besides, he's not much more than a boy."

"Yes, yes," Primus chanted. "So you say, so you say, but he sure *looks* like a man to me, with them strong arms and big shoulders of his."

Celine held her tongue. She knew that when she got into a debate with Primus, she invariably lost. To her mind Nathan Hale *was* a boy, but he did have the body of a man. She had first met him at a reception given by George Washington at his quarters in the Kennedy House, at 1 Broad Way. The general had been in residence here since coming down from Boston last year, after the battle of Bunker's Hill, to take command of the Continental Army.

That battle, Hale had told Celine, changed the way the British ministry viewed the disturbances in America. The British had suffered almost a thousand casualties—enough to convince London they were not up against a "New England mob," but a tough, determined force. Thereafter they considered the matter not a police action, but a full-scale military venture.

During the past twelve months General Washington had given many receptions and balls at the splendid mansion that had belonged to Captain Archibald Kennedy of His Majesty's service, of late the customs collector of the Port of New York. When the rebels took over the city and Captain Kennedy fled, the army appropriated the mansion—first for the commandant of the city, General Israel Putnam; and then, upon his arrival, for General Washington. Just as he was moving in, a mob of rebel soldiers and civilians pulled down the heavy statue of George III that stood in the Bowling Green park in front of the house. More than forty thousand bullets were made for the Continental Army from the four thousand pounds of lead yielded by the melting down of the statue—all of the statue, that is, except the head. Someone had lopped that off, and it had disappeared into the mob. The general ordered the city searched for the image of the king, but it was not to be found. "If that lead head turns up in England, it'll be hard to tell it from the original," Jan de Kuyper commented.

Some found it strange that Washington hosted so many social gatherings in a time of trouble, but the general claimed he did it for the morale of the troops. "It does their hearts good," he was fond of saying, "as they tramp their posts on the walls of Fort George, to see my guests coming and going." There were those with differing opinions, of course, but he was a new general with a new army, and they let it pass. Besides, with the arrival of the British army, Washington no longer remained in the city, but had moved his headquarters to Harlem Heights.

Celine had become a fixture at these gatherings, partly because she came from the cream of the city's society, but mostly because she was a sparkling guest, and the general had seemed infatuated with her since meeting her at her father's house when she had been only fifteen years old. Perhaps a romance might have flowered, despite the fact the general remained, as far as anyone knew, a faithful husband in a time when such a thing was a rarity; but whatever the general's intentions, Celine had no interest in such a liaison. "I'm not very keen about famous men," she confided to her friend and cousin Mary Beekman Delafield. "They're too busy with other things to give enough of themselves to their women."

Mary, who at thirty-three was beautiful enough to turn men's heads, but who had remained resolutely faithful to the husband she disliked, enjoyed living vicariously through her cousin's adventures. "But think of the satisfaction after such a conquest," she said, almost breathless at the thought of such a thing happening to herself.

"I'm more interested in the satisfaction *during* the conquest," Celine blithely replied.

Mary Delafield couldn't understand her cousin's attitude. "If you're going to do these things, I mean, why not do them with someone worth gossiping about?"

"I like men when they're young and hungry, and haven't yet acquired all the polishing that dulls them."

Young Hale was still unpolished enough for her. It had been Washington himself who had introduced them at one of his receptions. "One of our brightest young officers," the general had said. That had been less than four months ago, at the beginning of June, and since that evening the captain had been her admirer and companion. In the beginning she had thought the affair would last only a week or two, but as time went on she learned to appreciate Nathan's tenderness and kindness. When his duties as a captain in the Knowlton Rangers permitted, he took her driving in a carriage, escorted her to the theater and to dinner parties, and even procured a small boat to take her sailing on the river.

Now all this had changed, of course: ever since the British had moved their army from Staten Island to Long Island and, only three weeks ago, routed Washington's forces in the one-sided battle of Brooklyn. These days most army officers had no time for anything except preparing the defense of Manhatan, but somehow Captain Hale still managed to call at the Place—the name she had come to accept for her house near the river. It was shortened from Beekman's Place, the name used by old New York hands in recognition of the Beekman family's onetime ownership of all the land in the area.

Celine had also noticed that Hale was undergoing a change of late. He was grumpy and moody a great deal of the time—quite a departure from the easygoing fellow with a ready smile. Celine tried to get him to talk about whatever was bothering him, but with no success. Once, even though she hated herself for doing it, she picked up some papers he had left on the table in his bedroom. But to her chagrin, Hale kept his notes in Latin, a language of which she knew hardly a word.

She was still seated at the table, sipping her tea, when her son, seven-year-old Peter, clumped down the stairs and came into the kitchen. He was a sturdy little boy, tall for his age, with dark, brooding eyes and a stubborn jaw. Primus brought him a glass of milk and a slab of buttered toast.

"Is that soldier still here?" he asked, his mouth full of toasted bread.

"Why do you call him 'that soldier' when you know perfectly well his name is Nathan?" Celine asked in annoyance.

"I don't like him," Peter said, stuffing another large piece of toast into his mouth.

"Don't talk with a mouthful of food," she said, assuming her parental role. "And what's this nonsense about not liking Nathan?"

Peter finished the piece of bread before he spoke. He looked straight at his mother. "He's always giving me presents."

Celine's eyebrows lifted. "What's wrong with that? *I* like it when people give me things."

"He only gives them to me because of you," the boy said.

Startled, Celine shook her head, and realized she had better be more discreet around the boy.

"Nonsense, he gives you things because he likes you," she said. The answering look on her son's face told her he believed her as much as she believed herself.

"Finish your breakfast," she said, standing to signal that the conversation was ending. "Remember you're going down to Grandpa's house this morning."

Peter's eyes lit up. "He promised I could go aboard one of his ships."

"Only if you were good."

"I'll be good," he said sullenly; but even such an unattractive promise as this was not enough to vanquish the delight he felt at the prospect of being on a ship.

Celine patted him on the shoulder as he twisted away. She left the kitchen to return to her room. Her son's interest in ships hardly surprised her. Almost all the men in her family had been interested in only two things—shipping and banking. It was as if when God made de Kuypers He forbid them to have thoughts of any other profession or business. The Rhinelanders and Schermerhorns might produce doctors and teachers, and the Brevoorts and Van Wycks could breed men who ran breweries and ironworks; but a true de Kuyper never deviated from his love of ships—and of controlling the disposition of money. It had proven to be a most useful combination. There were many ships sailing under the de Kuyper colors, and these had usually been financed with de Kuyper money.

But all this was apart from Celine's personal world. She had never taken much part in her family's affairs. It wasn't because she was a woman—her own mother had taken an active role in the business—but because commerce and trade had never interested her. Her place had been amid the social life of the city, and it was in this sphere that she flourished.

It had never occurred to Celine that she was being flighty or avoiding responsibility, because she lived in her world—and a very orderly one it was. Everything had its place, and it annoyed her when things were not as she expected them to be.

Of late, unfortunately, that world had been tumbling down about her. First the rebels had thrown out the British, and now the British appeared to be coming back to throw out the rebels. It was making a shambles of her plans for the coming winter season, but she realized there was nothing she could do about it. These men and their stupid games! she thought as she hurried up the stairs to her bedroom. Why can't they find something better to do with their time? Of what use was all this fighting and troublemaking?

She entered the bedroom expecting Hale to be asleep, but he was already half-dressed and standing at the window, using a spyglass to look at the river beyond the lawns and fields that sloped to the water's edge. He heard the noise of the latch and spun around, then smiled grimly at Celine and went back to looking out the window. The sun was peeking over the horizon, and the day promised to be clear and humid.

"What are you looking at?" she asked, admiring his lean, muscular torso, naked to the waist. Hale was just over six feet tall, with blue eyes and light-brown hair. His very slender waist made his chest and shoulders appear even broader than they were.

"Look over there," he said, pointing across the river to Long Island. "British frigates getting underway."

Celine came to the window and peered through the spyglass. She saw several ships sailing from Newtown Creek. "Ships have been sailing in and out of there all week," she said. "So what?"

"Supply barges, yes, but these are frigates and they're forming into line."

"What does that mean?"

"Usually an attack."

Celine shook her head and walked away from the window. "What are they attacking? Do they plan on sinking the island? Good luck," she said as she opened the door of her large wardrobe to select the day's clothes.

"The frigates will probably be used to give cover to the barges carrying troops. . . . So it's finally going to happen."

There was a tremor in his voice, and she saw that his body too was trembling. This was most unlike him. She dropped the dress on the bed and went to his side. As she placed her hand on his bare shoulder, he jumped.

"You've seen fighting before," she said quietly, hoping to ease his nervousness.

"It's not the fighting that bothers me," he said in a whisper. "It's what I must do afterward."

"Tell me about it."

"Some things are to be kept secret."

"For God's sake, Nat, I'm the woman who just spent the night in bed with you. Don't you trust me?"

He thought about it for a moment, then nodded in agreement as he turned to stare intently into her eyes. "Haven't you noticed anything strange?"

"Like what?"

"Like I haven't been wearing my uniform all week."

She looked puzzled.

"When everyone else is donning a uniform," he continued, stressing the point, "I suddenly stop wearing mine."

"I hadn't thought about it, but yes, it does seem odd."

"I'm a spy," he said quietly, and turned his gaze from her. He sat down on the window seat, watching as the five frigates moved out into the river to form their line. He had seen them many times in the recent weeks—the *Rose*, the *Roebuck*, the *Phoenix*, the *Orpheus*, and the *Carysfort*.

"A spy?"

"I've been picking the places that will go if we fail to stop the British attack."

"Places that will go?" she said, still confused. "What the devil are you talking about?"

"The general staff believes it a mistake to allow New York to fall into the hands of the British. If we can't hold it, they want to burn it."

"What!"

He nodded in misery. "The general staff claims that most rebels have already fled New York, and the people who remain are loyalists—"

"That's not true!"

"—and why should we leave the city for them and the British invaders? The staff wants to retreat and leave nothing behind."

"And General Washington agrees with this outrage?"

Hale looked at her and shrugged. "No. He's spoken out

against it several times. But he wants as little dissension as possible among his staff, so he's going along with it."

"And this, of course, is what's been upsetting you."

"Yes," Hale admitted.

Celine could well understand. To stare at a building and imagine what it would look like when it was in flames; to close one's eyes and see the people shouting and cursing as they fled for their lives—it was hideous.

"I don't care what your orders are, you can't do it," she said, and her hand gripped his arm with such strength that her knuckles turned white. "You've *no right* to burn New York."

Hale looked dumbly at her. In his heart he agreed, but he was a soldier and had sworn an oath to carry out his orders.

"What you've been writing down in that notebook of yours are the best places to burn? Is that it?" she asked.

"Yes. And I also made notes and sketches of the defenses. They'll be helpful when we counterattack."

"*After* you burn the city," she said with contempt.

"Dammit, Celine, I'm a soldier and I have my duty," he said fiercely, and then immediately softened. "But I may not have to do it at all. Washington told me to go ahead with the plans, but to not actually start any fires until I received a direct order from him."

"Then there's a chance you'll not do it?"

He nodded. "The general was quite explicit. The city is to be burned only on his *direct* order. Even if Old Put himself ordered me to do it, I'd refuse. You don't know how miserable all this has been making me," he complained as he sat down on the edge of the bed. "I've learned to love this city as if I'd been born here."

Celine, city born and bred, could well understand the attachment someone like Nathan Hale could develop for New York. He was a farm boy who had attended a school as rustic as himself—a place called Yale in New Haven, where there had been all of sixty students in attendance when he graduated, in '73. A young farm boy, suddenly given a commission as an officer, who became a confidant of men like George Washington, General Gates, and Benjamin Franklin; and then to be thrust into the heady milieu of New York, with all its glamour and activity: a lot of tea for his small cup, and no wonder he felt overwhelmed. He had just begun learning to cope with an expanded world, and now he was suddenly being ordered to burn it down.

"I can understand how you feel," Celine said. "But I still say you can't do it, no matter what your orders are."

"But General Washington himself—"

"Go to him and explain. I'll go with you if you wish," she said. "I have some influence there."

A hint of a boyish smile crossed Hale's lips. "So I hear. There are a number of rumors about the two of you, you know."

She dismissed his teasing response with a flick of her hand. "There's nothing to those rumors. Besides, I've met his wife, Martha—'dear Patsy,' he calls her—and I wouldn't be accused of stealing a man away from such a mousy creature."

"I won't need your help with the general," he said stiffly. "I can stand on my own two feet."

"You must convince him it would be idiotic to burn New York."

"And if he won't listen?"

"Then don't do it anyway."

"I swore an oath," he protested. "I made a solemn promise."

"Promises are like loaves of bread," Celine said. "They're made to be broken. Now, get the rest of your clothes on and get to your general."

Hale reached for his boots. "He's up at a house on the Harlem Heights. Quite a place it is, too."

"It isn't the Roger Morris house, is it?" Celine asked, and continued when he nodded agreement. "I've been there many times. The house is all right, but the furniture is awful—great big cumbersome pieces, just like most of the Morrises themselves. And all those porches, and the ponds with the ducks. Dear God! I never heard so much quacking in my life. And you know, of all the times I've been there, they've never served duck?"

The captain hesitated before pulling on his boots. "When shall I see you again?"

She looked at him with amusement. How young he was! One moment babbling about his duty and his honor, and the next wrapped up with her. "I suspect you might have a busy week ahead," she said wryly.

"Maybe we'll get lucky and destroy the British as they try to take the island. We have thousands of armed men dug in along the shores of the East River," he said, visualizing the men along the embankment. They *had* to beat back the attack, because if they didn't, and Washington ordered him to burn the city...

How could he burn the city that was the home of the woman he loved?

There was a lost look in his eyes. Celine saw it, was moved, and wanted to comfort him. Her slender hand reached out and touched the side of his face. Then it moved down until it made contact with his bare shoulder. A slight shudder ran through his body, and goose bumps studded his skin. He reached for her, and their bodies came together as they kissed with a passion born of the understanding that a long time might pass before it happened again.

"Celine, I . . ."

"Shh."

"I . . . I want you . . ." he murmured as he nuzzled her neck with his moist lips.

Gently, she pulled him back on the bed, and before he could see how it happened, she too was naked from the waist up. Then their flesh seemed to blend together and their hands hungrily explored each other's bodies.

"Now," she said huskily. "Now!"

The ships in the river and the men along the embankment were forgotten as Nathan Hale made love to Celine de Kuyper Murray.

Earlier in the day, a less tender scene was played out farther south, in the city proper.

Clang! Clang! Clang!

Dick Goelet thought a cannon was going off next to his head; he had no idea where he was. He tried to jump to his feet, got tangled in the bedsheets, almost strangled himself, and finally fell back, choking, on the straw-stuffed pallet.

"Ah, you're awake!"

His initial shock over, Goelet sat with a dazed look on his face as he regarded the Barbados girl standing beside him with a tin plate and a wooden spoon in her hands.

"I tried shaking you," she said in a matter-of-fact tone, "but it didn't do any good. The plate and spoon did it."

"Did it!" Dick said indignantly. "They almost did me in!"

"It was his idea," the girl said, jerking her thumb toward the door, where, in the feeble light, stood Andrew de Kuyper, fully dressed, neat as a pin, and smiling broadly. "Come on, Dick. Let's go, lad," he said pleasantly. "The day's a-wasting."

Day? Dick thought, looking out the window at the still pitch-black night. He looked back at the girl, who was also smiling. Was this the same girl who had been so accommodating the night before?

"Should I give it another whup?" she asked, bringing the plate closer to Dick's ear.

"No, no!" he said quickly. "I'm awake, I'm awake."

Drew nudged the pair of boots closer to the side of the bed. Dick sighed and heaved his legs off the pallet, giving up. His cousin wanted him to rise, and once Drew made up his mind, he could be quite stubborn.

"Did you have a good time last night?" Drew asked the girl, ignoring Dick as he hunted around for his clothes, which were strewn over the floor.

"Oh, yes," she said. "He was very sweet. You was with Elsie, wasn't you?"

"Yes," Drew said. "And she was very sweet, too."

"Not as nice as this one with me, I'll bet."

"All a matter of taste, my dear," Drew replied blandly. "But you're probably right, everyone always calls Dick sweet."

Dick glared up at the two as he scrabbled about on the floor.

"He is a bit hard to wake, though," Drew added.

"Do you always have to use this?" the girl asked, giving the plate another rap with the spoon. Dick winced; it was almost possible to see the pain of his hangover searing through his brain. As he dressed, he looked at his cousin and mentally shook his head. Drew had had every bit as much to drink the night before, but here he was, perfectly sober. Dick had often wondered about this inequity. Drew had tried an explanation a few months ago. "You're two years younger and lack experience," he said, but Dick knew Drew was only trying to make him feel better. True, Dick *was* two years younger—nineteen to Drew's twenty-one—but the older cousin could drink just as well two years ago as he could today. Maybe it had something to do with size, he thought. Drew stood six feet tall; Dick was five inches shorter—the shortest male in the family.

"Thank you for waking my cousin," Drew said, reaching into his pocket and bringing out a few coins.

"That's not necessary, sir," she said, not meaning it. "It was my pleasure."

Her pleasure! Dick thought. What kind of monster takes pleasure in almost killing a man to wake him up? "Yes, a great pleasure for *all* of us," he said with as much sarcasm as he could muster. "We must all do it again soon."

"Of course," she answered, taking the money from Drew and placing it in her pocket. "Anytime you want."

There was a fly-specked water pitcher and a basin in one corner of the tiny room, and Dick splashed some water on his face, then ran his wet fingers through his hair. Finally he was ready, after a fashion, to face the world. He took out a few more coins and placed them on the bed next to the girl. Drew's sour look told his cousin he thought he was being stingy, so Dick added a few more bits of copper to the pile. The girl smiled and gave the tin plate a little tap to indicate her happiness, causing Dick to wince again and hurry to the door.

They left the small, stuffy bedroom on the third floor of the Queen's Head tavern—which of late was referred to as Fraunces Tavern, after the man who owned it—and made their way downstairs to the taproom on the ground floor. Oil lamps were burning, and even though it was before dawn and a Sunday, there were dozens of men scattered about at various tables, drinking from pewter mugs and pottery cups, all engaged in hushed conversation. The same room that had seemed so cheery to Dick the night before now, with his hangover, seemed to be made of sour smells and unfriendly faces.

The cause of all this predawn activity, of course, was the war with the British. People tended to get up before the chickens, listening to the latest gossip, hoping to learn something that would help them decide whether to stay or to flee the city. The whole town, if the truth be admitted, was a place gone mad, with half the residents already gone and the other half wondering what to do.

Sam Fraunces, the tavern's owner, was already up and about, and, even before he could be asked, he set two mugs of steaming coffee in front of the two young men. "Hot bread is on the way," he said, patting Drew on the shoulder to signify he was a favorite. "And what gets you buckos up so early?"

Drew took his coffee mug in his hands and stretched his long legs before him as he sprawled in the chair, looking as comfortable as a cat. "Just interested in seeing the sunrise, Sam," he said. "Nothing more than that."

Sam Fraunces's brow contracted into furrows, but he accepted the answer and didn't press further. It was dangerous to ask too many questions these days, because those who did were suspected of being Tories, and that could lead to all sorts of trouble. Only last week three men who were suspected of being loyal to the king had been tarred and feathered, and sent across the river on a rail in the middle of a longboat. It was the sort of thing that made a man stop before he began to appear nosy.

Fraunces was a very dark-complexioned man, and born on a Caribbean island, so the rumors about his being part black were probably true. It didn't hurt his business, though, and his tavern was among the most successful in New York. If you were *black* black, there was little chance of being accepted in New York. But if you were mostly *white looking*, with only a hint of Negro blood, the suggestion of color would rarely stand in your way. For example, take young Alexander Hamilton, who was a big hero with the Sons of Liberty. Everyone believed he inherited some black blood from his great-grandmother, but you didn't see it holding him back.

Dick was slurping away at his scalding coffee. Not that the weather was cold—it was, in fact, one of those warm, muggy days that often afflicted New York in September; he was simply trying to dilute the effects of last night's rum and gin.

Fraunces came back with the hot bread and some freshly churned butter. "I hear the lobsterbacks have been building up their forces at Newtown Creek," he said.

"It's true," Drew replied. "And Dick here has a good explanation for it."

Dick spluttered as he nearly choked on his coffee. Fraunces looked expectantly at him while Drew looked away to hide his smile. The younger man hadn't the slightest idea why the British were collecting troops at Newtown Creek, except for the obvious one that they were preparing to mount an attack, but he attempted to play the game. "Well, if memory serves me," he said, and paused, making up his story as he went along, "it seems Lord Howe has a birthday coming up and the lobsterbacks are planning to throw a big party for him."

"Yes, true enough," Drew said blandly, having decided not to let his fish off the hook. "But why exactly at Newtown Creek?"

"That's easy," Dick said, now easily slipping into the role Drew had forced upon him. "The British are planning to invite Washington and his officers, and it's an easy row across the river from Kip's Bay to the head of the creek."

It took only a split second for Fraunces to see the absurdity of this. He scowled and threw his hands up in the air. "That's what you get for asking a serious question of the younger generation," he said in disgust, walking back toward the bar to continue stacking the mugs that would hold his customers' ale. Not that he had to do this kind of chore himself; the Queen's Head was a very successful enterprise. It was housed in a beautiful building that had once belonged to the De Lancey family, but they had sold it when the area around Broad and Pearl streets became too commercial for their tastes. The tavern was a three-story affair, with five dry cellars and fourteen fireplaces. In normal times Fraunces employed over a dozen people, but now here he was, at the crack of dawn, cleaning and stacking his own glassware and mugs. "You'll never make a good liar, Dick Goelet," he called out as he went about his work.

"I don't know," Drew said, eyeing his cousin carefully. "He might have the makings."

They sat for a few more minutes; then Drew broke the silence. "Let's go. We've got a lot of riding to do."

Dick finished his coffee as Drew laid a few coins on the table. Good British coins they were, and none of this scrip that was now being issued by the Continental Congress and was looked upon with suspicion even by the most zealous rebel. Most people accepted the new paper money grudgingly, because it wouldn't look good if they refused it, but proffering it in payment was often a surefire way to make an enemy.

As they left the tavern, it was filling up with early customers. A good many were sailors hoping to find a berth aboard a departing ship. Not that there was a chance of any such sailings, with British warships infesting the bay, and most of the sailors would be falling-down-drunk by noon.

The two young men saddled their horses, then started up Queen Street at an easy trot. They passed through Hanover Square, where the old men of New York seemed to congregate—*poor* old men, who slept in drafty lofts and dank cellars and lived on next to nothing. They would sit in the square in all kinds of weather, saying little and staring off into space. One wondered what they saw. One empty day following another? An echo of better times? The debris of a used-up life?

The old men chose the area because it was close to the docks, and this proximity gave them the chance of earning a little money doing odd jobs. It also gave them a chance to do some stealing, but most people felt sorry for the old fellows and looked the other way when they snatched a loaf of bread or a handful of greens.

They made their way past Wall Street, with its fine houses and big oak trees, and came to Maiden Lane. Drew followed a still unnamed path until he came to John Street and that small rise of land known as Golden Hill. The cousins reined in their horses and stood side by side. In the faint light of the coming dawn, the hill began to look as golden as its name.

"Years from now people will look back and say this is where the revolution began," Drew said.

"The Bostonians will disagree," Dick said.

"The hell with them," Drew said. "Somebody will have to tell the truth." He reached over and grabbed his cousin's arm. "Maybe that's a good job for you. To write the true history of the rebellion, and tell how it all got started here in New York in 1770."

Dick looked startled, and Drew smiled. "You've a knack with words, Dick. Remember all the poems you used to write as a lad, and the short stories; you could do worse things with your life than to become the historian of New York."

"I'll think about it," Dick said, entertaining an idea that had never before entered his head.

"Just remember you're standing on the spot where the rebellion started. And that my grandfather died the next day because of it."

"I knew he died about that time," Dick said. "But not because of the fighting."

"Grandfather James watched the battle from that doorway right over there," Drew said, pointing to a house on John Street. "It belonged to a Quaker friend of his. A stray bullet hit the man and he fell dead at Grandfather's feet."

The thought seemed to make him angry; his eyes blazed. In this attitude, he was even handsomer than usual. His nose was straight and set between the wide-spaced eyes characteristic of the de Kuypers. He was powerfully built and wore his hair on the long side, tied in a queue in the style of the day.

"Grandfather went home to the house he kept on Wall Street," he continued. "He remained a loyalist to the end, and contended the rebels were in the wrong. He and my father got into a terrible row because, as you know, Jan is a dedicated rebel even if he does believe we can win without bloodshed.

"Grandfather was crushed by the fighting, and the death of his Quaker friend. He went to bed that night seeming normal, but they found him dead in the morning."

Dick had only the barest memories of those times. The battle of Golden Hill had taken place in September 1770, when he had been only thirteen. The Sons of Liberty—a radical group he and his cousin now belonged to—had erected a tall "Liberty pole." Some British soldiers had come along and knocked it down. The Sons came out of a tavern and beat up the soldiers.

The fight raged onto Golden Hill, and the shooting began when a British lieutenant panicked and ordered a volley fired into the crowd. The deadly battle began, and when the smoke cleared there were a half dozen people dead and almost fifty wounded.

"In a way it was a kindness that the old man died then, in his sleep," Drew said. "He belonged to a different age and wouldn't be able to understand what's happening today."

"He was of my blood too," Dick said quietly. "Don't forget I'm a direct descendant of *his* grandfather."

Drew smiled. "You came along through the de Witt-Goelet side of the family," he said. "The bad side."

"We'll forget that when I write my history," Dick said, and grinned. He was beginning to enjoy the idea. "But we *will* remember that the battle here happened two months before they had their massacre in Boston."

The two men continued their journey until they came to the point where Bowery Lane led into the Boston Post Road. They left the city and followed the Post Road for a mile until it split. The left fork became the Bloomingdale Road, which wended eastward until it ended at Harlem Heights, near the North River. The right fork continued on the easterly side of the island until it reached a point where it became known as the King's Bridge Road, after the oldest bridge across the Harlem River. Their destination was the shore of the East River near Kip's Bay, which, Drew argued, was where the British would make their landing.

The American generals obviously didn't agree with him, because they had fortified the lower end of the island as well as the northern shore along the Harlem. Drew claimed they had spread themselves too thin.

"So you think they'll land near your sister's house," Dick said.

"Yes," Drew said maliciously. "My sister likes parties at old Beekman's Place, and maybe she'll enjoy this one."

Dick smiled, because, like everyone else, he was aware of the animosity between Celine and her brother. They were both strong-willed people, and while Drew might be easygoing about

THE CITY INVADED

many things, he could become very testy about matters concerning his sister.

As the two men rode north along the Post Road, they began to pass groups of soldiers—some going south and some going north, all moving sluggishly in a most unmilitary way. It didn't seem to make any sense, and Drew stopped and scratched his head.

"Where are you going?" he asked a pasty-faced militiaman whose hat sported the green cockade of a lieutenant.

"We've been ordered south to join the forces of the commander of Fort George," the man replied. Drew asked the same question of a man tramping north, and he said he was coming *from* Fort George.

Drew looked at his cousin in astonishment. "Troops going north. Troops going south. It doesn't give a man much confidence in our generals, does it?"

"They're all we have," Dick said with a shrug.

Drew sighed. "A shame. I guess my father was right after all," he said, and Dick knew what he meant. Jan de Kuyper claimed the Continentals couldn't withstand a British attack for more than a few days—which was why he had Drew and Dick out riding every morning. The de Kuypers had four ships docked along the North River, and Jan planned on sending them out to sea the moment the British attacked Manhatan. He hoped that in the confusion they'd be able to slip past any British warships on patrol.

They continued riding north as the new sun began to bathe the world in light.

Celine ran the tips of her fingers over the chest of the naked, panting man.

Nathan Hale was covered in perspiration. As usual, Celine had managed to drive him to a frenzy of lovemaking, a sort of madness he had never known before. It always amazed him that her slender body could have such power and stamina. More than his own, he confided to himself.

He took her hand and began to kiss Celine's fingers, when the first British cannon fired and sent its iron ball whizzing toward the shore of Manhatan. The rumble of the first gun was still reverberating when the second gun fired, and then the third and the fourth, and then it became impossible to distinguish the sound of a single cannon as the five frigates on the river began in concert to pound the shoreline. They had moved into line and anchored facing Kip's Bay, their lead shot pounding the earth and mangling men.

Nathan Hale leaped from the bed. He stood at the window and watched as the guns poured a continuous rain of iron and the smoke began to obscure his view of the river. A gentle wind lifted this gray presence and carried it toward the island.

Celine came to Hale's side, and they watched in mute horror for a few seconds. It was she who first broke the spell that held them. "Nat, get your clothes on. I think they mean business."

The sound of the bombardment rolled across the land and reached the ears of Dick and Drew. It was like thunder, and they realized it was coming from the East River.

They spurred their horses into a gallop and fairly flew down the road, toward the secondary lane that led to Kip's Bay. As they turned off the Post Road, they were only a hundred yards from the bay, and galloped past dozens of soldiers' encampments.

There was a great deal of commotion at these camps as the men came from their tents and lean-tos or, in many cases, from under nothing more than the trees, and stood about looking in the direction of the river. Some were dressing and others were checking their weapons, but disorganization prevailed. There were officers among the men, recognizable by the colored cockades in their hats, but they behaved as ineffectually as everyone else.

The closer the two cousins came to the river, the more confusion they encountered. Now they began to pass soldiers who were retreating from their positions along the shore. Some were bloodied and wounded, but most were simply panic-stricken and fleeing from the punishment being meted out by the British guns.

Drew and Dick crested a hill, and stopped as they were met by the sight of the river spread out before them. They watched in awe as the five frigates kept up their ferocious barrage. The American troops along the shore weren't even bothering to answer the fire, but were quitting their positions and retreating inland. The ground along the path of their retreat was littered with abandoned equipment and weapons, and the bodies of the unlucky.

Drew pointed across the river at a number of barges emerging from Newtown Creek. Most were filled with men wearing the red coats of British soldiers, but one barge, in front of the others, was filled with men in green.

"Greencoats?" Dick said in surprise.

"Hessian jaegers," Drew said, and both men became more concerned at the sight. Everyone was terrified of these strange troops, because it was said they preferred to kill with bayonet rather than musket or rifle. The very thought of being spiked on a bayonet point sent a chill up men's spines.

The barges moved slowly and ponderously, but even at that rate they would be touching the shoreline at Kip's Bay within twenty minutes—and there would be nothing to stop them once they arrived, because the cannon barrage had the American troops literally crawling over one another as they retreated.

Drew reined his horse about. "Let's get to Celine's place," he shouted over the din.

As they galloped toward Beekman's Place, they passed amid the retreating militiamen. Many of them were only boys, and if the situation hadn't been so tragic, their frantic disorder would have looked amusing. Some of them began throwing away their packs and muskets because the weight was slowing them down. Here and there an officer tried to rally them, but it was a hopeless task.

The two riders reached the gates of the Place and, from their position on the hill, looked back over the scene. A thick haze of smoke hung over the river as the frigates continued to fire away. The servants and farmhands from the Place were gathered outside, their eyes wide with fear as they watched the destruction below.

As Drew and his cousin were tying their horses to the hitching rail, a man dashed out the front door of the house. "Hello, de Kuyper!" he shouted as he passed.

"Who's that?" Dick asked.

"Captain Nathan Hale."

"*Captain?* Queer uniform he's wearing."

"Knowing my sister, he's lucky to be wearing anything at all."

The first person to greet them as they entered the house was Primus Gerait, coming down the stairs with Peter in tow. "Mister Andrew," he said, "you sure picked the right time to call."

"Where's my sister?"

At that moment Celine appeared at the top of the stairs, and she descended them so quickly she almost tripped.

"I've got to get back to the city to see to our ships," Drew said. "You and Peter come with me."

"No, I intend staying here," she said. "But I suppose it would be best if you took Peter."

"Why do you want to stay?" Drew protested. "The British will be all over the place in a few hours."

"This is my home and I'm staying," Celine said defiantly. "And since when do I take orders from you?"

"Soon you'll be taking them from the British."

"I have my reasons for staying here."

"Sure, you do," Drew said angrily. "You're probably planning to hold a dance for their officers."

"Look, little brother," Celine said with a nasty gleam in her eye, "General Washington is going to need time, and anything that can be done to delay the British will be welcomed. If I stay here, I may be able to do something."

At that moment Mary Delafield came down the stairs. She looked shaken.

"You're here, too, Mary?" Drew asked. "Maybe you'll come back to the city with me."

"Mary's my houseguest, and she can do anything she wants," Celine said. "But I wish you'd stay, Mary, because I might need your help."

"Won't the British be here soon?" Mary asked.

Celine nodded. "And that's when I may need your help."

"I'm not a very strong person," Mary said. "But if you think I can be of some use, I'll stay."

Drew swore beneath his breath and grabbed his nephew's hand. "Stay if you like," he said as he started for the door. "But the consequences are on your own heads."

"Aren't they always?" Celine said.

Drew rode his horse down the road, with Peter on the saddle in front of him. Dick Goelet followed. The sounds of the big guns continued, and when they reached the Post Road, they found it choked with men. As before, some were going north and some were going south and nobody seemed to be in charge.

At one point a group of fear-crazed soldiers set upon them and tried to steal their horses. One man grabbed at Dick, but he brought the butt of his pistol straight down into the man's face and he dropped like a stone in a pond. Drew, holding his nephew tight against him, reared his horse and scattered the attackers for a moment, giving himself and his cousin the chance to gallop down the road.

"They're like a pack of wild animals," Drew shouted as they raced toward the city.

They rode furiously; and after a time the sound of the guns became muffled; but they could still be heard at the northern end of Bowery Lane. By now the entire city knew what was happening.

Dick Goelet had no time now to think about a career as a historian: when one is living history, one has little time to reflect on it.

Captain Patrick Blakely stood at the bow of the heavy barge that was carrying the Hessian jaegers. It was his intention to be the first man ashore.

The captain had a score to settle with the Americans.

He had been in the fighting at Lexington the previous year, and after the doctor had removed the lead slug from Blakely's leg, he had limped painfully for six months. During that time he had built up a smoldering hatred for the rebels, not so much because they had the temerity to defy the king, but because they had caused Blakely himself such personal pain. Now he was accompanying the British army as deputy provost marshal of the troops that would occupy New York. He was especially pleased with this post, knowing that his chief, the provost marshal, Colonel Cunningham, would allow him to pursue his duties in whatever manner he chose. He could hardly wait for his revenge, and it was for symbolic value that he wanted to be ashore with the first wave, even if it meant going with the Hessian troops.

General Howe was fond of sending Hessians in the forefront of an attack, because he recognized that it was almost impossible to break their iron discipline. The green-coated jaegers always went first, fanning out almost in the manner of Indian scouts. They carried rifles, not muskets, and were crack shots at any distance up to one hundred yards. If the resistance stiffened against the jaegers, they would step aside and let the blue-coated Hessian grenadiers move past in their tight formations. The grenadiers were armed with musket and bayonet, but relied mostly on the latter in their terrible work. They marched with their muskets in front of them, and nothing short of death itself could stop them. It wasn't that they were braver than other men, but each Hessian knew he was being watched by every officer from General Knyphausen and Colonel von Donop down to the lowest subaltern. Any man who broke ranks was accused of cowardice, and faced the unpleasant fate of being lashed to death with a lead-tipped cat-o'-nine-tails. Such harsh discipline had created a force of the fiercest fighting troops on earth.

Patrick Blakely was a tall man, a bit over six feet, carrying one hundred and ninety pounds on a strong frame. His features were darker than those of most of the British officers, but that was because of his Irish blood—the notorious Black Irish that had been created after sailors from the defeated Spanish Armada had swum ashore on the Emerald Isle and there found Celtic wives, a permanent home, and a new nationality.

The captain was tall and good-looking; the sort of looks that caused women to turn their heads and stare after him. There was a smoldering quality to his eyes—detectable despite the boredom usually written on his face. He had that jaded look of a man who has too often seen the darker side of human nature.

He stood at the bow and looked north, noting the bristling American defenses at Horn's Hook, where the land jutted into the East River. He was amused, because he knew those defenses would be useless on this day. The Americans had accepted the bait when General Howe sent several companies to garrison on Buchanan and Montressor Islands, in the middle of the river. They assumed these were advance troops for the invasion that would take place along the Harlem. In preparation they made a strong artillery position at the Hook, thinking they would be able to blast away at the frigates and troop barges as they passed. Alas, thought Captain Blakely, but we will never pass the point, and those guns will lie idle while we storm ashore at the more southerly position.

"The rebels are retreating," Colonel von Donop said as he stood at Blakely's shoulder.

"We'll chase them right across the island and dump them in the other river," Blakely replied.

"We should have done that weeks ago when we had them pinned down back there," the Prussian said, jerking his thumb toward Long Island.

The two officers looked on with satisfaction as the heavy barge came closer and closer to the shore. They could see that most of the positions previously occupied by the American militia already lay abandoned. Men in a wide assortment of makeshift uniforms were escaping over the hills, trying to put

THE CITY INVADED 25

as much distance as possible between themselves and their attackers.

Captain Blakely looked around and was comforted by the sight of the dozens of other barges trailing his own. Howe had scheduled four thousand troops for this initial invasion force, and from the looks of things they would be more than sufficient. And even if they didn't prove to be enough, the general had another thirty thousand men at his disposal—almost all of them well-trained troops, as opposed to the rebel force, which was about eighteen thousand strong, but composed mostly of ragtag militiamen and untrained youngsters.

Now the barge was reaching its goal, and the coxswain steered toward the left of the spit of land that jutted out into the middle of the bay like a widow's peak. The flat underside of the boat hit bottom, ground ahead for a few more feet, and then stopped. Blakely leaped over the gunwale, dropped into two feet of water, and began wading ashore as the Hessian jaegers came tumbling out of the barge to follow him.

In minutes a half-dozen barges were nuzzling the shore and the troops were wading ashore. Green-coated jaegers and blue-coated Hessian grenadiers fell into ranks next to red-coated British grenadiers. The Englishmen looked especially splendid on this day, with their bright coats, and straps and belts freshly whitened with pipe clay. A few critics had mocked this fastidiousness of battle dress, but Blakely knew it signified British discipline and helped terrorize their opponents.

The jaegers quickly spread out over the countryside, meeting little resistance and handling without problems whatever they did encounter. The British grenadiers formed into lines and marched forward with a precision that seemed more appropriate to a drill field than to a hostile shore. The Hessian grenadiers formed into lines on the southern portion of the bay.

The captain strode to the top of the small hill overlooking the bay and watched as the Americans retreated in panic. The occupation of the island was going to be easier than anyone had imagined. He could count hundreds of men running away as far as the Post Road. The only sign of resistance was in a cluster of trees near a side road, where a group of rebels had taken a position and were firing their muskets at the advancing jaegers.

A group of grenadiers wheeled in that direction and marched forward at a steady pace. They stopped once to fire a volley, but this was more for effect than for anything else. The jaegers were crack shots, but the marksmanship of the Hessian grenadiers was notoriously poor, and they kept advancing until they could close with the enemy and use their real weapons—the bayonets. The rebels at the cluster of trees were commanded by a young officer who stood in the open, bravely firing his pistol. Here and there a Hessian would topple over, but the rest kept moving until they came to the trees. The massacre was swift and merciless. The rebels who stood their ground were impaled on the iron spikes and their bodies tossed aside while the Hessians searched for more victims. The brave young officer drew his sword and managed to fend off the bayonet of one enemy, but then two men pierced him from either side. The double bayoneting had the effect of keeping him on his feet for a few seconds, but he was dead while still vertical.

Blakely watched as the Hessians moved among the wounded on the ground, performing a ritual killing rather than taking prisoners. He was fascinated by the cold-blooded way the Hessians went about this business—the manner of it forbidden to the British troops, as it was considered something of an atrocity.

The captain thought such squeamishness to be out of place in battle and had argued for the bloodier policy, but General Howe had been adamant in forbidding it. Most likely, Blakely thought, the fussbudgety general would have preferred to forbid the Hessians to kill their prisoners; but the Hessian prince had made a contract with the English king, and there were certain things that were left to the devices of the German soldiers.

Within a few hours, the commander of the assault force, Lieutenant General Sir Henry Clinton, son of the former royal governor of the province, had achieved his objective. He was in control of Kip's Bay and the surrounding area all the way to the Post Road. His troops fanned out from the bay in a semicircle until they controlled a large beachhead area from below Sunfish Pond to the south, extending to the Post Road, on the east, and to the edge of the large manor house of Celine Murray, to the north.

At this juncture General Clinton, on the orders of General Howe, called a cessation of the advance, and his troops settled down to hold their positions. The tactic was sound. A first wave of men was sent to secure the objective and make it safe against counterattack; only then was it prudent to bring over the main body of the invasion force. Of course, the plan pre-

THE CITY INVADED

supposed that the enemy would offer resistance and attempt a counterattack.

Captain Blakely quickly realized the Americans not only had abandoned their defenses, but were in such a state of disarray and panic that no counterattack would be coming. "We ought to keep after these rebels," he complained to Colonel von Donop.

The thickset Hessian nodded in agreement. "We should continue right across the island and cut their forces in two. Divide and conquer, divide and conquer."

The two officers returned to the beach and waited for the barges bearing horses. Neither was accustomed to going about on foot, but General Howe had decreed there would be no horses in the first barges. He had been expecting a pitched battle, with the American forces dug in along the shore, in which horses would only get in the way.

Blakely shook his head. We could have come ashore on elephants, he thought. He stood on the shore and watched as more barges ground to a halt and soldiers disembarked. The sixth barge to arrive contained the horses. General Howe and a contingent of senior officers arrived on the seventh. Colonel Cunningham, the provost marshal, was with this group, and Captain Blakely eased his way to his chief's side. The two exchanged glances as they listened to General Clinton's report to the commander.

Blakely disliked General Howe. In the first place, Howe was an aristocrat, born to a class that seemed to look down on everyone else, especially someone with Irish blood. In the second place, he seemed far too eager to pursue a course of peace rather than settling the rebels' hash for good. Blakely's solution to the rebellion was simple: kill or lock up anyone who so much as spoke against the Crown.

"I recommend we continue our advance," General Clinton was saying as he concluded. "Now that we've got them on the run, let's keep it that way."

Howe shook his head. "Before we advance, we'll bring over the next wave of nine thousand men. In the meantime I'd like to inspect our perimeter."

General Clinton disagreed, but held his tongue. He believed in reasonable caution, of course, but what was there to be cautious about in this situation?

General Howe gestured that he wanted Clinton and the provost marshall to accompany him. Cunningham nodded at

Blakely that he was to join them. Accompanied by a sergeant and a detachment of men, the four officers rode out to the perimeter. The soldiers they passed all had faces flushed with victory. They went along the southern flank, then rode north on the Post Road.

"I take it I made an unpopular decision to delay pressing the attack?" the general asked Colonel Cunningham.

Cunningham cleared his throat. He was a large, meaty man, much happier in a barroom brawl than in conversation with his commanding general. "It's not for me to say, sir."

The general smiled. "Most battles are lost in the planning stage," he said. "I always follow the advice of Caesar Augustus—make haste slowly."

"Yes, of course, sir," the colonel replied, racking his brain to recall ever hearing of this Caesar Augustus, and failing.

"Sometimes one can be too cautious," General Clinton said. "A battle can be lost because of that."

"Maybe there won't be many more battles," Howe said hopefully. "Perhaps the rebels will realize they have no chance of winning and will come to terms with us. These people aren't really enemies, after all, only misled cousins."

Captain Blakely, riding a length behind his superiors, made a sour face. This was just the sort of coddling he disliked. But what else could one expect from a general who took six weeks to move his troops from Staten Island to Long Island? And then another three weeks to follow up after his victory in Brooklyn? After that battle, the Americans had fled back to the shores of the East River. If attacked immediately afterward, they would have surrendered, to a man. But no, the good general—*General Willie*, as he was called behind his back—let thousands of defeated troops slip away in hundreds of small boats.

Another example of the general's folly, as Captain Blakely saw it, was the inexcusable delay in attacking Governor's Island, where Washington had stranded over two thousand of his troops. *General Willie* did nothing while a fleet of rowboats came from the Battery and took the men and over forty pieces of heavy artillery off the island. To compound this foolishness, the very next day British warships were ordered to bombard the island with gunfire. They gave it a heavy and sustained cannonade—the only problem being that there was no one left on the island to take the punishment.

God save us from our leaders! the captain swore beneath his breath as they came to a halt at a bend in the road where sixty downcast rebels were prisoners of a company of red-coated grenadiers.

"You'll have to find some place to hold these men," the general said to the provost marshal.

"Yes sir. As soon as we take the city, we'll find a proper place," Cunningham replied.

"I wouldn't want to hear of their mistreatment," the general warned.

"They're dangerous rebels," the colonel protested. "We must take precautions to keep them from escaping."

"Yes, of course, precautions. But nothing more."

The colonel exchanged another look with his deputy, and then shook his head. More coddling.

They came to the point in the road where a smaller, secondary road led up to the cooling shade of the porches of Celine's house. The general stopped and allowed himself the pleasure of taking in the sweeping lawns and gardens that spread in all directions from the house.

"What a splendid home," he said. "Do you know who owns it?"

Captain Blakely took a map from his dispatch pouch and studied it for a moment. "It seems to be known as Beekman's Place, but the owner is a Mrs. Murray."

"And would her tendencies include loyalty to the king?"

The captain looked at the provost marshal for advice, but received none. "I wouldn't know, sir," he said.

"Let's find out, shall we?" Howe said, and the group turned up the road that led to the house.

Celine was looking out through the parlor window, with Mary beside her. Several anxious servants stood behind them, whispering nervously among themselves. Primus Gerait kept himself apart from them, and wore a look of disdain for the worriers.

"They're coming here," Mary said nervously. "What should we do?"

"Two of them are wearing the uniforms of generals," Celine said. "I doubt we'll have any trouble from them."

Mary remained unconvinced. "I've heard awful stories about how soldiers act during a war."

"Only the riffraff act like that," Celine assured her. "These are generals, and they—"

She stopped as a sudden thought entered her mind. Nathan

Hale, she hoped, had gone to General Washington to talk him out of burning down New York. He could probably use all the time he could get. If she could delay these generals, if only for an hour or two, it might help.

She turned to Mary. "Look, I'm going to invite them in for a drink."

"Really, Celine! A drink?"

"It's important. Now, I want you to be your usually charming self."

"There's a war going on. We can't just invite the enemy generals in for a *drink*," Mary protested.

Celine smiled devilishly. "Remember when we were girls, how we used to pretend we were giving a tea party for the king? Well, that's what we'll be doing now—pretending to be entertaining them, but really spying on them."

"Spying? What are we trying to find out?"

"Leave that to me. Just be flirtatious, and the more outrageous the better."

A conspiratorial grin came to Mary's face. "Well, if you put it that way..."

"Good."

General Howe reined in his horse in front of the main door of the house. He was aware of a group of field hands and servants standing at the far corner of the building, looking as if they were prepared to take flight. Not a promising beginning. And then the door opened, and he smiled when he saw the two good-looking women who came out.

"Good day," Celine said in a cool voice. "It's a warm day, and I was wondering if I could offer you gentlemen a glass of Madeira?"

General Howe beamed. "Indeed you may, madam," he said as he swung down from his horse.

Soldiers stepped forward and took the horses as the other officers dismounted. The general led the way up the steps, and the men accompanying him, as well as those left behind, exchanged mystified glances. The middle of an attack, and the commander was stopping to have a drink?

"I'm General William Howe, madam," he said with a courtly bow. "At your service."

Celine, who had been well schooled by Nathan Hale, knew who her visitor was, but pretended to be flustered. "Oh, *General* Howe... but I thought you were an admiral... and an older man."

If the general had been a cat, he would have purred. "The Admiral Howe you speak of is my brother. And I *am* a younger man."

"Of course, how silly of me," Celine said with a titter that caused Mary to smile behind a judiciously raised hand. Celine certainly knew how to put on an act. "I'm Celine Murray, and this is my cousin, Mary Delafield."

The general kissed both extended hands and then introduced his officers. The ensuing rash of hand-kissing made Colonel Cunningham very uncomfortable, and his face turned beet-red. Celine invited them into the house, where it was cooler and the wine awaited. The grenadiers remained outside, sweating in their heavy coats under the broiling midday sun. They shifted from foot to foot as they stayed in ranks, complaining bitterly about their officers, and envying them.

As General Howe took a glass of wine from Celine, he seemed to have forgotten about everything else. While he drank, chatted, and relaxed, the other three officers wondered why the attack wasn't continuing. The fifteen thousand soldiers who waited in the sun were mystified. Why weren't they being allowed to continue the rout of the rebels?

On a hilltop less than a mile away, another man was wondering the very same thing.

General Washington had come down from his headquarters on Harlem Heights. He passed the retreating rabble that was supposed to be his army, appearing to take it calmly that they were going the wrong way. At first he gave dignified orders for them to turn and make a stand, but they were deaf to his commands and left the roads, fleeing north through field and forest. The general lost his composure and cursed his men, calling them cowards and scum and worse—but this vituperation had no more effect than his first commands. Then he got down from his horse and took a few swings at his men, but most managed to duck his large fists, and continued north as fast as their trembling legs could carry them. As a final gesture of disgust the general took off his hat, threw it down into the dust of the road, and trampled it.

And now he stood on a hill looking toward the mansion at Beekman's Place, where he could see the detachment of idle British troops. General Putnam's aide, Major Aaron Burr, stood at his side. Washington's face was flushed with rage. Burr had just informed him what happened to the reinforcements sent up from the city to Kip's Bay. It seemed the commander of this force had taken the wrong road, turning left at the fork onto the Bloomingdale Road, away from the fighting, and by now was as far north as Harlem Heights.

This last piece of intelligence had turned the commander speechless with rage. Half his army was filled with cowards, the other half with fools.

What he didn't know at this moment, as he took off his hat to smash it on the ground again, was that this combination of cowardice and foolishness would be the major reason his army would regroup to fight another day.

The three riders reached the de Kuyper house on Maiden Lane, and Drew turned his nephew over to Dick Goelet with instructions to stay with him inside the house. The swift ride through the city had convinced Drew the streets would soon be unsafe. People were packing up and trying to get out before the British arrived, clogging the streets with wagons and carts, panicking and knocking down anyone who got in their way. Meanwhile, columns of Continentals streamed through the streets, heading north even as other soldiers staggered south, some bloodied, dazed from the British attack.

Drew spurred his horse and rode down to Wall Street, where he turned right and headed for the North River. The magnificent oaks on both sides of the street gave him some protection from the hot sun. Even on this respectable street there were people who were piling their possessions onto carts, abandoning their homes to the mercies of the invaders.

At least a third of the houses on the street were already boarded up, their inhabitants having fled. It was the same throughout the city. A good many people known to be rebels had decided they wouldn't fare well under the British. People like the de Kuypers, of course, thought of the city almost as an extension of their own flesh and blood, and remained even though they were ardent supporters of the revolutionists. As far as they were concerned they *were* New York, and they weren't about to abandon it for any reason.

He crossed Broad Way and went down Little Stone Street to the docks. The de Kuyper packets were moored together, and as Drew jumped from his horse, they were already preparing to get underway. Philemon Peabody, one of the de Kuyper company senior employees, was on the dock.

"Hello, Drew," Peabody called out as the younger man ran up to the group on the wharf.

"Philemon," Drew said grudgingly. "I see you beat me here." He resented that he had been unable to be on hand to do his job—and besides, he just plain didn't like the furtive little man.

"Jan wants the ships to head north to Albany," Peabody said.

Drew peered out into the bay and saw a pair of British frigates patrolling. "They'd be safer if they got into the ocean," he said. "But I suppose those frigates would try to stop them."

Peabody nodded his head. "Best they try Albany."

"I'd hate to try to outrun those frigates," one of the captains said.

"All right, Albany it is," Drew said. "But do it quickly. I've just come from Kip's Bay, and our men didn't hold up the redcoats for five minutes."

The captains strode for their ships, shouting orders to their crews as they went. The British might capture the city, but they would find no de Kuyper packets at their berths.

"Coming back to the office?" Peabody asked.

"Of course. We all have to get our marching orders from my father," Drew said with grim humor. A year ago Jan had announced he was semiretiring and turning over the day-to-day running of the business to another cousin, David de Witt Sackett. The only problem was that Jan had given up hardly any control. David Sackett was a patient man, with an orderly mind trained in the law, but Jan was driving him toward an early grave.

Drew and Philemon Peabody made a contrasting pair as they walked from the dock to where they had left their horses. Peabody was fair-haired and five feet four inches tall. He was slight of build and walked with mincing steps.

He was now thirty years old and held an important position in the de Kuyper company. He had arrived in America only twelve years before as an eighteen-year-old indentured servant. His new master had met him as the ship docked in New York and planned on taking him to Philadelphia, where he lived. They stayed overnight at an inn, and the fast-talking Peabody had convinced the innkeeper that he was really the master and the man sleeping in the back room was the indentured servant. He proceeded to sell his master to the innkeeper and, taking both horses, went back to New York. Naturally, there was hell to pay when the innkeeper announced to the Philadelphian that he owned his services. Things were eventually sorted out, and the Philadelphian returned to New York with fire in his eye.

What might have happened when the irate master caught up with his servant would never be known, because Peabody had a rare bit of good luck befall him. As he was walking down Whitehall Street toward the docks with the intention of finding a sailor's berth and fleeing the city, a frightened horse threw its rider and came galloping wildly down the street. He was making straight for a gray-haired man just emerging from a building.

Peabody wasn't remotely a hero, but acting out of sheer instinct, he pulled the older man out of the horse's path.

The rescued man was Jan de Kuyper, and he was grateful to the lad who had saved his life. He offered a reward, but Peabody sensed he had aided a powerful man who could solve his problems. He poured out his own, revised version of the incident at the inn, and Jan didn't hesitate in his response. He sought out the Philadelphian and bought Peabody's contract of indenture—for double what it had cost. Then he tore the paper to pieces in front of Peabody and told the young man he was free.

Realizing he had made a powerful ally, Peabody asked for a job with the de Kuyper company. Jan, of course, hired him on the spot. From that time on, Peabody made many enemies because of his addiction to trickery, but Jan refused even to listen to any complaints. "If it wasn't for Philemon Peabody," he would say, "I wouldn't be here today." And that was that.

Over the past dozen years Peabody had risen higher and higher in the company and now stood very near the top. His official duties were not well defined, but everyone understood he acted as a personal assistant and advisor to Jan. David Sackett disliked him for his influence over Jan, and Drew simply couldn't like any man he couldn't trust. But Peabody remained: Jan insisted on it.

Drew and the smaller man rode their horses down to the Battery, where a great commotion was going on as a colonel of militia attempted to organize three hundred soldiers into some semblance of ranks.

"This is the mob that's going to protect us from thirty thousand Englishmen and Hessians," Drew said in contempt.

"We're in a lot of trouble," Peabody agreed nervously. "We could all go down with them."

Drew didn't bother answering. Even when there was a disaster in the making, all Peabody could think of was his own welfare.

The red-faced colonel continued to shout orders to his men as the two riders passed, and he looked up at them distractedly, desperation evident on his face. Drew was embarrassed.

They arrived at the old building on Whitehall Street and took their horses to the stables in the rear. Drew washed the dust of the road from his face and hands at the watering trough, and the two men went inside the building.

"The ships get away?" Jan snapped as they entered his office.

"To Albany," Drew said.

"We wanted to send them out in the ocean," Peabody said quickly, knowing this had been Jan's first wish and wanting to cover himself on the point. "But two frigates were blocking the way."

Jan accepted the explanation, much to Peabody's relief. He was now in his late sixties, and looked vigorous and trim. His once dark hair was now gray, and the weight of his years seemed to have made him shorter—although this was probably an illusion caused by his slight stoop. He wasted no time on past business, but went immediately to what else had to be done. "I want you to get some men and board up our grain warehouse," he said to his son. "There may be plundering."

"You don't think there's a chance our troops may hold them off?" David Sackett asked, more in sheer hope than in anything resembling faith.

"Not a chance," Drew answered. "Our troops threw down their guns and ran away."

"That bad, eh?" Jan said, cocking his head to one side, the way he usually did when he was annoyed. It was a trait he had passed on to his children.

"Terrible, terrible," Peabody intoned.

"It's hard to believe our men are so ill trained," Jan said.

"It isn't hard for me to believe," David Sackett said with a laugh. He was a stout man with a florid face, and his laughter caused his entire body to shake. "As a representative of New York, I've been going to meetings of the Continental Congress, and if the army is as disorganized as Congress, we're really in trouble. Just a few weeks ago old Ben Franklin seriously suggested arming our soldiers with bows and arrows because a man can shoot arrows faster than he can fire and reload a musket."

"You made that up," Jan said in amusement.

David smiled. "I'm not that clever. You've got to spend time with Ben to understand him. One minute he's brilliant, and the next he sounds like a crackpot. Take that meeting we had with General Howe a week ago."

"The one on Staten Island?" Drew asked.

"Yes. Besides Howe there was Franklin, Sam Adams, and myself. Instead of concentrating on peace terms, old Ben kept carrying on about how good the claret was, and how much he preferred cold ham to cold mutton."

"Ben always was a trencherman," Jan said, remembering a few memorable evenings he had spent with the old man, and how much food and drink they had consumed.

"He got in a few good licks at the meeting, though," David said with a chuckle. "'If America should fall,' Howe said, 'I would lament the loss as if it had been my brother.' Well, old Ben looked the general straight in the eye and said, 'We will use our utmost endeavor to save Your Lordship that mortification.'"

"Did Howe offer any specific peace terms?" Jan asked.

"No, it was the damnedest meeting, nobody seemed to want to talk about anything. I asked Adams if he could figure out what Howe was up to, and he said, 'It's impossible to discover the designs of an enemy who has no designs at all.'"

"Sometimes I think His Lordship doesn't want to win this war," Jan said, pouring himself a mug of the hard cider commonly known as Jersey Lightning.

"He's sure acting like he wants to win it today," Drew said.

"So nothing came of the peace talks?" Peabody asked.

"Nothing," the lawyer said. "Oh, yes, Sam Adams caught a cold. He and Franklin shared a room. They argued about leaving the window open, and Sam fell asleep as Ben was lecturing him about the necessity of sleeping with fresh air. Sam woke up in the morning, the window still open, and he had the sniffles."

"And Ben?"

"Healthy as a horse," David said, joining Jan in a glass of the fiery cider. "So what do we do now? Join the army, or stay here in the city?"

"I'm too old to be joining armies," Jan snapped. "And so are you."

"*I'm* not," Drew said quietly.

"You might do more good by staying here. Washington is going to need supplies, and we've got ships."

Drew smiled. "I recall reading in the family chronicles that we've been privateers before."

"There's a lot of money to be made in that line," Peabody said.

"Jesus Christ, man!" David exploded. "We're talking about fighting for our lives and you speak of making profits!"

Jan, still thinking about his son's future, ignored the altercation between the other two men. "If you go into the army," he said to Drew, "you'll only be one of thousands carrying a gun. If you stay here, you might have an opportunity to do something unique."

"I'll think about it," Drew said. "For all we know the war may be over tomorrow."

"Fair enough," Jan said. "And now get started on that warehouse job."

Drew started to leave, then halted, remembering. "I brought little Peter to your house."

"And Celine?"

"She stayed up at her house."

"What for?"

"God knows," Drew said. "Maybe she plans on holding a fancy dress ball," he added, and left the room quickly, because he knew his remark would irritate his father.

"Children!" Jan said to David.

"You should talk," David said with a sigh. "Those twins of mine would test the patience of a saint."

Jan poured two more drinks. "I've a great fear that we're about to suffer a defeat at the hands of the British. Maybe we rushed things along too quickly."

"If we waited for the king to accede to our demands, we'd be waiting forever."

Jan sighed. "New York being attacked by an invading army—hard to believe. It's the first time it's ever happened, did you know that?"

David nodded. "Yes, I did."

Jan explained for the benefit of Philemon Peabody. "The English took it away from the Dutch without firing a shot. The Dutch took it back the same way. It became English again by treaty. Well, we've had a hundred and fifty years of peace here. Maybe when this is over, we'll have another hundred and fifty."

David nodded toward the bottle. "That Jersey Lightning is turning you soft in the head."

"Maybe this is a good time for it."

David stood up. "I'd better get home and find out what mischief Jemmy and Jenny are up to."

Jan smiled. The Sackett twins had reputations as terrible troublemakers; God knows what they might do now. "Maybe they're planning on blowing up your house as a protest."

David sighed. "Keep an eye on them while I'm away, will you?"

"You're leaving town again?"

"I must. The Congress is meeting in Philadelphia in two days. It's up to you to look after things."

"Let's hope there'll still be something left to look after by then," Jan said glumly.

It was noon, and Drew was sweating as he placed the last of the boards across the doors of the warehouse on Beaver Street. A group of horsemen galloped madly down Broad Way. He recognized the leader as General Israel Putnam—Old Put, as everyone called him behind his back. Drew was aware that Putnam had been up north at Washington's headquarters, and he wondered what had brought him back here now. Were they planning on a defense of the city?

He decided this was something worth finding out. He slammed the last nail into the wood and went to get his horse. He followed the riders down to the Battery and saw the militia officers gathering about the general. Drew got off his horse and edged his way closer to the center of the throng.

General Putnam was patiently explaining what had happened and how, plainly, the events made it impossible for them to hold the city. Therefore, he announced, he was planning to go north with every last man to join the remnants of Washington's forces at Harlem Heights.

"The British will have spread over the island by now, so we'll probably have to fight," the dour old general said. "And it's about time we showed the British the American army knows how to fight."

A cheer went up from the men, and the general waved his arm for silence. "The time to cheer, lads, is after we've won the battle."

THE CITY INVADED

He gave orders for all the troops in the city to gather at the Battery and be prepared to march north in force. Then he called for volunteers to go ahead of the main force to scout the enemy's strength. He said he wanted men who knew every inch of ground between the Battery and Harlem Heights.

"I know this island like the back of my hand, sir," Drew called out. "I'll go."

The general looked at the young man and noted he was not wearing a uniform. A cloud of suspicion crossed his mind. "And who are you?"

"Andrew de Kuyper, sir."

Recognition flickered in the general's eyes. "Related to Jan de Kuyper?"

"My father."

The general accepted these credentials. "Now tell me, what would be our best line of march?"

"Since the British attacked from the east, sir, I'd say the best route would be up the Greenwich Road until it comes to the river. Then follow the shoreline north."

"Tough going once the road ends," the general said. "Speed is important, you understand."

Drew understood. "The fastest way would be to take the Greenwich Road to the Bloomingdale Road, which goes right up to the Heights. The problem is, the British have probably advanced that far by now."

"Unfortunately, you're probably right," the general said. He turned to Major Aaron Burr, who was a pace behind him. "Alert all commanders we march in two hours. If they're not here by then, it's too bad."

Burr nodded and looked at Drew, whom he knew slightly. "Finally got you in the army, have we?"

"Not yet," Drew said. "I'm not overly fond of uniforms."

"Get ready to see a lot of red ones."

"I know, I was up at Kip's Bay this morning."

Burr looked surprised. "And you're still willing to scout?"

"Someone's got to do it."

Burr held out his hand. "We might even become friends."

"I wasn't aware we'd been enemies," Drew said, accepting the other's hand.

Burr laughed, and suddenly realized the general was giving him a smoldering look. "On my way, sir."

* * *

Within two hours over three thousand men had assembled at the Battery. General Putnam ordered the bulky equipment left behind, because, as he said, it was speed that was going to save them. Drew rode out ahead to scout the terrain as the main body began to march north.

He went up Broad Way until he came to Cortlandt Street, turned left, and proceeded along Cortlandt until he came to the Greenwich Road, which paralleled the North River. It was eerie now to be riding through the familiar streets; they were almost deserted. Many houses were boarded up, and it saddened Drew to find the usually bustling city silenced.

He followed the pleasant road through the village of Greenwich. A few people were out in the dusty streets, and they looked queerly at him, as if wondering why a lone rider was going north when the rumor was that thousands of redcoats were up that way.

Greenwich Village had become a favorite place for New Yorkers to spend their summers. Here were many shade trees and cooling brooks that twisted and purled their way down to the river. To the north of the village there were large green fields, dotted with black-and-white cows who stolidly munched their way through the grass, war or no war.

When he reached the estates of Oliver de Lancey and William Bayard, he became more cautious: he was sure he'd soon be encountering his first British soldiers. But he saw nothing as he continued north until he picked up the beginnings of the Bloomingdale Road where it forked off the Post Road.

He stopped and considered the situation. By now, surely, the British must be spreading across the island. But where were they? If they hadn't yet reached the Bloomingdale Road, it might be possible for Putnam's column to make use of this speedy highway. They could save many hours getting to the Heights. He rode to the top of a small knoll, which afforded a good view of the road for more than a mile.

Not a redcoat in sight. He thought for another moment, and then rode recklessly back in the direction he had just come. Within twenty minutes he came upon the advance troops plodding along the road. He rode past them, found General Putnam, and reported what he had seen.

"It doesn't seem possible," the general said. "My God, man, the British should have taken that road hours ago."

"But they haven't," Drew said. "I saw it with my own eyes."

"Well, the hell with *why* they haven't taken it," Putnam

THE CITY INVADED

growled. "We'll take advantage of it. You go up ahead, and let me know the moment you see a sign of the British."

"Yes, sir," Drew said. He went past the column of sweating men and returned to the Bloomingdale Road. He went north until he was parallel with Kip's Bay; still no sign of the British. They could have come this far if they had *crawled,* he thought.

What in God's name were the British doing?

"Surely you'll have another glass of wine," Celine said as General Howe gallantly held out his arm and helped her up the steps to the back porch of the Place. "Your throat must be parched from all this heat."

"Perhaps another small one, Mrs. Murray," the general said, touching his hand to his throat. They were returning from a tour of Celine's flower gardens at the rear of the house, and the afternoon sun was making him uncomfortable under his heavy tunic.

They went into the coolness of the house and returned to the parlor, where Mary sat with the other three officers. General Clinton and Colonel Cunningham looked annoyed, but Captain Blakely sat next to Mary. He seemed to be enjoying himself thoroughly; Mary seemed amply pleased with the attention he was paying her. Celine noticed and frowned; she had only met this captain, but there was something *deadly* about him.

"There you are, Howe," General Clinton said dryly. "We thought you might have fallen into the hands of the enemy."

"But he has, you see," Celine said brightly. "After all, I'm an American."

General Howe laughed and permitted himself the liberty of squeezing her hand. He was a tall, handsome man with dark, penetrating eyes. It was said of him that he liked his glass, his lass, and his game of cards. During the past year in Boston, his affair with Mrs. Joshua Loring had become the scandal of the British army. However, since he was a second cousin of the king, no one had been foolhardy enough to openly question his dalliance.

He accepted the glass of wine from Celine and allowed himself the pleasure of a long look into her eyes. She managed to make her eyelids flutter, and then moved to refill the other officers' glasses.

"Really, Mrs. Murray," General Clinton protested. "It's time we were about our business."

Celine would have none of this. "After all you went through today, you deserve a rest."

Clinton pointed to a large grandfather clock on the wall opposite the fireplace. "It's already four o'clock, madam."

"Four o'clock?" General Howe said in surprise. "I had no idea it was so late."

General Clinton placed his full glass down on the table and got to his feet. "I must get back to my troops, sir."

Colonel Cunningham also rose, but Captain Blakely was openly staring into Mary's eyes. "It appears we are going," he said.

"So soon?" Mary asked, reaching out and touching the captain's hand. She had been told by Celine to be flirtatious, but found there was no need to pretend to find the captain attractive.

"We must press on," Clinton said.

"We've already accomplished a good day's work," General Howe said. "We'll hold our present positions for the night."

"And not take advantage of the situation?" Clinton asked in wonder.

"The situation will be the same tomorrow," Howe assured his second-in-command. "We'll take advantage then."

"In that case, why don't you dine with me?" Celine said, looking directly at Howe. "All of you, of course," she added.

"I accept," Howe said.

"My staff expects me back," Clinton protested.

"And I have much work to do," Cunningham said; and then he noticed the way Blakely and Mary were looking at one another. *"We* have much work to do," he amended.

"It seems I must go," the captain said to Mary. If it was obvious she was attracted to him, he in turn made no secret of his interest in her.

"Perhaps another time," she replied.

"Well, General," Celine said, "it looks as if I'll have you all to myself at dinner."

"Let's try to muddle through, shall we?"

As the three officers were departing, the colonel told General Howe that he was leaving the sergeant outside with a detachment.

"Perhaps you could post guards around the perimeter of this farm," the general said.

"Perimeter guards, sir?"

"Yes. I may wish to make this house my temporary field headquarters."

Cunningham wasn't clever enough to conceal his emotions, and a look of indignation came over him. "Yes, sir," he said stiffly, and left the house.

The general went to the window and watched his officers depart. Celine came to stand at his side. "They seemed a bit peeved with you."

"By the time one has become a commanding general, my dear, one has learned that everyone is always peeved with you. It's because the commander gets to make all the decisions, and what else is life but an endless string of decisions?"

"But some are more important than others," Celine said playfully.

"Yes, that's true," Howe said, suddenly in a serious mood. "Before we go any further, Mrs. Murray, let me express my regrets about this war. We are one family, speaking one tongue and worshipping one God. It is an unnatural war."

Celine immediately realized why it had been so easy to dally with this man and detain him. He had *wanted* to be detained — and not just because of her. She dropped her lighthearted attitude. "Maybe everyone will come to their senses and bring it to a halt."

"My most fervent wish," he said, and then a smile returned to his lips. "And now, perhaps, Mrs. Murray, you would be good enough to get out a deck of cards so we can get down to a serious game of whist?"

In the waning hours of the afternoon, as Celine and General Howe sat in her parlor playing whist, the main column of Putnam's army was making good time northward on the Bloomingdale Road. Drew, as scout, ranged a quarter mile ahead and to the east, because if a British threat materialized, it would come from that direction.

As he rode his horse through the rolling hills of Manhatan, he noted the thick late-summer brush and realized the rough terrain would confine the British columns to the roads. By the same token, the rugged countryside would favor troops who took up defensive positions. He guided his horse around an outcropping of rock, forded a small stream, and followed a narrow valley until the ground rose and he came to the crest of a hill. From this position he looked west and saw the first troops of Putnam's column moving along the Bloomingdale Road.

But what startled him was the view eastward: another column was going north up the Post Road. The crimson coats identified the troops as British.

Drew could hardly believe his eyes. Here were two large columns of troops from opposing forces making their way north on almost parallel courses. He realized the Americans were unaware of the British, but it appeared the British were equally unaware of the Americans. The two columns were only a half mile apart, yet the hills completely hid them from each other.

He whirled his horse about and made his way back to the Bloomingdale Road, where he again sought out General Putnam. The general listened intently as Drew made his report.

"The roads come closer together up north," Drew said. "At the rate the two columns are moving, we have the edge. I think we can get through McGown's Pass before the British arrive."

"What's the significance of that?"

"The land becomes steeper at the pass—it's the beginning of Harlem Heights. The hills close in on the road, so it's a natural place to leave a rear guard."

"Good enough," Putnam said, and he was impressed by the young man's knowledge of terrain and his awareness of military tactics. When his troops filed through McGown's Pass, he left a detachment of Marylanders to take up defensive positions, thus protecting the rear of his retreating army.

Drew, as scout, was the first man from Putnam's column to reach Washington's encampment, and the commander was delighted to learn the bulk of his southern forces had escaped the clutches of the enemy.

"What's your name, lad?" he asked.

"Andrew de Kuyper, sir."

"De Kuyper? Oh, of course, Jan's son. And how is your sister, Mrs. Murray?"

"I'm not sure, sir. Her home isn't far from Kip's Bay. I'm sure she's in the hands of the British."

The general frowned. "Well, the British aren't savages. I'm sure they'll not harm women."

"I hope not," Drew said, suddenly realizing how much he cared for Celine despite their lifelong sniping and bickering. She had always assumed the role of the older, wiser sister, and it had galled him. But now that she might be in danger...

He was still with Washington when Putnam arrived. He listened as the crusty old fellow informed the commander-in-chief of the day's events. It was a grim situation, with hardly a glimmer of good news. The single bright spot of the afternoon came a bit later, when a messenger arrived with the information that the Maryland rear guard had skirmished with the British at McGown's Pass, and the British had withdrawn.

"It was this young man's idea to leave the rear guard there," Putnam said, acknowledging Drew's contribution.

General Washington nodded in appreciation and looked a bit more closely at the man. Drew had shown brains and a quick responsiveness, two qualities the general found sorely lacking in his army.

The general, however, had little time to waste on past events, and turned to the more pressing need of planning the defenses of the following day.

Drew drifted away in search of something to eat. He was a young man with a young man's appetite, and had eaten nothing since the toasted bread at Fraunces Tavern early in the morning. He managed to come across a soldier who had an extra ration of deer meat and was willing to share it with him. In this he was fortunate, because food was scarce and more than half the men went to sleep that night with no more than a crust of bread or a potato in their stomachs. There was a shortage of tents, and thousands of men were forced to sleep under the open sky. This wouldn't have been a problem, except a sudden rain squall fell at dusk and many men were soaked to their skins, Drew among them. At least, he thought, trying to find some comfort in the situation, the rain washed away the muggy heat that had plagued him all day.

Before he had a chance to get any sleep, he was approached by Lieutenant Colonel Thomas Knowlton, the commander of the Rangers. He asked many questions about the strength of the British column. When the colonel was satisfied he had learned as much as he could, he offered Drew the opportunity to go with his unit the next morning.

"We'll be out before dawn," the colonel said. "We should be the first to make contact with the British."

Drew jumped at the chance, because if there was anything resembling a glamour outfit in Washington's army, it was the Rangers.

It was still dark when Knowlton led his men down the bluffs to flat land. The Rangers were composed of some one hundred and twenty men, mostly from Connecticut and Massachusetts. They were a rough-and-ready group and moved cross-country rather than yielding to the convenience of the roads.

Drew remembered that his sister's friend Nathan Hale was a member of the Rangers. He asked the colonel about him.

"Hale's on a special mission," Knowlton replied tersely.

"He was at my sister's house yesterday when the British attacked," Drew volunteered, hoping to learn more of the special mission.

"Your sister's house?" the colonel said, failing to hide his surprise. "What was he doing there?"

"Personal reasons, no doubt."

"Damn the man!" the colonel muttered. "He's supposed to stick to business."

Drew attempted to press the issue and find out what this business was, but Colonel Knowlton remained closemouthed. "It's not a matter I wish to discuss," he said, firmly ending the conversation.

The Rangers moved easily over the land until they came upon their first British troops—a series of pickets guarding the head of the Bloomingdale Road. Knowlton moved his men forward with no attempt at concealment. The British began firing, and the Americans returned the fusillade. This, in turn, caused more British troops to leave their bivouac and come forward to engage the Americans.

The two lines were too far apart from each other to do much damage, because the most common weapon on both sides was the cumbersome English flintlock known as the Brown Bess. Unlike the long-barreled rifles made by German and Swiss immigrants in eastern Pennsylvania, the Brown Bess was a most inaccurate weapon. One rarely aimed it, but merely pointed it in the general direction where the lead slug was supposed to go, and tried to keep from flinching too hard when the weapon went off with a belch of flame. General Washington had been begging the Congress for more of the long rifles, but they were scarce.

Besides being accurate, the Pennsylvania rifle was also easier and quicker to load. The rifle ball could be rammed down to the powder with a slender wooden rod, because the one-ounce slug fit loosely and was accompanied by a piece of greased linen that facilitated its passage. On the other hand, the heavier musket ball had to fit very snugly; consequently a great deal of strength was needed to pound it home with a heavy iron rod and, as was sometimes required, a mallet.

A good man could be expected to fire a musket four times in four minutes, whereas a good rifleman could get off eight or nine shots in the same time. The advantage the musket had was that its heavier slug packed more punch; but this advantage was more than offset by the greater accuracy of the lighter weapon.

Drew found himself actually enjoying the skirmish. After the tediousness of making his way up the island the previous day, at last he was involved in something exciting!

The fighting was broken off when Colonel Knowlton heard the skirl of approaching bagpipes. They signaled the arrival of a detachment of the Royal Highland Regiment of Foot—the famous Black Watch. The Watch was the most feared unit in the British forces. Most of the men were wild Highlanders, who spoke only Erse and were picked for their height. They wore kilts, short red coats, white vests, goatskin pouches, and Highland bonnets, and wrapped themselves in a twelve-foot length of distinctive tartan. They always entered battle accompanied by the sound of pipes.

Knowlton realized his small force couldn't stand up to an entire regiment, and prudently called the retreat. The Rangers moved back across the countryside, climbed back up the bluffs, and made their report to the commander.

General Washington had spent a sleepless night making his plans. The troops under General Greene moved down the bluffs and began to form a line of defense. They were joined by detachments of Marylanders and New Yorkers. In addition, Washington put together a special unit composed of almost three hundred men, which he placed under Colonel Knowlton's command. This unit was to go into the rough terrain to the east and attack the British from the flank as they moved against the American main force.

Washington's plan was to keep his main front deceptively small. A detachment was sent out in front of Greene's force, and this small group would be the first the British came upon. The idea was to get the enemy to think there was little opposition. They would move forward, and the Americans would fall back. The clever part was that when the British finally did get to Greene's main force, they would be moving uphill. The Americans would have the advantage of looking down on their enemies.

The British took the bait, and soon they were struggling uphill to engage the enemy. At this point Washington ordered more units down the hill to increase the pressure.

Drew, in the meantime, was traversing the hills to the east

with the Rangers, moving slowly south to bring them around to the flank of the British. It was a good plan, but unfortunately a few of the Rangers became trigger-happy, and alerted the enemy to their presence. The British responded by sending out a flanking party of their own, and the Rangers found themselves face to face with the enemy instead of being able to fall on them from the side or the rear.

The greatest loss of the day came when Knowlton stood on a small ridge to get a better view of the British positions. Drew was standing two feet away when the musketball struck the colonel in the back. He cried out in pain and fell to the ground. Drew went to the wounded man's side. "You'll be all right, sir," he said, trying to give the colonel, and himself, some hope. But then he looked at the gaping wound and knew all hope was in vain.

"Don't worry about me," the colonel said through clenched teeth. "Get on with the fight."

The decision was made to pull the Rangers back and abandon the flanking attack, since it was now impossible to gain surprise. When they finally rejoined the main force, Knowlton was dead.

The Rangers added their strength to the units engaging the British in a large cornfield near the North River. The battle swelled until there were over four thousand men involved.

The fighting waged back and forth, and Washington became alarmed at the appalling waste of precious gunpowder. Then, after two hours, the British decided they had had enough and went into full retreat. The hotheads among Washington's officers wanted to pursue the enemy, but the general wisely allowed the British to go on their way. He was well aware there were tens of thousands more British troops farther down the island, and his men were in no condition to face a fresh army. The buglers called retreat, and the Americans made their way back to the relative safety of the Heights.

The commander-in-chief came to pay his last respects to the fallen Colonel Knowlton, one of the finest and bravest men in his command. After saying a short prayer over the body, he looked at Drew, who had remained with the dead man after bringing him back to camp.

"Were you with him when it happened?"

"Yes."

"We can ill afford to lose a Knowlton," the general said quietly, and Drew's heart filled with compassion for this man who faced each day knowing he must accept the deaths of men who were his friends as well as his subordinates.

"I'd like to join your army, General," he said with a sudden surge of patriotic zeal.

Washington looked surprised. "I assumed you already were with the army."

Drew explained the circumstances that had brought him to the Heights. He also told the general what his father had said about being of greater use in another capacity.

"Your father is right," the general said.

"But, sir..."

"Hear me out. Go back to the city. Pretend to sympathize with the British. In fact, have your father do the same. With your family's resources, you'll be in an excellent position to help our cause."

"If that's what you wish, sir."

"It is," the general said. They spoke for a little longer, and Drew's curiosity got the better of him and he asked about Nathan Hale and his secret mission.

The general studied him for a moment. "I've been looking for Hale and haven't been able to find him," he said, without adding a word of amplification.

"My sister might know where he is."

"I want you to deliver a message to him. Come to my tent in an hour," the general said, turning and leaving Drew as mystified as ever about Hale's mission.

An hour later he stopped at the commander's tent, was given a sealed message, and started on his way down to the city.

He kept off the roads, and although he caught sight of many British soldiers on his trip down the island, he managed to avoid contact with them. He arrived in the city: here too there were many British soldiers, but from their fresh-looking condition it was obvious they had encountered little resistance. There was a relaxed mood in the air, a far cry from the atmosphere of the battlefield up north. He rode to Maiden Lane, took his horse to the stable in back, and entered his father's house.

"Where the hell have you been?" Jan greeted him as he stepped through the double doors opening into the parlor.

"Up north with Washington," Drew answered. "There was a big battle and we won."

"We won?" Philemon Peabody said in surprise. The little man was seated in a chair in the corner.

"I know it's difficult to believe, but we fought well and the British finally retreated."

"Not like down here," Jan said in disgust. "The British just walked in without having to fire a shot. I figured the revolution was all over."

Drew related his conversation with General Washington, telling how the general asked him to remain in New York instead of joining the army.

"A bloody spy, that's what he wants you to be," Jan said.

Drew poured himself a glass of Madeira. "You were the one who said I might be of more use in the city. Well, apparently the general agrees."

"And you'll hang if they catch you," Jan said. "Spying wasn't exactly what I had in mind."

"Earlier today they were trying to shoot me. What's the difference?"

Philemon Peabody had been listening as the other men talked, and his fertile brain was mulling over the possibilities. "I think we have a rare opportunity here," he finally said. "If you act sympathetic to the British, it should be possible to also do business with them. But we'll have Washington as a customer as well. Can't you see what kind of profits we might make from such an arrangement?"

"Christ Almighty!" Drew said angrily. "Now you plan to bleed Washington and the Continental Army!"

"Not as much as we'll bleed the British," Peabody said, looking to Jan for approval. "What's wrong with making money?"

"How you make it is important," Drew said.

"I tell you we can take most of it from the British. After all, they've got more to spend," Peabody said. "What do you think of that?" he asked Jan.

The older de Kuyper looked away from his son. As usual, his protection of Peabody was alienating him from other people, but Jan de Kuyper was a most loyal man. "In a way, when we drain money from the British we'll be helping Washington," he said, finding a rather weak defense.

"It seems immoral to me," Drew said.

"As you grow older, you'll find nothing immoral about making money," Peabody said.

"We can make money off the British, and donate our services to Washington," Jan said.

"That's not what I had in mind," Peabody said quickly.

"I still have the final say around here," Jan said with an edge to his voice. "And that's what we're going to do."

"Of course, Jan," Peabody said, adopting a subservient mien now that Jan had made up his mind about the project.

"So what are you planning to do?" Jan asked his son.

"The first thing I must do is find Captain Nathan Hale. I have a message for him from the general."

"Nathan Hale?" Jan said, his brow furrowing. "I don't think I know him."

"Your daughter does," Drew said. "The last time I saw him, he was running out of her house."

The reminder of Celine worried Jan. "We've got to get her down here. I've heard some stories about how these Hessians act. She'll be safer with us."

"I'll go up to the Place and see how she is," Drew said. "Maybe she can tell me something of Hale."

"What's his connection with Celine?"

Drew smiled. "She's your daughter. If you haven't figured out her connection with men, you never will."

Jan scowled. "When the hell is she going to settle down?"

"She tried that once. I don't think she liked it."

While Drew and his father dealt with family matters, Philemon Peabody poured himself a glass of ale and concerned himself with thoughts he considered more important. It was all well and good for the de Kuypers not to worry about making great profits; they were rich men who didn't have to worry about such things.

But Philemon Peabody didn't have enough money to suit his tastes. Nor would he ever have enough, he admitted to himself. The stink of his boyhood poverty still haunted him, and drove him on in quest of riches. He had known what it was like to cry himself to sleep because he was hungry. He had known what it was like to sleep in doorways and alleys and gutters.

Well, it was never going to happen again. The de Kuypers could forgo all the profits they wished, but he had no intention of doing so. While they concerned themselves with the course of the war, he would handle the money and keep the books. It would be a fairly easy matter to insure that a reasonable share of that money ended up in his own pocket.

The problem with the de Kuypers, he decided, was they had been born with money and had never learned to appreciate its importance. To them money was something that was always around and easy to get. They couldn't really understand there were people in the world who did not know the luxury of possessing an extra penny.

This new situation of pretending to be friends of the British could be his big chance, he thought. People would certainly be spending money in unprecedented ways.

Maybe the war would turn out to be the best thing that ever happened to him, he concluded.

Earlier in the day, as the two armies clashed in the north, General Howe enjoyed a splendid lunch with Celine on the verandah of the Place. Chilled wines were served along with warm bread, fresh vegetables, and duck in aspic. Generous slices of a luscious cold melon were served with the port. The general settled back in his chair and smiled at his hostess. She was quite the loveliest thing he had seen in a long time.

"If you wish to smoke a pipe, you may," Celine said. "I find the scent of tobacco quite manly."

"Your fondness of the odor is almost enough to make me take up smoking, madam. However, until this moment it has never appealed to me."

"Don't take it up on my account," she said. "I don't want to be accused of getting the commanding general to take up bad habits."

"But is it bad?" he asked. "Seems perfectly harmless. Unless, of course, you fall asleep while smoking in bed and burn the house down."

"If you smoked, would you smoke in *bed?*"

"Not as a rule," the general said in amusement. "I normally go to bed with something else in mind."

"Sleep, no doubt."

"No doubt."

"Are you teasing me, General?" she asked. "Having been married, I'm something of a worldly woman. I know all about men."

Howe smiled again. This was coming along more easily than he had thought possible. "But not all men are the same, Mrs. Murray. I wonder if you're aware of that."

"How do they differ?"

"Some men never learn to appreciate the finer qualities of a woman."

"My late husband, I'm sorry to say, was like that," Celine said. "All he cared about were his horses. He went out at the crack of dawn and came home exhausted at night."

"Not a very perceptive man."

"Whereas you are?"

"I do my best, madam."

"If you had been my husband, then, you would have acted in a different way?"

"Of course."

"How?"

It was like playing chess, he thought. She had offered a move. He countered with one of his own. "When a man is offered gold, he should no longer concern himself with lead."

"I guess my hair could qualify as gold."

"And the rest of you as well."

"Your *tongue* is golden, general."

"Perhaps, then, we have much in common."

"There is very little common about you, sir. But then who would know that better than you yourself?"

"Perhaps a woman as intelligent and perceptive as you," he said, delighted in being able to cap her remark and continue building their word pyramid, which was becoming more attractive moment by moment.

"To perceive the obvious is hardly a sign of a distinguished intelligence," Celine said as she refilled their wineglasses.

It was the general's turn, but the game was interrupted by the arrival of Captain Blakely. He had been sent by Colonel Cunningham to inform the commander that the city had been taken without resistance.

"Prisoners?" the general asked.

"Several hundred, sir. Rebel soldiers who remained in the city."

"You plan on setting up a prison?"

"Yes, sir. It's necessary."

The general glanced at Celine. "Only a temporary measure, my dear," he said in a calming voice. He looked back at the captain. "I want no prisoners abused, do you understand."

"Yes, sir, I understand."

"Make sure Colonel Cunningham understands as well. We will not make martyrs out of these prisoners."

"The colonel has a question concerning yourself, sir."

"Yes?"

"Does the general intend to remain overnight in this house?" Blakely asked, and pointedly looked at Celine.

Damn the man! the general thought, his anger rising. He has no respect for anyone or anything. But Blakely continued before Howe could voice a reprimand.

"I'm only asking, sir, because Colonel Cunningham wishes to add men to the guard here if those are your plans."

The general looked at Celine. "This is your home, Mrs. Murray. It would be unseemly of me to force myself upon you as a guest."

"There can be no force when the invitation has already been extended," she said.

The general smiled, and then remembered the captain was still in the room. "Inform the colonel I'll remain here," he said.

"Very good, sir," Blakely said. "Have a good evening, sir," he added blandly as he left the room.

"Impertinent chap," the general said in annoyance. "Half the time I think he's sneering at me. But a man in his line of work must have some form of relief, I suppose, because he sees far too much of the dark side of human nature."

"And generals do not?"

"Heavens no, my dear," Howe said with a chuckle. "Generals are like little boys playing with wooden soldiers. They move this regiment here, and that battalion there, and then call for ships to form a blockade. It all comes down to a game, because generals must forget they are dealing with real human beings. Far from dealing with the dark side of human nature, we completely forget there *is* such a thing as human nature."

"I don't believe that about you for a moment," Celine said. "You've far too much compassion not to care about the men who serve under you."

"You've found out my secret, my dear," the general said. "It is the bane of every commander's life that he must send his men into battle knowing many of them will die. To protect his sanity he *must* begin to pretend they are only numbers, not flesh and blood. Otherwise, I'm afraid, he could never face himself in the mirror."

"You chose a strange profession for a man who thinks the way you do."

"Actually my profession chose me. The Howes have been serving our king in military service for hundreds of years. My eldest brother, who's dead now, chose the army, the second brother the sea, and I elected to take the army. I've often thought how different my life might have been had I been born into a different sort of family. But then, of course, I would have been denied one of the greatest pleasures of my life."

"And what is that?" Celine asked.

"Meeting you."

Celine smiled and excused herself. She went to her bedroom and was running a brush through her hair when Mary Delafield knocked on the door.

"We have our guest for dinner again tonight," Celine informed her cousin.

"Must I retire early again, and leave you two alone as I did last night?" Mary asked.

"Not tonight," Celine said. "The general behaved like a perfect gentleman last night, because that was the impression he was trying to make—that he *is* a perfect gentleman. I think he'll be a bit more randy tonight. So stay with me."

"You want me around for protection?"

"I'm perfectly capable of taking care of myself," Celine said archly. "Having you around will make him anxious."

Mary was sitting on the edge of the large bed, and she shook her head. "How did you ever learn so much about men? I wouldn't know where to begin in a situation like this."

"Now Mary Delafield, I saw you making eyes at that handsome captain."

"He *was* good-looking, wasn't he!"

"I have a hunch he's as dangerous as a snake. Watch your step with him."

"Don't tell me you didn't find him attractive."

"Attractive, yes," Celine said honestly. "But not really my type. He *did* get to you, though, didn't he?"

"There was something about him that... well, it made me churn inside," Mary said, and then sighed. "But I'm a married woman."

"What does that have to do with it?"

"Really, Celine, you know how I feel about marriage... even when it isn't what you'd hoped it would be."

"The trouble with marriage is it takes the mystery out of everything. It's really a bore."

Mary shook her head. "It's a sacred institution."

"Because a dried-up prune of a dominie says so?" Celine asked. She snapped her fingers. "That's how much I care for his opinion."

Mary giggled. "And you look so pious in church."

"I go only because of my son," Celine said. "When he's old enough, he'll make up his own mind about church. If he has any sense, he'll forget about it."

Mary threw her hands up in mock horror. "I'm afraid to stay in the same room with you. The lightning may hit me, too."

Celine finished combing her hair and put the brush back on the dressing table. "Remember to stay with me to the bitter end tonight. I want the good general to lie awake all night thinking of me. Maybe a lack of sleep will cause him to make wrong decisions that will help our own army."

She started for the door and paused. "You know something? I'm really beginning to like Mr. Howe. Wouldn't it be ironic if I fell in love with a British general?"

"You couldn't!"

"Why not? Beneath his uniform he's just another man—but probably better than most. I might even marry him."

Mary laughed. "At this point your father would be glad to see you marry *anyone*."

"But don't hold your breath," Celine said, and slipped out the door ahead of Mary.

As Captain Blakely left Celine's house, he was annoyed with himself; he had not presented his case for getting tough with the prisoners. The general obviously intended to coddle them. They were rebels, dammit! Rebels against the Crown.

He rode his horse down the sweeping path and came to the gate, where two soldiers were on duty. One of them snapped to a rigid attention, but the other moved slowly and slovenly.

The captain was delighted to find someone to vent his wrath on. "You!" he snapped. "Is that the best you can do when an officer approaches?"

The man jerked his body to a ramrod position, tucking his chin down in a tight brace.

"Ah, so you do know how to come to a proper attention. You just like to take your time about it." He turned to the other guard. "Fetch your sergeant."

The guard saluted and took off on the double toward the barn, where the guard had established its command post. The captain sat silently on his horse, all the while glaring at the soldier who had offended him. Within moments the other guard returned with his sergeant.

"What's this man's name?" Blakely asked the under-officer, ignoring the man's salute.

"Hibbs, sir," the sergeant said after a quick glance at the braced soldier.

"Hibbs has forgotten how to stand at attention. Three dozen lashes should help him remember."

"Yes, sir!"

There was a short pause, but nobody moved.

Blakely looked down at the sergeant. "Well?"

"Beggin' the captain's pardon, d'you mean *now*, sir?"

"Of course I mean now."

"Again, beggin' the captain's pardon, but we've only arrived here and not set up a proper place for punishment."

"Dammit, man! Take him into the barn and tie him to the side of a stall."

The sergeant saluted. "Hibbs, follow me!" he barked.

Captain Blakely rode his horse into the barn and remained in the saddle while the unhappy soldier had his shirt removed and was tied to two thick posts that supported the side of a stall. The sergeant had a nasty moment when he couldn't find the baize bag containing the cat-o'-nine-tails. He was acutely aware of the dirty looks he was getting from the captain, and it was with great relief that he spotted the bag in a field trunk containing cooking equipment.

The vicious-looking cat emerged from the bag, and the sergeant snapped it to work the stiffness out of the leather. The nine strips of leather each held a half-dozen knots. When the sergeant was satisfied the whip was limber, he handed it to a stout corporal. "Three dozen, well laid on."

The corporal took up his position behind the mute but trembling soldier, ran the thongs through his hand several times, brought the whip back over his shoulder, and whirled it around with all the strength in his body.

"One!" the sergeant intoned.

The knotted strips of leather made nine tracks of blood appear on the man's back as if by magic. Hibbs grunted in pain.

"Two!"

This time he grunted louder and chewed on the lead bullet the sergeant had given him to keep him from biting his tongue.

"Three!"

"Four!"

"Five!"

Hibbs's control snapped, and he screamed. The lead slug dropped from his mouth to the dirt of the barn floor. His back was now a mass of cuts and welts, and dripping blood that seeped down into the tops of his trousers.

The lash kept hissing viciously through the air; now the leather knots were landing on flesh that was already an open wound, and the man was screaming in agony.

"Twelve!"

"Thirteen!"

"Fourteen!"

Celine was leaving her bedroom when she heard the screams coming from the barn.

She went downstairs and out onto the porch to listen. There was no doubt. She could hear the crack of the lash as it landed on human flesh, followed by another scream. She grabbed the edges of her long skirt and started across the lawn toward the barn.

General Howe was still in the parlor, and he too heard the screams. He went to the window and saw his hostess hurrying across the closely cropped grass. Without hesitating, he walked to the front door, opened it, and went after Celine.

"Twenty-one!"

"Twenty-two!"

The screams were no longer strident, but were now more like choking sobs as the man's strength diminished. The half-dozen soldiers who were watching had seen a great deal of this sort of punishment, and were aware their comrade would be unconscious by the time the last stroke was delivered.

"Twenty-three!"

"Twenty-four!"

"Stop that!"

The corporal, who was now sweating from the exertion, paused with the lash over his shoulder. He saw the woman in the doorway and looked hesitatingly at the sergeant.

"I forbid you to hit that man again," Celine said angrily. "This is *my* barn, and we'll have none of that here."

"Sir?" the sergeant said, looking to Captain Blakely for instructions.

The captain hesitated. He knew he was well within his rights in ordering the lash as punishment. But this woman was very friendly with the commanding general. It was a touchy situation.

"This is purely a matter concerning discipline in the British army, Mrs. Murray. Please don't interfere."

"You will not touch that man again."

The soldiers in the barn suddenly stiffened to attention as the imposing figure of General Howe walked in and stood beside the woman. "What's going on here?" he asked.

"This man is receiving punishment, sir," the captain said.

"And it will cease here and now," Celine said.

"Now, now, my dear," the general said in a conciliatory tone. "Discipline must be maintained."

"There will be no whippings on my property," she insisted.

The general looked at her flushed face and knew his budding friendship would never bloom if he permitted the punishment to continue. On the other hand, he clearly understood that to a considerable extent his army's efficiency was maintained through strict discipline. The situation clearly called for tact.

"Mrs. Murray's point is well taken," he said to Blakely, who was seated stiffly in his saddle. "No more punishment will be delivered on her property."

The captain grimaced.

"Don't look at me in that manner, sir," the general said testily. "It's a simple matter to move the man elsewhere for punishment."

"Yes, sir," the captain said.

Celine turned and walked back toward the house. "Take him out of here," the general said, indicating the whipped man. He then hurried after Celine to soothe her ruffled feelings.

Captain Blakely nodded, and two soldiers stepped forward to untie the bleeding figure.

"Shall that do it?" the sergeant asked.

"I believe I ordered three dozen," the captain said.

"Yes, sir."

"Take him off this blasted woman's land and finish the job."

"Yes, sir."

The whipped man was still conscious, and he winced. By the time he was taken elsewhere and tied up again he would have completely revived; he would not enjoy the boon of being unconscious for the final dozen.

The captain rode out of the barn and continued his journey down to the city. There was work to be done. Colonel Cunningham was establishing the provost marshal's offices in the prison building at the head of the Commons. There were many orders to be issued and many arrangements to be made to take control of the city.

As he rode south, he passed various units of the army. They looked fresh and untested. Blakely had heard reports of the fighting at the northern end of the island, but obviously none of it was occurring down here.

He became angry at the thought of that damned woman interfering with the punishment. And the general! He was determined to treat the rebels with kindness. Maybe there was a way to change his mind. If the general could be convinced of the rebels' treachery, he would have no course of action but to allow Cunningham a free hand. That was it: the general had to be convinced that harsh treatment was the only way to keep these people in line.

But what would be convincing to the commander? What would make him change his mind?

The captain wasn't sure what was needed, but he knew the answer existed and it was up to him to find it. He wouldn't stand about waiting for something to happen; he would go out and *make* it happen.

He arrived in the city and went to the prison, where dozens of soldiers were fixing up the rooms to be used by the provost marshal and his staff. He found Colonel Cunningham in his office, working even as two men at his back hammered a table together.

"We've about four hundred prisoners right now," Cunningham said. "But I expect a lot more to be coming down from the north."

"Are we to prepare their baths?" Blakely asked sarcastically.

The colonel grimaced. "I've no mind to coddle prisoners, but you know the general's orders."

"Maybe he'll change his mind."

"I don't know about that. This General Willie acts like he'd rather be having the rebels to tea than fighting them."

"Maybe something will happen to change his mind."

"What would that be?"

"I'm not sure. Yet."

The colonel was a direct man, and he had learned his deputy could be far more devious than himself. Most of the time, however, the captain's intricate schemes were beyond his ability to decipher. "Are you planning something?"

The captain shrugged.

"I don't want to know about it," the colonel said with a

wave of his hand. "Even after it's happened I don't want to know about it, do you understand?"

"All right with me."

"But do me a favor, Blakely. If you're going to make something happen, do it soon."

Blakely left the office with a smile on his face. The colonel was being himself: he never wanted any part of something that required thought. He walked down the corridor and came to a courtyard, where many prisoners were standing about.

At this moment two British soldiers came in with a large cooking pot; they were staggering under its weight. The prisoners came forward eagerly to get the thick soup that was being passed out in wooden bowls. It was the same soup served to the British troops.

"Good grub," a prisoner said to the captain as he walked by licking his lips. "Better than we get in our own army."

The captain left the prison in disgust. He walked across the grassy Commons and headed down Nassau Street. Walking always helped him think, and he needed an idea that would bring the general around to his way of thinking.

He never doubted for an instant that he would come up with something.

Early the next day, Dick Goelet breakfasted with Peter in the kitchen of the de Kuyper house on Maiden Lane. His own house was a few blocks away, on Wall Street, but it had been boarded up ever since his father had died, two years ago. His mother had passed away years before that. Rather than live alone, Dick had elected to stay with his relatives.

"Can we go down to the docks?" the boy asked.

"Most of the ships are gone," Dick said.

"Can't we at least go to the river?" Peter asked unhappily.

"All right," Dick agreed.

When Marie Therese heard about the excursion, she warned the two to be careful. "There's a lot happening on the streets," she said.

"We'll be careful, Grandma," Peter said.

"I'll keep a good watch on him," Dick reassured her.

The morning was fresh and cool as they walked toward the East River. The arrival of the British seemed to break the hot, muggy spell that had plagued the city. They came to the Fly Market on the slip at the foot of Maiden Lane. The market consisted of two wooden sheds where the merchants sold their wares. Ordinarily the place was a beehive of activity, but today it was almost deserted. A detachment of British soldiers stood to one side, their firearms stacked in a neat pile. These men stood around, joking and talking as if they didn't have a care in the world. And well they could act this way, for all the resistance they had met. Most of the American soldiers they had encountered in the city had surrendered without a fight. They had been rounded up and taken to prison.

The streets around the area of the Fly Market contained many shops: there was Wilson, the dealer in dry goods; Philip Livingston, who sold everything from rum to furs to marble chimney pieces; the Dutchman Rapelje, who imported exquisite delftware from the Netherlands; the Buchanan Brothers, who sold the finest boots in the city; Dietrich, the German butcher, who leased his building from Jan de Kuyper and was always complaining about the rent.

A short way down Queen Street was where the Frenchman Peter Lorillard had his tobacco shop. Near by was the store of the druggists, Caswell and Massey, where people always stopped in to smell the wonderful aromas of their great variety of soaps.

On nearby Hanover Square Dick's uncle, Peter Goelet, had his ironworks and hardware store. Dick didn't particularly get along with his uncle. The young man liked to read and dream, and Uncle Peter was more interested in making nails and horseshoes. They saw each other on certain holidays, and avoided each other at all other times.

"You're right," Peter said, looking down the docks. "There aren't any ships."

"Hard to imagine New York without ships, isn't it?" Dick said.

"No. All you have to do is look around," the boy said, quite logically.

A group of men were gathered near the Old Slip. Most of them were merchants, and they stood about and worriedly discussed the plights of their businesses. Several recognized Dick and nodded curtly.

"Good morning," Dick said. "Although there seems to be little that is good about it."

"Aye, that's the truth," said Seth Cuyler, the sugar dealer. "What's Jan de Kuyper planning to do about the situation?"

Dick Goelet had already been informed about General Washington's wishes. The de Kuypers—and that meant him as well—were to let everyone think they were going along with the British. Dick cleared his throat and spoke the words expected of him. "Jan plans to go ahead with business as usual," he said. "What else is there to do?"

The men looked sharply at him. "Jan's starting to sound like a loyalist," Seth Cuyler said with a dark edge to his voice.

"No," Dick said. "He's not a loyalist, only a realist. The British are here—for the moment, at least—and that's a fact we're going to have to live with."

A few of the men muttered to one another, and they weren't praying for the soul of Jan de Kuyper and his relatives. Dick decided it would be prudent to soften his stance.

"The truth is," he said, lowering his voice and looking around furtively, "it won't do any harm to give the British a few reasons to relax."

"Why?"

"If they let down their guard, who knows what might happen?" Dick said with a wink.

Seth Cuyler laughed and clapped him on the back. "Perhaps you've a point, lad."

"Smart bugger, that Jan de Kuyper," Seth said to the other men, and they relaxed their posture toward Dick and Peter. The conversation turned back to business, and Cuyler did most of the talking. A big bear of a man, with a beard and a pair of mighty arms, he had worked his way up from being a common laborer.

As they talked, they became aware of a man walking toward them. He was a British officer, and so the conversation subsided. By the time the officer reached the group, there was utter silence.

"My name is Captain Patrick Blakely, deputy provost marshal," he said. "Who are you?"

"Seth Cuyler's my name," the big man said. He introduced the others and ended by saying, "and we're all men of business. As a matter of fact, we've been discussing what's going to happen to our businesses. You wouldn't happen to know, would you, Captain?"

"As of now the city is under martial law," Blakely said. "All merchants and traders must register with the provost marshal's office. No business can be conducted until you're registered."

"But after that we *will* be permitted to do business?" Dick asked.

"If we grant approval."

"And what would keep you from doing that?" Cuyler asked.

A grim smile came to the captain's lips. "That's our business."

"It seems to me it's ours too," Seth said.

"All traders and shopkeepers must hand over lists of their inventory," the captain said to the group, ignoring Seth's last remark.

"What for?" Seth persisted, even though he could see the Englishman was becoming annoyed with him.

"The army may need what you have. If so, they'll commandeer your inventories."

"Without payment?" Dick asked. Not that he, particularly, had anything to lose; he was a curious chap.

"If your sympathies lie in the right direction, you ought to be pleased to aid the Crown," the captain said sarcastically, knowing full well that no matter where a businessman's political sympathies lay, his first loyalty was to his purse.

Seth, beginning to sputter, argued that it was immoral to take away a man's goods. Nothing much might have resulted, except for the remark he made to conclude his harangue. "And as for the British army's needs, sir, to hell with them! I'd rather burn my sugar than turn it over for nothing."

Captain Blakely looked over at the soldiers standing on the other side of the pier—unofficially known as Rotten Row, because of the eternal fish smell that hung over the place. He waved his arm, and a sergeant trotted over with two soldiers.

"Take this man to the prison and lock him up," the captain said.

The soldiers grabbed Seth from both sides. "And what exactly am I being charged with?" he asked.

"Treason," the captain said. He turned to the rest of the group. "Would any of you care to accompany your friend?"

A few men mumbled, but no one agreed to share Seth's fate. The captain waited another moment, and then turned disdainfully and led Seth Cuyler away.

Dick and Peter returned to the house and found Marie Therese preparing breakfast. There were a number of servants in the house, but she always insisted on preparing Jan's breakfast herself. She brought a mug of cocoa and placed it on the table in front of Peter.

"Would you like anything, Dick?" she asked.

"Some coffee, if it's no trouble."

Drew entered the room. "I'll get your coffee, too," Marie Therese said.

Marie Therese was in her sixties, but retained the sparkle of over twenty years ago. Her body was slender and her skin was clear, her hair a lustrous gray. Quiet-tempered and calm, she was the steadying influence in the family. The others tended to quickly take offense, and were prepared to defend their rights as they saw them; Marie Therese moved through the fray with tranquility and ease. Once, when a friend remarked that he couldn't understand how she put up with the rest of the family, Jan spoke what was probably the truth. "Don't worry about Marie Therese. She's the toughest of us all."

Drew joined the others at the table. "They arrested a man at the docks," Peter announced.

"Seth Cuyler," Dick said.

"What happened?" Jan asked.

"This Englishman—deputy provost marshal, he said he was—told a group of merchants he wanted a list of their inventories."

"So?"

"So Seth Cuyler objected and they arrested him for treason."

"Seth never did know when to keep his mouth shut," Jan said. "Serves him right."

"Will you say that if they hang him?" Drew asked.

"Who said they were going to hang him?" Jan said. "What did he say that made them arrest him?"

"The Englishman said they might confiscate goods without payment. Commandeering, he called it. Seth said he'd destroy his sugar first."

"They couldn't hang a man for that, could they?" Marie Therese asked, a worried look in her large eyes.

"They'll probably lock him up for a few days to scare him," Jan said. "After all, the British aren't barbarians."

"No?" Drew said, taking up the gauntlet. "Then why are we fighting and dying to get them to give us what's ours in the first place?"

"Because we haven't been able to convince them this isn't their land," Jan said tartly. "But I still maintain we can come to a peaceful solution."

"We've all heard that before," Drew said hotly. "The only way they'll leave is at the business end of a rifle."

"Haven't you two had this argument before?" Marie Therese asked pointedly.

"Many times, to be sure," Jan said.

"Too many times," Drew added.

"Exactly," Marie Therese said. "By now you should be smart enough to realize neither of you can convince the other he's wrong. So why don't you both stop making so much noise and enjoy breakfast?"

Jan chuckled and winked at his son. "I think the answer is to send your mother to negotiate with the limeys."

"Sorry, Mother," Drew said. "We'll remember to have our disagreements when you're not around."

"I like it when Grandpa and Uncle Drew fight," Peter said.

"We do not fight, boy. We merely take opposite sides of an issue," Jan said.

"Extremely opposite," Drew added, and then looked away when he saw the warning look in his mother's eyes.

After a few more minutes Jan left the house, and Marie Therese disappeared with Peter.

"I've got to find Nathan Hale," Drew said. "Would you care to help me?"

"Sure," Dick agreed.

"I'm going up to the Place in case Celine knows where he is. Why don't you start to look for him here in the city?"

"What do I tell him if I find him?"

"A good question," Drew said, and looked puzzled. "All I plan on doing is handing him Washington's message."

"Too bad you don't have two messages," Dick said, unable to refrain from sarcasm. "One for each of us."

"I have an idea," Drew said brightly. "Why don't I open the message, and we can pass it on verbally?"

"I don't know about that. The message is from the general to Hale."

"The general never told me *not* to open it."

"He never told you not to stab Hale in the back, either. He just assumed you wouldn't do it."

Drew began pacing the room, a habit of his when he was lost in thought. After a bit, he stopped and faced his cousin. "Look, under normal circumstances I wouldn't do it, but since we'll have twice as much chance to deliver the message if we both know it, I say we open it."

Dick hesitated, then nodded. "All right, you make a good point."

Drew reached into his pocket and brought out a folded piece of paper that had been fixed with a pair of wax seals. He broke the seals and read the message. "I don't believe it," he said in astonishment, and let the paper fall on the table.

Dick picked it up, and his eyes widened as he read.

Hale,

My generals and my staff, almost to a man, are in agreement to burn New York to the ground. I waver, but trust to God that I am pursuing the proper course of action in ordering you *not* to carry out your plans for the destruction of the city. I take full responsibility for this decision because, in good conscience, I cannot see how destroying New York will aid our cause.

                                                  Washington

"Jesus Christ!" Dick hissed. "They were planning on burning down the city?"

"So it appears."

"That's insane," Dick said, the blood rushing to his head; he gripped the top of a chair to steady himself. "The crazy, dirty bastards!"

"Calm down," Drew said. "If you've read the same message that I did, you see Washington doesn't want to do it anymore."

"But even to *think* about doing it—Christ, it's enough to make me go over to the British!"

"I'm glad we opened it," Drew said calmly. "It's more important than ever to find Hale. We've got to tell him not to burn the city."

Drew left the house and went to the stable. Within minutes he was galloping north toward his sister's house.

Dick was about to leave the house when he realized the letter was still on the kitchen table. It would hardly do to leave it there, so he retrieved it and put it in his pocket. Then he went down to the tip of the island and began nosing around the old fort. He wasn't sure about Hale's habits, and decided to leave nothing to chance.

For more than six hours he haunted every tavern he knew, cautiously inquiring about the missing captain. No one knew anything about the man, and Dick decided he was hunting for a ghost.

When he got to the Swan & Bear tavern, it was past three in the afternoon and he was hungry. Instead of his usual routine of asking a few questions and leaving, he sat down at a table and ordered a cold mutton chop and a tankard of ale. Caleb

North, the owner of the tavern and a fellow member of the Sons of Liberty, saw him and joined him at the table.

"Nathan Hale?" he said in response to Dick's question. "No, don't know the man. What do you want of him?"

"I have a message for him. It's important."

"I'll ask around," North said. Then he looked around to make sure no one was listening, and poked his head close to Dick's. "There's a rumor going around that Washington plans to march down and retake the city."

Dick didn't believe it. "The British have too many troops. And from what I hear, Washington's army is in sad shape."

"I don't believe it either," Caleb North said. "But I've heard it from more than one man."

"Wishful thinkers," Drew said.

Caleb North chatted with Dick as he ate his chop and washed it down with the refreshing ale. He was just finishing when Captain Blakely entered the tavern.

The Swan & Bear was usually a noisy place, but when the Englishman walked through the door, it was possible to hear a pin drop. He walked around, looking from face to face, finally stopping at a table only three away from Dick and Caleb North. The two farm boys seated there looked as if they'd been enjoying a good deal of liquid refreshment. The captain stood looking down at the two boys, who began to squirm in their chairs.

"What are two healthy lads like yourselves doing out of uniform?" the captain asked. "I should think Washington would want you in that rabble he calls an army."

"No, sir," the first farm boy said. "I ain't never been in an army."

"Me neither," the other one chimed in. "I don't like uniforms."

"Do you dislike mine?" the captain asked pleasantly.

"No."

The captain's attitude changed in a flash. "Stand up when a British officer addresses you," he snarled.

The boys scrambled to their feet. They were about twenty years old, drunk, and now scared. The captain signaled for the sergeant, who stood in the doorway with two soldiers at his back. "Search them."

The sergeant went through the lads' pockets. On the first he found a few coins, a knife, a short piece of rope, and a few nails. But on the second he discovered a leaflet printed by the

Sons of Liberty. It was a common one that advised good citizens how to deal with loyalists.

The captain took his time reading the leaflet, finally handing it over to the sergeant. "Reading treason, are we?" he said to the now terrified farm boy.

"Please, sir, I can't even read hardly. Someone gave that to me the other day. I . . . I forgot I had it."

"I don't believe you," the captain said coldly. "But what difference does it make? You were taken with treasonable material on your person. Take them outside, Sergeant Taggert. Two more for the prison."

The first farm boy, very drunk, began to argue. Sergeant Taggert didn't hesitate. He had a club in his hand, and he brought it down on the boy's head. He fell to the floor, and the two soldiers behind the sergeant came forward, grabbed his arms, and dragged him across the floor as if he were a butchered calf. The second farm boy followed without a word of argument.

The captain resumed his walk around the taproom. He looked at Caleb North; then at Dick Goelet, and stopped. "Didn't I see you earlier today?" he asked.

"Yes, sir, down by the Old Slip."

"Yes," Blakely said, remembering. "When I arrested that troublemaker."

"He does talk too much, sir," Dick said.

This seemed to placate the captain, and he walked on, stopping at a table down the way. A strong-looking man was seated alone. The captain smiled. "Those are the boots of a soldier," he said.

The man shrugged, and then stood up, looking uncertain. If he had kept his head, he would have realized the captain had no way of proving by his boots that he was a soldier. There was no general issue of boots in the Continental Army. But the man was afraid, and decided the best thing to do was to make a break for it. He bolted for the door, and kept going through it when the sergeant shouted for him to halt. He might have gotten away, except he had the bad fortune to stumble over a gnarled tree root, and twisted his ankle. He got to his feet, but he could no longer run, and several of the soldiers from the captain's detachment fell upon him. They clubbed him with their rifle butts, then dragged him back to where other soldiers were guarding the farm boys. Sergeant Taggert stepped up and crashed his fist into the man's mouth. He fell back against the two soldiers who had been holding him, and they again began to use their butts as clubs. Finally the man collapsed in a heap, and the beating stopped.

The captain had remained in the taproom. "Who owns this place?" he asked.

"I do," Caleb North said, and the captain returned to the table where North sat with Dick Goelet.

"It's your duty to report rebels," the captain said. "If you don't, you'll wind up in prison with them."

"I understand."

The captain was about to pass on, and then looked back at the tavern owner's companion. "What's your name?"

"Dick Goelet."

"You ever been in the army?"

"No, sir."

"Are you a coward?"

"No!" Dick said in indignation.

"You look like a reader to me," the captain said. "Do you read much?"

"A fair amount."

"Rebel reading?"

Dick hesitated.

"Search him," the captain instructed his sergeant.

Remembering he had Washington's note to Nathan Hale in his pocket, Dick felt his heart seem to leap to his throat. But it was too late: Sergeant Taggert found the note and handed it to the captain.

Blakely read it, then reread it, then smiled. "I believe we'll take this one, too," he said to the sergeant. "*Especially* this one," he added as he folded the note and placed it into his own pocket.

"Yes, sir."

"Make sure we keep him," the captain said. "I look forward to having a long chat with Mr. Goelet."

Sergeant Taggert was a burly man, and he towered over the slight figure of Goelet. "Let's go," he said, grabbing Dick's arm in a grip that resembled a bear trap.

On the walk back to the prison, Captain Blakely positioned himself so he was only a few feet away from his latest captive; the note had given him preeminence among the new prisoners. When they arrived at the Provost, the other prisoners were led away to the common lockup, but Dick was brought to the captain's private office.

"So you're a courier for Washington," Blakely said, wasting no time on preliminaries.

"No, I am not."

"And the note?"

"I found it on the street."

"Yes, of course, and women don't have tits," the captain said. "Now let's be honest. Where is this man named Hale?"

"I don't know."

"If you have a message for him, you must know where to find him."

Dick could no longer contain himself. "If I knew where he was, I'd find him. New York is my home Captain. Do you think I want to see it burned to the ground?"

"How do I know New York is your home?"

"My name is Goelet. I'm related to the de Kuypers and the de Witts and the Sacketts. Our families go back to the beginnings of the Dutch settlement. No one is more of a New Yorker than I am."

"De Kuyper," the captain said, mulling over the name. "Isn't that Murray woman a de Kuyper?"

"Celine, yes, her maiden name is de Kuyper."

The captain thought for a moment. "I'm inclined to believe that you want to find Hale. How were you planning to do it?"

Dick heaved a sigh of relief. "I was going to look around. Ask people about him. A man must leave some sort of trail."

"Yes," the captain agreed. He sent for Sergeant Taggert and, when the man arrived, ordered him to take Dick to an isolated cell in the lowest cellar.

They went down the stone stairs and entered a narrow corridor. Dick was locked inside the last cell, and no one was permitted near him. The sergeant's footsteps echoed as he walked away, leaving the prisoner to his thoughts.

What was the captain planning to do? he wondered.

One thing was for sure. Dick could hardly give Nathan Hale the message about not burning the city. And if the man went ahead and lit the torches, how much of the blame would rest on his own shoulders for failing to deliver Washington's message?

Earlier in the day, Drew had arrived at the Place. He was met with suspicion by the guards at the gate.

"Where d'you think you're going?"

"To the house."

"As easy as that, eh? This is General Howe's headquarters."

"It's also my sister's home."

The senior guard grudgingly accompanied him to the front door, where he was greeted by Primus.

"Mister Andrew!"

"You know him?" the guard asked.

"This gentleman is Mrs. Murray's brother," Primus said stiffly.

The guard wasn't impressed; he turned away and walked back to the gate.

"These British sure take a lot of airs on themselves," Primus complained.

"Where's my sister?"

"In the sewing room with Mrs. Delafield."

Drew was so delighted to see that his sister had come through the invasion that he grabbed her and hugged her. She was too flustered to say anything about this uncharacteristic show of brotherly love.

"How is Peter?" she asked.

"Fine. Mother is taking good care of him."

"I'd like him with me," Celine said. "But I guess he's better off in the city."

"Besides, things have been pretty lively around here," Mary said, and then reddened at Celine's warning look.

"The main reason I came here is to find Nathan Hale," Drew said, getting down to business.

"What do you want with him?" Celine asked suspiciously.

Drew hesitated, and then decided he needed to convince her of his mission's importance. "He has orders to burn New York."

"I know."

Drew was surprised, but explained that General Washington had issued an order telling Hale not to burn the city.

Celine explained that Hale's orders had been to do nothing until he heard from the general. "So there's really nothing to worry about," she said.

Drew was relieved. "I still want to talk to him and make sure he knows the general's wishes."

"He'll show up here soon," Celine said, and then invited her brother to join her for lunch with General Howe. Drew was glad to accept; it fit in perfectly with his plan to make the English think the de Kuypers were cooperating with them. He debated with himself about telling his sister of this, then decided against it. It wasn't that he didn't trust Celine—he knew she would never purposely do anything to harm the family—but he considered her flighty and injudicious. Who could tell when her tongue would slip and she'd say the wrong thing to a man like General Howe?

"What sort of man *is* Howe?" he asked.

"Nice," Celine said, but offered nothing more.

"Celine's quite taken with him," Mary said. "But not as much as he is with her."

"Another conquest?"

"Look, little brother, there are some things that are my business and no one else's. Is that clear?"

"Am I still invited for lunch?"

"If you can behave discreetly."

"And if I don't, what do you plan on doing? Tell the general I'm a secret member of the Sons of Liberty?"

Primus supervised the serving of lunch, and fussed over the wine that had been brought up from the deepest part of the cellar—chilled perfectly by the blocks of ice placed there under straw the previous winter.

The general raised his crystal glass and proposed a toast. "May all my wars be waged in such marvelous surroundings with such charming companions."

They drank, and it was Drew's turn to propose a toast. "May the present hostilities quickly come to an end."

"Indeed!" the general murmured warmly.

Thin slices of cooked beef were served on a bed of spiced wild Indian rice, along with fresh beans and a salad of leafy spinach mixed with bits of tender crab meat and walnuts. The talk was harmless chitchat at first; then Drew steered the conversation to the general's business at hand. Who knew what one could learn?

"My personal feelings are that the die-hard rebels are few," the general said. "Under their misguidance, the colonies are being disrupted by this unnecessary war."

"There are a few hotheads," Drew admitted.

"Exactly, *only a few*, and yet they are influencing everyone else. You're an intelligent young man; you can see we're all Englishmen under the same English king. It's in our best interests to band together and present a united front against the French and other natural enemies."

"If the king would only make a few concessions, it might

allow the reasonable men to ignore the hotheads," Drew said, not believing himself.

"He will, he will," the general assured the others. "But he's only human. When the rebels hold a gun to his head, he no longer wants to listen to reason, but, like any other man, becomes angry and wants to strike back at those threatening him. Remove the gun and the king will come around to see your point of view."

"Unfortunately," Drew said, "this invasion will harden many hearts against the king."

"It is a necessary unpleasantry," the general said. "But perhaps you've noticed our measured pace of advance?"

"Sir?"

"My wish is not to destroy this land and its people. Just the opposite, in fact. After the battle of Long Island it would have been an easy matter to immediately cross the river to Manhatan. I delayed because I wanted to give your leaders a chance to think. It must be obvious that our strength is far too much for General Washington to cope with. We captured most of this island without losing a man. Surely Washington understands that his position is hopeless, and that he should bow to the inevitable and make peace."

"Is that what you'd like to happen, sir?"

"My fervent wish," the general said, and it was clear he was telling the truth.

"What *are* your plans for the city?" Celine asked.

"That everyone should get back to a normal way of life as soon as possible. What advantage does the Empire gain by holding our natural cousins in bondage? By bickering among ourselves, we invite attack from some other quarter. Europe is in a state of unrest, and the future of the British Empire demands that its various parts be at peace with one another."

"I agree," Drew said, managing to avoid his surprised sister's eyes. She was well aware of his true sentiments, and they had nothing to do with being at peace with the British Empire. "It's time that men of reason on both sides work to get things back to normal."

"If everyone thought as you, we would have the most powerful empire that ever existed," the general said.

"My father has asked me to tell you that the de Kuyper company plans to cooperate with you. Our ships, if you wish, will begin carrying supplies for your troops."

"Splendid," the general said. "Something tangible like that

THE CITY INVADED

will prove to the king we're dealing with reasonable men, and not savages as some of his advisors inform him."

"There are still men in England who think of us that way?"

The general made a sour face. "There are men who think anyone who lives five miles from the center of London is a savage. It's an outdated view held by fools. There's too much at stake, however, to continue to let fools have their way."

Drew was impressed by the general's outspokenness. He must have made many enemies in London. But he was related to the king and above reprisal, as kings were markedly tolerant about the foibles of their relatives.

Lunch ended, and Drew thought it had been time well spent. He was certain he had won the general's confidence. It would stand him, and the de Kuyper family, in good stead to be on friendly terms with the commanding general.

It amused him to think that in the space of two days he had communicated personally with the commanding generals of the two opposing forces.

A group of officers arrived for consultations with Howe, and he excused himself and retired to the parlor. Drew was in the kitchen talking with Celine when Robert Delafield showed up and noisily chastised his wife for remaining in the country rather than returning to their house in the city.

"But I was afraid to travel," Mary protested. "It seemed safest to stay here while there was a British general living in the house."

Delafield looked at Drew and sneered. "A British general, eh? Pretty quick to jump to the other side."

Drew held his temper in check. He tolerated Robert Delafield only because he was married to his cousin. The man was in his early forties, bald, overweight, and a loudmouth. He snorted when he laughed, belched in public, and was as mean and tight a man as there was in New York. He had money, the Delafield family having made a comfortable niche for themselves as dealers in wines and teas. Over the past ten years, however, since Robert had taken over from his father, the business had not fared well. Most people disliked him as much as Drew did, and took their trade elsewhere.

"I'd watch my tongue if I were you," Drew said in a low voice, cocking his head to one side.

"I'm only saying what everyone else is thinking. The British are here only a few days and the de Kuypers are hobnobbing with their general. Traitors!"

"Your wife is a Beekman," Celine said icily. "That means she's part of the family, too."

"Worse luck for her. And me too."

"If you're going to be your usual unpleasant self, I wish you'd remove yourself from my house."

"Gladly. I only came to collect my wife."

"Until things settle down, this is the safest place to be," Celine said to Mary.

"She's right," Mary said to her husband.

"You're my wife and you're coming home with me," Delafield insisted.

"You might find it difficult to get home with a broken leg, Delafield," Drew said, his voice low and menacing.

"Are you threatening me?"

"Yes."

"Oh, don't bother yourself with this ass," Celine said to Drew, stepping between them and taking her brother's arm.

"Mary decides for herself whether she stays or goes," Drew said.

"She stays over my dead body," Delafield replied.

"Don't tempt me," Drew said.

"I'm leaving," Mary said, anxious to end the scene. "Robert is correct. A wife belongs with her husband."

When the Delafields were gone, Drew crashed his closed fist down on the table. "One of these days I *will* break his leg! The fat pig!"

"Don't let him bother you," Celine said. "Nobody takes him seriously, you know that."

"It's hard not to take it seriously when someone comes into your own sister's house and calls your family traitors."

"Speaking of which," Celine said, "that's more or less what you were sounding like when you were talking with General Howe. And what's this about Father wanting to cooperate? Does *he* know anything about that?"

"Yes."

"I don't get it," Celine said, looking perplexed. "One minute you're a wild-eyed rebel, and the next you're telling the general how nice it is to have the British back. What are you up to?"

Drew smiled. There was nothing wrong with Celine's powers of deduction. He told her about Washington's idea and how the family was going to pretend to be friendly with the British.

"Clever enough," Celine said. "I just hope you can handle it."

"*I* can handle it," Drew said heatedly. "I just hope you can handle this general of yours. Don't get burned."

"Don't worry, he's only a man," she said, and walked out of the room.

Drew allowed himself to smile. Celine really *was* a beauty, he thought, and really *did* have a head on her shoulders. General Howe might have been a man of the world, but he doubted the poor man had ever before encountered a woman like Celine.

As he was leaving, Primus accompanied him to the door. "You take good care of her," he said.

Primus sighed. "That's more of a job than an old man like me can handle."

"You do it better than anyone else."

"Known Missy since she was born. Got to learn something in that amount of time."

Drew shook hands with the black man and left the Place.

Primus watched until he rode out past the guards at the gate, then closed the door and went down to the kitchen. He began to prepare a dish that was the pride of the Place; pea soup made with bits of lean pork. A colander of fresh peas stood next to the water pump, and there he cleaned the tiny, bright-green balls. Next he put them in a large pot half filled with water and placed it over the fire to simmer gently. He added a generous amount of Madeira and a few dashes of brandy. Then he began to add bits of pork, followed by several pungent spices and herbs. It was a concoction he had learned from an old slave woman when he had been a young boy. He never shared the recipe with anyone, and he took care that no one was around when he made the soup.

He was suddenly startled when he realized someone had come through the back door and was standing in the middle of the room, watching him.

It was fifteen-year-old Elizabeth Henry—Beth, everyone called her. She stood silent, her feet spaced apart, and looked very alert.

Primus placed his spoon down and went over to her. "Why, child, is something the matter? What are you doing here?"

"I came up to make sure Celine and Peter were all right," Beth said. "I also thought I might stay here for a while."

The old man put his arm about her shoulders. "Why, of course you can stay here. This has always been your second home, and no one is more welcome."

"Thank you," she said, and smiled for the first time.

Beth was a tall girl, and very slender. Her beautiful brown eyes were large, and her long, dark hair cascaded down past her shoulders. She had a thin, perfect nose and wore a perpetual look of self-assurance. The big surprise, however, came when she spoke. It was startling to hear the deep, sensuous voice that issued from that angelic face. Her complexion was dark enough to reflect the Indian blood that had trickled down from both sides of her family—the Cléments and the Henrys.

Her mother and father, Theo Henry and Louise Clément Henry, had both been stricken, two years before, when a mild plague once again visited the city. Not many people were lost, but two of those who died were Beth's parents. She had remained alone in the Henry house on Rutgers Hill with a pair of servants to look after her. Not that she needed much looking after.

"Nothing happened at your house, did it?" Primus asked.

"No."

"A young lady's got to watch herself with all these strange soldiers wandering about."

"I keep my eyes open," Beth said.

Primus had a sudden thought. "How come the soldiers just let you come up to the house by yourself? They're mighty touchy with that general staying in the house."

"I came through the fields," Beth said. "I made sure they didn't see me."

Primus smiled. "That Indian blood in your veins can be a handy thing to own, at times."

"When I was a little girl, Primus, my mother would tell me to forget about my Indian blood. She said that people didn't respect Indians."

"Now, why did she say such a thing?" Primus said, clucking his tongue on the inside of his mouth. "We got to admit to what we are. Imagine what it would be like if I went around trying to be a white man. Only person I could fool would have to be blind."

Beth's teeth gleamed white as she smiled. "I like being part Indian," she said. "After all, we once owned the whole country."

"That's the way to think of it," Primus chuckled. "These white folks here, they're just your tenants."

"That reminds me, Primus—what bedroom can I take?"

"Take one of the guest rooms on the second floor. Not the blue one. That's where the general is staying."

"I'll take the rose one on the north side," she said.

As she was making her way up the stairs, she chanced to meet

General Howe, who was returning to the parlor after getting a dispatch case from his bedroom.

"Hello, my dear. I'm William Howe," the general said, "and at your service."

"My name is Beth Henry."

The general regarded one of the most exquisite faces he had ever seen. Celine, of course, was a stunning woman, but she knew a great deal about the world and her face and attitude reflected her sophistication. This girl, on the other hand, had a natural beauty untainted by cynicism. Her eyes were those of a startled doe, he thought. And that voice!

"Are you part of the family, my dear?"

"My father and Celine's father called each other cousin," she said. "But they weren't really cousins, just good friends. My grandfather and great-grandfather were the managers of the de Kuyper property in Westchester."

"You must be as close as family."

"Yes, we are."

"Why haven't I seen you before?" the general said mischievously. "Don't tell me Mrs. Murray has been hiding you from me?"

"I only just arrived."

"Then we'll surely be seeing more of one another," the general said, and smiled.

She returned the smile, although not in as grand a manner, and continued up the stairs.

He watched her until she disappeared from view. Amazing, he thought. Beautiful women keep popping out of the woodwork around here.

He suddenly remembered the dispatch case in his hand, scowled at the thought of the work to be done, and descended the stairs.

"Let's get on with it," he growled to the half-dozen officers in the parlor who had been waiting for his return.

2

The City In Flames

1776

IT WAS EARLY IN THE MORNING, WEDNESDAY, SEPtember eighteenth. Captain Blakely strode across the Commons toward the Provost, the name given the headquarters and prison by Colonel Cunningham.

The captain was delighted: he now had the idea he had been looking for—the idea that would convince General Howe that harsher methods were needed to handle the rebels.

He was going to burn down the city of New York and blame it on the rebels.

It had to be done cleverly, to appear to be the work of the rebels. The key to this was the capture of Captain Nathan Hale; and he had to get to him before the man learned he was not to burn the city.

The captain increased his pace. He had sent for a dozen hand-picked men, and they would now be waiting at his office. Their orders would be to find Hale, to capture him and some evidence—or create some. It was important to act swiftly. If he waited too long, the destruction of the city would be meaningless and he would lose his opportunity to get Howe to see his point of view.

He returned the salute of the guard at the main door and made his way down the corridor to his office. A dozen men were waiting. Within ten minutes they had their orders and were gone, off to scour the countryside and the city for Nathan Hale.

Blakely now turned to another problem. He had to find a number of trustworthy men—at least twenty of them—who would do the actual burning. They would have to be men who

THE CITY IN FLAMES

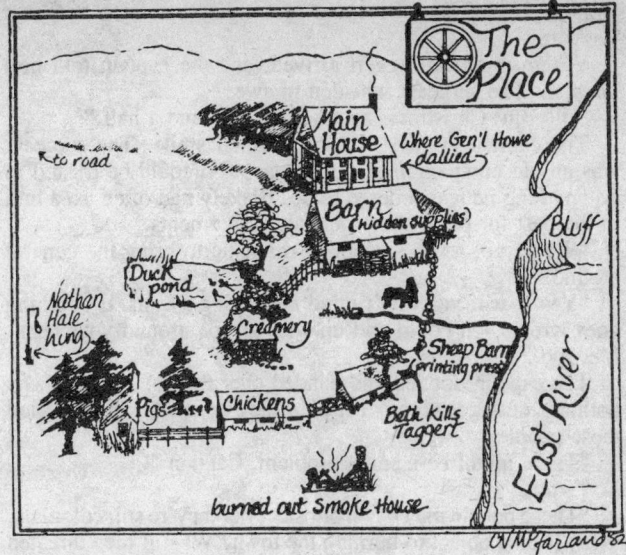

would blindly follow orders and keep their mouths shut. He went to his desk and took out a folder containing a list of known sympathizers. It would be much better to use loyalist Americans than British soldiers. If a soldier were caught, it would be hopeless to attempt to blame the fire on the rebels. A loyalist, however, could suddenly prove to be not a loyalist at all, but a secret rebel.

There was a certain immorality to this, of course, Blakely thought. A loyalist would hardly appreciate being abandoned by the very people he was being loyal to. But there was no other way to do it. The captain would not enjoy hanging a loyalist, but he would not hesitate to do so if it meant the success of his plan. In time of great need, anyone was expendable.

The captain's list gave not only the loyalist's name, but also quite a few details about him or her. The women especially interested him: a woman would arouse less suspicion than a man for the activity he had in mind.

After a half hour of poring over the list, he came up with a new list of twenty-five loyalist New Yorkers, seven of them women. He left his office and sent a guard to fetch Sergeant Taggert.

Within minutes Taggert arrived, and the captain told him his plan. The sergeant whistled in awe.

"Bleedin' Christmas, sir, that's a plan and a half."

The captain allowed himself a small smile. The sergeant was an old companion of his, a man who could be trusted to do anything he was ordered to do. Blakely had often used him in the past for particularly delicate assignments.

"We've got to do something dramatic to bring the general around."

"Yes, but if you don't mind me saying so, sir, if anything goes wrong you could end up with a rope around your neck. Me, too."

The captain nodded and handed over the list. "That's why nothing must go wrong. I'll plan the fire; your job is to find these people."

"There might be a small problem, Captain."

"What?"

"These people may be on our side, but they're still colonials. What if they object to burning the town? What if they threaten to talk?"

"We'll offer each one a bribe of ten pounds."

"And if that isn't enough?"

"Do I have to spell it out for you, Taggert?"

The sergeant nodded. "I'll bring along a pair of bully-boys."

"Whatever you need."

"I best be about it right away," the sergeant said.

After he was gone, the captain studied maps of the city, noting places with clusters of wooden buildings that would be ideal for fires. He was happily engaged in this work when a guard informed him he had a civilian visitor.

"I'm Andrew de Kuyper," Drew said as he stood before the desk. The captain did not offer to shake hands. "I understand you arrested my cousin, Dick Goelet."

"That's correct."

"On what charge?"

"I don't need any charge to arrest a rebel soldier."

"Dick's not a rebel soldier, and never was."

"Really?" the captain said, carefully watching Drew for a reaction. "I've always considered couriers as soldiers."

The second Drew heard the word *courier*, he knew that Dick had been arrested with Washington's note on his person.

If this captain suspected he knew anything about the note, he'd be locked up along with Dick—and would hardly then be in a position to help him. "Courier?" he said, putting as much amazement as possible into his voice. "Where did you get that idea?"

"From a note I found in his pocket," the captain said, his eyes never leaving the other man. "It was a message from General Washington."

"I don't understand. What could Dick Goelet have to do with Washington?"

"Do you have any idea what was in the note?"

"How could I?" Drew said.

"That remains for you to say. Next you'll be telling me you're a one hundred percent loyalist, I suppose."

"Not exactly. But yesterday, at lunch, I was telling General Howe that—"

"You had lunch yesterday with General Howe?" the captain interrupted, it being his turn to be surprised.

"Yes, I was visiting my sister, and the general is her houseguest."

"Ah, Mrs. Murray is your sister."

"Yes. Anyway, the general and I had a long chat about the affairs of New York. I've never claimed to be a loyalist, only a realist."

The captain sat back in his chair. That damned interfering Mrs. Murray! And this was her brother. Which meant trouble with General Howe if things weren't handled properly. The fellow locked up down below became an even hotter issue.

"I'm sorry about your cousin," he said. "But there's nothing I can do for him. He was caught redhanded with a message from Washington—and that makes him a rebel soldier. My orders are to lock him up. Those, by the way, are orders from General Howe."

Drew understood. Getting caught with the note had been a big mistake on Dick's part. Something could be worked out, he was sure, but not right now, and not with this captain. Perhaps a direct appeal to General Howe would be the best answer. Besides, Dick's imprisonment was only part of the issue; there was still the problem of finding Nathan Hale.

"Very well," Drew said. "We'll find a way to sort this out. If you have any doubts about our family, feel free to ask the general. He's aware of our sentiments."

"Perhaps I'll do just that."

"I don't suppose it's possible for me to see my cousin."

"No, it isn't permitted."

"Thank you for your time, Captain," Drew said. He turned to leave Blakely's office, but the captain stopped him before he passed through the doorway.

"A word of advice, Mr. de Kuyper. Your cousin is marked as a known rebel. Too much activity to help him might make people suspicious about you."

"I'll try to remember that, Captain," Drew said coldly, and then he was gone.

Blakely thought about his visitor for a few minutes. He decided the man knew about the note and its contents. As soon as it had been mentioned, his manner had changed, almost as if he knew he would be fighting a losing battle on his cousin's behalf.

He decided it might be a good idea to keep an eye on the activities of this young de Kuyper. Who knew where his trail might lead?

The two commanding generals ate their dinners that night under very different circumstances.

Washington sat on a rickety camp stool eating cold mutton and cabbage off the top of a crate at the front of his tent. The canvas was still sodden from the rain, and the place had a sickly, stale smell. A single oil lamp provided light. Sharing the meager repast with the commander were Generals Nathanael Greene and Israel Putnam, and Major Aaron Burr. Each man had a stool of different size and height, giving the group an awkward, disheveled appearance.

"I dislike saying it, Your Excellency," Greene said, addressing Washington. "But our forces are incapable of holding off a sustained British attack."

"We did all right the other day," Putnam growled.

"A lucky fluke," Greene said.

"Even so," Washington said thoughtfully, "the victory did wonders for morale. It's as if we suddenly had a new army."

"I agree," Putnam said.

"All the more reason to avoid a major defeat," Greene counseled.

"So what do you suggest?" Washington asked, scratching the top of his hand.

"That we begin planning a retreat across the Harlem into Westchester."

"What's to keep Howe from following?" Putnam asked.

"Nothing," Greene admitted. "But if he follows, his lines of supply will be drawn out. He's bound to be weaker than if we sit here and wait for him to hit us in full strength."

Washington considered both sides. "I believe you make the most sense, Nat," he finally said.

"Where will we find a stronger position than here?" Putnam protested. "I say we stay."

General Greene smiled. "Are you looking for another chance to get off a line like 'Don't fire 'til you see the whites of their eyes?'"

Putnam seethed, but Washington lightened the moment by laughing. "Put," he said, "assuming our side wins this war, you'll go down in the history books for that one."

"I'd rather go down in the books as a general who won some battles," the crusty old fellow said. "What do you think about this talk of retreating?" he asked his aide, who had been quietly picking at his food, maintaining a discreet silence while his superiors argued.

Now that he was called upon to talk, Aaron Burr didn't hesitate. "The state of training in our army is miserable. I think General Greene is right—we should get away from here. In fact, I'd carry his thoughts even further. After we get Howe to chase us into Westchester, we should cross the Hudson and make him follow us down through New Jersey."

The major was rewarded by a black scowl from General Putnam, who had expected his own aide to support his position. The general wasn't too surprised, though, because he had learned the young major had a mind of his own and wasn't afraid to speak out.

"By the time we do all that, winter will be upon us," Washington said in a low voice, as if he was thinking aloud. "I doubt if Howe will mount a winter campaign. That would give us several months' respite to train our men."

"I don't like retreating," Putnam said.

"Better to retreat," Greene said, "than to endure another horror like the one on Long Island."

"I suggest we sleep on it, gentlemen," Washington said. "Maybe one of us will have a flash of brilliance by tomorrow."

While Washington was sitting in his stale-smelling tent, his opponent, General Howe, was in Celine's brilliantly lit dining room, enjoying a meal served on fine bone china from a table covered with a lace cloth from the Netherlands. The menu, too, differed from Washington's cold mutton and cabbage.

There was pommes soufflées, calvados; potage à la Florentine; pâté de foie et de porc en brioche; marmite aux fruits de mer; and côtes de veau braisées aux champignons. To round off this gourmet's delight, Primus proudly presented a charlotte Jamaïque en flammes. A variety of excellent chilled wines from the cellar accompanied the food.

"Mrs. Murray," the general said as he held his glass by the stem and twirled it, swirling the wine. "You keep as fine a table as I've ever sat at. And, madam, I have dined with princes, kings, and emperors."

"It's important to keep up a soldier's spirits," she replied playfully.

"Do you often dine like this?"

"Why do you ask? Are you one of these Europeans who think colonials eat only bear meat stew?"

The general chuckled. "There was a time in my life when I suppose I did. But never again, after tonight."

He was feeling extremely mellow and pleased with his situation. His plans for taking control of New York were going very well, with only a few mild setbacks. It was only a matter of time before his forces thoroughly routed Washington's army. Meanwhile, he was living in a fine house, enjoying splendid food, and monopolizing the company of two beautiful women. He was smitten with Celine, but Beth Henry fairly took his breath away.

She wasn't even a woman yet, he thought, as he studied her over the dessert, and yet she had a face that could *haunt* a man, it was that beautiful. It was more than her looks, though; there was something in her manner that made him want to throw out his chest and strut. There was so much *female* in her. The best part about it, he thought, was that the girl didn't seem to be aware of this power she possessed, still retaining a shy innocence.

"Are the soldiers going to stay in New York for a long time?" she asked in her throaty voice.

"Only until the war is over, which should be very soon."

"The sooner the better," Beth said.

"Do they frighten you?"

The girl looked the general straight in the eye. "No, why should they?"

"Sometimes women, especially young ones, imagine bad things about soldiers."

"How many of them have hunted a bear with a bow and arrow?" Beth asked.

"Have you done that?" the general asked.

"Yes."

The general looked at Beth with new respect. "Forgive me for misjudging the situation, my dear. I should be warning the soldiers about you."

"When the soldiers leave," Celine asked, "does this mean we'll be losing your company as well?"

"I plan on making my permanent headquarters in the city. I'm sure we'll have an opportunity to enjoy one another's company."

"That'll be most agreeable. But I don't see why you can't make your headquarters right here."

"Protocol must be served," he said with a sigh. "The commanding general must have a place in the city."

"You won't have any trouble finding one. So many people have fled that half the houses are empty."

"Only rebels have fled, no doubt, leaving nothing but loyalists."

"Not everyone who remains is a loyalist," Beth said.

The general assumed a look of mock horror. "Does this mean I'll actually get to see some rebels face to face?"

"What does that mean?"

"Until now I've seen only their backs as they've run away."

Celine bridled. "You claim we're your cousins and want to win our affection. Do you think, sir, it helps when you call us cowards?"

The general accepted the rebuke. "I stand corrected. Forgive me for making a crude joke."

Celine smiled politely, and reminded herself she was supposed to be playing the role of one who accepted the British as a fact of life. Most of the time it wasn't very difficult, because she really couldn't understand what all the fuss was about. Things hadn't been so bad for her under British rule.

After a time Beth excused herself and went upstairs to her room, and it became obvious the general was most interested in bringing his relationship with Celine to a greater intimacy.

But Celine was good at playing this game. She knew that a man was most vulnerable when he was spurred on by desire, rather than basking in its fulfillment. At this moment it was important to keep the general vulnerable. She smiled. She laughed at his jokes. She let her hand linger on his when she touched him. She tossed her hair in the languid manner she knew was admired by men.

And then she allowed him to kiss her hand—and went off to bed by herself.

She snuggled under the bed sheet and wondered what the general was thinking at this very moment. Did he have a vision of her face in his mind? Was he remembering the line of her shoulders and her graceful neck? Would he sigh and toss for hours as sleep eluded him?

She fell asleep quickly, smiling.

Tendrils of patchy early-morning fog drifted by as the sixteen-foot flyboat sailed across the North River to New Jersey.

Drew was with his cousins, Jeremy and Jennifer Sackett, David's children, known by everyone as Jemmy and Jenny. The twins were a year younger than Drew—exactly twenty. They were short, sandy-haired, and startlingly alike, down to the devilish twinkle ever present in their eyes. Neither was married, nor seemed to be interested in the idea; an outsider would be an intrusion on the life they had developed with one another.

"Would you mind telling me why I'm here?" Drew asked for the fifth time.

"You'll see," Jemmy said, his hand on the tiller and his eyes searching for a break in the gray mist.

"We want it to be a surprise," Jenny chimed in.

Drew drummed his fingers on the gunwale. He was regretting that he had allowed himself to be dragged from Fraunces Tavern before dawn. He had been enjoying the affections of Elsie, the cheerful Dutch serving girl with whom he'd been dallying for several months. Elsie was getting married soon, to a sailor whose return was expected daily.

They didn't ask much of one another—a little affection and a lot of lovemaking. He always left a sum of money under the pillow, although neither ever mentioned it. Elsie was happily hoarding this money, planning to use it to furnish the home she would share with her new husband. This morning when Jemmy had shown up to fetch Drew, he had been lying in Elsie's arms with his cheek on her ample bosom, dreaming about floating on a cloud of whipped cream.

He doubly—triply—regretted being here on the river: Dick

was still in prison, and Nathan Hale had yet to be found. Drew's frustration on their account had been a big reason why he had sought the comforts of Elsie last night.

Like everyone else, though, he found it almost impossible to resist his cousins. Whatever they were doing was always "the most important thing in the world," and they refused to take no for an answer. Their own father always referred to them as "a pair of crackpots," and his definition was widely accepted.

The twins were always concocting wild schemes, most of which didn't work, but nevertheless showed lively, inventive imaginations. They had designed an eight-sided wheel, which they'd claimed would work better in the mud; it didn't. And they were credited with designing a complicated mechanism that slowly pushed a candle up its holder so the flame wouldn't go out as the wax burned lower. Unfortunately, the device pushed too quickly and toppled lit candles onto the floor, once almost burning down a house.

The twins' combination spoon-fork met with little acceptance. The same was true of their "instant field tether," whereby a horse could be tethered in the open by tying his tail to a hind leg. The farmer they talked into trying it got kicked, and walked about with his arm in a sling for weeks, muttering and threatening to commit mayhem on the twins.

None of these defeats, of course, dampened their enthusiasm in quest of scientific advances.

There was a break in the fog, and Drew could see the settlement on the shoreline at Paulus's Hook—a collection of ramshackle wooden docks and covered piers, with a few houses dotting the low-lying hills farther inland. It amused New Yorkers that the people living here claimed they would one day compete with New York. They had begun calling the place Jersey City. Drew estimated there were more squirrels and raccoons in this city than there were people. Besides, he was a New Yorker, and New Yorkers always thought of the western side of the river as the wrong side.

Jemmy eased the little boat against the dock and dropped the sail. It was a uniquely structured gaff-headed sail designed by Jemmy himself. No one else dared to use it, because it had a tendency to break off in a stiff wind. This didn't deter Jemmy, who claimed it would only be a matter of time before he "worked out all the bugs."

Jenny led the way to a small roofed pier that looked old and ready to collapse. They went inside, and Jemmy lit an oil lamp. He went over to the edge of the water and held up the lamp.

"Isn't she a beauty?" he asked.

Drew didn't know what to say, because he wasn't sure what he was looking at. The thing looked something like the open top of a long barrel that went straight down into the water with only a small part remaining in the air. A domelike hatch could be closed to seal the interior. Three small air vents in the top of the hatch could be shuttered to complete the seal.

"What is it?"

"The world's first subwater boat," Jenny said proudly.

"Subwater boat?"

"Yes," Jemmy said. "It moves under the water instead of on top."

"*Under* the water?"

"Yes."

"How does it do that? And why, for godsake?"

Jemmy took the lantern and quickly disappeared down the ladder that was inside the boat. Drew peered down through the open top as Jemmy explained the various mechanisms. A collection of lead weights kept the boat balanced in the water. If the driver wished to remain below the surface for a sustained time, a canvas breathing tube with a cork top could be floated to the surface. When submerged, the driver could steer the boat with a compass illuminated by the glow of foxwood. For propulsion the subwater boat used a hand-cranked, twenty-four-inch wooden screw. Another screw, on the bottom, moved the vessel vertically.

"And it goes along under the water?" Drew asked, not really believing any of this. "What if it sinks?"

"It won't sink if you keep the lead weights properly balanced," Jenny explained, using a tone of voice one would use when speaking to a not-too-bright child.

"The idea is to keep the boat balanced so the screws can move the boat forward, backward, or up and down," Jemmy added more tolerantly. "And you don't want to get so heavy that you can't come up for air."

"Yes, I can understand that," Drew said dryly. "Having no air would be a bad thing."

"Exactly."

"But what is this . . . what is it supposed to *do?*"

"Win the war."

"*What?*"

THE CITY IN FLAMES

"Look at these," Jenny said, tapping her hand on two bulky objects on the dock. "Floating bombs. The subwater boat takes them out near a British ship, floats them toward her, and *boom!*"

"Boom?"

"They blow up the ship," Jemmy said impatiently.

Drew looked from cousin to cousin, waiting for them to admit it was a joke. But no, the two cherubic faces were in deadly earnest.

"Think how surprised the British will be when their ships begin to explode mysteriously," Jemmy said gleefully. "We'll blow up their entire fleet and they won't be able to do a thing about it."

"Take it a bit slower, Jemmy," Drew said. "Have you ever tested this thing?"

"What's to test?" Jenny said, speaking for her brother. *That*, Drew reminded himself, was another exasperating thing about the twins: they always acted as if they were one person. When a man dealt with them, they came at him from both sides until his head was swimming.

"Something, just possibly, might go wrong," Drew suggested.

"Well, we'll find out in a short time," Jemmy said. He climbed out of the tubelike craft and, with his sister's help, moved it to the end of the dock. He opened the gate and peered into the fog that drifted lazily over the water.

He went back aboard and climbed down the ladder again while Jenny held on to the boat. "We wanted you to be the first to see this," she said. "We figured you might help us build more."

"Does your father know about this subwater boat?" Drew asked.

"No," Jemmy said. "He wouldn't understand it."

That was an understatement, Drew thought.

The hatch was lowered until it fit tightly over the top of the boat. Jenny tied the two bombs to the back of the craft and pushed them into the water, where they trailed behind, supported by their own cork floats. She signaled Jemmy that all was ready by knocking on the side of the boat. It began to move slowly forward in the water.

"It works," Drew said, scratching the back of his head.

"Of course it does," Jenny said.

The subwater boat and the two bombs moved out into the

bay, looking for all the world like a family of turtles, and disappeared into the fog. Jenny walked out of the shed and stood on the shore, pointing down the coast. "There's a frigate anchored about a half mile south. That's the ship he'll blow up."

Drew grunted and sat down on a flat rock. My God! he thought, was Jemmy going to get himself killed? The British weren't stupid. They kept lookouts on their ships. Surely they'd become suspicious when they saw several large turtles coming toward them. A sudden thought occurred to him.

"What makes the bombs go off?"

"We've rigged a flintlock trigger inside. When the bomb hits an object with sufficient force, it springs the trigger, which sets off a charge that blows up the whole thing."

At least that part made sense, Drew thought. "How much force is needed?"

"We haven't worked that out yet," Jenny said blandly.

Drew lapsed into silence and brooded about being here when there was so much else to do. After a while Jenny interrupted his thoughts.

"Jemmy said when he dragged you out of bed, you were with some floozy."

"She's not a floozy," Drew said indignantly. "Besides, it's none of your business."

"You don't have to be ashamed of acting naturally."

"A man has instincts," Drew said.

"What makes you think a woman doesn't have the same instincts?" Jenny asked, and Drew was embarrassed. This was not the sort of conversation one had with a woman, especially a woman relative.

"I've fooled around a few times," Jenny said, somewhat proudly. "And I like it."

"We're not supposed to be talking like this."

"Why not? Because I'm a woman? What is a woman supposed to talk about? Baking pies? Mopping the kitchen floor? Listen, Cousin Andrew, all this talk that only men enjoy sex is a lot of bull."

Drew managed to change the subject, and they talked about family, friends, the war—anything at all, as far as he was concerned, as long as it was relatively noncontroversial. It was three hours before Jenny finally spotted a turtle in the water. "It's Jemmy! He's back!"

They went into the shed, and within minutes Jemmy expertly

THE CITY IN FLAMES 93

guided his boat to the dock. When the hatch opened, he emerged, drenched in sweat, exhausted. "These hand-cranked screws wear a man out," he said.

"What happened?" Jenny asked. "We didn't hear any explosions."

"The bombs didn't go off," Jemmy said. "Then the tide turned and carried them upriver, away from the frigate." He peered out across the water, which by now was almost free of fog. "There they are out there. Going north."

Drew saw the two bombs, merrily bobbing in the water. They were about a quarter mile from shore, and two men in a small fishing boat were rowing toward them.

"What are those fishermen doing?" Drew asked.

"Just curious, I guess," Jemmy said.

Drew tried again. "If they fool around with those things, couldn't they get hurt?"

"Umn," Jemmy said, as if the idea hadn't occurred to him before this moment. He walked out to the shoreline and began calling to the men in the boat. But there was a stiff wind, and it prevented his voice from carrying. The fishermen were already alongside the first bomb and were using a gaff hook to bring it to their craft.

"They'll blow themselves up," Jenny said, showing her first sign of concern.

The fishermen inspected the bomb, and presumably couldn't figure out what they had found. One of them began beating it with his gaff, and the three watchers on shore held their breath. Nothing happened. Finally the fisherman stopped hitting the bomb. He gave it a shove and watched it float away from the boat.

Drew let his breath out. He watched the object float steadily away from the boat. "That's some bomb," he said deprecatingly.

"I don't understand it," Jemmy said.

The bomb was almost a hundred feet from the fishing boat when it exploded with an ear-shattering blast. A spout of white-flecked water shot up thirty feet into the air. Bits and pieces of the bomb flew up, then splattered back into the bay. The two fishermen were far enough away to avoid harm, but they looked with disbelief at the spot where the bomb had exploded.

"I wonder what caused the delay?" Jemmy asked, puzzlement written on his face.

"It might be a faulty trigger mechanism," Jenny offered.

"Or the gap spring needs adjustment. Maybe it just works

itself loose and blows up when it wants to," Jemmy said in a matter-of-fact way.

"That could be it," Jenny said, and nodded sagely.

"You mean to say that damned thing could have gone off at any time?" Drew asked in horror. "Even when we were standing next to it in the shed?"

"In theory, yes," Jemmy admitted.

"I don't believe it," Drew said angrily. "You drag me over here to look at some dumb thing you've dreamed up, and now I find out it could have killed us all!"

"You've got to experiment with these things, otherwise you'll never know if they work," Jenny said. "I should think you'd understand *that* much, at least."

"Take me back to the city," Drew said between clenched teeth. "Right this minute."

"All right," Jemmy agreed. "Jen and I have to experiment with the trigger before we try again."

"Before you try again..." Drew seethed. "Listen, you lunatic! Before you *try again*, I want you to post notices so everyone can hide in their houses while you're out blowing yourselves up!"

"I never knew you had such a temper," Jenny said mildly. She looked at her brother. "Did *you* know about this side of Cousin Andrew?"

It was Friday morning.

Again Drew was up before dawn. After the Sackett twins had brought him back to Manhatan, he had spent the remainder of the day and evening in a fruitless search for the missing Nathan Hale. He decided he would use today to continue his search. There was no sense in going up to the Place; if Celine found Hale, she would send word.

He came to Hanover Square and watched as an old man shuffled across the open space to join three others who, like the first man, were dressed in mean, tattered clothes. They had started a small fire and were cooking soup of some sort in an old iron bucket. The old man nodded to the others, reached into his pocket, took out a few small vegetables—obviously his contribution to the common meal—and tossed them into the pot.

The four men sat silently, not having much to talk about even though an occupation of their city by a conquering army had just begun. It was of far more interest that they had collected enough meat and vegetables to cook a decent meal.

Drew suddenly had an inspiration. He walked over to Broad Street and pounded on the back door of a bakery. The baker came to the door, his hands and face white with flour.

"What do you want?" he growled, rubbing his hands together to shake off some excess powder.

"I want to buy four loaves of bread," Drew said.

"We don't open till seven."

Drew looked over the man's shoulder, saw a stack of fresh loaves, and pointed to them. "Now that you've opened the door, you might as well make some money."

The baker grumbled, but he walked over to the bin, grabbed four loaves and brought them back to Drew.

The four old men looked suspiciously at Drew as he approached them with the loaves in his arms. Without a word he handed a loaf to each man. The last one pinched the loaf, smelled it, and looked up in surprise. "This is fresh baked."

"Yes, within the past hour."

The old man smiled. One eye was covered with a black patch. "Thanks. Day-old bread is the best we usually manage."

"There's more," Drew said, reaching into his pocket and bringing out a few coins. He handed a shilling to each man. "I want to hire you to do a bit of work for me."

Suspicion crossed their faces. "What work?" the one-eyed man asked.

"Nothing dangerous or illegal," Drew told the four, and proceeded to enlist their aid in finding Nathan Hale. Older indigents were a common sight in New York, and they could wander almost anywhere without eliciting suspicion. People would speak freely in front of them as if they didn't exist.

"Meet me back here at six this evening and there's another shilling in it for you. A half-crown if you've learned anything."

"A half-crown for each of us?" the one-eyed man asked.

Drew nodded his agreement. The old men looked at one another, and it was the one-eyed man who made the decision. "All right, 'tis a bargain."

Drew walked away satisfied the old men would do as much as they could to find Hale. He decided he'd give each one a half-crown even if they didn't learn anything. It would spur them on to continue the search tomorrow, if necessary.

After two hours of walking, talking, and learning nothing, he found himself near Caleb North's tavern on Barclay Street, and his stomach reminded him he'd eaten no breakfast. He went inside and ordered a ham steak and coffee. Caleb North brought his own cup over and joined him.

"Thanks for getting word to me about Dick's capture," Drew said. "I went to the prison, but they wouldn't let me see him."

"Bad business," Caleb North said as he sipped his coffee.

"Tell me exactly what happened."

When the tavern keeper had related the incidents leading to Dick's arrest, Drew realized there was no doubt Captain Blakely had Dick dead to rights.

"Strange doings going on all around here," Caleb said. "Three men have been murdered in the streets, all of them not a five-minute walk from my own front door."

"The British?"

"The dead men were all known loyalists. Why would the British kill them?"

Drew whistled. "You think it's our people?"

Caleb shook his head. "It's not the Sons. I'd know if it were. Besides, who would want to provoke the limeys now? That'll only bring reprisals."

"Maybe it's only a coincidence."

"There's something fishy about it," Caleb said. "All three men had their necks broken. And not one man was robbed. They all had money in their pockets when they was found."

Drew finished his breakfast, left the tavern, and walked down Broad Way, turning left when he came to Whitehall. Along the way he saw constant reminders of the British occupation. Several times he passed squads of troops; twice he saw soldiers escorting unhappy prisoners north to the Provost building. In several places British soldiers were moving into houses they had commandeered. Most of the houses were already empty, having been abandoned by owners who had fled the city.

It was strange to be walking through his own town and know it had been taken over by conquerors—only most of the British didn't seem to be acting like conquerors.

"Good morning," he said on a whim as he passed an officer.

The Englishman didn't hesitate. "Good morning," he replied in clipped tones.

Drew looked up at the sky. "Going to be a dry day."

"Better than all that beastly rain. Bloody awful climate you have at times."

They continued on their respective ways, and Drew shook

his head. Men at war exchanging pleasantries about the weather: how odd!

A little way down the street, however, the realities of the war were brought home to him when he saw four Hessians dragging a man from an alley. The man wore the uniform of a Continental soldier. The Hessians shoved him along, and when he was a bit slow, one of them whacked the butt of his musket into the man's kidneys. The soldier grunted in pain and stumbled to the ground. For this he received several kicks, and then the Hessians dragged him down the street.

Drew arrived at the de Kuyper building. Half a dozen clerks were at work. They barely glanced at him, keeping to their ledgers and counting-books. Normally about twenty men worked in the big front room, but today there were only six. The de Kuyper business, like every other business in the city, was falling apart because of the war.

He climbed the stairs to the second floor and entered his father's private office. "What have you been up to?" Jan asked.

Drew unburdened himself. He told his father about Washington's note to Nathan Hale, and about the capture of Dick Goelet with the note on his person. Jan listened glumly as the tale unfolded.

"Well, Dick's in a mess of brine, that's for sure," he said. And then Drew recounted his conversation with Caleb North and how the tavern keeper was puzzled by the murders of the three men. It puzzled Jan, too, and he walked over and looked out the window. A flash of heat lightning zigzagged across the sky. "It's going to be a scorcher," he said, loosening the neck of his shirt. "None of the dead men were robbed, you say?"

"None of them."

"And they were all loyalists," Jan mused, and a shrewd look came over him. "If someone was looking for a good way to provoke the British, I'd say they found it. On the other hand, maybe the British themselves are looking for ways to make it *appear* they were being provoked."

"Do you think they'd do something as nasty as that?"

"Why not?" Jan said.

Drew nodded. "It does make sense."

"It's also a bit frightening in light of what you've just told me," Jan said grimly.

"What do you mean?"

"If the British are looking for ways to prove they're being

provoked, what better way than to find this Nathan Hale and show that he was planning to burn down New York?"

"Good God!" Drew said, coming to his feet and walking to the window to stand next to his father. They both watched as more heat lightning filled the sky.

"You still don't know where Hale is?" Jan asked.

"He must've fallen into that hole that goes to China," Drew replied.

The heat lightning crackled in the sky as Nathan Hale looked out the narrow window of the boatman's shed. The waters of the East River looked calm and flat. By standing at the extreme right of the window, he could peer out at the small sloop that was to carry him to Westchester. From there he intended to make his way west to Spuyten Duyvil, come back across the Harlem, and join Washington's army.

The boat shed and dock were a mile north of Kip's Bay, opposite Blackwell's Island, in a tiny cove that gave it some protection from the turbulent waters of the swift-flowing river. Hale glanced up at the sky, and from the position of the afternoon sun knew it was time to go. He picked up a corded fishnet, placed a fisherman's cap on his head, and walked out of the shed. To a casual observer he was simply another fisherman going about his business.

He may have appeared to be calm, but his thoughts were in turmoil. He had procrastinated about going to Washington, fearing the general would order him to burn the city—a thing he had decided he would not do under any circumstances. Now he wanted to see the general, explain his position, and accept the consequences.

There were about a dozen small boats in the cove, some at the dock, some anchored close to shore. Other fishermen were working on their boats and equipment. Hale spotted the fisherman who had agreed to take him north, and he nodded in recognition. The man returned the silent greeting, and soon the two were moving side by side toward the dock. Several strangers stood at the head of the pier. Despite their civilian dress, they had the look of soldiers.

"One moment," one of them said as Hale and the fisherman walked out on the wooden planking.

"Yes?" the fisherman asked, looking annoyed. "What's the matter?"

The stranger peered closely at Hale. "Are you a fisherman?" he asked.

"Yes."

"Been at it long?"

"Long enough."

The stranger looked at Hale's hands, then at the man standing next to him. "Do these look like the hands of a fisherman?"

Hale self-consciously looked down at his hands, then at his fisherman companion. The other's hands bore many mementos of slips by sharp knives, but his own were without a single scar. He found himself between two tall men who had closed in on him. For an instant he thought of plunging into the water, but quickly dismissed the idea as foolishness.

"I think we'll go back to the shed and talk," the stranger said, and Hale felt his arms gripped by the men at his side. They went to the shed, where Hale was subjected to a body search. The plans and drawings of New York's defenses were quickly discovered.

"Quite a collection, Captain Hale," the Englishman said, reading Hale's name on several of the papers. "I think you had better remain here."

The man posted a guard inside at the door, and left. Nathan Hale breathed a sigh of relief. The most damning evidence of all had not been discovered: the papers referring to his mission to burn New York. These were hidden beneath a strip of leather in his left boot. He wished he could take them out and hide them somewhere in the shed, but the guard's eyes followed his every move. All he could do was hope no one would think of searching the insides of his boots.

It was getting darker when he heard a horse ride up and stop outside the shed. A few words were exchanged, and then a dark-haired British officer entered through the low door.

"Captain Hale?" the new man asked.

There didn't seem to be any reason to deny who he was. "Yes, I'm Nathan Hale."

"Captain Patrick Blakely," the Englishman replied. He had the papers that had already been found in Hale's possession. The man who had taken them entered the room and waited silently while the captain glanced through the lot. "This is all you found?" he finally asked.

"Yes."

"You searched him from head to toe?"

"Yes.... Well, we didn't look in his boots."

"Take them off," the captain said to Hale.

As the soldier stepped forward to implement the captain's order, Hale lashed out and caught the unwary man on the jaw, knocking him backward into the arms of the surprised guard. As the guard struggled to get his fellow soldier off his chest, Hale hit him on the side of the head and plunged toward the open doorway.

He almost made it, but Captain Blakely was too quick. Just as Hale was passing through the doorway, the butt of the captain's pistol caught him on the back of the head and knocked him unconscious.

When he woke, he was bootless and sprawled in a corner of the shed. Blakely sat on a barrel. It was dark now, and the interior was lit by a single candle.

"That was a stupid thing to do," Blakely said.

Hale sat up, moved his head from side to side, and winced as a jolt of pain reminded him of the crack he had taken on his skull.

"So you planned to burn the city?"

"Only if I received a direct order. I never got it."

"What if you did?"

"I decided I wouldn't burn New York."

"You'd disobey a direct order?"

"That one, yes."

"They'd hang you."

"Better to hang than to burn the city. I couldn't live with that on my conscience."

Blakely admired the other man's courage. In a way he felt sorry about what was going to happen; men like Nathan Hale were rare. But the captain needed a sacrificial lamb, and Hale filled the role quite nicely.

He left the shed and gave orders that Hale was to be kept inside, and alone. "Don't let anyone near him. Keep him here for at least twenty-four hours." He mounted his horse and started back toward the city in the darkness. Within an hour he was back in his office with Sergeant Taggert.

"We're ready," the sergeant informed him.

"Any problems?"

"Three of the men I talked to refused to burn the city. They got very unhappy about it."

"And?"

"They won't be getting unhappy anymore."

The two men sat talking for over an hour, referring to maps

THE CITY IN FLAMES

and lists. At the end of their discussion the sergeant left to get ready to carry out their plan.

The captain sat back in his chair, put his boots on the desk, and allowed himself the luxury of a mug of tepid beer. If all went as planned, he would be working under a different set of circumstances on the following night. The coddling and pampering of prisoners would cease. The rebels would learn the true price of their folly.

A few hours before Captain Blakely was making his final plans with Taggert, Drew had walked over to Hanover Square to meet the old men he had hired to search for Hale.

"Not a trace of him," the one-eyed man said. "And it wasn't because we didn't give you your money's worth. I damn near wore my feet out walking around the town."

Drew brought out some money and handed each of the four men his half-crown. The men smiled and sent one of their number off to buy a bucket of beer.

The one-eyed man took Drew aside. "There's queer doings going on," he said.

"What do you mean?"

"Three men were murdered over on the west side near the river. Strangled, they were. A navvy I talked to claimed he saw one of them being done in. Claimed it was British soldiers who did it."

Drew remembered Caleb North's telling him about these murders, and what his father had said about them.

"Maybe the British want it to look like someone's trying to make trouble," the old man said. Drew was startled. It was exactly the same thought as his father's. He looked at the old man more closely.

"That's an interesting theory," he said.

"Until a better one comes along."

"What did you do before you moved here to the square?"

"Printer. In Boston," the man replied. "A good one, too."

"How did you wind up here?"

"Got into a brawl in a tavern one night. Lost an eye. After that everything seemed to go wrong. Felt sorry for myself and drank too much. Let my business fall apart."

"What's your name?"

"Around here names don't count for much."

"Tell me."

"I've given myself a new name since I moved to the square. Call me Sisyphus."

Drew smiled at the allusion to the mythical Greek king who had been condemned to push a rock to the top of a steep hill only to have it topple down to the bottom again. It was the fate of Sisyphus, because he had offended Zeus, to repeat this unsatisfying task for all of eternity.

"If I could find you a living, Sisyphus, would you take it?"

"Depends," the old man said thoughtfully. "Here on the square I manage to retain some dignity."

"I wouldn't do anything to change that."

"If you can find honest work that suits me, I'll consider it."

Drew nodded. "In the meantime keep looking for Nathan Hale. If you hear anything, go to the de Kuyper building on Whitehall Street and leave word for Drew. That's me."

"You're a de Kuyper?" the man asked.

"Yes."

"Shipping people, aren't you? Well, if you find me a job, make sure it's on solid land. I've been pushing that rock uphill so long I wouldn't know how to act on the water."

He returned to his companions, who were fussing over their bucket of beer and preparing their supper of vegetable soup.

"You'll be good, won't you?"

"Yes, Mother," Peter said dutifully, happy he was being allowed to stay at his grandfather's house on Maiden Lane. There was a great deal going on in the city, and he wanted to be part of it all. Celine had come down to spend the day with him, but was now preparing to return to her own house.

"Be careful," she said, putting her arms about him. He made a face and endured the hug. Finally she let go, and he quickly retreated to another room.

"Don't worry about Peter," Marie Therese said. "We'll take good care of him."

"I know."

"I wish you'd stay here with us, too, Celine," Marie Therese said.

"I can't. For one thing, I've got that British general as a houseguest. And Drew wants me there in case... well, in case someone shows up."

"Nathan Hale?" her father said, looking up from the book he was reading. He was amused by her surprised look. "I know all about the captain and his mission. Drew told me."

"Then you know why it's important that I be there."

He shook his head. "I agree with your mother. You'd be better off if you stayed here than up at Beekman's Place with British generals and whatnot."

"It's not called Beekman's Place anymore, Father," Celine said with a touch of exasperation. "It *used* to belong to the Beekmans, but now it's mine."

"Oh yes, I forgot," he said with a chuckle. "Now it's simply known as the Place. Very elegant."

"Stop teasing Celine," Marie Therese said. "She's got enough on her mind without contending with you."

"Getting so a man can't talk with his own daughter," Jan complained.

"Talking with her is one thing. Picking on her is another."

"I'm going to take my after-dinner walk," Jan said, putting down his book and rising from the chair. "Think I'll take Peter with me. He likes going down to the docks."

He came over and kissed Celine on the cheek. He might not approve of the way she lived, but Jan loved her as much as any man loved a daughter. He could pick on her, yes, but woe betide any other man who tried it. She patted his hand in affection, and waited in silence until he had left the room.

"He worries about you being up there alone," Marie Therese said.

"I have Primus and the other servants," Celine said. "Beth is staying with me. And then there's a British general who comes with two dozen armed guards. That's being alone?"

"You know what I mean," Marie Therese said. "It would be different if you had a husband."

"Let's not start on that again."

Marie Therese nodded agreement. It *was* a topic that had been overworked the past few years. She shifted subjects. "Your son is certainly turning into a bright young fellow."

"He can be scary at times."

"So were you when you were his age."

"And look how *I've* turned out," Celine said in mock horror. "If you don't believe how awful I am, ask your husband."

"Your father's bark is worse than his bite," Marie Therese said, with a wave of her hand. "Always has been."

"Peter told me he likes to stay here because he sees more of his Uncle Drew. He really worships him."

"A boy likes to pattern himself after a man," Marie Therese said. "It's natural."

"Is that another hint?" Celine asked suspiciously.

"No. We agreed to drop the subject of marriage. I'm merely making an observation about your son," Marie Therese said. "You're a big girl, and I won't try to lead your life for you."

Celine smiled. "I know. Even when I was a *little* girl, you rarely told me what to do. You just let me go ahead and make my own mistakes."

"Sometimes we learn more from our mistakes than from anything else," Marie Therese said.

"Not many people are wise enough to understand that," Celine said. "But then not many people think as clearly as you do."

"The trouble is most people are never *taught* to think clearly. I hope I didn't fail in teaching you or your brother."

"Maybe I turned out all right, but I'm not so sure about him," Celine said teasingly. She kissed her mother on the cheek. "And now I must get going. You know how much Primus hates to drive in the dark."

"Take care of yourself, my dearest," Marie Therese said, a slight mist coming across her eyes. She understood that children grow up and go off on their own. But even so, she occasionally longed for the days when Celine and Andrew had been little and had looked to her for everything and had spent every night sleeping in their rooms down the hall.

"What could happen on such a quiet, pleasant evening?" Celine replied.

The fire began shortly after two o'clock in the dark hours of Saturday morning.

Sergeant Taggert, dressed in farmer's clothes, personally started the first blaze, in the cellar of an abandoned dram shop at the foot of Broad Street. It was an ideal place, because the floorboards reeked of the whiskey and ale that had been spilled there over the years. The heavy stink of alcoholic spirits was still in the air. To make certain the flames would spread, the sergeant fed the fire with pine sticks that had been dipped in pitch. Within minutes, the cellar was engulfed in flames that shot up through the rickety floorboards of the old building, licked the dry walls, caught there too, and raced to the rooftop.

Several homeless men and women had been using the upper floor of the dram shop as a place of shelter. They were wakened by smoke and crackling sounds as the wood smoldered, blackened, and burst into flames. They made their way to the stairs, choking and gasping as the thick smoke swirled about, and were finally stopped by a wall of flames shooting up the open stairwell. An old woman began screaming hysterically.

"Here! Stop that!" an old man commanded.

"But we're going to burn!" the old woman sobbed.

"You're going to do that in the next world anyway," the man said, shoving her out of his way.

As the heat drove them back, the terrified people retreated into a room at the front of the building. But now the flames were devouring the entire structure, and the smoke and heat in the room became too much to bear. The first man leaped through the window and landed with a sickening crunch on the paving stones of the street below. The others followed quickly. Three died immediately. Two lingered for a time, until death ended their pain. Somehow, four others survived and managed to crawl away from the burning building. Only one person failed to jump. The hysterical old woman, felled by the smoke, lay on the floor, too weak to get up by herself. She had implored the others for help, but they were too busy trying to save their own lives, and left her to burn as the building turned into a torch. In the din of the fire and the commotion of the street, no one heard her last, feeble screams.

A southerly wind was prevailing, and the flames quickly spread from the dram shop to the buildings connected to it. As it consumed more fuel, the fire grew hotter and more voracious, and began spreading north and west up Broad Street. Leaping from roof to roof, the flames spread over to Dock Street, Beaver Street, Stone Street, and Marketfield. Soon the conflagration was a single wall of fire howling and roaring its way to Broad Way.

As the fires reached Bowling Green there was a shift in the wind and the flames jumped northward, leaving untouched the buildings inside the fort; the Kennedy mansion, which the British were preparing as Howe's new headquarters; and the houses immediately north of the mansion. In fact the entire block of four- and five-story houses between the Battery and Morris Street was spared.

Sergeant Taggert's men started many other fires, beginning at Pearl and Whitehall Streets, all the way west to the fort. The prevailing winds fanned the flames, and soon the entire southern part of the city, except for the little pocket near the Battery, was hellish with flames. The smoke rolled through the streets like a thick fog at sea.

New York was a city of wood, and as houses burned and the flames raced out of control, people tumbled out into the street. Many carried bundles—sheets and blankets filled with their most valuable possessions. They dashed this way and that, looking for an escape route, and often not finding any. In the melee several were trampled to death, some by their friends and neighbors who were too terrified to realize what they were doing.

The various volunteer fire departments were handicapped, because General Washington had removed all the fire bells, which might otherwise have been used to alert the people. He had taken them to melt them down to make bullets for his soldiers' muskets. The bells were used not only to call the volunteer firemen, but also, depending on the number of rings, to tell them where to go. On this day, many firemen didn't know where their services were needed most.

Philemon Peabody was sleeping in his bedroom on the third floor at the back of the de Kuyper building. Another bachelor, a clerk named Wilson, slept in the next room. Both men dressed quickly and ran down to the street. While Peabody stood a little distance away, shivering from fright and all but biting his nails, Wilson went back into the building, opened the cabinets, and came back outside with a set of record books. He placed them on the street, covered them with a piece of heavy canvas, then brought bucket after bucket from the water barrel to wet the canvas. When he was satisfied it was wet enough, he went back into the building to get more books.

All the time Wilson worked, Philemon Peabody stood to the side, frozen in his tracks, too frightened even to think of helping.

The flames came to Broad Way, paused at the wide gap for a moment, then shot across the street and began working their way west to the river. Soon the many fires in this section blended into a single huge one, and the monster moved steadily northward.

When the flames came to Trinity Church, they seemed to pause for a moment before attacking this imposing edifice; then they pounced on it with a vengeance. In minutes the interior was ablaze and the church, valued at the staggering sum of twenty-five thousand pounds sterling, began to disintegrate. The magnificent organ, which alone had cost eight hundred

THE CITY IN FLAMES

and fifty pounds, began to burn, its elegant brass tubings melting as Trinity turned into a huge furnace.

The fires reached across the narrow green sward and attacked the parsonage of Trinity's rector, the Reverend Dr. Inglis, who was forced into the street in his nightshirt and cap. He watched in helpless frustration as the flames worked their way to the top of the hundred-and-forty-foot wooden steeple of the church, turning it into a beacon that could be seen for miles around. It finally weakened and crashed to the ground, killing an unwary man who was frantically searching for his family.

The good Reverend Inglis wept as he watched the Lutheran church, on the opposite corner of Rector Street, go up in a blaze.

The great fire spread. Panic swept across the city. Drew was asleep in his second-story bedroom on Maiden Lane. The great columns of smoke advanced, and he was awakened by what sounded like distant gunfire. He leaped out of bed and looked out the window. Seeing the red blaze reflected against a dark sky, he slipped into his clothes and went down to the main floor of the house—to find that his father was also dressed and getting ready to go out into the night. A frightened Marie Therese stood to the side, holding little Peter by the hand. The boy's eyes shone with excitement.

"It looks like the entire city is on fire," Jan said.

Drew looked at his father, and they both had the same thought. "Nathan Hale?" Drew asked.

Jan shrugged. "Who knows?"

Jan grabbed a couple of wooden buckets and handed them to his son. A servant appeared with two more, and the older man took these for himself. "Maybe we can be of some help."

"Don't take any chances," Marie Therese cautioned. "May God be with you."

"Can I go?" Peter asked.

Marie Therese grasped his hand more firmly. "Certainly not," she said. "I don't think even your grandfather and uncle should be going."

"If it was our house, we'd be grateful for help," Jan said as he opened the door. "If it looks as if the fire is coming this way, we'll be back."

Marie Therese touched her son's shoulder. "See that he

doesn't get into more trouble than he can handle," she said, nodding her head toward Jan.

Drew nodded. He looked down at Peter. "You stay here and watch over Grandma," he said.

"I'll do that," Peter said.

The de Kuypers—father and son—quickly strode to Broad Way and began to make their way south. They were staggered by the great wall of flame that hovered over the southern end of the city. The flames kept appearing and disappearing behind the ever-growing clouds of smoke that blew northward on winds that fanned the flames to greater intensity.

The wooden walls and floors and the shingled roofs of the western sector of the city kept adding fuel to the fire, and it swept unchallenged until it came to the grassy sward at the southern edge of King's College on Barclay Street. Here a unit of volunteer firemen had set up a bucket brigade, and the men grunted and sweated as they passed the heavy water buckets. Their efforts were proving successful, and the fire failed to cross the green, sparing the college and all the buildings to the north of it.

Miraculously, St. Paul's Chapel was spared even though the buildings around it burned and crumbled into hot, smoking embers. Quick-thinking members of the congregation had gone up onto the flat roof, which had a balustrade on the eaves, and stamped out the hot embers as they dropped from the sky. A new bucket brigade was organized, and thousands of gallons of water were poured on the roof, preventing it from heating and bursting into flames like other buildings in the vicinity.

Ugly incidents began to occur.

A squad of British soldiers pounced on a man they claimed had put a torch to the wooden stoop of a house. Whether the man was innocent or guilty would never be known, because the soldiers beat him to death. No one came to the man's defense.

A man tried to loot the de Kuyper offices, but the clerk Wilson drove him off. Again, Philemon Peabody stood motionless to the side. Wilson berated him, but Peabody didn't answer.

Looters were active everywhere, and the sound of gunfire became commonplace as people tried to defend their property.

On Whitehall Street alone, three men and two women—one not much more than a child—were killed, their bodies left in the street and ignored.

Robert and Mary Delafield lived at 7 Broad Way, just north of the Kennedy mansion, in the block of houses that was spared. They stood outside their front door, fearfully watching the flames and hoping their luck would hold. Robert paced back and forth, cursing under his breath and, in general, acting as if the fire had been started to interrupt his personal night's rest.

"Damned British did it," he said.

"How do you know that?" Mary asked.

"Use your head!" he snapped. "They're punishing us for rebelling."

"It's crazy to burn the city."

"Maybe you're precious relatives won't be so pleased with the British now," he said.

Mary knew the reason the de Kuypers were acting so accommodatingly to the invaders, but Celine had sworn her to secrecy and she held her tongue.

At that moment a man came running down the street, pursued by several soldiers. They caught up to him in front of the Delafield house and began beating him.

"Hold on!" Robert said loudly, walking straight into the midst of the angry soldiers. "What right do you have to beat this man?"

"Starting fires, he was," a soldier said, and aimed a kick at the man who had fallen to the ground.

Robert Delafield wasn't a clever man, and he was something of a bully, yet he was brave in the way of a foolish man; that is, he acted without considering the consequences. He grabbed the soldier and started to pull him away. The soldier responded by swinging his musket around, slamming the butt into Robert's stomach. Then he reversed the butt and hit Robert a glancing blow on the side of the head. He fell unconscious to the ground.

Mary ran to her husband's side.

"If he belongs to you, missus, best tell him to mind to his own business," the soldier said.

A servant came from the house and helped Mary carry the unconscious man back inside. She took wet towels and tried to revive him.

* * *

Drew and Jan joined a bucket brigade just south of St. Paul's, and when this fire seemed contained, they moved farther south to help out wherever needed.

Drew saw a small child, a girl about three or four years old, hugging a rag doll to her chest, crying and looking around in bewilderment. "There, there," he soothed as he picked the child up and held her in his arms.

He looked at his father. "We can't leave her here. Maybe I should take her home."

Jan scratched his head. "Her family's probably looking for her right now. If we stow her away in our house, they'll think the worst for sure."

"What are we going to do with her?"

The problem was solved when a woman's voice cried out. "You've found her! You've found her!"

It was Alice de Witt, the wife of Enoch, a cousin of theirs. Drew looked at the child in his arms. Of course, it was little Elly—his own kin, but so covered with soot and ash that he hadn't recognized her!

"Elly, is that you hiding beneath all this dirt?" he asked, jiggling the child in his arms.

"Thank God you found her," Alice said, taking Elly and holding her tight against her breast. "I was worried to death."

"How come she was all alone out here in the street?" Jan asked.

"We were afraid our house was going to burn down, so we went outside. Enoch fell down, and while Jacob and I were helping him, little Elly just wandered off."

"Enoch fell down," Jan said, repeating her words, but giving them a world of meaning.

Alice looked at him and blew a wisp of hair from in front of her eyes. She was a thin woman, almost painfully so. She had once been quite pretty, but the ravages of impoverishment and worry had set upon her and diminished her beauty. "Yes," she said with a great weariness. "He was drunk again."

Drew had to look away. His cousin, Enoch de Witt, was, at the age of forty-two, a hopeless drunkard. The family seemed always to be finding him jobs, which he would promptly lose because no one would put up with his drinking for long—no one but Alice, who remained loyal despite the pain he brought to her life.

"Has your house burned?" Jan asked.

"A bucket brigade was working on it the last I saw," Alice

said. "Maybe they'll save it. We don't own it anyway, we only rent."

That was typical of Enoch, Drew thought. The man never saved enough money to own anything. If the de Kuyper-de Witt-Sackett-Goelet family had a black sheep, it had to be Enoch. "You'd better take Elly and go to our house," he said.

"Yes," Jan added. "Marie Therese will be glad to see you."

Alice looked skeptical. "Enoch might not like for you to take us in. You know how he can be."

Jan nodded in understanding. Even though Enoch had made a shambles of his life, he was still very proud. He knew what the other members of his family thought of him, and avoided them. He rarely went to their houses, and never invited them to his.

"Enoch can't have any objections now," Drew said. "Not with all that's going on."

"I guess you're right."

"Good. It's settled, Alice. You go to our house," Jan said.

"I should look for Enoch and Jacob."

"You take care of Elly," Jan said firmly. "If we see her brother and Enoch, we'll tell him where you are."

They watched as Alice took Elly in her arms and hurried north toward Maiden Lane. "If we find Enoch, I'd like to beat some sense into him," Drew said, releasing some of the anger he had repressed because of Alice's presence.

"You never knew my cousin, Ned Goelet. He was the same as Enoch for many years. Then he straightened out, and died a hero."

"Poor Alice," Drew said. "She puts up with a great deal."

They continued down Broad Way. Every step was fraught with danger. Embers rained down from the sky. Crazed horses dashed about, killing several people who weren't nimble enough to get out of their way.

A line of trees on New Street caught on fire. The flames shot up through the leaves, devouring them in an instant; the trunks were giant torches rooted in the ground.

The docks along the North River began to burn, and the ships themselves were not spared, except those few whose captains were alert and swift enough to slip their cables and drift out into the sluggishly moving waters. Better to be adrift and at the mercy of the tide than to remain at the docks and burn.

The de Kuypers struggled down to Beaver Street. Jan grimaced when he looked at the remains of what had been their warehouse—a heap of burning embers and hot ashes. "And I had you board it up to keep the British out!" he said.

"We lost a lot of money this night," Drew said.

"We didn't lose as much as he did," Jan said, pointing toward a blackened corpse that lay next to the remains of a burned wall.

Beaver Street was a disaster; not a single building was left untouched. The cloth that Drew placed over his nose and mouth didn't do much good against the awful stench that emanated into the air.

"A warehouse for storing hides used to be here," Jan explained. "They must have burned like tinder."

"What a smell!" Drew complained. The stench was choking him and making his eyes tear.

"There's an even worse smell in the air," Jan said grimly. And it was a horrible truth that the smell of burning flesh could be detected. Many horses had been trapped in their stables, and Jan had no doubt that a good many human beings in their homes had been trapped as well.

When they finally arrived at Whitehall Street, they were surprised to find their building in perfect condition. A number of other buildings in the immediate area had also escaped the conflagration. A shift in the wind had helped; so did a bucket brigade that was still working to keep the roofs wet.

Philemon Peabody saw Jan and Drew and hurried to meet them. The clerk Wilson, having saved the records, was now working in the bucket brigade.

"I think we're going to be all right," Peabody said. "As long as the wind doesn't shift again."

"What's that?" Jan asked, pointing to the canvas-covered heap in front of the main door of his building.

"Our records," Peabody said. He looked around quickly to make sure Wilson was out of earshot. "I rescued them in case the building caught on fire," he added.

"Good man!" Jan said.

"Yes, good thinking," a surprised Drew added grudgingly.

"Now we'll have to put them back," Peabody said.

"Let Drew do it," Jan said, clapping his arm on the little man's shoulder. "After all, you did all the work getting them out here."

That seemed fair enough, Drew thought as he uncovered the stack of ledgers and books. He started bringing them back inside while his father and Philemon Peabody stood surveying the damage to other buildings on the street.

A half mile away a group of soldiers captured another man who seemed to be one of the incendiaries. The man protested innocence, of course, but the soldiers refused to listen and began beating him with their fists and boots. The fellow was battered for a few minutes, and then Sergeant Taggert came upon the scene.

The man spotted him. "Sergeant!" he cried. "Tell them who I am!"

Taggert recognized the man as one of those he had hired to start the fires. He realized the man was about to betray their secret.

"Please, Sergeant," the man whined. "Explain why I was doing this."

There was no time for explanations, and Taggert didn't bother looking for any. He came up to the bleeding man. "One of the lousy bastards who's burning the city, are you?" he shouted.

He held his pistol by the barrel and brought the butt down on the man's head with all the force in his arm and shoulder. The wooden stock was thick, but even so it shattered into a dozen pieces as it crunched down into the man's skull, splintering bone and pulverizing the flesh.

"That's what we do to arsonists," Taggert shouted to the ring of soldiers. Several cheered, but others looked with dismay at the crushed head of the dead man at their feet.

The horizon to the east began to show the first signs of the new day, but it hardly brought joy to the people who were forced to continue fighting the flames. It was an exhausting and depressing task. While they were extinguishing the fires in one place, new ones would spring up elsewhere.

When the sun finally brought enough light to see, it was half obscured by drifting columns of smoke. People couldn't tell who was who, so covered with ashes and soot were they. The only clean parts of their faces were their eyes, and these had the haunted look of people who had seen their homes burn and their worldly possessions destroyed. Even so, the ones who lived counted themselves as lucky; there were enough charred bodies lying about the streets to convince them of that.

As the sun moved higher in the sky, Captain Blakely stood

on the front steps of the Provost, noting the night's work with grim satisfaction. It was a disaster of the first order; the fires were continuing to spread in the central parts of the city, from Dock Street, across Duke and Mill Streets, from Broad Way over to the fringes of the East Ward. From the looks of things, it would take all day to put out the remaining fires—but not before many more buildings were destroyed.

He walked around to the back of the building and got his horse from the stable. Accompanied by a detachment of mounted men, he rode over to the Post Road. The next phase of his plan was about to be put into operation.

After Drew had brought all the records back into the building, he allowed himself to rest for a few moments in a chair in his father's office. Philemon Peabody and Jan rested with him. Peabody's eyes shone with excitement.

"This fire is going to cause a shortage of everything," he said. "We ought to start making our plans."

"What do you mean?" Jan asked.

"We ought to get word to our ships at Albany. Have them load up with food and rum and get back here as fast as they can. Think of the profits we'll make."

"Profits!" Drew exploded. "People are dying and you talk of profits!"

"If we don't make them, someone else will," Peabody said. He turned to Jan. "Besides, the people are going to need these things. It's our *duty* to use our ships to supply the city."

"You're right," the elder de Kuyper said. "But Drew's also right. Let's have no talk of profits at a time like this."

Peabody nodded. He had gotten what he wished. Their ships would start bringing cargoes to the city. If the de Kuypers didn't want to be apprised of the profits to be realized, all the better for him.

Their rest was interrupted when a nearby building suddenly burst into flames.

They went back into the street, and Drew volunteered to be the lead man of the bucket brigade on the roof of the burning building. As he stood there, grabbing buckets and hurling their contents into the fire, he could feel the heat through the thick soles of his boots. After a time, the heat and smoke became too much and he began to choke and gasp for air.

Several men half dragged and half carried him back to safety. It was ten minutes before he was able to see or talk. While Drew was being tended for, the men gave the building up as lost and concentrated on soaking down the adjoining buildings to keep the fire from spreading.

So it continued throughout the day. When it seemed all the fires were out, a new one would erupt and the exhausted men and women were forced back to work.

When the last fire was finally extinguished, people were not yet aware of the extent of the disaster. They would soon learn that over five hundred buildings had been destroyed. Hundreds of horses and other animals had perished. The toll of human lives would never be known exactly, but even the conservative guesses put the number at close to one hundred.

But these were only numbers, and could not begin to measure the agony of men and women who had seen their hopes and dreams go up in a cloud of smoke.

Celine glanced out the second-story window and saw the approaching horsemen. The Irishman, Patrick Blakely, was the first rider. When she saw Nathan Hale riding between two British soldiers, obviously a prisoner, she gasped and her hand moved inadvertently to her mouth.

The men rode up to the front door, dismounted, and entered the house. Celine went to the head of the stairs and watched as Hale was led into the parlor being used by General Howe. The captain looked up and saw the anxious woman. He tried to affect a brave smile, but Celine wasn't fooled. Hale was in a great deal of trouble, and knew it.

She hurried down the stairs and went to the kitchen at the back of the house, where she found Primus chopping vegetables to make soup. He told her that a man had just come from the city to inform them the de Kuypers had come through the fire unscathed.

"And the house?" Celine asked.

"That's fine too," Primus said. "Your father said not to worry about anything."

Celine was relieved. She had been planning on going down to New York, because she was worried about her family, especially little Peter. But now that she knew there were no major problems, she could stay here and deal with the problem of Nathan Hale.

"Probably only want to question him," Primus said when she told him what she had seen.

Her hand shook as she held the kettle to pour herself a cup

of tea. Primus took the kettle from her and poured the tea himself.

"Now, now," he soothed. "If he hasn't done anything wrong, they're not going to hurt your young captain."

"But what if they say he *has* done something wrong?"

Primus shrugged. "That's different. But then you have a fine friend in this General Howe."

"Yes," she agreed. "That might be important."

She sat in the kitchen, sipping her strong tea, wondering what was going on in the parlor.

Howe sat in a comfortable chair as Blakely, his prisoner in tow, reported on the capture of Nathan Hale and told the general about the man's mission.

"Well, sir," the general coldly addressed Hale when Blakely had concluded. "Is this true? Were you the man who planned this damned burning of the city?"

"I didn't do it."

"The man lies," Blakely said. "Half New York is in ashes."

"Not by my hand," Hale insisted.

Captain Blakely took out the papers Hale had concealed in his boot. He handed them to the general. "These indicate the best places to start fires," he said.

The general glanced through the papers and began to scowl. He finally dropped them on the table. "With this evidence, do you really expect me to believe you?" he asked.

"I expect you to believe the truth, sir," Hale said.

"The truth," Blakely sneered. "The truth is the rebels decided to destroy what they were unable to hold. The truth is you burned the city and killed a great many people."

He turned his back on Hale and looked at the general. "Look at his clothes, sir. A captain in a civilian costume. I say he's a spy and should hang."

"If you want to hang me for being a spy, then do it," Hale said. "But don't say I burned the city, because I didn't."

"I suppose the fires started by themselves?" Blakely asked. "And the papers we found on you don't exist?"

Hale shrugged. "The papers exist, and there was some talk of burning the city. But we never implemented the plan."

"I suggest you look at the city and tell me there was no fire," Blakely said. "I say we hang him, sir."

General Howe looked at the prisoner. He liked what he saw: a handsome young officer in the prime of his life, respectful without being subservient. There was nothing of the cringing toady about him. He appeared to be just the kind of young officer the general liked to have in his own command. He sighed, because such speculation was as painful as it was useless.

"I'm sorry we're on different sides, lad," he said in a not unkindly voice. Then he looked at Captain Blakely. "Hang him at dawn."

The Irishman managed to conceal the smile of triumph that was forcing itself on him. "Yes, sir, at dawn. And now, with the general's permission, may I make another request?"

Howe's eyebrows lifted, and Blakely continued. "Now that we've evidence of the rebels' vindictive nature, isn't it time we started cracking down on them? If we continue to be soft, there'll be more burnings and loss of life, sir."

"I suppose Colonel Cunningham is in sympathy with this view?"

"Yes, sir."

"And, no doubt," the general said ironically, "you already have a few ideas about how to 'crack down.'"

"Quite a few ideas, General."

Howe sighed again. "Well, go ahead. I suppose we must get tougher in the light of what's happened."

"Sir, you must believe me," Hale protested. "Neither General Washington nor I had anything to do with the fires."

"Enough," the general said. "The evidence condemns you. Take him away."

After Blakely left with the prisoner, the general walked to the window and brooded. Damned, nasty business! He had hoped to convince the rebels their cause was hopeless. If it were up to him, the war would end and everything would go back to normal. The trouble was, the rebels weren't being cooperative. Burning their own city! What were they trying to accomplish?

There was a knock on the door, and Celine let herself in.

"What a delightful surprise," the general said with unfeigned enthusiasm.

"Do you have a moment?"

"For you? Of course," he said, coming forward and kissing her hand.

"I noticed you had an American visitor a few moments ago."

"Captain Hale."

"Is he in trouble?"

"My dear, these are unpleasant times. We are all in trouble."

"Nathan Hale is a friend of mine," Celine said. "I have an interest in knowing what's happening with him."

The general became unhappy. More complications, he thought. Well, there was no use in evading the issue. "Captain Hale is a spy. He's also responsible for the burning of New York. I had no choice but to order him hanged in the morning."

Color drained from Celine's face, and she stepped back several paces.

"My dear!" the general said with concern, and he took her arm lest she collapse.

It had been impossible for Celine to conceal her emotions. She looked at the general in horror. "You're going to hang him?"

"A terrible business," the general said. "But this *is* war, and he *is* a spy. I'm sorry he's a friend of yours, but there seems to be no alternative."

Celine had collected her thoughts. There was nothing to be gained by becoming angry and rejecting the general's friendship. In fact there was, conceivably, a great deal to be lost. On the other hand, she didn't want to fail to do whatever she could to save Nathan Hale from the hangman.

"You don't have to explain your actions to me, General," she said.

"I insist. I don't want you thinking of me as an ogre who likes to hang people."

"It would never occur to me to think of you as an ogre. It's just that Hale is such a young man, with his whole life before him. Must you hang him?"

A shadow crossed the general's mind. As commanding general, he could easily stay the hanging. He could simply order the man held in prison for an indefinite time. What problems could he cause in a cell? Ah, yes, he thought, many problems, among Howe's own officers. Especially Cunningham and Blakely. If he called off the hanging, he would have some outraged officers on his hands, and nothing could be worse during a time of war. As much as he wanted to please Celine, he couldn't risk destroying the morale of his subordinates. As much as he wanted to show his compassion to this woman, he had to remember his responsibilities as a general.

"I'm afraid we must indeed hang him," he said quietly.

"I see," Celine said, unable to keep the coldness out of her voice. "Would it be possible for me to have a private conversation with the captain before..." She was unable to continue.

"Of course," the general said, grateful to be able to offer some concession. "Anytime you wish."

"Right now, if I may."

The general walked to the door of the parlor. "I shall accompany you myself."

"That isn't necessary."

"I insist."

Nathan Hale was alone in a stall at the far end of the barn. Extra boards had been nailed to the sides of the stall, creating an effective prison cell.

General Howe ordered the soldiers away from the stall, and then withdrew himself to allow the prisoner and Celine their privacy.

When she was certain no one was watching, she threw her arms about Hale, kissed him, and looked into his eyes. "Nat, Nat, Nat," she breathed as tears rolled down her cheeks. "Why did you let them capture you?"

"I didn't do it on purpose," he said caustically.

"And now they're going to hang you!"

He held her hands in his own. "They're convinced I started the fire. They blame it all on me."

"But you didn't do it—did you? My brother had a note from Washington telling you *not* to."

"I never saw the note, but it wouldn't have made any difference. I'd decided I would never do it. The question is—since *I* didn't burn New York, who did?"

"Some of your friends?"

"No friends that I know of."

She kissed his hand. He was so young and handsome, so proud-looking, she wanted to drop down and make love to him on the floor of the stall. "There's still one chance that I can save you," she said. "Don't give up hope."

"What can you do?"

"Never mind," she said, giving her head a nervous toss. "I'll do what I can to keep you alive."

"That makes two of us that want me alive. Now, if we could only convince General Howe..."

"Maybe he can be talked to," Celine said, averting her eyes. "Maybe he'll listen."

"I doubt it," Hale said. "He's damned angry about what happened. As long as he thinks I did it, I'll hang."

"We'll see. In the meantime, is there anything I can get you to make you more comfortable?"

"Something to eat. They haven't fed me all day," he said, and then his old roguish smile returned. "Maybe they aren't planning on hanging me, after all. Just going to let me starve to death."

His smile caused Celine an almost physical pain as she recalled the happy hours they had spent together, in bed and out. She suddenly realized just how much he had come to mean to her, and it was far more than she had imagined. To discover this just as he was about to die was awful! She had to do anything she could to save him.

"I'll have Primus cook you the meal of your life," she said, and then kissed him again. It was a long kiss, a fierce one, as if both felt it might be the last one of their lives.

Celine wiped her eyes, but they retained a redness, and the general noticed it as they walked back to the house. Celine said nothing, and he too was silent, now well aware that Nathan Hale was more than a passing acquaintance of hers.

Celine withdrew to her bedroom, and soon afterward sent a servant down to the city with a note for her father, explaining what had happened to Hale and urgently requesting that he do something to save the man before the British hanged him in the morning. Then she went to the kitchen and started Primus on the preparation of a magnificent meal.

"I want you to leave me alone with the general after dinner," she said to Beth.

"All right."

"I'm pulling out all the stops tonight. Maybe I'll be able to do something for poor Nat."

Beth looked at her curiously. "Do you intend to sleep with General Howe?"

"I'll do anything if it will save Nat's life. Why do you ask? Do you object?"

"No. Anyway, it's not my place to object to what you do."

Celine looked at the girl. She was always so self-contained and sure of herself. "Tell me," she said on a sudden impulse, "if you were in my place, would you sleep with him?"

"It's an impossible question," Beth said. "I'd have to be

experiencing your emotions to really know. Besides," she admitted, "I've never slept with a man."

Celine could hardly remember when she might have said the same. "Are you curious about what it's like?"

"Yes."

"Have you ever thought about doing it? And with any particular man?"

"Thought about it, yes. With anyone in particular, no. There's plenty of time for that."

Celine nodded. Beth had plenty of time for everything. Unfortunately, the same could not be said for Nathan Hale, unless she could do something for him tonight.

She was determined to hold back nothing if it would save her friend's life.

That evening, in the cellar of Jan de Kuyper's house, there was a hastily convened secret meeting of a select group of the Sons of Liberty. Among those present were Drew, Caleb North, and Alec Seixas. Seixas, a notorious patriot and hothead, was the son of Gershon Seixas, the rabbi of the Jewish temple.

After receiving Celine's note, Jan had rounded up this group to see if anyone had any ideas about saving Nathan Hale. If they could prove he hadn't started the fire, they had a chance.

Drew related his conversation with Sisyphus, and how the old man had claimed he had talked to a navvy who had told him the murders could be laid to British soldiers. "If they'd murder to create an incident, they'd hardly be above starting fires," he concluded.

"This man who told you this is a homeless vagrant?" Jan asked.

"Yes."

"I doubt if his word would mean much to Howe," Jan said sourly.

"Yeah, what makes you think Howe would listen if we told him his men were going about murdering people?" Caleb North said to Drew.

"Maybe we ought to start doing a bit of murdering ourselves," Alec Seixas said.

"I think we ought to talk sense," Jan said quickly. "Fact: Hale says he didn't burn the city. Fact: somebody did. Question: who?"

"Another fact," Drew chimed in. "We have only until dawn. After that it will be too late."

"What makes you think it wasn't Howe himself who's behind the whole thing?" Alec asked.

"My sister claims the general was very upset about the fires. If he'd started them, he wouldn't have reacted that way, would he?"

"It wouldn't be the first time we've dealt with a two-faced limey," Alec growled.

"We need some proof to show Howe," Jan said. "And we don't have any."

"Maybe we could bribe some British soldiers. They might know something," Caleb North said.

Jan shook his head. "By the time we found the right man or men to bribe, Nathan Hale will be dead and buried."

"Well, we're not going to find out anything sitting around here," Alec said as he stood up.

"Let's get out in the city and start asking questions," Caleb North suggested.

"Well, I haven't any better ideas," Jan said reluctantly. "Let's get to it."

One by one the men left the cellar and spread out into the devastated city. They talked to men and asked them questions, but no one really had any hope of success.

Except one man. He knew what he was going to do to save Nathan Hale, and went quickly about his task. He told none of the others what he had in mind, because Alec Seixas believed in keeping his own counsel.

General Howe enjoyed another splendid dinner with Celine and Beth. Word of it, of course, filtered back to his officers and troops. The officers grumbled about their commander's dilettantish attitude and his hesitation to pursue the attack on Washington's forces on Harlem Heights. The common soldiers took a more amused view of it all. A rhymist invented a ditty that passed through the ranks until it had been heard by almost every British soldier in the New York area.

> Awake, awake, Sir Billy,
> There's forage in the plain.
> Ah! Leave your little filly,
> And open the campaign.

If William Howe ever heard this rhyme, he made no mention

of it, but continued to take his time in developing the campaign against the rebel army.

"I understand your house was spared in the fire," he said to Beth as he allowed a servant to add claret to his glass.

"Yes. I was lucky."

"Many people were less fortunate," he said.

"The general thinks he's captured the man who started the fires," Celine said, and Beth picked up the cue as Celine had instructed her to do.

"How do they know he's the one?"

"We found a great deal of incriminating evidence on him," the general said. "But must we talk about something so unpleasant at the dinner table?"

"Do you plan on hanging him?" Beth asked.

"Yes, we do."

"The question is, Beth," Celine said, "have they captured the right man? If they're not absolutely positive, don't you think they ought to wait a bit before they hang him?"

"Yes. You can't bring a dead man back to life," the girl said.

"The point is, we *are* absolutely positive," the general said. "Everyone except you, Mrs. Murray."

"I still think you ought to wait."

"The man is responsible for countless deaths and endless destruction," the general replied. "He deserves to hang."

Celine caught Beth's eyes and indicated it was time for her to take her leave. Beth wiped her mouth daintily with her linen napkin and stood up. "I'm really tired," she said. "Please excuse me."

The general stood and bowed. "Until the morrow, Miss Henry."

Celine and the general chatted for a short while, carefully avoiding the subjects of Nathan Hale and the fire. She was more the coquette than usual, and he responded with an eager gallantry. Finally there was a long period of silence, and they sat staring at one another. It was Celine who spoke at last.

"My bedroom is the one with blue doors at the far end of the corridor to the right of the stairs," she said, and with that left the room.

The general continued to sip his wine. He swirled it around in the bottom of his glass and seemed pleased by the little bubbles that appeared.

So! It was finally going to happen. He had come to the

conclusion that it never would. Being a gentleman, he had accepted his fate with good grace. It wouldn't do for a man of his standing to act like a whining, puling schoolboy. Too many men made asses of themselves over women.

He took his gold watch from his pocket and set it on the table. Another part of being a gentleman was that one never rushed the lady. He decided to stay at the table for ten minutes. They were going to be, he realized, ten very long minutes.

Once in her room, Celine wasted no time in getting out of her clothes. She stripped down to her bare flesh and rubbed her body first with a damp cloth, then with a thick, soft towel. She put on a flimsy green nightgown, and went to the mirror to begin brushing her silky blond hair.

It had been a simple decision to make: if she could save Nathan Hale by making love to the general, she was going to do it. But she had never before used her body to curry favor, and she wasn't delighted with herself.

Celine finished brushing her hair and went to the dressing table. She opened a vial of perfume and dabbed some behind her ears and beneath her breasts. Then she put out all the lights except one. She stood by the open windows and allowed the gentle night breezes to caress her body.

A few minutes later the door opened and William Howe slipped inside. His eyes were bright with anticipation when he saw the woman standing at the window. He walked across the room and stood at her side. After a few moments he placed his hand on her shoulders and looked into her upturned face. His kiss was soft and gentle.

Celine put her arms about him and kissed him back, enjoying the sensations she felt suddenly. The silvery moonlight rested on her face.

"You're beautiful, my dear," he whispered. "You fairly take my breath away."

"And I find you, General, most attractive," she murmured, looking up at his rugged face and feeling the strength in his body. Her reason for this tryst was to save a man's life, but now she found herself wanting this general for himself. She stepped back, confused, and her lip trembled.

"What's the matter?"

"I have a confession to make," she said quietly. "I have an ulterior motive for wanting you here."

Howe sighed. The ulterior motive could be only one thing. "Yes?"

"I want to save Nathan Hale's life."

"A lucky man, to have a woman willing to do so much for him."

"But I can't do this to you. I...I care too much."

He was touched. "And I care for you, too. But even so, in the matter of Hale I can do nothing."

"If I could show you positive proof he wasn't the one who started the fire, would you do something then?" she asked.

"What proof?"

"If I could show it to you, would you at least delay the hanging?"

"I must ask again—what proof?"

"There was a note sent by General Washington to Hale. It ordered him not to carry out the burning. Hale's orders were to wait for a direct order to burn or not to burn. Since he never received any order, he did nothing."

"May I look at this note?"

"I don't have it," Celine said.

"I see," the general said.

"I know this sounds strange, but you must believe me, the note exists. My...someone I trust told me about it," she said, wanting to bite her tongue for almost implicating her own brother.

"Someone *told* you about it?" the general asked. "You mean you've never seen this note yourself?"

"No," she admitted, realizing that her case was looking weaker and weaker. "But I trust the one who told me about it."

"But you won't tell me his name?"

"I can't. It would mean betraying a trust. Would you want me to do such a thing?"

"No, my dear, and it was churlish of me to ask," the general said. "But you do see the dilemma you're putting me in. How can I do something that will antagonize my officers? If you had real evidence of Hale's innocence, I wouldn't hesitate for a second. But as it is..."

Celine looked out the window, because she realized she was beginning to cry. She had been willing to make love to this man to save Hale, but in the end she couldn't do it. Besides, the general probably had too many scruples to take a woman under such circumstances.

He noticed her tears and brushed one away. "Don't cry," he said.

"I feel like a fool. This whole thing was done to save Nathan. Even if I went through with it, you wouldn't change your mind about him, would you?"

He shook his head slowly. "Mrs. Murray...Celine...I would gladly give you anything within my power to give. But this calls for a breach of honor. Surely you wouldn't ask me to do that?"

"No," she said. "I wouldn't ask you to do that. But there is one thing I can ask."

"And that is?"

"Don't hang Hale in the morning. Give me two days. I'll see if I can have the note in that time."

"I can't give in even that much. When a commander gives an order, he must be firm about it."

"You can't take my word about the note?"

"*I* can," he said meaningfully. "But my officers won't."

"Promise me you'll at least think about it," she said, now grasping at any straw, however flimsy.

"I can't," he said, quietly but firmly, and Celine knew the discussion was over.

"Now that we've settled the matter, my dear, I think it time for me to go to my own bedroom," he said. He took her hand and kissed it, then started for the door.

He stopped at the opening and looked back at her. There was a longing in his eyes, and a sadness. "Good night, my dear. The important thing is, in the end, we were both honest with one another."

He closed the door behind him.

Shortly after three o'clock in the morning, a sentry at the fence post near the end of Celine's barn thought he saw a movement in the bushes.

"Halt! Who goes there!"

The heavy musket ball that returned in reply caught the sentry in the chest and knocked him backward to the ground. Several men jumped out of the bushes and ran toward the barn. In the lead was Alec Seixas.

When the meeting of the Sons had broken up, he had independently recruited several like-minded men, and they arrived at the Place with the intention of freeing Nathan Hale by force. Alec knew exactly where to go, because he had sent a spy ahead to reconnoiter while he enlisted the other men.

But the British were not caught napping. Captain Blakely

had posted triple the usual number of guards against the chance of just such a rescue mission. Several redcoats raised their muskets and fired toward the source of the commotion. One of Seixas's men fell to the ground and began screaming in pain.

Captain Hale had been asleep when the nearby blast shattered his reverie. He tried to peer out through a narrow opening between the slats of his prison, but could see nothing in the darkness.

"Here!" he cried, hoping to guide what he assumed were his rescuers. "Here I am!"

Alec heard the cry and continued running toward the barn, keeping his body low to present a smaller target. A sentry suddenly appeared in front of him, and Alec fired one of the three pistols he was carrying. The sentry dropped immediately.

He'd made it almost to the barn when a fusillade of musket fire killed two more of his men. The remaining three turned and fled back toward the safety of the nearby woods.

Alec fired another pistol and was rewarded by a scream of pain, but he realized there was nothing left to do but retreat. He ran, and within seconds was swallowed up by a thick growth of trees and brush. He kept going until he emerged on the road that led to the river. He followed this for a ways, hiding in the bushes once when a cavalry patrol galloped by. Then he resumed his trip back to the city without further interruption. His plan had failed, but at least he had tried to do something, while almost everyone else had gone to bed.

The commotion at the barn wakened Celine.

She came to her full senses immediately. Gunfire! The barn! Nathan! She ripped the sheet off her body, wrapped it around herself, and was out of the room, running toward the head of the stairs.

She wasn't the only one awake in the house.

Primus came from his first-floor bedroom, in the wing behind the kitchen. He heard the sound of bare feet pounding on the stairs and came into the foyer in time to see Celine open the door and run out of the house. His eyes opened wider when he realized she was clad only in a bed sheet.

General Howe was awake—indeed, he had not been able to fall asleep at all. He had tossed and turned, his mind filled with visions of a beautiful blond creature that was part Celine, part a figment of his imagination. He slipped into his boots, hastily put on his trousers, and was into the hallway a few seconds after the woman. He was in time to see her going down the stairs, and followed.

Celine ran across the lawn. Soldiers were shouting and running in all directions. She ignored them, stopping only when she came to the barn. She was panting from the exertion, and the sheet slipped from her shoulders. She clutched it to keep it from falling completely.

Captain Blakely, fully dressed and looking as if he hadn't slept at all, came around from the side of the barn. He stopped and regarded Celine with something that was almost amusement.

The general arrived. He was bare from the waist up, and his usually carefully groomed hair was in wild disarray. Captain Blakely stepped forward, started to salute, then stopped, realizing the gesture was out of place while the general was only half dressed.

"Yes, yes," Howe said impatiently, annoyed by the pleasure it seemed he was giving to the captain.

"They tried to rescue the rebel, sir. Two of our men are dead. Another two wounded."

"And Hale?"

"We still have him."

"Damned rebels!" Howe said angrily. "I'll be glad when this hanging's over."

"Yes, sir," Blakely said, not unhappily. He was delighted that the rebels had tried to rescue Hale. The death of the two soldiers would harden the general's heart.

Celine caught her breath audibly on hearing this exchange. The general stepped to her side. He put his arm about her, and their naked flesh touched.

"I'm truly sorry about this, Mrs. Murray. Truly sorry."

Celine's flesh came alive with goose bumps as she felt the warmth and smoothness of his skin against her own.

The tableau was frozen as Primus arrived from the house, carrying one of Celine's robes. He held it close to her body and stared at the general.

Howe realized his arm was in the way. "Sorry," he mumbled in embarrassment as he withdrew it.

Celine allowed Primus to place the robe over her shoulders. She had never seen him look at her in this way. What was in his eyes? Displeasure, certainly. But more: reproach. Why? What was the matter with him?

And then she realized Primus had been looking at a half-naked general holding a half-naked *her* in the circle of his arm. Primus must have thought that...

She wanted to explain to the black man—to assure him that he had misunderstood, that this was harmless, nothing—but immediately knew how foolish it would all sound, how absurd; and anyway, from the look in his eyes, he wouldn't believe her.

Rather than become angry, she felt a great warmth and compassion for the black man. She understood he was reacting out of love; and felt closer to him than at any other time in her life.

"I'll be all right, Primus."

"Hmn."

"Really... everything is *all right*."

"I hope so," Primus said, and his usual sense of humor was notable by its absence.

"Do you wish to be present at the hanging, sir?" Captain Blakely asked the general, bringing them all back to reality.

Howe hesitated, then answered. "Yes."

"Very good, sir."

"And now, my dear Mrs. Murray..." the general began, but Celine—a rather bedraggled figure in a sheet covered by a robe—was already walking back toward the house, with Primus at her side.

The general lowered his head and followed after.

Captain Blakely's face betrayed the contempt he felt for all of them.

Celine paced back and forth in her room, still clutching the bed sheet. Sleep was out of the question. A thousand images ran through her mind; none of them made sense.

The door opened.

General Howe stepped inside. He was still dressed only in his boots and trousers. He closed the door behind him and stood still, watching her, *devouring* her.

He knew, she thought.

He had felt what *she* had felt when their flesh touched; and he knew what had been in her thoughts, because her thoughts were his too.

He stepped forward and put his arms about her. The sheet dropped to the floor. A surge went through him; his skin actually tingled.

His hands roved downward across her smooth back; he

found the curve of her rounded buttocks. Her breasts were pressed against his chest, and the nipples hardened.

"No," she murmured.

He shook his head. "You don't mean no."

She wanted to tear herself away; and couldn't.

"This is what we want," he said.

Her voice was hoarse. "We want it for *us*. There's no other reason."

"No other reason."

He picked her up in his arms and carried her toward the soft, waiting bed.

The sound that came from her throat was half ecstasy, and half sob.

A rooster crowed. The darkness began to soften.

Captain Blakely led a detachment of ten men to the barn. They opened Hale's stall. The prisoner came out and stood between the soldiers, who had formed two lines. All marched out of the barn with military precision.

In deference to Celine, the general had ordered the hanging to take place off her property. The execution detail left her land and went to another part of the old Beekman's Place, a farm currently owned by the British colonel Rutger.

A rope was tossed over the branch of a stout apple tree, and a ladder set up beneath it. The prisoner was led to the ladder and made to climb halfway to the top. The hangman dropped the noose over Hale's neck and tightened it. He stepped back and waited.

The general arrived. Captain Blakely saluted. The general looked irritated and uncomfortable. He looked up at the face of the man with the noose about his neck.

"Do you have any last words?" the general asked.

"I only regret that I have but one life to lose for my country."

The general nodded. The hangman kicked the ladder out from under the prisoner.

Justice was done.

Dick Goelet had been alone in his cell at the Provost for almost a week, and was beginning to think he'd spend the rest of his life there. No one talked to him, not even the guard who brought food or the old man who emptied the slop pail.

The cells at the other end of the corridor had begun to fill up, but Captain Blakely had ordered Dick to be isolated from everyone. Even so, he heard scraps of conversation and knew that a terrible fire had swept the city. There was no way he could find out whether it had been started by Nathan Hale.

The food in the prison took a sudden turn for the worse. At first Dick and the other prisoners had been fed a reasonable amount of well-cooked food, but now the men received only one meal a day—a bowl of unappetizing gruel or watery soup. The big challenge was to find a bit of meat in the soup. Coffee had been available at first, but that also had been stopped.

The attitude of the soldiers toward the prisoners hardened. If a man was slow about following an order, the soldiers used their musket butts freely. One poor fellow was beaten to death just yards down the corridor from Dick's cell. The body lay on the cold stone for two days before it was removed.

The architect of the new rules, of course, was Captain Blakely. He finally sent for Dick. When he arrived at the captain's office, his presence wasn't acknowledged, nor was he offered a chair. He remained standing in front of the desk.

"Nathan Hale never received your message, Goelet," the captain finally said. "So he burned the city."

Dick didn't know it was a lie. He felt terribly sad that his failure might have brought about the destruction of his city; he said nothing.

"You have no response to offer?"

"I've been downstairs in a cell for a week, Captain. How could I know who burned the city?"

Blakely opened the drawer of his desk and pulled out Washington's note. "Hale never received this order. It's obvious he went ahead with his plan. More's the pity for you and the rest of your people."

"But you know what the note says," Dick blurted out. "General Washington never intended to burn the city."

"The road to hell is paved with good intentions."

"What's to become of me?" the prisoner asked, shifting nervously from foot to foot.

"I'm locking you up with the rest of the rebel scum," the captain said.

Dick nodded. At least he wasn't going to be shot. Thank God for small favors. "Did you ever find Captain Hale?"

"Found him and hanged him. His last words were that he regretted he only had one life to lose for his country," Blakely said mockingly. "Too bad he doesn't have more lives than one. I'd be happy to oblige him."

"At least he died a hero," Dick said.

"Which brings us to you," the captain said meaningfully. "I want you to forget you ever saw this note. If you start talking about it, I'll see that you join your friend Hale."

Dick nodded. He was in the lion's den, and it made no sense to twist the nose of the big cat. "I don't know anything about that note, Captain," he said.

The next day he was taken from his cell and brought with several hundred other prisoners to the old Sugar House, on Crown Street. It was a tall building with seven main stories, two below ground, and an eighth floor under the eaves of the roof. The walls were thick and formidable, with bars set in the windows to make it a fortress of a prison. Years ago it had been used to store raw sugar and molasses.

The ceilings of the building were low, and a very tall man was forced to stoop when he went through a doorway. All the doors inside had been removed, and the British made no attempt to assign the prisoners to specific places. They could go anywhere they wanted—as long as it was inside the building.

Despite the conditions, Dick was relieved to be back among his fellowmen. A great deal of the conversation, naturally, was about the fire. He learned that the British blamed the rebels for it and this was the reason for their harsh treatment of the prisoners.

He was seated on the floor with his back against a rough stone wall when Seth Cuyler spotted him.

"Well, Dick, my lad, I see you've managed to land in this mess of porridge, too."

Dick was surprised—and delighted—to find someone he knew. "It happens to the best of us."

"This damned old building," Seth said, looking around at the mottled walls, so damp in places that there was a fungus growth. "I've been here on business dozens of times, but I never thought that one day it would be my home."

"How long do you think they'll keep us here?" Dick asked. There was an edge of horror to his voice. He had been in the Sugar House for less than an hour, and already he hated it. What if they kept him here for weeks? Or months? Or—God forbid!—years?

"They'll keep us locked up as long as Washington is in the field with an army," Seth said. His stomach suddenly growled, and he laughed. "I'm not used to getting by with so little food. But I suspect I'll have to adjust."

If the men had any doubts they would be living on short rations, they were dispelled that afternoon, when the British passed out to each man a loaf of bread, a pound and a half of raw pork, a half pint of uncooked rice, and a quart of raw peas.

"Is this for one day, or two?" Dick asked.

The soldier who was passing out the rations smiled and jabbed his companion in the ribs. "Listen to His Majesty here. Wants to know if this is for today. No, you rebel scum," he said with a sudden scowl. "That's four days' worth, so don't eat it all up at once."

Dick walked away realizing things were going to be very difficult indeed.

He approached a window and stared out through the iron grate. Another unhappy thought occurred to him. How could they cook their food? He posed the question to Seth.

"They're passing out the pots," the big man said. "We'll cook our food together and be a team."

The shortage of pots caused a great deal of arguing, but finally the men agreed to combine their food and cook it as several units. The real problem was getting wood to make a fire. The soldiers were extremely uncooperative, but finally enough wood scraps were produced.

Dick had been accustomed to eating his fill, something that was no longer possible. However, he soon learned it was possible to bribe the guards to get more food. So did the other men, and bribery became a way of life. It was that or near starvation.

There were over nine hundred men jammed into the Sugar House, and since there were no provisions for bathing, they let their beards grow and began to stink. The prisoners themselves grew accustomed to the smell, and they began to take a perverse pleasure in their inspections by British officers. The noisome odors obviously bothered the Englishmen.

The Sugar House became a jungle, with every man out for himself. The only rule agreed upon by all was that there could be no stealing of food. The punishment for that sin was established on the third day, when almost everyone had run out of provisions and there would be no more for another day.

A bully named Simpson spotted a chunk of bread in the pocket of a smaller man. Without ado, he snatched it from the weaker man and cuffed him in the mouth when he complained.

"You can't do that," Seth said, standing up to the bully.

"Who's going to stop me?"

"I am," Seth said quietly. He was a big man, as big as Simpson and very strong. He grabbed the bully, knocking the bread out of his hands. Simpson threw a roundhouse punch and missed. Seth belted him in the mouth and stunned him. Then he stepped behind him and grabbed the man's head in both hands. "This is what happens to anyone who steals food," he said.

With a vicious twist he broke the bully's neck. A gasp went up from the watching men, and Dick Goelet's eyes almost popped out of his head.

"Give me a hand," Seth said to him, and the two men carried the body to the front door, which was guarded by a heavy iron grate. "This one's dead," Seth said to the guard.

"How did he die?" the soldier asked.

"Fell down and broke his neck," Seth said. "Always was a clumsy bastard."

The soldier shrugged and unlocked the grate. "Dump him over there," he said, pointing to a spot just outside on the street. And that was it. The death of a man in the Sugar House was about as important as the death of a fly.

The word about Simpson passed through the building in minutes, and most men agreed that his had been a fitting punishment. Only a few weeks ago the idea of killing a man for stealing a hunk of bread would have been unthinkable to most of these men. But now they had been reduced to a different level of existence, and they were adapting; their instinct was to survive.

As the days passed and the men settled into their new routines, they learned there were other prisons like their own throughout the city. The North Dutch Church, on William Street, and the Middle Dutch Church, near the Commons, were being used to hold thousands of men. The North Church alone held eight hundred prisoners, which made it even more crowded than the Sugar House.

The British had also taken the Friends' Meeting House, on Pearl Street, and turned it into a hospital for their own wounded; and the old brick church on Beekman Street was half prison, half hospital. Actually, the latter was, for many, the last resting place before the grave. When a prisoner became too sick to stand or eat, he was shoved into the hospital and allowed to starve there. The bodies were disposed of in mass graves.

Dick and Seth got their first taste of Hessian humor the second week they were in the Sugar House. Captain Blakely had decided that Hessians, being meaner and more primitive than regular British troops, made better jailors. Half the guards were now Germans, and they shouted at the prisoners and harangued them in a guttural language few could understand.

When the Hessians became bored, they played a game with an unlucky prisoner. The first man so honored was Seth. One of the Hessians gave him an order in German, and Seth, not understanding the words, made no response. The Hessian whistled up several of his cohorts. Together they stripped Seth of his coat and shirt, then used these very articles of clothing to strangle him until he passed out. They revived him with rum and slaps on the face; then they strangled him unconscious again. They did this five times before they tired of the game and left the man alone.

"The rum almost made it worthwhile," Seth said when he finally regained consciousness.

He and Dick had become great friends. Seth brought physical strength and discipline to their unit; Dick provided the ingenuity, always managing to scavenge food and firewood.

The incident with the Hessian stranglers made Seth Cuyler a passionate hater of the mercenaries. He vowed that when he got out of this pesthole he was going to kill every Hessian he laid his hands on. Dick tried to reason with Seth, because he thought his friend's rage would only get him killed. He might have succeeded, but for the news of a personal tragedy that was brought into the Sugar House.

A new prisoner sought out Seth and found him seated on the floor next to Dick. "I hate to be the one to bring you bad news, Seth," he said. "But I guess I've got to tell you."

"What?"

"There was an incident at the Battery the other day. Soldiers opened fire on some people. Killed three of them. One was your son."

Seth passed his hand over his eyes. His son had been only sixteen. "The soldiers who fired," he asked, "were they Hessians?"

"Come to think of it, they were," the man said.

Seth's hatred now became an obsession. He would watch the German guards and pretend he had a musket in his hands. He would aim and pull the trigger, then smile and count another enemy dead.

The fall weather began to turn colder. There wasn't a boarded window or pane of glass in the Sugar House, only iron bars and grates. The prisoners complained they needed blankets, but the guards ignored them.

The only amusement the men had was to gossip and pass rumors. There was one that Washington had taken his army off the island of Manhatan and was somewhere in Westchester. It was also said that General Howe had followed with an army. The one thing the rumors had in common was that they were always bad news.

New prisoners brought tales of rebuilding in the city, and sometimes a message from one's family was smuggled in. Dick tried to learn something about his own family, but wasn't successful. It was Seth Cuyler who finally found a guard who was willing to carry a message to the outside.

"You bribed him?" Dick asked.

"How else? He's going to see my wife and tell her I'm all right. He'll do the same for you."

The English guard turned out to be a slight, ferret-faced man who didn't look as if he could be trusted. But Dick had no choice. He started to give instructions, but the man held up his hand.

"Let's see your money first."

Dick reached into his pocket and pulled out a single coin. "Not much," the Englishman said with a sneer.

"It's enough," Dick said, determined to hold the remaining two coins in his pocket for a dire emergency.

"All right," the man snarled, grabbing the coin and shoving it into his own pocket.

Dick instructed the man to go to the de Kuyper house on Maiden Lane and inform the people there that he was alive and held prisoner in the Sugar House. "Tell them I'd like to see them."

"Want visitors, do ye?"

"Yes," Dick said, and then, with a sudden craftiness born of his new way of life, added, "They'll bring more money and maybe you and I can do more business."

The suggestion had the desired effect on the Englishman. He grunted. "I'll get to these people straightaway."

For the first time since he had been thrown into prison, Dick began to feel there was some hope. He began to whistle a tune, and the men about him looked up astonished.

* * *

"Look, Captain," Drew said, fighting back his anger, "There's no reason to keep holding Dick Goelet a prisoner."

"There's every reason in the world," Blakely replied.

"My family is trying to cooperate with you people. We've already got ships hauling grain for your army. We need Dick in the business."

"He should have thought of that before he became a courier for Washington."

It was the second time Drew had come to the captain to plead for his cousin. He was having no better results this time than last. The only concession the captain had made was to allow Drew to visit the prison once. At least on that occasion he was able to give Dick a supply of food and some money.

But no prisoners were being released; the captain was adamant on this point, although the temporary prisons now held thousands of men and were filled to overflowing. The British were desperately looking for a solution to this problem, which was draining resources and manpower.

"The conditions in the Sugar House are appalling," Drew complained. "The men are jammed in there like peas in a pod."

The captain was unmoved. "They asked for it."

"There *is* such a thing as compassion."

"Was it compassion that drove them to rebel against the king? Was it compassion that made them burn their own city?"

Drew gave up and walked to the door. "General Howe claims he wants to win us over to his side. Is this any way to do it?"

"The commander approves of what we're doing," Blakely said.

Drew walked out into the crisp November air. He tried to think of other ways to help his cousin. Maybe a direct appeal to Lord Germain would do it; the minister for foreign affairs could override orders issued by General Howe or Captain Blakely. Jan had met Germain several times—maybe he could write a letter, Drew thought.

Drew walked through the streets, which seemed alive with the sounds of saws and hammers as the townspeople and soldiers tried to patch up the wreckage caused by the disastrous fire. With the cold breath of winter on their necks, they worked as fast as they could to assure themselves some protection during the coming months.

As they worked, they talked of current events. In general, the news was bad: Washington and Howe had fought an inconclusive battle at White Plains during October, and now the Continental Army had retreated across the North River and was fleeing south. General Howe, as usual, was taking his time with the pursuit; but also as usual, his plans were professional and complete. Compared to the Americans, with their ragtag methods, the British army was a marvel of efficiency. The sloppiness of the Americans, in fact, had caused the British to begin referring to them as a rabble-in-arms. The epithet stung Washington and made him swear under his breath.

Several carts holding prisoners came rumbling by. The men looked battered and wore hangdog expressions. More prisoners from Westchester, Drew thought. Soon the whole city would be nothing but a prison camp; they might as well fence in the whole damned island.

He stopped to watch a group of people as they erected the side of a damaged house. The men used long poles to stand the already completed wall against the house; the work was done swiftly and expertly, as men swarmed up ladders and began nailing the wood in place.

Drew was almost at Maiden Lane when he met David Sackett coming from the other direction. "Good morning," he said, somewhat surprised, because the lawyer spent most of his time in Philadelphia as a member of Congress. "What brings you home?"

"Business. Have you heard the latest news from up north?"

"I hear nothing *but* news," Drew said. "What bit are you talking about?"

"Our friend General Howe has chosen not to follow Washington into New Jersey. Instead he's turned south and is moving against Greene's position at Fort Washington. Greene's men are the last American troops on the island."

"How many men do we have at the fort?"

"Two or three thousand. And Howe has fifteen thousand. How do you like those odds?"

Drew grimaced. "General Washington was counting on Greene to protect his flank. If Howe captures Greene, the commander is in real trouble."

"He's in real trouble now, nephew, make no mistake about that. This war is just about over. And on top of everything else, I'm on my way to complain to Colonel Cunningham."

"About what?"

"The damned navy has commandeered the de Kuyper dock near the Whitehall Slip. They've tied up a powdership there.

A powdership! If anything goes wrong—boom!—there goes our dock."

"Do you think the colonel will listen to you?"

David threw up his hands. "Who knows? But I've got to try. And then it's back to Philadelphia."

"How are the sessions of Congress going?"

"Don't ask," the lawyer said, and was on his way again.

Drew arrived at his father's house and entered through the front door. Peter, eating an apple, was walking down the hall. Sounds of a heated debate issued from the dining room.

"What's going on in there?" Drew asked.

"Grandpa and Enoch are having another argument," Peter said, and bit down through the juicy red skin. "As usual."

Drew debated avoiding the situation, but told himself it was a family problem and he was part of the family and therefore it was his problem too. He went to the dining room doors, opened them, and stepped into the next room.

Enoch de Witt was a heavyset man, forty-two years of age, his hair a mixture of dark blond and gray. His flushed face showed the ravages of the heavy, longtime drinker. He and his family had been living in Jan's home since their own house had burned down in the fire, and his presence had precipitated one argument after another.

"I'm a grown man," Enoch said. "I don't see that it's any of your business how much I drink."

"It's my business as long as you're living in my house and it's my rum and gin you're swilling," Jan said.

"Then I'll leave," Enoch said. "I won't stay with my family in a place where we're not wanted."

"Who says *they're* not wanted?" Drew asked.

"All everyone does is complain about me."

"Not about you," Jan snapped. "About your drinking habits."

"I've managed to survive."

"Yes, but at what cost to your family?" Jan said angrily. "Your wife is harried almost to her grave. Your son is ashamed of you. And poor little Elly—what's she to think?"

"I'm going out to look for a house right now," Enoch said. "When I come back, I'll take my family away."

He angrily made his way out of the room, swaying unsteadily. Jan shook his head. "If his father could see him, he'd turn over in his grave."

"Don't let him upset you," Drew said. "He's not going to change."

"I don't give a damn about Enoch," Jan said. "He's related to me—and to you—by blood, but it's his family I'm concerned about." He thrust his hands into the air. "Family! Why is it everyone in the family is suddenly going crazy! What the hell is going on?"

Drew was surprised by the outburst. "What else is happening?" he said.

"Your sister is what else is happening."

"What's she done now?"

"She took one of our ships."

"Celine? Took one of our ships?" Drew asked in disbelief. "What for?"

"It was the *Pearl*," Jan said. "Came down from Albany last night loaded with corn—corn that Philemon Peabody had already promised to the British."

"How on earth did she take a ship?" Drew asked.

"When it docked she went to the captain and identified herself as my agent. She gave him new sailing orders, and off they went together. She's with that crazy Alec Seixas."

"Obviously they plan on bringing the corn to Washington," Drew said. If Alec was involved, that had to be it, because he was one of the biggest smugglers in New York. He was also a patriot, and now smuggled only for the rebel forces.

"I don't mind that part of it," Jan said. "It's just that I don't like my daughter playing pirate."

"She's not exactly a pirate," Drew said in her defense. "After all, she's being a patriot, and Washington has promised to pay for anything he gets."

"Sure," Jan grumbled. "But he'll pay us in continentals, and you know how much they're worth these days."

Drew smiled. Once a businessman, always a businessman. Continentals were issued by Congress in Philadelphia, and this American paper money was rapidly becoming worthless. Not long ago it could be exchanged for sterling at a rate of about two and a half to one. But with a British victory appearing closer, the rate now stood at forty to one, and was widening.

"What's gotten into Celine?" Drew wondered aloud. "She never took an interest in the rebellion before."

"I've talked to her a lot since she moved in with us," Jan said. "The death of Nathan Hale affected her. Now she wants to see us win the war."

"We're doing our best, maybe we should let her do hers in her own way."

"I'm not always sure we *are* doing our best," Jan complained. "Every time I hear we've made another delivery to the British, I wince."

"We only give them enough to make them *think* we're cooperating," Drew pointed out. "Besides, a lot of that food goes to feed the prisoners—and they know we're on their side. After all, our own Dick Goelet is one of them."

Jan nodded. "Yes, yes, I know we can justify everything we're doing. But I still have my sleepless nights. Take Dick. Isn't there something more we can be doing?"

"Not without arousing suspicion. You must be easier on yourself, Father," Drew said gently. "After all, this pretending to cooperate with the British is General Washington's idea. He's the commander. What else can we do but follow orders?"

"Some orders are easier to follow than others."

Drew nodded, and decided to get his father away from such a sore subject. "Where did Celine and Alec take our ship?"

"She didn't tell me," Jan said. "My daughter the patriot pirate!" he added derisively. But even so, there was a look of pride on his face; his daughter was doing more than most people.

"There's another way to look at it," Drew said.

"What's that?"

"You're always complaining Celine spends her time engaged in frivolity."

"That's the truth."

"Now she's becoming more serious. Maybe it's a sign she's settling down."

Jan burst into laughter. "Maybe you're right, but how do I explain that to anyone? Yes, my daughter's finally 'settling down,' yes; she's become a pirate."

He put his arm about his son's shoulder, and their laughter reached into the kitchen, where Marie Therese sat with Alice de Witt.

"They seem to be enjoying themselves," Marie Therese said.

"Enoch must have left," Alice said. "They don't laugh much when he's around," she added, and there was a soft wistfulness to her voice. Alice always acted as if she was afraid she might break something.

"I'm sorry we're such a bother to you, Marie Therese, but we'll be getting another house shortly."

"You're not a bother at all. I love having you and the children in the house."

"And Enoch?"

"He can be somewhat trying," Marie Therese admitted. "Alice... please forgive me for this question, but have you ever thought about leaving Enoch? I'm not trying to cause trouble—Lord knows Enoch causes enough by himself! But maybe if you left him, it would be the jolt he needed to start straightening himself out."

Alice's smile was a sad one. "He wouldn't even notice I'd gone. As long as there's a bottle on the table, he doesn't care about anything else."

"Then why stay?"

"I need him," Alice said. "I'm terrified to be alone. I have nightmares about it. Enoch may not be much, but he's something—and I guess he's enough."

"I think you're wrong," Marie Therese said firmly. "You'd be better off alone than with a man who abuses you."

"He's never hit me."

"There are other forms of abuse. Some can be worse than hitting."

"He's all I have," Alice persisted.

"You're a good-looking woman—or you would be if you took better care of yourself. There'd be other men."

Alice shook her head. "Not for me," she said miserably.

Marie Therese sighed. Unless a woman had some appreciation of her own worth, there was nothing to be done for her. She felt like crying. It was a terrible thing to watch Alice de Witt being destroyed—especially since she was destroying herself.

The *Pearl* had eased out of her mooring on the North River long before dawn. The captain, a dour Scot named MacBourne, was certain he was on a fool's errand. But this Celine de Kuyper Murray *was* a de Kuyper, and the family owned this ship, so it was hers to command.

He glanced over at her as she stood at the rail with Alec Seixas, and made a face. Taking orders from a woman! He shook his head and ordered the sailors into the shrouds to set the sails. The ship picked up way and headed down through the Narrows. They passed a British frigate at anchor, but since the *Pearl* seemed on legitimate business, the frigate's lookouts didn't give her a second glance.

MacBourne brought the ship down to the southern tip of Staten Island, followed the shoreline, and entered the mouth of the Raritan River.

"We'll come to a place known as Signal Rock," Seixas said to Celine. "There's a dock there. Men will be waiting to unload the ship."

The more time she spent with Alec, the more she learned about the elaborate system of rebel spies and smugglers. "How do they know we're coming?"

"Smoke signals."

Celine was impressed. She was pleased with her new involvement with this man, whom she had sought out to thank for his attempt to rescue Nathan Hale. As they had talked, both realized they might be of use to one another. The result was this voyage with a cargo of corn for General Washington.

It was nothing new for the Seixas family to join in a venture with a de Kuyper. Years ago, during the French and Indian War, Levi Seixas and Ned Goelet had worked together as privateers in the Gulf of St. Lawrence. Ned had died in battle, and Levi had enjoyed privateering so much that he took up pirating after the war ended. He was finally caught and hanged by the French on the island of Martinique.

"This is all going so smoothly," Celine said with satisfaction. "We ought to do it again."

"Anything to make life miserable for the British," Alec agreed.

"I can be of great use to the cause."

Alec smiled. "Forgive me, but your reputation has been mostly as the belle of the ball. You're quite surprising."

"I have good connections," she said. "Maybe I can find out about things *before* they happen."

"That kind of information could be invaluable," Alec said, and found his respect for this woman growing steadily.

They sailed down the river until they came to Signal Rock. The captain expertly guided the ship to the rickety dock and tied up. Within minutes the cargo of corn was being unloaded and taken away in horse-drawn carts.

"It'll take them all day to unload," the captain said.

"We have the time," Alec said.

Captain MacBourne walked away muttering to himself. It was bad enough to be taking orders from a woman, but now to be pushed around by a Jew! He decided he was going to quit his job the minute the ship got back to New York. He was a patriot, yes; but this was too much.

During the day a man arrived with the news that Fort Washington had fallen and Howe had captured two thousand men.

"That means two thousand more prisoners to be jammed into those foul holes," Alec said.

"We've been unable to get Dick out of there," Celine said.

"They won't let anyone out. It's the work of this Captain Blakely," Alec said. "He's a devil."

"We've got to get rid of every last British soldier."

Alec, who had heard a few choice rumors, looked quizzically at her. "Even General Howe?"

"Even him," she answered without hesitation.

The next morning the lightened *Pearl* sailed down the Raritan on the tide and came back into the open waters of New York Bay. By nightfall she was snugly tied at her berth on the North River. The first delivery of supplies from New York City to General Washington in New Jersey had gone off without incident.

Beth Henry was in her house on Rutgers Hill.

It had not been badly damaged by the fire. The fence at the front had been knocked down by a confused cartman during the conflagration, and there were a few scorch marks on a southerly facing wall, but to all practical purposes the house had not been touched.

She was in her room packing a trunk, preparing to move in with the de Kuypers. Because Beth lived alone in the big house except for two servants, the British had commandeered it as a billet for a dozen naval officers. She was to move out by the afternoon so the gentlemen could take possession by nightfall. Her petitioners had been polite about it, but quite firm. Her house would be an officers' quarters for the duration of the hostilities. Of course they would pay her for this use; on this point the British were fair. If something belonging to a loyalist, or even a neutral, was taken over, they made suitable payment.

In a way she was happy about the move, because the house was far too big for her. It had been left to her by her parents, and she kept it in their memory. The paintings, the candlesticks, the knickknacks—all the curios that had belonged to her mother—were staying in the house. Beth was also leaving behind the two servants—partly because the British offered to pay them, and partly because they could keep an eye on Beth's possessions.

She put the last of her clothes in the trunk and closed the lid. She left the room, went down the corridor, and entered what had been her mother and father's bedroom. It seemed so huge and empty without their presence. On the wall over the mantelpiece was a painting, her father's favorite portrait of her mother. It was a full-length study showing Louise Clément Henry in the buckskin garb of an Indian maiden; a reminder of her half-French, half-Indian heritage.

Beth opened her mother's closet. Most of the clothes had been stored or given away, but several outfits were still on padded wooden hangers. One was the buckskin outfit in the painting.

She took out the buckskins, held them up, and then, on an impulse, undressed and put them on. She donned the trousers and jacket, then slipped her feet into a pair of deerskin moccasins. She stood in front of the mirror and studied herself. The hair was wrong, so she spent a half hour arranging it in long braids that hung down in front of her shoulders. Then she placed a circlet of beads and leather about her head.

The mirror reflected an Indian maiden, a beautiful one with large, unblinking eyes. She smiled at herself. Satisfied, she left the bedroom and went to the parlor, where Mary Delafield was packing the last of the silverware. Mary was helping Beth move, and it was her idea not to tempt the British officers by leaving the silverware.

"You look just like an Indian," Mary blurted out when she saw the way Beth was dressed.

"That's because I *am* an Indian," Beth said. "At least as much an Indian as I am a white."

"But why are you dressed like this?"

"I felt like doing it. Don't you like it?"

"You look beautiful," Mary admitted, but she was not quite sure of her own words. She was very conservative, and dressing like an Indian at least bordered on poor taste, she thought. "I guess you can get away with it because you're so young."

"As opposed to being an old crone like yourself," Beth said with a laugh.

"Be amused," Mary said, looking closely at the girl and realizing she could not compete with her in the eyes of most men. Beth had a dark, brooding beauty that made her unique.

"Are we taking the candlesticks?" Beth asked, pointing to a pair of silver holders on the mantel.

"Yes, all the silver."

They were almost finished when Captain Blakely appeared. "I beg your pardon, ladies," he said. "Just a routine inspection that the house is in order." He looked straight into Mary's eyes. "A pleasure to see you again, Mrs. Delafield."

Mary felt a shiver go up her spine. What did this man have that made her react so to him? She introduced Beth to the captain, and he was polite, but it was obvious he was much more interested in Mary than in the beautiful younger woman.

"I suppose you like taking people's homes away from them?" Mary asked, being spiteful in order to fight the other emotions whirling about inside her.

"Not particularly," Blakely said. He looked at Beth. "And we *are* reimbursing you handsomely."

"I have no complaints," Beth said.

The captain studied her for a moment. "You are part Indian, Miss Henry?"

"Yes."

"You wear it well," he said. He turned back to Mary and focused his most intense gaze upon her. "It's a shame we almost never see one another, Mrs. Delafield."

His words and his brazen stare made their impact.

"It's been difficult to lead a normal life," she said, striving to conceal the sudden breathlessness she felt.

"Unfortunately," he said. "But who is to say what will happen in the future? And now if you'll both excuse me, I'll inspect the rest of the house."

He smiled at Mary and left the room.

"I'd watch my step with that one," Beth said.

"I find him fascinating," Mary said, and then her hand flew to her mouth. "What am I saying? I'm a married woman!"

"I don't think that would bother him."

Beth moved into the de Kuyper house, and that afternoon wandered into the parlor. She inspected the paintings. There was one of Jan, another of Marie Therese. Near the fireplace was her favorite—a painting of Jan with her own father, Theophilus Henry. How handsome he had looked as a young man!

She sank into a high-wingbacked chair and was studying the painting when the door opened and Drew entered the room. In the poor light of the late afternoon, he didn't see her. He went to the sideboard and poured himself a glass of Madeira. He walked to the window and looked out broodingly.

Beth's eyes remained fastened on Drew. He was about the same age as Theo was in the painting. As much as she admired her father, she thought Drew to be even better looking. A strange emotion came over her as Drew walked back to the sideboard for a refill. Her skin tingled; it rose into goose bumps. What was going on?

Suddenly Drew sensed that someone else was in the room. He turned around, startled. "Who's there?"

She moved in the chair and he saw her. "Who the devil is there?" And then he stepped forward and could see her features. "Beth! . . . It seems you like to give me a start."

"I didn't mean to," she said, standing up and moving into the light. "I was just sitting there."

He saw the Indian outfit and was startled anew. "Why the costume?"

"It belonged to my mother. I thought I'd wear it," she said in a voice that was smaller and less sure of itself than usual.

"Celine said you'll be living here," he said.

"Yes."

"That's nice," he replied, his interest diminishing with his curiosity. "Well, I must be about my business."

He was gone, and Beth stood alone in the middle of the room. It was obvious he still thought of her as "little" Beth, the daughter of his father's friend. His impression of her had probably been reinforced when he saw her "costume."

But she was not a little girl. When she had looked at Drew, she could feel a stirring inside her. He was a man, and she was a woman and she knew it.

She was no longer little Beth.

3

A Terrible Winter

1776–1777

"A TEMPORARY SETBACK, THAT'S ALL IT IS, TEMporary. An accident." Philip Van Cortlandt, a patrician-looking man wearing a powdered wig, was annoyed. He rubbed his forefinger along the side of his nose. A silk handkerchief crept from the sleeve of the uniform coat that identified him as a lieutenant-colonel in the loyalist militia.

"But what's to prevent such an accident from occurring again?" Jan de Kuyper asked, baiting this man he had known for thirty years and detested for as many.

"Washington's victory at Trenton was a fluke, luck, a one-in-a-thousand chance," Van Cortlandt insisted. "The man ignored the rules of warfare and, by all rights, ought to have lost."

"Ah, but he didn't lose."

The two men stood along the far wall of the ballroom of the Kennedy mansion, now the residence and headquarters of General William Howe. Only a few months ago this building had housed George Washington, but now a different flag hung from the second-story flagpole: the banner with the red cross of St. George on a white field, and diagonally the Scottish white cross of St. Andrew on a blue field. Over two hundred people were gathered at the mansion on this evening of December thirty-first, the last day of the year 1776; they were here at the invitation of the commanding general to join him in ringing out the old and heralding the new.

Half the men in the room were in uniform—a cross-section of the highest ranking British, Hessian, and loyalist officers in the province. The civilians, for the most part, were important New Yorkers, loyalists favored by an invitation from the commander. For some it was a dubious honor. The latter were men who seemed to be going along with the British occupation, but whose hearts weren't in it. Jan de Kuyper, for one, came because to have refused would have aroused British suspicions. But that didn't mean he had to suffer graciously the pomposities of a loyalist ass like Philip Van Cortlandt. Beneath the veneer of politeness existed a great depth of hostility.

The women in attendance were mostly wives and daughters, the men having recognized the commanding general's house as hardly the proper place to bring a mistress or a camp follower. The ladies were dressed in long gowns and wore silk pumps, and precious jewels adorned wrists, hands, and necks. A few women wore tiaras studded with diamonds and emeralds. In the fashion of the day, most of them carried exquisite fans made of silk and ivory.

General Howe moved among his guests, welcoming them, putting them at their ease, making them feel at home. He had a prodigious memory, and wherever possible he would mention something personal, and the guest would be gratified to know this important general took time to know about their own affairs. Passing thus through the room, he came upon Jan and Van Cortlandt in the middle of their argument.

"Any man who ignores the fundamental rules of warfare," Van Cortlandt was saying, "as does this George Washington, in the end is bound to be defeated."

"You speak of fundamental rules," Jan countered, "but surely tactics that are correct on an open plain do not apply in the mountains. The forests of America are not the fields of Europe."

"War is war," Van Cortlandt said. "Damme, sir, I don't understand how you can take the side of a man who's won only a single battle in a year and a half of warfare."

"Yes, but we must remember that the battle he won happens to be the last he fought."

General Howe, still unnoticed by the arguing men, winced at these last words. How true they were! His army had swept Boston. His troops had easily defeated the rebels on Long Island. He had run Washington off Manhatan, chased him out of Westchester, and pursued him down through New Jersey. He had compiled victory after victory, until it had begun to look as if the rebels had no chance against him in the field.

And then came Trenton.

Howe had assumed the year's campaigning was over, and ordered the bulk of his army to return to New York for the winter. He left a picket line of garrisons at New Brunswick, Perth Amboy, Bordentown, Princeton, and Trenton. The Trenton garrison consisted mostly of Hessians under the command of Colonel Johann Rall. On Christmas night Washington crossed the ice-choked Delaware River nine miles north of the town. He divided his troops into two units and, at eight o'clock on the morning of the twenty-sixth, attacked Trenton from the north and northeast.

The Hessians were taken by surprise and routed. The Americans killed thirty, and took over nine hundred prisoners while suffering only five casualties.

The mortified British tried to blame everything on the Hessians. The Hessian commander-in-chief, General Wilhelm Knyphausen, in turn attempted to place all blame on the Trenton commander, Colonel Rall—which gentleman, conveniently, had been killed in the fighting and was therefore in no position to defend himself.

But no matter what was said or what accusations were tossed out, General Howe was a realist, and he understood what had happened. The British had become complacent and overconfident and had underestimated their enemy.

Howe's field commander, Lord Cornwallis, hadn't even been in New Jersey when the rebels counterattacked. He had been in New York waiting to take the next trip back to England for the duration of the winter. Those plans had been quickly changed, and there was no more talk of the campaign's being over. Washington's lightning victory had put an end to that notion.

The general therefore was none too pleased to hear mention of all this under his roof during what was supposed to be a social interlude.

"Yes, Washington won the last battle," he said, attracting the attention of the two men. "But the important thing is, who will win the next one?"

"Good evening, sir," Philip Van Cortlandt said with a smile. "Is it possible for any intelligent man to have doubts?"

"A lot of intelligent men said the same thing a week ago," Howe answered sourly.

"But surely we have nothing to fear from a little enemy—"

The general interrupted. "There is no such thing, sir, as a little enemy."

"As I was pointing out to de Kuyper," the flustered Van Cortlandt continued, "it was an accident, General, a mere fluke."

"A well-planned fluke," Howe said, turning his attention to Jan. "Tell me, Mr. de Kuyper, is there more to Washington than meets the eye?"

"I suppose that could be said of any man."

"Yes, but you apparently think highly of the fellow's capabilities."

It was Jan's turn to smile. "It doesn't much matter what I think, does it? He won the battle."

The general was glum. "And just when I thought all this unpleasantness was going to end. I can't see that anyone is gaining from this affair."

"The rebels will be taught to respect the laws of the king," Van Cortlandt said, piously repeating the standard loyalist line.

"Yes, Trenton certainly proves that," Jan said, knowing he was crossing the line of propriety as well as that of discretion, but not caring. The general looked sharply at him, but his attention was diverted by what he saw over Jan's shoulder. "Ah, your daughter, Mr. de Kuyper."

Celine had entered the main room. She stopped, and let her eyes drift about the room. She looked very striking in a low-cut gown of green silk. Her fine blond hair was tied in a series of knots and was artfully arranged to show her snow-white neck and shoulders to full advantage. She knew the impression she made by the looks on people's faces. The men wanted her; and the women hated her.

Two men were standing to the left of the doorway. "Good evening, Mrs. Murray," Captain Blakely said.

"Captain," she murmured, and he brushed his lips over the top of her hand and then introduced her to his companion, General Wilhelm Knyphausen.

"A pleasure, madam," the Hessian said. His deep voice had such a thick accent it made everything he said sound as if it was accompanied by a belch.

The Hessians had done nothing of late to alter their reputation for savagery, and as she turned her gaze to the stout general, Celine felt both revulsion and amusement. She couldn't suppress a smile at the sight of the huge paw Knyphausen extended. When he kissed her hand, his mustache tickled it and she almost stepped back, but managed to check her response.

"Where is Mrs. Delafield?" Blakely asked.

"She's not feeling well and decided to stay home," Celine lied. The truth was that Robert Delafield would no more set foot in an Englishman's house, or allow his wife to do so, than he would jump off the roof. Mary tried to get him to control his temper, but without luck.

"A shame," Captain Blakely said. "I was looking forward to seeing her."

"A *nize* party here," General Knyphausen said, trying to insert himself into the conversation. His breath smelled of beer and sausage.

"It would be far better if Mrs. Delafield were here," Blakely informed him.

"I'm sure you'll see her again," Celine said. Blakely smiled and made a little bow, and she was again struck by his good looks. And his charm, she thought, even though his reputation for brutality was now well known. While Colonel Cunningham might be the provost marshal, a good many people were beginning to realize that the man who really ran New York was Captain Blakely.

General Knyphausen said something more, but his accent was so thick that Celine was unable to decipher a single word. Captain Blakely grinned. "The general is asking about your husband," he said.

"There is no Mr. Murray, General," she said. "He died several years ago."

The general was dutifully saddened by this news, but he brightened at the thought that this attractive woman was a widow and might be available. "Ach, a zorrow to be zhure, but life must go on," he said.

Celine noticed that General Howe had left her father and had gone to the table laden with food. She excused herself and walked across the room.

As Captain Blakely watched her go, a sardonic smile played about his lips. He wasn't fooled about the reason for Mary Delafield's absence. His spies had told him enough, and he had Robert Delafield marked down as a troublemaker—one of those hardheads who couldn't accept reality. Perhaps the man's stubbornness will be what brings his wife to me, he thought further. He wasn't quite sure what it was about Mary that fascinated him, but fascinate him she did. The few times they had met, he had felt his hands grow moist and his heart beat faster.

"That's quite a woman," General Knyphausen said, admiring Celine's bare back. He wiped a bit of perspiration from his chin.

"A good friend of the commander's," Blakely said dryly.

The message took a few seconds in penetrating the Hessian's mind, but then he beamed with understanding. "Zo? He has good taste, *nein?*"

"Indeed," Blakely said.

"Good evening, General Howe," Celine said. The smile that came to his face was genuine. He bowed and kissed her hand in a formal manner, then turned and introduced her to the man he had been talking with.

"The famous Lord Cornwallis," Celine said. "We hear much about you, but you never seem to spend any time in the city."

"Being a field commander, I leave the city to the commander-in-chief, my dear," Cornwallis said smoothly.

Charles Cornwallis was thirty-eight years old, stocky but not fat. He had a healthy, ruddy complexion, sensuous heavy-lidded eyes, and an aquiline nose. He was bright and affable, and might have been considered handsome except for the unfortunate squint in his left eye. It was the legacy from a field hockey accident suffered while he was a student at Eton.

"The best field commander in our army," Howe said warmly.

"Not that flattering a distinction," Lord Cornwallis said with some distaste. "We have too many officers whose only qualification is the size of their purse."

"And as long as they pay, they hold the jobs," Howe added.

"I don't understand," Celine said, mystified by the general's statement. "Officers in the British army *buy* their places?"

General Howe coughed. "I'm afraid so, my dear. A man without a private income can't afford to be an officer in our army."

"Just to become an ensign of infantry costs four hundred pounds sterling," Cornwallis complained. "To buy the same appointment in the cavalry costs almost a thousand."

"That's terrible," Celine said.

"It's worse than that," General Howe said. "To become a lieutenant colonel in a famous Guards regiment costs six thousand pounds. Do you believe that? I'm ashamed to tell you,

Celine, but that's twice as much as the pay of the First Lord of the Admiralty."

"But try to get any money out of the government to spend on the troops!" Cornwallis said. "Only last year I wanted new coats and breeches for my men. I couldn't get a farthing out of the treasury people, so I spent a thousand pounds of my own money." The subject was a sore point with him, and the squint of his eye seemed to worsen as he thought about it.

They continued to talk about army affairs, and Celine was surprised at the way they openly discussed matters in front of her. Apparently they didn't think it necessary to be cautious in front of a woman. She became especially interested when they discussed the new plans that had been drawn up since the debacle at Trenton.

In the morning Cornwallis was going to New Jersey to take command of the army. His plan was to move a great number of troops to Trenton, build up a strong front, and then crush Washington and the rebel army in a single overpowering attack.

"What I want to do is take my time," he said. "When I'm certain I have the advantage, I plan to attack and capture this pesky man. Bag the fox, so to speak."

"Keep your supply lines strong," Howe said. "And set the battle at the time and place of your choosing, not Washington's."

"I'll box him in at Trenton," Cornwallis said. "Let's just hope he stays there."

"The site of his great victory will also commemorate his final defeat," Howe said.

"Nicely symbolic," Cornwallis said, and as the conversation drifted into the more technical aspects of the coming campaign, Celine excused herself.

She wanted to leave the mansion, but didn't want her departure to be obvious. It was important that she send her brother off to warn Washington that the British were planning to trap him at Trenton. Surely the American commander would make good use of this information and escape.

Once she looked across the room and saw Howe smiling at her. He was a true gentleman. They had never spoken of their night together, nor repeated it. They shared the memory; it was enough.

She found herself accepting a glass of Madeira from a servant at the same time a handsome man in civilian clothes was taking one from the other side of the tray. Their eyes met, and when the servant walked away, they were left standing in front of one another.

The man held up his glass. "To the new year."

"To the new year," Celine said, and they both sipped a bit of wine. She looked at the man and wondered who he was. Certainly she would have remembered meeting him, because he was a remarkably handsome fellow, tall and lean, with pale yellow hair cut a bit on the long side. He had deep-blue eyes and the whitest teeth she had ever seen. Little lines converged into wrinkles around his eyes when he smiled, as he was doing now.

He nodded his head to indicate a man across the room. "I wonder if the major is getting enough to eat these days," he said.

Celine saw he was referring to an English officer, a fat man heaping more food onto an already overladen plate. In between the forkfuls he dropped on the plate, he crammed others into his mouth, extending his jowls and looking like nothing else so much as a happy pig.

"Poor fellow looks underfed," Celine said.

"Yes, war can be a trying experience. As witness all *those* poor men."

At his gesture, Celine looked at the others gathered at the food table. None was as obese as the major, but most were on the heavy side. The war might be causing privation in New York, but certainly not among the British officer corps.

"Are you from New York?" the man asked.

"Yes; and you?"

"A visitor. Actually, I would like to think of myself as a guest. But since this city is your home, that is for you to decide," he said. "Like any good guest, I try not to abuse whatever hospitality I receive."

Celine found herself taken by this charming man with the dry sense of humor. From his accent she deduced he was English, and from his clothing that he was not a member of the military; probably a commercial attaché, or some kind of diplomat. She had never seen him before, and concluded he had only recently arrived.

"You mean you wouldn't act like the fat major? Or his German friend?" Celine asked, noticing the major had been joined by General Knyphausen, who was eating a turkey leg without observing the nicety of a plate.

The blond man smiled again. "General Knyphausen is one

of the jewels in the crown of the prince of Hesse-Cassel. Surely you can't be referring to him?"

"I have yet to meet a German with manners. Wouldn't you think London would choose their mercenaries from more agreeable people?"

"You have a low opinion of Germans?"

"They're uncouth," Celine said. "With the manners of peasants."

"Ah, but there's a reason for that," the man said, now thoroughly enjoying himself.

"And that is?"

"They *are* peasants. But there isn't enough land back home for them to farm, so the prince rents them out. They do make good soldiers, you know."

"I've heard they're even better at looting and stealing."

The man shrugged. "A European tradition for centuries. Such soldiers consider loot and booty to be part of their pay."

"And you approve?"

"As a matter of fact I don't, but there's not much I can do about it."

Celine realized she had been pressing the man, and without cause. "I'm sorry, I didn't mean to imply it was your fault. After all, what have you to do with the Germans?"

"Yes," he said seriously. "I try to avoid the Germans at all times."

"Wise of you," Celine said. "They're not really our sort of people."

A British cavalry major was walking by, and he nodded a greeting. "Good evening, Colonel."

"Good evening."

Celine stared at the man at her side. "Colonel? You're in the army?"

"Yes, madam, but whenever possible I wear more comfortable clothes. Let us say that at heart I am a civilian."

Celine laughed. "Maybe we'd better introduce ourselves," she said. "I'm Celine Murray."

The man bowed. "And I am Franz von Lossow, colonel in the service of the prince of Hesse-Cassel." He winked. "Actually he's my cousin, but we never did get along."

Celine's mouth dropped open. "You're a German!" she accused.

He looked around furtively, then brought his finger to his lips. "Shh. I won't tell anyone if you don't."

"That wasn't fair... letting me go on about the Germans like that."

"Why not? You only spoke the truth."

"But your accent is... so English."

"My father is a very odd German. He sent me to England for my education. I read at Balliol for several years."

"Balliol?"

"Oxford, you know."

"Will you ever forgive me?" Celine asked.

"Only if you will permit me the honor of a dance."

She smiled, and a few minutes later they were taking part in an elaborate minuet known as the Royal George. The colonel wasn't a very good dancer, but if his feet kept moving to the wrong places, he never lost his composure. When the music ended, they walked to the side of the room.

"I hope I didn't embarrass you," von Lossow said. "I never did learn to dance well. But then we Germans are barbarians and who can expect elegance from us?"

"Stop that," she chided. "You're anything but a barbarian, and you know it. Going to school in England seems to be the answer for you people. Now, if you could only get *all* of you to go..."

He laughed. "Can you imagine General Knyphausen having tea at four every day? Balancing a little china teacup on his knee?"

"No, but I can see him with a mug of beer and a platter of pigs feet," she said lightly. "Tell me, do you always make fun of your superiors?"

"That depends, madam, on what they are superior at," he answered.

They chatted for about a half hour, and Celine learned that the colonel was thirty years old, unmarried, and owed his rank to being the prince's cousin. She was thoroughly enjoying the company of this engaging Hessian, but was also anxious to get back to her house and talk to her brother. She decided to wait until just after the old year had passed into the new.

At midnight she stood at Colonel von Lossow's side and toasted the beginning of the year seventeen hundred and seventy-seven. They clinked their glasses and smiled at one another. He leaned over and kissed her, and she was aware there was more than mere friendliness in the way their lips lingered. He murmured that he wanted to see her again, and she agreed that it might be possible. And then she forced herself to stop thinking about him.

Soon she had said her good-nights and asked her father to take her home. They came out into the night. Primus was waiting near the warmth of a blazing fire that had been started by the coachmen, who were forced to remain outside while their masters and mistresses drank and danced.

Jan and Celine got in the trap, and Primus flicked his whip to start on the short ride back to Maiden Lane. The pair huddled under a blanket, doing their best to thwart the frigid air that swirled about them. The streets were dark and the buildings looked cold and ominous. In many places where houses had burned down in the great fire, there were scores of hastily erected tents. Hundreds of dispossessed people lived under these canvas coverings because they had no other place to go. For them the onslaught of winter was proving to be a terrible test indeed.

Wood was becoming scarce as the British troops swelled in numbers and commandeered whatever they needed. Many people in the city could no longer buy firewood; the price had risen beyond the limits of their purses. In many houses and tents the only thing that could be burned for heat was body fat, and there was precious little of that.

Food prices were rising, and many people found themselves eating less and less as each week passed. For families lucky enough to own a cow, the only answer was to butcher it and hope that the meat lasted through the winter. For those without animals, the situation was worse. People were reduced to begging on the streets, and it was becoming impossible to walk a few hundred yards without someone tugging on one's sleeve, begging for money or food or anything tangible. Some men were too proud to beg, and most of these turned to crime. Only a fool went abroad at night without a weapon in hand.

As Primus drove the trap, he kept a musket balanced on his knees. Jan kept a pistol in his hand as he huddled beneath the blanket, a precaution not only against desperate men, but also against the Hessians, who were fond of robbing men and raping women. General Howe had ordered scores of lashings and dozens of executions, with little or no deterrent effect on the German soldiers. As Franz von Lossow had observed, they were peasants and had been raised in a culture where such pastimes were permitted to a conquering army.

Celine felt pleased with herself as she rode in the trap. She finally had gotten some information that would be of use to Washington. She was also pleased that she had met Colonel von Lossow. Things were looking up.

When Primus let them off at the front of the house, Celine went directly to Drew's bedroom and woke him from a sound sleep. She told him what she had learned, and he agreed it was important to get to Washington as soon as possible. He dressed, went around the corner, and came back a few minutes later with Alec Seixas. He'd decided it would be safer if he had a companion, and who could be better than the tough Jew?

It was only a few minutes after two o'clock in the morning when Drew and Alec tramped out into the arctic streets and made their way toward the docks on the North River, where they could take a small boat across to Jersey. The snow crunched beneath their feet, and several times the sound of their passing woke shivering men who were trying to sleep in unheated tents.

They went into a covered dock at one of the de Kuyper piers, untied the frozen lines that held a small rowboat, and made their way out into the blackness of the river. The water was running smoothly, as the ice had not had a chance to build up significantly. Low-lying clouds moved across the sky, obscuring the stars, making it difficult to see where the river ended and the Jersey shore began.

They manned the oars, putting their backs to the task, using the work to stay warm as much as to move the craft.

If the rebel army was to have a chance of survival, it was imperative they reach Washington and tell him of Cornwallis's plan to entrap him at Trenton.

"I hope they don't get into trouble," Jan said to his daughter as the two of them sat before the hearth in the kitchen, warming themselves with the flames and with cups of scalding coffee liberally laced with rum.

"Me too—but what choice did we have? It's important that Washington get the message," Celine said.

"What I'm wondering is why the general was so open about giving you the information." Jan said thoughtfully. "He must trust you."

She shrugged her shoulders. "I notice you're rather chummy with him yourself."

"It's the price we pay so the British will allow us to keep

in business. What makes it hard is that an idiot like Philip Van Cortlandt thinks we're on the same side."

"Poor Daddy," she teased. "It really kills you to be nice, doesn't it?"

"'Daddy'? I can't remember the last time you called me that. Do you want something?"

"Nothing I can think of."

"I meant to ask you—who was that blond chap you were dancing with? I don't recall seeing him before."

"One of their officers," Celine said evasively. "He was a terrible dancer."

"You looked as if you were having a good time."

"All part of the game," she said, getting to her feet. "And now if you'll excuse me, I'm tired and want to crawl into my bed."

"How do you like being back in your old room?"

She grinned. "You like having me there, don't you? I like it too."

He sat alone by the fire for a few minutes. Yes, it was nice having his daughter back in the house. And his grandson. It made them seem to be one family again. His only regret was that it had taken a war to do it. A man must take the good with the bad, he told himself; and his head began to nod. The fire was toasty and the rum was warming his insides.

Marie Therese came into the room a half hour later and found him fast asleep. She thought of waking him, but decided he looked too comfortable. She brought another heavy blanket and wrapped it around his shoulders. Then she kissed him on the forehead and smiled.

Before she went to her own room, she stopped to look in on Peter. The boy was buried under a mound of blankets. She picked up one corner to allow some air under the heap. Her grandson's steady breathing assured her he was all right.

She stopped outside Celine's door and paused. She felt the same as her husband: it was good to have their daughter back with them. It wouldn't last, of course, because Celine was a grown woman with a life of her own. But even for a little while, it was a pleasant thing.

She went to bed and got under the heavy down-stuffed quilt. It seemed strange to be in bed without Jan. It would be, as always, comforting to have him at her side, reassuring to feel the heat of his body warming the sheets. But she preferred to let him sleep in the kitchen rather than wake him up and make him clump exhausted up the stairs.

She said a little prayer for her son, because she knew he had left the house. It was a nice family she had, and for the thousandth time she gave her thanks to God.

As the de Kuypers drifted off to sleep, a man in dark, nondescript clothes made his way through the frozen streets until he came to the Delafield house on Broad Way. He stopped, looked around, and satisfied himself that he was unobserved. He opened a small can of paint, scraped away some ice, and dipped his brush in the red liquid. With quick, deft strokes he painted the letter *R*—for Rebel—on the front door of the Delafield house. He stepped back to admire his handiwork and grunted with pleasure at the sight of the two-foot-high letter. It was an ominous new note being introduced to New York—the painting of a red *R* on the doors of men suspected of being rebels. The sight of an *R* on a door was certain to bring trouble to the owner. Several men so honored had been beaten up.

The man replaced the top of the paint can and hurried through the dark streets toward the Provost. He made his report to the officer who had sent him on his mission, and left.

Patrick Blakely was pleased. If the way to get to Mary Delafield was through the orneriness of her husband, fine. The captain was pleased to do his bit to enhance that orneriness.

Who knew what could happen?

It was almost noon, but even at this hour patches of cottony mist still hovered close to the frozen ground. The two horses Alec had taken at Paulus Hook were exhausted. Drew himself was hardly in the best of condition.

They had ridden down along the shore of Newark Bay, passed Elizabethtown, forded the Rahway River, crossed a bridge over the Raritan, and now were skirting the British encampments near Princeton. Within hours they would be in Trenton.

"These horses will never make it," Drew said as they stopped for a brief rest.

"We'll get two more."

"How do we do that?"

"Steal them," Alec said.

"We can't keep stealing horses," Drew protested.

"We'll steal them from the British," Alec said. "That should make you feel better."

The morality of it troubled Drew. And the risk. If the British caught them stealing horses, they'd be hanged. If he was going to die, he wanted to go out as a patriot, not a horse thief.

They rode a bit farther and came to a barn. It was an old building, unpainted, standing at the end of a field. A short distance away was a farmhouse. They dismounted and quietly went to the side of the barn. Alec looked inside and smiled. "There are three or four soldiers asleep in the hay," he whispered.

They drew their pistols and crept inside the building. Four Englishmen were curled up in a pile of hay in the center of the barn. Their horses were tethered in stalls along the left wall.

Alec went to the nearest soldier. He cocked his pistol and brought it to the man's head. The ominous noise was sufficient to wake him, but the man remained mute as his eyes widened at the closeness of the gun's muzzle. Alec brought his finger to his lip, indicating he wanted silence.

Drew went to the others one by one and poked them in the ribs with his pistol. They woke bleary-eyed, sleepy, and frightened by the guns in their faces.

"Now, lads," Alec said, "if everyone stays calm, no one will get hurt."

"On your feet. And no funny business," Drew said.

The four men stood up and gingerly wiped the hay from their uniforms.

"You two take off your clothes," Alec said to the soldiers on the right. He proceeded to tie the other two men with ropes that he found hanging from pegs.

"Why are they undressed?" Drew asked when the two soldiers had stripped to their underclothes.

"It'll be easier for us to continue if we look like British soldiers, won't it?"

Drew nodded. Clever idea, he thought. The last two soldiers were tied up. Now that they were no longer a threat, Drew and Alec put on their uniforms.

"You make a good lobsterback," Alec said as Drew finished buttoning his crimson tunic.

"You're not so bad yourself," Drew said, admiring his friend's getup.

They took fresh mounts from the barn and started down the road to Trenton. They passed several detachments of British troops, but were looked upon as two cavalrymen in the midst of the British army.

In the later afternoon, as the sun was hovering over the western horizon, they crossed Shabbakonk Creek and came to the outskirts of Trenton. They saw a great deal of activity as the British were bringing up hundreds of troops to oppose the rebels who held the town on the banks of the Delaware. It looked as if Celine's information was correct: the British would try to trap the rebels with their backs to the river.

The sun was almost gone from the sky. They were riding down the Princeton road alongside an apple orchard when a shot rang out and a lead slug whistled past Drew's ear. Several ragged-looking American militiamen were coming out of the orchard with muskets in their hands.

"Don't shoot!" Drew cried. "We're Americans!"

The suspicious militiamen didn't lower their muskets, but they stopped shooting.

"Americans?" the gangly leader asked.

"Yes. We're looking for General Washington."

"They sure don't look like Americans, do they?" the gangly leader said to a short, stubby man at his side. He spit a wad of tobacco juice from the side of his mouth.

"I say we shoot 'em," the short man said.

"We stole these uniforms," Drew explained. "So we could pass through the British lines."

"I say it's a trick," the short man said, and he started to raise his musket, but the gangly man restrained him.

"Know anybody who can vouch for you?" he asked.

"General Putnam knows me," Drew said. "And Aaron Burr."

The gangly man scratched his head. "Old Put's not here, and I don't know this Burr."

"How about Alexander Hamilton?" Drew said. "Is he here?"

"You know Captain Hamilton?"

"A little," Drew said. They were hardly close friends, but had known each other through the Sons of Liberty. "He'll tell you who we are."

"I guess we better take them to Hamilton," the gangly man said.

The short man was disgusted. "Shoot 'em, I say."

The militiamen made Drew and Alec dismount, and the group walked into Trenton. They passed through the middle of hundreds of rebels, who looked at them with a mixture of curiosity and hostility. Their neat British uniforms were in sharp contrast to the shabby buckskins and nondescript, piecemeal uniforms of the Continentals. Finally they stopped in front of a squat building that was normally the shop of a leather worker. The gangly man went inside and returned with Captain Alexander Hamilton.

Hamilton took one look at Drew in his uniform and burst into laughter. "Well, de Kuyper, your true politics have made themselves known at last."

"Alex, don't play games," Drew said. "Just tell these gentlemen with the guns that we're okay."

Hamilton nodded to the militiamen, and they walked away, rather disappointed that their prisoners had turned out not to be British. Drew quickly explained his mission, and Hamilton took Drew and Alec to the tavern that Washington was using for his headquarters.

"Nice," Alec observed. "Right in the middle of all the rum."

Hamilton shook his head. "Not too much rum—or anything else—to be found. The damned Hessians looted the place. Rotten thieves."

A roaring fire was blazing in the tavern's hearth, and Drew rubbed his hands in pleasure as he stood before the flames. General Washington sat on the other side of the room. In front of him was a table strewn with maps and papers. Hamilton went over and spoke briefly to the general. Washington looked up, seemed surprised at the presence of two "redcoats," squinted, then nodded in recognition and motioned for Drew and Alec to join him.

When Drew finished reporting Celine's information, the general looked at Hamilton. "If this is true, we can't stay here."

"We could build a strong front," Hamilton said.

"Not strong enough to withstand the entire British army," Washington said. "Besides, I don't like having my back against the river."

"We could withdraw back across the river," Hamilton suggested.

"That might be wise," the general admitted. "I just hate to retreat after we've won a victory."

A large map of the New Jersey countryside was spread on the table, and an idea was forming in Drew's mind. "We just came through the British lines, General," he said, and pointed to the map. "They're building up along this front."

"So?"

"So instead of staying here, or retreating, why don't we outflank them and go north?"

The general held his chin in his hand as he thought. "It might work. If the British think we plan on making a stand here, it might be possible to slip around them."

"And hit the supply depots at Princeton," Hamilton said with excitement. "Think of all the gunpowder! God, how we need gunpowder!"

"We saw wagons that looked like they might be carrying powder," Alec said. "Seems to me that if that's what you need, then up north's where we ought to go."

The general spent a few more moments in thought. "All right," he finally said, and looked at Hamilton. "We begin moving north after midnight," he said, tapping the map. "We'll go right up the Princeton Road. As long as we're taking a bold step, we might as well be really bold."

"May I make a suggestion, sir?" Drew said, and continued without waiting for an answer. "Have some men start building an earthwork right now. That will convince the British you're planning to stay here."

"And keep them from getting suspicious," Washington said with a nod. He looked at Hamilton. "See to it."

"I'll give the job to the Massachusetts men," Hamilton said. "It'll keep them too busy to complain," he added.

Washington smiled grimly at the captain's inadvertent reminder of the constant bickering going on in his army. Hamilton, as a New Yorker, disliked the Massachusetts men. The Rhode Islanders disliked the Marylanders, who, in turn, distrusted anyone from Virginia. And so it went, right down the line.

After Hamilton had gone, the general looked at the two haggard messengers and suggested they get some sleep.

"First I'd like something to eat," Alec said. "And drink."

"There's precious little of either around here," the general complained. He took a tin cover from a plate. "This was supposed to be my supper, but you can have it."

Alec and Drew nibbled at the scraps of deer meat that rested in a cold, thick, syrupy gravy. They washed it down with flat beer from an old pitcher. As they ate, the general resumed studying his maps.

Drew, only a few feet away, had an excellent opportunity to study this man upon whose shoulders rested most of the American hopes. Washington was tall and prepossessing, but what struck Drew most was how confidently and quickly his eyes moved from one part of the map to another. The general seemed strong and ready to accept a challenge.

As they were preparing to take a nap, Washington reminded Drew and Alec that they were still wearing British uniforms, and suggested they change clothes.

"Maybe we should keep them on, General," Alec said. "We can ride at the head of the column tonight. If an Englishman sees us, he might be fooled into thinking we're part of his own army."

The general chuckled. "All right. And from now on I'll refer to you as my British battalion."

It was the hour after midnight when Alex Hamilton shook Drew's shoulder. "Time to go," the young captain said. Alec Seixas was already awake.

They had been sleeping in a small storeroom, and now came back into the taproom of the tavern. It was a beehive of activity as the officers came to get their orders from Washington. The general stopped the two men in British uniforms and told them to go with General Hugh Mercer, who was leading the line of march with troops from Maryland and Virginia.

The scene outside was also one of great activity, yet it was all conducted in a strange silence, as if in a dream. The wheels of the heavy cannon carriages were wrapped in thick hides and canvas to cut down on the noise they would make as they rumbled over the frozen ground.

Drew's breath came out in great clouds of steam. He stamped his feet to restore circulation and rubbed his hands together, wishing he had gloves. Apparently they were very hard to come by, Drew noticed; most of Washington's men simply wrapped rags around their hands, or stuck them inside their coats.

Alex Hamilton was doing a wonderful job of convincing the British that the army was digging in for a long stay. Dozens of cooking fires had been started. Sixty men labored away with picks and shovels as they pretended to be building an earthwork. They would continue to do this until the last possible moment. Hamilton and his hand-picked men would bring up the rear of Washington's column.

The army started on the move.

The men followed a road that skirted the eastern edge of Trenton. There were no British patrols to challenge them. They

A TERRIBLE WINTER

moved forward in a ghostlike silence, keeping a close eye on their left flank: if the British came, they would come from that direction.

Drew and Alec marched at the forward point with General Mercer. It was a dark night, and the road zigzagged through thick stands of trees. It became a struggle to keep the heavy cannon carriages moving between the stumps and rocks that were everywhere.

The ground was icy, and men and horses slid and floundered. Now and then the weight of a cannon carriage would break through the crust of ice, and it became an ordeal to keep it moving. Men got their feet wet; soon the water turned to ice, and they clomped along on elephantine feet.

But despite all the hardships and obstacles, the men kept moving forward until the entire column had passed the limits of Trenton. Only once did they encounter any English troops—a patrol of four.

The first men they saw were Drew and Alec. "What's going on?" one of the Englishmen asked.

Drew was suddenly next to him, holding a cocked pistol in his face. Then Alec came up, and in another moment the four Englishmen were surrounded by a dozen men.

"Not a sound out of you," Drew warned, and the Englishmen took one look at the odds they faced and said nothing.

"Just what we need," General Mercer complained. "Prisoners."

"We can let them go in a couple of hours," Drew said. "By then we'll be too far north for it to matter."

"I can't believe we're getting away with this," Mercer said. "The damned British never even considered we'd go north."

"They're too sure of themselves," Drew said. "It's what'll beat them in the end."

The column continued to plod northward, and during the hour before dawn the cold took on a real presence. Drew suffered in silence, knowing that every other man in the march had to cope with this deadly enemy.

The first men crossed the Quaker bridge over the Assunpink as the first hint of dawn appeared on the horizon. They forded Stony Brook Creek and followed the road that paralleled it. They came to a fork and followed Washington's plan: to send the main body ahead on the primary road to Princeton while Mercer's troops took the left fork and the secondary road. This meant that Princeton would be under siege from more than one direction.

Drew and Alec went with Mercer and his three hundred and fifty troops. They wound their way around a copse whose trees and bushes glistened with frost. The icy snow crunched beneath their feet, and the ground cracked as the sharp hoofs of the horses split its skin. Soon the two columns were out of sight of one another.

An unexpected factor was added: a British detachment of several hundred men under Lieutenant Colonel Mawhood left Princeton on a *third* road on the far side of the village, proceeding south to join their army at Trenton.

Colonel Mawhood, riding at the head of his troops, was suddenly surprised to see another column of troops moving north on the primary road. What troops could be moving north? the colonel wondered.

He rode to the top of a hill to get a better look—and that was when he spied Mercer's troops winding their way around the copse. Rebels! The colonel was an experienced soldier and realized the purpose of the two columns. If he acted swiftly, he could attack Mercer's troops and keep that road, at least, open to Princeton.

He was angry with himself. Only last night, General Cornwallis had passed through Princeton and told him he wouldn't be needing any defenses there because they were going to trap Washington at Trenton. Accordingly, the building of Princeton's defenses had been halted. There were only a single earthwork and two old artillery pieces in front of Nassau Hall. Not even enough to stop a battalion, much less the entire rebel army.

Colonel Mawhood brought his column about and within minutes was in sight of Mercer and his men. Both groups stopped and took stock of the situation; and both commanders decided on a frontal attack.

The British troops were seasoned veterans. Mercer's Marylanders and Virginians had little training, were unaccustomed to fighting in the open, and were now exhausted from the long march. While the British advanced in well-formed ranks, the Americans proceeded more in the fashion of a mob.

Both groups approached an apple orchard, and it looked certain the battle would be fought there. Drew, riding with General Mercer, noticed there was a hill overlooking the orchard. "We ought to get our artillery up there," he said.

"Damn steep," Mercer complained. "How can you drag guns up there?"

"I can try."

"Go ahead," the general said without enthusiasm.

Drew took Alec and went back to where some of the men were struggling with two heavy gun carriages. "We're taking them up there," he said to the sergeant in charge of the detail.

The sergeant looked at the steep hill. "Is the friggin' general out of his friggin' mind?"

Drew didn't bother to tell the sergeant it was his idea and not the general's. "Well, it's an order and we've got to try," he said.

The sergeant grumbled, but started to carry out the order. A dozen extra men were put on the ropes, and two extra horses were tied to each carriage. Slowly, very slowly, the guns began to ascend the hill. The men swore and bit their lips, but they put their backs into it, and suddenly the impossible was beginning to look possible.

Down on the flat land of the orchard, General Mercer had managed to create some order among his men. At least he had them all heading in the right direction.

When the two forces had come to within fifty yards of each other, the Americans opened fire. As usual, the muskets weren't highly accurate. The balls flew out of the muzzles in the general direction of the British, but did little to stop their advance.

Colonel Mawhood ordered a bayonet charge. With their weapons in front of them, the redcoats came forward and attacked the Americans. Suddenly the orchard was filled with hundreds of milling, shouting, fighting men. The British bayonets did their deadly work against the Americans, who were not equipped with such a weapon. Muskets continued to be fired, and soon the cold ground became strewn with more and more bodies.

The ferocity of the bayonet charge broke the spirit of the Americans. The battle became a rout as the rebels turned their backs and ran from the carnage in the orchard.

While that was happening, Drew and the other men managed to manhandle the two artillery pieces to the top of the hill. They wheeled them into firing position.

It was a good piece of timing. The last of the Americans had fled the orchard, and the British had halted to reform their ranks. The American guns boomed and their deadly missiles whizzed down into the British. The guns were loaded with chain—two iron balls held together by iron links—making an effective weapon against men in the open.

The guns fired a second round, and the British were having their first bad moments of the battle. Colonel Mawhood ordered his own artillery brought up, but that would take time. Since he was a prudent man, he ordered his troops to retreat.

This gave the Americans the precious minutes they needed to regroup. General Washington himself had heard the beginnings of the battle and was riding to investigate. He reached Mercer's retreating troops, which had been joined by a regiment of newly recruited Pennsylvania militia. These fresh troops had seen the splashes of blood on the tunics of Mercer's men and panicked, joining in the retreat although they hadn't had any contact with the enemy.

Washington dashed among the troops and halted the retreat. In a short time he had them turned around. A regiment of New Englanders came up, and the beginning of an American counterattack was under way.

Drew stayed on the hill with the cannons and helped keep up a steady fire toward the faltering British ranks. They had to stop when Washington appeared with his troops and once again the orchard was filled with friend as well as foe.

Within twenty minutes the aroused Americans slashed through the enemy ranks and another rout ensued—only this time it was the British who were in retreat. Washington stopped for a moment and surveyed the orchard. There were many dead Americans, among them General Hugh Mercer.

But now nothing stood between Washington and the tiny garrison at Princeton.

The American army moved into the town. There was sporadic fighting, but most of the garrison troops realized they were vastly outnumbered and fled.

One pocket of resistance was at Nassau Hall. A group of British soldiers took up positions inside the stately twenty-year-old building, knocked the glass out of the windows, and began shooting at the oncoming Americans. The advance halted momentarily.

Drew and Alec came down the road, accompanying the crews dragging the guns that had served at the apple orchard. They immediately positioned the guns so they could be used against Nassau Hall.

A TERRIBLE WINTER

The first shot missed the building and crashed into a fencepost to the left, terrifying a tethered horse. The crazed animal reared back, snapped the rope, and galloped off into the fields as the second gun blasted away.

This shot was more accurate. It flew through the window into the prayer hall, decapitating a statue of George II, the long-dead grandfather of the present king, whose policies had caused this war. Several more rounds pounded into the building, punching holes in the walls and creating chaos inside.

"A pity to destroy such a fine building," Drew said as another round blasted away a piece of window casement.

"Then let's stop and go in there!" Alec shouted above the roar of the cannon. "Hell, there can't be more than a dozen of the bastards!"

"Let's go in!" Drew shouted to the New England militiamen who were watching the bombardment with interest from behind the cannon.

But the soldiers inside the Hall had had enough. As soon as they saw the Americans running toward the building, they ran out the back door into the fields. The Americans went right through the building and into the fields after them. The battle of Princeton was turning into something that looked like a foxhunt.

Alec was the first man to enter the building. He walked down the main hall, carefully watching for the enemy. There was nothing; only the sounds of his comrades behind him.

He came to a room where a cheery fire blazed in the hearth. A long table was placed in front of the fire, and Alec smiled when he saw it was set for breakfast. He sat down in a chair, poured himself a cup of steaming tea, and began to butter a piece of toast. Drew entered the room and stopped dead in his tracks.

"What are you doing?"

"Having breakfast."

"Breakfast?"

"Pull up a chair," Alec said as he chomped on a piece of toast. "There's plenty."

Drew sat down. He took toast and tea, then removed the top of a pewter dish, revealing a dozen cooked sausages. "Mmm," he murmured as he helped himself to the tasty pork morsels.

"Thoughtful of the British to do this for us," Alec said.

"Have some?" Drew asked, offering the sausages.

Alec shook his head. "Jews don't eat pork."

"Why is that?" Drew asked as he filled his mouth with a large bite of the delicious smoked meat.

"An old tradition. It goes back thousands of years."

"But why?"

Alec shrugged. "Who can figure out religions? First, *you* explain the Inquisition—then I'll figure out about pork."

"But you're not religious about anything else," Drew said.

"I know, but when I was little my mother drummed into my head that I shouldn't eat pork. I tried one time, and I almost choked to death. Now I don't try."

Drew nodded. He looked over the table. "No eggs," he complained.

"You can't have everything."

While Drew was happily stuffing himself with sausages, Alec wandered around the room, opening doors and drawers, looking inside closets. In one he found a silk-lined British officer's coat, brand new, with paper wrapping still protecting the silver buttons. He carried it to his chair and draped it over the back.

He returned to the same closet and came back with several buckskin trousers and jackets. He selected one of each and, after removing the British uniform he was wearing, put them on.

"Much better," Drew said.

"These should fit you," Alec said as he handed over the other buckskin clothes.

Drew continued to eat as he changed clothes. When he was finished, he picked up both discarded British uniforms and threw them into the fire. Then he tried to remove most of the black that was on his face from firing the cannon.

In another closet, Alec found a barrel of flour. He rolled it out into the room and stood it near the fireplace.

"What are you going to do with that?" Drew asked.

Before Alec could answer, a group of townspeople appeared in the doorway, timidly inspecting the Hall. Two women were among them.

"Look at this," one of the women said, pointing to a place in the wall that had been gouged by a cannonball. "It's going to take a lot of work to get everything back together again."

"The whole town is like this," the second woman complained.

"We're sorry," Drew said.

A TERRIBLE WINTER

"It wasn't you," the woman said. "It was the Hessians. They took everything."

"Do you need flour?" Drew asked, suddenly remembering Alec's latest find.

"Of course."

Drew pointed to the barrel. "Help yourselves."

"The women spread their aprons and began to fill them with the fine white powder. "We'll tell the others about this," one of them said. "They need flour, too."

The women left, and Alec scowled. "We could have sold that flour." He picked his British officer's coat from the chair. "Oh, well, at least I have this."

As they left Nassau Hall, the streets were becoming crowded with the balance of the arriving army. The two found Washington at yet another temporary headquarters—a room that had been a library, but was now a scene of destruction.

"And they call *us* barbarians," the general complained to Drew when he saw him. He waved his hand, and Drew looked at the shelves where hundreds of mutilated books were scattered.

"The Hessians again," Alex Hamilton said. He picked up a book, regarded its broken spine and torn cover, and let it drop to the floor.

"The Hessians!" the general said, throwing up his hands. "I'm beginning to wonder. There aren't enough of the buggers to be doing *all* the damage. I think the British are just as much to blame."

"They just help themselves to whatever they want," Hamilton said.

Drew was about to mention that the Americans were doing the same, but decided it wasn't the sort of thing Washington wanted to hear.

The truth was that all groups—Hessians, British, and American—were acting as if they were invading a foreign country. The Hessians did it because it was their way of life in Europe. The British did it because they saw the Hessians doing it. And the Americans were doing it to survive—particularly because the Congress was stingy about supplies.

"I understand it was your idea to take the cannons to the hill above the orchard," Washington said to Drew.

"There were others involved," Drew said modestly.

"But it was your idea. Thank you."

Drew was embarrassed, and the general dropped the matter.

He began discussing the question of winter quarters for the army. Several officers made proposals, but it was Hamilton's idea the general favored.

"Morristown is the place to go," he said. "It's easily defended on all sides. We'll winter there."

"Coming with us?" Hamilton asked Drew.

"Do you want me?"

"I'm sure the general will be happy to give you and Seixas a commission," Hamilton said.

"Not for me," Alec said quickly.

"Nor for de Kuyper either," Washington said. "We had this talk once before. You can be of far more use in other ways."

"Then I guess we'd better start back for the city," Drew said. He looked toward Alec, who nodded his agreement.

Hamilton walked them to the door of the building. "Until now I don't think there was a man in the army—except the general, of course—who really thought we could win."

"We have a long way to go," Drew said cautiously.

"Yes, but now we know we *can* win," the ebullient Hamilton said. "And other people will know it, too. By spring we'll have ten thousand more volunteers in the army."

They went into the street as a column of bedraggled British prisoners moved past under the watchful guards.

Hamilton made a face. "I don't know why we bother capturing them. We can't feed them. We'll just turn them loose in a day or two."

"They'll rejoin their army," Alec said.

"What choice do we have?"

Alec silently drew his finger across the front of his neck.

Hamilton was shocked. "What do you think we are, Hessians?"

Alec was silent for a moment. "Only having a little joke," he said, and Hamilton relaxed. But Drew knew there was a dark side to his friend; Alec was perfectly capable of killing any man who stood in his way.

"Thank you for the help," Hamilton said. "I'm sure you'll be of use to us again, and together we'll drive the redcoats back to London."

Drew was impressed by Hamilton's strong convictions, and thought about them as he and Alec made their way across New Jersey. Hamilton was right. If Washington could defeat the British twice, he could do it again—and again and again until he won the final victory.

They arrived at the shore of the North River without further incident. They looked across the water and saw the brooding hulk of New York. The city seemed to be hugging the ground against the onslaught of the frigid winds that blew from the ocean.

It was dusk by the time they found a fisherman willing to take them across the river, and dark when they reached their homes. Their return to the city was as discreet as their exit had been.

Dawn.

A dark figure stirred in a corner of the tiny shed. A tattered wool blanket was slowly drawn aside, and a face appeared. It was an old man, the ex-printer who styled himself Sisyphus. He looked at the other shapes crowded into the shed. Holding the blanket about his shoulders, he crawled to the opening at the other end of the shed, carefully keeping his hands and knees from disturbing the other sleepers.

At the entrance he pushed his way through several layers of canvas and emerged into the arctic air of the new day. He grimaced as he straightened to a standing position, his muscles and joints causing pain as they unwound themselves from their cramped sleeping position. He looked back at the shed: not much bigger than a kennel for a large dog.

The ground was covered with drifts of newly fallen snow. Beneath the snow was a thick layer of ice, and beneath that the frozen earth. The cold penetrated into the bones of the earth even as it seeped into the old man's bones. He stomped his feet and pulled an old woolen muffler tighter about his neck.

The shed stood near the back of an old mansion near Hanover Square. Now the building was being used by the British as their naval headquarters. Not thirty feet from where Sisyphus lived in poverty, British admirals and their guests dined on succulent roasts and chops, washing it all down with fine clarets and burgundies. Even in the midst of a war the admirals made sure their larder was well stocked.

Most of the people of New York, however, lived closer to Sisyphus's style than to the admirals'. The hand of winter gripped the city, and was crushing the life from it as never in the past.

There were shortages of everything—housing, food, clothing, firewood, even honest work. Supply ships arrived regularly, but most of these cargoes were commandeered by the

British military forces. New York had become their winter headquarters, and the authorities tended their needs before those of the civilian population. This attitude was turning many a loyalist into a rebel.

Sisyphus looked up at the still-darkened sky and decided to go down to the docks to see if he could earn a meal. Often when a ship arrived, help was needed to unload it, and the captains would hire men they found along the shore. These along-the-shore-men, or longshoremen, as some called them, could earn a few pennies and some food by hauling the cargoes from the holds. Not that Sisyphus had the strength to put in such a day's work; but he would do it for an hour, groaning and complaining that he was an old man and would soon collapse. Usually the captain would take pity, pay the promised wage, and release him from his labors. There were a few hardhearted souls who would fail to do so, of course, but Sisyphus was philosophical about the sorts of men one met during the course of a lifetime.

The streets leading to the docks were deserted and unfriendly. The diminishing supply of firewood made it impossible for all but a few privileged people to keep fires burning in their houses throughout the night. The people who slept in tents and sheds didn't even dream of such luxury. With wood scarce and outrageously priced, the vast majority could use it only to cook their meager meals, and often several families had to pool their resources to do even that.

Sisyphus stopped at the corner of Dock Street, peering closely at a still form next to the side of the building. A dog, it was—died during the night and frozen stiff. The old man shook his head. Sometime during the next hour the dog's body would be discovered by someone whose hunger exceeded all other considerations, and the dog would be scooped up, taken home, thawed, cooked, and eaten.

Well, why not? he thought. What's wrong with dogflesh? Why should it be differentiated from the flesh of cows or pigs?

The wind moved steadily up the East River, whistling and sighing its way through the rigging of the ships tied at the docks. There weren't as many vessels as in the days before the war, but Sisyphus saw a goodly number just the same. Of course, many were British warships, and he had learned to ignore them. The sailors were forced to do everything for themselves, and there was no work for outside helpers.

Down near the Fly Market, which was open every other day

during these hard times, as opposed to every day during normal times, he noticed a newly arrived ship—the *Anthony*—tied up at the wharf. He came closer and recognized the pennant flying from the mizzenmast. The ship belonged to the de Kuypers.

Sisyphus had made a practice of going to Drew in the pretense of looking for work. Sometimes he was given a task, but more often than not he was given a handout without any work attached to it. He considered himself a printer, and if he couldn't get work in his own trade, then he was content to get no work at all.

The sight of a de Kuyper ship pleased him. He walked down the dock until he came to the steep gangplank. He climbed aboard and peered about the deck. Not a soul was to be seen. He made his way aft, toward the main cabin. He stopped when he came to the starboard hatch that opened on the ladder leading below.

He hesitated before entering. The captain might not be too friendly if he found an uninvited guest prowling about his cabin. But, Sisyphus reasoned, he could always claim friendship with Drew. He passed through the hatch and descended the ladder to the lower deck. Doors leading to individual cabins lined the bulkheads. All were closed, except the one on the far right. Sisyphus could see the yellow gleam of an oil lamp filling the cabin. He made his way down the passageway, stepping around the boxes and crates that littered the deck. The captain, in his desire to bring as much precious cargo to New York as possible, had wasted no space, utilizing even the passageways.

He came to the slightly opened door and stopped. He heard a voice within and listened.

Philemon Peabody was with Captain Blakely.

"It's too bad the Crown must commandeer this cargo of wheat," Peabody said. "New Yorkers are in desperate need."

"So is the army."

"Mr. de Kuyper will not be pleased."

"Perhaps he'll be allowed to keep the cargo of the next ship."

"And if not, maybe the one after that," Peabody said with a chuckle. "As you say, the soldiers must be fed first. And a good thing it is for me and you."

"That will remain our secret," Blakely said. There was an edge to his voice.

Sisyphus was puzzled. He understood the part of the conversation about the British commandeering ships. But he recognized Peabody's voice, and knew he worked for the de Kuypers: why was such activity a good thing for him? He kept listening, and learned.

"Shall I tell Mr. de Kuyper the Crown is paying the usual five shillings a hundredweight?" Peabody asked.

"Yes."

"And what is the actual amount you'll receive from the Crown treasury?"

"Ten."

Peabody whistled. "We get ten and give five to Jan. That's a good profit. Maybe we should only give him three."

"Don't get too greedy," Blakely said.

"My books are clean," Peabody said. "Nobody could prove a thing."

"I could," the captain said.

"Ah, yes," Peabody said lightly. "But you share the profits. Why would you *want* to prove anything?"

"Are we finished with our business?" the captain asked.

Peabody looked at the papers in his hand. "I have your order commandeering the *Anthony*. And the government's payment order—where you've thoughtfully left the price blank."

The captain's chair scraped on the deck as he stood up, and Sisyphus became frightened. If these men knew he had overheard their conversation, his life wouldn't be worth a farthing. He looked around in panic. The ladder leading to the deck was at the far end of the passageway. Before he could reach it, the men would be out of the cabin.

He quickly decided on the single course of action that might save his life. He crawled a dozen feet down the passageway, rolled himself halfway behind a barrel, laid his head on the floor, and pretended to be asleep. Now, if the men saw him, they might not think he had been listening. He closed his eyes and came as close to praying as he had done in forty years.

"I'll go ashore with you," Peabody said as they stepped into the passageway. "I've got to get to the office and file your commandeering order."

The two men came down the passageway. "Here, what's this?" Blakely said when he saw the inert form of Sisyphus. He cautiously poked it with the toe of his boot. "I didn't see him before."

The captain rolled Sisyphus over. The old man put on an act, snorting, rubbing his eyes, and mumbling.

"He's drunk," Peabody said.

"Get on your feet," Blakely said.

"Huh!"

Blakely was a great deal younger and stronger than Sisyphus, and he dragged him to his feet and propped him against the bulkhead.

"Whassamatta, huh?" Sisyphus said, slurring his words and rolling his eyes.

"An old rummy," Peabody said with distaste.

"What's he doing here?"

"How do I know?"

"Do you think he overheard us?"

Peabody laughed. "Him overhear us? Good Lord, Captain, the man can't even stand on his own two feet."

Sisyphus thought this was a good idea. He allowed his knees to buckle, and his body slowly slid down the bulkhead to the deck. He pretended to be unconscious again.

"He's just an old drunk who wandered aboard by mistake."

"Looks like that's the case," the captain agreed.

The two men resumed their walk down the passageway. They went up the ladder, and Sisyphus could hear the tromp of their boots across the deck. He waited ten minutes before he moved. Then he got up and went to the foot of the ladder. When he heard nothing, he climbed up to the main deck. A heavy fog diffused the rays of the early morning sun, and the dock was gripped in a murky gloom.

The printer had one scare when a figure walked past. But there was no cause for alarm. It was a sleepy sailor, beginning the first of the morning's chores. He didn't even see the other man.

Sisyphus made his way across the deck to the gangplank. What if Peabody and Blakely were still on the dock? But then more sailors started to come out on the main deck, and he had no choice but to leave.

He reached the bottom and stood on the dock. Not a soul in sight. He sighed with relief and hurriedly walked away from the *Anthony*. No one saw him as he crossed Dock Street and disappeared into an alley that led to Hanover Square.

He had learned something very interesting—and very dangerous. It was a fearful burden on his mind. His young friend, Drew, would certainly like to know what Peabody was doing. At the same time, Sisyphus realized, Peabody and the English officer would slit his throat in an instant if they found out what he knew. Was it prudent to tell young de Kuyper? Or was it best to forget the entire matter? What could he get for this information? A few shillings? Was it worth it to risk his life for that?

Anyway, what did he care if *these* people were stealing from *those* people? And what did he care about the bitter struggle between the English and the rebels? Things had been bad for him no matter who was in control.

But beneath it all he was troubled. Despite himself, his pride—which he had thought was all but dead—had been stirred when the Americans threw the English out of New York. He had straightened his shoulders and held up his head when he saw the Continental flag flying at the fort. It was *his* flag, and they were *his* people. Of course, it hadn't lasted long, and the British had returned under General Howe, but while it *had* lasted, he had been proud.

He came to the alley off Hanover Square and saw that several of his friends were up and about, tending a new fire in the old iron bucket that served as their stove. They stood close to it, welcoming the warmth.

"Where you been?" one said to the printer.

"Looking for work," Sisyphus said.

"Find any?"

"No."

"Hm, not surprising."

"A ship came in, but there was no one about, so I came back," the printer lied.

A sallow-cheeked man whose complexion matched the color of the fog drifting through the streets bobbed his head up and down like a bird. "Nothing going on on Broad Way either," he said. "No work, I mean. I just came from there. Only thing happening they was dragging a man from his house."

"The British?"

"Who else is dragging people from their homes these days?"

"Who was it?"

"Big blustery chap, don't know his name. He was yelling and shouting and saying they had no right to arrest him. Ha! A lot of good it did him. They clubbed him on the side of the head and dragged him away like he was a sack of grain."

Sisyphus moved closer to the fire. He didn't know the man who had been dragged away, but what difference did it make? Another warm body for the prisons.

His problem concerned the information he had learned this morning. If he told young de Kuyper, would he get a big reward? Or would he wind up in the street with a knife in his back? Or maybe both?

The older printer stood by the fire. His body shivered with cold and fear as he tried to work it all out.

Robert Delafield was an early riser and had been in the kitchen, sitting close by the miserly fire, drinking weak tea from a china cup. It was foul-tasting stuff, not the sort of brew he was accustomed to, but it had become next to impossible to get anything better in the past month. One of the servants had gone to the front of the house to brush the accumulated snow of the night from the stoop, and had rushed back to inform his master of the big red *R* painted on the door.

Robert had stormed to the front of the house, taken one look at the mark, and proceeded to have a tantrum. His tirade awakened the entire household, and Mary had come downstairs, pulling on her heavy wool robe to protect herself from the numbing cold.

Robert went to the tack room of the stable at the back of the house. He returned with a chisel, which he began to use to scrape away the paint. He continued to blather and swear as he worked.

"Who did it?" Mary asked.

"Some sneaking gallows rat, and if I ever find him I'll break his bloody neck!"

"Can't you let a servant do this?"

"It was meant for me," he said stubbornly, "and I'll remove it myself."

Mary knew his thickheadedness. She sighed. "I'll make some more tea," she said.

As Robert worked, a patrol passed up Broad Way on its way from the fort to the Provost. The leader of the patrol was Sergeant Taggert.

When the sergeant saw the man chipping away at the large *R*, he stopped. His lips curled into a sneer. "Well, well, another damned rebel!"

Sense was not a commodity Robert Delafield was known for. He defiantly folded his arms. "Yes, a rebel, and what the hell are you going to do about it?"

The sergeant smiled. He loved troublemakers. "Bust in your face, that's what."

"Try."

Taggert didn't hesitate. He jumped forward to grab the man,

but Robert could be formidable when angry. His right fist struck a glancing blow on the sergeant's head.

The sergeant responded by taking his pistol and using the butt as a club. His first blow caught Robert on the arm, crippling him. The next found his head and the fight was over.

The commotion brought Mary back to the door. She screamed when she saw her husband's prone body and bloody head.

"Let's have none of that," Taggert warned her. He turned to the watching soldiers. "Take this one to the Provost."

Mary's face was ashen white. "What did he do?"

"Struck an officer of the Crown. Resisted arrest," Taggert said. "Enough to put 'im behind bars."

She tried to go to Robert, but the sergeant restrained her. She leaned against the doorway as two husky soldiers marched away, dragging her husband between them. She bit down on her knuckles, almost hard enough to draw blood.

Dear God! she thought; dear, dear God. Robert had an awful temper. What would happen to him in prison? She had heard terrible stories about those places.

Tears came to her eyes as she stepped inside and closed the door. Most of the time she wished she had never married Robert. But he was her husband, and now that he was in serious trouble, she wanted to help him.

She went to her bedroom and dressed. The house, aside from the kitchen, was unheated and as cold as a tomb. She could see her own breath as she pulled on her woolen stockings.

She left the house on her way to see the one person who might know what to do—Celine. She was oblivious of the falling snow, and the drifts that made her walk a zigzag path. She didn't even remember it was cold.

Drew sat on a stool in the kitchen near the fire. His father sat in a high-backed chair, and a few feet away, the printer, John Holt, relaxed in an identical chair. A messenger had just come from Philemon Peabody informing them of the commandeering of the *Anthony*. Jan was fit to be tied. The men sat in silence for a time, the only sounds being the sputtering of the logs in the fireplace and the steady ticking of the great spring-wound clock next to the door that led to the pantry.

Drew reached for the canister to make tea, and found only a small amount left. "Do we have any more?"

Jan shook his head. "But there's more coffee in the cellar."

"The English had better stop commandeering all our ships," Drew said. "We're running out of everything."

Alec Seixas entered the room, helped himself to a glass of sack from the sideboard, and sat down on the parson's bench along the wall. "I hear they took another ship," he announced.

"Bad news travels fast," John Holt said.

"The English are trying to beat us by starving us," Jan complained.

"It's robbery," Drew said. "They can't keep doing it."

"It's the law," the printer said.

"We've had crazy laws in New York in the past," Jan said with a smile. "We've survived. Governor Cornbury once passed a law placing a tax of five shillings on anyone who wore a pearl ring."

"Don't tell that to the provost marshal," Drew said. "They'll revive the law."

"Cornbury was a character," Jan said. "He decreed that any man who reached the age of twenty-five and was still a bachelor would have to pay a tax of two shillings, five pence."

"Cornbury was a madman," John Holt said. "Nobody took him seriously. But we aren't dealing with a madman. We're dealing with cold-blooded officials who are taking away all our rights."

The other men listened, because John Holt commanded respect. He had been the founder and publisher of the *New York Journal*, the first paper in New York to embrace the rebel cause. He was not a man given to idle statements. Holt was slight and dark-haired, and his massive head seemed too large for the rest of his body. He had thick lips, and when he ruminated he would pop them against each other. Jan had frowned at his son when Drew remarked that Holt gave the impression of being a highly intelligent frog.

Until 1774 his paper had carried the king's arms on the masthead of the front page. In that year Holt discarded the arms and substituted a snake cut into pieces. Beneath the chopped-up snake was the motto:

UNITE OR DIE.

The British weren't pleased with him, but elected to leave him alone. Then, in an issue of the *Journal* printed in January, 1775, the snake was suddenly made whole, with his tail in his mouth and coiled to form a double ring. On the body of the snake, beginning at the head, were the words:

> United now, alive and free—
> Firm on this basis Liberty shall stand,
> And, thus supported, ever bless our land,
> Till time becomes Eternity.

In editorial after editorial Holt attacked the British and expounded the cause of the men who favored separation from the mother country. Eventually the British closed him down. These days he lived a secret existence, because they had a price on his head and would have thrown him in prison had they been able to find him. He was protected by the Sons of Liberty and was hidden in their houses.

"Dammit," Drew said. "We just can't let them keep taking our ships!"

"Our family's been in the smuggling business before. Maybe we should go back to it," Jan said.

"Let's become *pirates* if we must," Drew said. "The British are taking our lands, our cities, and our ships. If that isn't piracy, what is?"

"Why not?" John Holt asked, and his lips popped furiously as he considered the idea. "Why not become pirates to fight against the biggest pirate of all—mad George who squats like a beetle on the throne of England!"

Jan had mixed emotions. He was a staunch proponent of independence, but had always envisioned that it would come about peacefully and evolve into a *union* of two countries. He had never favored severing all ties with the mother country.

"The king doesn't squat like a beetle," he said. "He's just being given bad advice by his ministers. Get rid of them and George will come to terms with us."

"I think you're absolutely wrong," Drew said heatedly. "The king surrounds himself with yes men. He's a tyrant with a tyrant's ways!"

It occurred to Jan that he was reliving the arguments he used to have with his own father. In those arguments he had been the firebrand and his father the conservative. Now it was men like his son and John Holt who were spelling out what was beginning to look like the new reality. The rebellion against the Crown had started as an economic complaint, but now there was an antagonism toward the very *idea* of allegiance to a distant sovereign. To men like Drew, being bound by the laws of the king and his parliament was anathema, because it meant accepting the rule of a *foreign* government.

John Holt neatly summed up the argument of those who were determined to fight for a new order. "It is intolerable that a continent like America should be governed by a little island three thousand miles away."

Drew slouched back on his stool. All this talk about the king was very well and good, but in the meantime there was a more pressing question. "What can we do about the British taking our ships?" he asked.

"Why not take them back?"

Alec spoke quietly, but the question stopped the other men, and they looked at him.

"What do you mean?" Jan asked.

"If the British can take them from us, why can't we take them from them?" Alec said. "Why don't we start with the *Anthony?*"

"Take a ship back from the British right here in New York?" Jan asked.

"Why not?" Drew said as he came to his feet. "Why not take a ship right from under their noses?"

The men stopped talking for a moment when Celine and Mary Delafield entered the room. But the women went to a table on the other side of the room, and the men resumed their conversation. That two groups of people, holding separate conversations, would occupy the same room in a de Kuyper home was an accommodation to the citywide lack of firewood; the kitchen was, as in most houses in the city, the only room made livable by a warming fire. The remainder of one's house was almost as cold as the outdoors, and if people had nothing to do, they often stayed in bed under a load of blankets and coats.

Mary recounted what had happened to Robert, and Celine tried to buck up her spirits. "He'll be all right," she said.

"You know what he's like," Mary said, shaking her head. "God knows what they'll do to him."

An image of Robert Delafield in prison flashed through Celine's mind. Yes, she knew what he was like. He'd cause trouble and a couple of guards would probably beat him to a pulp.

"Can you speak to General Howe?" Mary asked.

"Yes," Celine said, but she didn't think much would come of it. She had once talked to the general about Dick Goelet, but the man had deftly sidestepped the issue by claiming he didn't have any right to interfere with the operations of the provost marshal. Celine had dropped the subject. "I wouldn't get my hopes up about the general doing anything," she added.

"Well then, I've thought of someone else we could talk to," Mary said.

"Who's that?"

"Captain Blakely. He might do something if I asked him."

Celine looked at her cousin and couldn't decide whether Mary was being truly naïve. Celine had seen the way the captain looked at Mary, and she had also seen the way Mary looked back. Such boldness was definitely not in keeping with her character.

"Dealing with the captain might be playing with fire," she said, deliberately understating her feelings.

"It might be worth a try," Mary said hopefully.

Celine was sure she knew *who* it was worth a try for, but she let it pass. "The first thing we should do is find out where they've taken him. And then we'll try to see him," she said.

As the women talked, the men discussed the *Anthony*. Alec made it sound like a simple thing to do. "We take a dozen armed men aboard, kick the crew off, raise sail, and get the hell out of the harbor."

"Just like that!" Jan said sarcastically.

"Sure. It's the last thing the British will be expecting."

"You know, he's right," John Holt said.

"Where will we take the ship?" Drew asked.

"Wherever you want," Alec said.

Drew mulled it over. The obvious course was to sail the *Anthony* down through the Narrows and take her to Philadelphia, which was still in American hands. But that would hardly keep the cargo of grain in the area for the local population.

"I say we take it someplace nearby and unload the cargo," he said finally. "Then we take the ship away."

Jan nodded in understanding. "The British will never dream that we'd unload the ship around here. The question is, *where* around here?"

"Kip's Bay," Drew answered without hesitation. "We can store the grain at Celine's—the old Beekman Place, where the British will never think of looking."

"Aren't there soldiers up around there?" Holt asked.

"Not anymore," Alec said. "Once you get out of the city, you won't see a redcoat until you get up to Harlem."

Celine had become more and more distracted by the conversation of the men as they discussed the use of her house and property. Now she interrupted them. "Alec's correct about that. Ever since Howe moved to the city, the British don't bother about anything up there."

"But why Beekman's Place?" Jan asked.

"It's not *Beekman's* Place anymore," Celine said wearily. "Just the Place."

"All right," Jan said, allowing his daughter her whimsy. "But why must it be the Place?"

"It's out of the way," Drew said. "It's big and roomy, and it's only a couple of miles from the city."

"Smuggler's paradise," Alec added.

"Don't you think you ought to ask the owner if you can use it?" Celine said indignantly.

"We all must make our little sacrifices, Celine," Drew said. "Seriously, you *will* let us use it?"

"Of course."

"When should we take the ship?" Jan asked.

"What's wrong with right now?" Alec said. "I can round up the men in an hour."

The immediacy of the plan brought silence to the room. It was one thing to talk of hijacking a ship from under the noses of the British, but another to plan to do it within the hour.

"Well, if we're going to do it, what's *wrong* with right now!" Drew agreed.

"Get on with it," Jan said.

Alec left to get the needed men, and the other three discussed ways of moving grain from the Place to the city. As they talked, Beth came into the room. The men nodded at her, but continued talking. Beth allowed her eyes to linger on Drew for a few seconds, but he didn't notice. She went past the men and sat with Celine and Mary.

"I feel so useless," John Holt was complaining. "What's a printer without a printing press? The British took mine and melted it down for bullets."

"But there's one hidden in the city," Drew said. "It was stashed away before the British came."

"If I could get that press, I'd start fighting my own war with the British," the printer said with feeling.

"We'll get it for you, Holt," Drew assured him.

Beth kept watching him out of the corner of her eye. Celine noticed her interest, and for a moment was startled. Beth had always seemed like part of the family, and her sudden attraction to Drew seemed almost to approach incest, Celine thought. But then she thought a moment more, and smiled.

Finally it was time for Drew to be on his way to meet Alec and his men at the dock. Jan and John Holt wanted to join him, but Drew insisted they stay out of the affair. Alec's men were used to danger, he said, and older men would only get in the way. Jan found himself gritting his teeth at the "older men" reference, but he kept his peace because he knew his son made sense.

"Take care of yourself," Beth said to Drew as he started for the door.

"Sure," he said. "This will be a piece of cake." And then he was gone.

"We'd better get going to the prison," Celine said. "Maybe we can take a basket of food for Robert."

"They won't let us see him," Mary said. "I know it, Celine."

"Don't be pessimistic."

"I'll go with you," Beth offered.

"It might be dangerous," Mary said. "It's not your problem."

"I'm making it mine," Beth replied.

Mary looked doubtful, and looked to Celine for support.

"Let her come," Celine said with a shrug. "Beth's a big girl now."

Colonel Franz von Lossow awoke in the frigid room on the second story of the building whose main floor housed the Crown & Thistle tavern. Every bed of the inn was occupied by a British or Hessian officer. He went to the wash stand and made a face when he saw the crust of ice covering the water in the pitcher. He took his ceremonial officer's dagger and poked a hole in the ice, then poured the frigid water into a bowl and splashed some on his face. The shock made him gasp. He did it again, and within seconds his skin began to tingle. He stretched his arms, still tired from only a few hours' sleep, but pleased that his body was responding well.

The colonel had arrived late last night from an inspection tour of the Hessian forces in the New Jersey area. As he had listened to the firsthand accounts of the battle of Trenton, he was appalled by the lax precautions of his countrymen. It was just as well Colonel Rall had died of his wounds. If he had

A TERRIBLE WINTER

lived, he would have faced the ugly prospect of a court-martial, and probably the hangman's noose.

A great deal of his time had been wasted by officers eager to prove that they, and they alone, had played a heroic part in the battle. After a dozen such interviews, the colonel was concerned about the level of honesty among the Hessian officer corps.

And the English officers he had talked with had been no better. According to *their* version, the Hessians had acted like swine, but they themselves had been heroes. The colonel hadn't bothered to point out that the Hessians now being maligned were the same troops commended for bravery by General Howe for their performance during the battles of White Plains and Fort Washington.

Now he was back in New York preparing to report his findings to General Knyphausen. How the Old Man would rant and rave when he heard what the English said about his soldiers! How he would shout and threaten to take the whole lot of them back to Europe! Not that it would happen, of course, because the English king had already paid the Prince of Hesse-Cassel a great deal of money for the services of his troops, and von Lossow knew how his cousin felt about money.

He went to the window, scraped off its icy frosting, and looked down on the white street. A sudden gust of wind blew down the road, lifting the snow into the air, swirling it about, then driving it into the building.

And they said this was a *temperate* climate, he thought. My God, it was as bad as Germany! Worse. At least the houses at home were built solidly of stone and earth; they weren't cheap wooden frame buildings like these that abounded in New York—firetraps no better than the sheds his family used to house pigs back home.

His thoughts were interrupted by the sudden squealing of a woman in the next room. The high-pitched sounds pierced the thin wall; it was as if the woman were in his own room. He was momentarily alarmed, then quickly realized the squeals were of ecstasy. One of his fellow officers and a woman were having a wonderful time. The squeals slowly changed to low moans, and then the urgent grunting of a man could be heard. The grunting and moaning blended, intensified, and finally climaxed. Once again there was silence from the next room.

Colonel von Lossow was both excited and disturbed by the incident. It had been a long time since he had had a woman—

far too long. But the ones he had met in New York—the ones that were obviously available—held little interest for him. Mostly they were tarts or slatternly serving girls, and he was offended by the idea of coupling with them. Not that it made much difference physically, he told himself. You just closed your eyes, and then what the hell difference did it make who the woman was? But he hadn't convinced himself: he was something of an aesthete and had need of better goods than were being offered.

He thought of Celine. Ah, now there was a woman he could pay attention to, a great deal of attention. She had everything—looks, charm, brains, manners. *There* was a woman who could make a man throw capes over puddles, and toss flowers at her feet.

He went to the chest and took a book from the top drawer. It was a small, leather-bound edition of the poems of John Donne. The drawer also contained a volume of Shakespeare's sonnets, Milton's *Paradise Lost,* and *Volpone, Or the Fox,* by Ben Jonson. All the books were in English, a reading habit the colonel had picked up during his school days at Oxford. Even if there had been no other differences between him and the other Hessians, this peculiarity set von Lossow a world apart from them. Most of the officers knew only enough "military" English to get by in the field; and the common soldiers couldn't speak even decent German, much less any foreign language.

He opened the book and looked for "The Dreame," for in truth he had dreamed about Celine several times since he had met her at General Howe's New Year's Eve party. Exciting dreams they were! He found what he was looking for.

> Deare love, for nothing lesse then thee
> Would I have broke this happy dreame,
>   It was a theame
> For reason, much too strong for phantasie,
> Therefore thou wakd'st me wisely; yet
> My Dreame thou brok'st not, but continued'st it,
> Thou art so true, that thoughts of thee suffice,
> To make dreames truths; and fables histories;
> Enter these armes, for since thou thoughtst it best,
> Not to dreame all my dreame, let's act the rest.

He closed the book. Then he closed his eyes and conjured up a vision of Celine. Yes, to make dreams truths . . . and enter these arms... to see her coming to him: the golden hair, so soft; the white shoulders; the sensuous mouth; the curve of—

He opened his eyes and shook his head to clear the spell his imagination had been spinning.

Lord, she was a lot of woman—worth that damned tedious voyage across the ocean.

But the colonel was honest with himself about her availability. She came from one of the best New York families; although such status didn't mean much to an old-world Teutonic aristocrat, it meant something to her, and that was what counted.

He placed the book back in the drawer and returned to the window to stare out at the street. A lone man was passing the tavern, all bundled up. A heavy red muffler covered most of his face, making him unrecognizable.

Poor devil, the colonel thought, wondering what brought a man out so early on such a day. Perhaps a baker on his way to work. Or a drayman. Or maybe a seaman heading toward his ship. Or a thief on his way home after a good night's work.

It was a little game he liked to play—guessing people's line of work by their appearance. He decided he couldn't see enough of the man in the long red muffler to come to any conclusions. Yes, there was one he could make; a man who wore a red muffler must have an imagination.

The colonel would have been most surprised to know the man with the red muffler was the brother of the very woman he had been thinking and dreaming about. He would have been even more surprised had he known the nature of Andrew de Kuyper's business on this cold winter morning.

Drew arrived at the alley where he was to rendezvous with Alec Seixas. As he stopped where the alley terminated at Dock Street, a hand reached from a doorway and touched his shoulder.

"They didn't even post a guard," Alec sneered, pointing across the street to where the *Anthony* was berthed.

Drew studied the ship. There appeared to be almost no activity. Once a sailor hurried across the deck, but he seemed to be on some common errand.

The snow was falling even more heavily than before, making visibility even poorer. It was not the best time to be taking a ship into the river, and Drew said so.

"The poor visibility also hides us," Alec said.

"Who's going to captain the ship?"

"I was going to do it myself," Alec said, and it was true he was a fair seaman. "But on a day like this I'd thought it best to get some help." He signaled, and a short, squat man stepped out of the doorway. "This is Nils Nissen. He knows every inch of the harbor and shoreline."

"I've seen you around the docks," Drew acknowledged.

"Aye," Nissen said. "Lots of captains hire me as pilot when there's fog. I've kept many a ship off the rocks."

Drew felt reassured about the safety of the *Anthony*. Nissen was one of a new group of men who called themselves harbor pilots—men who met ship master's qualifications, but preferred a shoreline berth. Their speciality was knowing every inlet, sandbar, and current in the harbor. There were only a few of these pilots, but they had been proving their worth. Ship owners were learning that the expense of hiring such a man was very little when compared to the cost of a ship foundering on rocks or sandbars.

"We best be getting on with it," Drew said.

"Not 'we,'" Alec said.

"What do you mean?"

"I mean that you're not coming with us. Many of the crew members probably know you—after all, it is your father's ship."

That was sensible, but Drew didn't give up easily. "I'll wear a mask."

"We're all masked anyway, what with all this cold-weather gear we're wearing. But there's another job for you to do. Go up to the Place and make sure everything is ready for us. Get wagons. Have them standing by the bay. Figure out where we can store the grain."

Drew surrendered. "All right. I guess I am the best one for that job."

Alec squeezed his arm. "Best you get away from here. In a short while there'll be a lot of unhappy sailors in this street."

Drew took a last look at the *Anthony*, then turned and walked back toward Maiden Lane. As he returned past the Crown & Thistle, a blond Hessian officer was coming out into the street. The men looked at each other, but made no greeting. The German recognized the man in the red scarf as the one who had been going in the other direction only a short while ago. That was quick, he thought, whatever it was the man had to do.

A TERRIBLE WINTER

For his part, Drew didn't give the blond man a second thought. Just another Hessian, a mercenary, one of the king's hired animals. Well, their time was limited, he thought, and they'll all be leaving—either in a ship back across the ocean, or in a pine box that went six feet into the ground.

After Drew had gone, Alec led his men aboard the schooner. They captured her without firing a shot. The crew was rounded up under gunpoint and held on the main deck. The lines to shore were taken in, and at the last moment the crew was forced to jump from the ship to the dock. Three sailors fell into the water and almost froze to death before their mates could haul them up onto the wharf. The captain of the *Anthony* stood shaking his fist at the pirates as the ship was swallowed up by the dense fog and mist.

The pilot, Nils Nissen, ordered a limited number of sails set, turned the ship around in the middle of the river, and slowly began to move north with the tide. The heavily laden vessel inched forward under the light spread of canvas, her Danish captain pacing back and forth on the quarterdeck, issuing crisp orders to the helmsman. Alec was satisfied he had picked the right man for the job.

It suddenly occurred to him that, surely, the finest sailors in the world lived right here in New York. Wouldn't it be possible to get them to sail under the banner of the new nation? On ships that were bound to the American Congress?

It was ironic, he thought, that America had the best sailors, but no navy. Maybe it was time for General Washington to have a naval force to support his army. The more he thought about the idea, the more he liked it. He made a note to talk to Jan de Kuyper about the matter. They could use one of his ships to start the New York navy—no, the *American* navy, because it would be working in the interests of all the colonies.

Nils Nissen stopped his pacing and watched Alec as he cleaned his fingernails with the point of a wicked-looking knife.

"Don't cut your finger."

"Just sail the ship."

"You're not paying much attention to how I do it."

"*You're* supposed to know the how of it," Alec said.

"But what if I ran the ship on the shore?" Nissen asked, accustomed to teasing frightened owners.

"It would be the last one you'd do it to," Alec said quietly.

The Dane laughed. "Relax, Seixas, you don't have anything to worry about."

"I am relaxed."

Drew arrived at the Place. He organized the servants, and soon several workhorses were harnessed to heavy sleds for work in the snow. The back of the haybarn was cleared and made ready to hold the cargo from the ship. They piled a mound of hay in the middle of the barn so anyone looking in from the front couldn't see what was stored in back. Of course, if a suspicious visitor went into the barn and went beyond the hay, he would see what was there. But, Drew reasoned, if someone was that suspicious, the game would be up anyway.

When everything was readied and waiting, Drew went to the main house and sought some refreshment. He took a pewter pitcher and filled it to the two-thirds point with beer. Then he added half a pint of rum and half a cup of sugar. He went to the fire and withdrew a red-hot poker. He plunged the rod into the pitcher, and the liquid sizzled and bubbled as the heat from the iron spread through it. After a full minute he withdrew the poker and poured a mug of the liquid. It was warm and delicious as it coursed down his throat. The heated iron gave the rum-and-beer punch a burnt taste, almost bitter, yet very pleasant.

It was a popular winter drink in New York. But the potent brew often led to fighting, and sometimes the combatants would hit each other with the very pokers they had used to heat their drinks. Since another name for a fire poker was *loggerhead*, the expression "to be at loggerheads" meant a violent brawl.

In Drew's case the effect of the punch was to calm him.

It was almost dark when Alec arrived at the Place; and by the time the last of the grain had been taken from the ship and hauled inland on sleds, it was the next morning. Drew stood exhausted on the deck of the *Anthony*. He had been awake for over twenty-four hours.

"It's time to get the ship out of here," Alec said.

"Where are you taking her?"

"Somewhere off the Jersey shore. Anywhere so they don't suspect we unloaded her here."

"Yes, I trust we'll be doing this again," Drew said. "Let's leave a note for the British."

He went into the captain's cabin and found paper, a quill pen, and a bottle of ink. He scribbled away for a time, then handed the note to Alec, who read it, smiled, and then laughed aloud.

To the English Commander:
Thank you for the grain we found aboard this ship. I am certain I will put it to better use than yourself. You, no doubt, would give it to Germans, whereas I will see it gets to members of our common Anglo-American family.
  You remain, sir,
  my humble and obedient servant,
  G. Washington

"I'd love to see Howe's face when he reads this," Alec said, continuing to chuckle.

"He'll especially appreciate the remark about the Germans. I've heard he isn't particularly fond of them."

"Then why the hell does he have them in his army?"

"He doesn't have anything to say about it. The king doesn't seem to be able to recruit enough loyal Englishmen to fight his war, so he's forced to hire foreigners who fight for pay."

"That's what happened in Rome," Alec said. "The Romans became fat and lazy, and Gauls and other barbarians were hired to do their fighting for them. It was the beginning of the end of the Roman Empire."

"You seem to know your history," Drew said.

"One of the advantages of being Jewish is when you're a little kid they stuff your head full of history: and then they destroyed *this* temple, and then they erected *that* temple, and the houses were razed and the people led into captivity. Somewhere along the way you actually learn something. It's interesting because you can make comparisons."

"Are you telling me the British are turning to Roman-style debauchery?"

Alec laughed. "Of course they are. And as soon as America is free and on her own, she'll start down the same road. Nations are like people—the moment they're born, they start to die."

"That's cynical. And depressing."

"Not really. Look at it this way: if life ends in death, then death must end in life. It's all a big circle, with no end. But enough philosophy," Alec said. "I've got to get this ship over to New Jersey."

"It seems odd to be giving her back to the British," Drew said, letting his eyes rove over the deck of the handsome schooner. "After all, she does belong to my family."

"The British will hand her back to you. Then you can get more grain. The British will commandeer it. And we'll steal it again."

Drew smiled. "You're right about life being a circle."

The *Anthony* raised anchor, and Drew walked back to the Place. The air was freezing and the footing treacherous. When he returned to the warmth of the kitchen, he treated himself to another mugful of heated rum and beer.

Alec Seixas was certainly a surprising character. Complex. A man of action. Obviously also a man who spent time speculating about mankind and his fate. It made him a person who commanded respect; a man who contemplated history would have a better understanding of what was happening in the present; yes, and what might happen in the future, too. Human nature doesn't change very quickly, and a man who studied the changing currents of Roman history would also gain a well-informed opinion about what was happening in eighteenth-century America.

As he half drifted off to sleep by the fire, his thoughts turned again to Dick Goelet. Nothing he had done had been helpful in getting his cousin freed from prison. He sipped his mellowing punch and wondered what Dick had to eat and drink. Was it any good? *Was it enough to keep him alive?*

He decided he would pay another visit to the provost marshal's office and see if there was anything to be accomplished. He owed Dick that much.

And then he worried no more about it. His eyes closed and his head fell toward his chest. His dreamless sleep was that of a man who had put in a hard but satisfying day's work.

"It smells in here," Peter said, rubbing his nose and looking with distaste at the discolored walls of the shabby hallway.

"Shh," Marie Therese said. "You don't want to hurt Alice's feelings."

"I wouldn't say anything to her," Peter said. "Just to you."

"Don't say anything at all," she admonished. She knocked on the door at the far end of the hall. After a short pause, Alice de Witt opened it a crack. She peered out suspiciously, then saw who was there and opened the door wide.

"This is a surprise," she said, smiling.

Marie Therese took the wicker basket she was carrying and

placed it on a table. "I brought a few things for the children. Meat, bread, a few vegetables, some other things. We have more than we need for ourselves."

"Thank you," Alice said, glancing toward the closed bedroom door, behind which the sound of loud snoring could be heard. It was ten o'clock in the morning, and Enoch was still sleeping off his previous night's drunk. "Enoch won't like me taking charity, but we're so low on everything I can't refuse."

"It's not charity when it comes from your own family," Marie Therese said firmly.

"My husband doesn't look at it that way."

Enoch had moved his family out of the de Kuyper house and into these wretched three rooms at the back of a house that had been broken up into flats and rented out to poor families. The house was old and drafty, the floorboards slanted, the roof full of leaks. Even so, it was better than living in a tent. The rent wasn't much, although Enoch was always behind and the landlord constantly threatened to evict the family.

"How's little Jacob?"

"About the same," Alice said with a shrug. Her eight-year-old son had contracted a severe chest cold and was confined to his bed. "He's in the other bedroom asleep."

Little Elly was near the tiny stove playing with a doll. She smiled at the visitors, and Marie Therese realized the girl was doll-like herself. She had curly blond hair, wide blue eyes, and a perpetual impish smile.

"Elly looks well," she said.

The thin woman managed to smile. Since it was a rare thing for Alice to do, it appeared to be a painful experience for her. "She's the strongest of us all. Nothing hurts Elly." She suddenly looked distressed. "Oh, dear, here you've come to visit and I can't even offer you a cup of tea, because we don't have any."

"There's some in the basket."

While Alice made tea, Marie Therese looked about the room and was appalled. She knew that many poor people in New York lived like this, but these were *relatives*. There were only a few sticks of furniture in the tiny room. The walls were a leprous green, and the floors were bare wood. The single window allowed light to come through only one pane, because the rest of the glass had been broken and the hole covered with wood. But despite the abject poverty, the place was spotlessly clean.

"I wish you'd let Elly stay with us through the winter," Marie Therese said. "It would be healthier for her."

"I wouldn't mind, but you know how Enoch feels about it."

"She might get sick like your son."

"Enoch says he'll get well."

"How can he be sure about that?" Marie Therese asked. She also wanted to ask how Enoch knew anything at all, since he passed most of his time in a drunken stupor.

Elly came over and showed her doll to Peter. He inspected it with all the boredom a seven-year-old boy can show for anything connected with a four-year-old girl.

"Nice," he said and handed it back.

"Do you have a doll?" Elly asked.

"Boys don't have dolls," he said indignantly.

"Take Elly for a walk," Marie Therese said to her grandson. She wanted to talk openly to Alice, and didn't want the boy to hear.

Peter made a face, but led the little girl from the room.

Alice brought the tea, and Marie Therese sat in a rickety chair, half afraid it would collapse. "Has Enoch had any work?" she asked.

"Once in a while he works for a day or two on the docks. But nothing steady."

"What do you do for money?"

"I clean a British officer's house two days a week. But he also lets me do his laundry."

"So it's really you who supports the children," Marie Therese said, and paused. "I'm sure Enoch buys whiskey with every penny he makes."

Alice looked glum. "I'm afraid that's how it is."

"I hope this doesn't offend you," Marie Therese said, coming to the real reason for her visit. "I talked to Jan, and he could use help in keeping his office clean. It would be full time."

"Why would I be offended?" Alice said. "I'd be delighted to take the job. Having a steady income would take a load off my mind."

"Then it's settled," Marie Therese said, pleased that she hadn't injured the other's pride. "I'll tell Jan and you can start whenever you wish."

"I'll start tomorrow," Alice said happily.

A few minutes later Peter and Elly returned, and the visitors took their leave.

A TERRIBLE WINTER

As Marie Therese and her grandson walked home, the boy was curious. "Why doesn't Enoch work?"

She hesitated. Peter was a bit young to be learning about drunks and their habits, she thought. "He isn't well," she said.

"Grandpa told me he drinks too much."

"Your grandpa has a big mouth," Marie Therese said, and then became honest. "But he's right, Enoch drinks too much."

"I don't like beer," Peter said, making a sour expression.

"A little won't hurt you. It's when you drink too much. Like Enoch."

"I won't drink too much," Peter promised. "I don't want to snore like Enoch."

Marie Therese smiled and held her grandson's hand as they turned down Maiden Lane toward their house.

Dick Goelet was having a miserable time in the Sugar House prison.

The snow blew through the barred windows and settled on the prisoners' bodies as they tried to sleep. If a man didn't move once in a while, the stuff would cover him and he would freeze to death. It had happened to dozens of unlucky men in this godforsaken place.

With the coming of winter, the prisoners' rations had been cut. Each man was given two pounds of hard biscuit and two pounds of pork a week. For anything else, he had to depend on his wits and imagination; or his friends on the outside. Prisoners were allowed to get packages, but they had to pass through the hands of the guards, who always took about half the contents for themselves. It didn't do any good to complain; the guards would only laugh. And if a man complained too much, usually he would turn up dead.

The guards also sold things to the prisoners, at outrageous prices. Dick tried to buy a candle that was little more than an inch long, but the guard wanted a whole guinea.

Dick and Seth Cuyler had become very close. At the moment they were resting with their backs against a wall near a window, the snow sifting down on top of them. "We're going to freeze if we stay here any longer," Seth said.

"It's our time to go inside anyway."

Seth nodded and stood up. Dick joined him and they spent a painful minute stretching to restore their circulation. They went into the adjoining interior room. These windowless rooms were the warmest places in the building, and much sought after.

The prisoners had set their own rules, the main one being that after two days in an interior room, a man must move to one of the outside ones.

Dick followed Seth inside. He went directly to two men who were seated against the wall. The room was jammed with bodies.

"You've been here for two days," Seth said to the men. "Time to change."

"You've got it all wrong, mate," the man said. "We only got these places this morning. Try someone else."

Seth wasn't a man to waste words. He grabbed the man by his jacket and hauled him to his feet. "I've had my eye on you. Now beat it."

The man sized Seth up, looked at his friend and shrugged; and then he and his companion left the room.

"Welcome to your new home," Seth said.

"For two days at least," Dick agreed.

He sat down and pulled his blanket over his shoulders. It had been given to him only a week before by Drew, who had bribed a guard. It was standard procedure in the prison.

"Look who's coming," Seth muttered, and Dick looked up to see Robert Delafield making his way across the room. Robert had been in the prison for only a short while before he was alienating almost everyone by his manner.

"Do you have anything to eat?" Robert asked.

"No," Dick said.

"I'm starving to death."

"So are we all," Seth said.

"You don't look as if you are," Robert complained. "I'll bet you have something in your pocket."

"Not a thing," Dick said truthfully.

"I don't believe you."

"Look, Delafield," Seth said, moving his large frame as if ready to get up. "Things are bad enough without you calling people liars."

Robert squatted down and fingered Dick's blanket. "Where'd you get his?"

"Leave him alone," Seth growled.

Robert switched topics. "Have you made any plans to escape?"

"How can you escape from *this* place?" Dick asked.

"You can't just sit here on your asses, and let them get away with it."

"You escape," Seth said. "I promise not to tell anyone."

"Some patriots," Robert sneered, and walked away.

"I almost prefer the Hessian guards to him," Seth said.

"He's married to my cousin Mary," Dick sighed. "That makes him sort of a relative."

"Better keep it to yourself," Seth grunted. He closed his eyes and imagined he was eating a good meal. There were ham, turkey, and a large joint—all smothered in a thick gravy.

Dick was thinking, too, but not about food. He was planning the book he was going to write when the war was over, *if* he managed to survive the Sugar House. The tentative title was *The War As Seen Through the Eyes of One Who Was There*. At the moment he was scanning the faces in the room, trying to memorize them so he could write about them. Within days, several of these faces would be gone. Almost fifty men a week died in the Sugar House, but they were quickly replaced by new ones.

Both men's thoughts were interrupted by a fight that broke out on the other side of the room.

"You stinkin' bastard! That's my biscuit you have in your hand!"

A small Virginian stood with his jaw thrust out as he screamed into the face of a much larger fellow. Another fight over food. It happened all the time.

"Go on with you, it's my biscuit," the large man said. "And shut your mouth before I shut it for you!"

The little man trembled, then threw himself at his antagonist. The big man easily fended off the flurry of blows, but then the plucky little Virginian brought his knee up into the other's groin.

"Bastard!" the big man shouted, his face registering pain and anger. He lunged forward, but the Virginian jumped aside and his would-be assailant plunged into a group of men. That's when the free-for-all broke out. This man bumped into that man, someone else threw a punch, and suddenly the room was filled with scuffling prisoners, all shouting and yelling.

Dick and Seth stood up and, trying to stay out of the melee, flattened themselves against the wall. Once someone tried to hit Dick, but Seth tossed the man back into the crowd.

The fight didn't last more than a couple of minutes. A dozen Hessian guards came running into the room, swinging heavy clubs without discrimination. There were many Hessian guards now, because Captain Blakely had grown ever fonder of their brutality.

Within minutes the fight was over. A half-dozen prisoners had been knocked unconscious, and the Hessians left them on the floor. The big fellow who had started it all had been clubbed so hard he died that night. His body was taken to the front entrance and left there until the death cart came the next morning and took him away to the Jewish cemetery, where his body was tossed into an open pit. The dead man's final resting place had nothing to do with his religion. The British authorities used the Jewish burying ground simply because it happened to be convenient. Rabbi Seixas had complained of this to Colonel Cunningham, but to no avail.

A week passed, and Robert Delafield finally found the trouble he had seemed to be looking for.

Sergeant Taggert liked to amuse himself by going to the prison and personally distributing the boxes and cartons that had been brought to the prisoners. He made a great game of it, baiting the men and turning the whole affair into a spectacle of degradation. The English and Hessian guards would gather around and laugh as the prisoners came to get what remained of their goods.

"Where's Penworthy?" Taggert called out. A tall, nervous man with a horrible scar on his cheek came forward to claim his package.

Taggert peered into the carton, smiled, and looked at the guards. "Lookee here," he said, showing that the box contained four small potatoes. "Maybe enough to keep Mister Penworthy alive for at least another week." He took one potato and shoved it in his pocket. "I'll give this one to my pig."

This sally was met by hoots and laughs from the guards; then, after it had been translated into German, the Hessians rewarded the sergeant with a second round of applause.

Taggert shoved the package into the wretched Penworthy's stomach, knocking the wind out of him. The fellow barely noticed as he grasped the precious box and scuttled to the back of the crowd. He hardly minded that most of the contents had been stolen. He had a few potatoes, and a bit of food was a bit of life.

More names were called and more jokes made. One man received a small hunk of hard soap, and this occasioned great hilarity among the guards—especially the Germans, who didn't seem to know what the gift was for until it was explained. Taggert elaborately mimed the act of taking a bath, using the soap to wipe all parts of his body, especially the private parts.

"Now we have something for Delafield," Taggert said when he had amused himself sufficiently with the soap. He brought forward a handsome wicker hamper tied with a large blue ribbon.

Robert came foward, looking angry.

"Know what's inside?" Taggert asked.

"Just give it to me."

"Tsk-tsk. Is that any way to talk to a man who's giving you a present? And such a pretty one!"

"It belongs to me," Robert said, making a move as if he intended to snatch the hamper.

Taggert held on. "First you have to guess what's inside."

Robert smoldered silently.

"Well?" Taggert asked.

"Food," Robert said grudgingly.

"What kind?"

"Potatoes, meat, bread."

"D'you think those are good guesses?" Taggert asked the guards.

"Do I receive my goods or not?" Robert said.

The sergeant handed over the basket and winked at the guards. Robert opened the hamper. His face blackened with rage. "Empty!"

The sergeant peered inside. Then he smiled. "Someone sent you *nothing*," he said happily. "The people on the outside think as much of you as we do."

Robert went berserk. He raised the wicker hamper over his head and brought it down with a crash on Taggert's head. The braided wicker split and flew all over the place. For a moment it was amusing to look at the startled English face poked through the top of the hamper.

The amusement didn't last long.

The other guards, outraged at the temerity of this prisoner, began to beat him with their clubs. Taggert pulled the hamper from his head, his face emerging scratched and bleeding from the sharp wicker. He grabbed a club and began to beat Robert with a fury.

The prisoner tried to defend himself, but the rain of blows knocked him to the ground and rendered him unconscious. It was Dick's quick thinking that saved his life.

"He's dead!" Dick cried loudly.

Taggert hesitated and then lowered his club. He shoved his boot under Robert's chin. "Dead, is 'e?"

"Yes," Dick said, coming forward and holding Robert's head.

"Damned rebel bastard," Taggert growled, touching his own face and staring at the blood that came off on his fingers. He gave the inert form a parting kick and left the room to care for his own wounds.

"He's still alive," Dick said to Seth. "Let's get him over to a corner."

"Man's a damn fool," Seth muttered as he helped place Robert on the ground against the wall.

Dick began to wipe the blood away from Robert's face, and the unconscious man began to stir. Dick didn't like Robert, but he had come to his aid in time of need. At this moment they were two prisoners with a common enemy; they were brothers.

"The third ship pirated in less than a month!" Colonel Cunningham raged as he pounded his huge fist on the desk top. "Stolen right from the dock! What are we, fools?"

Captain Blakely sat in a chair on the other side of the desk, calm and collected. The way to handle the colonel was to let him expend his anger.

"I tell you, Blakely," the colonel continued, "this has got to stop. Someone is tipping off these pirates. They know about ships the instant they arrive. I want action on this! *Fast* action!"

Captain Blakely crossed his legs and remained unperturbed. It was true that pirates were taking ships from the very docks, but he refused to accept any blame for it. If the navy would provide adequate protection in the harbor, the problem might be solved. But the stuffy admiral refused to become involved. "The ships are docked, sir," the admiral had said, "and the docks are on land, and what happens on land is of no concern to the navy."

The problem was compounded when General Howe refused to send his soldiers to guard the docks. He was as stubborn as the admiral. "It's clearly a job for the navy," he said. "Let them handle it."

Since neither the navy nor the army would provide shipboard guards, the pirates had an easy time of it. Captain Blakely decided that if the admiral and the general wished to squabble, they would have to accept the consequences. The pirates could steal the whole city as far as he cared.

"So what are you going to do about it?" the colonel asked.

"I can't do anything until you get me either soldiers or sailors to stand guard."

"I can't convince the damned admiral and I can't convince the damned general," the colonel said. "But can't you come up with *some* idea?"

Suddenly the captain had an idea, but saw no reason to discuss it with Cunningham. He got to his feet. "I'll give it some thought," he said.

The colonel grunted, and the captain departed for his own office. He sent a soldier to fetch Philemon Peabody. Within a half hour the little man, looking nervous, came into the room.

"The pirates are upsetting Colonel Cunningham," Blakely said.

"What's that got to do with me?"

"You're well known as a shipping man. I want you to join these pirates. They should be pleased to have someone with your qualities."

"You're not serious."

"Quite serious."

"I'm not a pirate," Peabody said huffily. "I don't steal ships."

"I don't want you to steal ships. I want you to find out who's already doing it."

"So you want me to become a spy."

"You'll probably be good at it."

Peabody started to protest, but the captain cut him off. "I don't want to discuss it. As of now, you are to try to join the pirates."

"And if I won't?"

The captain brought his hands together and clapped. "Bravo, Peabody! But enough of courage. If you don't do what I say, I'll ruin you."

"How can you do that?"

"I'll expose you as a cheat. You cheated your own employer and defrauded the Crown. It's enough to get a rope around your neck."

Peabody forced himself to laugh, albeit uneasily. "Then we'll hang together. You were in on it, too."

"I don't know what you're talking about."

"The two prices. The one the king paid, and the one the de

Kuypers collected—with you and me splitting the difference. Surely you haven't forgotten about that."

"My records show what the king paid for the de Kuyper cargoes," Blakely said. "I also have receipts signed by you for those exact amounts. If they differ from the amounts you gave your employers, that's your problem."

Peabody was puzzled. "I never signed any receipts."

The captain unlocked his desk drawer, opened it, and withdrew a stack of receipts. He held them up for the other man to see. At the bottom of each page there was a number and the signature "Philemon Peabody."

The little man blinked his eyes. It *was* his signature—not really, of course, but an almost perfect forgery. "I never signed those! And those numbers saying how much was paid—they're wrong!"

"Of course they are," Blakely said, putting the receipts back in the drawer and locking it. "But the only people who know are you and me. If it comes to a trial, they'll have to take your word or mine—the word of a British officer or that of a former indentured servant. Who do you think they'll believe?"

Peabody felt trapped. The damned captain was correct. He wouldn't stand a chance in a trial. Damn! He slumped down, and his body seemed to deflate. "All right. What would you have me do?"

"Find the pirates."

"Will you give me those receipts if I do?"

"Perhaps."

Feeling like a cornered rat, Peabody stepped into the street. He tightened the scarf about his neck and trudged onward, his boots clumping on the icy, hard-packed snow. He rounded a corner and started to pass a group of men erecting a wall on the side of a building. The owner of the house was directing the operation. Several workmen assisted him; also helping were a half dozen of the old vagrants who could be seen on almost any street in the city. For a pence or two they were willing to pitch in on odd jobs.

Peabody was about to continue on his way when one of the vagrants stepped back to take a better look at what was happening. There was something familiar about the old man, Peabody thought, something that—

He took another step and stopped dead in his tracks. Suddenly he knew he was looking at the old drunk who had been asleep in the passageway aboard the *Anthony* just before it had been taken by the pirates. He wondered if the old man had anything to do with that event.

And then he had another thought.

If the old man hadn't been drunk, there was a good chance he had overheard the conversation between Peabody and Blakely. If so, the fellow also knew the captain was as guilty as Peabody himself of stealing money from the Crown.

The old man could be his salvation!

He moved across the street in order to remain inconspicuous. He was going to follow the man and find out more about him.

Sisyphus was too involved with the work to notice the bystander whose eyes were glued to him.

Drew went into the barn at the Place and walked behind the mound of hay. He stopped and scratched his head when he saw the crates and boxes that represented the booty from the last ship taken by Alec and his pirates. Unlike the cargoes of the first three ships, which consisted mostly of food and soft goods, this last cargo contained weapons.

He placed his hand on an opened crate and peered inside at twenty neatly stacked muskets. The crate was one of four hundred. Near by were scores of barrels containing black gunpowder. There were boxes and crates of rifle balls, musket balls, and cannonballs ranging from three-pounders to twelve-pounders. The barn had been turned into an arsenal.

Quite a cache, he thought. And then his brow furrowed as he pondered: what the hell was he to do with all this stuff? It would be foolish to send it down to the city. What would civilians want with all this weaponry. Obviously it should be given to General Washington, but the problem was, the matériel was on the eastern shore of Manhatan and Washington was at his winter quarters in Morristown. Between the supplies and the army there lay a big river and thousands of British troops.

He'd been mulling over the problem for two days and was no closer to the solution than when he had begun. He had asked Alec for advice, but Alec wasn't much help. "My job is to pirate the stuff. It's your job to figure out what to do with it," he said.

He had thought about sending a message to Washington that would hand over the problem to him, but decided against it. There were spies in Washington's camp, and he didn't want to take a chance on one of them finding out that Celine's Place was being used as a storage depot. It had proved to be an excellent choice—quiet, out of the way, ignored by the British.

It was frigid in the barn, and he went back to the main house. He was making tea when two visitors arrived—Jemmy and Jenny Sackett. They took off their heavy outer clothes and joined him at the fire.

"Some people can afford to have a nice fire," Jenny said. There was an accusation in her voice.

"It's easier to get firewood here than in the city," Drew explained.

Jemmy glanced at his sister, and his look contained a warning that they hadn't visited their cousin in order to insult him.

"What brings you here?" Drew asked.

"Depends."

"Depends on what answers you give us," Jemmy said, imparting further mystery to his sister's cryptic reply.

"Ask the questions," Drew said.

"You're involved with the pirates who take the ships from the docks," Jenny said. It wasn't a question, but a statement of fact.

"And you use this place as a storehouse," Jemmy added.

"True?" Jenny said, finally asking the question.

Drew hadn't the slightest idea how the twins had gotten this information. But they were his cousins, and he trusted their loyalty if not their good sense. He admitted it was the truth.

"It wouldn't have done any good to lie to us," Jenny said blandly. "We already knew."

"I don't lie to you, Jenny," Drew said. "Tell me a time when I did."

"If I wanted to, I could."

Jemmy grabbed his sister's arm. "No fights." He turned back to Drew. "The last ship you took was loaded with guns and ammunition, correct?"

Drew was startled. "How do you know that?"

"We know," Jemmy said.

"And it's all still here," Jenny said.

"And you're wondering what to do with it," Jemmy said.

Drew laughed. "And knowing you, I suppose you've come here with a solution to my problem."

Jemmy smiled and looked at his sister. "See, I told you he was pretty smart."

"All right," Drew said, folding his arms. "How do I get it to General Washington?"

Jemmy nodded. "I'm sure you've thought about the problem. Getting a shipload of guns and ammunition through the British lines won't be the easiest thing in the world."

"Yes, the thought has occurred to me," Drew said in his driest tone.

"The British patrol the North River."

Drew nodded his agreement. So far his cousins were thinking correctly.

"Of course, you could always take the stuff up north, cross the river miles from the nearest troops, and then come back down through Jersey," Jenny said.

Drew had considered this possibility, but discarded it for practical reasons. With the land in the grip of winter, the northern roads were all but impassable. He was about to say this, but Jenny cut him off.

"We hoped you weren't thinking of trying anything so dumb," she said, and Drew fought to remain calm.

"So we've come up with a plan with minimum risk and every chance of success," Jemmy said.

"Actually, it's all his idea," Jenny said grandly. "I only listened and agreed with it."

"No, that's not true," Jemmy said. "It was your idea about going down to the city."

"But if you hadn't come up with the original idea of British uniforms, I wouldn't have been able to add to it."

"An idea isn't any good until it's complete. Without your help this one would've gone nowhere."

"It still started with you."

"For the love of God!" Drew interrupted. "Will you two stop all this blather and tell me what you have in mind!"

"Get *him*," Jenny said derisively.

Jemmy smiled. "Here it is. We load the guns and ammunition onto wagons. Then we dress up the drivers in British uniforms. *You* dress up as a British officer, and *you* lead the wagons down to the city. The British have troop barges docked at the Battery. You hand the guards an authorization for a barge. You load the wagons aboard and go to New Jersey. You drive the wagons off the barges, thank the British, and take the stuff to Washington."

"What if the British stop me?"

"They won't. To them, you'll be British too."

Drew was silent for a time, and then he erupted. "You're

absolutely mad! That's the craziest idea I've ever heard, even from you two! It'll never work! I won't do it!"

Jenny looked at her brother and smiled.

Drew felt foolish in his British cavalry lieutenant's uniform as he rode his horse to the docks at the Battery. Six heavily loaded wagons followed, each with two "British" soldiers on the driver's bench. They were, of course, Alec Seixas's men.

He reined his horse up at the end of the dock as two Hessian guards came to block the way. They held their muskets diagonally across their chests. Drew reached into his tunic and withdrew papers that purported to be his orders. They had been forged by Jenny. *Badly* forged, Drew worried. Again he cursed himself for allowing the Sacketts to talk him into this insane scheme.

The Hessian glanced at the document, told Drew to wait, and went to the guardhouse shack. He returned a moment later with a British corporal.

The Englishman saluted, took the papers from the Hessian, and perused them. Reading, obviously, was not one of his major accomplishments, and after a few moments of squinting at the documents, the corporal returned them to Drew and saluted again.

"Very good, sir. And what exactly is it that you require?"

Drew suddenly realized the corporal couldn't read at all, and his performance had been a sham. However, there was no reason to antagonize the man. "As you read in the orders, Corporal, I'm to load these wagons onto a barge and take them to General Cornwallis."

"Yes, sir," the corporal said. He looked at the wagons with a critical eye. "Beggin' your pardon, sir, but you'll never get that lot onto one barge. Best take two."

"Two it is," Drew said in the clipped English voice he was affecting.

The corporal was very helpful as the wagons were loaded onto the barges. He showed them how to lock down the wheels, and how to tether the horses securely. He gave the Hessian oarsmen their orders. When the barges were ready to leave, he looked at Drew.

"Shall I cast you off, sir?"

"By all means, Corporal," Drew said in a friendly manner. "What is your name? I should like to send your commander a note about your cooperation."

A TERRIBLE WINTER

The corporal beamed with pride. "Melrose, sir. Corporal Jack Melrose."

"Very good, Melrose, carry on."

The heavy barges drifted out into the river, and the Hessian oarsmen strained their broad backs as they rowed through the ice-strewn waters. Drew stood at the bow of the first barge and was joined by Jemmy and Jenny, both dressed in British uniforms. Drew shook his head when he looked at Jenny. "Even with your hair rolled up under that hat, you look like a girl."

"I am a girl."

"You shouldn't have come."

"And miss all the fun? Don't be silly."

Drew gave up. He looked across to the Jersey side. "I hope things go as smoothly over there."

"They will," Jemmy said with assurance. "The British will help us unload and send us on our way to Morristown."

"Where, no doubt, Washington's guards will think we're British and shoot us."

Jemmy smiled. "No they won't, because you're going to ride ahead and tell them we're coming."

"*I'm* going to ride ahead?"

"The officer always goes first," Jenny said, smiling.

Drew grumbled and walked away. Madness! And yet this crazy plan seemed to be working. Where Jemmy had gotten all the British uniforms was a mystery, and Drew hadn't asked, because he was afraid of knowing the answer. The wagons had been no problem, nor the ride to the city. In fact everything had gone exactly as predicted, and it looked as if the rest of the journey would go as smoothly.

Jenny noticed her cousin was brooding. Deciding to comfort him, she came to his side. "Are you worried, as usual, about failing?" was her opening remark.

Twelve hours later a cold and miserable young man was escorted, on foot and under armed guard, into the presence of George Washington. The four Pennsylvanians who accompanied Drew had halted him on the road, forced him to dismount, threatened several times to shoot him, and finally, after a long discussion, agreed to take him to the general and let him decide if this man in an English lieutenant's uniform was telling the truth about his identity.

The general was at a staff meeting in a large tent when they arrived, and Drew was told to wait outside. One of the Pennsylvanians went into the tent and returned a few minutes later with Washington.

The general took one look at Drew and grinned. "Ah, de Kuyper, my favorite British officer. A dragoon this time, I see."

Drew smiled weakly and nodded his head toward the Pennsylvanians, who were still eyeing him suspiciously. "I don't know if they get the joke."

The wagons finally arrived, and the general was enthusiastic about this windfall of guns and ammunition. "By God, this will put us in fine shape for a while."

"I trust you'll put them to good use, sir."

The general invited Drew into the large tent and offered him a drink. The other officers were highly complimentary about Drew's accomplishment.

"You don't suppose you could do this again soon?" Washington asked.

"We'll have to wait and see," Drew replied.

The general chuckled. "The next time would you mind dressing as a Highlander? It would be amusing to see you in a kilt."

Drew smiled through his teeth.

"And you might round up a bagpiper. He could pipe you right through the British lines in style."

The greatest storm of the year descended on New York in early March. The gray and leaden skies dumped immense quantities of snow on the already buried terrain. The winds howled on, and men caught in the open became lost, went in circles, and froze to death. Travel was halted, and people stayed in their homes for days on end, going outside and doing battle with the forces of nature only in the direst emergencies.

The ice on the rivers thickened, and in many places it was possible to walk across from Manhatan to Long Island, or even to Jersey.

As drifts piled up against the barns and buildings, the roofs groaned under the weight, a number of them finally surrendering, burying people and animals in a quiet death. The drifts filled the streets of the city and covered the surrounding fields. Entire houses disappeared from view, and their inhabitants were forced to dig themselves out before the lack of air caused them to suffocate. Others were not so lucky. People who fell asleep without knowing their houses were buried drifted peacefully into eternity.

Old Sisyphus had picked up enough odd jobs to move from the miserable shed off Hanover Square. He now rented a small room off Beaver Street in the house where Enoch and Alice de Witt lived.

He hated to leave his room on such a day, but he knew he had a day's work if he ventured a trip to a farmhouse near the Collect. He needed some money to pay his rent, and he was hungry, so he decided to brave the elements. On his way out he met Enoch de Witt in the hallway. For once the man seemed sober.

"Who are you?" Enoch asked.

"I live here," Sisyphus said. "And we met before, but I guess you were too drunk to remember."

"I find it easier to get through each day if I have a few."

It was none of his business, and he knew it, but Sisyphus had taken pity on the thin, wan-looking woman who lived down the hall and put up with so much. "That's a lovely wife you have, man," he said. "Why don't you straighten out your life?"

"Another would-be preacher who's worrying about me," Enoch said. "I wish you'd all shut up and leave me alone."

"It's not you I'm worrying about. It's your wife and kids. Can't you stop drinking?"

"I've tried," Enoch admitted. "But I don't have the willpower. And right now I have a bigger problem. I have nothing left to drink and no money, and my sweet little wife won't give me any. You wouldn't want to make a man a loan, would you? A loan, mind you; I'll pay it back."

Sisyphus shook his head angrily and went out into the polar street. As he walked along, the wind whistled through his clothing and bit at his flesh. He walked northward until he came to the frozen Old Kill, the stream that connected with the Collect.

A group of boys were skating on the ice! He rubbed his eyes to make certain they weren't playing tricks on him. No; in the middle of a blizzard, a dozen youngsters were having a wonderful time on the ice. Attached to the bottoms of their boots were long, shiny beef-rib bones. The polished bones were highly slippery. With one under each foot, a boy could glide along the ice at a breathtaking speed. The snow fell on the ice, of course, but the rib bones sliced through the drifting powder with ease.

"You'll freeze out here," Sisyphus said as he came up to several of the boys, who were taking a break near the banks of the frozen stream.

"We keep warm by moving around," one boy answered.

"Besides, it's fun."

"*You're* the one who'll freeze," one of the older boys said. "Why are you out today, anyway?"

"I have a job."

"Have you eaten?"

"Not today," Sisyphus said.

The boy had strips of dried meat in his pocket. He handed several of them to the man. It was a common event these days in New York, this sharing of food.

"We're going to skate over to the Little Collect," the boy said. "That's where the best ice is."

Sisyphus watched the youngsters skate off, and resumed his struggle to get to the farmhouse. He had a lot on his mind. Should he, or should he not, he asked himself for the hundredth time, go to young de Kuyper and tell him what he knew about Peabody and Blakely?

Suddenly the thought of the skating boys gave him courage. They were mere youngsters, and look how brave *they* were.

He'd tell de Kuyper.

Yes, he was going to find Drew and tell him what was going on behind his back. *Tomorrow*. No sense rushing to get it done today. Tomorrow would be a better time.

While old Sisyphus was coming to his decision, the men in the prisons suffered the tortures of hell; not the hell described in the Good Book, to be sure, but rather, a frozen hell.

The Sugar House saw more deaths in two weeks than it had seen in the previous two months. Normally, the number of men confined to the old building was slightly over nine hundred. Their number was now below seven hundred. Men who had been clinging to life gave up the ghost before the raging gales and bone-piercing cold. Their bodies stiffened and turned to ice before they could be taken to the front gate for removal. Nor did their presence bother the living, whose only concern was for themselves. Where Death is a constant companion, his presence becomes taken for granted.

Dick Goelet and Seth Cuyler huddled in each other's arms under their combined blankets, and when one weakened, the other offered encouragement. It was the same with men

A TERRIBLE WINTER

throughout the Sugar House. They held on to existence and fought the storm—not with any thought of defeating it; that was too ambitious—no, the only idea that could sustain a man was the desire to live through the next hour. The very idea of enduring this frozen agony for a greater period would make a man give up, and soon afterward the breath of life would pass through his lips and he would die.

Beth Henry was far better able to cope with the storm.

She was hunting. There was hardly any meat left in the house on Maiden Lane, and she was out for a deer. She was tracking an animal through the stubby hills of central Manhatan while Primus waited back at the sled, shivering and complaining even though he was buried under the weight of a half-dozen bearskins.

For years deer had been scarce this far south on the island, but Beth reasoned that the heavy late-winter snows would drive the animals far afield in their search for food. Nor was she mistaken.

As she silently passed through white-shrouded trees and snow-mounded boulders, herself a snowshoed wraith of the forest, she had come upon the tracks of a deer. Following the prints for half an hour, she came within sight of a buck. He was an eight-pointer in the prime of life, but made almost scrawny by the hard winter.

Staying downwind, Beth moved closer and closer until the buck was in range. She raised the highly accurate grooved-bore rifle to her shoulder, sighted, then held her breath and squeezed the trigger. The shot, muffled by the snow, reverberated softly through the hills. The buck jumped high in the air, took several steps, and fell to the snow-covered ground.

Beth moved to the animal's side. He was dead from the clean shot. She dragged his body onto the extra snowshoe she had been carrying on her back. Using a short rope, she started pulling the carcass back toward the horse-drawn sled.

It took her the better part of an hour to make the journey. The terrain was rough, and in places the drifts were taller than she was. But Beth expertly used the snowshoes to bring herself and the deer down from the hills. A grown man with twice her strength but only half her skill would not have been able to make it.

"Lot of trouble just to get some meat," Primus grumbled as he helped Beth shove the deer aboard the sled.

"We need meat."

"Get along just fine without it," he said. "Man like to freeze to death out here! Never find his body 'til spring."

As Beth and Primus were returning home with their deer, Jan paced back and forth in his Whitehall office, half to keep warm, half to help himself think.

It was uncanny, he pondered, the way the British knew all about the movements of his ships, and about the cargoes they contained. Before a ship even docked, the British knew what was aboard, and commandeered it. There was only one conclusion to draw from this: he had a traitor in his company—a spy who tipped off the British. But who?

A spy! he thought, and the thought made him angry. Spies—damn them! One spy could cause more trouble than two regiments of infantry.

Jan's thought was shared by a gentleman seated inside the kitchen of the farmhouse serving as winter headquarters for the Continental army. General Washington too was plagued by spies.

The basic problem with ferreting out a spy, the general decided, was that you couldn't guess the motive unless you knew the nature of the man. Some men would do anything for profit. Others acted out of spite, still others out of patriotism as *they* saw it. There were even—God forbid!—men who would do such things just for the excitement of it.

The door to the kitchen opened and two men hurried in, the snow and wind blowing at their backs. They quickly closed the door when they saw the black look they were receiving from the commander.

"Nasty weather out there," Captain Alexander Hamilton said as he removed his thick muffler.

"Good morning, General," Benedict Arnold said.

General Washington gestured toward the chairs near the fire. "Best place to sit to get the chill out of your bones."

"Chill?" Brigadier General Arnold said with a chuckle. "If this is only a chill to you, sir, you're one of the great optimists of all time."

"If I wasn't, I wouldn't have taken this job," Washington said.

"Anytime you're tired, I'll relieve you," Arnold said with another chuckle. Washington smiled, but half wondered whether the other man was being serious. Arnold was a strange duck, he thought. He had distinguished himself at Ticonderoga, and his epic march through the north woods to Quebec, where he had started with a thousand men and arrived with only six hundred still alive, was already a legend. Arnold was brave and clever, but Washington had not been able to figure what it was the man truly wanted—the Continental victory, or the personal glory.

"The brigadier is here to discuss the coming summer campaign in the north," Hamilton said.

"And also to ask why I haven't been made a major-general," Arnold complained. "I'm long overdue for promotion."

Washington's eyes narrowed. He appreciated ambition in a man, but perhaps at this moment he was seeing too much of it. Well, better to have that sort of man than one who wants to surrender and go home to pet his cat.

"What do you think of our chances in the north?" he asked.

"Splendid," Arnold said with enthusiasm.

The commander nodded. He listened to the brigadier for a few moments, then proceeded to outline his own ideas for the months ahead. This was exactly the sort of information the British would love to get their hands on. Well, no problem here; as their histories had proven, Hamilton and Arnold were two of his most loyal and devoted officers.

Soon after Arnold and Hamilton joined Washington, there was a caller at the de Kuyper house on Maiden Lane. Celine answered the door.

Colonel Franz von Lossow, resplendent in a new uniform, stood outside. He bowed. "I was passing by and thought I would pay a visit," he said.

Celine looked past him and saw a cart standing in the street. It was heavily laden with firewood. Two Hessian soldiers sat on the driver's bench. "Is that yours?" she asked.

"Yes."

Celine bridled, making no attempt to mask her displeasure. "Is this a form of Hessian humor? To lord it over civilians by displaying your vast supply of wood?"

"You misunderstand, Mrs. Murray. The firewood is for you. Tell me where you want it and I'll set the men on the job."

"Oh, I'm *sorry*, Colonel. Obviously, I wasn't expecting such generosity. And I really must stop making such a fool of myself at your expense!"

He smiled at her, then took her hand gently and kissed it. "We chopped down some oak trees on Wall Street," he explained in his Oxford accent. "I thought you might make good use of some of them."

Celine told him where she wanted the wood, and the soldiers began unloading their cart. Celine invited von Lossow into the house for a glass of wine.

"There is a motive behind the gift of wood," the colonel said.

"And that is?" Celine asked, tilting her head saucily to one side.

"I needed an excuse to see you again."

She was amused by his candor. "The conquering hero come to look upon the vanquished?" she teased.

"Hardly that. It just seemed that time was passing and I was doing nothing about fostering our friendship. If one waits too long, the opportunity passes."

"Ah, yes," Celine said. "There is a tide in the affairs of men..."

"William Shakespeare."

"You *are* an unusual German. How come you know the great English bard?"

"You forgot my Oxford schooling. As I recall that passage:

"'There is a tide in the affairs of men,
Which, taken at the flood, leads on to fortune;
Omitted, all the voyage of their life
Is bound in shallows and in miseries.
On such a full sea are we now afloat;
And we must take the current when it serves
Or lose our ventures.'

"Isn't that it?"

"I'll take your word for it," Celine said, acting blasé to conceal her admiration for the man's learning and his memory.

"There's another matter I wanted to talk to you about," the colonel said. He stretched back in his chair and placed the heel of one boot on the toe of the other. "A very important one."

"What is it?"

"How loyal are you to the Crown?"

It was a most awkward question, and Celine didn't know what to say.

"Before you answer, let me say something about myself,"

A TERRIBLE WINTER 219

the colonel continued. "I like America. I like Americans. I think I am going to forswear allegiance to the British king and go over to their side."

It would have been possible to knock Celine over with a feather.

While Franz von Lossow talked with Celine, Mary Delafield was hurrying through the cold streets to the Provost building. She had come to a decision.

She was going to see Captain Patrick Blakely. Maybe he could do something to help Robert.

Her cheeks were a rosy red as she entered the building. A guard directed her to Captain Blakely's office, and she went down the dingy hall, plagued by all sorts of fears about what she was doing, and why.

The captain looked up, and smiled on seeing his visitor. "Mrs. Delafield, a charming surprise."

"I hope I'm not interrupting."

"Of course not. May I offer you a glass of wine?"

Mary didn't know if this was a good time to be drinking, but a bit of wine might calm her and give her more courage. "That would be nice," she said.

He poured two glasses, and they sat in two chairs by the side of his desk. There was a long silence, during which they watched each other as if waiting for something to happen.

"I guess you know why I'm here," she finally said.

"Perhaps you'll tell me."

"It's about my husband."

He nodded. "You'd like him out of prison, wouldn't you?"

"Yes."

"I can do nothing for him," the captain said. And there was another long silence. He sipped his wine and looked at her. "Now, isn't there another reason you came to see me?"

He knew.

And now she had to admit it to herself. She had come here to see the captain, to find out more about the strange stirrings he caused in her.

"I feel the same way about you," he said, without waiting for her reply.

She felt like an animal. A very happy animal.

She was under the heavy covers next to the sweat-stained body of Patrick Blakely. They had come to his quarters and had been making love for over an hour, and she still wanted more. It had never before been this way for her. Sexual relations with Robert had been a bore.

For the first time in her life, at the height of their lovemaking, Mary had experienced a wonderful eruption inside her body. She had never dreamed anything could be so glorious, and screamed in ecstasy. They continued making love in a frenzy, finally being forced to rest when their bodies could take no more.

He reached out and touched her smooth skin. He put his mouth near her ear. "We both knew it would be like this."

"*How* did we know?"

"Does it really matter?"

She began to pet his chest, barely touching it with the tips of her nails. She surprised herself—where had she learned this? He moaned, and she gloried in her newly found power over a man. Her hands went lower and lower, and she held his manhood, stroking and touching it and feeling it harden again. She moved on top of him, and he guided himself inside her body. Her thighs squeezed his body, and she began to move in a slow, sensuous way. She put her arms about him, and her nails began to dig into his back.

4

The Year of the Asp

1777

SPRING.

The city had survived the terrible winter. The snows melted, and bubbling rivulets wound their way to the rivers, lakes and bays. The frozen ground softened, and the sound of songbirds filled the air. New buds appeared on trees and bushes. The grass once again rustled in the wind. A sigh passed across the land as those who remained alive after the harshness took hope from the return of nature's gentler hand.

Dick was still a prisoner in the Sugar House, and although conditions were awful, at least now he wasn't freezing to death. He was standing at a window, looking out on the street through the bars. The spring rains had begun and the thawed earth turned to mud.

He was smiling as he looked down on a Hessian whose wagon was stuck in the mud. The stupid fellow kept yelling at his horse, threatening him and flailing at him with a whip. The terrified beast pulled and struggled in his traces, but the wheels only dug deeper into the mud.

"Look at that kraut," he said to Seth, who came to stand by the window.

Seth laughed. He liked nothing better than to see a Hessian having trouble. "Stupid lout! *Dummkopf!*" he shouted through the bars.

Several other men looked out and began jeering at the German. He shook his fist at the prisoners, but they were behind bars and there was no way he could get at them.

"Are you going to miss this place?" Seth asked.

Dick's mouth opened. "Are you crazy? Miss the Sugar House?"

"It may be better than where we're going," Seth said.

"A ship's got to be better than this place!" Dick responded.

Today was the day the prisoners were being transferred to the ships that had been prepared for them. The British had too many prisoners and not enough prison space. To solve this problem they had taken several of their older ships-of-the-line, dismasted them, and anchored them permanently in Wallabout Bay on the Brooklyn side of the East River.

The prisoners were moved under heavy guard toward the river. The Hessians pushed and shoved the men, keeping them herded together like a pack of animals. Boots and musket butts were used freely to enforce order.

Many townspeople came out to watch the prisoners, and a more ragged, smelly group of human beings it would be hard to find. Many of these witnesses had stern looks on their faces, as if they disapproved of the prisoners for *being* prisoners.

The line of march was down Crown Street to Broad Way, then down to the Battery. It was the first Dick had seen of the effects of the great fire. He looked at the scars left on many of the buildings.

"Look at all the tents," he said to Seth.

"I guess people lost their homes in the fire and this is the best they could do."

"They must have had a winter as hard as our own."

Seth shook his head. "No! They were still free. That makes a big difference."

"Who am *I* to say this, but—notice the stink!" Dick said. He was astonished he could still be offended by odors after spending over half a year in the confines of the Sugar House. "Why does it smell so bad?"

Seth pointed toward a pile of garbage that obviously had been there all winter, but had bothered no one until the spring thaw. "Normally the pigs would have taken care of that," he said.

"The pigs!" Dick said, looking about him. "Of course, that's it, the pigs!"

Seth nodded his agreement. In normal times New Yorkers allowed their pigs the freedom of the streets. The animals wandered about, scavenging everything edible. This practice kept the streets fairly clean, and it saved the owners the expense of feeding their pigs. It had been a common sight to see swine rooting in piles of garbage.

But the pigs had been eaten during the winter by the hungry people, and now New York was turning into one big, smelly garbage heap.

The prisoners went past the Battery and turned down Whitehall Street. Jan de Kuyper was standing outside his building with Drew and Mary Delafield. They were eagerly scanning the faces of the passing men.

Robert was walking a few paces ahead of Dick and Seth when he saw his wife. *"Mary!"* he called.

She turned and looked in the direction of the voice. She looked straight at her husband, but there wasn't a flicker of recognition in her face.

"Mary, it's me!" Robert called again.

She looked at him blankly, then gasped and stepped back. She would have fallen if Jan hadn't stepped up and grasped her arms.

"Look at him!" she wailed.

"There's Dick!" Drew said, spotting his cousin behind Robert Delafield.

It was Jan's turn to gasp. "Good Lord!"

"Dick Goelet, keep your spirits up!" Drew shouted, and Dick started to wave, but a Hessian nudged him with his musket and he was forced to move on.

Mary's face was white, and she looked ready to collapse. Jan kept her in his firm grasp. "Did you see Robert? What have they done to him?"

Drew had never liked Robert Delafield, but even he felt sorry for the man. His face had looked as if it had been hit by a runaway coach.

"And we've been complaining about our lives," Jan muttered to his son.

"We've got to *do* something," Drew said.

"They're all going to die," Mary said dully.

The file of men turned onto Dock Street. Dick looked around in bewilderment at the still-unrepaired damage left by the fire. This street, which once had been lined with shops and crammed with goods from the four corners of the earth, was now only a shell of its former self. Half the remaining storefronts were boarded up, their owners driven out of business or dead. The lack of stores meant a lack of goods, and prices had gone berserk. A four-pound loaf of bread that used to cost a penny now cost two and a half pence, and most people couldn't afford the bread even if they could find it.

Suddenly a man bolted out of ranks, knocking down the nearest Hessian, and ran up an alley that led to Hanover Square. The guards began shouting, and instantly there was chaos. Several of the Hessians took off after the fleeing man. They would have shot him, but there were too many civilians about and they couldn't get a clear shot.

The prisoner burst into Hanover Square, which was crowded with people because it was the day of the week when an open market was held there. The prisoner shoved and stumbled his way through the crowd, followed by the yelling Hessians. People were pushed and knocked about as they scrambled to get out of the way of the running men.

Alice de Witt was in the crowd with her sickly son, Jacob. With the coming of good weather, she had made a practice of taking the boy for walks, hoping the sunshine would help bring him back to health. Indeed, he was looking a little better with every passing day.

They were directly in the path of the fleeing prisoner and the Hessians. She tried to shield Jacob with her body, but the prisoner inadvertently brushed her aside. The Hessian chasing him crashed into the little boy, knocking him into the air, and kept going without breaking stride. The boy flew through the air like a rag doll, and landed headfirst on the street of paving stone.

Alice cried out, got to her feet, and rushed to her son's side. She knelt down and began weeping, but they were tears without hope, because the condition of the little boy's skull told the story. A man picked the boy up and offered to carry him home, but Alice snatched her son away. She, and no one else, was going to carry him. The sympathetic crowd was so intent on this drama that they paid almost no attention as the Hessians dragged their captured prisoner back across the square.

Bearing Jacob's limp body in her arms, Alice walked mournfully toward her home.

The prisoners were taken to the Old Slip, where a small flotilla of longboats awaited them. The boats were packed to the gunwales, and British sailors rowed them across the river to Wallabout Bay.

Dick was next to Seth as they first set their eyes on their new home, the prison ship *Devon*. The masts were gone; there was no rigging. The sides had been built up, and most of the portholes were sealed. Two anchors were set from the bow, and two from the stern.

"Doesn't look so bad," Dick said hopefully.

Seth shrugged. "Wait and see."

"At least we'll get more fresh air here."

"Wait till winter. Then we'll see how much you like fresh air."

Dick blanched. Winter? Another *year* in prison?

Dick and Seth, along with Robert Delafield and twelve hundred other prisoners, were taken aboard the *Devon*. Guarding them were a captain, two mates, a steward, twelve sailors, twelve British marines, and thirty Hessian soldiers. None of these guards lived aboard the ship; they thought it bad enough they had to do their tour of duty there.

The *Devon* was a spacious ship, formerly a sixty-four-gun ship-of-the-line. There were other ships pressed into this odious service, and the people of New York would learn to know their names well. The *Prince of Wales*, the *Strombolo*, the *Hunter*, the *Kitty*, the *Bristol*. There were others whose very names made a mockery of their purpose—the *Good Hope*, the *Good Intent*, and the *Providence*. There were the *Whitby*, the *Falmouth*, the *Scorpion*—and the *Jersey*, the ship that would come to epitomize the brutality and sadism of the prison-ship system....

Twelve hundred men were crammed into a sixty-four-gun ship, and no one who had never been aboard such a vessel could have the slightest idea of what life would be like. Most of the portholes were sealed, so the six below decks were in a perpetual stygian gloom. Only one hundred men were allowed topside at any one time. The rest were crammed below, where they couldn't find a place to sit or lie down without touching someone else's body.

Within days, of course, disease became a way of life, and the men suffered from typhus, dysentery, and smallpox. Many deaths ensued, but conditions remained crowded: when a dead body was removed, a live one was brought aboard to take its place.

The Hessians were brutal guards, but the British marines were just as bad. Every morning a marine sergeant would order the hatches opened. "Rebels! Throw out your dead!" he would shout. And not a day passed when there weren't at least six or seven corpses.

As the bodies came topside, the sadistic sergeant would inspect the men carrying them. "I'll be seeing you carted up soon," he would say to a gaunt bearer. Or, "Why don't you join the corpses now? Why wait?"

At night, when it was time for all prisoners to get below, a marine would shout, "Down, rebels, down!" and then smile and shout again: "Down, dogs, down!" And there was truth in his cry, because in this place not only was a rebel treated no better than a dog; usually he was treated worse.

Dick learned the true horror of the *Devon* on his second night aboard. It was late, and he woke with an overpowering urge to urinate. He made his way to the hatch and asked permission to go topside to relieve himself over the side of the ship.

He had to wait.

The sadistic warders had instituted a rule that only one man at a time could go on deck at night to relieve himself—*one man* aboard a prison ship in which twelve hundred men were confined below decks, many weakened and almost too sick to stand on their own feet.

While Dick waited, he thought how terrible it would be if there was an epidemic of dysentery among the men. *If!* he immediately thought in horror: there was no "if" about it; under such conditions it would be impossible to avoid an outbreak of dysentery. And there wasn't a single privy or outhouse below decks.

At the last moment, just as he was sure he couldn't contain himself any longer, the marine guard signaled it was Dick's turn to go topside. He rushed up the ladder, went to the side of the ship, and emptied his bladder.

It had been close, and he knew there would be nights when he wouldn't be able to wait—even as tonight there were men below who couldn't wait, and so added to the general stench and misery suffered by all.

As if this wasn't enough, Dick was soon plagued by a new worry. A ferret-faced prisoner named Conners decided he was Dick's friend. He had once worked for the de Kuypers on the docks, and decided this near acquaintanceship was a bond between them.

"There's your old friend Conners," Seth would tease, and Dick would shake his head.

"He's no friend of mine."

"That's not what he goes around telling everyone."

The trouble was, Conners was always toadying up to the guards, and many of the prisoners suspected him of being an informer. Dick did his best to avoid guilt by association with the man, but ducking Conners wasn't always easy on the crowded *Devon*.

Generally the nights aboard ship were worse than the days. At least during the daylight hours there was some access to fresh air. Several men thought they could jump over the side and swim to Brooklyn, but the British had placed sharpshooters in a tower on the main deck. They easily picked off the poor fools in the water as they tried to swim for shore.

Below decks was a constant misery, containing tightly packed, smelly bodies. Lice plagued the men. Mites and chiggers bit them, and the air was almost too fetid to breathe. And then there was the constant noise: men snored, cried out in their sleep, wheezed, coughed, and babbled incoherently. Most men were able to fall asleep only when they became thoroughly exhausted.

Not all the tortures were physical.

At the beginning of the second week aboard the *Devon*, Dick stood on the main deck and looked across the bay at the little village of Brooklyn. There were only about forty or fifty houses. Behind them and off to both sides was the lovely countryside, with its attractive farms and cultivated fields. Dick suddenly realized how odd it was to be standing at the railing, filthy and ragged, surrounded by dozens of other filthy, ragged men, looking at the village and seeing normal people walking down the streets and going in and out of clean, neat houses.

He wasn't more than a half mile away. But his degraded existence made it seem like a thousand. He could see attractively dressed women, and the very thought seemed strange. *Women*. Did such exotic creatures actually exist? In this world of the prison ship, it was difficult for Dick even to imagine them.

After a while he stopped looking at the village; it made him too sad.

It wasn't long before Robert Delafield got himself in trouble again and was given a fierce beating.

He was standing topside, holding his tin cup of watery soup. A Hessian thought it would be amusing to knock the soup from his hand. Robert didn't think the German's move was funny, and he clouted him. Other guards saw this, and they tied up the rash prisoner. They lashed his arms to the stub of a mast, then took a long, thick rope and beat his bare back unmercifully. It looked like raw meat when they were finished.

Dick did his best to patch up the wounded man. If nothing went wrong, Robert would live. But, Dick wondered, was this living? How long would a man *want* to go on living like this?

He felt like shaking his fist at the sky; cursing the God who allowed such a place to exist. But that would be a futile gesture, he told himself; life itself was almost a futile gesture here.

The only thing was to go on from day to day. And hope. There was nothing else left.

The small coffin containing the body of Jacob de Witt was lowered into the ground at the cemetery of the Dutch Reformed Church. The dominie read from his prayer book in a monotone voice. A small group of mourners stood at the graveside, watching as the small pine box disappeared beneath the soft dirt being shoveled on top of it.

The onlookers included Alice and Enoch de Witt. Jan and Marie Therese were present, as were Drew, Celine, and Peter. Jemmy and Jenny Sackett stood beside them, among other relatives—de Witts, Goelets and Sacketts. Primus Gerait was there.

"He hadn't even begun his life," Alice said. She wasn't crying, because she was beyond tears. "He didn't live long enough to have even a taste."

"He's in heaven," Marie Therese said. "Looking down on us at this very moment."

"I'd like to believe that," Alice said.

Enoch was sober. It was the first time in years many of the people at the grave could remember seeing him that way.

"I guess I haven't been much of a man," he said to Jan. "I've made the family ashamed of me."

"This isn't a time to worry about that, Enoch," Jan said kindly. "We all share your sorrow."

When the grave was covered over, the dominie gave his final blessing, and the entire group walked back to Jan's house, where a lunch awaited them. It was an old Dutch custom to toast a departed family member with a meal of honor.

"He was so tiny," Jenny Sackett said to Celine as they walked along, side by side. "It's sad when a life is snuffed out before it's had a chance to be anything."

"Very sad."

"Why couldn't it have been Useless himself?" Jenny added.

She nodded her head toward Enoch, who was walking ahead of them between his wife and Jan.

"Shh," Celine warned. "This is a time for charity."

"Charity!" Jenny said in derision. "This family has given Enoch nothing but charity for years. What good has it done?"

"Not today, Jenny," Celine said, more firmly now.

But Jenny liked to have the last word. "He ought to have some charity for his wife. Look at her. He's putting her in an early grave."

Celine winced at the word *grave*, but finally decided the best way to argue with Jenny was to say nothing.

Strangely enough, as some of the mourners commented to one another, Alice looked better on this day of the funeral of her son than she had in a long time. She was wearing a neat black dress, and her hair was combed back and held in place by bone stays. She seemed to be holding her head higher than usual. Perhaps little Jacob's death had removed at least one burden from her shoulders; it gave her one less thing to worry about.

Peter walked beside his Uncle Drew. "Why do people die?" he asked.

Trust Peter to come up with the tough ones, Drew thought. "Because God only gives each one of us so much time on earth," he said.

Peter thought about that for a moment. "But why do some people live a long time, and others only a short time?"

"That's the way God wants it, I guess," Drew said, knowing even as he said it that it wasn't much of an answer—certainly not enough of an answer for someone with a mind as quick as this youngster's.

"*Why* would He want it that way?"

"Life isn't always fair," Drew said, and he could see the wheels in Peter's mind turning and digesting this bit of information.

Jan took hold of Enoch's arm as they walked along. "Maybe it's time you came back to work for the family," he said.

"Aren't you forgetting what happened all those other times you gave me jobs?"

"We all make mistakes, Enoch. But we're your family, and we'd like to stand by you."

"It's nice to hear that."

"I mean it," Jan said. "And the offer of a job stands."

"Let me think about it."

Alice had been listening as she walked at her husband's side. "Stay sober while you're thinking," she said sharply. Jan was surprised by her tone of voice. This was not the Alice he had known.

"I'll try," Enoch said.

"Trying's not good enough," Alice responded, quickening her pace and walking away from her husband. She fell in alongside Marie Therese and Jemmy Sackett.

"My father is in Philadelphia with the Congress," Jemmy said to Alice. "I know he'd have liked to be here."

"David is a kind man," Alice said. "I know he'd have come if it'd been possible."

After a short pause, she looked at Marie Therese. "I've come to a decision. Either Enoch straightens out his life or I'm leaving him."

"Good for you," Marie Therese said.

"It's about time," Jemmy said. "Enoch may be a blood relation, but I'm on *your* side."

"I think of you as family, too, Jemmy," Alice said, and patted his hand. She turned back to Marie Therese. "I've always tried to hold us together because of the children. That's done a lot of good, hasn't it?" she said bitterly.

"It's not your fault," Marie Therese said.

"I've got to start thinking of Elly. She's my whole life now."

"She's enjoyed staying with us the past few days," Marie Therese said, glancing at the other woman. "You wouldn't consider letting her stay on a bit longer, would you?"

"No," Alice said firmly. "I want her with me."

Marie Therese nodded. She could tell the other woman had made up her mind and there would be no talking her out of it.

They arrived at the house and were subdued as they ate lunch. Enoch made it a point not to drink anything, but Jan noticed he looked yearningly toward the sideboard, with its many bottles of liquor.

He knew Enoch was serious about trying to change his life. He only hoped he was strong enough to do it.

Enoch was thinking the same thing.

Philemon Peabody had discovered that the old man called himself Sisyphus, and that he lived in a house off Beaver Street. He was waiting there for him now.

In his pocket was a letter detailing Blakely's involvement in the theft of money from the Crown. It was a damning document, and he was going to get the old man to make his mark on it.

Peabody was waiting for about an hour when he saw him coming down the street.

"A moment of your time?"

"Are you going to offer me work?" Sisyphus asked, not exactly pleased with the prospect. It was too nice a day to spend in drudgery.

"You might put it that way," Peabody said.

"What's the job?"

Peabody reached into his coat and took out the letter. He opened it and coughed. "First I'll read this document to you."

"Read." When a man was as poor as himself, he was forced to endure the stupidity of others.

"To whatever parties are in possession of this letter," Peabody said, reading from the paper. "I admit, of my own free will and without being coerced, that on October the twenty-third of the year of Our Lord seventeen hundred and seventy six..." He paused and looked up. "That was last year."

"I'm aware of the year," Sisyphus said dryly.

Peabody resumed reading: "...seventeen hundred and seventy six, I was aboard the schooner *Anthony*, a ship owned by Jan de Kuyper, and whilst aboard I heard a conversation between one Philemon Peabody and one Captain Patrick Blakely. The nature of the conversation told me that Peabody and Blakely were partners in a crime against the Crown. To wit: they commandeered ships, receiving monies from the Crown. The owners of the ships received only a portion of these monies, while Peabody and Blakely kept the difference for themselves. I swear to this, so help me God."

Peabody stopped. The old man was staring at him as if he were the Devil himself.

"Now, put your mark at the bottom."

"What are you talking about!" Sisyphus cried. "I don't know anything about stealing from the Crown!"

Lord, he thought, it's come back to haunt me! He had procrastinated about informing Drew of what he had learned. He always had the best intentions, and had been going to tell de Kuyper *tomorrow*. Always tomorrow, but somehow tomorrow never came—and now here was this little weasel with his piece of paper.

"You were aboard the *Anthony*."

"I don't know what that is."

"A ship. You pretended to be drunk, but the truth is you overheard everything we said."

"No!"

Peabody pulled out a pistol. "You have thirty seconds to make your mark, or I'll blow your brains out."

"This paper doesn't sound legal to me," Sisyphus said.

"It's not meant to be used in court, only to make a certain captain keep his mouth shut," Peabody said, but now he looked sharply at the old man. "And how would someone like you know about the law?"

"I won't sign it."

"Ten seconds."

Sisyphus looked at the gun next to his head. It seemed as large as a cannon. He was no hero. "All right, I'll sign."

Peabody took a box from his pocket. It contained a quill pen and a small bottle of ink.

"Make your mark."

Sisyphus took the quill and dipped it into the ink. "I'll make no mark," he growled, and wrote his name with a flourish.

Peabody was surprised that the man could write. He looked at his signature. "James Richardson? There was a well-known printer in Boston named James Richardson. But he died a few years ago."

"Do I look dead?"

Peabody blew on the paper to help dry the ink, then folded it and put it back into his pocket.

"So you're going to blackmail this English captain?"

"You know too much for your own good."

"But you'll not be the man to do me in," the printer said. A cunning expression crossed his face. "In fact you're now the one man in the world who has an interest in seeing me stay alive."

Peabody thought about it, and concluded Richardson was correct. If it came down to it, he could always use the old man to help blackmail Captain Blakely.

"So what?"

"You're going to have to help me stay alive. I need money to live. From what I know, you have plenty of it. Stolen from the Crown. Where's my share?"

Peabody reached into his pocket, brought out a shilling, and handed it over.

Sisyphus handed it back. "Half a crown or nothing."

Peabody grumbled, but he found a half crown and handed it over. "Don't push me too far."

Sisyphus chuckled, stuffed the half crown in his pocket, and walked into his house. He was pleased with himself. He had found a new source of income. And with no work attached. He was certain he could drag a half crown a week out of Peabody.

He left his house after a little while and walked to a bakery, where he bought two large loaves of bread. Then he walked over to Hanover Square to give the bread to men who were less fortunate than he. It gave his spirits a boost to know that he had taken a big step up in the world: from a man who wasn't much more than a beggar, he had risen to one who *fed* beggars.

Captain Blakely reread the letter on his desk. It was from Philemon Peabody. It quoted the text of another document that Peabody claimed he had in his possession—a document, the man hastened to make clear, that he was keeping in a secret place.

The facts were clear to the captain.

One, the note existed.

Two, it had been signed by a man named James Richardson.

Three, this Richardson was the old drunk they had found asleep on board the *Anthony*—only it was now clear he hadn't been asleep, but had been eavesdropping.

Four, Peabody was using the old man to blackmail him.

The fifth, and determining, fact was that the captain had no intention of letting Peabody get away with it. Who did that little rat think he was?

He sent for Sergeant Taggert.

"Yes, sir?"

"Do you know a man named James Richardson?"

"No, sir."

"Find him."

"Yes, sir. Can you tell me anything about him?"

"He's about sixty, sixty-five years old. Gray hair. Looks like a bum."

The sergeant scratched his head. "A lot of old geezers look like that. That's not much to go on."

"If I see him again I'll recognize him."

"You want me to bring the suspects here, sir?"

"Yes."

"Would it help if I knew why you wanted this man, Captain?"

"No, Taggert, thank you, that's all."

The more the captain thought about Peabody's letter, the more annoyed he became. The first thing was to find the old man; then he would tend to Mr. Peabody.

He walked across the room and picked his hat from the rack. He looked at himself in the mirror and was pleased with what he saw. He left the Provost to go to his quarters, where Mary Delafield would be waiting for him.

On July 4, 1977, the first anniversary of the signing of the Declaration of Independence, Drew made up his mind that he would attempt to get his cousin out of prison.

He went to the docks, found Alec Seixas, and talked of his ideas as the two of them walked back to Maiden Lane. "If we don't do something, he won't last the year. He looks like hell."

"What do you have in mind?" Alec asked.

"Can you get a schooner and a crew together?"

"Yes."

"We'll go out at night and board the *Devon*."

"Isn't that somewhat ambitious?" Alec asked.

"You're the one who's supposed to be willing to try anything. Lost your nerve?"

"No, nor my senses. History is littered with the bodies of men who acted precipitously."

"There aren't many guards aboard those hulks at night. We'll take forty or fifty men, hit them fast, grab Dick, and get away."

"Where do you plan to go?"

"Anywhere. Out through the Narrows. We'll hide along the southern shore of Long Island."

Alec considered the plan. Taking a hulk might not be that difficult. But what then? The British usually had several fast frigates around, and they always patrolled the southern shore of Long Island.

"I think we have to come up with something better," he said, and the two men walked a ways in silence.

They turned up Queen Street, passing an open-air market where several farmers had set out their wares for sale. A few merchants had joined them, adding their goods to the display. Drew stopped, asked a question of a merchant, scowled, and walked away. "That thief wants six shillings for a pound of coffee," he complained.

"I liked your old-time thief better," Alec agreed. "He just put a gun to your head and demanded your money."

Suddenly two men got into a fight over the price of a chicken. The farmer insisted his price was fair, and his prospective customer, a big blacksmith, objected and clipped him on the side of the head.

Other men got involved, but Drew and Alec kept walking. Food riots were not uncommon, and neither man wanted to take part in one.

"You seem more worried about your cousin than you did a few months ago," Alec said.

Drew nodded. "I was shocked when I finally saw him. And a few months ago I didn't think the war would last much longer. But that's all changed. Washington's army has taken the field. We've another army up north. Last month Congress gave us a new flag..."

"Nice looking," Alec said. "Thirteen stripes, thirteen stars."

"Ben Franklin has gone to France to seek her help against England—and from what I hear he's already gotten some money out of the French. So what it all means is this war will probably drag on for a long time."

"And as long as the war continues, the British will keep the prisoners locked up."

"Exactly."

"Howe is planning a campaign to take Philadelphia," Alec said. "Everyone knows that. What if he does capture it? That might end the war."

Drew shook his head. "They took New York, didn't they? That didn't end the war."

"All right, let's say the war goes on and we want to get Dick out of prison. I still say it's crazy for us to raid the *Devon*. We'd never get away."

"You have any other ideas?"

"No."

"Then we have to try it."

"Ignorance is bliss," Alec said.

They arrived at the house and sat in the kitchen while Primus told his tale of woe about being unable to buy fresh vegetables. They hardly heard a word he said, because both were pondering the problem of taking the *Devon*.

* * *

While their son sat with Alec in the kitchen of their house, Jan and Marie Therese were out for a walk. Jan hadn't been feeling well lately; it was nothing he could identify, just a general feeling of weakness and lethargy.

"Old age creeping up on me," he grumbled.

"Nonsense," Marie Therese said. "It's simply that we're living in such trying times."

They came to the little park at the Battery, and Jan smiled. "My own father was one of the men responsible for giving us this park," he said. "Years ago he and some friends talked the city council into creating it."

"I used to enjoy coming to the park when my family first moved to New York," Marie Therese said. "But I never knew your father was to thank for it."

Jan nodded. "The old boy loved New York, even though he didn't like to admit it. Always claimed to prefer the country."

"Maybe that's why he wanted this park—to bring a little country to the city."

They continued to walk, and Jan scowled when he noticed the British flag flying over the fort. "And to think I used to regard that flag as my own!" he said contemptuously.

He stopped and coughed for a moment, and a look of concern came over Marie Therese. "Maybe we ought to go home."

"Nonsense," he said, straightening himself to his full height. "I'm fine. Fresh air'll do me good."

He took her arm, and they continued their walk. But Marie Therese was concerned. Her husband had become so preoccupied with the war that he seemed to take its indignities personally.

She felt a sudden, cold fear that all was not right with Jan. It was a horrible thought, and she quickly banished it from her mind. But its essence remained to trouble her.

Colonel Franz von Lossow and Celine had become lovers. It had begun with quiet, flirtatious meetings on Maiden Lane. Of course it was impossible for any intimacies to occur in that house; Celine had to think of her mother and father. And the colonel's quarters in the tavern were not exactly the place to bring a woman of her quality.

So on a pleasant summer day Celine asked Franz to take her for a drive and, without telling him what she had in mind, brought him to the Place.

The servants, well versed in the ways of their mistress,

acted as if nothing unusual was happening, and went out of their way to avoid the couple. The colonel had had the good sense not to wear his Hessian uniform, and it was impossible to tell his nationality from the way he spoke English. Celine referred to him as the colonel, a title immediately picked up by the servants, and if they wondered what he was a colonel of, they had the good sense not to ask.

The couple enjoyed a light lunch with chilled wine. Afterwards Celine casually offered to show her guest the house, and it seemed only natural she would include her bedroom in the tour.

There was a longing in her eyes when, in the middle of the room, she turned and faced him. The longing was more than matched by his own.

In the arms of Franz von Lossow that afternoon, Celine experienced a tenderness she had never known. There had, perhaps, been wilder times; more erotic passion. But this was good, and fulfilling, and more. It felt natural; it felt like something that was meant to be. After the lovemaking was over, they talked for a long time. It came easy.

Eventually the talk turned to von Lossow's dissatisfaction with the British. "I guess today solves any problems I had," he said.

"What do you mean?"

"I had mixed feelings. But now I have *you*. I want to stay with you. Be like you. Be an American."

"You really mean it?"

"This country has been like a breath of fresh air to me. And so have you. I want to live here."

"Don't get carried away because of *this*," she said, patting the bed. "One of these days you might want to go back to your home."

"I could live my whole life without seeing my royal cousin again and be very happy. But you must understand—I'm *excited* by this country! It's so new—anything is possible."

Celine was pleased. It had made her a bit uncomfortable to feel so good about an enemy. "I'm glad," she said. "What do you plan to do?"

He shrugged. "Find Washington and ask him if he'll have me in his army, what else?"

Celine had a quick mind, and she was using it now. "Maybe you can be of more use if you do something before they know you've defected?"

"Do something?"

Could she trust this man? *Really* trust him? Well, there was one way to find out. "My brother has a problem," she said. "He told me about it and asked for my ideas. I didn't have any. Maybe you will."

"Tell me about it."

Celine told him of Dick Goelet's imprisonment aboard the *Devon,* and of Drew's determination to rescue him. She revealed her brother's plan to attack the prison hulk with an armed schooner.

The colonel shook his head. "It's a mad plan."

"That's what I think. But I can't think of anything better."

Von Lossow got out of bed and started to dress. "You had better get up, my lovely Celine," he said.

"Why?"

"We're going back to the city. I want to talk to your brother."

"What for?"

"I have an idea about saving Goelet that just might work," he said, and proceeded to tell her about it. When he was finished, she whistled.

"It *might* work."

"It will work."

"It had better, or we'll all hang together."

"I couldn't have picked nicer company," von Lossow said.

General William Howe—*Sir* William since he had been invested in the Royal Order of the Bath as a reward for conquering New York—studied the map hanging on the wall behind his desk. Within two weeks he would embark from New York with over fifteen thousand troops. The ships would take him down to Philadelphia. The general believed the rebels would surrender once he had captured their Congress.

The general still hadn't given up hope of bringing about a peaceable settlement; he still believed the Americans and British to be cousins.

His spies had informed him of the position taken by Washington. The rebel forces were concentrated along Brandywine Creek, so it was obvious that was where the battle would take place. And he was not underestimating Washington: he had done that before, and the result had been Trenton. And Princeton.

This time he was going to win, and decisively—as General Burgoyne was claiming to do up north. There hadn't been a

THE YEAR OF THE ASP

single large-scale battle up there, but messengers kept coming down to Howe with reports of Burgoyne's smooth advance. He had captured Ticonderoga and Mount Defiance and, according to the last dispatch, was moving swiftly toward Skenesborough and Fort Anne. The rebels, he said, were melting from his path like butter on a hot stove. "Nothing but forests as far as the eye can see," Burgoyne had written. "But not many of these damned rebels."

General Howe studied his map. He would take Philadelphia; Burgoyne would clean out the area from New York to Montreal. With all that territory solidly British, it would be only a matter of time before the rebels capitulated. How could they continue to fight against the greatest armies ever to take the field in North America? It was ludicrous for them to even imagine they had a chance.

He turned his mind to a problem that, as far as he was concerned, was more difficult. What would happen after the rebels surrendered and normalcy returned to the colonies? Lord North was taking a hard stand about making the Americans pay for the war. By the prime minister's own estimate, the war was costing £350,000 a year. It was Lord North's intention to make the Americans repay every last farthing. The thought of what would happen when they were presented with this bill made the general very uneasy. They'd probably go into rebellion again. God save us from our politicians! he thought. Lord North was a stubborn fool, with perhaps as much vision as the average shopkeeper. If he thought he could squeeze millions of pounds from the Americans, he was very mistaken. Didn't the ass realize it was excessive taxation that had caused all the trouble in the first place?

His thoughts were interrupted by the arrival of Colonel Cunningham and Captain Blakely.

"You wanted to see us, sir?" the colonel said.

The general nodded. He took his time before bringing up the subject to be discussed—the prison ships. He had been receiving a great many complaints. But the situation was touchy. The prime minister had made it clear he wanted to punish the rebels. The minister for colonial affairs, Lord Germain, was even more adamant. Many rebels captured at sea were being held in England at the naval prisons of Portsmouth and Plymouth. On specific orders of the colonial minister, these prisoners were being treated not as honorable opponents, but as traitors. Conditions in the prisons were extremely harsh.

Therefore the general was well aware that his superiors in London were not willing to listen to complaints about injustices to captured rebels. Since it was imprudent to oppose North and Germain directly, the general preferred to ease conditons in the American prisons by moving quietly, without bothering to inform London. To do this, he needed the cooperation of the provost marshal. Of course, he could always *order* Cunningham to do anything he wanted; but if the colonel didn't like the orders, he would find a way to get the news back to London. The general was having enough trouble with North and Germain without adding more fuel to the fire. And yet he wanted to alleviate the misery in the prisons.

"I hear many complaints about our severity with the prisoners," he said as an opening gambit.

If Colonel Cunningham had known something about chess, he would have realized the general was opening the conversation with a feint. "Too severe, sir?" was all he said.

Captain Blakely, however, was an excellent chess player, and understood the similarities between that game and diplomacy. He countered the general's opening move with one of his own. "Is it permitted to ask from whom the general is receiving these complaints?"

The general switched his attention from the colonel to his deputy. "That hardly matters, does it Captain? The question I raise is—are we being too severe? Are we going further than is necessary with the prisoners?"

"One must then ask, what is further than necessary?" Blakely said.

It was a good move, but the general refused to accept it. "I hear these prison ships of yours are charnel houses with a staggering death rate. Do you believe such horrors will endear us to the Americans? Or will they, as I believe, anger our cousins even further, and stiffen their determination to fight?"

The captain realized his defense wasn't working, so he switched to the attack. "Are you suggesting we coddle them, sir? I don't believe this is the position taken by the colonial minister."

"Don't tell me about the colonial minister's positions, sir, his positions are directed to me."

"Yes, sir." The general's anger told Blakely he had scored a point.

"I didn't call you here to bicker. I want to know how,

without sacrificing security, we can make conditions more humane on the floating prisons."

"We can look into the matter, sir," Colonel Cunningham said, but all that meant was that he would leave the job to his deputy.

"Can you be more specific?"

The colonel looked at his deputy. "We can increase the food ration," the captain said.

"That's a start."

"As soon as we receive a greater allotment from the treasury," the captain added, burying that suggestion. All three men knew there wasn't the slightest chance of getting more money out of London for the prisons. As it was, London was complaining about costs.

"To combat the overcrowding we can add more ships," the captain said, making it sound as if it were a realistic suggestion.

"I'm sure you're aware the navy claims it doesn't *have* any more ships," the general said dryly. In a chess game this would be check.

"I've heard that, Your Lordship, but you know the navy. Who can believe anything they say?" Countercheck.

General Howe sighed. It was all too true. Sometimes the British navy acted as if the British army were the enemy.

"Is there any way we can put these men to work?" he asked.

"We've talked about that, sir," Colonel Cunningham said. "It's not practical while most of our soldiers are in the field. We'd need thousands of them just to guard the prisoners."

"Any other ideas?" the general asked impatiently.

"We might send all the prisoners out of America," Blakely said. "I believe that was a suggestion of Lord Germain's."

"Have you thought about a place to send them?"

"Yes, sir. We have a fort at Senegal. Lots of open space around there. The big advantage is they wouldn't be here, so no one here could make any more complaints." Another bold move to check.

The general studied the deputy's face to see if he was making a joke at his expense. He could read nothing in the captain's expression. Senegal! Good Lord! The man would send American prisoners off to the jungles of Africa.

"I don't think that's a very practical idea," he said, barely managing to restrain his temper.

"Just a suggestion, sir," the captain said blandly.

"Any more ideas, Colonel?" the general said, knowing only

too well the provost marshal always left his thinking to his deputy.

"None the captain hasn't stated, sir."

So there it was. Checkmate. He was not going to get cooperation from the provost marshal's office. To make changes, he would have to start doing things that would infuriate the London crowd. At the moment he needed their cooperation in running the war, not their antagonism.

"It would seem there's not much to be done," he said sarcastically.

"At least we tried to think of something, sir," Blakely said, and this time the general knew he was being mocked. But it was done so subtly he would appear a fool if he got angry.

"Thank you, gentlemen, I'll not detain you any longer."

"Sir!" the colonel said in a voice so loud it startled the other two men. The general looked at Blakely, and the hint of a smile crossed the captain's face.

The moment his subordinates left his office, the general went over to the window and looked out on his garden. The flowers filled it with every color of the rainbow. Beyond the garden was a path that led to the narrow beach on the North River. It was so beautiful and peaceful. A butterfly flew past the window, and he envied the innocence and freedom of the creature. Was the butterfly at war? Did he care which flag flew over the fort?

He was peeved with Captain Blakely, but knew he would do nothing about it. Blakely *was* the provost marshal's office. The basic trouble with the man was that he was Irish, the general decided. They were all alike, these bloody Irishmen, glib with their remarks and insults; troublemakers.

Not for the first time did the general think it had been a mistake for England to include Ireland in the empire. It would have been better to leave the damn place alone. Let the Irishmen continue to paint themselves blue and speak in that idiotic language of theirs. They could worship stones, kill fatted calves, dance under a full moon, and hold each other's hands as they all went straight to hell, as far as he was concerned.

A group of senior field commanders arrived, and the general began going over his plans for the forthcoming invasion of Philadelphia. Once again he was a military commander, working in the world he enjoyed most. It was a world without intrigue and politics and men who trafficked them.

As he planned the coming battle, the plight of the prisoners receded in his mind.

Drew and Alec Seixas were in the kitchen of the de Kuyper house on Maiden Lane. The more they worked out the details for taking the *Devon*, the more skeptical Alec became.

The door opened, and Celine entered the room with a tall blond man. "This is my brother Andrew, but everyone calls him Drew," she said. "This is Alec Seixas. And this is Franz von Lossow."

Drew extended his hand, but on hearing the "von" attached to the name, he hesitated, then finished the handshake. Alec nodded from his chair, and he didn't look pleased.

"Actually, it's *Colonel* Franz von Lossow," Celine said.

"In the service of the prince of Hesse-Cassel," von Lossow added, lest there be any doubt in the minds of the other men.

Drew exchanged glances with Alec. He ignored the German and looked daggers at his sister. "We're busy. Would you mind leaving us alone?" His sister and a *Hessian*, for the love of God! Was she mad?

"Yes, I do mind," Celine said. "The colonel and I want to talk to you. To both of you, as a matter of fact."

"What could we possibly talk about?" Drew asked, cocking his head to one side and looking much like his father.

"To begin with, we might talk about your rescue of Dick Goelet," the colonel said in a soft voice tinged with amusement.

There was a hushed silence in the room. Alec's hand strayed down to the boot where he kept a sharp knife.

"I've told Franz all about your plan to rescue Dick," Celine said blithely. "He doesn't think you have a chance."

If the silence had been leaden at first, it was now deadly. It was Alec who spoke first.

"You know about our plans, Colonel?" he asked mildly, but his very mildness caused Drew to catch his breath. He knew the violence Alec was capable of.

"I know," the colonel said. "And as Celine said, you haven't a chance of pulling off such a scheme."

"Perhaps I should explain about the colonel," Celine said, delighted by the effect of the bomb she had dropped in the room. "He's planning to desert the British and join Washington. I'm sure the general will be most pleased to have him."

There was a slight release of tension, but Drew was still wary. "Interesting, but why should we believe you?"

"For one thing, Mr. de Kuyper, I plan on becoming your brother-in-law. For another, I have a plan that might get your cousin free. Are these two reasons enough to make you believe me?"

Celine was startled by the first statement, but Drew and Alec were more interested in the second.

"Please tell us more, Colonel," Alec said.

"Can we have a drink first?" Celine said, and Drew was pleased to see that his sister was flustered. He guessed it was the first time the subject of marriage had been mentioned. His sister's rare discomfiture was almost enough to make him like this German.

They poured drinks and sat down at the table.

"Celine told me how you plan to board the *Devon*, subdue the guards, and take your cousin," von Lossow said. "I think you might get that far, but after that..."

"That's what I've been saying," Alec agreed. "The frigates will be on us like a cat on a mouse."

"Exactly," the colonel said. "Instead of saving your cousin's life, you'd probably be throwing it away. With your own as well."

"So what do you suggest?" Drew asked.

"Can you get a longboat and have six men dressed as British sailors at the oars?"

"Yes," Alec said.

"I'll prepare documents stating that Dick Goelet is wanted for questioning at the provost marshal's office. I'll take the longboat out to the *Devon*, present the papers, and they'll turn your cousin over to me."

"Just like that?"

"Yes. I have access to the proper documents. It will be a simple matter to forge the signatures. And, as far as anyone outside this room knows, I'm a loyal officer serving the British king."

Alec and Drew again exchanged glances. The plan seemed logical and simple, even workable. The question was: could they trust this man, a Hessian?

"After you take Dick off the boat, what do you do with him?" Drew asked.

"Take him someplace safe."

"Take him to the Place," Celine suggested. "That other stuff up there seems safe enough."

Drew looked sharply at his sister. Talking about stolen supplies in front of a Hessian officer? She *was* crazy.

"I know all about the stores you have there," von Lossow said.

Drew was astonished. "Just how much have you told him?" he asked his sister.

"As we were leaving, I showed him the barn," she said, and then her temper flared. "He's one of us. Why can't you accept that?"

"She's telling the truth," the colonel said. "Once I help free your cousin, I'll be a wanted man myself."

"It's going to take some getting used to," Drew said. "The history of German mercenaries in America is not a pleasant one."

"I apologize for my countrymen's behavior," von Lossow said. "But you must remember it was your English king who brought them here."

"He isn't my king," Alec said.

"Nor mine," Drew said. "All right, I'm willing to take you at your word, Colonel. However, I do insist on one thing."

"Which is?"

"That I go with you when you board the *Devon*. To make sure we rescue the right man."

"And also to keep an eye on me, no doubt."

"No doubt," Drew said, holding out his hand to seal the bargain. This time there was more warmth in his handshake.

"Are we also to shake?" the colonel asked Alec.

"I'll wait till Dick is safe," he said.

"As you wish," the colonel said. "You'll learn to trust me."

"Especially if you're to be my brother-in-law," Drew said, looking toward his sister. Now that the hard business was over, he could afford to be playful.

Celine was not the sort to repress her emotions for long. She whirled on the German. "As far as *that* goes, I suggest you consult with me first."

He smiled. "I'm ready to do that now."

Peter came in the room. "Look what happened," he said, holding up his hand. There was a scratch and a little trail of blood.

Celine took the hand and looked at it. "We'd better wipe it with alcohol and put on a bandage," she said.

"That stuff stings," Peter protested.

"I know, but it cleans out the dirt. How did it happen?"

"The cat who lives next door. We were playing. But she didn't mean to do it."

"Let's take care of it," Celine said. She took her son by the hand, and they left the room. Soon afterwards Beth entered, and smiled when she saw Drew.

"Can you give me some help?" she asked.

"Sure," Drew said. "What is it?"

"I've been trying to stack some straw-filled sacks. One person can't do it alone."

"Straw-filled sacks?"

"For target practice with my bow and arrow," she explained.

Von Lossow was looking at the girl, admiring her beauty. "You shoot a bow and arrow?" he asked in surprise.

Drew laughed. "Beth can hit the eye of a fly at fifty paces," he said.

"I'm not that good," she said, but looked steadily at him even as she denied what he had said.

"Come on," Drew said. "Let's get your target set up."

They went back behind the stable and started to work. Drew, intent on the task, scarcely looked at Beth. But she didn't take her eyes off him.

Drew was strong, capable, and pleasant to be with, she thought. It was odd how her perception of him had suddenly changed. Not long ago he was like an older brother. Now? Well, her thoughts were hardly sisterly. It might only be an infatuation, but she doubted it. There weren't too many things she wanted, but a desire for young Andrew de Kuyper was rapidly growing in her mind and heart.

"We'll have this fixed in no time," he said.

"There's no hurry," she said, not at all anxious for him to be finished; while he was busy working, she was free to study him as much as she wanted.

Unmindful of the attention, Drew continued manhandling the sacks.

Alec and von Lossow had been left alone in the kitchen. The first man poured another drink for himself.

"Still not convinced about me, are you?" von Lossow asked.

"Not quite."

"My motives are simple. I think your cause is just and you should be a free people. I want to join you because I want to stay here in America. Since I'm willing to adopt you, you should be willing to adopt me."

"We'll see."

The colonel sipped at his glass of sack and studied the other man. "Seixas is an unusual name."

"It's Jewish," Alec said.

The colonel nodded. "Is Alec a Jewish name as well?"

"No, that's the name I gave myself. My father's name is Gershon. He named me Solomon Maimonides. I didn't want to go through life with that around my neck."

The colonel laughed. "My full name is Wolfgang Franz Gunther Christian Serlow Michael von Rhinebeck und Metlow von Lossow. I fully appreciate your problem. As you can see, I've cut my own name down."

"Do you know any Jews back in Hesse?"

"No, I don't," von Lossow admitted.

"People are more tolerant of us here than in Europe," Alec said softly. "Does that bother you?"

"People are more tolerant of *everything* here, Mr. Seixas. It is one of the things I find most attractive about America."

"There is no place for Old World prejudices here."

"How large is the Jewish community in New York?"

Alec smiled for the first time. The Jewish *community*, he thought. Why are Christians always so quick to lump us together? Why must they always think of us as a group rather than as individuals?

"I'll give you your first lesson about Jews in America, Colonel," he said. "To begin with, we are the despair of European Jews who visit our shores. We have no duly ordained rabbis. And the Jews you meet here come from everywhere—England, the West Indies, Brazil, the Netherlands, Spain, Portugal, and even your own country. Some, like myself, were born here.

"Our Jews come from vastly differing backgrounds, and we have many of the problems Christians of differing backgrounds would have—maybe even more. Our European visitors are appalled when they hear us reading our prayers. Apparently we don't even pronounce the Hebrew words correctly. Some of us can't even read the written language. And yet you speak of us as a community. You know, Colonel, sometimes I think the only thing that holds the Jews together as a people are Christians. 'What the hell,' a man like my father will say, 'if they think of us as one people, maybe we ought to go along with it.'"

"But you don't?"

"Yes and no. I'm certainly not ashamed of being a Jew," Alec said. "On the other hand, I much prefer to think of myself as an American. For *that* name, I'll fight."

Von Lossow measured the man: wide shoulders, a stubborn jaw, large hands covered on top with black hair. He was a picture of strength and power. This, from all appearances, was not a man who could be broken. Killed, perhaps, but not broken.

"You and I will get along," he said.

"I'll let you know after we rescue Goelet."

Drew returned to the kitchen and pulled up a chair.

"That was quite a surprise about becoming my brother-in-law," he said to von Lossow. "It surprised Celine, too."

"I meant it."

"She's not used to letting someone else make her decisions for her," Drew said.

"There are some decisions a man must make for a woman."

Drew looked at Alec and smiled. "Yes, I'm sure my sister will enjoy having her decisions made for her."

Alec shook his head and returned the smile. "Provided you keep her unconscious."

Von Lossow wasn't certain he understood. "But Celine believes—at least I *think* she believes—that many decisions should be made by a man."

"What makes you think that?" Drew asked.

"She is so... feminine... so sweet—"

Alec snorted. "Sweet, eh? 'The two noblest of things are sweetness and light.'"

"Jonathan Swift," von Lossow said immediately.

Alec was impressed. "So, Colonel, you are a literary man."

"I have read a few things."

"When Swift made his observation, he didn't have the slightest idea about a woman like Celine."

"What do you mean?"

"When she starts acting sweet," Alec explained, "it's time to look out. Big trouble is brewing."

"We'll see," von Lossow said, not at all convinced the other really knew Celine.

Drew found himself liking this Hessian. Any man who dared even to *think* he could control Celine was all right with him. But he wasn't ready to bet against Celine, at least not yet. He would just sit back and watch what happened.

"When do we get Dick?" Alec asked, bringing them all back to the more immediate problem.

Von Lossow shrugged. "I can have the necessary documents in two days. Any time after that is all right with me."

"In two days I'll have a longboat and men dressed as British sailors," Alec said. "Let's add one day just to give ourselves a little breathing room. This is Tuesday. We do it on Friday. Unless someone has an objection."

Drew looked at the colonel. "Why not? The sooner the better, as far as I'm concerned."

"Do you have a British officer's uniform?" von Lossow asked.

"Yes. I'm a dragoon," Drew said dryly.

The colonel looked puzzled. "Oh, I understand, some sort of joke," he said with an uneasy laugh.

"If you're going to become an American, you have to develop a sense of humor," Alec said.

"Yes, of course," the colonel answered, but he was uncomfortable, and the other men exchanged smiles. The German sense of humor, or rather the lack of it, was a joke in New York these days. One story making the rounds of the taverns was about a German lieutenant who had attempted to be amorous with a barmaid. "Go jump in the lake," the girl told him. He returned an hour later complaining he had been unable to find the lake. The girl felt so sorry for him, at least so the story went, that she took him to her room to spend the night and tried for an hour to explain her remark, but without success.

Drew stood. "Well, gentlemen, in three days—"

"In three days your cousin will be a free man," von Lossow said.

"For your sake, Colonel, as well as his, I hope so," Alec said.

Celine returned and took von Lossow away. Alec decided he would wait until the next day to get the boat and the men he needed. He left the house with Drew, and the two men walked down to Fraunces Tavern. It was the best place in town to relax and hear the latest rumors.

Fraunces greeted them as they entered.

"Hello, Sam," Drew said. "Hear any good news?"

"Just the usual. Howe is going to Philadelphia, Howe *isn't* going to Philadelphia. Washington will *win* the battle, Washington will *lose* the battle. There won't *be* any battle. A normal day." He shrugged.

They sat at a table, and Elsie came to take their order. When the buxom barmaid returned with their beers, she pressed her thigh against Drew and smiled at him.

"Where's your husband, Elsie?" he asked. It had been quite a while since she had been available, since her sailor boyfriend had actually shown up and married her.

"Off on a ship again. Be gone for months this time, I expect," she said, and then breathed a long sigh. "I get so lonely, by myself in that room upstairs."

"I thought you and your husband found a house?"

"We did. But when he's gone, I stay upstairs," she said. "Alone."

Drew could see the smirk on Alec's face. "That's too bad, Elsie," he said with a straight face. "But I'm sure your husband will be back before you know it."

She looked crestfallen, but he shielded his mouth from Alec and mimed "Later." She broke into a generous smile.

"Oh, yes, I'm sure you're right, he'll be back soon," Elsie said and was off to wait on another customer.

"I'm surprised she hasn't smothered you with those tits of hers," Alec said.

Drew smiled. "What are *you* doing for amusement these days?"

"Mention the sin, but never the sinner," Alec said.

They drank their beer for a few minutes, conversing about harmless topics in case they were being overheard. Drew's eyes wandered about the room, and suddenly narrowed when he saw Enoch de Witt seated at a table on the other side of the room. He was glassy-eyed and had a silly smile on his face. A bottle of rum sat before him.

"That damned Enoch!" Drew said. "I thought he'd sworn off the stuff."

Alec didn't bother to hide his contempt. "A man who lets himself go like that deserves everything he gets."

"He's been doing odd jobs for our company. My father says he's not a half-bad worker."

"When he's sober, maybe. Which, at the moment, he is not."

Drew walked across the room and stood in front of his cousin's table. "Enoch, I'm surprised to see you here."

"Andrew de Kuyper! Sit down. Have a drink," Enoch said, slurring his words.

"I thought you'd stopped drinking," Drew said, pulling up a chair and sitting down.

"I did. Will again."

"How many times in your life have you said that?"

"Lossa times," Enoch said pleasantly. "Mean it every time."

"I don't think you do mean it."

"Oh, but I do! Came here to have just a beer. There was a man at the next table. Drinking rum, he was. Got to wondering if it tasted the same as the rum I used to drink, so I ordered some. Yes, it does."

"Does what?"

"Tastes the same, it does."

"I think you ought to go home to your wife."

"In a li'l while, dear cousin, li'l while."

Drew went back and sat with Alec. "I guess I'm going to have to cart him home," he said unhappily.

"He looks comfortable enough here," Alec said.

"I'm thinking of his wife."

Alec nodded. "I'll take him home."

"He's my cousin."

"Yeah, but don't you have plans with the Dutch girl?"

"Sure, but I can come back."

As it turned out, they both took Enoch home, because he passed out and it took the two of them to carry him. Alice just shook her head when she saw the condition of her husband.

"I guess I'm going to leave him after all," she said.

"You still won't stay with us?" Drew asked.

She shook her head. "It's important that I stand on my own two feet. I'll just live with little Elly for a while."

Drew looked around the shabby room and felt ashamed that he could do nothing to help the woman. But she had a stubborn streak, and refused to let anyone do anything for her if she believed she could do it herself.

"Come back to the tavern with me?" Drew asked after he and Alec had come outside.

"No, I think I'll go home."

Drew walked back to the corner of Pearl and Broad and thought about his family. What the hell was happening? One cousin in jail. Another a drunk. His sister carrying on with a German.

He shook his head and went into the taproom and had a few

drinks. They made him sleepy, so he went upstairs and found the bedroom at the back.

A few hours later, when Elsie had finished her work downstairs, she joined him in the narrow bed. At first he was still half asleep and hardly knew what was happening. The world seemed to be a jumble of breasts and thighs, lips and fingers. And then it just began to feel good, and he stopped wondering what was happening. And he stopped worrying about his family.

He let himself get into the spirit of the thing.

Dawn on the prison ship *Devon*.

The hatches were opened, and the marine sergeant shouted for the first group: "Get your asses up on deck!"

Dick and Seth were not in the first group of the day, so they remained below, wondering when they would be fed. The British had started giving the prisoners bread every day. The stuff was hard and fairly infested with weavils, but it was at least some concession on the part of the provost marshal's office to accommodate General Howe's wishes. Along with the bread there was usually some watery soup containing potatoes, stringy vegetables, and an occasional bit of meat. Dick once discovered a shoe buckle in his bowl. He complained to Seth, who told him he should look on the bright side of things. "Lad, the shoe was probably made from deerskin, and that skin was once part of a deer, and a deer is meat, isn't it?"

There was a shout near the hatch as the prisoners climbed up. A Hessian guard had spotted some infraction and began kicking a man.

"Damned Hessians!" Seth said. His hatred, banishing his good humor of a moment ago, was as great as ever. To him "Hessian" was the same as "mad dog."

Dick pointed out it wasn't only the Hessians who acted like brutes; the prison ship made all guards that way. "Look, every man has a savage side to his nature," he said. "Ordinarily it's held in check by the laws, the church, the desire of a man to win the approval of society. But none of that applies here. The guards think of the prisoners as cattle. They kick and beat us and no one tells them to stop."

Seth shook his head. "No. And none of your philosophy for me, if you please. *Hessians*—all of them—are animals!"

They sat on the deck and waited for their turn to go topside. About two hours later several men descended to their deck.

The group was led by a marine sergeant. Colonel Franz von Lossow, Drew, and two guards followed.

"Richard Goelet!" the sergeant called. Dick looked up—and saw Drew. He rubbed his eyes, and looked again in disbelief. He was dumbstruck.

"Answer up, stupid," Seth said, giving him a sharp blow in the ribs."

"Here!"

Drew glanced over at his cousin, but controlled his emotions. For all anyone could tell, the dragoon officer was looking at a stranger.

Dick rose, and the Hessian colonel came over and stood in front of him. "You are Richard Goelet?"

"Yes."

"You are wanted at the provost marshal's office for questioning." He looked at the sergeant. "Bring him on deck."

"Come along, you," the sergeant said.

As Dick followed the colonel up the ladder, his mind was working at a feverish pace. If Drew was supposed to be a British officer, who was this Hessian colonel? *Was* he a Hessian?

He quickly concluded that if Drew was involved, it must be some plot to rescue him—and the colonel was part of the plot! And then he realized that if he escaped, he would be leaving Seth Cuyler. They had been through so much together. If they rescued him, they must save Seth as well.

But what could he do?

Whatever he was to do, he had to do it quickly. They had come to the top of the ladder and emerged on deck. The faces of a hundred curious prisoners were turned toward them. In a world of boredom, anything that deviated from routine was a major event, and they didn't want to miss a thing.

Dick touched the Hessian colonel's arm. "Sir—I must speak to you."

"All right," von Lossow said reluctantly. The idea now was to get off the ship as quickly as possible.

"I know why I'm being taken to the provost marshal's for questioning," Dick said. "I believe they will also want to question the man who was with me at the time of the incident."

Von Lossow looked at him blankly. "What are you talking about?"

Drew had come up and overheard. He caught on quickly. "There were two of you involved in that incident?"

"Yes."

"Who was the other man?"

"Seth Cuyler. He's down below."

Drew turned to von Lossow. "We'd better take the other man with us as well. Save us a trip back here."

"Get this other man," von Lossow said to the sergeant.

"Your orders only mention one man," the sergeant protested.

"Don't presume to tell me what my orders say, Sergeant," von Lossow snapped. "Get the other man!"

"Yes, sir!"

"Seth Cuyler," Dick repeated for the benefit of the flustered sergeant.

The officer ran toward the ladder. As Dick stood with Drew and von Lossow in silence, the crowd of men watched them. On some faces there were signs of pity for the poor man being dragged away. On others there was envy. Any place would be better than the hulk.

One of the onlookers was Robert Delafield. He stared at Drew, and there was no doubt he recognized him. Dick noticed Robert and his heart almost stopped. Christ! The man was capable of ruining the whole escape!

The little toady Conners, who had worked for the de Kuypers on the docks, was standing next to Robert. He too was staring at Drew with recognition. In another moment, Dick saw him. It was all over, he thought. Conners would sell his own mother for a handful of corn.

The sergeant returned with Seth, and Conners nudged Robert with his elbow and pointed at Drew. He was about to step forward and give away the plot, but Robert's big paw of a hand came around and clapped itself over Conners's mouth. No one but Dick noticed, because all eyes were on the arrival of Seth and the sergeant. The little man struggled briefly, until Robert brought his other fist down on top of Conners's head with a resounding smash. He let the body drop to the deck.

The thud caused everyone to look in his direction. "Poor devil collapsed," Robert said. There was a slight smile on his face as he stared straight at Drew.

"Are we ready?" von Lossow asked.

"Yes," Drew said.

"Then let's go. We're late as it is."

Within a short time Dick and Seth were seated side by side on a bench in the middle of a longboat. Drew and von Lossow sat on the next bench, and six sailors began rowing them away from the *Devon*.

Drew was the first to speak, although he pretended to be talking with von Lossow; hundreds of pairs of eyes on the *Devon* were still within sight.

"Well, Dick, my lad, you certainly look a proper mess."

Dick glanced uneasily at the Hessian.

"He's one of us," Drew said. "And the ones on the oars are Alec Seixas's men."

"Welcome home," von Lossow said.

"If you were going to get someone to impersonate a Hessian, you might at least have gotten a man with a better German accent."

"I *am* a Hessian," von Lossow protested.

"A Hessian!" Seth hissed.

"Take it easy," Dick said. "He just saved your life."

"Franz is a Hessian, but he's one of us," Drew said.

"Damn it all!" Seth growled. "Here I've been making promises to kill every Hessian, and the first one I meet saves my life. Where the bloody hell is the justice in the world?"

When they were far away from the prison hulk, Drew leaned across the bench and embraced his cousin. Then he shook Seth's hand as Dick shook von Lossow's. The colonel then held his hand toward Seth.

It took great effort on Seth's part, but he finally accepted the extended hand. "A Hessian," he mumbled, still disbelieving.

"Where are we going?" Dick asked.

"Celine's house at Kip's Bay."

"Beekman's Place?"

"Don't let her hear you calling it that."

"Oh, yes, forgive me. The Place. Period."

And then Dick suddenly realized he was free. It had taken this long for the truth to sink in. He stared at Seth, who was coming to the same understanding. The two bearded, dirty men in tattered clothes put their arms about one another and began to cry.

Drew had to look away, because he could feel the tears starting to run down his own cheeks.

Sergeant Taggert was frustrated and angry. For weeks he had been scouring the streets and alleys of New York in search of the missing old man. He had paraded almost a hundred candidates before the deputy provost marshal, only to be told he didn't have the right man. And now he was hard pressed to find men who even remotely fit the description. The six men at the other end of the room were his last hope—and a poor hope it was, he thought, as he looked at his latest haul.

One man had reddish hair, not gray. Another was one-armed, and a third looked part-black.

Captain Blakely entered the room, barely glanced at the waiting men, and turned to the sergeant. "Really, Taggert, is this the best you can do?"

"I've searched everywhere, Captain. That old man can't be in the city."

"Enjoying a holiday somewhere, is he?" he said acidly.

"I didn't say that, sir," the sergeant said, more annoyed with himself for his failure than with the captain for his sarcasm. "Maybe he's dead."

Blakely shook his head. "I've personally been checking the paupers' graves. You can let them go," he said. "Especially the black one," he added, casting his most withering look at Taggert.

The sergeant looked sheepish. "Yes, sir."

He dismissed the detained men and walked back to the guardhouse. He was going to get a detail of men and have another crack at finding the missing man. The old bastard's vanished into thin air, he grumbled to himself.

Dick arrived with the others at the Place, and he first realized how terrible he looked when he saw his image in the ten-foot-tall pierglass mirror that stood in the main hallway. He saw a bearded, bony, filthy stranger. Then Seth stood beside him, and together they stared into the glass for a long time.

The two shaved off their beards and rested for several days. Their stomachs were unaccustomed to normal quantities of food, and they couldn't hold down a big meal. They nibbled and snacked through most of their waking hours.

On the fourth day, Dick entered the parlor and found Drew seated with an old man. They were drinking beer. Drew introduced the man as Sisyphus.

"Sisyphus?" Dick asked.

"A private joke," the man said. "My real name is James Richardson."

Dick was a bit surprised at the old man's appearance; he looked like one of the vagrants who hung out around Hanover

Square. But then why should one be surprised? he thought. Just yesterday Drew had shown him the barn, with its mounds of stolen supplies, and told him the Place was being used as a depot for weapons and other goods taken from the British. After that, why would anything at all surprise him?

"Tell him the story," Drew said to the old man.

Sisyphus told Dick how Philemon Peabody and Captain Blakely had been partners in theft, and how Peabody now was trying to blackmail the Irishman.

"I noticed a funny thing happening in the city the last few days before I came to Drew's office," he said. "Soldiers were rounding up men every day—older men like myself. I managed not to be picked up, but one of my friends was. He told me what happened at the Provost. He and the other men were personally inspected by the deputy marshal—Captain Blakely himself.

"Maybe it's only my imagination, but I got the feeling he was looking for me. After all, Peabody had shown me his blackmail letter, and I know Blakely has good reason to want to see me dead. So I went to see Drew and told him the story."

"And I believe it," Drew said. "I brought Sisyphus up here to hide."

"That bastard Peabody!" Dick said. "Stealing from Jan, after all your father's done for him."

"We've got to figure out what to do with him."

"Kill him," Dick said.

"All that time in prison has softened your brain," Drew said. "We're not barbarians. We don't go around killing people."

"Do you have any other ideas?"

"How about if we forge a note?" Drew said. "From General Washington to Peabody, thanking him for sending him supplies."

"A note," Dick said skeptically. "It was a note that got me thrown in prison."

"We won't let you touch this one. We'll see it falls into the *right* hands."

"The British will think Peabody's the pirate," Sisyphus said, immediately grasping Drew's idea.

"We'll let them take care of the little rat."

"I don't know if it's such a good idea," Dick said. "Peabody has been awfully close to your father. If they think Peabody's a pirate, they might get suspicious about Jan."

Drew nodded. "Maybe we better think about it a bit more. Right now we've got to decide about you and Seth."

"What about us?"

"You can't go back to the city. Maybe you'll want to stay here."

Dick shook his head. "Seth and I have talked it over. We both want to join Washington's army."

"Franz is going across the river tomorrow. You could go with him, I suppose."

"After what happened to me in prison, I want to go somewhere I can take a gun in my hands and starting shooting back. Seth feels the same way."

"I understand," Drew said. "Sometimes I feel the same way myself. But right now I've got to stay here and get supplies for the army."

"It's important you do that," Dick said, reassuring his cousin. "But with me it's different. All I've been doing is getting clubbed and kicked. I want to start giving some of it back."

"All right, it's settled. You and Seth go with Franz tomorrow. In the meantime I'll give more thought about that note to Peabody."

Two days later, before Drew had made up his mind about the note, his problem with Philemon Peabody was solved—in a most unexpected way.

Captain Blakely was angry. They had failed to find the old man. He decided the next best thing was to throw Peabody himself in jail.

"You stupid fool," the captain said when the man was brought to his office under guard. "Did you really think I'd let you get away with blackmail?"

"I was only protecting my interests," Peabody protested, but he felt the panic rising within him; he realized he had gone too far.

"No, you weren't protecting your interests," the captain said. "You were scheming against me. Well, you're not going to get away with it."

"What are you going to do?" Peabody asked, and his hands were trembling.

"I ought to break your neck. That's the surest way of making sure you keep your mouth shut."

"You're going to kill me?" Peabody asked, his voice cracking.

"I ought to," the captain repeated with a smile. "But I don't think I'll do it. Not just yet."

"What, then?"

"Throw you in the darkest cell in the lowest level of this building and keep you in isolation. You can tell your story to the rats who'll come to visit you at night."

"How long will you keep me there?"

"Until you rot."

There was a knock at the door. A guard appeared. "Colonel Cunningham wishes to see you, Captain."

"What now!" Blakely complained. He went to the door and stopped in front of the Hessian guard who stood outside. "Make sure my guest waits here for me."

"Yes, sir."

Peabody was alone in the room, and he paced back and forth, his brain racing over the latest events. What a fix he was in! To languish in some hole in the bottom of the building! Peabody had no illusions about the captain's compassion. He *would* stay there until he rotted.

He went to the window, but the heavy iron bars ruled out any escape in that direction. He went to another door and opened it. It was a closet. An officer's tunic hung from a peg. There were several pairs of trousers, a spare hat, even a sword and trappings.

He had an inspiration. If he dressed up in these clothes and could get past the guard—he could picture the fellow's face— dull, stupid-looking; a Hessian idiot, a peasant...

It was insane—but what else was there to try?

He quickly took off his own coat and trousers and put on a pair of trousers from the closet. They were Blakely's, and far too big for the little man. He grabbed a belt and tightened it to keep the trousers from falling down. He donned the tunic and felt like he was swimming around inside it. But it would have to do. He put on the hat. Big, but not too bad. He took the sword and adjusted the strapping around his waist.

He grabbed a pile of papers from the desk and went to the door. He took a deep breath, opened the door, and stepped halfway into the hall. The guard looked at him and frowned. Peabody looked back over his shoulder. "Wait here. I'll be back in a few minutes," he commanded the empty room. He closed the door, hefted the papers under his arm, and looked at the guard.

"Make sure the prisoner stays here until Captain Blakely or I come back."

"Yes, sir!" the Hessian said, and brought his heels together in a loud clack.

Peabody walked down the corridor, pressing his right hand against his side to keep the baggy trousers from slipping down. The sword banged against his legs, almost tripping him, making him scuttle along like a crab. He felt like a fool. Any moment now someone was going to stop him and end the masquerade.

To his amazement, no one questioned him or even bothered to look at him. He walked out the front door past a yawning guard, turned the corner, and disappeared down an alley.

He hurried to his room, got out of his oversized costume, and dressed quickly. He shoved a pistol under his belt and covered it with his coat flap. He went to the back of his closet, pulled up several floorboards, and took out a metal box crammed with money. He carted his box out of his room and left the building.

It could be only a matter of minutes, he told himself, before Blakely returned to his office and found him gone. Patrols would be sent out to scour the city.

Only he didn't plan on staying in the city. Blakely would be furious and would tear the place apart to find him.

He went down to the Fly Dock and found a fisherman standing on the wharf next to his small sailing craft. "I want to hire you and your boat," he said.

"For how long?"

"I want to go to Philadelphia," Peabody said. Since that city was still in American hands, he would be safe from Blakely.

"Philadelphia?" the fisherman said in disgust. "I haven't time to waste on foolishness."

"I'll pay you fifty pounds sterling."

The fisherman almost choked. Fifty pounds! He could fish all summer long and not make that much. Peabody had transferred some money to his pocket before leaving his room. He pulled it out. "I'll pay you half now," he said holding out twenty-five pounds. "But we must leave this minute."

"But I have a partner," the man protested. "He'll think I've stolen the boat."

"When you return with all this money, he'll forgive you."

The fisherman nodded. "We go now."

Peabody held his precious money chest tightly as he climbed into the boat. The fisherman raised one sail and undid the lines holding the boat to the dock.

He raised a jib when the boat came into the middle of the river, and the little craft sped down the bay toward the Narrows. They passed a frigate, and Peabody worried for a moment. But the frigate sailed majestically past them; small fishing boats were a common sight on the bay.

Suddenly Peabody began to laugh. It was a high, nervous laugh, and the fisherman looked startled.

"What's the matter?" he asked.

"I was just thinking," Peabody said, as his eyes filled with tears of laughter. "Thinking about what a certain English captain will have to say to a certain Hessian guard. Especially after he looks in his closet."

The fisherman grunted. He sailed the boat, but kept one eye on this strange passenger during the entire journey.

Marie Therese was in the garden at the back of her house, playing dolls with Elly de Witt. The little girl often spent her days on Maiden Lane while her mother was working at Jan's Whitehall office.

"Here, Elly. I've changed the dress on the blond doll," she said.

The child took the doll and studied it. "She looks pretty," she said. "Like you. And my mommy."

"Yes, like your mommy," Marie Therese said with a smile. She enjoyed having the child around. At first she had thought Elly's company would be nice for Peter, but the boy was almost nine and had no interest in a five-year-old girl. He much preferred the company of other boys his same age. There were quite a few of those in the neighborhood.

"Your mommy should be here soon," Marie Therese said.

"Are we staying for supper?"

"I don't know. That's up to your mommy."

"I like eating here," Elly said. "The food is good."

The honesty of a child! Marie Therese thought. She hoped Elly never said such things to Alice.

Alice had left Enoch and moved to a small house only a block away, on Crown Street. She had half the house, and the other half was lived in by the owner and his wife. Actually, the man no longer owned the house; Jan had secretly bought it and made arrangements for Alice to pay a rent she could afford. She paid the rent to the former owner, and he kept Jan's secret. It wasn't a large house or a grand one, but it was far better than the place in which she had lived with Enoch.

Peter came into the garden through the back gate. He looked dirty, disheveled, tired, and happy.

"Hello, Grandma," he said, ignoring the little girl.

"You look as if you've been having fun," Marie Therese said, amused at how messy boys could get in almost no time. It had only been an hour ago that he had gone out, washed, neatly dressed, his hair combed. Now he had mud on his pants and shirt, a tear in one of his stockings, and dust on every exposed inch of his skin.

"We were playing kick ball," Peter said. "Our side won," he added proudly.

It was a form of an old Dutch game boys had been playing on the island since before the days of Peter Stuyvesant. Two sticks were set up close together at both ends of a field. The object was to kick the ball through the sticks. No hands could be used. The other team, of course, tried to block the shots and kick the ball through their goal at the opposite end of the field. There were no rules other than that the game be kept going until one side scored a goal. Then the ball would be brought to the middle of the field and play would resume again. This went on until everyone was exhausted, and agreed to quit. The ball itself was made of hard wood, and at the end of the game there were many black-and-blue thighs and bruised shinbones.

"Better clean up," Marie Therese said. "You know what your mother will say if she sees you looking like this."

Peter made a face. "Where is she?"

"In the sewing room."

"I can clean up in the kitchen," he said, and went into the house. He hadn't even glanced at Elly.

"Why doesn't Peter like me?" she asked.

"He likes you," Marie Therese assured her. "It's just that boys act strange around girls."

"I like *him*," Elly said plaintively.

Jan arrived home, and Alice was with him. He came out into the garden and smiled when he saw Elly. He held out his arms. She ran toward him, and let herself be caught and lifted high in the air.

"Have you been a good little girl?"

"Yes!" she squealed.

"And what do good little girls get?"

"Candy!"

Jan put her back on the ground. He folded his arms. "Now which pocket is it in?"

Elly took her time deciding, and finally pointed to the pocket on the left side of his coat. He let her reach in, and she giggled when she brought out a wrapped piece of hard candy.

"You guessed the right one again," he said, not telling her that he always put candy in both pockets so as not to disappoint her. "Now let's go inside and get old Grandpa a drink."

Alice and Marie Therese had been watching this ritual with amusement, and when Jan took Elly's hand and went inside, Alice turned to the older woman. "Thank you so much for taking care of her."

"I love having her here," Marie Therese said. "She's so good, and she gets prettier every day."

"I'm just afraid I'm inconveniencing you."

"Put that out of your head," Marie Therese said. "I love hearing a little girl's laughter in the house. It's been a long time. Now, you *will* stay for supper?"

"Oh, no," Alice said quickly. "I've got everything ready at home. It just has to be heated up."

Marie Therese didn't argue, because she admired Alice's fierce pride even as she was dismayed by it. "Well, the least you can do is take home some pie. I baked it earlier and promised Elly she could have a piece."

"That's fine," Alice said with a shy smile, knowing Marie Therese was working out a compromise on the supper issue. "You bake the best pies in New York."

"Tell that to my husband. He claims I didn't know how to boil an egg when we were first married. Speaking of husbands, do you ever see Enoch?"

"He came around last week to see Elly. He was sober," she added quickly.

"Maybe he's learned his lesson," Marie Therese said, but she knew it wasn't true. Jan had been keeping an eye on Enoch, and he knew the man spent almost every night in a tavern. He worked here and there at odd jobs for Jan and others, and spent all his money on whiskey.

"We'll see," Alice said quietly. "In the meantime I'm better off without him."

That was true, Marie Therese thought, even though New

York was not the best place for a woman without a man. Such women were usually looked down upon, and men thought of them as fair game.

After Alice got Elly and took her home, Marie Therese wandered into the parlor, where Jan was fixing his second drink. "Want one?" he asked.

"All right," she said, and after he had handed it to her, she sat on the arm of his chair and took a few sips. "I'm worried about Alice," she said at last. "I don't like her living alone."

"She's not exactly alone. There's another couple living in the house. And she has Elly."

"That's not what I mean."

"Alice has been hurt, my dear. By Enoch. By the death of her son. These things take time to work themselves out."

"I'm starting to think of Elly as my own grandchild," Marie Therese said.

"No harm in that. Her own grandparents are dead. Anyway, you make the best-looking grandmother in town."

She put her arm around his shoulder and kissed his forehead. "And you don't make a bad-looking grandpa."

He held her hand and smiled. "Later, after dinner, you want to go upstairs and fool around?"

"You old goat," Marie Therese said, but there was laughter in her eyes, and love.

In the middle of September, Mary Delafield came to see Celine. She was upset and worried. Celine made her a cup of tea and added a dollop of rum. They sat in the parlor, near an open window overlooking Maiden Lane, and let the air cool them. It was one of those typical muggy days of late summer in New York, hot and sticky; even the slightest exertion caused perspiration to bead on the skin.

"I have a problem," Mary said.

"What is it?"

"You know I've never had any children. Well, I always blamed it on me and not Robert."

"Yes?" Celine said, suddenly having a premonition about where this conversation was leading.

"Now it looks as if it wasn't my fault after all."

"What exactly are you trying to say?"

"I think I'm expecting a child."

It was a simple situation to grasp. Robert Delafield had been in prison for almost a year; Mary had not been with him. "Who's the father?" she asked.

"Patrick Blakely."

"No!"

"I know you warned me about him," Mary said. "But... well, it happened."

"What do you mean it *happened?* Did he force himself on you?"

"No, no, nothing like that. It just, well, I *wanted* it to happen, and it did."

"Let's go back a bit. You said you *thought* you were expecting a child. Do you think, or do you know?"

"I know."

"How far has it gone?"

"Three months."

"You have another month before anything really starts to show, maybe two. Then what?"

"That's why I'm here," Mary said with a wail. "I thought maybe you could figure out what to do."

Celine swore under her breath. Dear, sweet Mary, who never did anything wrong, had certainly pulled a corker this time. "Well, you can't stay in the city," she said. "That's out of the question. You'll have to go someplace else to have your baby."

"Where?"

"That's what we have to decide."

"Maybe I could stay at Kip's Bay. At the Place," Mary suggested.

Celine thought about it. What if Blakely found out Mary was staying there? Would he want to see her? And the child? The last place in the world Celine wanted the deputy provost marshal was at her house. All those stolen supplies...

"I don't think that's a good idea," she said.

"But the Place is quiet—isolated. What's wrong with it?"

"It's not isolated enough. Do you want your English officer visiting you? What if Robert found out? How do you think he'd feel?" Celine asked, even though she was enough of a realist to know that he'd probably find out anyway. How long could one keep such a thing a secret?

"I don't want Robert to find out," Mary said. "I feel bad enough as it is."

"How did it happen?"

"How did what happen?"

"How did you wind up in bed with Blakely?" Celine said, exasperated.

"There was something in his eyes, something that drew me to him. Something I couldn't resist," Mary said with fervor. "If I tell you a secret, will you promise not to tell anyone? Ever?"

Celine nodded.

"For the first time in my life I knew what it was like to be a woman. He made me feel that way the first time, and I couldn't stop."

"Captain Blakely is probably the most hated man in New York," Celine said. "You *can't* see him anymore."

"But—"

"You have to start thinking of the child. People will know Robert isn't the father, but they *don't* have to know it's Blakely."

"Yes, I understand," Mary said meekly. "I must think of the good of the child."

Beth came into the room, and the other two women stopped talking and looked at her.

"I'm sorry. Am I interrupting?"

Celine shook her head. "We might as well tell Beth," she said, and explained the problem.

Beth thought about it for a moment. She had several relatives who maintained farms north of Pell's Point, on the old de Kuyper manor founded by Jacob Adam. Over the years the manor had been split up and several sectors sold to members of the Henry family.

"I have a cousin named Noah who has a farm way up in Westchester," she said. "He's always been a good friend. I'm sure he'd be happy to take Mary in. When do you want to do this?"

"The sooner the better," Celine said.

"We'll go tomorrow," Beth responded.

"So soon?" Mary complained.

"Why not?"

"But the house... there's so much to do..."

"I'll see to everything," Celine said.

"It's a long journey," Beth said. "And the roads in Westchester are rotten. There's an inn called the Porridge Pot just across the Harlem, near the King's Bridge. We'll spend tomorrow night there and be at Noah's before nightfall the next day."

"Do you want me to go?" Celine asked.

"I can handle it," Beth said.

"Should I tell Patrick?" Mary asked.

"I don't want you to see that man again," Celine said firmly.

"He'll have to know I've gone."

"I'll tell him."

Mary went home to pack some things for the journey, and Celine thanked Beth for her help.

"You'd do it for me," Beth said.

"Yes, I would. Only I have a feeling you wouldn't let yourself get into such a situation."

"I wouldn't mind getting into that kind of trouble with your brother," Beth said with a smile. "But it's not likely."

"He still doesn't really notice you, eh? He must be blind."

"Well, at least there's plenty of time...if that will help."

Drew returned to the house with Peter. They were hot and sweaty from working on the docks, helping to re-rig a river packet.

"What a day to be working," Drew said as he wiped the sweat from his brow. "Got something cold to drink?"

"Me too!" Peter said.

"Peter learned a lot about rigging a ship today. It's getting so he can do a man's work."

"Drew taught me," Peter said affectionately.

Celine brought cold beer and apple juice from the cellar, and the man and the boy took their drinks over to the window to let the slight breeze help cool them. The two were drawing very close to each other; Drew was becoming something of a surrogate father to the boy. It was beginning to annoy Celine. She wasn't sure she liked the idea of her son being fonder of her brother than of her.

The two women were a distance away, and Celine spoke in low tones in order not to be overheard.

"Maybe Drew should go with you and Mary tomorrow."

"Why?"

"It might be better if there's a man with you."

"I can take care of things," Beth said.

"I thought you might appreciate being thrown together with him."

"It's got to be his idea."

Celine sighed. "Sometimes a man can be quite blind, you know. A woman has to do something to open his eyes."

"I understand," Beth said. "I'll do it, if he doesn't, when the time is right."

Drew decided to be sociable and join the women. "Well, dear sister and little Beth, anything new happening?"

Beth and Celine exchanged knowing looks.

"Not a thing," Celine said.

The next morning Beth drove a trap-and-horse to Mary's house, picked up the woman and her luggage, and drove north.

It was late in the afternoon when they crossed the King's Bridge and came to the Porridge Pot. Beth made arrangements with the innkeeper for a room for Mary and herself. Ordinarily there were two beds in each sleeping chamber, and it was customary for two people to share a bed. Beth, however, insisted that the two have a room to themselves, claiming her companion was ill and given to tossing and moaning in her sleep. The inn wasn't full, and the innkeeper agreed.

After resting in their room for an hour, Beth and Mary went to the taproom of the inn. They ordered two glasses of sack, and portions of the beef stew for dinner.

The taproom of the Porridge Pot was typical of the sort found in inns along the roads, serving as office, tavern, dining room; general gathering, loafing, and dozing room. A bar of polished oak ran half the length of the room along one wall. Pewter mugs and tankards hung from pegs behind the bar. There was an array of bottles and kegs. The far end of the room held a large fireplace; this served as the kitchen for the cook, who was also the innkeeper's wife. A low fire was burning, and delicious aromas wafted from the copper pots and cauldrons set near the flames to keep their contents simmering.

Other travelers were eating their suppers. They were all men, and the two women were the objects of many secretive, and some not-so-secretive, glances. Mary and Beth ignored the men, but it became more difficult to do so.

A burly woodsman ambled over to their table, pulled out a chair, and sat down. "You two ladies wouldn't object to a bit of company now, would you?"

Mary blushed and looked to her companion.

"Why don't you take a bath?" Beth said. "You smell."

The other men smiled. A few sniggered. This had the makings of a fine entertainment.

"A bath, she wants," the woodsman said, looking at his

companions and smiling. He turned back to Beth. "Maybe it's that you don't know what a real man smells like, eh?"

"Go away," Beth said calmly.

"And if I don't?"

Beth started to take another bite of stew. The woodsman reached out and grabbed her wrist. "Come on darlin', let's be friends," he said pleasantly.

Beth smiled and this encouraged the man. He leaned closer across the table. Suddenly his smile changed to a grimace of fear as he felt the point of a sharp blade touching his throat. It happened so quickly he didn't know where the knife came from.

"If you don't leave us alone I'm going to slit your throat from ear to ear," Beth said.

"Uh...uh..." the man uttered as the sharp point drew blood.

"Will you go away?"

"Y-yes..."

She took the knife from his throat. "Good."

The woodsman touched his neck and saw a trickle of blood on his fingers. He got up, knocking over his chair, and stumbled to the bar. He took out a filthy piece of cloth and held it against his wound. The innkeeper poured him a large portion of Barbados rum.

"It's not right," the woodsman complained after taking a goodly swig from his glass. "She looks so young and harmless."

"Best keep clear of that one," the innkeeper said.

Mary sat horrified in her chair.

"Eat your dinner," Beth said mildly, as if nothing unusual had happened. She daintily speared a piece of meat. "I always get terribly hungry when I travel."

David Sackett, along with other members of the Continental Congress and the fledgling government, left Philadelphia before the advance of Howe's army. The majority, including David, were now in Lancaster, Pennsylvania.

He had been surprised recently when Philemon Peabody had shown up in Philadelphia, but when David questioned him about his presence, the fellow had been very secretive. Of course David soon learned of his perfidy, but there was nothing to be done about it in Philadelphia. Peabody immediately set himself up as a trader. Within a week he made a handsome profit by buying a shipment of rum and shrewdly selling it to a sea captain who took it to Boston, which had a shortage of drink.

David was staying in a Lancaster tavern with other members of Congress, and at the moment was in the taproom enjoying a tankard of ale and a dish of mutton with Richard Henry Lee. Lee was one of the prime movers behind the Declaration of Independence, and a member of the committee that gave George Washington command of the Continental Army. Their conversation as they ate, as always these days, was about the course of the war.

"Howe thinks he's taken Philadelphia," Lee said. "But he'll soon find out it's Philadelphia that's taken him."

David smiled at the witticism, and knew there was some truth in it. Howe was winning battles, yes, but the longer the war went on, the more it favored the Americans. Howe's original plan was to take Philadelphia, and then move north and join his army with Burgoyne's forces. But Washington was keeping his army on the move and avoiding a total defeat. The British were beating the Americans in battle, but it was also arguable that the very size of America herself was beating the British.

Howe had landed at a place called the Head of Elk with over fifteen thousand troops. Washington had over ten thousand men, and they took up positions along Brandywine Creek. On September 11, Howe attacked, sending Knyphausen's Hessians directly against the rebel force, but also sending Lord Cornwallis around to the right in a clever flanking movement. Washington and his generals, Greene and Sullivan, fought valiantly, but the flanking movement proved their undoing. They were forced back, and the British army marched toward the City of Brotherly Love. David and the other members of Congress fled the city, and now it looked as if Howe and Washington were getting ready to clash again near the main British encampment at Germantown.

News of the war in the north kept reaching the Congress, and for a time offered no encouragement.

General Burgoyne had a force of over eight thousand men—British regulars, Hessians, Canadians, and Indians. He moved steadily across the land, taking what he wanted as he willed. Many stories trickled down from upper New York about atrocities being committed by the general's Indian allies, and these tales angered many an American who had previously harbored loyalist emotions.

But then the news began to change for the better.

Word came through about the battle fought at Bennington, where the American general John Stark had engaged a British force and soundly beaten them. The entire British detachment of over seven hundred men were either killed or taken prisoner. Burgoyne tried to save this detachment by sending reinforcements, but they arrived too late and were, in turn, routed by the Americans. After losing a third of their number, these reinforcements fled back to the protection of Burgoyne's main army.

"I hear our northern army is planning to attack the British at Saratoga," David said.

"And we'll beat them," Lee said. "More and more men are signing up with the army. The British made a big mistake when they decided to use Indians."

"Civilized men shouldn't resort to such tactics," David agreed.

The conversation drifted to another topic. "I think we've got to put more pressure on the French," Lee said. "They've got to give us more aid."

"I agree."

"What's even more important is that France officially recognize us as an independent nation."

"What more can we do to push them?"

"That's what I wanted to talk to you about, David. My congressional committee wants to see more privateers on the water. We need ships that will harass the British and take them on where they're supposed to be strongest—the sea."

David nodded. Easier said than done, he thought, and waited for Lee to continue.

"We want to send another envoy to France to assist Ben Franklin. This new man's job will be to beg, borrow, or steal ships from the French and outfit them as privateers. We need a man who knows ships, who's young and daring, and who can be charming with the French. Do you know of anyone like that in New York?"

David mulled it over. Certainly Jan de Kuyper knew as much about ships as any man in the city. But his health wasn't all that good, and anyway he was too old. He silently considered a few more names, and discarded them. He came to Drew. Young, yes—and daring. And his knowledge of ships was extensive.

"Yes, I believe I know of such a man," David said. "My nephew, Andrew de Kuyper."

Lee's eyebrows arched upward. "We've had problems with nepotism," he said. "Ben Franklin gave his own nephew a job. The man's done nothing properly, and there's been holy hell to pay."

"Drew may be my nephew, but he also fits your particulars. I don't think he should be penalized simply because he *is* related to me."

"I see your point," the congressman said. "If you think he's the right man, then so be it. I'll draw up a commission giving him the appointment. It's up to you to convince him to take it. What's his full name?"

"Andrew de Kuyper."

"Ah, the Dutch are still among us," Lee mused. "Good stock."

"I suppose I should attend to this immediately."

"Yes, and I'll draw some money from the treasury. Your nephew can deliver it to Franklin in Paris."

"How much?"

"A thousand pounds."

"Not much to start a fleet of privateers."

"You misunderstand. This money is for expenses. We'll be counting on your nephew to get the French to *give* us the ships. God forbid that we have to pay for them."

"I'll leave for New York in the morning," David said.

"I like a man who gets right to work," Lee said.

David smiled. "Maybe I've been inspired by you. I've heard the story of the horseflies."

Richard Henry Lee looked startled, and then laughed. He knew David was referring to that session of Congress during which members finally passed the Declaration of Independence. Several congressmen had been endlessly arguing over minor points, delaying the vote. Lee conspired with Ben Franklin to open all the windows in the stuffy room. It was spring, and a plague of horseflies came inside. The members soon were scratching and swatting as the persistent insects bit through their silk stockings. Finally, so the tale went, a vote was hastily taken and the motion approved, in good part because the men wanted to get out of the room and away from their tormentors.

"It's a true story, David," Lee said. "We declared our independence with the help of horseflies. I like to think they were put there by God to guide us in His wisdom," he added with a wink.

The next morning David boarded a coach to New Jersey. He was forced to spend two days at Trenton before he could find an ongoing coach. The war had interrupted all scheduled coaches, and those that did run followed their own whims. Six days after leaving Lancaster, David arrived at Paulus's Hook on the western bank of the North River, where he paid a waterman to take him to New York.

He arrived in the city only to learn that Drew was up at the Place, so he went to his own house and had dinner with his son and daughter. Jemmy and Jenny, finishing one another's sentences as usual, informed him of all the smuggling activities, and for the first time in a long while he felt his children were doing something practical. That night he slept the dreamless sleep of an exhausted traveler.

The next morning he was up early and drove to the old Beekman's Place. On being greeted by Drew, David reached into his coat and brought out the congressional commission. He handed it to his nephew. "Read that, then we'll talk."

Drew read the document, his eyes widening as he realized the enormity of the task being entrusted to him. The commission granted him extraordinary powers to do whatever necessary to get hold of fighting ships. It allowed him to select captains and issue sailing orders. He was authorized, if necessary, to commit funds that would be supplied by Congress. Nominally he was to take his orders from Benjamin Franklin, but since that gentleman was so busy with other matters, essentially he would have a free hand.

"Quite a piece of news!" he said when he finished reading.

"Are you pleased?"

"How could I not be? It's a lot of responsibility, and an honor."

"We'll find a French ship and book you on her," David said. "The first one out."

Drew agreed he should leave quickly. With winter approaching, the weather was becoming more and more unpredictable. In very foul weather the ships wouldn't even be sailing. It was an odd fact, considering there was a war going on, but these days the port of New York was busier than ever. Even taking into account that a good many ships were carrying

British soldiers and war supplies, there was a surprising amount of normal traffic.

A French brigantine, the *Alizé*, was found in port, due to sail in a week's time for Le Havre. The name meant "tradewind," an indication the vessel had spent most of her time in the Indies.

Drew went back to the house on Maiden Lane to attempt to tidy up his affairs, David having warned him he might be away as long as a year.

Alec asked to go with him. "I want command of one of those privateers," he said.

Drew agreed. Alec was a veteran with both ships and fighting, and would make a good privateer captain. "All right. We go together."

The night before they left, the family and Alec gathered for a farewell dinner at the house on Maiden Lane. In addition to the people who lived in the house, there were David Sackett and the twins, Alice de Witt and little Elly. Enoch was invited, but didn't show up.

A new problem had been added to their lives: Jan had contracted a mysterious debilitating disease. Only a few months ago he had been robust and healthy, but now he seemed tired and listless all the time. The very flesh seemed to be melting from his bones. He had already lost almost forty pounds, and his skin hung loose and flabby.

It pained Drew to be leaving him at such a time, but he knew he had an important job to do; besides, there was nothing he could do for his father.

Marie Therese pretended there was nothing wrong on this last night that her son would be in America, but Drew could see that when she looked at Jan, her eyes were full of worry and sadness.

Of all those present, only Jan was utterly honest about his condition. He knew he was failing, and accepted it. "We need you here in New York," he said to David. "I'm not fit to run the company anymore."

"You'll snap out of it," Sackett said. But he, too, was a realist. "I can arrange to spend more time here, though. You should rest more."

Jan looked at his wife. "I spend half my time in bed as it is, and he tells me to rest."

After dinner the family went into the parlor.

"Watch out for those French girls," Celine said to her brother. "I hear they're wild."

"There are wild enough women right here," he said.

"Yes, I've heard about some of your escapades," she said.

"None are as famous as yours."

"Have fun, just don't marry a foreigner," Jemmy Sackett said.

"I'll leave that to my sister," Drew said blandly, and looked at Celine. "How *is* Franz these days?"

"With Washington," Celine replied, unruffled. "I received a letter from him the other day. He mentions Dick and Seth Cuyler. All three are well."

"I'll miss you, Drew," Peter said as he stood beside his uncle. Indeed, he had spent the entire evening at Drew's side.

"And I'll miss you," Drew said honestly. He had been enjoying his unasked-for role of mentor to the boy. It had added a new dimension to his life, making it richer. "I'll write to you," he added.

"Will you write to *me*?"

It was Beth Henry. Drew smiled. "Certainly. I'll tell you all about Paris. It's supposed to be a wonderful city."

"I'd like to see it someday," she said.

"When the war's over, you probably will."

"I'd like to see it with you," she said boldly.

Drew, startled, looked at her, and for a moment began to see her exquisite face as others saw it. He met her deep, moody eyes; this was a lovely young woman. But in another moment Peter spoke and the budding realization was dispersed.

"Beth, will you take me hunting with you?"

"If you like, Peter."

"And there's a job for you while I'm gone, Nephew," Drew said. "You take care of Beth, because with me not around you have to start doing a man's job."

"All right," Peter agreed, and straightened his back.

"You're in good hands, Beth," Drew said, and winked at her.

"Among the best, I'm sure," Beth said.

Drew wandered away, and smiled when he saw little Elly sitting on Jan's lap. His father was telling her a story about a wolf and a bear, and the little girl was believing every word of it. Jan had always been fond of children, and it pleased Drew to see his father enjoying himself.

"God be with you," Alice de Witt said to Drew, interrupting his reverie.

"Thanks, Alice," Drew said. "And from the way you're looking, I'd say God was with you these days."

The separation from Enoch was doing wonders for the woman. She had put on weight and lost almost all trace of gauntness. Her eyes had life in them, and she smiled now and then, a phenomenon that had been a great rarity in the old days.

"There's less tension in my life," she said. "I just take each day as it comes."

Neither spoke directly of Enoch, since her husband was a topic that made them both uncomfortable. "Where's Mary Delafield?" Alice asked. "I'm surprised she's not here."

"Celine told me she had to go to the country for her health," Drew said. "I don't know any more than that." It was the truth. The only people in the family who knew about Mary's problem were Celine and Beth; not even Marie Therese had been told.

Caleb North showed up to say good-bye to Drew—and to bring some tremendous news. "Burgoyne has been beaten by General Gates!" he said. "An American victory! Word has just come down that Burgoyne has retreated to Saratoga with our army in pursuit. This time we even outnumber the British!"

"Do you think we'll win?" Jan asked.

"Yes," Caleb said. "Just a matter of time."

"Wait until *that* news gets to Lancaster," David said.

"I'd love to bring it all the way to Paris," Drew said. "Maybe I should delay my journey and take the next ship."

David shook his head. "It's important for you to get there as soon as you can."

"Besides," Jan added. "If Burgoyne is thoroughly beaten, the news will surely reach Paris."

"But it would be nice if I could bring Franklin news of a great victory," Drew said. "Surely it would lift his spirits."

"His spirits will be lifted enough when you arrive," David said.

"Still the glory hound, aren't you, Cousin!" Jenny Sackett said to Drew.

"Well, I was wondering when you were going to get around to wishing me a safe trip," he said sarcastically.

"Oh—I *do* wish you a safe trip, Drew. I just don't seem to know how to say it."

She threw her arms about his neck and kissed him. When she pulled her head back, Drew saw tears trickling down her cheeks. Unless his memory was faulty, it was the first time he had ever seen her cry.

"See to it you take care of yourself," Jenny ordered him, and he was touched.

He was going to miss the people in this room.

It was before dawn, the morning of October eighth. Drew went to his father's bedroom to take his leave before departing for France.

"In a few months you'll be your old self again," Drew said. But his father's sallow complexion and thin face told him otherwise.

"Don't let old Ben Franklin lead you around by the nose," Jan said. "Stand up to him. He'll like that."

"I'll watch out for myself. You do the same."

Jan put his hand on his son's. "Maybe this is a time to be honest. I'm not getting any better. Just the opposite, in fact. And you'll be gone for at least a year."

Drew suddenly felt drained and bit dizzy. He knew what his father was going to say next.

"This may be the last time we'll ever see one another. At least on this earth. I just want to tell you that I'm proud of you and you've been the son I wanted. And the man."

Drew fought back the tears. "And you've been the best father a man could ask for."

"I've led a full life," Jan said. "And a happy one. So don't feel sorry for me. My only regret is that I won't live to hold your children on my knee. But a man can't be greedy," he added with a sad smile.

Drew was beyond words. He kissed his father on the cheek, and left the room. His mother was waiting for him. They walked to the front door.

"Take care!" she said in a fierce whisper.

He nodded. It was still too painful for Drew to talk. His father's face swam before him—the face of a man he loved above everything else in the world; the face he might never see again.

"You have your work to do," Marie Therese said. "You can't be worrying about Jan."

He nodded.

She grasped him by both shoulders. "You have to carry on for him, be the man he would be if he'd taken on the job," she said. There was pride in her voice, a strength that came from deep within.

"Be your father," she said, and smiled.

He nodded, and kissed her very gently.

She was still smiling as he left the house and walked down the street. He was too far away to see when the tears began rolling down her cheeks and her smile faded away.

Alec was waiting at the corner for Drew. They hurried through the streets toward the docks. It was a brisk morning, with hoarfrost on the bushes and ice glazing the ground. Their breath puffed out in great clouds of steam.

They arrived at the East River dock where the *Alizé* was berthed, went aboard, and were shown their quarters—a tiny cabin amidships.

They were back on deck as the ship was getting under way. Sailors scampered up the ratlines, into the rigging, and out onto the slender spars. The lines were shipped, and as the sails were raised, they began to fill out and snap into place.

Drew suddenly noticed two small figures standing on the receding dock. He squinted his eyes to make sure he wasn't seeing things. The smaller of the two was Peter. The other was Beth. He smiled and waved his hand. The two figures waved back.

"I wish I was going with him," Peter said.

"So do I," Beth whispered. "So do I."

Out in midriver the tide and wind took the ship. It puffed out the sails, and the *Alizé* began to move purposefully through the water toward the distant twin hulks of the Narrows. They passed several patrolling frigates, but their ship carried the flag of France and was a neutral not to be disturbed.

Drew looked back at the skyline of New York. "Maybe the next time we see the old place, a different flag will be flying from the fort."

"Get me a good ship and I'll do my part," Alec said.

"The first one we get is yours," Drew said. "I promise."

Alec held out his hand. "It's a deal."

They clasped hands tightly for a long moment. The circumstances of the past year had brought them close to one another. Both felt richer for the experience.

After a turbulent, storm-wracked ocean crossing, the *Alizé* finally arrived at Le Havre. The usual way to get from the port city to Paris was to take a boat down the Seine, but both young men wanted a rest from boats. They were forced to spend two days in Le Havre before they could arrange passage on a coach.

Rather than fret about the delay, they explored the city, practicing their new mastery of French, learned during long daily lessons taught by the captain of the *Alizé*. They had become good friends with the seaman, and as he taught them the language, he also educated them about the people and the land.

Le Havre was a lively port, with ships coming from all parts of the world to tie up at the docks. Drew was accustomed to the polyglot of peoples to be seen on the New York docks, but it seemed that Le Havre boasted an even greater variety of human types. He saw tall, blond Scandinavians, intrepid seamen from the cold, northern climes. There were swarthy Turks and other traders from the Levantine, come to Le Havre with their gold, silver, and brilliant diamonds. Persians and Arabs, wearing great flowing robes, walked the streets and dealt in precious stones, Damascene swords, and beautiful carpets. There were Armenians, Egyptians, ebony-skinned men from the northern regions of Africa; Malays, Chinese, and turbaned Hindus from far-off India passed Greeks, Dutchmen, and sharp-eyed Catalans. The English came here, as did Germans, Austrians, Italians, Flemings, Netherlanders, and even an occasional visitor from Muscovy.

Le Havre made Drew aware of America's isolated geographic position. New York might be a great city, but it was far removed from the hub that was Europe. Now more than ever, he understood that America was an entity to herself and it was truly wrong that her people were forced to pay allegiance to a king who lived thousands of miles away, on the opposite side of a mighty ocean. Now more than ever, he was certain it was America's destiny to stand alone, a proud, independent nation where men could breathe free air and set the course of their own lives.

Drew and Alec helped themselves to liberal servings of the wide variety of food they found and washed it all down with copious amounts of good wine. For two robust young men who had been dining on the tasteless food served aboard a ship at sea, Le Havre was a treat.

The captain of the *Alizé* dined with them on the second night, and after dinner took them to a house without telling them what he had in mind. It turned out to be a brothel. Suddenly Le Havre was an even more wonderful treat.

The next morning they felt at once eager and satisfied as they boarded the coach and set off on a bouncing journey across the French countryside. A new snow had fallen, and the earth looked pristine. They passed through herds of sheep whose thick wool looked yellow against the perfect whiteness of the snow. Farmers walked along the roads tending these flocks, but Drew noticed that unlike their counterparts in America, they didn't wave at the coach. This was a far older and more settled land than America, and a passing coach didn't represent a momentous occasion.

They spent their first night at a roadside inn, and became celebrities when the other travelers discovered they had a pair of Americans in their midst. Drew's command of French got better with every hour, as he was forced to express more and more complex ideas. Alec, on the other hand, seemed content to know only enough to get by.

"The Indians, are they as savage as we've been told?" one Frenchman asked.

"Most of the ones who live near white people are fairly civilized."

"My mother's cousin," another man said, "once visited Quebec City. He said the Indians use axes to cut off the top of an enemy's head. Is this true?"

"It's called scalping," Drew admitted. "And yes, it has happened. Only last year, as a matter of fact. The English hired Indians to fight against us."

"They loose savages like that upon you!"

"Yes."

"Bah! The English are no better than pigs!" the Frenchman said, and reeled off a sizable vocabulary of curses that had not been a part of Drew's French education.

"Would you mind repeating those words?" Alec asked. "I want to make sure I get them straight." And for the next twenty minutes, Drew and Alec were treated to a complete course in very basic French.

But there was also a serious side to these conversations, and Drew and Alec made converts of a good many of the French. That most Frenchmen hated the English simply because they *were* English made the task considerably easier.

* * *

They continued their journey in the morning and were fascinated by the neat, manicured countryside, so unlike the wilder land that was their own home. They traveled for two more days, endured a final change of coaches, and arrived at the outskirts of Paris. Because they were Americans and therefore oddities, the driver of the coach went out of his way in order to deliver them to their final destination.

Bejamin Franklin had established his residence in Passy, near the Seine, in a separate wing of the Hôtel de Valentinois, owned by his friend and admirer Ray de Chaumont. He thought it better to live apart from the ostentation of Versailles, even though it was to that vast complex of palaces that his duties took him.

When Franklin heard of the two new arrivals from America, he hurried out to greet them. He was dressed in dazzling white linen and a brown Quaker coat that had a definite colonial cut. No Frenchman wore anything like it, and he wore it as a badge of his identity whenever he ventured out of his house. Since Franklin's reputation in France was greater than that of any other American, including George Washington, a ripple of recognition would both precede and follow him whenever he walked through the streets. Men smiled at him and doffed their caps, and women curtsied.

It was for this very reason that Congress had sent him to Paris not long after the outbreak of hostilities in America. If anyone had a chance of winning the French to the American cause, it was the gentleman from Philadelphia.

Now he came walking from the hotel to the paved brick courtyard. The Americans exchanged greetings, and Franklin inspected the papers authorizing Drew's commission.

"Big job for a young man," he said. "How'd they pick you?"

Drew explained his connection with David Sackett, and how the congressman from New York had been asked to select a man for the job.

"Ah, yes, I know your uncle," Franklin said. "Admirable man, Sackett, admirable. So you got your job through influence, did you?"

It was a challenge, and Drew knew it. "I got the job because the Congress thinks I can do it," he said evenly, remembering what his father had said about standing up to the old gentleman.

"Can you?"

"Yes."

Franklin broke into a big smile. "Come inside, the both of

you, and tell me all the news from America," he said, and placed his arm around Drew's waist.

Ben Franklin's parlor was obviously used more as a workroom than a place of entertainment. Piles of books and papers were scattered everywhere. He pushed aside a stack of documents, found a tray with glasses and a bottle of wine, and poured a libation for himself and his guests.

"Tell me of the war," Franklin said. "But only *good* news."

"We defeated Burgoyne's army at Saratoga," Drew said. "A total victory."

Alec's eyebrows lifted at this. The last they had heard was the American army under Gates was moving to attack Burgoyne. He and Drew had sailed before the outcome of the battle was known. Drew was conveniently inventing the victory.

"What?" Franklin exclaimed, scarcely able to believe his ears. "You mean Gates has beaten Burgoyne? Beaten the entire British force?"

"Easily," Drew said.

Franklin's joy was contagious. He happily explained the French policy had been one of appearing to remain aloof, while secretly supplying and arming the Americans. This was done to pacify the English and prevent a war with them. It was Franklin's contention that the longer the American war dragged on, the deeper the French would be drawn into the conflict. Now that the Americans had won a great victory, it might be possible to press the French to sign a treaty with the new nation.

"So you can see what your news means, my boy," Franklin said. "Tomorrow we go to Versailles to see the foreign minister. De Vergennes is really on our side, although he pretends to be neutral. I don't know how he'll be able to overlook *this* bit of news."

Later on, while Franklin was busy informing others of the great American victory, Alec took Drew aside. "Why did you lie to him about Saratoga?"

"We've got to have reasons for the French to give us ships."

"But what if Burgoyne actually won that battle?"

"It didn't sound like he was going to."

"But what if he did?"

"What if the earth opened up under your feet and you dropped a hundred miles?"

The next morning after breakfast, Drew and Franklin drove to Versailles in a large enclosed carriage pulled by four horses.

"I've already sent word that I have some good news—I didn't tell them what," Franklin said. "They'll be waiting for us with open arms."

Drew almost told the old gentleman the truth, then decided he would do it later. Maybe the French would make some commitments they couldn't take back. At any rate, Ben was so pleased it seemed a shame to spoil his day.

"Look at this," Franklin said with a trace of anger as he took a piece of folded paper from his inside pocket. "It's from that pompous ass Stormont."

"Who's he?"

"The British ambassador to France."

Drew took the note, unfolded it, and read.

> The King's Ambassador receives no application from rebels, unless they come to implore His Majesty's mercy.
>
> Stormont

"That's the response I got back to a note of mine suggesting we exchange prisoners," Franklin said in disgust. "The bastard refuses even to see me." Then he chuckled. "I'd love to see his face when de Vergennes tells him about Saratoga—and he *will* tell him, because the foreign minister despises Stormont almost as much as I do."

"De Vergennes sounds like our friend at court," Drew said.

"He's been a big help," Franklin admitted. "Let me tell you about one way. Have you ever heard of a firm known as Roderique Hortalez et Cie.?"

"No. Should I have?"

"Not many people know of it, but they've already helped us with guns and supplies worth over a hundred thousand pounds. And they haven't made a penny in profit. *Lost* money, in fact."

"How do they stay in business?"

Franklin laughed. "Roderique Hortalez et Cie. is a front for the French government. It's the brainchild of a very strange fellow named Caron de Beaumarchais. A wild man, this Beaumarchais, but a solid supporter of our cause. The government allows him to buy weapons from their arsenals, and he ships them across the ocean to us. De Vergennes himself supplies Beaumarchais with the money to finance the whole operation."

Drew's head was spinning. Business could be pretty complicated over here. "And the British know nothing about all this?" he asked.

"Oh, they know about it, but since the French government has no *official* connection with it, they do nothing about it. The British are pains in the ass, but they're also sticklers about protocol."

Franklin went on to inform Drew about the goings-on at the court of Louis XVI. The young king was only twenty-two years old, with a rather narrow view of the world; he preferred spending his days as a locksmith to attending affairs of state. His strong-willed but uninformed wife, Marie Antoinette, didn't help matters. All she cared about were balls and parties and dances and her affairs, including one with the king's younger brother.

"The king had two good ministers," Franklin said. "Malesherbes and Turgot. The first resigned last year, and the second was driven from office by the noblemen who didn't like the reforms he was sponsoring. Like our tyrant George III, these men like things the way they are—everything for the ruling class and nothing for anyone else.

"The only reason we have French support is that these nobles believe our war is weakening the British Empire. As long as Britain is at war with us, the French think it helps their own cause."

"Who cares about their reasons," Drew said, "as long as they continue to help us!"

"Ah, spoken like a true diplomat," Franklin said, his eyes twinkling. "You're going to get along here just fine."

"I hope so."

"You must meet Beaumarchais. One of the more interesting characters in our little drama. Which is not surprising, since he is a dramatist himself. I don't suppose you've heard of a play called *The Barber of Seville?* No? I guess this sort of news doesn't get back to America. Who has time to go to plays? Anyway, Beaumarchais is the author of the comedy. He's also a watchmaker, a philosopher, a wine connoisseur, and a master of disguises. My kind of man," Franklin added warmly.

"Will we see the king today?"

"I doubt it. The foreign minister is the one we deal with. Louis spends his days with his locks, or hunting. You'll get to meet him one of these days. Just smile and agree with anything he says, because five minutes later he won't remember a word of the conversation."

"Why is it," Drew asked, genuinely puzzled, "that the kings of the world seem among the most stupid of men?"

"Ah, my boy, that's because a king has one of the few jobs in the world a man can get without accomplishing anything. It simply depends on how clever he was in picking his parents."

"I see what you mean," Drew said. "I wasn't clever enough to figure that out when I was being born."

"And a good thing for you," Franklin said, wagging his finger. "The way the French court is arranged, it's almost impossible for the king to be anything but an idle buffoon. A man needs challenges to help him expand his mind. The biggest challenge Louis faces is which gold spoon to use on his morning egg."

Drew's attention was half on the streets of Paris as the carriage made its way to Versailles. They were filled with life, and the many stone buildings contrasted to New York, a city of wood. The streets were dirtier than New York's, but the Parisians seemed content to ignore the offal and refuse at their feet. It was also a common custom to pitch garbage out windows, and this practice didn't make negotiating the streets any more pleasant for pedestrians.

The carriage passed through the narrow streets into more open land, following a broad avenue that would take them to Versailles.

They finally came to the seat of the French government. The carriage passed the Place d'Armes, went through a gilded iron gate and a stone balustrade—and then Drew saw it.

He was stunned, and barely heard Franklin's words as he pointed out highlights of the miracle that was Versailles.

There were heroic statues all about, the most colossal being one of Louis XIV on horseback. To the right and left stretched the long wings of the palace. Beyond extended the Royal Court, and beyond that the smaller Marble Court. To the north, south, and west stretched the central buildings. Beyond were the stupendous gardens that were a true wonder of the world. The Grand Canal was two hundred feet wide and a mile long, and it ran as straight as an arrow. There was the Orangery, with its central gallery alone containing over twelve hundred orange trees, in addition to three hundred other varieties.

The elegance and opulence of the French court crashed into Drew's senses. The manicured gardens lay under a thin blanket of snow, but even so, it was possible to appreciate the Herculean effort needed to keep them as beautiful as they were.

The scale of everything amazed him. These edifices rendered puny by comparison every other building he had seen. Versailles was made on a plan for giants.

The carriage went to a vast palace and stopped in front of a pair of immense doors. The guards' uniforms glittered in the sun. An officer recognized Ben Franklin and saluted.

The old gentleman seemed quite at home in these grandiose surroundings, and, waving aside a liveried would-be escort, led the way into the sprawling palace. Drew was almost afraid to put his boots down on the shining marble floors. The ceilings were high, the walls hung with paintings and tapestries. Hundreds of candles burned in crystal chandeliers, even though it was daytime, and grandly dressed men and women swept up and down the halls, chatting, laughing, and taking all the magnificence for granted.

Franklin led the way through a bewildering series of corridors and rooms, until Drew was hopelessly lost. Even in his wildest dreams, he had never thought to set foot inside such a building. Everything gleamed, and reflected light from the candles and from the sun streaming through the tall windows. Some had stained-glass sections, and the light that came through these made beautiful patterns of color on the floors.

They finally arrived at the place Franklin had been seeking. Entering a high-ceilinged antechamber, he was effusively greeted by a bewigged secretary. The man then scurried into an inner room, and returned almost instantly with news that the foreign minister would be delighted to see the honorable gentlemen from America.

The comte de Vergennes was an impressive man, with a high forehead and intelligent eyes. He was pleasant, but somewhat distant as Franklin introduced Drew and told of the young man's mission to secure privateers to set against the English fleets. Saving the best for last, Franklin finally told the foreign minister the news of Saratoga. Now de Vergennes was far less distant. He grasped Franklin's hand.

"But Mr. Franklin, how marvelous!"

"Yes, we think so."

"They must be shedding many tears in London," the count said with relish.

"Not half as many as they will before we're through with them," Franklin promised.

"Such a great victory!" the count said. "And over one of their greatest generals."

"Now don't you think this might bring about a change in our... ah, arrangements?"

"Sir?"

"Formal recognition of our country *as* a country. And with France as our ally," Franklin said, being blunt as he pushed for the most important goal of his mission to France.

"I believe you have a stronger case than before, Mr. Franklin. I shall bring it up at the meeting of ministers."

"Will you champion us?"

"We shall see, we shall see," the count purred. He had been a diplomat for many years, and was adept at handling petitioners.

The minister's secretary entered and informed them the king had heard of Mr. Franklin's arrival and desired to see him.

"Come along, my boy," Franklin said to Drew. "I hadn't supposed you'd meet the king so soon, but now's as good a time as any."

The foreign minister led the way this time, down another confusing series of corridors. Drew's eyes widened even more, because, if possible, the splendor of the palace increased by degrees as they came closer to the royal apartments. Louis XVI, King of France, ruler of millions of people, one of the richest men in the world, received his visitors in a workshop off his bedroom. Incongruous as it seemed, the king had outfitted the entire room as a carpentry workshop—even to the point of covering the beautifully painted wall panels with rough-hewn planking. Only the hand-painted ceiling hinted at how the room had looked before His Majesty had his way with it.

"Ah, Franklin," the young king said. "How timely of you to stop by. We wanted to ask your opinion about something that puzzles us."

Franklin bowed. "Your Majesty, it gives me great pleasure to introduce my countryman, Andrew de Kuyper. He is... *brave comme votre épée, plein de courage, et de zèle pour notre cause*... and he brings news of a great American victory."

The king looked at Drew. "Do you know anything about locks?"

"No, sir, not very much."

The king's brow contracted into furrows. "Not many people do, it's a shame. Now look at this," he said to Franklin, holding up a complicated-looking brass lock. "The locking mechanism should slide easily at this point, but the bolt keeps sticking. Can you help us figure out what's wrong?"

Franklin took the lock from the king and carried it over to the window in order to have better light. He jiggled the bolt back and forth for a few moments, then held it open for the king to see. "Look at that pin down there, that's the problem. It has to be driven in tighter so this part of the bolt has a clear path to the end of the shaft."

Louis peered inside the contraption, and then a big smile lit his face. "Yes, we see! How stupid we were! That little pin is causing the trouble. How can we ever thank you, Franklin?"

Franklin smiled back. "By assuring me of France's continuing support of the new American nation."

"We enjoy being your friend."

"Perhaps Your Majesty would be interested in knowing about the great American victory," Count de Vergennes said. "They wiped out the entire army of the English general Burgoyne."

"Really?" the king said, showing a mild interest. "An entire army, think of it."

"Yes, Your Majesty," Franklin said, quickly taking advantage of the opening. "And I also think it means it is time for France to formally recognize our country."

The king cocked his head to the side and looked at Franklin the way a sparrow might eye a bit of seed. "That could make trouble for us with the English. What do you think, Vergennes?"

"I believe that America will win her independence with or without us, Your Majesty."

The king's eyes brightened. "Yes, we see, and if they can win without us, why should we bother causing trouble with England when it isn't necessary?"

Drew was impressed. Beneath all the silliness, the king had the ability to reason.

"Perhaps this is so, Your Majesty," Franklin said smoothly. "But when we finally throw off the British yoke, we will gratefully remember those who helped us most in our time of need."

His barb was directed at the foreign minister, and it found its target. It was a tenet of Vergennes's policy to regard a strong, independent America as a first-line defense against British aggression. If France openly helped America and she won, France would have made a grateful ally. If she did not help and the Americans still won, who could tell what would happen? Therefore, in the light of America's latest victory, it might well seem prudent to please the Americans, and to hell with what the British thought.

De Vergennes said as much, but by this time the king was back at his workbench, attempting to fix the errant pin in the brass lock. He had no more time for international affairs.

The group took its leave and retired from the royal chambers.

"They're going to recognize us and sign a treaty," Franklin said to Drew as they drove back to Passy. "I've learned to read their minds. Your news of the victory at Saratoga was what did it. That made all the difference."

Drew coughed. "Yes, sir, about that, you see..."

"Wonderful timing, de Kuyper, wonderful timing!"

"Yes, I guess, but..." Drew stammered, trying to screw up his courage.

"You've given me one of the happiest days of my life, my boy. What do you say to that?"

Drew was miserable. How could he tell Franklin the truth? "That's wonderful, sir," he said, hunching down in his seat, feeling like a traitor.

Drew could understand why Ben Franklin approved of Caron de Beaumarchais. The man had a mind almost as restless and far-ranging as Franklin's own.

"This one is a beauty," the Frenchman said, pointing to the dark hull of a three-masted brigantine at the dock in Le Havre. At Franklin's urging, he was helping the Americans pick out the ships to be used as privateers.

Drew and Alec slowly let their eyes wander over the ship, approving of her raked-back masts and sharply angled bow. She was a ship built for speed.

"Would you care to inspect her now?" Beaumarchais asked. "Or would you rather wait until after we've had lunch?"

Drew was becoming accustomed to the French obsession with food. No matter what business needed attending, when it came time for lunch, everything stopped while the French dined.

"I'd like to see the ship," Alec said.

Beaumarchais slipped a gold-encased watch from his vest pocket. "Mmm, we don't have much time before lunch. Why not wait until after? Then we can do a proper inspection."

Drew knew that if they tried to inspect the ship now, the Frenchman would be hurrying them through. It would be just as well to wait. "We'll eat," he said, and the relief his host felt was evident.

They went to a cozy tavern where Beaumarchais was well known. Over a delicious lunch of vegetable soup and a dish of braised veal and potatoes cooked in cream, accompanied by hard, crusty bread and a superb wine, they discussed many things—the war, the problems of starting a new country, what made good theater, how inventors worked, and why French bakers made the best bread in the world. Alec said almost nothing. Drew commented a few times, but it was the Frenchman who carried the conversation, jumping from topic to topic with barely a pause for breath, as happy discussing the various vegetables in the soup as he was theorizing over which form of government was the most durable.

"It's only a matter of time before we have a revolution in this country too," he said. "The conditions in the countryside are most intolerable. Rich landlords take all the profit from the peasantry, usually not leaving them enough to live decently. So the peasants leave the land and drift into the cities. But what do the cities have for them? Nothing but more poverty and pain."

"The countryside I've passed through looks very beautiful," Drew protested. "And I saw many cultivated fields. Surely France produces food in quantity."

Beaumarchais waved Drew's observations aside. "You've been only on main roads leading from one city to another. Go into the back country if you want to see what's really happening. Don't you think this veal is delicious?" This last remark was directed toward Alec.

"Umn."

"You don't get this kind of cooking in America, I'll wager."

"Well, I don't know if—" Drew began.

"Most people eat to live, but we French live to eat," Beaumarchais resumed. "Now tell me, after you win the war, how does your Congress plan to divide the lands belonging to men who remained loyal to the British king? But before you answer that question, how much does this land amount to?"

And so the conversation went, until finally they returned to the ship. When they agreed it was a worthy vessel, Beaumarchais promised he would come up with the necessary funds. In the meantime Drew and Alec could proceed with the selection of a crew.

The next ship they bought was the *Alizé*, the very one that had brought Drew and Alec to France. Alec decided this was the ship he wanted for himself. The names of all the ships were changed. The *Alizé* became the *Freedom*. The other two ships they received were renamed the *Liberty* and the *Avenger*. Alec stayed in Le Havre to prepare the ships, and Drew went back to Paris.

His arrival coincided with news that came as a great relief to him. That morning a man had arrived from America reporting a great victory at Saratoga, and the capture of General Burgoyne.

"I've known about it for over two weeks," Franklin told the mystified man. "Next time bring fresh news."

It was drawing close to Christmas, and he was working night and day to get the French to sign a treaty. Things were looking very good, he informed Drew, and it would only be a matter of weeks. "They'll sign, you wait and see."

Drew knew the treaty would have one important effect as far as he was concerned. With France pretending to be a neutral, her ports were supposedly closed to foreign combatants. That meant—in theory, at least—that American privateers could not use French ports for supplies or repairs. With a signed treaty, however, the ports would be open to American ships. Drew would have less trouble supplying his privateers.

On Christmas Eve, Beaumarchais arrived with a carriageful of presents from Versailles. Franklin received a gold watch, a silver-headed walking stick, two cases of wine, a scarf, and a pile of books.

"Just what you need," Beaumarchais said blithely. "I picked these books out especially for you. Here's one by Christian Huygens—in Dutch of course, but you'll have no trouble understanding the language."

"No, none at all," the old gentleman dryly replied.

Even Drew received a present from the king—a fur coat. "See," Beaumarchais said with glee, "you must have made a good impression on him."

Count de Vergennes sent a beautiful scroll that conferred upon Drew an honorary commission as a lieutenant in the French army. This gift elated Beaumarchais.

"Ah, don't you see what this means?"

"He's being friendly."

"More than that," the Frenchman said. "It means solidarity in arms. The minister is saying that even as he calls you into the service of France, you will soon be permitted to call the arms of France into *your* service."

"We'll celebrate when the foreign minister puts that in writing," Franklin said blandly.

New Year's Eve, 1777...

The last day of the year had arrived. The passing of the old year meant many different things to different people. Nor did everyone look to the coming year with similar hopes and expectations.

Peter, now almost nine years old, loved the outdoors. He spent the day in the woods north of the village of Greenwich with Beth. Beth was soon to be seventeen, an age when most young ladies of New York had long given up such pastimes as tracking rabbits through snowy woods.

With Drew's departure a void had opened up in the boy's life. He needed someone to look up to and admire—and found Beth, who was living in the same house as he.

For her part, Beth enjoyed the woods and was happy to teach Peter all the tricks she had learned. It was important to walk without making a sound; it was important to know where the wind was coming from so a hunter could remain downwind; and one had to know the places where rabbits were likely to be found. All this and more she imparted to the boy as they snowshoed across the countryside.

Peter was an avid student, and much more interested in the woods than in studying the books his grandmother made him read.

"Tracks," he whispered as his sharp eyes detected a set of markings on the curve of a sloping hill.

"Squirrel," Beth said. "We want rabbit."

"How can you tell the difference?" he asked.

She knelt down, and with her fingers traced a set of markings in the snow. "These are squirrel. See how they resemble the real ones you found?"

The boy compared the tracks and nodded.

"These are rabbit tracks," she said as she scratched a new set of marks in the snow. "The squirrel jumps like this"—she gestured—"but the rabbit bounds. See how the toes make different shapes."

Peter studied the markings and memorized them. "I know them now," he said.

They continued through the woods, finally coming across the trail of a rabbit. They followed in silence.

Beth spent a lot of time thinking about Drew—Andrew, as she always referred to him even in her thoughts. He had only been gone a few months, but to her it seemed like years. She had yet to get a letter from him. That didn't bother her, because she knew it often took the better part of six months for communications to reach from one side of the ocean to the other. She wondered about his life in France...his friends...the women he met.

The two hunters were moving around an outcropping of rocks. They came to a clearing that in the summer would be a grassy glade. Now it was a flat bit of snow-covered land. She stopped, and Peter stopped at the same moment.

There, in the center of the clearing, was a fine, plump rabbit. Beth nodded her head almost imperceptibly, and they moved as one body as they circled closer to the animal. Quietly they moved to within forty feet, and stopped again. The rabbit had seen them and was watching warily, but so far they had made no threatening movements, so he held his ground.

Beth indicated it was the boy's rabbit, and he slowly fitted an arrow into his bowstring. Taking a deep breath the way Beth had taught him, he drew the bowstring back, sighted slightly above the target to allow for droppage, and paused for a moment. The trick now was to hold the bow steady and slip his fingers off the string without shifting the direction of the flight of the arrow.

Just as he released the arrow, a bird in a nearby tree squawked. The noise startled the rabbit, and he bounded forward. The arrow flew true and sliced into the snow at the exact spot where the rabbit had been. Too late: the animal was gone, leaping through the woods in a swift, zigzagging pattern.

Peter shook his head. "I thought I had that one."

"You did," Beth replied. "But a hunter sometimes needs good luck as well as a good eye."

They resumed their hunt, and for them it was a fine way to spend the day of New Year's Eve.

On this day Marie Therese sat at the table near the fire in the kitchen of her house on Maiden Lane. She was writing a letter to her son. She paused for a moment to allow her cramped fingers to relax. Not too many years ago she could have written far longer before the stiffness set in. Old age gets all of us, she thought to herself. She reread parts of the letter.

> ... We have had the same problems this winter as last. Not enough of anything. But I shouldn't complain, because we're really better off than most people in the city. The British have cut down the remaining trees on Wall Street, and I hate to walk there because it looks so barren. Your own Grandfather James planted some of those trees, and now they're gone. A shame....
>
> Peter misses you. He looked up to you and tried to do what he thought you would approve of. I think he needs a man to guide him. Celine and Beth love Peter and spend time with him, but they're women and a boy needs the love of a man too. Sometimes I almost wish you had taken him with you. He might be better off outside New York anyway.
>
> I don't like to write bad news, but I've always been honest with you, and I can't honestly say your father is getting better. He spends many days in bed now. Then all of a sudden, he'll feel better, and even goes for walks. But then he usually suffers a relapse.
>
> At least he doesn't have to worry about business. David has taken over and is doing as well as can be expected during these trying times....

Marie Therese's fingers felt less stiff, so she picked up the pen again. She debated writing about Beth. Celine had told her the girl was in love with her son—and that her son was hardly aware of Beth's existence.

She didn't plan on interfering, but the thought of her son and Beth was an attractive one. She remembered the first time she had met Beth's mother. Louise Clément had been a serving girl at her father's tavern in Nova Scotia. She was half Indian, and a beauty. She had married Theo Henry, moved to New York, and spent her life ignoring the small-minded people who sneered at her because she was a half-breed. Louise had taken it all in stride. No doubt her daughter had inherited this strength. She would make someone a fine wife. Her own son? ... If he was lucky, she decided.

Primus came over and set a cup of tea on the table next to her letter. "Time to warm up your insides," he said.

"My insides, yes," she said, and sighed. "But Primus, I'm getting so old nothing can warm up these fingers."

The black man chuckled. "I'm lucky that way. Never did learn to write."

"Come have some tea with me."

The man got himself a cup and sat down on the other side of the table. "Writing to Drew?" he asked.

"Uh-huh. I wish I could send him only good news, but it seems we have a great deal of the other kind."

"When we get old, maybe that's the only kind we can see," Primus said thoughtfully. "You take little Peter, he seems happy most of the time. Maybe we can get him to write to Drew. Let him tell him what he thinks."

Marie Therese appreciated the black man's insight. "Maybe you're right. Two old fogies like ourselves shouldn't be telling young people our view of the world."

"Two old fogies," Primus chuckled again. "Yes, indeed, that's sure what we are, two old fogies."

Marie Therese laughed. "Things aren't all that bad when you can admit the truth to yourself."

Not far away, at the Provost building, Captain Blakely walked back from Colonel Cunningham's office to his own. He had just received more bad news. And on the last day of the year. Was this prophetic?

The supplies promised by London were being delivered at half the expected rate. This meant shortages. It was hard enough to keep order as it was, and shortages could only result in an angrier populace.

As if this wasn't enough, two more ships had arrived with troops. That meant another six hundred soldiers with not much to do until the following spring. In the meantime they must be housed and fed, and given firewood to keep them alive.

Firewood had become a hated word to the captain. It was in desperate need and very short supply. Recently he had sent gangs of men to chop down trees on Staten Island. It was slow going. Freezing weather made the task difficult. And then there was the problem of carting the logs aboard ships back to Manhatan. The whole thing took time, and the supply of wood never met the demand.

When the captain returned to his office, he found a report waiting on his desk. It told him that a prisoner named Robert Delafield was still alive and confined aboard the *Devon*. The report marked the man as a troublemaker.

The captain's interest in Robert was not prompted by humanitarian instincts; quite the opposite. He was aware that Mary Delafield was to have his child. As long as her husband was alive, there was a possibility that he would some day come looking for revenge.

The solution to the problem was simple: another death aboard a prison ship would be unremarkable. But the captain was in no hurry to have Robert killed. With conditions the way they were, there was a good chance the man would die anyway.

Mary Delafield, he thought, and his face relaxed as he remembered the moments they had shared together. He would have liked to see her again; he would have liked to help comfort her about the prospect of having their child.

But that bitchy Celine Murray had come to his office and told him Mary was going far away to have the baby. Where was 'far away'?

One thing he knew for sure—she wasn't in the city. His spies had told him that much. But knowing she was out of the city was hardly a help, because America was a vast land. He didn't know where to start looking.

He thought about Mary and the child and wondered whether it would be a boy or a girl. What name would Mary give the infant? What would it look like when it was a year old? Two years? Ten?

For the moment the captain ceased to be the deputy provost marshal of the city of New York. For the moment he was only a man worrying about a woman and her child.

Farther south, toward the tip of New York, Celine spent a quiet evening at 1 Broad Way with a small group of people, guests of General Howe. This New Year's Eve made a stark contrast with the previous one. Last year there had been a great ball, a feeling of imminent victory among the Englishmen, and a gala celebration of the general's appointment to the Royal Order of the Bath.

This group was more subdued.

Celine almost hated herself for coming. She was living a lie. Her sentiments were with Franz von Lossow and the rebels, and with her brother, who was working for them in faraway France. But she had come, because there was still a masquerade of friendship with the British.

"You are the most beautiful woman in the room," the general said to her when she arrived. "As ever."

She was dressed in a pale green gown with a revealing

neckline, but because even the general conserved on firewood, she wore a fringed woolen wrap about her shoulders. "A smaller party this year," she observed, looking around the room and quickly estimating the number of guests.

"We have less to celebrate, my dear. In fact, less than nothing."

She took a glass of wine. "The course of the war displeases you?"

"Our losses almost equal my frustration."

"But you're only up against a—and this is an expression I've heard your own officers use—a rabble in arms."

The general smiled. It was something he did very little of these days. "They are hardly that. Any armed force that can defeat Burgoyne and six thousand British troops can no longer be referred to as a rabble. They are an army, and one well suited to this country."

"You sound pessimistic."

"Celine, can I tell you something in confidence?" he said, lowering his voice almost to a whisper.

She nodded.

"I've asked to be relieved of my command. I expect I'll be called back to England soon."

Celine was surprised. "Things are that bad?"

"I've never approved of this war," he said. "It looks like it's going to drag on, and I don't want any part of it."

"What do they think about this in London?"

"I've been having a tiff with London for years. This is just more fuel for the fire," the general said. He took her hand in his. "I will miss you."

"I'll miss you, too," she said automatically.

He shook his head sadly. "You and I had our moment, and it passed. Perhaps if I were a wiser man I would have pursued it, but I did not. I sometimes think it was the greatest mistake of my life."

"We'll never know, will we?"

"No," he said sadly. "No, my dear, we shall never know."

A little while later she studied him from a distance as he played the part of a charming host with his guests. He was a handsome man, she thought, a man of feeling and tenderness. When he had been the great general, the conquering hero, she had played a deadly game with him as an equal. Now he was unhappy—an idealist defeated by his own ideals—no longer the conquering hero. She felt an impulse to go to him, comfort him, hold him in her arms, be a woman for him again.

It couldn't happen, she realized. Nor did she really want it to; the thought was enough.

General Howe with problems was a much more sympathetic character than General Howe without them. She wondered if she would ever see him once he'd returned to England. And at that moment she found herself not really caring. She realized how much Franz von Lossow had brought to her life, and how much he meant to her; there was no room in her heart for any other man.

At any rate, she was pleased she had come to this party. She had picked up an interesting bit of news to pass on to the rebels. Wouldn't Washington be pleased to hear it!

The highest-ranking British general in America had just admitted he no longer had the stomach for this war—and that the Americans could probably win.

David Sackett was enjoying a quiet little gathering at his home. Besides his children, there were Alice and Elly de Witt, and Caleb North. A fire blazed in the kitchen hearth, and everyone was gathered near it, drinking heated mulled wine and enjoying the aroma emanating from the plump goose cooking in a large pan.

Jenny Sackett was basting the goose, and little Elly stood at her side, watching with great interest as the hot drippings were spread over the top of the bird.

"Why do you do that?" she asked.

"To make the skin crisper," Jenny said.

The girl nodded. "So it goes crunch when I bite it."

"Yes, so it goes crunch," Jenny said. "Do you think you can eat your share of the goose? It's almost as big as you are."

"But not nearly as pretty," said David, who had been listening to the exchange between the little girl and his daughter.

Elly was very serious as she studied the goose. "I think he's very pretty. And I'll eat my share, because that makes my mommy happy."

Alice was seated near by, between David and Caleb North. She was wearing a trim-fitting blue dress with sleeves that came down to the tops of her wrists and a neckline that reached to her throat. Her cheeks were full, and rosy now from having been out walking with Elly in the crisp air.

Caleb was telling her about business at the Swan & Bear.

"It's not as good as it used to be, but I get by. At least my customers are American. The British have their own favorite taverns."

"It's almost like there are two New Yorks," Alice said. "We have ours and the British have theirs."

"David was telling me that he made you a clerk at his office," Caleb said. "Isn't that unusual?"

"A woman clerk? Certainly it's unusual. I must be the only one in the city," Alice said with a shy pride.

It had happened recently. At first Alice had cleaned the de Kuyper offices. One day she looked at a column of figures and told David they were wrong. He checked the arithmetic and found she was correct. He gave her a little series of tests, and she scored so well he promoted her on the spot.

David was seated at her left. He leaned forward and spoke to Caleb. "She's as good with figures as any man," he said.

Alice blushed. "I like to work with numbers."

"How would you like to keep the records for the Swan & Bear?" Caleb asked. "I never get my books to come out even."

"Would you really want me to do that?"

"If you have some spare time," Caleb said. "After all, I don't want to be stealing you away from David."

"You could work for Caleb on Fridays, Alice, if you like," David said, willing to accommodate his old friend.

"I'll do it—if you really mean it," Alice said.

"Really mean it?" Caleb said happily. "Of course I mean it!"

"All right then," Alice agreed. "I'll start next Friday."

Jemmy made another pitcher of mulled wine and refilled all the glasses. He proposed a toast. "To George Washington!" There was enthusiastic approval all about the fireside.

As the food was brought to the table, David was standing next to Caleb. They had known each other for years, and ever since Caleb's wife had died, several years before, David had more or less adopted his friend into the family at holiday times.

"Alice is a handsome woman," Caleb said as he watched her help Jenny carry the goose to the table.

"She's also very surprising," David said. "She's changed a great deal, has much more confidence in herself."

"Breaking away from Enoch is what's caused it."

"He's the skeleton in our family closet," David said with resignation. "But one can never choose one's relatives."

"He treated her very badly."

"Yes. But then he treats himself badly," David said.

"I'd know how to treat a woman like that," Caleb said thoughtfully.

"Let's eat!" Jemmy said, surveying the table.

"Let's eat!" little Elly parroted.

They sat down to a bountiful meal. It wasn't often that New Yorkers ate as well as this. Alice became aware that Caleb was watching her whenever he thought he wasn't being observed. At first it made her uncomfortable, but after a while she rather liked the idea.

Farther up on the island, two men sat before the kitchen fireplace at the Place. John Holt and Sisyphus were lamenting that they were not practicing their trade as printers.

"If only I had a press," Holt said. "We could put out tracts that would sizzle the Englishmen's skin."

"The smell of ink gets in your blood," Sisyphus agreed.

Holt nodded. "And you can never get rid of it."

They were drinking a combination of heated rum and beer. Both men had moved to Celine's home because it was a good place to hide from the British. They were charged to be caretakers of the stolen supplies that still arrived regularly at the Place. The pirates and smugglers had continued to operate after Alec Seixas had gone to France, and the Place had become a secret storehouse for George Washington.

"Here we are, two printers," Holt said sadly, contemplating the powerful drink in his hand. "And all we are, really, are a pair of storekeepers. It's important work for now, I guess. But a printer has to be printing, or else he's not happy."

Something started to click in Sisyphus's mind. His physical appearance had changed drastically since his days on Hanover Square. His hair was trimmed, his face shaven. He no longer looked like a vagrant. And he had gained weight, because he was eating his fill these days. Indeed, sitting as he was on top of a mountain of stolen goods, he was eating better than most people on the island of Manhatan.

"I remember something you told me once," he said.

"Yes?"

"That young de Kuyper said there was a press hidden somewhere in the city."

"Yes," Holt said. "But he's in France, and who knows where it's hidden?"

"We can find out. We'll start with his sister."

"She won't know where it is."

"But she can put us in touch with other men, and eventually we might find someone who knows."

Holt nodded. It wasn't the best of plans, but *any* plan that would get him a printing press was better than nothing. "We'll send word to Mrs. Murray tomorrow," he agreed.

"And we'll be printers again," Sisyphus said.

"Printers again!" Holt toasted his companion and himself, and took another long drink of the potent beverage.

Within the hour, both had had so much to drink that they fell happily asleep, dreaming of their new press.

George Washington, at Valley Forge, sat in his headquarters building, warming himself before a small fire. For dinner the general enjoyed a half-gill of rice and a tablespoon of vinegar. He had managed to get a bottle of wine, but it tasted somewhat sour. He refused to accept any food that was better than that shared by the poorest of his soldiers.

He was reviewing the past year—not as good as he had hoped, but not as bad as, at times, he had expected. And now there was the cold, cold winter to get through before the new campaign could begin in the spring; now there was nothing to do but build the army's strength and improve its training.

He considered himself fortunate to have obtained the services of a number of experienced military men from Europe. Baron von Steuben had been an especially valuable addition. The baron had become the army's drillmaster. He taught the men to fire in volley, to load and shoot as a team, to hold ranks when necessary. The Prussian joked about it and had told Washington the men were "learning to like his plate of sauerkraut."

Other foreign officers had joined Washington. Some, such as Pulaski, Kosciuszko, de Kalb, and Lafayette, had proven very valuable. They brought something sorely needed in the American army—discipline. These Europeans were appalled at the casual relations that existed between American officers and the men under their command. The Americans, in turn, sneered at the Europeans for their stiffness.

Washington sighed. If only he could get these two groups to meet somewhere in the middle! *Then* he would have an army.

The general's aide, Alexander Hamilton, came in and warmed his hands by the fire.

"You want some wine, Alex?" the general asked.

Hamilton took the glass and sipped it. "Not bad," he said.

"Not bad, around here, means it won't kill you," the general said.

"Von Steuben wants more bayonets," Hamilton said.

"We'll ask Congress for a supply, although I don't know how much good that will do. They sent me a trunk of money to pay the troops today."

"Continental money?"

"What else?"

"That stuff isn't worth the paper it's printed on," Hamilton complained. "But we'll get by."

The general nodded. It was almost a miracle, but despite the losses of last summer and fall; despite the bitterness of the present winter; despite everything, the men were in better spirits than ever before. There had developed a general feeling, almost a euphoria, that the Americans would eventually win the war.

"Have some more wine," Washington said, as he pulled his little dish of rice closer. "It helps wash down this elegant supper."

Less than a hundred yards from the general, three men sat around a small fire, cooking their own supper. It was, in fact, a better meal than the one being consumed by Washington. In addition to rice, they were enjoying a bit of freshly roasted deer meat. The aroma of their feast drifted through the air, causing their nearby comrades to have visions of themselves committing mayhem. Seth Cuyler, Dick Goelet, and Franz von Lossow blithely ignored all the dirty looks they received. The meal was worth every one of them.

"Where did you get the meat?" Franz asked Seth.

"Don't ask," Dick interjected. "Sometimes you don't want to hear the answers."

Seth smiled. "I traded for it."

"What did you trade?"

"Oh, some things."

"Things?" Franz said.

"Uh-huh."

"It was the same in prison," Dick said. "I'd have starved if it hadn't been for his trading."

Franz shrugged. "No more questions. This is the best food I've ever eaten. Who cares how we got it?"

The three men finished their supper, then pulled their blankets about their shoulders and sat close to the flames. Their tent was just behind them.

A strange thing had happened. Seth, the hater of all Hessians, had become a close friend to von Lossow. Franz felt the same way about him. It had surprised Dick, but pleased him. Apparently Seth had finally come to the conclusion that there were good Hessians and bad Hessians.

"I don't know if I can take another winter like the last one," Dick said.

"There are several months of this one left," Seth reminded him. "Take it easy, you'll live longer."

"Amazing!" Franz said.

"What's amazing?"

"Last year at this time I was at a New Year's Eve party at General Howe's house, and it was when I first met Celine. Last year I served King George. This year I fight against him."

"Last year Seth and I were prisoners. This year we're free men," Dick said.

"See, life gets better and better," Seth said contentedly.

"Enjoy your walk?" Noah Henry asked as the snow-dappled figure of Mary Delafield came through the door of his house.

"The air is wonderful!" Mary said as she unwound her long scarf. Her eyes were bright as she walked to the fire to warm herself. Her swelling stomach clearly told of the budding life within her body.

"You shouldn't go out in weather like this," Sarah Henry complained. "'Tis no good for the baby. How many times do I have to tell you that?"

Mary said nothing. In the long weeks she had stayed with the Henrys, she had learned not to listen to Sarah. The two women were about the same age, as was Noah, but Sarah behaved like a sixty-year-old, and a cranky sixty-year-old at that. She was never satisfied with anything, always finding fault, always looking on the dark side of things, and certain that no one but herself was doing things properly.

"What's wrong with a bit of fresh air?" Noah asked.

"Don't you take her side," Sarah warned.

"I'll take her side when she's right," Noah replied.

The Henrys made the strangest couple Mary had ever known. Noah was open, easygoing, and always ready to smile. Sarah never stopped complaining. She was pinch-faced, stringy-haired, and mean. She always looked as if she had been sucking on a tart fruit.

Noah was tall and stockily built. He had straight dark hair, brown eyes, white teeth, and a pronounced but handsome nose. He was a woodsman and a farmer, and when in the forest he was the picture of stealth and strength. It was Noah who had taught Beth much of what she knew of forest lore.

"Another year is ending," he said as he went to the fire and poured rum into a pewter pitcher. He jammed a red-hot loggerhead into the liquid. It bubbled and hissed. "A nice mug of hot rum will do fine to toast the new year."

"None for me," Sarah said. "Rum is of the devil. And you shouldn't have any either," she griped to Mary. "'Tis not good for the child."

Mary smothered a smile as Noah winked and handed her a mug of the aromatic liquid. "Ah, Sarah," he said, "if anyone listened to everything you said, they'd just give up the ghost and lie down to die."

"Some people just want to poison their bodies," Sarah sniffed, and swept out of the room.

Mary sat down on a chair near the fire while Noah squatted on the hooked rug that lay directly in front of the hearth. "You're starting to look more like a mother every day."

"Carrying this belly around is starting to make me feel like one."

"It'll be grand to hear the sound of a baby in the house," Noah said. "For reasons known only to the Lord, Sarah and I have never been blessed with one. And now maybe it's getting a bit late in our lives."

"That's what *I* thought," Mary replied. "Now look at me!"

They sipped their hot drinks, taking care not to burn their tongues. It was odd, she thought, but she was almost content. She knew it didn't make any sense. Her husband was in prison, and she was carrying another man's child. But it was good to escape the turmoil and straitened circumstances of life in New York, and having the peaceful woods to walk in and Noah to talk to made her life very pleasant.

If only Robert had Noah's temperament, she thought, how much better their lives would have been! She didn't feel she was being disloyal to her husband by thinking this way. Their life together simply had not been a good one, and she didn't miss him at all. Oh, she was sorry he was in prison, and she hoped he would be released. But what then?

Her protruding stomach reminded her that nothing could ever be the same for the two of them. Perhaps Robert would simply abandon her. Good, she thought; even abandonment was better than the life they'd had in the past.

"More rum?" Noah asked.

"I'm fine for now," she said. "You know, I was just thinking what a nice New Year's Eve this is."

Noah smiled. "I haven't had a better one in years."

Drew celebrated his New Year's Eve in Ben Franklin's apartments at the Hôtel de Valentinois. The loquacious Caron de Beaumarchais was with them. Drew regretted that Alec could not be with them, but he was at sea aboard the *Freedom*.

The dining-room table groaned under the weight of the food supplied by Beaumarchais. A second table was used to hold all the wine and liquor bottles. A number of other guests were expected, mostly Americans who looked to Franklin as the leader of their group.

"Come, my friends," Beaumarchais said. "Let us drink a toast to the gallant American army as they rest in their winter quarters, gathering strength and girding their loins for the glorious battles to come."

"If it's anything like last year, they're all freezing their behinds off," Drew said.

"And hardly enjoying such a supper as this," Franklin added, his eyes running over the smoked goose, the pigeon pies, the large slabs of pâté, the roasted joints of lamb, the curried rice, the ducks, and the rest of it—truly, it was a groaning board.

"Ah, my friend, don't make me feel guilty for bringing these tokens," Beaumarchais said. "I take pleasure in doing what I can to make your lives more enjoyable. If I could bring you victory, I would do so. But, alas, I cannot. Have you tried this baked squab?" he said, switching topics in that disconcerting way of his, without a pause for breath.

Before Drew could answer, Beaumarchais was off again. "Try it, try it—the food of the gods! A friend of mine has a house not far from here, and this is the specialty of his cook. He insisted I bring it when I told him who the meal was for. Ah, Ben Franklin, my friend, you are a famous man! A beloved man! All France would lie at your feet and listen to your wisdom!"

"All I wish is that France sign a certain paper, and lay that at my feet," Franklin said.

"She will, she will," Beaumarchais promised; and then he was off to greet several arriving guests, although these were not his apartments nor this his party.

"Sometimes I'd like to strangle that man," Franklin said. "But then I remember how much good he does for us, and I curb my temper."

Drew smiled. "He's a big help."

"Yes, I know, so I grit my teeth—what's left of them—smile, and pretend I enjoy it when he claps me on the back and stuffs a baked fig in my mouth."

"You are a true patriot, sir," Drew said, managing to keep a straight face.

"And you are a rascal," Franklin said. "And we must think of what work to put you to next."

"I'm supposed to get ships..."

"Yes, and you have three of them, but not much chance of getting more crew members for a while, or at least that's what you told me."

Drew felt like kicking himself for having told the old gentleman the fact that American sailors who could be depended on were hard to find. But it was true.

"I have a job for you," Franklin continued. "I want you to go to a place where you will learn more, and by learning more be able to do more."

"Where is this place?"

"England."

"England?"

"No doubt you've heard of it."

"But we're at war with England," Drew protested. "If I showed up there, they'd put me in jail!"

"Nonsense. The English play the game of life by strange rules. I've been in communication with Dr. Templeton, who is the chaplain of the Earl of Westbourne. The earl would be delighted to extend his protection to you, and have you as his houseguest. You'll find that a good number of Englishmen disagree with their king's views. So what do you say?"

Drew wanted to say no, that he wanted to go aboard a privateer and fight the war the way his friend Alec Seixas was fighting it.

"Whatever you think best, Mr. Franklin," he said mildly.

"Good," Franklin said, clasping his surprisingly strong arm around Drew's shoulder. "We're going to look back and remember this past year. We'll remember it was the year Lord

Stormont made his prediction that the British Empire was going to crush the life from the American worm."

Ben Franklin had a grim smile on his face. "He will learn that this worm has turned out to be an asp. And the asp's bite on the empire's throat shall be fatal."

5

The Tides of Change

May, 1778–December, 1779

DREW WALKED WITH LADY JANE MIDDLETON AND her daughter, Althea, in the gardens of the Earl of Westbourne's estate, the great house called Chatsmill.

"Mr. de Kuyper," Lady Jane said, "Sir Michael has often entertained the idea of visiting our colonies in America, but for sundry reasons my husband has never availed himself of the opportunity."

"One visit would be worth a thousand of my words, Lady Jane," Drew said, in the fencing, diplomatic manner of speech he had acquired since coming to Europe.

It was the last week in May, and he had been in England for almost three months. In that time, as guest of the earl, he had met hundreds of influential people—here at Chatsmill, at other estates, and in London. As Ben Franklin had predicted, many of these people favored the American cause. Many others, while not in favor of the cause, were rather more bewildered than hostile. Lady Jane was fairly typical of the latter group.

"What I can't understand is why you want to break away from the empire," she said. "Good heavens, it's the same as if Liverpool decided to become independent. Can't you people see that?"

"It isn't quite that simple, Mother," her daughter said, coming to Drew's rescue.

"Fiddlesticks!" Lady Jane said. "God has given us the king, and we must accept him."

"Many would disagree, my lady," Drew said with a charming smile. "The French, for example."

"I meant," Her Ladyship said frostily, "that God has given the *English* king to the *English* people."

Althea broke into a silvery titter. "Oh, Mother, Mr. de Kuyper knows quite well what you mean, where's your sense of humor?"

The young Englishwoman had very fair skin, and reminded Drew of a fragile bird. Althea was of average height, but she wore her blond hair piled high and augmented it with a matching wig, so she appeared taller than she really was. The Middletons had been houseguests of the earl for almost a week, and since she was close to his own age, Drew found himself seeking Althea's company. Her brittle aristocratic manner was tempered by a certain softness, and the combination appealed to him, mostly because he had never encountered its like before.

"Almost time for tea," Lady Jane reminded them. "We'd better return to the cottage."

Drew smiled. The cottage, indeed! It made no difference to Lady Jane that Chatsmill was an imposing stone pile containing two hundred and fifty rooms and over a hundred fireplaces. Chatsmill was in the country, therefore it was a cottage.

The house was situated to the north and west of London, in Buckinghamshire, on a hill giving it a commanding view of the Thames.

The rolling English countryside spread out in all directions, lush and green and inviting. In the distance there was a picturesque village. From a mile away it looked like a fairyland, but upon closer inspection Drew had discovered it was pockmarked with poverty and despair. In England, as in France, the ruling classes saw to it that a few took the most, while the many took the least.

As they walked across the close-cropped grass toward Chatsmill, a half dozen gardeners paused in their labors to remove their caps and bow stiffly. Drew had once counted forty gardeners, and he doubted he had gotten them all.

But the gardeners were only one group of servants serving the earl. There were butlers and under-butlers, serving maids, chambermaids, upstairs maids, downstairs maids, cooks, cooks' assistants; silver polishers, bakers, pastry chefs, footmen, drivers, outside men, inside men; cobblers, tailors, seamstresses, account keepers, blacksmiths, coopers, tanners, cattle drovers, keepers of hounds, stablemen, swineherds, chimney sweeps, artisans, architects, carpenters, and more—all members of the more than three-hundred-servant "family" that served the earl, his family of five, and his guests.

Here was a display and a use of wealth on a scale unknown in America. Here was the manner in which the ruling class of England had grown accustomed to live, and it was this very way of life that made it impossible for them to imagine the ideas and feelings of people who lived on the frontier of America.

Drew realized, to be sure, he had seen an even more extravagant display of wealth at Versailles, but that had been a symbol representing an entire nation to its own citizens and to the world outside. Here, in England, every landed baron, earl, marquis, and duke lived on a scale that approached that of a ruling monarch.

They arrived at the house and entered the informal reception hall to the left, where tea was being served. The Great Hall stood off to the right, but it was so mammoth and grand that it was used only at functions with over a hundred guests. The most imposing piece of furniture in the Great Hall was a large chair—a throne, really—that had been given to an ancestor of the earl in the late fourteenth century by Richard II. Former earls had sat in the chair as they listened to charges being read against offending serfs; and there they dispensed their justice, often in the form of whipping, branding, mutilation, or death. By now, however, these practices has been abandoned, and the earls of Westbourne treated their retainers with more benevolence.

As they sipped their tea and munched on sweet cakes, Drew was introduced to a newly arrived guest from London.

"Mr. de Kuyper, this is Mr. Ogilvy."

Philip Ogilvy was dark-haired and slight of build, and he carried himself with the careless ease of a born aristocrat. His left eyelid drooped, and he had a nervous habit of sniffing. Those who reckoned age by years alone would say he wasn't much older than the American.

"I must confess I'm not here by accident," Ogilvy said. "Lord North wishes to convey the terms of the latest peace treaty he is proposing. It is his understanding that what is said to you will reach Mr. Franklin."

"Quite so," Drew said smoothly, aware of Althea's admiring glance at him as he conducted affairs of state.

Ogilvy outlined Lord North's terms. Basically, he offered

to repeal the Tea and Coercive Acts, to impose no more revenue taxes, and to suspend most of the other unpopular acts that had been passed since 1763. In short, the terms were everything the Americans had unsuccessfully demanded only two years ago.

But Drew also knew these terms were no longer acceptable. The American Congress had decided to accept nothing short of full independence.

"Mr. Franklin would not be interested in these terms," he said.

"It is a tragic mistake," Ogilvy said.

"Our Congress does not agree."

"You mean these terms have already been offered to the Americans?" the earl asked.

"Yes," Ogilvy said.

"Then why are you reoffering them to this gentleman?"

"Lord North feels Mr. Franklin might be able to use his influence to sway the Congress," Ogilvy said.

"Foolish way to do business," the earl grumbled, and Ogilvy turned slightly red. As a matter of fact he felt exactly the same way, but Lord North had insisted on trying this route to peace.

Althea Middleton giggled. Her blue eyes had been following Drew's every move, and her obvious interest was not lost on him. Whenever he returned the gaze, she would bring her fan up to hide the lower part of her face. It was all very beguiling.

Philip Ogilvy was a persistent chap. "But why won't Congress accept our terms?" he asked Drew. "They're exactly what they've asked for in the past."

"It is a question of offering too little too late," Drew said.

"This is a senseless war," Ogilvy responded. "Both sides are being hurt."

"I know a way to end it," Althea said.

Drew and Ogilvy looked at her. "We should allow the Americans to become independent," she said. *"Then,* they should rejoin the British Empire of their own free will."

It wasn't all that silly an idea, Drew thought. As a matter of fact, it was very close to the position his own father had taken not long ago—a position held by a number of thoughtful Americans.

"Impossible," Ogilvy said, closing the door quickly. "The king would never agree to such a proposal."

The next day Ogilvy invited Drew to return to London with him. At first the American was reluctant, but the Englishman tempted him by promising a visit to the naval prison at Portsmouth, a place where many captured American seamen were being held. After discussing the matter with the earl, whom he had found to be open and honest about everything, and assuring himself that Ogilvy could deliver on such an invitation, Drew accepted. His only regret was that he was leaving at a time when his relationship with Althea Middleton was just beginning to warm up.

"I'm *so* unhappy that you're leaving," she said when he told her of his plans. "It will be so *lonely* here without you."

"I'm sure we'll meet again."

She became pouty. "All men say such things."

There was something about her that made him want to shield her from the world. She seemed so vulnerable and soft, yet kittenish and charming.

"But I mean what I say."

Instantly she put on a dazzling smile. "I know you do. I promise to think about you. Will you promise to think about me?"

He agreed, and then the conversation shifted as they were joined by Lord Middleton, an overweight gray-haired man who approved of Americans only if they kept their place. The place Middleton had in mind, Drew had learned, was somewhere below the salt at an Englishman's table.

The ride to London was bumpy, uncomfortable, and uneventful, but Ogilvy was a pleasant traveling companion. Drew learned to like him, and opened up a bit about himself and his family. The Englishman seemed impressed by the de Kuyper credentials, and said so.

"We've nothing like the traditions going back many centuries such as you have here," Drew said modestly.

"Ninety percent of our good families would love to have a recent family history as colorful and exciting as yours. They just wouldn't admit it.... Have you seen much of London?"

"Mostly the interiors of dining rooms," Drew admitted. "I haven't seen much of the city itself."

"I shall be your guide," Ogilvy said.

The Englishman owned a comfortable house off Drury Lane, not far from the Inns of Court. The house itself was handsome and tastefully furnished, but Drew was amazed by the filth and dirt of the streets around it. All London, so it appeared, was like this.

Not one hundred feet from the splendor of St. Paul's Cathedral, one could see a hovel where people in rags lived and died; one could see ragged children begging and, if this occupation was unsuccessful, stealing. When he asked Ogilvy for an explanation, the Englishman merely shrugged and said London was a city, and cities were like this. Drew's mind chewed on that one. New York was a city—not as old nor as large nor as famous as London, perhaps, but a city nevertheless—and New York did not have the filth and degradation that seemed a part of the very sinew and bones of London—not even during a war, while being occupied by the enemy.

Drew's host directed their coach down the Strand, past Charing Cross, thence down Whitehall to the city of Westminster and the famous Abbey of St. Peter, on the north bank of the Thames.

For the first time since he had come to England, he felt truly awed as he stood in the middle of the Abbey's transept; it was so vast and spacious. Drew felt almost mesmerized by the bright sun filtering down through a cloud of dust particles, and he gazed in silence at the heavy marble tombs and crypts beneath which the kings and queens of England slept a dreamless sleep of centuries.

Nothing in his nature or his background made him wish to venerate the dead rulers of this ancient land, but he paused and was touched by the brush of history as he stood above the spot where a Saxon king of the eighth century was said to lie buried. A thousand years ago this man ruled, and now he was a few specks of dust.

"Are you a religious man?" Ogilvy asked as he stood beside him.

"No," Drew answered, his voice a whisper, as loudness seemed inappropriate in this place.

"Neither am I," the Englishman said. "But when I come here, I always feel closer to God."

"I understand," Drew said. "It's a timeless place."

"Makes our wars seem inconsequential, doesn't it?"

They spent over two hours in the Abbey, then rode back in their carriage to St. James Square, where they were to have lunch "with a special friend of mine," as Ogilvy put it.

Drew wondered who this might be, because by this time he had learned more about his companion. Philip Ogilvy was the third son of the Earl of Devonshire. He was related in one way or another to half the nobility of England, and considered a bright young man with an unlimited future. He had a facile mind and a good imagination. He was a friend of the Americans and did not want to defeat them in war, but bring them back peacefully into the folds of the empire.

In this respect, Drew realized, Ogilvy was like General Howe and many other Englishmen. None of them were being realistic, however, because the days of reconciliation were gone, and now the war had to be fought to the finish.

They arrived at St. James's Square and entered a magnificent townhouse belonging to one of Ogilvy's uncles. The "special friend" turned out to be the third son of King George III.

William Henry, the Duke of Clarence, was an engaging lad of sixteen years. He had bright, alert eyes, a handsome profile, rather full lips, and a mind that was both inquiring and open. "Tell me something, Mr. de Kuyper," he asked soon after Drew was introduced as Ben Franklin's representative in England. "Do you think our trade with America would increase or decrease if your people were granted their independence?"

It was a sophisticated question. "I think, in the long term, it would be beneficial for both countries."

"And in the short term?"

"The United States of America, at first, would open new avenues of trade with other countries. Our markets, which have been exclusively England's, would then be open to the world. It might take some adjustments to recognize the new realities."

The prince smiled. "Very politely stated, sir. You are suggesting that Englishmen would have to stand on their own two feet and compete on equal terms."

"Something like that."

The prince turned to the other men gathered about. "I can't say I find that awfully distressing. Must we depend on captive markets?"

There was a murmur of consent, but it was difficult for Drew to tell if it was out of conviction, or deference to the prince's rank.

An older man, the Marquis of Ipswich, voiced the opinion that was more popular in conservative circles. "But Your Highness, we founded our colonies just so we *would* have captive markets. Otherwise why did we go to all that damned trouble?"

The prince nodded that he understood the marquis's position; after all, it was the very same as that taken by his royal father. He didn't want to get into an extended argument, because news of his position was certain to get back to his parent, with the usual row resulting. He changed subjects.

"You used a term I had not heard before. The United States, I believe you said."

"Yes, Your Majesty. The United States of America, a term our Congress adopted last November. It describes us quite well—a distinct and separate group of states existing in the Americas, united in a common cause."

"Quite straightforward," the prince said.

"Sounds impertinent to me," the elderly marquis complained. "And you, sir," he said to Drew, "are impertinent as well."

"If impertinence leads to freedom, I accept the charge," Drew said, following Franklin's instructions to stand up to fools who had closed corridors for minds.

"Just because you've had a few piddling victories, don't think you can withstand the might of the British Empire."

"Come, come Your Grace," the prince admonished. "You can hardly call their triumph at Saratoga a piddling victory. General Burgoyne totally capitulated to this Mr. Gates. Isn't that so?" he added, directing the question toward Drew.

"I know of no Mr. Gates," Drew said.

The prince looked confused.

"I know a *General* Gates, Your Majesty. Are you, perhaps, referring to him?"

"I stand corrected," the prince said with an easy smile. "General Gates it shall be. And now, bless me, my stomach tells me it's time for lunch. Shall we adjourn to the table?"

After lunch Drew returned to the house off Drury Lane and wrote a letter to Franklin telling him about the prince. It was a shame the young Duke of Clarence wasn't on the throne of England. He seemed to have a deeper understanding of America's problems with the mother country than his own royal father had.

But there was little hope of his assuming the purple, because George III was as healthy as he was difficult. Besides, he had two sons who led the young duke in the line of accession to the throne.

The next day Ogilvy made good on his promise, and Drew was taken to the prison at the naval base of Portsmouth.

The visit was nightmarish. The prisoners were kept in cold stone cells, the more troublesome men being chained to the walls. They were in rags, ill-fed, and mistreated by the brutal guards. None of this was done by accident. Since it was Lord North's policy, as well as that of Lord Germain, to consider the prisoners traitors, they were accorded the treatment usually given to those waiting to be hanged.

The British commandant was a very proper man, and Drew could tell he didn't approve of such a harsh policy, but he was an officer and followed his orders. He made certain, however, that nothing was held back and that Drew could see everything. He let him interview several men.

"How long have you been here?" Drew asked one thin blond man who looked as if he were about fifteen years old.

"'Bout six months," the lad said.

"How is the food?"

"Terrible."

"All the time?"

"The only thing worse is when there isn't any food at all."

"There are times when they don't feed you anything?"

"When there's trouble," the young man said. "Then they don't give us any food. Christ Almighty, we're half starving to death in this place!"

"We're working to get you out," Drew said. He knew it sounded like an empty promise, but there was nothing else he could say.

The young sailor smiled. Drew noticed he was missing several front teeth. "We've been told we'll never get out until our folks back home surrender. They want us to write letters to them, telling them to surrender."

"Have you done it?"

"When they give me something to eat, I do. They write the letter and I sign it with a mark. That won't fool my folks," the sailor said. "They know I can't write. And even if I could, I would never write about quitting."

The worst part of the prison was down below, where men were chained in small windowless cells. Some of the cells had ceilings that weren't high enough to allow a man to stand.

"This is an outrage!" Drew said.

"These are the ones who've tried to escape," the commandant said. "Troublemakers. They end up here."

"For how long?"

The commandant shrugged. "Until they die."

"Does that happen often?"

"All the time."

Drew peered into a cell and saw a man chained to the floor. His head lolled on his chest and saliva drooled from his mouth. His hair was matted.

"That one will go today or tomorrow," the commandant said matter-of-factly.

"And you'll do nothing to save his life?"

"My orders are to not lift a finger. When he dies, we'll wrap his body in a canvas sack, weight it, and drop it in the sea for the sharks."

"Why are you telling me this?"

"Because I hate what I'm doing," the commandant said with sudden feeling. "I've applied for other duty, and if a transfer doesn't come through, I'll resign my commission."

"I'd like to say I don't blame you for all this," Drew said, looking him straight in the eye. "But I can't."

"That's the problem," the commandant said sadly. "I can't even say it to myself."

"I've seen enough."

He went back to London and paced in his room for over an hour. There was a war going on, and men were fighting while he was chatting with Englishmen in their drawing rooms. Men were dying while he was having lunch with a royal prince. He was ashamed of himself, and decided he had spent enough time in England. He was going back to France to inform Franklin that he was through with being a diplomat. He was going to get into the war, get a ship, like Alec Seixas, and start striking real blows for the freedom of his country.

He attended one last garden party before departing for France. He didn't want to go, but Ogilvy insisted there would be important men in attendance, and who could tell what good Drew might accomplish by talking with them.

Drew was merely going through the motions of being polite, sipping a glass of chilled wine and consuming but not tasting the elegantly prepared morsels set out on silver trays. As he looked at the display of rich food, he thought of the emaciated American prisoners at Portsmouth. He felt like a traitor. He took a half-eaten crayfish and slipped it back on the linen-covered table. Not much of a gesture, he complained to himself even as he was doing it.

"So we meet again, Mr. de Kuyper."

It was Althea Middleton, dressed in white from head to toe,

soft and inviting. She suddenly looked sad. "Philip Ogilvy tells me you're returning to France. Is this true?"

"I'm afraid it is."

"I was hoping you would be staying for the fall season. We have many parties and balls, and such a gay time. I would have liked to show it all to you."

"I'm sure you'll not lack escorts," Drew said, suddenly envying the men who would be squiring her around.

"Yes, but you see I wanted it to be *you*. It would be so exciting to be making the rounds with an American," Althea said. "We'd be the talk of every party."

"I see," Drew said with less enthusiasm. What did she think he was, some kind of exhibit? "I'm sure you'll find some other conversation piece."

She looked surprised. "Now I've gone and offended you, haven't I? Being a conversation piece is just something extra. I wanted to be with you because of *you*. . . . Now you've gone and hurt *my* feelings," she said, tapping her toe and turning her back slightly toward him.

He wasn't sure exactly why, but he felt he had slighted her honor. "I'm sorry if I said something wrong, Miss Middleton . . ."

"You don't even like me well enough to call me Althea."

"Yes, all right, Althea . . ."

"And I'll call you Drew. Philip Ogilvy tells me that's what you prefer."

"Yes, that's correct."

"It *is* a shame you won't be here," she said. "It would have made my father furious. He thinks all Americans are really barbarians, and he was horrified when I told him I liked you."

"You told him that?" Drew said, suddenly aware that things had been moving along without him, and more quickly than he cared for.

"Yes," she said. "Even that I might be taking you rather seriously."

"But we hardly know one another," Drew protested.

"I know that, but I also know what I like. And I can be *very* determined when I want to be."

"Yes, I can see that," Drew said. He was discovering another side to the ethereal Althea Middleton.

"Papa thinks he knows what's best for me," she said. "He thinks I should get involved only with men who have titles.

It doesn't matter if the man's a complete ass or not, just so he's titled. Well, he has another think coming."

"You're accustomed to getting your way, I see."

"I usually do," she said, and her eyes looked up into his. "You *must* come back to us from France."

"I'll try."

"I want to make everything here wonderful for you," she said. Her wistfulness was back, and he had a sudden urge to take her in his arms and kiss her. He resisted the temptation.

He nodded gravely and walked away from her, his head swirling with conflicting thoughts. On the one hand, she was willful and stubborn, spoiled by adoring and indulgent parents. On the other, she combined an untouchability with a strong physical attraction. It was heady stuff, and he needed time to think about it.

He saw Ogilvy talking with a young dragoon officer, and went over to him. The officer's face froze when Ogilvy announced that Drew was an American. He nodded and walked away without a word.

"Unthinkable, his acting that way!" Ogilvy said.

"Maybe he thinks it his duty to hate Americans," Drew said with a shrug. He had met other Englishmen who had disliked him simply because he was an American. The surprising thing was not that it happened, but that it happened so rarely. Most Englishmen hated the rebellion, but not individual Americans.

"The man's a fool," Ogilvy said.

"I hope you and I will never hate each other," Drew said, and meant it.

"I don't think we will," Ogilvy said. "As a matter of fact I think our friendship will grow over the years. Shall I tell you my thoughts about your future and mine?"

"Please do."

"I have a suspicion that our countries will break apart from one another. I also think you will be an important man in yours, and that I will be in mine. When it comes time to deal with one another then, we will be able to trust each other more because we've shared this friendship."

Drew nodded. It made sense, but there was one point he wasn't certain about.

"The longer the war continues, the more bitterness it causes," he said. "What makes you sure our countries will have any dealings with each other after the war is over?"

"Of course we'll deal with one another," Ogilvy said with

great assuredness. "Right now you've made a treaty with the French. But how long do you think you can go on trusting them? The French, my dear Drew, have a long history of duplicity. Sooner or later America will regret having made an alliance with France. At that time, one might hope, we will resume the natural bonds existing between England and America. Like it or not, we are one people."

By the time he left the party, he knew one thing for sure: in Philip Ogilvy he had made a friend for life.

He left England, crossing the channel in a Dutch brigantine to Amsterdam. Then he traveled overland down to Le Havre, where he took another boat down the Seine to Paris. Arriving at the Hôtel de Valentinois, Drew was greeted exuberantly by Ben Franklin.

"Let me look at you, de Kuyper! A morning coat from a good British tailor. A silk shirt, silk cravat, brocade waistcoat. If I didn't know better, I'd think you were *from* the Court of St. James, instead of being one of those smelly rebels who are trying to overthrow it."

After telling Franklin of what he had learned in England, and encouraged by a few glasses of strong sack, Drew spoke with passion of his wish to ship aboard a privateer.

"Yes, yes, all in good time, my boy," Franklin said. "But right now I have a problem that needs immediate solving, and you're the perfect man for the job."

"More dinner parties?"

"No, no, no. The French have three old ships at Calais. Now that they've signed the treaty and are proper allies, they've given us the ships, but it's up to us to get them into proper shape. We need a man to supervise the job."

"Me?"

"You."

"But Mr. Franklin," Drew protested. "A job like that could take months. I want to do something... more active."

"Yes, yes, of course. You want to take a sword in your hand, stick a dagger between your teeth, and play pirate," Franklin said, making Drew's idea seem foolish.

"That's not exactly—"

"On the other hand, not more than a half-dozen Americans could get those ships ready, and you're the only one in France. Each of us must serve our country in the job where we can do the most good. Do you understand?"

"I suppose," Drew said grudgingly.

"So when can you go to Calais?"

"How about tomorrow?"

"Good, good, good."

"But when this job is finished, I'll want to get my privateer," Drew warned.

"Of course, of course," Franklin said distractedly, but he was already worrying about another problem, and left the room. Drew suddenly had a frightening premonition that he might spend the entire war doing odd jobs at the beck and call of Ben Franklin.

He sighed and went to make arrangements to travel to Calais. As long as he had a job to do, he might as well get on with it.

Grab a sword and stick a dagger between his teeth, indeed! And then he chuckled. The old gentleman had been absolutely right. That was *exactly* what he wanted to do.

Jan looked terrible.

Beth could hardly stand to look at him as he sat propped up in his bed. His face looked drawn and yellow. She placed the tray bearing tea and toast on the end table. The room was close and stuffy.

His eyes fluttered open. "Oh..."

"It's only me—Beth. With a cup of tea."

His eyes closed for a moment, then opened, this time remaining open. He managed a smile. "Thank you, my dear. A nice cup of hot tea will be fine."

She hated to see him this way, preferring to remember him as she had always known him—strong, happy, energetic. But she knew there was little hope he would recover, and suspected he was going quickly.

She smoothed the covers over him, and reached behind his head to fluff the pillow. His eyes caught hers and held them.

"You've grown into quite a woman," he said. "Theo would be proud, had he lived. And Louise, too. They were good people, your mother and father."

"They were always fond of you," she said.

"But they were taken away," he said with a sigh. "It happens to all of us eventually. And now it's happening to me."

"Hush," she said. "You just rest, and get your strength back. Soon you'll be up and about."

"I doubt it," he said, accepting the tea and taking a sip. He looked at her again and recalled that Marie Therese had been speaking of her only yesterday; it seemed the girl was in love with Drew.

"I understand you're fond of my son."

"Most people like Drew."

"I don't mean that," Jan said with a wan shake of his head. "I'm talking about something more important. Like love."

She blushed. "There's nothing between Drew and me."

"Too bad. If I had to pick a wife for him, I'd pick you. After all, you're like a daughter to me. What more could I ask for my son? Or for you, for that matter?"

She managed to hide her embarrassment. "He's very nice," she said lamely.

"I know what *I* see in him," Jan said. "But how about you? What attracts you to him?"

Beth was about to deny her feelings, and then stopped when she looked at the old man in the bed. He didn't have much more time left. It didn't seem right not to tell the truth.

"At first it was simply a girlish infatuation, I suppose," she admitted. "But as time passed I realized Drew was a very unusual person. Take the letters he writes to us. He obviously isn't too pleased with his work, but he stays with it because he knows it's the most important thing he could be doing. How many other people are willing to do what has to be done, instead of what they'd like to be doing?"

Jan nodded. "Very perceptive of you to understand such values. Drew's been taught to do what's right. I taught him that myself."

"He's also the most handsome man I've ever seen," Beth admitted, and now that she was telling her innermost secrets, it seemed easy to continue. "But it's more than looks—he's also the nicest person I've ever met."

"I hope he learns to appreciate you," Jan said kindly, knowing from his wife that Drew had so far ignored the girl.

"I hope so, too," she said ardently.

"Baby, baby," Noah Henry said, holding out his finger to the chubby infant in the cradle. Mary Delafield's son had been born at the end of March and was now five months old. She had named him David Beekman, after an ancestor of hers. But of this little David knew nothing, nor did he care. At the moment his tiny fingers were reaching out until they wrapped themselves around the man's finger. A look of happiness appeared on his face, and he chortled.

"Ah, smart little tyke, aren't you?" Noah said. He looked up at the child's mother, who was seated in a nearby chair. "A bright lad he is, Mary."

"And healthy, thank the Lord," she said. It had been her great fear that God would punish her for her indiscretion by giving her an abnormal child.

In the beginning things hadn't looked very good.

When Mary's time came, Sarah Henry refused to have anything to do with helping her. "The baby was conceived in sin," Sarah said, her face mottled red with anger. "And I'll have nothing to do with the birth of such a sinful child."

"The child is blameless," Noah protested.

"Sin is sin," Sarah said, putting on her heavy woolen scarf.

"The woman needs you," Noah said. "There's no one else to help her."

But his words did no good. Sarah hitched up a horse to a cart and drove two miles to the nearest neighbor's house. It was cold, and her fingers almost froze, but they weren't as cold as her heart. Her self-righteous neighbor said Sarah had done the proper thing in leaving Mary to her fate; they piously agreed with each other that it was the duty of good people to shun that which was evil.

It was up to Noah to help. He knew little about childbirth, but as it turned out, he knew enough. He boiled towels. He comforted Mary as her pains grew sharper and closer together.

It was a painful birth, and Noah was terrified, but he stayed with the woman and helped ease the child from her body. Almost by instinct he knew what had to be done next. When he heard the baby's first cries, he knew everything was going to be all right.

Young David was soon as happy and as healthy as any baby he had ever seen. Noah doted on the child, spending his free time playing games with him at the side of the cradle he had built with his own hands.

Noah was a kindly man, and it had been the bane of his life that his wife was childless. Having Mary's baby come into his house and life was almost as good as having his own child. Having helped bring him into the world forged the bond closer.

Mary had been embarrassed when she recovered from the ordeal of giving birth and remembered it had been Noah who had stayed at her side. She remembered screaming with the pain; she remembered the blood on the man's hands as they went between her legs and helped bring the new life into the world; she remembered more screaming on her part; she remembered it all. But the embarrassment wore off when she realized that had it not been for Noah, her baby would have died, and perhaps she as well. So when Mary saw him playing with the baby, she was pleased.

"You're going to spoil him," she chided gently, smiling.

"'Tis impossible to spoil a child at this age," he said. "All they need is love. The more you give, the better off they'll be later on in life. My mother used to tell me that when I was a runt."

"Then by all means spoil him," she said, continuing to sew the baby shirt she was working on. Mary was a more serene person these days; almost content. The only problem was Sarah.

She had returned the day after David had been born, and had never stopped complaining. "Seems to me," she would say to her husband, "that you spend more time with that child than you do with your own chores."

"Everything gets done," Noah replied mildly. "The baby likes to play with his Uncle Noah."

"Uncle, indeed!" Sarah sniffed. By this time, from a conversation she had heard between Noah and the new mother, she had learned the identity of the infant's natural father, and in her mind Mary was nothing more than a tart, a woman of the street, someone marked for the fires of hell. And the child as well, because a child born of sin *was* sin.

She started a campaign of complaining, with the idea of driving mother and child from her house, but Noah was adamant. It was *his* house, and Mary and little David were staying. Sarah had never seen him become so angry, and she retreated. If direct opposition wouldn't rid her of these people, she would resort to guile. Ever since she had learned the father was Captain Patrick Blakely, she had tucked away this information for use when needed. The day had arrived. Only last week she had written a short note in her crabbed and little-used handwriting. It was unusual for a farm woman such as Sarah to have such a skill, but her religious father had insisted on his children learning to read and write so that "God could reach them through His scripture."

She had carried the note miles to the south and handed it to a British sergeant who commanded a detachment at a small fort on the shore of Long Island Sound. She had been clever enough to hand him a silver coin with the note, and the note was promptly delivered to the city.

It was only a matter of time, Sarah gloated, as she worked in the keeping room, preparing a deer-meat stew for dinner. This reminded her of another of her complaints—that she had to do all the cooking. The Delafield woman, as she always referred to Mary, was useless in the kitchen. Spoiled, she was, Sarah mumbled under her breath, spoiled rotten, coming from a house filled with servants where she never had to lift a finger for herself.

It was mid-afternoon.

Noah was in front of the house repairing a broken harness trace, and Mary was in the rocking chair he had placed next to the door so she could sit and enjoy the sun. He saw the lone rider approaching first, but she was only a few seconds behind. The man wore the uniform of a British officer.

"Don't see many of them around here," Noah said, and they watched in silence as the horseman came closer. Mary suddenly turned deathly white. "My God," she whispered. "It's Patrick."

"Go in the house," Noah said. "I'll see what he wants."

As Mary disappeared into the squat building, Sarah was watching from a window. Her eyes gleamed with triumph, and she flicked her tongue across her lower lip. This must be him, she thought, this Captain Blakely who fathered the bastard, come at last to take the plagued woman and her brat away.

"Afternoon," Noah said as the Englishman reined his horse up before him.

"Are you Noah Henry?"

"Yes."

"You have a woman staying with you. Mary Delafield. I want to see her."

"What makes you think she'd be here? I live here with my wife," Noah said, measuring the other man. If it came down to it, he was ready to defend Mary, and with his brawny arms and iron back it would be no mean defense.

But it never came to that. The captain dismounted and tied the reins to the stout hitching post. "I'm not looking for trouble, Mr. Henry, but I must see Mrs. Delafield."

Noah thought for a moment, then shrugged. "I'll go in the house and tell her you're here."

"I'll go in. I prefer to see her alone," Blakely said evenly. There was no sense in forcing trouble. "As you wish."

Captain Blakely went to the door, opened it, and stepped into the house. He paused for a moment to allow his eyes to adjust to the relative darkness. Then he saw Mary on the other side of the room. An infant slept in the cradle beside her. He walked across the room and stared down at the child.

"Boy or girl?"

"His name is David."

"Is he well?"

"Very well."

"And yourself?"

"I'm doing all right."

"I'm sorry if I caused you trouble."

"I hated you when I first knew I was with child," she said. "But now that I have David, I wouldn't trade him for anything in the world. So I've stopped hating you."

"I tried to find you when you first disappeared. I've had no luck until now."

"Well, you've found me. What do you plan on doing?"

"Nothing," Blakely said. "I wanted to know if there was anything I could do for you."

"There's nothing more I want from you."

"Something for the child?"

"I'll take care of David."

"David," Blakely said softly, almost to himself. "David. A good name."

He looked down at the sleeping child and brushed his hand against the soft skin. "May he know peace and happiness," he said in a very gentle voice.

Mary was standing close to his side, also looking down at the sleeping infant. Instinctively she reached out and grabbed Blakely's arm. "Do me this favor, leave us alone. If people know you're his father, it will only cause him harm."

"I will do as you ask," he said.

"Thank you," she said. She gave his arm a squeeze and released it.

"It was love we had between us," he said quietly. "I don't think I'll ever have the same with anyone else."

She could feel her heart quicken, and the blood seemed to rush to her head. He was having the same effect he always had on her. She wanted to hold him in her arms, and kiss him, and feel him plunging into her body until she screamed in ecstasy. But it was over, finished forever, and she knew it.

"That's in the past," she said.

He smiled, because he could see her lower lip quivering and that was what always happened when they had almost drowned in the deep waters of mutual lust. "But we shall never forget."

"No, we shall never forget.... Promise me you'll never do anything to hurt your son."

"I'll hurt myself before I'll hurt him," the captain said, and the smile grew. He was a hard man, accustomed to brutality; his calling allowed him to see little else. But he was an Irishman, with that whimsical streak that runs through that strange race. It was a whimsy laced with madness, and when he made this promise, she knew he would keep it.

"I trust you," she said.

"And I trust you to raise my son to be a worthy man." He turned and left the room without another word. Mary was shaking as she walked to the window and watched him mount his horse and disappear down the road. The frightening part, to her, was that she knew she was shaking far more out of desire than out of any fear she might have for the captain.

Noah came into the house. "What did he want?"

"To see his son."

"That's all?"

"He won't be back again."

"You mean he's not taking you away from here?" Sarah screeched from the far end of the room. "You mean you plan on staying here? Where you're not wanted?"

"Wait one minute," Noah interrupted. "Who says Mary's not wanted here? Besides, I love the sound of a baby brightening up this place."

"Your wife doesn't want David and me here, Noah," Mary said. "It's her house as well as yours. We'll leave."

"But where will you go?"

"To my own house in the city. Or maybe to Celine's house at Beekman's Place. The reasons to come here were to have the baby and to stay away from Patrick. Well, I've had the baby, and I know Patrick will never bother us."

"I need you here," Noah said. He was close to tears, and the prospect was almost frightening in a man of his size and roughness.

"We must go," Mary said. "And as soon as possible."

Noah couldn't speak. He shook his head, gave his wife a withering look, and stomped out of the house.

"This is a proper house," Sarah said when she was sure

Noah was out of earshot. "Neither you nor that bastard of yours is welcome."

Mary was angry, but kept still. There was no sense in arguing with someone who had a mind as closed as Sarah's. She looked down at her son, who was beginning to stir from his nap. His eyelids fluttered. He looked up, and his mouth widened into a toothless grin when he saw his mother. He chortled and gurgled with happiness. She reached down and picked him up. It would be difficult to leave this place, she thought. Despite Sarah's constant backbiting and nastiness, Mary had felt at peace here.

Dear God, what *was* there to go back to?

Even if Robert came out of prison, she didn't want that life again. And there could be no more life with Patrick. And David; what about wee David? What would Robert say about him? What would others say?

She cradled her son in her arms, rocking gently back and forth, humming softly to please him and to calm her own fears about the future.

When Noah walked out of the house, he went to the barn and got his axe. He took it to the edge of the woods and began to chop away at a tree. He had been planning to cut down this particular tree anyway, but at the moment he simply needed a way to release the tension inside himself. He didn't want Mary to leave. Nor the child.

During the past months Mary had taught him of the soft and gentle side of a woman, something he had never known over all the years with Sarah. Having discovered this miracle, he was reluctant to see it pass from his life.

He chopped away at the trunk, pausing occasionally to measure the cut with his practiced eye to be sure the tree would fall in the proper direction. The sound of the axe rang in the air and was heard for miles around. When the tree was almost cut through, he leaned his shoulder against the trunk and pushed. The tree began to topple, slowly at first, then more swiftly until it crashed to the earth, sending reverberations through the forest, causing the deer to become wary and the squirrels to pause in their search for food.

He stepped back, sweat pouring from his brow, his shirt soaked to a darker color. He rubbed his hands together and felt better. But the problem remained.

What was he going to do without Mary and David?
What was he going to do with Sarah?
What was he going to do with his life?

* * *

Marie Therese's face was a chalky white as she walked out of the bedroom that belonged to her husband and herself. *Had belonged.* Only moments before, Jan de Kuyper had taken his last breath of earthly air. David Sackett waited near the door, saw her face, and understood. He put his hand on her arm as if to infuse the strength of his own body into hers.

"I'm sorry, my dear. I know how much you loved him," he said.

Marie Therese placed her own hand on David's. "No more than you did, David. Jan thought of you as his closest friend in the world."

"I'll miss him."

She managed to put on a brave little smile. "Yes, but we must remember he wouldn't want us to grieve too long. We must get used to life without him."

David was silent for a few moments.

"I'll make all the necessary arrangements," he said.

"Jan's been in pain for some time," Marie Therese said thoughtfully. "I'd like to think of this as his day of release."

Beth was standing at the top of the stairs. She saw David comforting Marie Therese and came over to her. She put her arms about the older woman. "I loved him as much as if he were my own father," she said, her normally husky voice even huskier.

"And you were as dear to him as Celine."

Beth nodded. "He told me that himself."

Peter looked out through the opened door of his bedroom. When he saw his grandmother being consoled by Beth and David, he knew what had happened. He was sad. He closed the door and stayed in his room, because he wanted to be alone. It was the best way he knew to handle sorrow.

Marie Therese went to the parlor and sat at her desk. It was her unpleasant duty to write to her son with the news. Dear son, your father is dead—Lord! What a thing to write, but in what other words could it be said?

Alone now, she allowed her eyes to wander about the room. That chair over near the wall: how many times had Jan sat in it, reading letters and business papers? And the stuffed chair near the fireplace where he loved to sit of a winter's eve, his feet propped up toward the flames, the warmth seeping into his body, his eyelids growing heavier and heavier until he drifted off to sleep.

The painting on the wall next to the desk; Jan as a younger man with an infant Drew in his arms. She could see the pride in his eyes as he held his firstborn son. How handsome he had been! The firm jaw, the penetrating eyes, the smooth lines of his forehead and cheek—the artist had captured them well, and Marie Therese gazed at them with the love of a lifetime.

Another painting, and an even younger Jan, with his daughter when she was three years old. Celine, even then, thirty years ago, had a look of impertinence.

She straightened the sheet of paper.

"My dear son," she began . . . and then the enormity of what had happened finally caught up with her. *Jan was gone. Gone. Gone.*

It didn't seem possible. Her life and his had been one for many years. Without him, everything would seem empty and meaningless. The only thing with meaning now was their legacy—Celine, Drew, and little Peter.

Jan was gone. She would never again see his face in the morning. Never again kiss his cheek at night. Never again talk quietly in their bed during those gentle moments before sleep came upon them.

She placed her head on her arms and began to cry.

Celine came in and found her mother like this. She sat in the chair at her side, wanting to comfort her, stop her tears. But she couldn't say anything, couldn't do anything; and then the tears began to come from her own eyes.

When Alice de Witt heard about Jan's death, she was distraught. It had been Jan, after all, who had helped her get back on her feet and start a new life. She owed everything to him.

She decided she would go to Enoch and see if there wasn't a way they could work things out. Not that she missed Enoch, but through her marriage to him, she had been related to Jan de Kuyper. Perhaps by trying again with Enoch, she would be paying a final tribute to her benefactor.

She had heard Enoch was living around Little Dock Street, and she went there to look for him. It had been many months since he had lived in the rooms they had once shared, because the landlord had finally tired of not receiving his rent and thrown him into the street.

She finally found a man who knew Enoch and told her where she would find him. It seemed he was living in one of the tents that stood in a lot where a house had been razed by the great fire.

Another man on the lot knew which tent was Enoch's, and now Alice stood before it, summoning her courage to find the right words to say to her husband. Finally she raised the flap and looked inside. An old man looked up and squinted at the unwelcome shower of light.

"What is it yer want?"

"Is... is Enoch de Witt here?"

"De Witt?" the old man mumbled. He thought for a moment, then jerked his thumb toward what looked like a pile of rags against the side of the tent.

Alice entered and returned the flap to its original position, plunged the tent into gloom once more. "You're sure that's him?"

The old man nodded. "That be him. I don't 'spect he'll have too much to say." He rummaged in the debris about him and came up with a half-empty bottle of wine. He uncorked it and began to drink straight from the bottle. Some of the wine slopped onto his cheek and ran down his neck, disappearing beneath his shirt. Paying no heed, the old man kept the bottle tilted in the air.

Alice looked down at the pile of rags. She could see the form of a man. Then she could see the face, and it was Enoch's. He almost looked happy.

"Enoch," she said softly, but there was no reaction.

She reached down and shook him. "Enoch."

He grunted. His eyes seemed to open, but they saw nothing. A wave of sour smells came up and assailed her nose. She pulled back. Enoch settled down in the rags and began to snore.

Alice fled from the tent.

I tried, she told herself. I tried, she told the soul of Jan de Kuyper. I tried, but I couldn't do it.

She would live her life for herself and her daughter. Without Enoch.

Jan was no longer among the living. Her own son had been killed and was no longer among the living.

As far as she was concerned, Enoch had joined them.

Celine was shaking her head as she came out the front door of the Place. She walked toward the sheep barn accompanied by her cousins, Jemmy and Jenny Sackett.

"You're actually making paper?" she asked, disbelief strong in her voice.

"Uh-huh," Jemmy said.

"It's easy," Jenny added.

"How did you learn to do it?"

"From a book," Jemmy said blandly. "Those two printers of yours—"

"They're not *my* printers," Celine objected.

"—needed paper, so I offered to make it for them."

Celine bit her tongue. Jemmy had a way of making everything sound logical even when it was crazy.

It had all started when the two printers, John Holt and Sisyphus, had tried to locate the hidden printing press. They had come to Celine, who knew nothing about it. She mentioned the missing press to Jemmy, and he conducted a thorough search of the city until, with Caleb North's help, he located it in the basement of a burned-out warehouse near the North River. From there, it was a simple leap of logic that led him into the paper manufacturing business.

Celine had moved back to the Place after her father died. She had insisted that Marie Therese accompany her, because she didn't want her mother moping about in the house on Maiden Lane, finding memories of Jan in every closet and behind every door. Besides, it was the middle of September, and the weather made it a joy to live on the East River.

It was, in fact, September 15—two years to the day since the British had attacked and occupied the island of Manhatan. Two years, she thought, *only two years*, and look at all that's happened!

General Howe had resigned and was no longer in New York. He had turned his command over to Sir Henry Clinton and sailed for England at the end of May. Publicly he maintained all was well, but privately to Celine and others he admitted his disgust with the war, and saw no end in sight.

Jenny interrupted her thoughts. "Our first batch of paper will be ready this morning."

"And then Holt and Sisyphus can begin printing," Jemmy said.

They arrived at the sheep barn and went inside. The two printers were working with the new equipment collected or built by the twins.

Celine looked around with distaste. In former times this building had housed a healthy herd of sheep, but now they were gone; the British had commandeered them to feed their army. She had been paid market value for her animals—the British remained fair in this respect to all except known rebels—but she would have preferred to keep them. Their baa-baaing and the tinkle of their bells were lovely sounds.

Jemmy had selected the sheep barn because it stood next to a small stream that ran down to the East River. At the far end of the barn he had constructed a waterwheel—the source of power needed to operate the press.

"Good morning," Jenny said to the printers. "About ready to produce our first samples?"

"I guess so," Holt said skeptically.

"I've done a lot of printing in my time," Sisyphus said. "But I've never made paper before."

"No problem," Jemmy said, briskly rubbing his hands together as he approached a series of trays and kettles. "Come here, Celine, and I'll explain it all."

"It really isn't necessary. I'll just observe."

"Nonsense," Jenny said, taking her cousin's arm and half dragging her to Jemmy's side.

"We take linen rags, cotton ends, and slivers of wood," Jemmy said. "We chop them all up, boil them in lye, then beat them until we get a nice pulpy texture like this."

He held up a handful of goop for Celine to see. "Fascinating," she said, averting her nose from the strong-smelling mess.

"The lye," Jenny explained. "You get used to it."

"Certainly," Celine said, almost gagging.

"Now we pour the pulp into this kettle of boiling water, stirring it constantly to keep it from settling," Jemmy explained. Dutifully, Sisyphus began stirring with a long wooden spoon. "Then we take a rectangular mold with a wooden frame and a bottom of taut wire," Jemmy continued. "The mold is passed through the water, where a quantity of the pulp is caught against the wire mesh. Now we take out the mold and shake it to get rid of the excess water."

He carried out the last procedure, in the process spraying everyone with water.

Celine looked at the wooden frame, which held the now flatly pressed goop. Oddly enough, it was beginning to resemble paper, she thought. It was soggy and grainy, with bits and slivers of wood to be seen, but paper nevertheless.

Jenny took over the narration as her brother continued to

demonstrate the paper-making process. "Now he removes the deckle, takes the mold over to a machine that's called a wet press—"

"I couldn't find one anywhere," Jemmy interrupted. "So I made this one myself."

"Damnedest thing I ever saw," John Holt contributed. "He figured out how to make a wet press without ever having seen one."

"It was just common sense," Jemmy said, playing down his accomplishment to save his modesty.

"He carefully empties the washed pulp from the mold onto a felt pad," Jenny continued. "There are a hundred and forty-four of these pads. On top of each goes a flat mold of pulp. When all the pads are covered, the press is brought down, and the pulp squeezed. This gets rid of the remaining moisture."

"I've previously placed a hundred and forty-three flat molds on the pads," Jemmy said. "So this is the last one."

He touched a lever, and the mechanism went into action. The water from the stream turned the wheel; the wheel turned a large wooden screw; the screw turned another and another, of varying sizes; and the top of the press moved down, causing water to run out on all sides. Jemmy reversed the lever, the top of the press rose, and he was ready for the next step.

He worked swiftly as he passed the now compressed and flattened pulp through a dip. "This gelatine mixture 'sizes' the paper and gives it a smooth texture," he explained. On finishing the sizing, he took the stack of one hundred and forty-four sheets and put them into a dry press, where they would be tightly compressed for an hour.

"The end result is over here," Jemmy said in triumph as he led the others to a second dry press. "We put this batch in an hour ago. Now I'll open it up and we'll have the first paper from our mill."

He held down a lever. The waterwheel turned the wooden screws of the press, and the top moved to reveal a stack of finished paper not unlike the one they had just seen made. Jemmy went over and tapped the pile. "Here, my friends, you see the results of our labors."

Sisyphus and John Holt became excited. Now they not only had a printing press, but paper as well. They were about to go to work.

"The honor of inspecting our first paper shall be yours, Celine," Jemmy said grandly.

"No, that's quite all right, Jemmy, I'll—"

"We insist," Jenny said.

Celine had a dubious look on her face, but she gamely reached to take the top sheet from the stack.

It didn't budge.

She slid her hand down the side of the pile, attempting to find a separation between any of the sheets, but without success. As a last resort, she picked up the whole thing. All one hundred and forty-four sheets were stuck together in a solid lump. "I think there's something wrong," she said.

Jemmy took the pile and attempted to pry off the top sheet with his fingers. Then he used a knife. Nothing happened. The sheets were held together as if they had been packed with mortar.

"Hmm," he said.

"Try dropping it," Jenny suggested.

The stack fell to the floor with a thud. Not one sheet moved even a millimeter. "Hmm," Jemmy said again.

"This means we won't be able to do any printing," Sisyphus said, his face a mask of anguish.

"Not with this batch," Jemmy said. "Now let's see, where did we go wrong?"

"The linen and cotton pulp—did you use the proper proportions?" Jenny asked.

"Yes. It must be something else."

"The water? The press? The wires?" Jenny threw out questions in rapid fire, but her brother kept shaking his head.

"I've got it!" he finally said, snapping his fingers. "The gelatine mixture must be wrong. Instead of making sizing, I think we created glue."

"Yes, glue could cause this reaction," Jenny said solemnly.

"I've got to get back to the house. Thank you for the demonstration," Celine said.

"We'll get it right," Jemmy promised, his mind already at work on the formula of a new gelatine mixture.

Celine walked back along the path from the sheep barn to the house. This used to be such a wonderful farm, she thought. The Place, where lovely parties were held, where men and women drank chilled wine and danced till the sun came up. Look at it now! The sheep barn held a printing press, for which that lunatic Jemmy Sackett was making four-pound sheets of paper. The horse barn was crammed with supplies stolen from the British. The creamery held hundreds of pounds of highly explosive black powder. What used to be the chicken coop was now an arsenal. The pigsty held no pigs, the duck pond was quiet, and the smokehouse had burned down.

And the main house! The two printers had rooms there, and spent half the night babbling away to each other in the kitchen—mother of God, what gabbing!

Mary Delafield now lived here with her baby. Peter and Beth had rooms, but they spent a great deal of their time hunting and fishing—so much time that Celine was beginning to fear her son would turn out to be an Indian.

There were two of Washington's couriers hiding in the upper part of the house—and when they left, they would probably be replaced by two more. And then, of course, there were the Hessians! This was something new. These peasants from Germany were discovering that America was a land of plenty. Many didn't want to go back to Hesse-Cassel, and so they deserted. The man who encouraged them was Franz von Lossow, and through his agents in the city he directed the deserters to the Place, where they could be hidden in the attic until it was safe for them to make their way across the North River to join Washington. Celine wanted to throw them out of the house, because all they seemed to do was get drunk on her beer. But she restrained herself out of consideration for Franz.

Franz... the brightest spot in her life. He had managed to cross the river twice to visit, and had promised to come again after the last campaign of the year. She looked forward to this time. How pleasant and comforting it would be to have him about; how nice to wake up in his arms! She would kiss his lips, and his eyelids until they opened sleepily; and then she would rest her head on his chest and listen to the steady beating of his heart.

When this damned war ended, she was going to marry him and live with him and be happy. Anyone who didn't like the idea of her marrying a Hessian could go straight to hell.

As Celine reached the house, she noticed a strange horse tied up outside. She went inside to find out who the visitor was. If it was another Hessian, she would scream, she promised herself.

It wasn't a Hessian, it was Caleb North.

When Alec Seixas had gone to France, the pirate gang was left without a leader. Several men had tried to play the role and failed, and now the mantle had fallen on Caleb. It seemed to be an excellent fit.

"Hello, Caleb," Celine said. "What brings you here?"

"A thorny problem."

"Let's have some tea while we talk," she said. "Or would you prefer something stronger?"

"A bit of ale might wash the dust of the road from my mouth," he said with a smile.

They sat at the kitchen table while Primus fussed about in the background making lunch. He kept complaining to no one in particular about the extra work he had to do because of the men hiding upstairs. Celine blithely ignored him as she got down to business.

"What's the problem, Caleb?"

"The British have brought an ordnance ship to the dock near the Fly Market. She's crammed with powder. I'd love to be able to take it for Washington."

"So? You've taken plenty of other ships."

"The British are getting smarter in their old age. It's Captain Blakely's doing. The ship is permanently docked. All the spars have been taken down from the masts, and the rudder's been removed. How do you steal a ship without a rudder?"

"I assure you I wouldn't know," Celine said dryly.

Caleb tugged on his forelock. "All that powder, and they'll use it against our people. It's a bloody shame."

"Well, if we can't take the powder, let's not leave it for the British," Celine said.

"What do you mean?"

"If we can't steal it, let's blow it up."

Caleb smiled. "You're a woman after my own heart. Blow up an ordnance ship right at the dock—why not!"

"I want to be there when you do it. It should make a hell of a noise."

"Ah, Celine, 'tis not fit work for a woman."

"And what is fit work, Mr. North?" Celine said, her temper flaring. "Tell me that."

"No offense intended, but you must admit that blowing up ships is not the usual pastime for a lady like yourself."

"Nor is hiding a bunch of krauts in my attic, but I'm doing it. Now let's get on with the planning."

Two nights later Celine was with Caleb and a half-dozen men in the back room of a tavern near the Fly Market dock.

They all listened intently as a small, wizened fellow named Jasper talked.

"I delivered a sack of fish aboard the ship and told them I'd be back with more. They think I'm making regular deliveries for the quartermaster, and they'll be expecting me."

"Good," Caleb said. "We won't disappoint them."

Twenty minutes later the would-be fish peddler went back aboard the ordnance ship. This time he was accompanied by two assistants, both wearing hoods and carrying what appeared to be sacks of fish on their shoulders.

A single sentry stood on the main deck at the head of the landing ladder. When he recognized Jasper's face, he relaxed.

"Evenin', mate," Jasper said.

"How come so much fish?" the sentry asked, jerking his thumb toward the assistants who were coming aboard.

"Maybe it's His Lordship's birthday," Jasper said. "Sort of a present he's giving to you."

"That'll be the day," the sentry said.

Caleb was one of the peddler's assistants, and as he passed the sentry, he dropped his sack and crashed his big fist into the man's face. The other assistant grabbed the unconscious sentry to prevent him from falling to the deck and making noise.

Caleb went to the railing and waved his arm. Immediately the rest of his men and Celine moved out of the shadows and quickly boarded the ship. Meanwhile, Jasper had gone to the hatch that led to the cabins and was listening to see whether their boarding had been noticed.

There was no indication that anyone below was aware of the intruders. Caleb moved to the hatchway. Jasper had told him there were only six guards aboard the ship—and no other crew. They already had one guard; that meant five more were below. With luck, they might all be asleep.

Celine came to the hatch and stood beside Caleb. Her blond hair was tied back and concealed beneath a close-fitting cap. She was masked, wore men's clothes, and carried a pistol in her belt. Her mask, along with those of her companions, was to prevent a chance recognition by one of the guards.

Caleb swore beneath his breath. He had pleaded—God Almighty, how he had pleaded—but nothing had made her change her mind about coming with him. He only hoped she wouldn't foul things up.

He motioned for two men to follow him below. They went down the ladder carefully and quietly. The other four men spread out on the main deck, taking up positions where they could surprise any unwary sailor or sentry who happened to come aboard. Celine had been given no orders, so she stood around for a moment and then decided to go below after Caleb.

The leader and the other two men made their way aft until they came to a hatch opening on the master's cabin. The hatch was ajar, and Caleb peered through the narrow opening. He saw four men; two appeared to be asleep, and a third was seated next to a porthole through which he was staring out at the moonlight playing on the water. The fourth sat at a table, where he cut away with his knife at a loaf of bread and a chunk of cheese.

There were supposed to be five, Caleb thought, and he wondered about the fifth man. He weighed his chances. He and his two companions could be through the hatch and into the cabin before the soldiers knew what was happening. They would be covered by pistols before they could do a thing. He decided to go ahead with this plan, ignoring that there was supposed to be a fifth man. Maybe he was ashore, or maybe Jasper hadn't gotten it straight.

He glanced at his companions and nodded. Moving swiftly, he kicked the hatch open and jumped into the room. The other two were right behind him. The three carried two pistols each, and the startled soldiers suddenly found themselves staring down the muzzles of six ominous-looking guns.

"The man who makes a move is a dead man," Caleb growled.

The unarmed soldiers stayed frozen.

"Hands in the air," Caleb said, and the soldiers wasted no time in complying.

Caleb looked around the cabin. There was no fifth man. That damned Jasper must have been drinking again.

"Cover me," he said, slipping his pistols into his belt. He took the coil of rope he had been carrying over his shoulder and moved toward the soldiers. "All right, lads, who'll be the first to be tied up?"

Three minutes later, each of the soldiers but one had his hands tied behind his back, a thick gag stuffed in his mouth, and a strip of cloth wound about his head and eyes. "And now you," Caleb said to the last soldier. He grabbed the man's arms and began to tie them.

"Hold it!"

Caleb saw the soldier standing in the open hatchway with a musket in his hands. The fifth man!

What might have happened next was a moot question, because at that moment a slight figure slipped behind the soldier and stuck a pistol in his back. "Drop it."

The startled soldier hesitated for only the briefest of moments, then let his weapon drop to the floor, where it landed with a clank. One of Caleb's men picked up the musket and motioned the soldier into the cabin.

Caleb smiled when he saw who had saved them—Celine. But there was no time to talk about it now. In quick order, the fourth and fifth sentries were bound and gagged and blindfolded. While they were being taken ashore to be locked up in a nearby cellar, Caleb and one other man went down into the hold to inspect the store of black powder.

"Is that stuff really so dangerous?"

Caleb looked over his shoulder and saw that Celine had followed him. "Get out of here," he said in a hushed tone, as if afraid that even a normal voice might be enough to set off the explosives. "This is very dangerous," he explained.

"I want to watch what you do," she said.

He took out a long length of slender rope that had been treated with pitch to turn it into a slow-burning fuse. He carefully placed one end into a powder keg that was surrounded by dozens of others. Then he backed out of the low-ceilinged hold, playing out the fuse as he went. When he was ten feet from the door, he reached the end of the fuse.

"Go topside and clear our men off the ship," he said to the man he had brought below. "And don't stay on the dock. Keep going. In three minutes I light this thing."

As the fellow scampered up the ladder, Caleb turned to Celine. "Your turn. And don't stop to look back."

"I'm staying with you to the end."

"Dammit! This isn't a game! You could get killed!"

"You were happy enough to see me when that soldier had a gun on you," she said, stubbornly planting her feet. Clearly, she had no intention of going anywhere.

"All right, have it your way," he said. "Two minutes to go."

They stood in silence, and Celine thought she could hear her own heart beating.

"One minute," Caleb said.

"I hope everyone is off the ship."

"They'd better be."

Another silent period of waiting, then Caleb knelt down in front of the fuse with his piece of flint and steel. He scratched one against the other. Sparks flew off the flint, but they failed to ignite the fuse. He grumbled, cursed, and worked on the flint again. After what seemed an interminable time, the end of the treated fuse hissed and a red glow began slowly to make its way along the length of rope.

"Let's get the hell out of here!" Caleb said.

They went to the ladder. Celine ascended first, and Caleb kept pushing at her buttocks to make her go faster.

"*Mr.* North, if you don't mind..." she complained, not at all pleased with this assault on her dignity.

"Keep moving, keep moving!"

They came out of the hatchway onto the main deck. Caleb grabbed Celine's arm, and they ran across the deck to the gangplank. On the way down, Celine's foot caught on a loose board and she almost fell into the water, but he managed to keep her on her feet. Then they were on the dock and running. None of their companions were anywhere to be seen. They came to the end of the dock, and Caleb headed for an alley. Celine stopped at the head of the alley, turned around, and stood watching the ship.

"Come on!" Caleb said. "She's going to blow any minute."

"Can't we watch?"

"Watch? Jesus Christ! That damned ship's loaded with powder!"

"So, we'll be safe here," she said, slapping her hand against the brick wall of the building at the head of the alley. "Seems pretty solid."

"Listen to me," Caleb said, his face turning red with exasperation. "You don't know how big an explosion that powder will cause."

"Educate me."

He started to speak, changed his mind, and was about to drag her away when the ship's magazine exploded.

The force knocked them to the ground. They were stunned, but had enough presence of mind to cover their heads with their arms. The sound of the blast was stupendous. The middle of the ship had *erupted*, hurling decking and masts high into the air as if they were sticks and twigs. Tons of water were scooped from the river and thrown up in the shape of a waterspout. Then the secondary explosions followed, one after another, and the ship seemed to disappear in a giant fireball.

The pressure wave from the blast blew out every window for a dozen blocks. It knocked down several buildings and killed two people a block away. It was as if a dozen thunderclaps had sounded all at once.

A fifty-foot section of the dock next to the ship disintegrated. One minute it was there, and then it ceased to exist. Two ships moored nearby had their sides caved in. They listed in the water as they started to sink.

The brick building that Celine had claimed would protect them didn't collapse, but a piece of its roof came crashing down into the street. Celine and Caleb were lying on the ground as the wreckage fell about them, and it seemed a miracle they weren't crushed.

The bright-red fireball diminished, and the awful noise and rush of wind subsided. Caleb grabbed Celine by the arm and brought her to her feet. This time she didn't need any encouragement to get moving as fast as she could. They were still half dazed as they stumbled down the alley, which by now was filling with other dazed-looking people, who were coming from their houses to find out what had happened. Many of them had literally been tossed from their beds by the force of the explosion.

Celine and Caleb didn't stop until they were a half mile away from the dock. They leaned against the wooden side of a house, panting, exhausted, grimy—and triumphant.

"Want to come the next time we do this?" he asked.

"I'll settle for your telling me about it," she said, gasping for air and suddenly realizing how dry her throat was.

Patrick Blakely was incensed when he learned the ordnance ship at the Fly Market dock had been destroyed. It had been his idea to disable her so she couldn't be stolen. At last he thought he had a plan that would thwart the pirates. He went to the dock and looked at the wreckage. What a mess! He vowed to make the rebels pay for what they had done.

The next morning he informed Colonel Cunningham he planned on using prisoners to repair the dock.

"Prisoners are not supposed to be used as laborers," the colonel said.

"They wrecked it, let them fix it," was the captain's answer.

"What if they try to escape?"

THE TIDES OF CHANGE

"I'll have enough guards to prevent an escape."

"And forget that you talked to me about this."

"I always forget that I've talked to you, Colonel," Blakely said, and he was amused by the bewildered, half-angry look on his superior's face. Cunningham was never quite sure when his leg was being pulled.

Longboats were sent to the *Devon*, where one hundred prisoners were selected and brought back across the river to Manhatan. They were ragged and filthy, men who had forgotten the smell of soap and the taste of good food. Their faces were dirt-stained, their hair and beards matted and tangled. Most had been incarcerated for less than a year, since the high rate of disease and pestilence constantly trimmed their ranks. A few stout souls, however, managed to go on and on. Among these men with strong constitutions and a stubborn will to live was Robert Delafield.

He no longer resembled the blusterer of old. No longer did he argue and sneer at the opinions of others. In fact anyone who had known him in the old days would have had trouble even recognizing him. He was seventy pounds underweight, with gaunt, hollow cheeks, and his eyes seemed larger because the flesh about them had melted away. Only half of his left ear remained, the rest having been torn off by the sharp edge of a club during a beating by a Hessian guard bent on teaching him to mind his manners. His nose had been broken; it lay flat against his face, giving him the appearance of an unhappy sheep. He walked with a shuffle, his head down, his shoulders hunched. He looked like a beaten man, a man who wanted no more from life than to be left alone.

With the other selected prisoners, Robert came ashore on Manhattan and was marched to the wreckage of the Fly Market dock. Their first task was to clear the rubble in the surrounding streets. It was hard work and they were weak men, so the task went painfully and slowly.

The area around the dock had been cordoned off, and more than fifty soldiers stood guard over the prisoners. Sergeant Taggert was in charge of this work detail, and the red-faced Englishman passed among the working men, issuing an order here, a shout there. If a man was slow to obey, he was hurried in his task by a kick, or a blow from a stout club.

Robert was one of the men assigned to work on what was left of the dock. His job was to remove the shattered timbers to make room for the new ones that would be installed. He was standing next to a piling, working a timber back and forth to loosen it enough to remove it, as Sergeant Taggert walked past, his eyes on the lookout for any malingering.

He looked at Robert, and it seemed to him that the prisoner wasn't working quickly enough. He cracked him on the shoulder with his club.

"More lively, here," he said. "Get your back into it." He continued on his way, thinking no more of the matter. It hadn't been an especially vicious blow; indeed, by the sergeant's standards it had hardly been a blow at all.

But to Robert it was the final insult, the last degradation he could endure. He had been given far worse beatings. He had been insulted and brutalized in ways that should have made the sergeant's blow seem like a love tap. But a man can maintain his sanity only as long as he is able to control his emotions. If the thread between his mind and the world becomes too frayed, it will snap and he will plunge over the edge of control into the abyss of madness—and this is what happened to Robert.

His eyes narrowed, and he looked about in shock after the sergeant had hit him and continued on his way. A look of rage swept over his face, his eyes blinked, and his lower lip trembled. Without a word he threw himself at the back of the man who had offended him.

Sergeant Taggert was taken by surprise. He suddenly found his throat encircled by a pair of hands that were trying to choke the life from him. He struggled in the grasp of his unseen assailant, flailing backward with his elbows in an attempt to hit the man's ribs and break his hold.

Robert was only a shadow of the man he had been. The sharp blows to his ribs made him gasp, and his grip weakened. The sergeant slipped out of his grasp and turned on him. He lashed out with his club, and it found the mark on the side of his victim's head.

Robert staggered backward, putting his hands before his face to ward off any more blows. He came to the jagged edge of the dock where it had been blown away by the explosion, and fell down into the water a dozen feet below.

By this time the men in the immediate area were in an uproar, all pushing and shoving forward to get a better look at what was happening. The guards were moving quickly toward the trouble spot, shouting and cursing at the other prisoners to get out of their way.

"The dirty bastard!" Taggert muttered as he looked down at his assailant. Robert's body was facedown in the water and slowly sinking.

"You lot, get down there and fetch him," the sergeant said to several nearby prisoners. The men rigged a platform consisting of a long plank at the end of two ropes. A prisoner stood on the board as it was lowered down to the water. The man managed to pull the inert body aboard. With much grunting and swearing, the other prisoners pulled the rig back to the top of the dock.

Robert was dead. The blow on the head, combined with the shock of falling into the water, had caused unconsciousness, and he had drowned. Taggert and a milling group of guards and prisoners were looking down at the body as Captain Blakely appeared on the scene.

"What's the trouble?" he asked.

"This bugger jumped me, sir," Taggert said. "I defended myself, and he fell in the water and drowned."

"Why did he attack you?"

"He must've lost control, Captain," Taggert said. "They do that from time to time."

"Do you know his name?"

Taggert shook his head. "I haven't a clue."

One of the prisoners coughed. "Begging the officer's pardon, but his name was Delafield."

"*Robert* Delafield?" Blakely asked.

"Yes," the prisoner said. "Leastwise I think that was his name."

"Robert Delafield?" Sergeant Taggert said, taking a better look at the face of the dead man. He shook his head. "He's changed a lot since I arrested him. Didn't even recognize the man."

Captain Blakely stared down at the body. So this was Mary's husband, he thought. And now he's dead and will never know his wife had another man's child. It was just as well.

"What will happen to the body?" he asked.

"It'll be dumped in a hole with the others who've died," the sergeant said. "That's what happens to 'em all."

"Give this one a separate grave," he said. Sergeant Taggert looked surprised, but nodded his assent.

The captain took a last look at the battered face of the dead man, then walked away. He was debating whether he should send word to Mary. On the one hand, she was bound to learn of it sometime; but on the other, he didn't want to cause her any more anguish. He had given her enough problems.

He remembered some of the things she had told him about her husband, and he knew she had never wanted to live with him again. Maybe it *would* be best to send word to her, so she would know she was free of an irksome burden.

Robert's death also raised another question in his mind. Mary had asked him to stay away from her and remain outside her life. Did her husband's death affect this decision?

He mulled this over, and finally determined that the entire idea of himself and Mary was a preposterous indulgence. Neither by inclination nor temperament nor occupation was he a candidate for domestic bliss. And, looking at it from her point of view, how could she openly be involved with an officer in the British army?

He felt sad about it, because he truly cared for Mary, and she had given him a great deal of pleasure. But pleasure was a fleeting thing, he told himself; one should enjoy it while it lasted and not mourn for it when it was gone.

He arrived back at the Provost and was working at his desk an hour later when Colonel Cunningham sent for him.

"I hear there was a riot among the prisoners on the dock," the colonel said in an accusing tone of voice.

"One man went mad and attacked Sergeant Taggert. It was all over in a minute."

"Only one man?"

"Yes—hardly a riot."

The colonel slammed his hand down on the desk. "All this blasted exaggeration! I was ready to call out the garrison. What happened to the prisoner who went insane?"

"He fell in the water and drowned."

"Still and all, it gives us an indication of what *could* happen. There *could* be a riot. There *could* be a mass escape."

"There *could* be a day when the sun doesn't rise."

"Better not to use prisoners as laborers," the colonel said, ignoring his subordinate's sarcasm.

"As you wish."

"This man who went insane and drowned, was he anyone important?"

"No."

"You know his name?"

"Robert Delafield."

"Delafield... Delafield... why is that a familiar name?"
"You met his widow the day we invaded Manhatan."
"I did?"
The captain nodded. "Remember how we wasted the afternoon in a house—I think they call it the old Beekman's Place—while General Howe made eyes at that blond woman?"
Cunningham's coarse features performed a series of contortions as he delved into his limited memory. "Yes, that pretty blonde who talked so much, I remember."
"Congratulations."
"And this man who died today was her husband?"
The captain shook his head. "Not the blonde. There was another woman there that day, a dark-haired one."
"Yes, of course," the colonel said. "A dark-haired one. Yes, yes, and now she's a widow, eh? Do you know what's become of her?"
"I haven't the slightest idea," Blakely said blandly.
"Ought to keep on top of things, Blakely," the colonel said smugly, being quite pleased with himself in getting the captain to admit there was something he didn't know. It was important to keep one's juniors in their place once in a while.
"I'll try, sir," Blakely said. "After all, I have you as an example of what an officer can become."

Dick Goelet found himself in the bizarre position of stealing pigs from the British army.
He was one of the thirty men under the command of Colonel Franz von Lossow, who had rowed two large flatboats across the Arthur Kill from New Jersey to Staten Island. Not far from the island's western shore the British kept a herd of swine, which they planned on using to feed their city garrison during the winter that was just settling in. Caring for the pigs were a pair of swineherds, who in turn were guarded by a half-dozen Hessians under the command of a British sergeant.
"Take half the men and circle around to the right," von Lossow said to Seth Cuyler, who was now a sergeant in Washington's army.
Dick went with Seth, and within ten minutes they were crouched on a hill looking down on the pens. Von Lossow and the other half of the men were on the hill on the opposite side of the little strip of flatland. Down below they could see the sheds where the swineherds and guards lived. There was no sign of activity.

"What do we do now?" Dick asked.

"Wait for Franz's signal," Seth answered. "He knows what he's doing."

Dick smiled. If only a year ago someone had told him Seth would wind up having a Hessian for a superior officer and a good friend, Dick would have called him a fool.

Until recently it would have been impossible to make such a raid as this one on Staten Island. Less than a month ago there were ten thousand British soldiers in these parts. And then Sir Henry Clinton had decided he was wasting his time chasing George Washington all over New Jersey and Pennsylvania, fighting battles that nobody really seemed to win, and occupying cities only to abandon them, as had been done with Philadelphia. General Howe had fought two great battles to take that city, but this past June the new commander in chief, Clinton, pulled all his troops out. It became an American city again, and the Congress returned to take up its business as usual.

Dick and Seth had been with Washington when he took the field against Clinton at the battle of Monmouth Courthouse. They served in a detachment commanded by von Lossow, and it was then the friendship between the Hessian and Seth developed.

The three of them had been together then, traveling with the new lighter packs Washington himself had designed. These gave the Americans far more mobility than the Hessians, who were loaded down by staggering weights.

It had been a hot and sticky day as the Americans slogged through swamp and forest, coming finally to a sandy marsh area where they caught up with the British. The latter army was staggering through a swampy ravine, plodding along like beasts of burden under their heavy loads, cursing and ready to sell their souls for a cold drink or a breath of fresh air.

The Americans went on the offensive, and von Lossow's men were at one of the points that made first contact with the enemy. The fighting was fierce, and Seth got whacked on the head and fell to the ground. A British soldier was about to run him through with his bayonet when Franz shot the soldier through the head. Then, while Seth lay on the ground trying to regain his senses, the Hessian stood over him with drawn sword and protected him from harm. From that moment, there was nothing but trust and affection between the two men.

It was during this battle that Dick saw a different, more human side of General Washington.

General Charles Lee, who was commanding Dick's sector, decided his Americans were losing. How he came to this conclusion was a mystery, because the British were in retreat. Anyway, Lee ordered his bugler to sound retreat, and the Americans began to pull back. It was a bizarre sight—two armies going in opposite directions in full retreat from one another.

Dick was about twenty feet away from Lee when Washington rode up, his look black with anger.

"What the hell are you doing?" Washington shouted at Lee.

"What, sir?" Lee answered, as if this was a sufficient explanation for his action.

"You boneheaded poltroon!" Washington roared. "Why are you retreating?"

"They were advancing," Lee said.

"And you were beating them, you dirty son of a bitch!"

"But—"

"You're relieved of command, you lousy bastard! Get your ass out of here!"

Dick looked at Seth and smiled. "I believe the general is upset," he said.

Seth chuckled. Washington always tried to maintain a posture of dignity, something that failed him on this day. The men, however, seemed to love him the more for being human even as *they* were.

If the commander in chief was changing, so was his army. The previous year it had been a motley collection of volunteers who thought of themselves primarily as Rhode Islanders, New Yorkers, or Virginians, rather than Americans. They had carried more or less the same weapons, enjoyed the same food, and had the same religious preferences. But that was no longer true, because the army was gaining an international flavor. One could hear French, German, and Dutch being spoken in the camps. Moreover, a French fleet had come into American waters, and now the new nation had an ally. The war was changing from a ragtag rebellion into a battle of equals.

But with winter upon them the battles were over for the year, and Dick was with the men on Staten Island who were about to steal pigs from the British.

Franz checked to see that his men were in place. Then he casually walked down toward the sheds on the flatland. He went to the biggest shed, whose chimney was belching forth a great plume of white smoke. He knocked on the door and spoke to the man who opened it, and within seconds the shed emptied. The six Hessian guards and the British sergeant looked up at the surrounding hills and saw they were covered by thirty men holding muskets. Franz spoke to the Hessians in their own language, explaining who he was and offering them a chance to desert the British and join the American forces. All six accepted. They tore off their epaulets, got their muskets, and lined up behind Franz.

This left only the British sergeant.

"Do you care to join us?" Franz asked.

"I'm loyal to King George," the man said with a strong Liverpool accent.

"But now you can become a loyal American."

"I'm an Englishman," the sergeant answered in an injured tone.

Franz told the Hessians to guard their former leader, and the rest of the men came down from the hills to take charge of the pigs. They were loaded aboard the flatboats to be taken to New Jersey and the larder of Washington's army.

Three men did not accompany them—Franz, Seth, and Dick.

Dick had received a communication that his presence was required in the city. Seth was his companion, and Franz was taking advantage of the situation in order to see Celine.

The three buckskin-clad men made their way to the northern end of the island and came to the village of Tompkinsville, where they found a fisherman who was willing to take them to Manhatan.

As the boat came closer to the Battery, Dick pulled nervously at a lock of his hair. "If they recognize us, they'll put us back on the *Devon*," he said to Seth.

"We looked a lot different the last time we were here."

"What exactly are your orders?" Franz asked.

"To find Celine. She'll tell me what I'm supposed to do."

Franz smiled. "I want to find her myself. I have one stop to make first, however."

"What's that?"

The German reached into his pocket and pulled out some paper money. "This is for a man who helps my Hessians desert the British. He's been very helpful."

"Continental money," Seth sneered. "Worthless."

Franz shrugged. "It's all we have for him."

"Who is this man?" Dick asked.

"A tavern owner named Caleb North."

Dick nodded. "I know him well. He's a good man."

The fisherman let them off at a dock near the Battery. They walked up Broad Way, approaching General Clinton's residence on their way to Caleb's Swan & Bear tavern. A group of mounted officers waited in front of the general's house. Just as the three rebels were passing, Clinton himself emerged. He looked very elegant in his cocked hat, lacy vest, and clubbed and powdered hair.

"Dick, could that be our great conqueror?" Seth asked.

"Off to chase hounds, no doubt."

"Shut up, you two," Franz whispered. "We're loyalists, remember?"

As the general mounted his horse, the others prepared to get under way. Their splendid uniforms told of the wide variety of soldiers serving the Crown in the New World. There was a lieutenant wearing the tall bearskin hat with the insignia of the Seventeenth Light Dragoons. There was an officer of fusiliers, in his distinctive scarlet, blue, black, and white uniform. Next to him was a bare-kneed Highlander, with his badger-head sporran. Two black-gaitered Hessians with blue coats and yellow waistcoats stood to the side a bit, conversing with the guttural tones of their native language.

Franz looked away as he passed these last two, because he knew they would recognize him if they saw his face. The three rebels continued up the street, went into the Swan & Bear, conducted their business with Caleb North, and then were on their way to the de Kuyper house on Maiden Lane.

It had been a long time since Dick and Seth had been in the city, and they kept shaking their heads as they passed rows of buildings that had been destroyed in the great fire and not replaced. The strangers were also depressed by the number of tents in which people lived because they could find nothing better.

They passed a wagon where a man was selling firewood by the bundle—and a paltry bundle it was—for six shillings each.

"Six shillings for *that?*" Dick asked in disbelief.

"A cord of wood now costs from ten to twelve pounds," Franz said. "Assuming you can find someone who'll sell you a full cord."

"Are all the prices like this?" Seth asked.

"Some are worse," Franz said.

"How do the people survive?" Dick said.

"Not very well," Franz informed him.

They came to Maiden Lane, but stopped a block away from the de Kuyper house. A man named Quigley, a rabid loyalist, was lounging on the front stoop.

Dick kept his back toward the house. "I know that man, and he knows me," he said. "He'll turn me in if he sees me."

"Quigley," Seth said in recognition. "He's sure to know me too. What's he doing at your cousin's house?"

Dick shrugged. "We'd better find out."

"I'll do it," Franz said. "He won't know me."

The Hessian went up to Quigley, had a brief conversation with him, and returned to his companions. The explanation was simple enough: the British had commandeered the King's College building for use as a hospital; and since Marie Therese was now living up at the Place, she was allowing the school to use her house temporarily.

"So we'd best get up to the Place," Dick said.

The three men walked north until they came to Queen Street. "Don't look now," Seth said. "But Quigley is following us."

Sure enough, Quigley appeared at the head of Queen Street, trying to remain inconspicuous. Seth gestured that they should turn up the next alley, and as they did, they disappeared from Quigley's view.

"The little rat's recognized us," Seth said.

"Maybe he thinks he'll get a reward for turning us in," Dick said.

"You two keep going," Seth said as he slipped into a doorway. "I'll take care of friend Quigley."

Dick and Franz walked to the end of the alley and approached Golden Hill Street. Quigley came scurrying down the alley, and halfway to the end he was grabbed from behind. Dick looked back and saw that Seth had Quigley. He hurried back to help out, but by the time he arrived it was all over. Quigley lay on the ground with a broken neck.

"Little bastard," Seth said.

"Where you find one spy or informer, you'll find more," Franz said. "Let's get out of here."

They continued up Queen Street toward the Post Road. Ordinarily it would have been a pleasant walk, but the wind picked up and it began to snow. Soon the snow was coming down in great flurries, and after a mile of steady slogging the three men began to tire. But on they went, their heads buried in their collars, three ghosts wandering through a landscape silent as death.

By the time they arrived at the Place, it was dark. Celine kissed them and took them into the kitchen, with its cheery fire. Primus immediately made mugs of steaming rum-and-beer. "This war is making you look older," he said to Dick. "I hope it's making you smarter too."

"Primus, what a thing to say!" Celine said.

Dick laughed. "He's known me since I was born. He's entitled to say anything he wants."

The three men drank from their mugs and began to thaw out before the fire. Dick brought up the subject of his visit. "Washington told me to see you," he said to Celine. "He said you had a mission for me."

Franz patted Celine on the hand. "The prettiest commanding officer in the army," he said.

"Actually it's not me who's to tell you of the mission, but Marie Therese. She'll be here in a minute."

"Do you know what it's about?" Dick asked.

"Yes," Celine said, but didn't elaborate. The men looked at each other in surprise.

Marie Therese came into the room, and the men rose to greet her. Franz bowed low as he kissed her hand in the European manner. "As charming as ever," he said.

"Mother, perhaps you'd like to be alone with Dick," Celine suggested. "It is something of a private matter."

"Secrets? Among old cellmates?" Seth said. "Now I'm really curious."

"I'll be happy to leave if you wish," Franz offered.

Marie Therese thought about it for a few moments, and then made her decision. "Both Franz and Seth are good friends, and men to be trusted," she said. "Besides, Dick may need some help."

"To do what?" Dick asked.

"Let's go down to the cellar," Marie Therese said, and started out of the room with the mystified men and Celine following her. They went down a narrow staircase, their way illuminated by candles held by the two women.

"Over this way," Marie Therese said when they reached the bottom. The dirt of the floor was hard, and the place had a musty smell. She went to the far end of the room, where there was a stout wooden partition built from wall to wall. A heavy iron lock was in the door. She took out a large key, and after a few seconds of metal grating on metal, the lock was opened and the door swung out. Celine led the way with her candle and the group entered the cubicle. Two dozen quarter-kegs were neatly stacked in two rows, their forms casting strange shapes against the back wall.

Marie Therese went to the first keg and removed the top, while Celine held her candle in a way that allowed the others to see the contents. Marie Therese dipped her hand in and brought it up filled with gold coins. She let them drop back into the keg. "There are twenty-four kegs," she said. "They're all filled with gold."

"Mother of God!" Seth hissed between his teeth.

"A fortune," Franz said quietly.

"What is this all about?" Dick asked.

"This fortune was once buried beneath our house on Maiden Lane," Marie Therese explained. "Last year Jan transferred it here. The only people who know about it are myself, Celine, Primus, and David Sackett. The three of you, of course, are now included in this little group."

Franz reached out and plucked a coin from the top of the pile. It was a gold Venetian zecchino, dated 1621. "I wish this coin could talk and tell us its story," he said.

"I can tell you part of it," Marie Therese said. "It was once part of the treasure collected from ships in the Indian Ocean by Captain William Kidd. He buried it on Gardiner's Island. My husband's father, James de Kuyper, dug it up and hid it beneath a theater on Maiden Lane. Jan transferred it, first to our house on that street, and then to here."

"But what am I supposed to do with it?" Dick asked.

"We've had a letter from Drew," Celine said. "He needs money to buy ships from the Dutch."

"Congress doesn't have any gold to give him," Marie Therese explained. "And the Dutch won't accept our paper currency."

"Smart of them," Seth murmured.

Marie Therese continued. "I told General Washington I could get gold and send it to Drew. That's your job, Dick— to take some gold to France."

"Captain Kidd," Dick said softly, his head spinning with the rumors he had heard about the old scoundrel and his buried treasure. And all the while it had been in the safekeeping of the de Kuyper family!

"It's a big job," Franz said. "And important."

"It was James de Kuyper's wish that the gold be used only to help New York," Marie Therese said. "I would think buying privateers to chase the English out fits into that category."

"Does Drew know about this?" Dick asked.

"Jan never got around to telling him about the treasure. The war sort of interrupted everything."

Seth laughed aloud. "The de Kuypers are the only people in New York who could sit on top of a mountain of gold and not say anything about it."

The next day they all ate a midday dinner together, joined by Peter, Beth, and Mary. Dick was startled to see how much Peter had grown since he had seen him last. The little boy was fast becoming a young man.

"You're going to France to see Drew?" he asked.

"Yes," Dick said. "He doesn't know I'm coming, so it'll be a surprise."

"I'd like to see him, too," Peter said wistfully. "We used to have such good times together."

Marie Therese was looking closely at her grandson. She often regretted that Drew was no longer around to be surrogate father to him. It was also obvious that Celine was infatuated with Franz von Lossow, and in the normal course of events would probably marry him, and then the boy would have a stepfather—but that wouldn't happen until the war was over, and God alone knew when that would be.

"Have you ever been to Europe?" Franz asked Dick.

"No, this will be my first time."

"It will be a good experience for you. I'm certain the average American has no idea of the vast differences between his country and the Old World. The conventions and customs are very ancient and different there. You will learn much about the world that you are not aware of now."

"Would it be a good experience for someone Peter's age?" Marie Therese asked innocently.

The German smiled at the boy. "He would learn more than any of you from such an experience. The younger the person, the more receptive the mind."

"Would you like to go with Dick?" Marie Therese asked her grandson.

Peter's eyes grew big, and he opened his mouth to speak.

"Now wait a minute," Celine interrupted. "He's only a boy, and it's up to me to make this sort of decision."

"It would be wonderful for Peter," Beth chimed in. "And it would get him away from this stupid war."

"And give him a chance to be with his uncle," Marie Therese said.

"You would be a man in no time," Franz assured the boy.

"I want to go!" Peter said.

"Hold it!"

Celine was on her feet. "I don't believe what I'm hearing. I'm his mother, and nobody's asking me what I think."

"Well, what *do* you think?" Marie Therese said sternly.

Celine was flustered. It had all happened so quickly she'd had no time to mull over the idea. Certainly it would be a broadening experience. And certainly it would be good for Peter to see his uncle. But he was her only son, and he seemed so young, and Europe was so far away...

"Can I go?" Peter said, interrupting her thoughts.

"Do you really want to?"

"Yes."

"Well...all right, then."

"I'll take good care of him," Dick said.

"Maybe I'd better go with you," Seth said to Dick. "Between keeping one eye on the gold and one on the boy, you might need help."

"An excellent idea," Franz said. "I'll tell the general when I return to camp."

"Then it's settled," Marie Therese said. But she averted her eyes from Celine, because she knew she had pushed her daughter into this decision. She was convinced, however, that it was in Peter's best interests, and had no regrets. She would make it up to Celine later.

"I wish I could go," Beth said, and then shook her head. "I had better stay here and help look after things."

Dick looked at Beth—and suddenly fell in love. He had always realized she was beautiful, but until this moment had never fully understood *how* beautiful.

"I wish you were coming, too," he said.

"Yes, I'd like to see Andrew again," she said.

Celine blew a wisp of hair from in front of her eyes. "Maybe he wouldn't be so blind this time."

Dick didn't miss the undercurrent, and was embarrassed.

If Drew and Beth were in love with each other, what kind of friend would he be to interfere? He looked longingly at Beth and was jealous of his cousin.

"What's all this about gold?" Peter asked.

"Dick is taking gold to Drew to buy ships," Marie Therese said.

"I didn't know we had any gold," the boy said.

"There are a lot of things you don't know," Celine said. She knew she had spoken sharply, and realized it was because she resented the way she had been pushed into agreeing to sending her son away.

"Now let's not get cranky," Marie Therese said, aware of what was going on in her daughter's mind.

"It will be a wonderful experience for the boy," Franz said, and his voice was tinged with iron. "If you try to hold on to a child too long, you do him a disservice."

Celine pressed her lips together in uncertainty, and suddenly was contrite. "You're right, of course. And I won't be cranky. Peter, come here and give your mother a kiss."

Peter wasn't thrilled, but he kissed Celine; it seemed to be the final seal on the bargain. Going to France and seeing Drew was worth the slight humiliation of having his mother kiss him and cry before all these people.

After dinner Mary Delafield brought little David into the room, fresh from his nap. She seemed radiant; happier than she had ever been. Dick, standing apart from the others with Marie Therese, said as much.

"I'm sure you're aware it was an ... unconventional birth," Marie Therese responded. "Sometimes a child born under such circumstances means more to the mother."

Dick wanted to ask the name of the father, but hesitated.

Marie Therese understood. "I don't know myself," she said. "And I hope to God I never find out. Some things are better off remaining a mystery."

"Mary seems happy," Dick offered.

"Happier than she's been in years," Marie Therese agreed.

As the evening wore on, people drifted off to their rooms. Eventually Franz made his way from his own bedroom to Celine's.

"I thought you weren't coming," she said.

"I didn't want to meet anyone in the hall."

"And *I* didn't altogether like your tone of voice when you lectured me about raising Peter."

Franz regarded her coldly, and then weakened. "Don't be afraid that I'll try to dominate you."

A smile crossed her lips. "I'm hardly afraid of that."

Franz had become well aware that while he had Celine's love, he would never have her submission. Nor, he told himself, did he want it. There was only one way to conquer this woman. He took her in his arms and kissed her. Her hands explored his chest and then moved around to his back. She and Franz took their time, never hurrying, prolonging the moment when they would begin to satisfy each other. Finally, when their hands could no longer stop moving and their bodies were almost out of control, they dropped down onto the soft bed and huddled under the covers.

"My God!" she said. "Do I want you."

In answer he brought his naked body against hers. It had been a long time for both of them.

Three weeks later the two men and the boy were ready to sail on a Dutch ship bound for Le Havre. Their luggage included six quarter-kegs of gold, and the precious burden made the men nervous. The kegs were marked "BALLAST LEAD," which would explain their heaviness and also make them appear worthless. Six quarter-kegs of gold was enough to bring every pirate on the seas down on them if they had known.

Before they left, Beth sought out Dick and asked him to give her regards to Drew.

"Tell Andrew we miss him," she said.

"Do you miss him more than the others?" Dick asked boldly.

"Yes," she admitted.

"He's a lucky man."

She smiled. "He doesn't seem to know it."

"I wish I was in his shoes," Dick said.

"You fill your own quite nicely," she said politely, and then switched subjects. "I want you to take good care of Peter. He's a wonderful person."

"I understand you've taught him to hunt with a bow and arrow."

"Yes, he's quite good with them."

"Maybe I should learn, too," Dick said. "Then maybe you'd pay attention to me."

Beth sighed. "I think you're very sweet, Dick. But there can be nothing between us as long as I feel the way I do about Andrew. If that ever changes . . . well, we'll see what happens."

It wasn't much of a promise, but it was enough for Dick, because it left the door to Beth slightly ajar. For the moment that was all he was going to get, and he had to settle for it.

The ship left the dock, and Celine stood at the very end, crying and waving her handkerchief. Marie Therese stood at her side with Franz, but nothing could stem her own flood of tears.

Peter stood at Dick's side at the railing and watched as the figures of his mother and the others grew smaller.

"Will you miss them?" Dick asked.

"Yes," the boy replied. "But I'm glad I'm going to France," he added.

"It's thousands and thousands of miles away," Dick said.

"I know."

"Do you know how far a thousand miles is?"

Peter eyed his companion coldly. "If we're to get along, you mustn't treat me like a child," he said.

Whew! Dick thought, this certainly was Celine's son. Ten years old and he was already putting people in their place.

Another keg of gold left the Place that very night. This one was smuggled back to Washington's camp by Franz von Lossow. It was an unexpected windfall, but the question was what to do with it. Should it be used to pay the troops? Or should it be sent to the Congress for their use?

Finally General Washington chose the latter course. It was Alex Hamilton who convinced him the soldiers would be content to accept the paper money issued by Congress even though everyone knew it was virtually worthless.

"These men are fighting for more than money," he insisted.

"But is it moral of us to hold back hard money from the men when we have it?"

"The men don't even know about it," the pragmatic Hamilton said.

"*We* know about it," Washington said tartly.

Hamilton shrugged. "Congress could use it to buy guns from the Portuguese. They take only gold."

In the end the young aide had his way and the gold was sent to Philadelphia, where a pleased Congress negotiated with the Portuguese to turn it into weapons. By a strange twist of fate, the middleman who arranged the deal was none other than Philemon Peabody.

For his part in the affair he was entitled to three and one-half percent of the total, but through adept juggling and trickiness, he managed to keep four and one-quarter percent. As he delivered the gold to the Portuguese, he congratulated himself on making a splendid deal.

It was only afterward that something about the gold coins struck him as odd. Almost every coin had been over a hundred years old. How strange. It was almost as if they had been buried for many years, and recently resurrected. Buried treasure? he mused, and could feel his pulse quicken at the very thought.

If the coins were buried treasure, he reasoned, then what he had handled might only be a part of it. There might be more—lots more. He decided it was worth looking into. The problem was, how to go about it? He could hardly go back to New York and start asking questions. In the first place, that blackguard, Captain Blakely, would hang him, and if he somehow slipped out of that, he'd have to answer to the de Kuypers.

He decided the best thing to do at the moment was to backtrack the gold: How did Washington get it, and from whom? That evening he visited a tavern on the Schuylkill River and looked up a man he knew. For a modest fee this man agreed to go to Washington's winter camp at Morristown and snoop about.

Philemon Peabody went home to bed satisfied that he had completed a good day's work. First a healthy commission on the Portuguese deal, and now, perhaps, a chance to sniff out the trail of a buried treasure.

A buried treasure! And if he ever found it, wouldn't *that* be putting one over on the high-and-mighty de Kuypers!

Caleb North was in his tavern, seated at the table nearest the fire and enjoying dinner with Alice de Witt. Little Elly was spending the night with Jenny Sackett, and Alice had a rare free evening. It wasn't the first time Caleb had invited her to dine with him, but it was the first time she had accepted.

They were discussing the recent arrival and departure of Dick Goelet and Seth Cuyler. "I don't think Seth feels comfortable in New York anymore," Caleb said. "Not that long ago, he was a prosperous businessman with a fine wife and a handsome son."

"Then he went to prison," she said.

"His business vanished. His son was killed by the Hessians.

And his good wife died last winter of the lung disease. No wonder he couldn't wait to leave this place!"

"He's suffered a great deal."

Caleb ate a few more mouthfuls of deer meat and washed them down with a quaff of ale. "You've suffered a great deal yourself, Alice."

She was silent for a moment. "I lost my son," she finally said. "And things were rough for a time. But I have a good home and a healthy daughter. And the de Kuypers and Sacketts have been wonderful to me. They're really Enoch's family, but they treat me as if I were one of their own."

The mention of her husband's name caused Caleb to make a sour face. Enoch de Witt was as hopeless as ever. Only a few nights ago he had come into the Swan & Bear already in his cups. He had two drinks and passed out. Caleb left him asleep near the fire. When he came back the next morning to reopen the tavern, Enoch was gone and had left the back door open.

"I hope you're not having anything to do with Enoch anymore," he said.

She shook her head. "I have nothing to do with him. I tried to help him, but there was nothing I could do. I don't mind the way things are for myself, but it bothers me to have Elly growing up with such a father. People can be very cruel."

"No one will blame Elly for Enoch. They won't blame you, either."

"I don't know," she said thoughtfully. "Sometimes I think if I'd been a stronger person, I might have been able to help Enoch."

"So what are you going to do with the rest of your life?"

"What do you mean?"

"You're a handsome woman," he said, looking at her with approval. "You've got a good head on your shoulders. Didn't it ever occur to you that another man might want to make you his wife?"

"My husband is still alive," she said in a very small voice.

"Barely," Caleb said with distaste. "And even if he is, what does he do for you? A husband is supposed to take care of his wife. Enoch can't even take care of himself."

Alice drank more of the wine in her goblet. It was a rich red, and strong enough to make her feel light-headed. It also gave her the courage to bring up a subject she had been avoiding for a long time.

"If I were an unattached woman, you'd be interested in me?"

"I'm interested in you now," he said without evasion. "You know that; I've certainly made no secret of it."

"Yes, I have known it for some time. And you're a free man. But we can't forget I'm not free."

"Being married to a man like Enoch is a joke," he said bitterly.

"May I make a confession to you?"

"Of course."

She took another drink before she spoke. "I find you to be a very attractive man, Caleb. A good man, too. I've even daydreamed about you. How nice it would be to be with you and Elly in a house. We could be a real family, Caleb, a happy family."

He reached out and took her hand. "I know it. And I can't think of anything I want more."

"Elly would be proud of her home. And proud of you. It would be wonderful for her to have such a life."

"Then why don't we come to grips with the issue?"

"Because just when the dream seems the most wonderful, I wake up and remember I'm a married woman."

"And so we'll continue to live this way and be miserable?"

"What else is there to do?"

They drank and ate in silence for a time. Alice kept looking at him, and it seemed she was having a struggle within herself. She finished her wine and allowed him to refill the goblet. Suddenly she smiled.

"You've invited me to dinner many times," she said.

"I know."

"And I've always turned you down."

"I know that, too."

"Do you know why?"

"Why?"

"I was afraid."

"Of what?"

"That I'd say exactly what I'm going to say now."

He looked at her, puzzled.

"Take me someplace," she said huskily. "Take me someplace and make love to me, Caleb North!"

Spring had come to Paris.
The dormant land, long asleep under winter's care, sighed

THE TIDES OF CHANGE

and came to life. The naked branches and twigs of trees burst into new buds and leaves. Color came back to the earth. Doors and windows that had been shuttered now opened, and bright streams of sunshine flooded into rooms that had been gray and musty.

The people awoke. It was now time to begin planting, time to drop seeds into the earth, seeds that would grow and bring a bountiful harvest in the fall. Spring: people loved to say the word. They would murmur it with a smile as they walked along the banks of the Seine, breathing the softened air, feeling the brush of tender grass under their boots. Spring, they thought: the chance for a new beginning.

Drew rode his horse along the road that followed the meanderings of the river. He was on his way back to Passy, filled with mixed emotions about the progress of his negotiations with the French and the Spanish. He was also concerned with the course of the war back in America.

The British had seized Augusta, and had successfully repelled an American offensive to recapture it. They were in possession of Savannah.

To counterbalance these losses, there had been two battles fought in South Carolina, at Port Royal and Kettle Creek, and both had been won by the Americans.

In New York, General Clinton was amassing an army to move north to test the American forces that had been so victorious the previous year over Burgoyne. It began to seem that a victory here was balanced by a loss there, the net results of a year's campaigning working out as a draw.

This was unacceptable to a man as young and impatient as Andrew de Kuyper. Three years ago, in 1776, he had been willing and eager to come to reasonable terms with the king. But after three years of fighting and bloodshed, three years of prisons and prisoners, three years in which hatreds were allowed to grow and fester, his position had hardened and he no longer wished to come to terms with men he considered his oppressors. Now the only acceptable solution was to drive every Englishman from the American continent.

He arrived at the Hôtel de Valentinois and left his horse in the stable. Ben Franklin was in his apartments enjoying a bath, and Drew was forced to wait half an hour before he made his appearance.

"A cleansed body means a cleansed soul," the old gentleman said as he joined Drew in the salon.

"Did one of the chambermaids help you with your bath?" Drew asked dryly.

Franklin chuckled. "The dark-haired one, the little one. When a man reaches my age, he finds it hard to scrub his back."

"I'm sure she did a good job."

"She always does, she always does," Franklin said, and Drew smiled, because Ben and his baths were infamous; he rarely took one without the help of at least one pretty girl. Indeed, the chambermaids at the hotel vied for the honor.

"I have good news about the Spaniards," Franklin said, getting down to business. "Yes, indeed, very good news."

"Yes?" Drew said with interest.

For over a year Franklin had been trying to draw the Spanish into the war on the American side. The wily diplomats from the Iberian Peninsula so far had refused to commit themselves to the cause; in fact they were less than happy about the idea of the American colonies winning their freedom from Britain. They reasoned that an independent America might inspire a similar revolt in their own American possessions, and this was clearly unacceptable. However, beyond all reason, the Spanish hated the English and their dominance of the seas, and were willing to suspend logic if it meant a British defeat.

So the Spaniards had proposed a deal.

"Give us Gibraltar," they said to the English prime minister, "and we will remain neutral."

The prime minister would not even consider such a proposal, claiming Gibraltar was far too vital to the interests of the Empire.

"Well, that was all that was needed to push the Spaniards into our camp," Franklin said. "The Spanish ambassador, in the presence of de Vergennes, informed me Spain would issue a declaration of war against England."

"Ben! You did it! Now we have both France and Spain in the war on our side!"

"There's a catch to it," Franklin said. "Spain has declared war on Britain, but she still refuses to recognize American independence. As far as they're concerned, that's a separate issue."

"What difference does that make?" Drew asked. "They've still declared war."

"Yes, but we have no assurances they'll continue to fight until we've won our war."

"You're the one who always told me you build a wall brick by brick. So now the Spaniards are laying bricks. What's to complain about?"

Franklin laughed. "The trouble with imparting wisdom to the young is they become smarter than oneself. All right, all right, I suppose it is something to be pleased about. Now tell me, how did your talks about money go with the French?"

Drew sat down in an uncomfortable high-backed chair. He placed one knee over the other and nervously jiggled his foot. "They're very pleasant, but they won't give us more money. Beaumarchais claims they haven't got it. Ben, I can't believe that. Even now—after how many visits?—when I go to Versailles I still blink my eyes at all that splendor."

"Ah, that's *Versailles*," Franklin said. "Look around at the rest of the country and you'll see our friend Beaumarchais speaks the truth. The wealth of the French nation is being siphoned off to maintain Versailles. For every French nobleman enjoying roast squab for breakfast, there are a thousand peasants going to bed hungry at night. The fact is, the country is going broke."

"That doesn't help us with our problem. We need money to buy ships from the Dutch. With them it's cash on the barrelhead and go hang yourself with promises."

The old gentleman was amused. "It would seem that a man with a name like de Kuyper should be able to appreciate the mercenary qualities of the Dutch."

Drew returned the smile. "When I was a little boy I used to ask my father for money. No matter how small a sum, he never gave it to me until I'd done some job for him. To gain a shilling I'd sweep the front steps, curry a horse, or carry in firewood. He claimed a man had to learn to work for his living."

"Exactly; and our friends in Amsterdam are saying that if we want their ships, then we'd better come up with the money. To tell you the truth, I'd rather deal with a tightfisted Dutchman, any day of the week, than listen to the emotional tirades of these bloody Frenchmen. If I hear one more speech about their 'histoire de gloire,' I think I'll scream."

"It's the price we must pay for their support," Drew said, amused by Franklin's posturing. "The problem is, they have too much *gloire* and not enough *pourboire*."

"Then we must do as my God-fearing New England ancestors would have done," Franklin said, bringing his hands together as if in prayer. "We must ask the Almighty for a miracle."

"And if we don't get it?"

"Then we steal it!" the old gentleman said as he slapped his hand on the table. "Only God knows where we'll steal it from. Maybe it's time you went back to England and tried your hand there again."

"Dammit, Ben, you promised I could stop playing the diplomat at this bunch of tea parties. I want to be more active."

"What could be more active than raising a fleet, my boy? You get the ships and we'll win the war."

"I wasn't meant to wear silk waistcoats and dance all night at some marquis's château," Drew complained. "At heart I'm a raggedy-assed colonial. I want to drink, smell like a bear turd, and fight in a tavern brawl."

"Admirable, admirable."

"I mean it!"

"Certainly, but in the meantime you'll continue doing the job I tell you to do, because it's the one that will help your country the most," Franklin said, and Drew recognized the tone as final.

He walked over to the window and glumly stared out at the blossoming garden. He wanted to tell Franklin he was going off to do what he damn well pleased. He also knew he would say nothing of the kind.

Of course, there were some compensations in this life he was leading—one of which had presented itself only recently.

He had been invited to dinner at the château of the Comte de Mirabois, and in the course of the evening had chatted at length with Juliette, comtesse de Villette. The comtesse was a sophisticated woman in her mid thirties, not quite content with her life as the wife of a man in his seventies who rarely left his vast estate near the river Loire. Indeed, the comte was possessed of such ill health he rarely left his bedroom. Which did not, of course, prevent the comtesse from spending a great deal of her time pursuing her various interests in Paris and at the châteaux of her friends.

At the moment she was a guest of the Comte de Mirabois, between lovers, indolent, and bored with life in general. When the young American diplomat entered the grand salon, she singled him out as someone deserving of her personal attention. She cultivated him by pretending an interest in life in America.

Drew was happy to talk about New York—what the people ate, what they wore, and the sort of houses they lived in. By the end of the first hour of their acquaintanceship she was holding his hand, looking deep into his eyes, and encouraging him to call her Ettie, the name, she said, all her closest friends used.

By this time in his life Drew was not exactly an innocent; nor did he act like a backwoodsman who had stumbled by mistake into the court of Louis XVI. Rather the opposite. He was an urbane young man who knew New York, London, and Paris, and conversed daily with men who wielded power in the world.

But even so, he was no match for the comtesse, whose life was a single-minded pursuit of pleasure and who allowed nothing to stand in her way when she wanted something.

Within two days the young American lay on her bed, naked and exhausted. The sweat glistened on his chest, and she ran her practiced hand over his skin, exciting him even though he knew his body was, at the moment, beyond further stimulation.

"A barbarian body," she cooed in French. "How much better than some fat marquis or jaded chevalier. You must never let yourself fall apart like that, my little cabbage; no, never."

At times there were soft, tender moments between them, but mostly their lovemaking more resembled a battle, with a great deal of biting and scratching mingled with the pleasure.

"Does that hurt?" she would ask as he felt her talons sinking into the fleshiness of his shoulders and drawing blood. And then he would hit her as she had taught him to do, and they would find ecstasy in the mixing of one sensual stimulus with another. Even when his body was exploding in an orgasm, she would find another pain to inflict, either with her nails or her teeth.

It was his introduction to the art of seeking pleasure without the slightest thought of its meaning anything more. With the other women in his life, there had always been something else—a tenderness, a caring, sometimes even a sort of patronizing. But with the comtesse there was no time for any of that, nor any place; there were only two naked bodies writhing on the sheets, straining at one another, working themselves into a frenzy.

"And now, my barbarian," the comtesse would say after he was certain he could not go on. "Let us see what will arouse you."

And she never failed.

"What are you thinking about?" Franklin asked, breaking in on his reverie.

"I was thinking about the fact that I will do as you wish."

Franklin nodded. "Thank you, my friend," he said to the young New Yorker who was half a century his junior.

"Perhaps things will change soon and we'll be able to spare your services," he added gently.

"You don't have to apologize, Ben. I know you're only thinking of what's best for America."

"Yes, but it still bothers me that you gnaw away at your insides because you aren't doing something more physical." A sudden smile brightened his face. "But speaking of the physical, I've heard you've become a good friend of the comtesse de Villette."

"Nothing of importance," Drew said with some embarrassment.

"Yes, yes," the old gentleman said with a chuckle. "I've heard a great deal about the comtesse, yes indeed. I'll say this for you, you don't pick the easy ones."

"Perhaps you'd care to take her off my hands?"

"No, no, I'm getting too old for that sort of woman. I like them poor and barefoot."

Drew smiled. Despite his disclaimers, the old gentleman was notorious for his womanizing. The French, of course, loved him for it, and in certain circles he was considered a pet. Some women gained a certain *cachet* merely by bragging they had dallied with him.

"But I'm willing to share this one with you, sir," Drew said.

"There are so many to be conquered. Why should I intrude on your territory? Anyway, I'd prefer not to be a rival to a man who has the advantage of youth."

"The lady who would prefer me to you has not been born," Drew said gallantly.

"Not even the Lady Althea Middleton?"

Drew's mouth opened. How in the devil had he found out about her?

Franklin looked delighted. "There's not much I don't hear about. She's quite lovely, as I recall. But watch out: these Englishwomen play a different game. With the French it's a case of *borrowing* your body; the English want to own it."

He turned suddenly to business. "I've had a letter from Stormont," he said, picking up a sheet of paper from the table.

"I thought His Lordship went back to England in a fit of pique after the French signed the treaty with us."

"He did. The letter came from London."

"What does he want?"

"To discuss an exchange of prisoners."

"That's good news. How do you plan to go about it?"

"I was hoping to send you."

Drew shrugged. Another sustained period as a diplomat. But it was important, because he would be able to help the poor wretches languishing at Portsmouth and Plymouth. He also would have the chance to see Althea again. Take the good with the bad, he thought. Aloud, he simply said, "All right."

The next day Dick, Seth, and Peter arrived in Paris, and because of what they brought there was no more talk of Drew's going off in haste to London.

Drew was in the little room he used as an office in the Hôtel de Valentinois when they descended on him. He looked up in astonishment as the porter announced his visitors, and could scarcely believe his eyes.

"This *can't* be Peter!" he said in mock astonishment. "Surely this young man is only pretending to be my little nephew."

Peter smiled. "It's been a long time," he said, and held out his hand in adult fashion.

"It must be hard on Celine to have such a big son," Drew said to Dick. "Reminds her of her own age."

"Mother looks as young as ever."

"I think I'll go back to the carriage and bring in the surprise," Seth said.

While the others waited for him to return, Dick told Drew some of the news from New York. He commiserated with his cousin about the death of Jan, but told him Marie Therese had taken it very well.

Drew asked about David Sackett and the twins. He wanted to know how Alice de Witt was faring, and whether Enoch had straightened himself out. He even asked about old Sisyphus.

"Don't you want to hear about Beth?" Dick asked.

"Of course," Drew said. "How is she?"

"Fine."

"That's good," Drew said, and passed on to another subject. Dick was amazed by his cousin's indifference toward the girl. He couldn't imagine that any man would be stupid enough to ignore the fact that Beth loved him.

Seth Cuyler returned with a hotel servant, who was helping him carry a heavy quarter-keg. They placed it on the floor with a loud thump. The servant withdrew after Seth handed him a small coin.

"Here, my boy," Seth said as he handed a chisel to Drew. "You do the honors."

Drew pried the lid open and gasped when he saw the glittering contents. "God Almighty," he whispered, and it was more of a prayer than an oath. He shoved his hand down, and it disappeared in the sea of coins. "Gold! The lot of it! You've brought a fortune!"

"There's more in the carriage," Seth said.

"Compliments of your mother, your grandfather, and Captain William Kidd," Dick said. "Not to mention the poor souls it was originally stolen from."

"I don't understand," Drew said.

Dick told him the story as he had heard it from Marie Therese. As a lad, James de Kuyper, Drew's grandfather, had sailed with the notorious Captain Kidd on a series of voyages when Kidd turned pirate. James was one of the three men who helped Kidd bury the treasure. After the captain was executed and the third sailor killed, there were only two men who knew the whereabouts of the gold—James and a man named Charles Lewis. They kept the secret for many years, finally digging up the treasure only when it looked as if the French were going to attack New York during the French and Indian War. The money had been used to buy ships to protect the city.

"It seems James had the idea that the money was ill-gotten and therefore should be used only for the public good, never as his private fortune," Dick said. "After his death, his son became the guardian of the remaining treasure."

"My father never said a word about it to me," Drew said.

"Circumstances prevented it, lad," Seth said. "I'm sure Jan would have preferred to be the one who told you."

Drew nodded, and liked Seth a great deal for speaking well of his father. He had not known there was such a gentle side to this burly man.

"When you wrote to your mother about needing money to buy ships," Dick continued, "she decided it was time to break out more treasure."

Drew picked up a small coin and held it to the light. The rays of the sun coming through the window bounced off and reflected a golden circle onto the wall. He held the coin out to his nephew. "You take this one for good luck."

Peter shook his head. "The gold is for New York. I can't take any of it."

Drew was impressed. Not many boys of Peter's age would pass up a chance at a gold coin. "Very well, Peter, it goes back with the rest to buy ships and cannons," he said, and tossed the coin back with the others.

Drew departed, and soon returned to the office with Ben Franklin. When he saw the treasure, the spectacles almost fell off the end of his nose.

"And you say this is a gift from your family?" he asked incredulously.

"From my departed grandfather," Drew said, putting his arm on his nephew's shoulder. "And Peter's great-grandfather."

After the explanations were repeated for Franklin, he stroked his chin with his hand. "James de Kuyper—yes, of course, I met him several times. In fact I once printed an article about those workhorses he was breeding. A splendid man. And he had Kidd's treasure all those years? My, my, my."

The old gentleman quickly decided what to do with the gold. A portion of it was hidden in the vault of the hotel, where it would be zealously guarded by the owner, Ray de Chaumont. A smaller portion was given to Dick and Seth, who were to return to Le Havre to find and sign up American sailors to crew the new privateers. The final portion was given to Drew, who was to go to Amsterdam and buy ships from the Dutch.

This business concluded, Franklin announced they would get to work on the morrow, but at the moment Beaumarchais was giving a dinner party, and they were all invited.

That evening, as they entered Beaumarchais's imposing Paris residence, Dick and Seth nervously kept putting their fingers inside the silk scarfs wound about their necks. The fancy clothes Drew had procured for them were not at all to their liking, especially in light of their years spent in prison and in the army. They were dressed in silk coats, waistcoats, and breeches. Shiny leather pumps with silver buckles adorned their feet. Young Peter was dressed in similar fashion, but was more comfortable; his mother had always insisted he be quite presentable at meals.

Drew, of course, now took such finery for granted, including the fresh flower in his lapel and the diamond-studded gold fleur-de-lis decoration that had been awarded to him by the comte de Vergennes for his "services to the glory of the king." Drew asked about these services, but could never find out exactly what they were. Ben Franklin told him to forget it. "When you leave France, you can sell the bloody thing and give the money to Washington," he said.

"You look like His Lordship himself," Dick said in admiration as he eyed his natty cousin from head to toe. "Not much resemblance to the old Andrew de Kuyper, late of the city of New York."

Franklin looked at his protégé with fondness. "He *has* adapted well, hasn't he? Well, it's about time. When I first started coming over here, these Europeans thought all Americans wore buckskins and carried tomahawks. Once they've seen a few more like Drew, they'll change their minds."

A majordomo announced their arrival, and Beaumarchais came over, as effulgent as usual in greeting his guests. "I'm positively delighted to have you visit my humble abode," he said, touching hands with the newly arrived guests from America. "Mr. Goelet, a great pleasure to welcome any relative of Drew's, a great pleasure indeed. He has become one of our favorites, you know, although I'm sure he's too modest to say such a thing. And Mr. Cuyler, a *very* great pleasure, sir."

Both Dick and Seth wore somewhat glazed expressions as the Frenchman turned to the boy. "And this is Peter. Let me look at you, young sir. Ah, may I live to see you turn out as splendidly as your uncle."

They walked into the main salon of the mansion, Beaumarchais with his arm about Seth's shoulder. "Now tell me, Mr. Cuyler," he was saying, "is it a fact that the American Congress decides everything by a majority vote? I must say, that is a splendid example of novel thinking, and I insist on hearing about it from you during dinner."

Drew smiled as Seth looked to him for rescue. He knew there was no hope, because once Beaumarchais picked a topic and a partner to discuss it with, there was no stopping him.

"And who is this handsome lad who bears such a striking resemblance to yourself?"

Drew turned, and saw he had been joined by Juliette de Villette, who was peering at his nephew through her jewel-encrusted lorgnette. "Could it be he is your son?"

Dick stared at the expanse of pearly flesh offered by the woman's décolletage. She looked at him and smiled, and his face reddened with embarrassment.

Speaking English, Drew introduced his cousin and his nephew. "His mother's name is Celine?" Madame de Villette said happily in her heavily accented, but understandable English. "How wonderful that your sister has a French name. *Bon!* I am beginning to think more and more of you Americans."

"Actually, Dick probably has some French blood in him from the Goelet side of the family," Drew said. "Perhaps a touch of Huguenot influence."

Fanning herself, the comtesse stepped closer to Dick. She lowered her eyes coquettishly and took a deep breath, which made her plunging neckline even more pronounced.

"Is this so, Mr. Goelet? If so, we must spend some time together *à deux,* so you can tell me all about it, *n'est-ce pas?*"

Dick turned an even deeper shade of red as he tried to stammer a reply. Fortunately, he was rescued by the majordomo, who pounded a gold-headed staff on the floor and announced that dinner was now being served.

Beaumarchais and his guests trooped along the Carrara marble floor of a long hallway that led into the dining salon. Minutes later, all fifty were seated at a series of tables formed into a large U. The plate and service was sterling and gold, the glassware the finest crystal, and the linen purest damask.

Dick felt like a true yokel as he gazed in bewilderment at the array of knives, forks, spoons, stemware, fingerbowls, and other items many of which he couldn't name, much less know how to use.

"Just start at the outside and work in," Drew whispered. He was seated between Dick and Peter. Ben Franklin sat on the same side of the U, farther down the table, between the Dutch ambassador to France and a voluptuous young girl who had a beauty mark on her left cheek and a penchant for laughing delightedly every time Franklin said something witty.

Beaumarchais sat in the center of the U, with Seth on his left and Juliette on his right. Throughout the meal Seth looked as if he wanted to jump up and run away from his host, while the woman kept glancing coyly at Drew and Dick.

"What's with her?" Dick asked.

"A friend," Drew said noncommittally.

"Is she a tart?"

Drew smiled. "A woman is a tart only if she doesn't have any money. Madame de Villette is very rich."

There was something in the way he said this that made Dick *know* something was going on between them. "How good a friend is she?" he asked.

"She's a far cry from a barmaid at Fraunces Tavern," Drew said. "You ought to try something like that yourself."

"I don't know," Dick said, attempting to sound casual. "My tastes run more to someone like Beth Henry."

Drew looked surprised. "Here you are in the land that invented love, and you're talking about some little kid in New York. Dickie, what's happened to you?"

"She's not such a little kid anymore," Dick said. He started to eat the first of the eleven courses, but his mind was back in New York. He conjured up the face of Beth Henry, and it made him feel warm and happy. If his cousin had no interest in her, then he could proceed to woo her without guilt. Oh, yes, he knew Beth claimed to love Drew, but after she realized he was rejecting her, her passion would wither—and then she could become interested in someone else. And who could that be? Why, none other than Dick Goelet, he replied in answer to his own question.

As they ate, Peter and Drew renewed their old friendship, and the boy spoke of his prowess at hunting and tracking. Drew was proud of his nephew, and they began to slip into the roles of former years.

"My mother is still seeing that Hessian," Peter offered.

"Franz? He's not a bad sort."

Peter shrugged. "If it wasn't him, it would be somebody else."

Drew almost choked on his soup. If only Celine could hear her son's observation on her mode of life. She'd want to break his head. "Oh, have there been other men?" he asked innocently.

Peter looked at his uncle as if he had just belched. "Mother doesn't really like to be alone," he finally said. "And so she usually isn't."

"Is that a fact?"

"Yes."

When the dinner had come to an end, a musical entertainment began. The comtesse de Villette made her way over to Drew. A devilish idea occurred to him, and within a few minutes he had managed to place her on the seat next to Dick. As

THE TIDES OF CHANGE 375

she warmed to the conversation and poor Dick became more and more uncomfortable, Drew took Peter and slipped away. The comtesse was so engrossed in the new American that she didn't notice the others leaving; she was informing Dick that he could call her Ettie.

"That woman smells," Peter said as they moved into the next salon.

"It's perfume. She wears a lot of it."

"I don't like it," the boy said. "I like a girl to smell the way Beth Henry smells."

Drew shook his head. What did this little girl have? Half the men and boys coming from New York seemed to be in love with her. He started to ponder his own question, but was interrupted by Ben Franklin, who wanted to have a chat with him and the Spanish ambassador. He thought no more about Beth Henry.

The next day, the time for play in Paris was over. Dick and Seth took their portion of the gold and, accompanied by the helpful Beaumarchais, set out for Le Havre to begin recruiting seamen for the new ships that would, they hoped, soon be in American hands.

Both of them left a bit reluctantly. Paris had taken them, in more ways than one, to her bosom. "These French girls are like rabbits," Seth said.

"God bless them," Dick said solemnly.

Drew planned on taking his nephew with him to Amsterdam, but since they had to wait a day for the coach to that city, Franklin suggested they show the sights of Versailles to young Peter.

Their carriage passed through the gilded iron gates at the head of the Place d'Armes, and Drew was amused by Peter, who kept craning his neck in all directions, and even so missed half what there was to see.

They walked down marble corridors and passed the rigid guards and chattering members of the court, who smiled and bobbed their heads when they recognized Franklin. The party of visitors turned at a grand salon and went down another long hall, which led to the offices of the Comte de Vergennes. There was a sudden commotion among the people in the hall, and then, without further warning, Franklin and his companions found themselves face to face with the youthful Louis XVI.

Franklin bowed and smiled. "An unexpected pleasure, Your

Majesty. Did you receive that fine old example of the Lombardy clockmaking art I sent over?"

Louis smiled. "Yes, and we know why you sent it," he replied in perfect English.

Franklin pretended innocence. "You do, Highness?"

The king wagged his finger under the old gentleman's nose. "It doesn't work. The mechanism has been sprung. Also, there's something wrong with the flywheel."

"Ah, of course," Franklin said, turning to Drew. "I knew if I could get His Majesty to look at that clock he'd figure out what was wrong." He shifted his gaze to Peter. "I want you to know, Master de Kuyper, that the king of France is also her premier restorer of valuable clocks."

"Second only to yourself, Franklin," the king said magnanimously.

"And now, Your Majesty, may I present Master Peter de Kuyper of New York, the nephew of my aide."

Peter cocked his head and looked with interest at the king. "You really fix clocks?" he asked. There was a hint of disbelief in his voice.

The chamberlain at the king's side was aghast at this lack of protocol and tact. "Boy, you are supposed to bow," he hissed.

Ben Franklin laughed. His sense of humor was his single greatest weapon with the French. "You may have the kings and queens of the world in awe of you, Your Majesty, but when it comes to a ten-year-old from cynical New York, you must still prove yourself."

The moment of tension broke as the king joined the old gentleman in laughter. "What's wrong with fixing clocks?"

"Nothing," Peter said. "But I thought all a king did was sit on his throne."

Louis sighed. "That's what they'd have us do, and then we would surely die of boredom."

"Then you'd better keep fixing clocks," Peter said.

"You understand that, do you?"

"Anything is better than dying of boredom."

The king turned to Drew. "What are your plans for your nephew, de Kuyper?"

"Today we're showing him Versailles, Your Majesty, and tomorrow we leave for Amsterdam."

"Must he go with you?"

"Not necessarily," Drew said. "Especially if Your Majesty has something else in mind."

"We would like to have him as our guest for a few days. We think we would enjoy his youthful candor."

Drew looked at Peter. "Would you prefer to stay with His Majesty?"

The boy thought for a moment. "Do you hunt?" he asked.

"Hunt!" the king exclaimed happily. "It's one of the things we do best. Would you care to hunt deer with us?"

Peter warmed considerably. "I know how to track a deer even in the dark. Beth Henry taught me."

"Then it's settled," the king said. "You shall be our guest while your uncle is in Amsterdam. We shall take good care of him," he added for Drew's benefit.

Drew bowed. "What could be safer than to stand in the radiance of the Sun of France."

"Ah, Franklin," the king said with a twinkle in his eye. "You have taught de Kuyper well. Even we are starting to believe his flattery." He took Peter firmly by the hand. "Now you must come with us, and we'll find some hunting equipment. Is there a particular type of rifle you prefer?"

"I usually use a bow and arrow," Peter said.

The king's eyebrows arched upward. "We've never done that. Come, boy, we must see if there are such things at Versailles."

"I don't like to be called boy. My name's Peter," he said evenly.

There were more gasps and outraged looks among the members of the king's entourage, but he dismissed them with a wave of his hand. "By all means, then—Peter it shall be," he said.

Peter walked at the king's side as they swept down the corridor, causing a swell of murmuring and bowing in their wake as if they were the prow of a ship cutting through the water.

"Peter will have something to talk about when he gets back to New York," Franklin said.

"I doubt if even spending several days with the king of France will impress my nephew very much," Drew said. "Unless, of course, the king proves to be an expert marksman with a bow and arrow."

"The equivalent of ten thousand guilders in gold," the heavyset trader, Van Hooght, said. "Soon she will be yours," he added, pointing out the window toward the dock, where a handsome three-masted brigantine was moored.

Drew had come to Amsterdam and had made rapid progress with the ship dealers of the capital of the United Netherlands—at least so far.

"May I take possession of the ship at once?" he asked.

"If it were up to me, *Mijnheer,* of course," Van Hooght said. "But the various guilds require certain statements about their wares, attested to by both seller and buyer and approved by a disinterested third party."

He took a sheaf of dog-eared papers from the table and handed them to Drew. "These must be filled out in the proper manner, and signed by the various designated authorities. Now *these* forms," he said, producing yet another substantial stack of papers, "are those required by the government."

"I must do all this before I can take possession of my ship?"

"Until it is done, she is not your ship. And then you must wait until all the papers are filed properly and approved. But don't worry, that's the way things are. While all that's being done, you can use your time in finding a crew," the Dutchman suggested with a conciliatory smile.

"I already have agents in Le Havre attending to the crew. Will you help me do all this paperwork?"

Van Hooght nodded. It would be his pleasure to accommodate the young American. It was the third ship he had contracted to buy, and it was simply good business to provide service for such a customer. In the meanwhile there was no sense in troubling him with the knowledge that identical piles of paperwork would have to be done for the other ships as well before the sales became final, and that the process involved normally moved along at a snail's pace. He would learn all this in good time, so perhaps it was a good idea to take his mind off such unpleasantness.

"And now, Mr. de Kuyper, perhaps we should retire to the guildhall tavern and enjoy some good beer and food," he said.

Drew nodded, and unconsciously patted his stomach. He had never eaten so much food in his life. It obviously was the custom among Dutch merchants to celebrate every transaction with an enormous meal. No wonder, he thought, they all became round as balls as they matured into their thirties or forties.

Amsterdam was a bustling city, a town of intense commercial energy and activity these days. For two hundred years the tiny nation of the United Netherlands had been sending her ships to the far corners of the world, exerting an influence upon the trade and traffic of the globe that was far out of proportion to her size and population. Of late this influence had been overshadowed by that of her much larger competitors, France and England, but she still managed to hold her own in many places. Dutch activity in the East Indies continued to be substantial, and trade with the Indian subcontinent continued to be brisk. In addition there was a constant stream of traffic to the West Indies, South America, and Africa.

The Dutch had joined the alliance with France and America, and declared war on England. Her confrontations with the enemy, however, were mostly confined to the North Sea, and her ships were never a factor in the New World—other than those she sold to America for her own use. As ship broker, she was making a difference in the balance of seapower. As they provided the Americans with a ready-made fleet that loomed more and more important in the war against England, the Dutch were proud of their accomplishment. They reveled in their revenge against the British for having excluded them from the lucrative North American trade.

The shipping offices of Van Hooght & Van Tilj had offices looking out on the old Brouwer's Graft Canal. Not far away was the tower known as the Schreijerstoren—the Crier's Tower, so named because it stood on the spit of land called Schriejer's Hook. It was from here that adventurous Dutchmen of the seventeenth century ventured from the European mainland to such places as Batavia, Ceylon, India, Brazil, and New Netherland.

Drew had gone to this bustling place several times, and stood watching the men hauling supplies aboard the ships. He had watched as heavily laden craft weighed anchor and slipped out toward the open sea. He wondered if it was from this very spot that his own great-great-grandfather, Pieter de Kuyper, had sailed to the New World more than one hundred and fifty years ago. What thoughts had passed through the mind of that young man as he stood on the deck of the ship and watched his homeland disappear over the receding horizon? What emotions had stirred in his breast as he thought of traveling thousands of miles to embark on a new life in a wilderness filled with savages?

Drew knew his family's history, which had been faithfully recorded and kept in ledgers stored in the de Kuyper building on Whitehall Street. His ancestor, Pieter, had initially gone to

America aboard the *Tiger*, under the command of Captain Adriaean Block, whose name was commemorated by the small island he had discovered off the eastern tip of Long Island. At the time, Pieter had been only a fifteen-year-old cabin boy. But in 1626 he had returned aboard the *Sea Mew* with Peter Minuit, not as a casual visitor, but as a permanent resident of the fledgling community of New Amsterdam, on the southernmost tip of the island of Manhatan.

From that day on the de Kuyper family had called the island home, contributing to its growth and wealth under both the Dutch rule and the English rule that followed. Drew's great-grandfather Jacob Adam, a tough-minded, hard-nosed trader, had taken the seeds planted by *his* father and nourished them, building a flourishing empire and a dynasty. Drew's grandfather, James, had contributed to the New World in his own way—in agriculture and in the breeding of superior workhorses, whose descendants could now be found in stables from Newfoundland to Georgia. And Drew's own father, Jan, had continued to build the de Kuyper fortunes; continued to help build America into a country that was now ready to take her rightful place among the free and independent nations of the earth.

And it all started here....

With a young man who was not content with his lot as an apprentice ironmonger, who would not accept the limited horizons of his ancestors. What a flight of imagination Pieter must have had, Drew thought; what a courageous thing to do! As he stood watching the activity of the port, he could feel a stirring within himself; an urging to emulate his great-great-grandfather, to strike out and change the world.

Well, he consoled himself, maybe by breaking away from Britain, that's exactly what we'll be doing.

Van Hooght took him to the tavern frequented by the shippers and traders of Amsterdam. They sat at a large table with a group of Van Hooght's friends and dined on roast lamb, noodles, sauerkraut, and generous helpings of juicy beans cooked in wine. Large pewter mugs filled with the heavy beer beloved in Amsterdam accompanied the food.

"When we heard that Benjamin Franklin had sent us a man named de Kuyper, we knew we'd do business," Van Hooght said with a smile as he wiped the beer foam from his upper lip.

"A good name, that," added a trader.

"Weren't you worried that I might be a sharper trader than a man of mere English descent?" Drew asked in amusement.

"Ah, we'd rather deal with a man with a name that makes us comfortable," Van Hooght said, and the other traders agreed. They asked many questions about the place they still referred to as New Amsterdam, and when Drew finished a long discourse on the richness and delights of their former colony, they all agreed it had been a sad day when Peter Stuyvesant had surrendered it to the English. By the way they spoke, an uninformed listener might suspect Stuyvesant had relinquished New Amsterdam out of spite, and that his act had nothing to do with the English fleet that was threatening to blast the colony into eternity.

One of the shippers mentioned he knew a man named de Kuyper, a solicitor who lived in Amsterdam. "I wonder if he could be a relative of yours?" he asked.

"My great-grandfather had a brother who was born in America, but who moved to Amsterdam," Drew answered with interest. "Maybe there's some connection."

Van Hooght offered to take him to where this Amsterdam de Kuyper had his offices. "You will need me not only to help find the place, but also, perhaps, to act as interpreter."

Drew grimaced. Since his arrival in the Netherlands, he had found that because his name was de Kuyper the Dutch expected him to speak their language. He explained that although his ancestor's tongue had been Dutch, that language had been discarded in New York for many years. Each generation had known less and less Dutch, until it came to Drew's turn, and he knew next to nothing.

"Maybe one of these days I'll learn to speak Dutch," he said apologetically.

The traders nodded their heads. "A very civilized language," they all agreed.

"Perhaps the *most* civilized," Drew said, and instantly made a half-dozen new friends.

The next morning Van Hooght took him through the narrow streets of Amsterdam, through a section of high-stooped homes that resembled the older houses of New York. They came to a substantial building that housed the offices of solicitors and business factors. They went up the stairs to the second floor of the building and stopped in front of a door marked:

STEENWYCK & DE KUYPER
Solicitors

They entered, and Van Hooght inquired of the clerk about the de Kuyper whose name was on the door. The clerk informed him the name referred to Gerrit de Kuyper, a partner in the firm. When told the visitors' names, Gerrit de Kuyper appeared immediately and ushered them into his private office.

He was a prosperous-looking man, about fifty years old, with light-colored hair that had turned mostly to silver-gray. He wore a rich waistcoat of silk, and had a habit of hooking his thumbs in the front pockets as he talked. A bit shorter than Drew, Gerrit de Kuyper had bright, piercing eyes, and he looked directly at a man when he spoke to him.

"A de Kuyper from America!" he said, and Drew thanked his good fortune that the Dutchman spoke a passable English. He had learned the language out of necessity, he said, because he was a specialist in maritime law and for many years now had dealt with cases involving English ships and English solicitors.

"Of course, there's not much business with them these days, now that our countries are at war," he added.

"I was wondering if we might be related," Drew said, and told his side of the family history. "We know that my great-great-grandfather had two sons. One was named Jacob Adam, and I'm his direct descendant. He had an older brother named Pieter. Our records tell us this Pieter returned to the Netherlands sometime in the 1650s. After that we know nothing about him."

Gerrit was astonished. "Pieter de Kuyper? The one who was born in the New World and who returned here?" he said.

"Yes. He left America as a young man, after building the palisade at Wall Street. His wall, as a matter of fact, was the reason the street got that name."

"But he was my great-grandfather!" Gerrit said. "He didn't leave us any records about his life in America, or make note of any family remaining there. What little we know suggests his experiences in the New World had not been very pleasant, and so he tried to blot them from his life."

"If he is your ancestor, then *his* father, the first Pieter, is our common great-great-grandfather," Drew said with excitement.

The older de Kuyper looked at this long-lost relative and

held out his arms. "Welcome home," he said, and they embraced. "I feel like I've gained a nephew this day."

"And I an uncle," Drew said.

It was a strange feeling to be clasping this man to his chest, a man he had never heard of until the previous day, and to realize they were sprung from the same flesh and blood. Despite their differences, these people and he shared a bond. Before America had even been dreamed of, their common forebears had tilled the soil of this land, fished its rivers and seas, hunted its woods, lived and died as one people.

That night Gerrit took Drew home to his house. Van Hooght was invited, but he made excuses, as he wished to leave the de Kuypers to themselves. The dinner was festive and, as usual in the Netherlands, more than plentiful.

Gerrit's son, Martin, was, at twenty-five, a year older than Drew, and a solicitor in his father's office. He was of medium height and handsome, with blond hair that settled just below his ear. His clear blue eyes and high cheekbones gave him a classic Dutch look. Martin rarely appeared anywhere without a pipe in his mouth. He was a serious young fellow, given to reading the classics in the original tongues. He liked to think things out fully before speaking aloud, and this caution gave him a slowness of speech; but it would have been a major error to regard his mind as slow. Despite his relative youth, he had already established his reputation before the magistrates of Amsterdam.

"You say Indians paddle their canoes right up to the same docks where ships from Europe tie up?" he asked in his slow drawl.

"They come to trade," Drew explained. "Furs and beads, mostly, but other goods as well."

"Are they good traders?"

"Terrible. The red man thinks only of the moment. He'll trade a fortune in furs for a few bottles of cheap rum."

"No wonder it was so easy to take their country away from them," Martin said. "I sometimes think people like that deserve to be taken advantage of."

They spoke of customs in the New World, and the Hollanders were delighted to learn that many of their own celebrations were kept in New York—Christmas, Easter, Shrove Tuesday. The Amsterdam de Kuypers also recognized the architectural styles Drew spoke of, as well as types of fishing boats—the old *vlieboots* that could be seen every day on the Zuider Zee as well as New York Bay. Their shoe buckles were of the same kind, and they used the same square-topped brooms and dozens of other household utensils.

"It seems a shame that the branches of our family have stayed apart for over a hundred years," Gerrit said. "I hope we don't wait another hundred before we come together again."

"Now that we've discovered each other, we must maintain the ties," Drew agreed.

Martin asked Drew his business in Amsterdam, and the American told him of his mission to buy ships, and of the problems he was encountering.

Martin smiled. "You need a good Amsterdam solicitor to help you."

"Well," Gerrit said to his son, "isn't that what you are?"

"Can I be of service?" Martin asked Drew.

"What can you do?"

"Well, for one thing I suspect you're finding out that paperwork can take a great deal of time in the Netherlands."

Drew nodded. "Much to my regret."

"I can speed up the process," Martin said. "Leave everything to me."

He was as good as his word. The titles for the ships cleared through the various guildhalls and government offices within three days. The Dutchman was a genius at knowing which clerk in which department to talk to, and which official to placate, or even bribe. Drew sat back and shook his head in amazement. What took Martin three days would have taken him three weeks, if not longer, he realized.

The ships finally belonged to Drew—which meant, of course, they belonged to the American Congress. Skeleton crews were hired to sail the ships to Le Havre, where Dick Goelet and Seth Cuyler would be waiting to take possession and properly staff them with full crews.

"The French also have a lot of stupid harbor laws and statutes," Martin said. "I'd better sail up with you."

Drew gladly accepted the offer. On the sixteenth day of August, 1779, the three ships weighed anchor, raised canvas, and headed into the Zuider Zee. They sailed north to the Wadden Zee, west until they came to the southernmost of the Frisian Islands, then south on the last leg through the Straits of Dover. They entered the wider part of the English Channel, and from there it was an easy sail to Le Havre.

Drew stood near the bow of the ship and watched the white water slap against the sharp prow and move out in widening patterns from the sides of the sleek brigantine. Now that he was out at sea, he felt like a new man. The sharp, clean air filled his lungs, and the tang of salt piqued his sense of smell. He felt alive, vibrant, ready for anything.

The only nagging disturbance was that he knew his exultation was temporary. In a short time he would turn the ship over to someone else, and then head back to Paris.

Martin joined Drew at the rail, and they presented a contrasting sight: the one tall and dark, slender as an arrow, smoldering with pent-up emotions; the other stockier, blond, and fair-skinned, a picture of calm with his omnipresent pipe between his teeth.

"I've never been to America," he said. "Le Havre, England—many times on business. But never the New World."

"You must come after the war is over."

"Yes, I think I will."

"Our home will be your home," Drew said.

"Are you married?"

"No."

"Neither am I," Martin said as he puffed away on his pipe. "I've always believed marriage is the end of youth. Seems a pity."

"Do you have a girl?"

"No, do you?"

Drew shook his head. "I've seen a number of women, including one in England. But there's been nothing serious so far."

"The moment a man marries, he becomes the chattel of others," Martin said. "He's owned by his wife, his children, the very servants in the house."

"Yet it would be nice to come home to a loving woman every night," Drew said.

"Yes, but how long do they stay loving?" Martin asked. "After a few years of marriage they grow fat and turn into shrews."

"You don't seem to like women very much."

"Why, cousin, don't misunderstand me. I love them—at a distance. When we get to Le Havre, I'll take you to a few places where the beer is chilled and the women are warm."

When the three ships entered the harbor at Le Havre, they tied up and were greeted by Dick Goelet.

"Well, Dick," Drew said. "Have you the crews to take them out to fight?"

"I do indeed. I've signed up over two hundred men with the gold we brought from New York."

The next three days were busy.

Dick, Seth, and the captains and crewmen of the newly commissioned ships—named the *Kieft*, the *Van Twiller*, and the *Peter Minuit* in honor of former governors of New Amsterdam—worked aboard them, familiarizing themselves with every last spar, boom, and belaying pin. Martin and Drew worked with the port authorities and quickly cleared the ships for sailing.

The night before the ships were to sail, Drew, Martin, Dick, and Seth dined together.

"The de Witts are important people in Holland," Martin said when he learned Dick had a de Witt ancestor as well as a de Kuyper and a Goelet. "Evert de Witt is the chancellor of the privy council and a good friend of my father's."

Dick looked at Drew as he asked the next question. "Would you say the de Witts are more important than the de Kuypers?"

"They do hold more important positions," Martin admitted.

"See, I told you," Dick said to Drew. "My side of the family has always been the best."

"I don't know about that," Martin said sourly.

"Don't mind Dick," Drew said. "He's annoyed with me because I've always had more luck with women."

"But not the right one," Dick said cryptically.

"The trouble with young men," Martin said, wagging the stem of his pipe in the air and ignoring that he himself was a young man, "is that they greatly exaggerate the difference between one young woman and the next. After a few years, what difference does it make?"

"Our cousin the cynic," Drew said.

"Since I've been in France, I've learned to love them all," Seth offered.

Dick smiled. Seth had been the most sober and faithful of husbands; and when his wife died, he grieved deeply and privately and long. But now Seth Cuyler had rejoined the human race—"with a vengeance," as Dick reported it to Drew, and some of the man's escapades in the brothels of Le Havre were fast becoming legends. "There's time enough to settle down when I get back to New York," was Seth's philosophy.

"Ah, then," Martin said with a gleam in his eye. "I think

I know a place where we can celebrate your departure in proper style."

Dick looked across the table at Drew. "Martin's a de Kuyper, all right."

Peter de Kuyper was disgusted. The king had taken him to the Grand Trianon Palace at the far end of the vast gardens of Versailles and was showing him a favorite pastime: hunting deer from the windows of the palace.

"We stay here with our rifle," Louis explained. "The gamekeepers let the deer loose at the far end of the building. They pass down this garden, and we shoot them from here."

"That's no fun," Peter complained.

"What do you mean?"

"The thrill is tracking deer through the woods and then using your skill to make the kill."

"This is too easy, eh?" Louis said, catching the drift of what his young companion was saying.

"This is like shooting rabbits in a hutch," Peter said, making no effort to mask his feelings. "When can we *really* hunt? I'll teach you everything I know."

The king pondered this for a moment. Shooting from the window had been the way he had been taught as a boy by his own father. It had always seemed natural, but now that he had been questioned by the youthful American, he began to see how unsportsmanlike it was.

"We see what you mean," he said. "Perhaps we should go down into the forests at Fontainebleau and do our hunting there."

"Real forests?"

"Yes."

"Take me there, and I'll show you how to track a deer so he'll never even know you're following him."

"We like that idea," Louis said, placing his heavy rifle on the bench next to the window.

Peter had been wondering why the king always sounded so odd when he spoke. He suddenly figured it out. "You never say 'I,' but 'we' or 'us,'" he said. "Why do you do that?"

"We are the king, and the king is France," Louis said in surprise. "Therefore, when we speak we're not speaking as Louis, but as all France. We're not one person, but many."

The king was pleased with his explanation until he saw the

look of scorn on the boy's face. "You don't think that quite makes sense, do you?"

"I guess it makes sense," Peter said. "But how can you have any friends if you can never be just you?"

"But the king doesn't need friends," Louis protested. "He's the king."

"If that's what you want."

"We don't like people to disagree with us."

"All right."

"And you're supposed to say Your Majesty when you talk with us," Louis said sternly.

"Yes, Your Majesty," Peter said sullenly.

"And it's all rather stupid, isn't it?"

"Yes, Your Majesty!" Peter answered, this time with a great deal more pleasure.

Louis smiled. "All right, my young American friend. We will no longer be 'we' with you. From now on," he said, pausing dramatically, "*I* will take pleasure in your company and friendship. I, me, Louis the person, not the collective spirit and soul of France."

"I like that."

The king put his arm about the boy and started walking toward the door. "Now, we must make arrangements to go to Fontainebleau. We—I mean *I*—can't wait for you to teach me this... how do you call it?"

"Tracking."

"Yes, tracking. Tracking the deer."

As they were preparing to leave in an elaborate carriage, much to the consternation of the court officials and majordomos, who wanted everything done according to strict protocol and schedule, the queen came by, accompanied by a dozen ladies-in-waiting. The king explained he was going to Fontainebleau to hunt, and the queen became angry.

"But we have several parties planned for this week," she complained, as she stood tapping her foot.

"You will carry on without us," the king said imperiously.

"We need you."

"That's enough," the king said, and Marie Antoinette recognized the hard edge in his voice.

"Yes, dear," she said meekly. Most of the time she was able to talk her husband into doing almost anything she wanted. Every now and then, however, a stubborn streak would emerge in Louis, and she was wise enough to back down. The king was usually a mild man, but when his temper was aroused, he could become a veritable devil.

She peered past the king into the carriage. "Who's that?" she asked.

"Peter de Kuyper from America. He's the nephew of Benjamin Franklin's aide. He's going to teach us the tracking of deer," the king added, with some amusement, because he knew his wife wouldn't have the slightest idea what he was talking about. He also knew she would be too proud to admit it; there was German blood in her veins.

The queen sniffed. "Very nice" was all she said.

Peter stared back at her openly. She was beautiful, he thought, but wondered why she covered herself with so much powder and scent. She would have been even more beautiful if she had been more natural. Like Beth, he reflected.

"I am ready," the king said to Peter. "Are you?"

"Yes."

"*I* am?" Marie Antoinette said, perplexed. "You speak to the boy in this manner?"

Louis smiled. "He's an American, and doesn't understand our customs. Besides, it's rather fun."

The queen shook her head. Louis could be trying at times. On the other hand, he had so many interests, he didn't object if she had a few of her own.

"How long will you be away?" she asked.

The king shrugged. "Three days...four days...who knows? Peter and I will come back when we're ready."

"Have a nice time, my royal darling," the queen said, reaching over to give him a friendly peck on the cheek. Her mind was already considering the possibilities presented by a handsome chevalier who had arrived at Versailles only this past week. "Stay as long as you wish," she added.

As the royal carriage passed through the great gates of the imperial complex, it was followed by two dozen more coaches carrying the people and appurtenances required to cater to the king. Two hundred mounted dragoons followed the entourage, their leader wearing a uniform trimmed with silver and gold thread.

As they passed through the countryside, Peter began explaining how one tracked deer. He told the king about staying downwind and taking care not to step on twigs.

"Sometimes the Indians make bird calls as they move, to disguise any sound their feet might make," Peter said.

The king of France, Louis XVI, was delighted to learn such useful information.

At about the time her son hobnobbed with royalty, Celine was involved in the more pedestrian task of watching the construction of another barn to hold the staggering amount of supplies that arrived weekly to be held for General Washington. The farm at the old Beekman's Place had become a major storage depot for goods brought from Europe. The British fleet patrolled the coast, but since New York was in their hands, they did not suspect anyone would be foolhardy enough to bring supplies in only a couple of miles to the north. It was the very audacity of picking the Place that made the idea work.

In addition, British control of the area—with the exception of the city itself—was slipping away. There had been a small skirmish recently at Paulus's Hook, and when the British withdrew across the river to New York, there wasn't a single redcoat left in New Jersey.

While the supplies arrived at the Place to be dispersed, the British garrison in New York sat on their hands and passed the time of day. The officers gave balls and dances, and the ordinary soldiers played at dice, drank, grumbled, and whored.

Celine was standing on a low-lying knoll, admiring the skill of the workmen as they raised one side of the bar in a single motion.

John Holt came by from the sheep barn. He was carrying a load of pamphlets. "Take one."

"I'll read it later," she said.

"It tells how our men are cleaning out the Indians all along the Mohawk River," the printer said. "The very latest news. Just came in last night."

"You don't waste any time, do you?"

"News can be as much of a weapon as a bullet," Holt said. "The people will be be happy to know we're taking care of those bloody Iroquois."

Celine nodded. The news from the frontiers had been especially unpleasant this past summer. The British continued to use the Indians as allies, and, predictably, there had been a number of massacres. One in particular had caused great outrage. It had occurred in the Wyoming Valley of the Susquehanna River, in Pennsylvania. A force of Iroquois combined with a group of Tory Rangers to surround a rebel garrison. The Americans, knowing they had lost, surrendered, fully expecting to be treated in a civilized manner as prisoners of war. The Indians, however, had other ideas, and proceeded to massacre all two hundred and twenty people. The killing was bad enough, but stories filtered back that many of the men were pitchforked and thrown alive into roaring bonfires. Others were tied to trees and killed slowly with the "death of a thousand cuts," a vile practice that supposedly had died out among the Indians, but that they had revived to entertain their British friends.

Such savagery was to be expected from the Indians, but what was not acceptable was that the British stood about without protesting while their red allies acted like beasts.

"A great mistake they made in hiring those Indians!" Holt said. "There isn't a settler in Pennsylvania or New Jersey who hasn't picked up his musket to defend himself. The whole countryside has turned against the king."

"Just make sure they don't catch you taking those handbills into New York," Celine cautioned. "They'll hang you if they do."

"I never go into New York," the printer said. "I'm a man with a price on my head. Sisyphus takes them down and distributes them."

Celine shook her head. "Well, then, tell *him* to take care."

"The old boy is as sly as a fox," the printer assured her. "They'll never catch him."

As Celine watched the men nailing the new barn together, a lone horseman rode up to the main house. He inquired of Mary Delafield. Primus wrinkled his nose at the man's rough deerskin clothes, and went to inform Mary of her visitor. Things weren't like the old days, the black man mourned. The Place used to be visited by men in velvet breeches and silk coats. Now? It seemed anyone was welcomed. The more ragged he looked or the worse he smelled, the more effusive his welcome—or at least so it seemed to Primus.

"Noah Henry!" Mary exclaimed in delight as she came into the parlor. "What a delightful surprise!"

Noah stepped forward, a bit embarrassed by the spacious room, the elegant furniture, and the well-dressed woman herself. "I came down to see how you and the boy are getting along," he said.

"David is well, and growing every day," Mary said. She

looked at Noah's dust-stained face and clothes. "First you must have a chance to wash up, then some lunch."

The water was still glistening on Noah's hair as he sat down at the table and gratefully accepted the mug of ale that Primus placed before him. He told Mary of the fine crops that had come in, and how the brown mare had foaled a sprightly colt. David was brought downstairs to play with the man for a while, and then taken back to his room for his nap.

"You came down just to see us?" Mary asked. "You have no other business?"

"I just wanted to see that you were all right."

She smiled and patted his hand. "As you can see, everything is going well for me. I'm quite content."

She did look content—and beautiful, he thought. When she had first come to his farm in Westchester, she had looked haggard and wan. Now her skin was smooth and her cheeks rosy, and she moved with alacrity and grace.

"Do you think of me once in a while?" she asked, rather innocently.

He could no longer maintain his pose of detachment. "Think of you once in a while? Mary, my dearest, I never *stop* thinking about you."

This was more than she had expected. "I see," she said coolly.

"I love you, Mary," he blurted out.

"Oh—oh my dear."

"There, now I've gone and offended you," Noah said as he rose from his chair. "I'd best be going."

"No, no," she said quickly. "I'm not offended. It's just that . . . well, you caught me by surprise."

"Ah, Mary, when you lived in my house I was a happy man. I looked forward to each day, to seeing you and playing with the baby. When you left, you took the soul out of that house, and out of my life as well."

"I enjoyed being with you, too, Noah, but—"

"I know, I know, you're a fine lady and I'm nothing but a back-country farmer. How could we ever get together? You don't have to tell me how insane it is."

"There's nothing insane about it," she said. "And I won't have you belittling yourself. Noah, you're the finest, gentlest, most considerate man I've ever known."

"Thank you," he said, confused. He reached for his ale and sipped it.

"We have problems."

"Yes, yes, I'm sure of it. Your husband..."

"Is dead. But how about your wife?"

It was obvious he was miserable. "I can't stand that woman anymore. Not after knowing you."

"But you're still a married man."

"Yes."

They sat in silence for a few moments, the only sound being his labored breathing. Both were lost in their thoughts, and neither could sort them out.

"Does Sarah know how you feel about me?" Mary finally asked.

"No. I can't talk to her. But she can't help it if she's not the woman I want. She's not to blame. She's—"

"Oh, stop it!" Mary said sharply. "I lived in your house for months. Sarah is the sort of woman who brings gloom into any room she enters."

"She does," he admitted. "She's never satisfied with anything, never happy, always crabbing. She couldn't wait until you were out of the house, and the moment you were gone she started cranking about something else."

"At least she missed me," Mary said sardonically.

"What are we going to do?" he pleaded.

"Do? There's not much to do, is there? You have a wife you don't want. And I have a dead husband and a bastard son," she said, showing bitterness for the first time.

He took her hand and kissed it. "Mary, let me give David my name. I helped bring him into the world. He'll be David Henry. I'll leave Sarah. I'll come to you. We can get married."

"Stop talking nonsense. You've a wife and there's nothing you can do about it."

They continued to talk, but went over the same ground again and again and accomplished nothing. Noah sat in his chair looking like a beaten dog. His chin rested on his chest, and he kept wringing his hands as if they were dirty and he was trying to get them clean. Finally he looked at her, and his gaze was steady. "Tell me one thing, Mary, and please tell the truth. Would it ever be possible for you to love me?"

She took her time and looked deep inside her heart. "Yes," she said in the tiniest of voices. "I could love you."

"Mary..."

"But what's the use of talking about such a thing? It's

foolishness, that's what it is. Noah, you've a wife, and that's that. I don't want to discuss it anymore."

"There's no need for more discussion," he said, suddenly very much in command of himself. He even smiled. "I've heard what I came to hear."

"What are you going to do?"

"Go back to my farm. Think about everything. The Lord has given me a burden, and I must bear it like a man."

"Noah..."

"Please, no more talk." He stood up and walked to the door. "Smile. I want to keep that picture in my mind."

She forced herself to produce a smile. It wasn't a very good one, but he didn't seem to care. He took one last look at her and then was gone.

Mary sat in the chair for a long time. Did she really think she could love Noah? Yes. Did she wish he was free to marry her? She wasn't sure. Nor could she be sure, she told herself, until she was faced with the real decision.

Celine came into the room and went over to the stove. She glanced at Mary and saw the faraway look on her face.

"What's the matter?"

"Nothing."

"You look strange."

"I was thinking about tomorrow."

"Tomorrow?" Celine said. "I thought we were taking little David down to the river to have a picnic."

"Not that tomorrow," Mary said dreamily. "The tomorrow when I must decide what to do with the rest of my life."

Celine paused as she was about to pour water from the kettle into the cup. *Now* what was going on? she wondered.

The elegantly dressed old man carried the large black leather bag of a doctor. With his beard neatly trimmed in the Flemish Van Dyck style, his lightly powdered wig, velvet breeches, and richly brocaded waistcoat, he appeared to be a respectable physician calling on his patients. Men tipped their hats as he passed, and women smiled. Even the British guards outside the City Hall, at the head of Broad Street, nodded. A physician held the unique position of being totally neutral, disease and injury not being partial to politics. Everyone treated such a man with respect, because they never knew when they would need his services.

The doctor shifted his heavy satchel from his left hand to

his right and stared at the doorway to the City Hall. The calm he reflected was in antithesis to the turmoil going on inside the meeting chamber in the building. And yet the two were related.

The "doctor" was really the printer, James Richardson, old Sisyphus himself. And the black satchel did not contain the medicines and salves of healing, but a batch of the latest one-page tirade against the Crown.

"This damnable press must be found and destroyed," Colonel Cunningham was raging at the assembled members of the Council of New York. "And the men who are printing these foul lies must hang!"

He held up a recent edition of the one-page newspaper, which appropriately called itself the *New York Instigator*. In large black type the headline said:

ENGLISH GENERALS ATTEND DINNER WHILE NEW YORKERS STARVE!

"Lies! Lies!" the colonel shouted as he paced in front of the twenty-four men who comprised the council and who, nominally at least, were in charge of conducting the business of the city. Actually, the council made no decisions and carried out no business, but was a tool used by the provost marshal. Cunningham decided what was to be done in New York, and the council automatically voted for it. Occasionally there was debate, sometimes quite acrimonious, but it was truly meaningless. Everyone knew that the provost marshal—and his deputy, Blakely—made the laws in New York City.

"I'm changing the curfew hours in the city," the colonel said with relish. "From now on people must be in their homes by six o'clock. Anyone found in the streets after that hour will be thrown into prison."

The council members looked at one another, but said nothing. What was there to say? A curfew had been in effect since the British had occupied the city, but it had rarely been enforced, except when there was a particular person they wanted to arrest.

"Do you think he means it?" the member sitting next to David Sackett whispered.

David shrugged. "Maybe he's trying to hold down the fires," he said tongue in cheek.

"What?"

"Why else would he be doing it?" David asked blandly.

His questioner shook his head and mumbled to himself. It was bad enough, he thought, to be putting up with the British and their wretched rules and laws, but now our own men are starting to act like fools.

But David, as he knew, was literally correct in his interpretation of what the curfew meant. Its origins began in France in the early Middle Ages, when most houses were constructed of rough-hewn timbers. The town marshal, or sheriff, would ring a bell at sunset, at which time all the inhabitants of the town were required by law to rake the live coals on the hearth, creating a pile that was then covered by a brass dome. The word curfew was a derivative of the Old French *covre feu*—to cover the fire—and the bell was known as the *covre feu* bell, or curfew bell. Originally the idea was to cut down on the number of fires in the highly flammable buildings, but eventually the curfew became a common practice to thwart highwaymen and other thieves who preyed on their fellowmen by night.

The English had brought the curfew to New York in an attempt to cut down on the townspeople's contact with the rebels—with a singular lack of success. The traffic in contraband had been increasing with every month. Washington's spies and couriers passed through the British lines as if they didn't exist. The situation was driving the provost marshal to distraction, and the publication of the *New York Instigator* was the greatest insult to date.

While the provost marshal ranted and raved at the indifferent council members, his face becoming red and veins sticking out on his neck, Captain Blakely sat at the rear of the room with Sergeant Taggert at his side. The captain was as bored as the members. He knew the council had no real power, and they wouldn't have used it to help the English if they had. The sergeant, however, was of a simpler nature, and believed what the colonel was saying if for no reason other than that the man was a colonel and his own superior.

"Maybe we should conduct a house-to-house search for the press," he whispered.

"Another search?" Blakely said. "We've already tried that."

"Maybe we didn't try hard enough."

The captain gave him a bored look and decided he didn't want to listen to any more of this nonsense. He left the room to get some air.

He stood on the steps of the City Hall and watched the respectable-looking doctor coming back down the street. In a way, he envied the man. A doctor practiced a trade that went on, inviolate, no matter what else was happening. At the moment it was an attractive, if somewhat boring, prospect.

The old doctor noticed the captain looking at him. He raised his arm slightly in greeting, and the officer returned the gesture. Sisyphus repressed a smile. If only the other man knew his identity! The thought made the old man chuckle as he continued down Broad Street until he was out of sight of the City Hall.

The captain thought about the problem of the printing press as he walked over to the East River. His men had thoroughly scoured the city and had not found a trace of it. Therefore, he concluded, the press was not in the city, but must be someplace outside it. But where? Farther up on Manhatan? In New Jersey, Connecticut, Long Island, Westchester? The possibilities were limitless, and a man could spend his life searching and still find nothing.

A blind search was not the answer; it would be a waste of time. He decided to use informers. This had been a successful method in the past, because it was always possible to find a man who would sell his own mother for a few pieces of silver.

Within the hour he had summoned two known informers and told them he wanted information about the printing press, adding that he was willing to pay extremely well for hard facts.

The informers went about their business, and within a few days they had widened their circle to include other men who trafficked in information. One of these men regularly made trips back and forth to Philadelphia, and in the course of his work he mentioned the reward to Philemon Peabody.

Peabody was doing well in the City of Brotherly Love. His trading deals were constantly adding to his coffers, and he had reason to be content with his new home. But the promise of accumulating greater wealth always drove him on.

So the deputy provost marshal of New York was willing to pay well for information about a printing press, was he? The wheels of Peabody's mind began turning.

He knew that Jan de Kuyper had been hiding a printer named John Holt, who had been wanted by the British for former treasonable printings. Jan, of course, was dead, and it was possible Holt too was in his grave. But it was also possible that Holt and the man printing diatribes against the British were one and the same. Moreover, he might still have some sort of connection with the de Kuyper family. It was a road that might be worth exploring, Peabody decided, and he paid the informer from New York to find out more about the de Kuypers and John Holt.

He wasn't sure what he would do if he found out anything. How far would he go for a few pieces of silver? Would he be willing to sell out his former employers to the British?

It was one thing, after all, to steal from them, but another to set them up for the hangman's noose. Well, he would face that decision when the time came. In the meanwhile he had more pressing business on his mind. One of Washington's men was in Philadelphia offering a generous commission to any trader who could arrange for a shipment of powder to be delivered to Delaware Bay. Peabody knew of a Portuguese captain who had slipped through the British blockade and claimed there was powder to be bought in Curaçao.

He hastened to the riverfront docks to find the Portuguese captain. Perhaps he could arrange a profitable deal. And if he couldn't deal with Washington's man, maybe he could find a way to sell the powder to the British.

Philemon Peabody believed in equal opportunity for all.

Dick Goelet was aboard the *Avenger* as it sailed through the Irish sea with the *Peter Minuit*, the *Van Twiller*, and the *Kieft*.

The American flotilla had sailed around the coast of Devon and headed across the Irish Sea until the sailors caught sight of the Old Head of Kinsale. Here the ships turned north to intercept the British squadron that was leaving Liverpool to join the blockade of the American coast. They knew about the British sailing because of information passed to them by cleverly placed spies who worked within the British government.

Dick was standing at the railing looking at the angry wind-whipped waters when he was joined by the captain of the *Avenger*.

"Maybe we'll have as much luck as John Paul Jones," Alec Seixas said as he stared out into the empty sea.

"I've heard he won some sort of battle," Dick said. "But I don't know any of the details."

"Jones was raiding along the eastern coast of England, raising hell and sending the locals into a state of panic," Alec said. "On September twenty-third he sighted a Baltic merchant fleet being guarded by the fifty-gun frigate *Serapis*. Jones was aboard the *Bonhomme Richard*, named, of course, in honor of our old friend, Benjamin Franklin.

"Jones's ship was badly outgunned by the *Serapis*, and

things weren't looking too good. The British captain saw the burning decks of the American ship, and in that supercilious way that only an Englishman can affect, he called out, 'Has your ship struck?' Meaning, of course, did Jones wish to surrender.

"Jones's answer is a classic," Alec said with amusement. "He stood on the quarterdeck and roared, 'I have not yet begun to fight!' His ship was burning, but he drove her straight toward the *Serapis* and caught her with his grappling irons. The two ships were attached bow to stern—in fact their cannons were nuzzling one another. The crews switched to swords and muskets and that was the start of the hand-to-hand battle."

"I'm glad I wasn't there," Dick muttered. He was short and not very strong, and well aware of these limitations.

"They fought all afternoon, and both decks were *awash* with blood," Alec said with excitement; it was obvious he would like to have been there with Jones. "The ships were locked in a death embrace within sight of the shore. Hundreds of people stood on the cliffs of Flamborough Head and watched the whole damned thing. It turned dark—and yet the crews continued to fight, because the moon was bright. Finally the Americans took the advantage, and the British captain decided to save the remainder of his crew. He struck his colors and handed over his sword.

"By this time the *Bonhomme Richard* was nothing more than a sinking hulk, so Jones transferred his crew to the *Serapis* and abandoned his own ship to the fishes. He sailed off with the British captain and the ship as a prize of war."

"What a wonderful victory!" Dick said.

"The idea that an American ship could defeat an English warship in English waters has caused tremendous repercussions. There've been fistfights in Parliament—"

"Ships ho!"

The lookout in the crow's nest had called out, and instantly the crew of the *Avenger* came alive. Alec used his glass to look at the ships on the horizon. "Six of 'em," he said.

"We're a bit outnumbered," Dick reminded him.

"Good," Alec said. "Maybe it'll be a fair scrap."

The wind picked up until it was blowing twenty-five knots, and it seemed the American ships were almost flying toward their rendezvous with the enemy.

Alec was delighted with the swiftness of his flotilla. "This wind will help us more than it will help them," he said. "We're quite a bit faster."

"Why are their ships slower?" Dick asked.

"They build them bigger so they can carry more guns."

"Oh," Dick said, now sorry he had asked the question. He wasn't delighted with the idea of going into battle on a floating pile of wood—which was the way he secretly thought of a ship.

Alec continued to peer through his spyglass. "They've seen us and are forming into line," he said. "Good, that's exactly what I expected them to do. The buggers have no imagination."

"What's forming into line?" Dick asked. He had heard the term before but wasn't sure what it meant.

"They like to fight in a single line, with each ship's bow following the stern of the one in front. Good enough tactics in a calm or light wind, but bloody stupid when they're in a roaring gale like this and up against a squadron of faster ships. Wait until you see what we do to them," he said with grim anticipation.

He ordered signals sent to the other ships, and the *Kieft*, the *Van Twiller*, and the *Peter Minuit* performed maneuvers as delicate as a gavotte, bringing them not bow to stern as the British, but parallel to one another. The howling wind sang through the rigging, straining the sails, and the American ships drove toward the enemy like four racing greyhounds.

They made a spectacular sight. Rake-masted and low-profiled, with a full ration of wind to strain the sails, they were ultimate examples of the shipwright's art, and they cut through the water like a hot knife through butter.

As the two squadrons drew closer and closer, Alec explained his battle tactics to Dick.

"See how they're turning broadside to us," he said. "That's so they'll be able to use their cannons. But all we're presenting to them are our bows, and that's a small target for a gunner on a pitching and rolling ship."

Dick had not failed to note the pitching and rolling. The heavy winds were whipping the sea into frothy whitecaps, and the ships dipped and bobbed.

"I'm going to sail between their ships," Alec said. "We'll pass through their line and both our starboard and port guns can fire at point-blank range. The British will have good shots only from their bow and stern guns. That's hardly a broadside."

"They still outnumber us," Dick said guardedly, not at all convinced about the wisdom of Alec's tactics.

"Speed is always better than sheer firepower," the *Avenger*'s captain said.

The ships closed.

The British began firing, and their cannonballs whizzed past the American ships. But, as Alec had foreseen, the heavy seas spoiled their marksmanship and they scored few hits.

Alec aimed the *Avenger* between two ships, the biggest of which appeared to be a sixty-four-gunner. As her bow crossed their line of advance, he ordered the gunners to commence firing.

Both batteries began firing, and it was impossible to miss. One cannon ball crashed into the base of the larger ship's mizzenmast, and it hung over at a crazy angle. Other balls tore into the decks and side plankings of the ship, and a shower of splinters raised hell among the English crew.

Alec had ordered his guns loaded with different types of shot. Some had conventional round shot, which punched holes in the enemy ship. But every fourth gun had grapeshot, which played havoc among the men and sails. A few guns were loaded with chainshot—two smaller round shot connected by stout iron links. These projectiles whirled around until they struck an object, and at close range were vicious killers.

He even had a few guns stuffed with langrage—a hodgepodge of lead and iron scraps mixed with bits of broken chain and glass. This was used to tear sails apart, but if a man was accidentally standing in the way, there wouldn't be enough left of him to bury.

As the *Avenger* passed between the two enemy ships, the other American ships were doing the same with their opposite numbers in the British line. They fired in unison, and then, when they were in the clear on the other side, swung around in unison to come back for another pass.

They came back toward the damaged British ships on the opposite tack, and the carnage continued. The British, of course, were now also scoring hits. One ball crashed into the starboard rail of the *Avenger,* tearing out stanchions, disabling a cannon, and killing three men. The other American ships also suffered hits, but none were crippling. The British ships were not doing so well: fire had broken out aboard three of them, and their decks were littered with spars and rigging that had been cut down.

The British admiral stuck to the book. The Americans were using the high winds to allow them to dash through his line of battle and cut his ships to pieces. But on he plodded, all ships remaining bow to stern, while the Americans yapped and snapped at their flanks like a pack of dogs gone mad.

The only time a British ship broke the line was when one of the heavy frigates took so many shots beneath her waterline that she began to list, and her hull speed was not sufficient to keep her up with her companions. The British admiral kept doggedly in line, abandoning the stricken ship.

"You don't intend to go back and take that wounded ship?" Dick was shouting to be heard above the roaring cannons.

Alec shook his head. "We have to keep running at top speed. It's the only advantage we have."

The battle continued for two hours, and the Americans gave the British an awful pounding. All the ships were in trouble to one degree or another, but the battle was broken off only because the fighting had been observed by a lookout on Holyhead and another British squadron was coming to rescue the first.

"Two small frigates and a coastal bark," Alec said as he peered at the fresh ships through his spyglass. "Also a ship-o'-the-line and two schooners. We'll break the engagement. The odds are getting too long."

Signals were raised, and the American ships broke away from the enemy and sailed toward the east coast of Ireland. "We'll head north and lose them past the Dublin coast. At this time of year there's always plenty of gray soup," Alec said.

As Alec had said, by the time it began to get dark, the ships were entering a sea of patchy fog. By ringing bells the American ships were able to keep track of one another, and they sailed through the night. When the sun came up, they were plodding along through heavy fog on winds that had died to whispers.

By eleven o'clock the last of the fog had been burned away by the frosty-looking November sun. The sea behind them was empty, without a glimpse of a British ship.

In the distance they could see the coast of Ireland, whose Mourne Mountains looked green and inviting in the morning light. The ships headed toward a medium-sized bay just to the south of the highest peaks.

"There's a small port at Dundalk," Alec said to Dick. "The

Irish will be more than happy to replenish some supplies—although they won't have any powder or shot."

"I thought Ireland was part of the British Empire," Dick said.

Alec nodded. "Yes, but the Irish people hate the British even more than we do. I guess they just don't know how to go about winning their own freedom, but they help us, because it gives them a sense of doing something."

"Why is it the British seem to alienate people no matter where they go?" Dick asked. "We hear stories about their problems in India and Ceylon. They seem to be troublemakers."

"The British have an innate arrogance," Alec said thoughtfully. "An Englishman always assumes he's superior simply because he is English. He looks down on everyone else. Who wants to put up with that for long?"

They anchored in the bay below the Mourne range. Seth Cuyler, who had been aboard the *Peter Minuit*, came over to the *Avenger* and was enthusiastic about the victory.

"We tore them to pieces," he said happily. "Did you see the way that one ship was sinking?"

"The other ships would have saved the sailors."

"I'd like to see all those rats drown."

Dick kept quiet. He did not think it amusing to see men thrown into the inhospitable waters of the Irish sea—even if they were Englishmen. But he knew this was an unpopular view, and said nothing.

The captains held services for the men who had been killed aboard their ships. Alec held a small, quiet service on the main deck of the *Avenger*. It didn't seem odd to anyone that a Jew read the last word over six Christians. Alec, after all, was captain, and to a seaman that counted for a great deal more than a man's religion. It was a curious fact, but seamen who faced death aboard a warship were religious without being pious. On land the parsons and dominies raved on darkly about the fires of hell, but aboard a fighting ship there was hell to see and feel, so the men communed silently with their God.

They rested for two days and took supplies aboard, helped by the friendly Irishmen, then headed south with the intention of taking up a position around the Old Head of Kinsale. The pattern of the war at sea was settling into periods of intense activity punctuated by long periods of boredom.

The last day of the year, 1779...
Celine sat beside Franz von Lossow before the fire in the

kitchen of the Place. They were drinking mulled wine and roasting thin slices of beef over the fire.

"Happy?" she asked.

He smiled and took her hand in his. "Except for the guilt I feel about being here while the rest of the army is over in New Jersey. Not everyone is enjoying a warm fire, good food, good drink, and the company of a beautiful woman."

She held out the toasting fork and offered him a slice of the crackling meat. "I don't know how much longer I'll be able to give you the fine food," she said. "Last January it was possible to buy a barrel of beef for seventeen pounds sterling. The latest figure I heard quoted was over two hundred."

Franz shook his head. "We bought a shipload for the army from a trader in Philadelphia, and his price was two hundred and forty pounds, eight shillings and sixpence a barrel."

Celine smiled. "You'd think he'd at least forget the sixpence."

"Business is business to these traders. The one I dealt with was actually from New York. He told me he had moved to Philadelphia only a year or so ago."

"What's his name?"

"Hmm. Peabody? Yes, I think that's it."

"*Philemon* Peabody?"

"Yes...yes, I remember, because it was such an unusual first name."

Celine laughed. "That crook! He used to work for my father, but it turned out he was stealing everything he could get his hands on."

"Well, I can assure you he hasn't changed, and is prospering in the city of Brotherly Love."

Celine became serious. She took his hand to her lips and kissed the tips of his fingers. "Franz...when this war is over...what's to become of us?"

"What's to become of us?" he asked playfully. "The eternal question, asked down through the ages.

> "'Time sweeps on,
> and old age creeps upon us
> in an unmarked chain of years;
> Days rush on
> Without a rein to check them.'

"That was Ovid's answer. In short, what becomes of us is that we grow old."

"I didn't mean what happens to mankind in the next century," Celine said in mock petulance. "I meant what happens to you and me."

He took her hand and placed it against his cheek. "I'm going to stay in America. We shall get married and grow old together."

"I like that," she whispered. "I like that a great deal."

He kissed her on the forehead, then the nose, and finally the lips. He held her face in his hands and contemplated the exquisite line of her cheek and chin, and her wide, intelligent eyes.

"I love you, Celine," he said huskily. "I love you with all my heart and soul. You have given me the meaning of my life."

She was deeply touched.

Love was not a new emotion to her; it had happened before, and it had always been good. Why deny it? But there was something unique about the love she felt for this man.

It was a love that could never quite be replaced. The other men in her life had come and gone, each filling the space left by his predecessor in more or less the same way. But all that had ended with Franz.

"I love you," she said simply. Anything more would have been embellishment.

6

The World Turned Upside Down

1780–1781

"WHERE IS SHE? WHERE'S THE HARLOT? SHOW HER to me!"

Celine stared at the red-faced, near hysterical visitor to the Place. "If you'd tell me who you are and what you're talking about, perhaps we could get to the bottom of this," she said calmly.

Only moments earlier, an agitated Primus had come to his mistress's sitting room on the second floor and announced that a strange woman was downstairs. She was carrying on in a loud, dreadful manner and made no sense to the black man. Celine had put aside her needlepoint and gone down to sort out the matter.

"Don't tell me you don't know what I'm talking about," the visitor screeched. "You're in league with the harlot!"

The madwoman Celine studied appeared to be in her late thirties or early forties, but had that sort of pinched-looking face that, at first glance, made her appear older. Her eyes were red from crying and rubbing, and her complexion was a mottled gray splotched with patches of redness. Her long dress was stained and fly-specked, and her shoes were muddied from the May rains that had been drenching the New York area for several weeks.

Celine's first inclination was to think the woman had wandered to the Place by mistake, and that she should be taken to a doctor. But then, she thought, it wouldn't do any harm to ask a few questions.

"Who *are* you?"

"Who am I? Ha! As if you didn't know!"

"I assure you, madam, I don't know," Celine said patiently.

"Sarah Henry be my name, and I'm after finding my husband, Noah, and that tart he comes here to visit all the time."

Now Celine understood. Since Mary Delafield had moved to the Place, Noah Henry had found excuses to pay frequent visits. Mary had confided in Celine, telling her of Noah's love for her and revealing that he was trapped in a marriage to some dreadful woman. This, obviously, was that dreadful woman.

"If you'd come into the kitchen, perhaps we can discuss this calmly over a cup of tea."

"It's not tea I want, it's my husband."

"But Noah hasn't been here in over a month," Celine protested. "I haven't the slightest idea where he is."

"As if I can believe that!" Sarah said in indignation. She put her hands on her hips and stuck out her jaw. "Take me to him!"

Celine managed to calm the woman to the point that she consented to come into the kitchen, where Primus served tea and toasted bread and then withdrew in relief.

The Place, as everywhere else in the New York area, had not yet recovered from the harshest winter anyone could remember. The snows had fallen without relief and the polar winds swept down from Canada. The North River froze over from shore to shore, and the British transported loads of wood by sled from Staten Island to the Battery. Children ice-skated from Manhattan to Paulus's Hook and thought it great sport. But they were the only ones who managed sometimes to enjoy themselves. Everyone bundled up in their heaviest clothing, trying to keep warm with the few miserable sticks of wood they were able to scrounge for the fire, and existing on the scantiest of rations.

The great stores of supplies that had been hidden at the Place had been exhausted. Everything had been sent to General Washington's winter camp at Morristown, and even that had barely kept the soldiers from starvation.

The lack of food and firewood had taken a heavy toll among the people as disease stalked the streets and houses, swooping down on the old, the young, and the weak, and several hundred people in the area had either starved or frozen to death. So when Celine served tea and bread to her uninvited visitor, she was hardly being parsimonious.

"The carryings-on in *my* house, 'tween my husband and that hussy!" Sarah hissed. "Shameful, they were, and don't think for a minute God wasn't looking down, watching and toting up the sins."

"From what I know, absolutely nothing went on between your husband and Mrs. Delafield."

"A lot you know! I was there!"

Finally, after a long and arduous series of questions, Celine learned that Noah had left his farm a month ago and had not returned. She had no idea where he was, but one thing was certain: he was not at the Place. She was eventually able to half convince his wife of this, and Sarah calmed considerably, contenting herself with grumbling and complaining.

"But if he's not here, where is he?" she wailed.

"Does he ever go down to the city?"

"Sometimes."

"Maybe that's where he is."

"But why didn't he tell me he was leaving?"

Celine shook her head. "That's something you'll have to ask him when you see him."

She looked at Sarah and realized the woman was exhausted. And almost starved, by the look of her; certainly the toast had disappeared in a hurry. Simple human charity compelled Celine to invite this disagreeable person to rest at her house. After a bit more food, it might be best if she went to a spare bedroom and took a nap.

"After you're rested, you'll see things from the brighter side," Celine said.

But Sarah Henry was not the sort of person to see the brighter side of anything. "Abandoned by my husband just as the spring planting is coming up—oh yes, yes indeed, I'll see the brighter side!"

Celine didn't bother arguing. She raided the much-depleted larder, quickly prepared some soup for the other woman, and then excused herself.

That turned out to be a big mistake.

While Sarah was eating her bread and soup, Beth Henry returned from an unsuccessful hunt. She was dressed in her forest buckskins and looked slender and beautiful. Sarah, of course, knew Beth was her husband's cousin, and also remembered she was the one who had brought Mary Delafield to her house in the first place.

"Another tart," she complained as she slurped at her soup. "Filthy tart."

"I beg your pardon," Beth said.

"I said, 'tis another tart living under this roof, and a fitting thing it is. A whole house of tarts."

"Hmn."

"You and that bitch you brought up to tempt my husband."

"I think you'd better be quiet," Beth said evenly. There was a nasty edge to her voice. Anyone who knew her well would understand it was a time to be cautious, but Sarah knew nothing about Beth, only that she was her husband's cousin and the cause of her trouble.

"Be quiet, the tart says! Listen to her! And whose husband are *you* stealing? Tell me that?"

If Celine had been in the room, she probably could have prevented what happened next.

Beth tried to ignore the woman at the table. She went to the kettle to get herself a cup of tea. Sarah regarded her slight figure and mistook Beth's willowiness for softness. "Look at you, you harlot!" she bellowed, working herself back up to a full rage. "Maybe what you need is for someone to beat some sense into you!"

Beth stared at the woman the way a snake might regard a fieldmouse it was contemplating for dinner. She poured her tea and started to leave the room. In a flash Sarah was up from her chair, barring the way.

"Not so fast, little tart!" she said, sticking her angry face close to Beth's. "Tell me where my husband is. And if you're not quick about it, I'll beat some sense into that empty head of yours!"

"I don't know what you're talking about," Beth said. "Get out of my way."

Again Sarah took the other's surface calm as a sign of weakness. She lashed out and knocked the teacup from Beth's hand. It fell to the floor and smashed into pieces as Sarah shouted anew.

"Are you going to tell me where Noah—"

Kick a wolf and he goes for you in self-defense: Beth's reaction was identical. No sooner had the cup hit the floor than her forearm struck Sarah across the throat. As the woman hurtled backward to the floor, Beth was upon her, delivering trip-hammer blows to Sarah's face. They hit the floor together, and Beth smashed her antagonist's head on the floor—once, twice, three times. The battle was over. She rose to a kneeling position and looked down at the unconscious woman.

Primus had been on his way to the kitchen with a load of firewood, and he dropped his burden and hurried indoors when he heard the commotion. "Merciful God!" he exclaimed as he saw the two women, the one prone on the floor, the other kneeling at her side. "Miss Beth, please, what's going on?"

"She hit me," Beth said.

Celine had also heard the racket. She came into the kitchen, and her hand flew to her mouth when she saw Sarah stretched out on the floor. She wet a rag with water and sponged Sarah's head while she listened to Beth's account of what had happened.

"She shouldn't have struck me," Beth said in conclusion.

"We've got to get her to bed," Celine said, observing that the welts on Sarah's face were already changing from red to black-and-blue. "You really clouted her."

"I'm sorry, but she asked for it."

The two of them, aided by a distracted Primus, who was still bundled in his customary three layers of woolen outerwear, managed to get Sarah up to the bed in a spare room. As Celine smoothed the blanket over the unconscious woman, it occurred to her that Sarah was the boniest person she had ever seen.

Noah's wife slept for ten hours. When she woke, she seemed normal enough, but later, when she was sitting at the kitchen table, chewing on a piece of bread and drinking tea, she began to cry. Nothing anybody said or did could comfort her.

Finally Celine and Beth got Sarah into bed.

When they returned to the kitchen, Mary Delafield was waiting for them. "Primus told me what happened," she said. "I feel responsible."

"Don't blame yourself. If anyone's to blame, it's Noah, for walking out of the house without telling her why he was leaving, or where he was going."

"Now that you've met Sarah," Mary asked, "do you blame him for walking out?"

"Hardly. But tell me, what's going on with you and Noah?"

"He told me he loves me," Mary admitted. "But I also discouraged him and reminded him he had a wife."

Celine sighed. "You don't think that would stop a man once he's made up his mind, do you?"

"He's got a wife."

"When a man tells you he loves you, he isn't talking with his brain," Celine said. "In fact, that's the last part of his body he's using."

Mary was embarrassed. "Nothing ever happened between us."

"Where do you think he is?"

Mary shrugged. "The last time I spoke with him, he told me Sarah was making his life impossible. I guess he just got fed up and left."

"Do you think he's in the city?"

"Noah doesn't feel comfortable in New York. He likes the outdoors better."

"If that's the case, then maybe we'd better start by checking the shacks and tents along the North River docks.... We should at least *look* for him," Celine insisted.

"I guess so," Mary agreed. "Sarah's been handled pretty roughly."

"Are you saying I did wrong?" Beth asked.

"You were a bit excessive," Mary said.

"Do you agree?" Beth asked Celine.

"I wasn't there to see what happened."

"If she acted the same way, I'd do it again," Beth said, and walked from the room.

Celine shook her head. "That girl has spent too much time in the woods. It's like living with a loaded cannon."

"Maybe she's right, and was only protecting herself," Mary said.

"Well, let's see about finding Noah."

But things were to move along a different course.

The next morning Sarah awoke before dawn. She dressed and went to the kitchen. Primus, as usual, was already up and about. Without a word, Sarah accepted the cup of tea he offered. After she drank it, she left the house for a walk in the mild spring air.

There was an unnatural calm about her. Her mouth no longer curled in a sneer, and she didn't seem to be looking at everything as if condemning it. She wandered into the barn, now empty for the first time in two years. There was no hoard of supplies waiting for Washington; only a few stacks of old hay and two horses in their stalls waiting patiently for their morning ration of oats.

She walked to the cemetery and peered inside. It was dark and cool, and she sat for a moment and patted the smooth surface of a large flat rock.

She walked down toward the stream and came to the sheep barn. Sisyphus and John Holt were already at work, printing a new edition of the *Instigator*. Both men were so involved with watching the press as it printed their latest diatribe they didn't notice the woman as she stood near the doorway.

It was difficult to tell from Sarah's expression what her thoughts were as she watched the two men scurry about their work. Did she comprehend what they were doing? Did she care?

Her face revealed nothing. After a while she left the sheep barn and wandered back to the house.

She entered the kitchen. Mary Delafield was at the table, and when she saw Sarah, she prepared herself for the worst. But nothing happened. Sarah accepted another cup of tea from Primus and sat staring at the crackling flames of the fire in the cooking stove. She finished her tea and left without saying a word to Mary. Indeed, she had not even acknowledged the other woman's presence in the room.

This strange behaviour went on for two days, and then Sarah disappeared.

By this time Celine had become concerned about her, because her actions were so erratic. Sarah had obviously been affected by the beating she had received from Beth.

"Where could she have gone?" Celine asked.

"Maybe she went home," Mary said.

"I hope that's it. Maybe Noah will be there."

"By the way, Celine," Mary said, "I haven't seen Beth around."

"She's gone off with Jemmy and Jenny. Something to do with Washington's camp, I think. I try to ignore anything that has to do with the twins."

Mary smiled. "I think they're fun."

"Fun, sure, like finding a snake in your bed. Did you hear what they were up to this winter?"

"I heard they built an iceboat and took it across the river."

Celine nodded. "They used thirty steer ribs on the bottom as runners."

"They sailed it across to Jersey, but couldn't stop it," Mary said as she giggled. "And the man who had paid them to take him across broke his arm. I'm sorry to be laughing, but I heard it was very funny."

"I'm beginning to wonder about you, Mary. A man breaks his arm and you think it's funny. No wonder you and the twins get along."

Mary tried to suppress her giggling, but failed. "I'm sorry."

"The iceboat was bad enough, but that's not what I was talking about."

"What else did they do?"

"I understand this other crackpot idea was Jenny's. Sometimes I think she's worse than her brother. After all, she's a grown woman now. Why doesn't she marry, have children, and stop all the nonsense?"

"Tell me what they did."

"Over in Pennsylvania there are places where some sticky black stuff comes out of the ground. It bubbles right up. Well, Jenny discovered that this black ooze burns. So she and her brother went to Pennsylvania and came back with a half-dozen barrels of it. They brought it to Morristown because they heard the soldiers were freezing. They figured the black ooze could be burned to keep the men warm."

"What happened?"

Celine smiled despite herself. "Jemmy rigged up a stove in the general's house and started burning the black stuff. Well, it burned, all right, but the smoke was enough to choke a man to death. It drove everyone out into the snow. Then the ooze leaked onto the floor and caused a fire. The general slept in a tent for two days before they could make his house livable again. He threatened to shoot any guard who let either of the twins back into his camp."

Mary laughed. "You must admit things aren't dull when they're around."

"Neither is it dull when there's a hurricane," Celine said. "But there's more to the story. Jemmy still had several barrels of the black ooze left, so he brought them back across the North River and took them to General Clinton's house and told the servants it was a marvelous new cooking fuel.

"That night the servants tried to use it while the general was entertaining the incoming governor, Robertson. The results were the same as at Morristown. Smoke filled the house, and the general and the new governor had to run out into the street. The servants managed to get the ooze out of the house before it started a fire, but the dinner was ruined because they had to open all the windows to get rid of the smoke. It didn't make things any more pleasant that it was one of the coldest nights in February."

"Maybe the twins have accidentally discovered a way to get rid of the British," Mary said gleefully.

"I understand General Clinton has *also* threatened to shoot anyone who lets them back into *his* house. Imagine! The Sacketts are the only people both sides would like to shoot."

Their conversation was interrupted by Primus, who came in with news of Sarah Henry.

"The stableman saw her walking toward the Post Road," he said.

"Did he see which way she went when she reached the road?"

"Nope," Primus said. "Just that she was going in that direction."

"Maybe she's on her way home," Mary said.

"She wouldn't go to the city, would she?" Celine asked.

"I don't think so."

"I'm sure she went home," Celine said.

But she was wrong.

"You've got to get him back, he's my husband, and he ought to be home, not out with tarts, oh he's not all that bad, just that he can't stay put, and I know he wants me, but that woman, *she's* the one who's taking him away, you've got to arrest her, yes, yes, arrest her and..."

Sarah carried on for many minutes in this manner, and Sergeant Taggert listened to her incoherent monologue with growing impatience.

Sarah had walked down to the city with a single idea burning in her mind. She would go to the authorities and condemn Mary and Celine and that terrible girl who had attacked her. She would tell what she knew about them and have them put in jail. Then Noah would be contrite and come home.

She arrived in the city and asked a shopkeeper where she could find the authorities who "would put someone in jail." The shopkeeper scratched his head, decided the woman was daft, and directed her to the Provost.

She arrived at the triangular park and stood in the middle of Murray Street near the corner of Vesey. There were several buildings, and she couldn't determine which was the Provost.

She finally went into a two-story gray building, only to discover it was the Almshouse.

There was a brief moment of confusion, because the Almshouse sergeant-at-arms took one look at her and thought she was trying to become a resident; only there weren't any places open. To many people the Almshouse offered a far better chance at survival than the streets.

"There are no more places," the keeper of the door said.

"No more places?" Sarah said, not knowing what he was talking about.

There was a man leaning against the wall just inside the doorway. He was unshaven and bleary-eyed. It was Enoch de Witt, who was now reduced to living in the Almshouse.

"What's all this about?" he asked.

"This woman wants a place here, but we haven't got any. Jammed to the rafters, we are," the guard said.

"She can have my place," Enoch said. "In this weather I can sleep in the park."

"What if it rains?"

"Then I'll have a bath."

The guard turned to Sarah. "Well, do you want his place?"

"What?"

"You won't get much sleep here," Enoch warned. "Everyone snores all night."

"Ha!" the guard exclaimed. "The way you drink they could hold a horse race next to you and you wouldn't hear it."

Enoch drew himself up to his full height. "Drinking is a man's God-given right."

The guard shook his head and turned back to Sarah. "So? Do you want his place, or not?"

"I want to get some people put in jail," Sarah said.

"Huh?"

"Tarts, they are."

"So what's that got to do with us?"

"They told me to come to the Provost."

Finally the mix-up was straightened out, and the sergeant-at-arms directed Sarah to the building next door.

"She looks crazy," Enoch said as the woman scuttled to the proper building.

"That means she'd fit right in with this crowd."

"I don't know; I may not be perfect, but I'm not crazy."

The guard laughed. "Maybe you'd be better off if you were."

"Maybe we all would," Enoch said.

* * *

The British soldier on guard at the Provost door looked at Sarah's swollen face and glazed eyes and shook his head. "You can't see the provost marshal. Colonel Cunningham is a busy man."

"Who *can* I see?"

The soldier tried to get rid of her entirely, but she became loud and difficult, so he decided to pass the problem along to someone else and had her brought to Sergeant Taggert's office, where she was now carrying on at great length.

"So when can you arrest the tarts?" she concluded.

"There doesn't seem to be any reason to arrest anyone, Mrs. Henry," the sergeant said. "And now, if you don't mind, I'm a busy man."

"But I explained how evil those women are, and how they're out to steal husbands, and how they—"

"Please, missus," the sergeant said, struggling to be polite, because it was obvious the woman wasn't in her right mind.

"I want them arrested. Them and those two men out in the barn with their papers. Printing up stuff they were, brazen as could be. I *know* they're in this thing with those women, the whole lot of them together..."

At this point the sergeant wasn't even listening, which was unfortunate for him. If he had paid attention, he would have been startled to hear the reference to the two printers Captain Blakely was so anxious to find.

"Missus, I must ask you to leave," he said, standing up from his chair and glowering down at the woman.

"You're in cahoots with them!" Sarah accused, her old shrillness now back in full force. "That's why you won't do anything to help! You're in it with them!"

The sergeant had had enough. One could be only so nice, even to a looney. He came around the desk, took Sarah by the arm, and began marching her toward the door. His grip was firm, but not hard enough to hurt. He wasn't interested in harming the woman, only in getting rid of her.

Something inside Sarah snapped. The face of the man escorting her to the door was no longer that of Sergeant Taggert. It became the faces of Celine and Mary and Beth, all wrapped into one. With a screech worthy of a banshee, she pulled her arm away from the sergeant and jumped him; her nails aimed at his eyes.

Taggert was strong, but not particularly quick, and the nails of her right hand dug into the flesh of his cheek, just missing his eye. A downward wrench left the tracks of five deep scratches that immediately began to drip blood.

The sergeant put his hand to his face, withdrew it, and stared in disbelief at the palm of his hand, which was wet and sticky with his own blood. "What in hell!" he roared.

She attempted to dig her nails into his face again, but this time the sergeant was ready. Grabbing her wrists, he spun her around so her back was toward him. He placed his knee in her back and wrenched her arms behind her. Sarah squealed in response to the sudden pain in her shoulders.

"Guard! Guard!" Taggert shouted as he held the woman harmless. The door was flung open and two Hessians entered, their muskets at the ready.

"Take this bitch to the women's cells and lock her up," Taggert commanded, giving the woman a shove in the small of her back. She fell right into the waiting arms of the Hessians.

"You're in it with the tarts! You're in it with the tarts!" Sarah kept shouting as the Hessians dragged her from the room.

The sergeant took a white cloth from his desk, went to the window to see his image in a pane of glass, and winced when he caught sight of the five scratches running from below his eye downward almost to his chin. "The dirty bitch!" he grumbled, placing the cloth against his cheek to stanch the flow of blood.

He went back to his chair and threw himself into it with such force the wood groaned and complained as if it were about to split. He picked up a quill pen, dipped it in ink, and began to write out an order for Sarah Henry's incarceration.

Five minutes later he took it to Blakely's office to get the necessary signature. The captain routinely signed all incarceration orders placed before him, and he treated this one no differently. He didn't even bother to read the name of the person being locked up. As he finished affixing his signature, he looked up at Taggert, who was still blotting blood off his cheek with the white cloth.

"What happened to you?"

Taggert pointed at the incarceration order. "This dirty bitch hit me when I wasn't looking."

"We're locking up another woman?" the captain said, glancing down at the paper. "I don't like locking up women. What's it all about?"

"The woman's daft, sir. She came in and wanted me to put

her husband in jail. As near as I can figure out he's got some doxie on the side and his wife thinks that's reason enough for us to lock him up."

Blakely smiled. "Infidelity is a serious business, sergeant, surely you agree with that."

Taggert was never quite sure when the captain was having his little joke. This *sounded* like one, but how could he be certain?

"Very serious, sir," he said straight-faced. "But it's not exactly a crime that concerns us in the provost marshal's office."

"You say she attacked you because you wouldn't agree to put her husband in jail?"

"Exactly, sir."

The captain shook his head. "A few days' confinement ought to teach her a lesson."

Taggert pointed to his cheek. "Look at this, sir. I'd say she deserves a few *months* for what she's done."

"Make it a few weeks. Is that good enough?"

The sergeant nodded. "If that's what you think, Captain, then weeks it shall be," he said, but his tone conveyed that he didn't think it sufficient punishment at all. He left the office, holding the cloth to his cheek and grumbling.

Captain Blakely smiled and thought no more of the matter. He had no idea he had signed an incarceration order for Sarah Henry, the woman who had once tipped him off about Mary Delafield's hiding place. If he had realized who the jailed woman was, no doubt he would have gone down to see her. After all, once she had done him a favor.

But he hadn't bothered to read the name on the incarceration order, and wasn't aware of who was locked up in his own jail.

He went back to the report he had been reading before the sergeant had come to his office.

Two weeks later, while Sarah Henry still languished in jail, a man a hundred miles away became interested in her.

A report from one of his spies had reached Philemon Peabody. The spy related that one of his woman friends—a prostitute and pickpocket by trade—had only recently been released from prison in New York. She regaled her friends and cronies with stories about events that happened while she was under lock and key; especially stories about the other people locked up with her. One of them was known as Crazy Sarah. This

Sarah had spent most of her waking hours telling a jumbled story about "a group of tarts," an "unfaithful husband," and something to do with "two men and a printing press."

The spy emphasized that a man couldn't put faith in what Crazy Sarah said, because she was obviously demented, but he was passing the information along, as he put it, "just so's Mr. Peabody can see I'm doing my job."

Philemon Peabody was equally ready to dismiss the story as meaningless, when at the end of the note the spy mentioned that Crazy Sarah's last name was Henry.

Henry!

Peabody knew the Henrys and the de Kuypers had always been as thick as mosquitoes on a hot summer's night. If this woman really *was* a Henry, there might be something to the story, and if he followed the trail it might lead back to the de Kuypers—which would, in turn, possibly lead to the printers and the reward.

It was a tricky business, Peabody realized, because the reward was being offered by the British, and he was wanted by them, or at least wanted by the deputy provost marshal. Captain Blakely, he was sure, had a long memory.

He thought about it for a long time. Was it worth the risk? The reward wasn't so much that he was willing to risk the present life he was enjoying. But there was more to it than the money, he realized. If Jan de Kuyper had only had the sense to understand that Philemon Peabody had been in the right, and had allowed him to make proper profits, none of this would have happened. He would not have been forced into stealing. He would never have gotten involved with Blakely. And he would never have been forced to flee as a fugitive from New York.

He decided he was doing all this not for the money, but for revenge. In his grave Jan de Kuyper would learn the penalty for bringing grief to Philemon Peabody.

He assumed the disguise of a sailor, added a false beard and flecked his hair with gray powder, hired a burly bodyguard, and set out for New York. They passed a number of detachments of American troops on the road, but didn't see a British soldier until they crossed the North River in a hired fishing boat and landed a few blocks north of the Battery. A few officers were playing at bowls in an alley off Greenwich Street, but they didn't give a second glance at two sailors making their way through the streets near the docks.

After a short conversation with his spy at the Bunch O' Grapes tavern, Peabody decided the only way he could be sure of anything was to talk with Crazy Sarah herself.

There were two ways to accomplish this. First, get her out of prison. Second, bribe someone so he could go inside and talk to her there. The second course seemed the easier, so his spy found a corporal of the guard who, for a fee, was willing to be helpful.

The little room off the cellblock was gloomy. A single narrow window allowed a minimum of light to pierce the interior, which was furnished with a rough-hewn table and several rickety chairs. Peabody nervously paced back and forth as he waited for the corporal to return with the prisoner.

The door opened, and the corporal motioned for the woman to enter. "You've ten minutes," he said. "Then I've got to get her back to her cell."

Peabody nodded, and the corporal left the room and closed the door. The woman stared at him strangely. She *did* look crazy, he thought.

"My name is Peabody," he said. "Are you Sarah Henry?"

She stared at him for a long moment, then went to one of the chairs and sat down. "I suppose you're in league with them too."

"Excuse me? And who might I be in league with?"

"Don't try to fool me."

Finally, however, he got her to admit her name, and say that her husband's name was Noah.

"Now tell me about these two men you saw working a printing press."

"At *her* house."

"Her?"

"With all her airs, a tart, that's all she is, a tart like the other one, and that little bitchy cousin of Noah's, tarts all of them, and don't think the Lord isn't watching, watching and toting up the sins, and biding His time until He sees them all roasting in the fires of hell."

"Of course, of course," soothed the exasperated man. "But exactly what is her name?"

"Celine Murray. Haven't you been paying any attention to me?"

"You say the printers were at her house?"

"I've already told you that," Sarah said indignantly. "And not *in* the house. The other place."

"Other place?"

"The barn."

"Really?"

"Now I'm tired of all this. If you don't plan on helping me with the tarts, I want to go back to my cell."

"Oh, I'll help you, but not this minute."

"Then I want to go."

Peabody went to the door and rapped on it. He told the corporal he was finished and handed him the second half of the promised money.

The corporal grinned as he pocketed the sum. "Anytime you want to see her again, just let me know."

Peabody made no reply as he stepped smartly out of the prison. It gave him the jitters to be so close to Captain Blakely; he was certain the Englishman was the vengeful type. The bright sunlight was a welcome sight as he exited into the street. He walked back to the Bunch O' Grapes to have a much-needed drink.

He would not have felt quite so relieved had he been privy to a conversation taking place in Captain Blakely's office at that very moment.

The corporal he had bribed was making his report. He was always available for such favors, but to protect himself, he always told the captain what was going on. It had proved to be a mutually beneficial arrangement. Right now he was telling the officer about the man whom he had admitted to talk to Crazy Sarah.

"Who would want to see her?" Blakely asked.

The corporal shrugged. "He didn't say why, sir."

"Get me the file on Crazy Sarah."

When the corporal handed him the file, he skimmed it quickly. Not much there: notice of arrest; incarceration paper; weekly report. And then he reread her name—Sarah Henry; and remembered who she was—the woman in whose house Mary had had her baby.

Mary Delafield! It was a small world, indeed, he thought. Now he began to wonder about the identity of the man who had visited her. From the corporal's description, it couldn't have been the man he had met the day he went to see Mary.

He became curious. "I think we ought to release this Crazy Sarah," he said.

"Yes sir."

"As of this minute you're detached from your usual duties. Keep an eye on her. I want to know where she goes, who she talks with, and what she does with every minute of her time."

"Yes, sir," the corporal said, pleased with the thought of such a departure from the routine.

When the corporal had gone, Blakely spent a few moments pondering his decision. What did he hope to learn? Was it worth all this bother?

He didn't know the answer. The only way he would know if this made any sense was to let the woman loose and watch what happened. If nothing happened, very well. In this case, he had discharged the debt he owed the woman for once having done him a favor.

But he had a strange feeling about this woman and her visitor. And often in the past his hunches had proved helpful.

In the meantime he could forget about it and get back to work.

The September reception at the Middletons' London townhouse was one of the first events of the new fall season. Lady Althea had invited Drew and Philip Ogilvy, and the two gentlemen stood along the mirrored wall that was known as Bachelor's Walk because it was the area where all the eligible young men seemed to congregate. It was a good place to observe the movements of everyone else and also had the advantage of being adjacent to the large bar, where three servants served champagne and an excellent variety of wines.

Drew had arrived in London at the beginning of summer on Ben Franklin's orders. His job this time was very specific and demanding. The new nation was desperate for money. The United States of America found itself in the odd position of being able to issue as much currency as it wished, and yet didn't have a farthing in gold specie to back it up. The result was inevitable, and the more money Congress printed, the more patently worthless it became. In the ports of Europe where Americans bought ships and weapons, the traders spurned the paper continentals, demanding payment in hard currencies. There were wealthy people in England who secretly supported the American cause and contributed generous sums of money. It was Drew's task to collect even more.

"Have no conscience," Franklin had instructed him. "When a man is willing to give a dozen pieces of gold, don't be satisfied with less than two dozen."

The old gentleman had waved a piece of paper in the air. "Look at this! Lord North's latest proposals for a peace. He becomes more and more generous."

"He doesn't seem to be listening to us," Drew said. "We've made it plain the only acceptable terms are evacuation of the colonies and recognition of our country."

"Ah, yes, Lord North's a remarkable man."

"He is?"

"Yes. Remarkable for his stupidity."

Drew was only one of several emissaries attempting to gather funds in European countries. Ben Franklin, of course, was the main money raiser in France, which had proven to be the most generous country of all. Even as Franklin kept getting money at Versailles, he confided to Drew that the king and his minister, de Vergennes, were bankrupting their country. "But you keep taking their money," Drew said, to which Franklin had a ready answer: "Of course I do, and more than that, I keep complaining that they're not giving enough."

With this fund-raising philosophy in mind, Drew had come to England to do his share. So far he had had good luck. John Jay was in Spain, and his efforts had met with only modest success, the Spanish being much more tightfisted than the French or English. John Adams was in the Netherlands, meeting with almost no success because the merchants of Amsterdam, Antwerp, and The Hague disliked the idea of giving anything away. The most they agreed to do was to supply ships, but then only for a price. It was true they kept the prices low, but a trait in the makeup of the Dutchmen prevented them from indulging in anything that remotely resembled charity.

"Beautiful girl," Ogilvy murmured as Althea Middleton swept through the open French doors on the far side of the room.

"She is, indeed," Drew agreed as he watched her make her way across the room, smiling at this guest, allowing her hand to be kissed by that one, being charming, witty, and most delightful.

"She'll make some Englishman a good wife," Ogilvy said.

"Why an Englishman? Maybe she'll marry an American," Drew said.

Ogilvy smiled. "Hardly, old boy. Her father will insist on bringing a title into the family."

It annoyed Drew to think this Englishman—a man who was supposed to be his friend—thought of Americans as second-class citizens. It also made the prospect of Drew's involvement with Althea even more attractive. Now it seemed he had something to prove.

"Mr. de Kuyper," said the lady in question, as she extended her hand. "So good to see you."

He brushed the top of her gloved hand with his lips. "And for me to see you."

"Isn't this exciting!" she said. "A whole new season is beginning. I *do* hope you plan on staying here."

"I'll do my best," Drew promised.

Althea moved closer to him, and her entire body seemed to be a subtle invitation for him to learn more about it. "It will be so good to get to know you, really know you."

"I say," Ogilvy said, interrupting the two of them. "That's Lord North himself over there."

"He's a friend of my father's," Althea said. She looked at Drew and smiled. "Imagine, Lord North and an American in the same room. You will behave, now, won't you?"

"Only if the prime minister does."

"Good. Don't let him bully you," Ogilvy said.

"I won't," Drew said. "Even though, according to you, I'm supposed to be intimidated by a title."

Ogilvy was embarrassed, realizing Drew was referring to his earlier remark about Althea's marriage prospects. "This isn't the same thing," he stammered.

Drew refused to let him off the hook. He looked at Althea. "We were discussing the chances of an American marrying a titled Englishwoman like yourself. Ogilvy doesn't think it possible."

"And why not?"

"I suggest you ask your father," Ogilvy said, trying to evade the issue.

"I don't have to ask my father about anything when I want to make up my mind!" she said heatedly. "I'll do as I please — even marry an American, if I want to."

"See, Ogilvy," Drew said. "I knew you had it all wrong."

"And now it's time for me to show you our garden," Althea said, linking her arm with Drew's.

She had never been so bold in the past, and it startled Drew. But then he relaxed and enjoyed feeling the warmth passing between them. "I'd like nothing better," he said.

"I have the most *divine* rosebushes," Althea said. "They're my specialty. Tell me, do you fancy flowers?"

"More and more," Drew said as the two of them walked away from the flustered Ogilvy.

The party continued, and Drew was introduced to Lord North by Ogilvy, who discreetly withdrew to allow the two men to exchange thoughts without worrying about what a third party might think.

"Ogilvy tells me you're associated with Benjamin Franklin," Lord North said. "Estimable gentleman, Franklin—yes, quite, that would be my opinion of him."

Hardly his opinion of you, Drew thought to himself, but aloud he was more diplomatic. "Your Lordship's reputation is well known in American circles," he said.

Lord North was a formidable-looking man. Heavy facial features set on a stocky body gave him, appropriately, the appearance of a stubborn bull. His lips were heavy, and he licked them often. He was nearsighted and squinted a great deal. He had a deep, clear voice that seemed pitched to addressing a crowded room. Indeed, His Lordship spoke as if addressing Parliament even when he was having a private conversation with one man—which was not surprising, considering that he had been in Commons since the tender age of twenty-two, when he had been elected as the member from Banbury. His tenure as PM had begun over ten years before, when he had succeeded Grafton in February, 1770.

The prime minister and the American sat in a small alcove in a hallway leading to the main salon. The other guests avoided them, tactfully respecting the private nature of their conversation.

"When is Franklin going to talk your Congress into coming to terms?" the prime minister asked.

"I believe Mr. Franklin has already expressed his views to you, sir. They are not substantially different from those of the Congress."

"But dammit, man, I'm willing to concede everything they've always wanted. What more can they ask?"

Drew shrugged. "Terms that might have been acceptable two or three years ago are no longer good enough. But I believe Mr. Franklin has made this clear to you."

Lord North was a bully. He didn't like the idea of acting as a supplicant to a young American half his own age. Instead of holding out a carrot, His Lordship decided to make use of his stick.

"I'm determined that next year will bring an end of this war," he said. "Until now I've shown restraint. But next year I intend to order our armies to capture and destroy that part of America the loss of which will be unacceptable to George Washington."

"Pray, sir, what part of the country is that?" Drew asked casually, wondering if Lord North was actually going to reveal his war plans for the following year.

"Washington comes from the colony of Virginia," North said, telling Drew exactly what he hoped to hear. "The last place in the world he wants to see ravaged is his own homeland. Therefore, I propose to carry the war to Virginia. When Washington learns of this, surely he'll sue for peace."

Drew was flabbergasted by the naïveté of the prime minister. Did he actually believe that George Washington was such a shallow creature? Didn't he realize the general considered all the United States to be his homeland?

Apparently not. "The war will be over this coming summer," Lord North assured him.

Drew wanted to shout the truth to this pompous Englishman, but resisted the urge. Let him believe this nonsense about Washington. Let him send his armies to Virginia: he'd soon find out that Virginia meant no more to Washington than New Jersey; that both meant *everything*. In the meantime the general would know his enemy's intentions and be able to make preparations against him.

"I truly hope Your Lordship is correct," he said. "An end of this war would be a blessing to us all."

Lord North nodded. "Good lad! I see you've a sensible head on your shoulders. Now, I want you to reiterate my terms to Franklin. I want to be certain he understands them, do you hear?"

"Yes, Mr. Prime Minister. I shall do as you ask."

The older man smiled, content that he had accomplished what he had wanted. He stood up and bowed, but he did it in such a way that it was almost a sneer. Drew stood and returned the favor.

While he waited alone in the alcove, allowing Lord North time to rejoin the others, he thought about the lack of understanding exhibited by the minister. North reminded him of an aphorism of Franklin's—all things can lead astray those so ill-inclined. The prime minister had convinced himself that an attack on Virginia would cause Washington to surrender. What stupidity!

His thoughts were interrupted by Philip Ogilvy, who approached with a familiar figure at his side. "Drew, I believe you know this gentleman."

"General Howe!" Drew said in surprise, because he had heard that since the general's return from America he had been living in seclusion on his country estate. Howe had become very popular with the Americans, because his views concerning the war were well known.

The general looked thinner and older than the last time Drew had seen him. Perhaps wiser as well, because he had been forced to deal with the antagonisms of his own countrymen.

"Young de Kuyper, so we meet again," he said, extending his hand. "Only this time you've shed your sheep disguise and come before us as the wolf you really are."

"I'll let you two alone," Ogilvy said.

"Thank you," Howe said, and he waited until the man was out of earshot before he spoke.

"I always knew you and your sister weren't loyalists," the general said.

"And I'm glad you've given up the futile task of trying to domesticate us," Drew said with a chuckle. He couldn't help liking this urbane Englishman.

"It was a task I never really wanted," the general said. "I've tried to convince Parliament they're making a mistake—not that I've made much of an impression."

"We thank you for trying anyway, sir."

The general nodded. The young man had acquired a great deal of polish since he had last seen him. "And how is your dear sister?"

"Well, as far as I know. And much the same. It will take more than four years of war to disturb Celine."

The general smiled. "She's a most notable example of how our culture has flourished in the New World. I've told disbelievers here in England they should spend an hour or two with your sister. That would convince them of the futility of trying to conquer you people."

"Don't let the prime minister hear you talking like this, sir. He's convinced he has the solution for a British victory."

"Yes, I've heard of his plan," Howe said sadly. "To believe

General Washington will put Virginia before the other colonies is to refuse to face reality."

"I suppose His Lordship must learn the hard way."

"Look, de Kuyper, there are many of us in England who realize the futility of this war. It must end. Can I do anything to help?"

"We need money."

The general's eyebrows lifted a bit. "A bit cheeky, isn't it, to ask a man to support the army that fights against his own country?"

"Yes, it is," Drew admitted. "But the sooner we can win this war, the better it will be for both Americans and Englishmen."

"I'd like to help, but my honor, sir, forbids it."

"I won't ask you to compromise your honor."

When they parted, Drew went back to the main salon, where he was joined by Ogilvy. "Well, did you collect money from the general?" he asked.

"I don't know what you're talking about," Drew said blandly.

"I'd like to make my own donation to your cause," Ogilvy said, ignoring the other's pretense of ignorance. "Five hundred pounds, will that be all right?"

Drew still wasn't certain about Ogilvy's motives. "Wouldn't you consider this a treasonable act? I'm sure I know what Lord North would think."

"What might be called treason today, will soon be accepted as recognition of reality. I make friends of you today. I can expect a favor from you tomorrow."

"Something like taking out insurance on a cargo?"

"Something like that," Ogilvy said.

During the next two weeks Drew saw Althea almost every day and every night. There were small dances and large balls, intimate dinners for a few, and crowded receptions for hundreds. It became the most natural thing in the world to see the two of them together.

Lord Middleton grumbled to his wife, but she shrugged his complaints off. Her Ladyship maintained that her daughter's interest in the American was only a passing fancy; His Lordship wasn't so sure.

"Isn't this the *best* ball you've ever been to, darling!" Althea said to Drew as they walked off the floor after an elaborate cotillion that he had only barely managed to negotiate, dancing not being among his major skills.

"Yes, it's nice," he agreed.

"Aren't you having a *wonderful* time?"

"Yes."

"Let's *do* have more wine punch. It's so *wonderful!*"

Drew had learned that Althea liked to speak in superlatives about everybody and everybody. She was always with the *best* people, in the *best* homes, doing the *best* things, and having the *best* time. Everything was always the *best* or the most *wonderful*, and sometimes it was both.

It didn't bother him, because he enjoyed watching her have a good time. But he could see she was spoiled and stubborn; and no wonder. For twenty years she had been an only child and the absolute darling of her father's eye. Middleton had wealth and position, and Althea had always gotten everything she wanted.

But she was a great deal of fun and obviously taken with Drew, and he just ignored what he didn't like about her and enjoyed what he did.

He didn't even have to feel guilty about having such a good time during the war, because at the places where he went with her, he met many wealthy and highly placed Englishmen who secretly agreed the American cause was just. Whenever he got an Englishman to admit this, it was then he asked the man to lend more tangible support. He surprised himself at the amount of money he was able to collect at a ball or a dinner.

For the first time in years, he was able to relax and not carry the burden of the war around with him.

But romances do not stand still; they either progress or fade away. His involvement with Althea was hardly fading. As they spent more and more time together, they got to know about each other and began anticipating what the other would want. Althea, of course, became very possessive, having spent her lifetime getting whatever she wanted. She no longer bothered to ask Drew if he would accompany her somewhere, but simply assumed he would.

After the first few days, they had begun to kiss one another. They shared little pecks on the cheek in the beginning, but eventually their lips met. Their kisses were intimate but not very sensual, although Althea's pretty face and trim young body were enough to stir Drew's imagination. Indeed, if she had been able to read his thoughts, at times she might have slapped his face. They held hands. They walked together. Occasionally he put his arm about her waist.

But it was all very subdued and proper—a courtship between a lady and a gentleman. It might have gone on like that until he had to return to France, except for what happened one night as he was taking her back to her house after a dinner. It was a gentle night and the Middleton townhouse was less than ten minutes away, so they had decided to walk.

Drew's boots echoed on the cobblestones as they walked along. The soft moonlight filtered down and gave them just enough illumination to see where they were going and to look at one another. There was a balminess to the air. It was a beautiful night for lovers.

And footpads.

They were almost in sight of the Middleton house when three men jumped out of the shadows. They wasted no time with explanations of their purpose. The first swung a club at Drew's head, but an acrobatic move saved him and the club whistled past, about an inch from his ear. The man was now off balance, and Drew slammed his fist into his face. The nose was smashed almost flat, and blood was all over the attacker's face as he stumbled to the ground.

Althea screamed for help as a second man ripped the strand of pearls from her neck and turned his attention to wrenching a jeweled brooch from her wrap.

Drew attempted to go to her aid, but the third man sprang to his back and began pounding him with his fists. With a burst of almost superhuman strength summoned up by Althea's screams, Drew reached back and pulled the man off his back. He held him in his arms, raised him above his head, and then slammed him to the ground with all the strength in his body. The man was out of the fight.

Now Drew attacked Althea's assailant, who was busy tearing at her clothes. The sight so outraged the young American that when he had knocked the man to the ground, he jumped on top of him, grabbed his head in his hands and began pounding it against the cobblestones. The man's head was hammered down half a dozen times, and then Drew realized someone was punching him on the back of his head.

He rolled to the side and came back to his feet as quickly as a cat—and now faced the man whose nose he had broken in the first moments of the fight. This one was bigger and stronger than his companions, and he lunged at Drew and clasped him in a bearhug. He was squeezing with every ounce of muscle he had when Drew's knee came up and caught him squarely in the crotch.

The man screamed, and Drew took advantage of his newly freed arms by slamming his fist into the attacker's Adam's apple. This produced a strangled sound that terminated when Drew knocked the man to the ground with another blow and then kicked the side of his head with the sharp toe of his boot.

The fight was over. All three footpads were on the ground—unconscious or dead, Drew couldn't be sure. He went to Althea's side and pulled her toward him as he tried to get her wrap back around her shoulders. The front of her dress was torn, and one of her breasts was exposed.

"Terrible, terrible," he said as he held her close against him as if trying to protect her from further harm.

She let herself be held for a few moments, then looked up at him with the hurt eyes of a little girl who has just learned of the loss of her innocence.

"Do you care for me?" she asked in a tiny, quavering voice.
"Of course I do."

She sighed. "I care for you more than anything else in the world. Oh, Drew, I was so frightened that those men would hurt you."

"It's over," he said reassuringly. "All over."

She tilted her head back, and they stared into one another's eyes. There was a look of hunger on her face, and he responded to it. He leaned forward and pressed his lips against hers—softly at first, then more insistently. His arms went around her and pulled her closer.

She didn't resist; rather the opposite. She allowed herself to be enveloped in his arms. One of her own reached up and around his neck. She grabbed a handful of hair and tugged.

The act was erotic, and he let one of his hands find her exposed breast and cup it. Their mouths met in a sudden urgency, and their tongues began darting, challenging one another.

They felt their bodies blending into one, and let their hands explore. The passion mounted, and they became breathless. Finally, with a willpower he wasn't aware he possessed, he gently pulled himself away from her.

Althea looked up at him, and her expression contained lust, wonder, and fear.

"We've got to get you home," he said in a shaky, but almost gruff, voice.

They had the kitchen of the Middleton townhouse to themselves, as the elder Middletons and the servants were in their beds. Althea had changed clothes, and the two of them sat before the embers of the fire, allowing the warmed rum to calm them.

"That was *something*," Althea said at last.

"I'm sorry about what I did," he said. "You felt so good, and I couldn't help myself. I—"

"Shh," she said, placing her forefinger on his lips. "There's nothing to be sorry about. When a man and a woman fall in love, they want each other. That's natural. I know all about it."

"You do?"

"My mother has been very open with me. You'd be surprised what I know."

He took her hand and squeezed it.

"How do you think we should handle this?" she said.

"Handle what?"

She looked puzzled. "Well, after what happened, we *are* going to get married, aren't we? And your friend Ogilvy wasn't all that wrong when he told you there'd be trouble if I tried to marry an American."

Marry? Had Drew said anything about their getting married? Wait, he wanted to say, wait, let's think about this. But before he had a chance to open his mouth, she went on in her blithest manner.

"Of course Papa will be dead set against it. And Mama as well, I suppose. But I can get around them. Especially if your family has a lot of money. They *do* have a lot of money, don't they?"

"Well, I suppose, yes..."

"Then that's one problem we won't have to face," she said, now taking full charge. "Do you have any disagreement that the children should be Church of England?"

"Children?"

"No objections?"

"No... But you—"

"I'd like at least one boy and one girl, and maybe two of each," she said. "Does *that* bother you?"

"Two of... Now let's—"

"All right, two it shall be. Now we have to decide where we'll live. Do you have a preference?"

"I never wanted to live anywhere but New York," he blurted out, finally coming to a topic he had given some thought to.

"Oh, dear, the Colonies. Papa certainly won't like that."

"But New York is my home."

"As London is mine."

"And my family business is there, and my work."

"That does put a different light on it," she admitted. "I suppose we'll have to give it a try. Let's do this, darling. We'll first live in New York, but if we find it *too dreadful*, we'll move back to London. There, isn't that fair?"

"New York isn't dreadful."

"So we'll give it a try, yes?"

"A try?"

"I'm glad you agree," she said. "We can have a fine town house right in the city, and an estate out in the country where we can go to relax. You *do* have a townhouse, don't you?"

"There's one that belonged to my father. I guess it now belongs to my mother and me."

"Is it a *big* townhouse?"

"One of the finest in New York."

"I'm sure," Althea said, and her tone implied that *that* wasn't saying too much. "I guess it will have to do."

Drew's head was spinning. What was this crazy Englishwoman talking about? His father's house was one of the best in New York, and here she was, sneering at it without ever having seen it. If you listened to her, you might suspect the de Kuypers lived in a shed near the docks.

"We can live in New York for a while," she was saying. "But we *must* get married here in England. At the chapel on our estate. After all, Middletons have been getting married there for *centuries*. You have no objections to that, I hope."

"No, no objections, but I—"

"A spring wedding would be nice, don't you think? May and June are such lovely months. All the *best* people always get—"

"We can't get married until the war is over," he interrupted.

Althea looked as startled as if he had slapped her in the face. Her lower lip trembled, and it appeared she was going to cry. "Here I am planning your future happiness, and all you can think about is the nasty war."

"No, no, that isn't it. It's just that we must be sensible about this. How can we get married when our countries are at war with each other? No one would understand."

She looked at him as though she were a pet sheepdog that had just been kicked by its master. "You're just looking for an excuse *not* to marry me."

"Now, Althea..."

"You only want to use my body."

"That's not true, I—"

"Use me and cast me aside."

"No, I hardly want to cast you aside," he said, almost desperate to make some sense out of all that was happening. "I want to keep you and—"

"Forever?"

"Yes, yes, you see—"

"And you *do* want to marry me?"

Drew opened his mouth, but no sound came.

"See! You can't say anything. You *don't* want to marry me."

"Look, Althea..."

"You've never *said* you want to marry me. If you really mean it, you'll say it."

There it was, he thought, the way out. *If* he wanted out. All he had to do was keep his mouth shut. He didn't have to think, didn't have to reason. Just keep quiet.

"You can't say anything," she said. "Because you don't want me."

It was the first tears that did it.

They seeped out slowly from beneath her big, beautiful eyes and slid down her alabaster cheeks. She looked so lovely, so appealing, so helpless.

Drew suddenly hated himself. What was he doing to this wonderful girl? he thought. Why was he hurting her? Why was he acting so damned selfishly?

"Althea, *will* you marry me?"

There it was. He had said it. Aloud, so she could hear. And he knew it was something she'd never allow him to take back.

"Yes, oh yes," she murmured, and snuggled up against him and put her head against his chest, where her gentle sobbing passed through both their bodies.

"Why are you crying?" Drew asked. "Didn't I just ask you to marry me?"

"Because I'm so happy, darling."

"I'll do my best for you."

"I know, I know," she cooed.

"And I must speak to your father about this," he said, accepting the new burdens he was taking upon himself.

"No, no," she said quickly. "I must talk to him first. I know him, and I know how to approach him with something like this."

"But it's my obligation to—"

"You can ask him later, *after* I make sure he'll say yes."

"How will you do that?"

She smiled. "Don't worry about it, darling."

After what had just happened to him, Drew felt a sympathy for Lord Middleton. Althea could wind a man up in knots before he knew what was happening.

"The best possible thing for you to do," she said, "is to make yourself unavailable while I break the news to Papa. He'll go through a period of temper tantrums, but if you're not around he won't be able to inflict them on you."

Drew nodded. She certainly seemed to know how to go about things. And it probably was for the best if he avoided a face-to-face confrontation with His Lordship. A shouting match hardly seemed the way to begin life with his new father-in-law.

"I should go to France anyway," he said. "I have... ah, business with Ben Franklin." Even if Althea was about to become his wife, she was, after all, an Englishwoman, and he *was* taking a good deal of money back to help her country's enemy.

"Good. And you must go right away. I'll wait until you're gone before I talk to Papa."

He gave it a moment's thought. Although France was only twenty-one miles away at the narrowest point of the English Channel, it wasn't that easy to get there: France, it had to be remembered, was at war with England, and neither country welcomed the ships of the other. It would be necessary to find a Swedish or Danish ship, Drew reflected, and that could, and most often did, take the better part of a week.

"My chances of getting a ship will be best at Gravesend," he said. "I'll leave London in the morning."

"Good. I'll have my little chat with Papa the day after tomorrow. Now, don't you want to kiss your future bride?"

He took her in his arms. She was soft and warm, and as their lips met he could feel the fires once again building inside his body.

There was nothing so bad about all this, he told himself. It certainly felt like a good thing.

The next morning he borrowed Ogilvy's carriage and driver and departed for Gravesend. He arrived late in the afternoon and went immediately to the docks. He was fortunate to find a Norwegian ship getting ready to embark for Le Havre. The captain accepted his passage money and told him to be aboard before midday on the following day. "We sail on the noon tide," he said.

After making sure the gold he was bringing to Franklin was safely stowed in the hold of the ship, Drew found a small inn near the docks, where he booked lodgings for the night. He retired to the taproom to enjoy a roasted joint and a few mugs of ale laced with rum.

It was only as he sat quietly at a table near the fire that he realized the enormous changes that would be happening in his life. Married to an Englishwoman, and a titled one at that! What would his mother think? And Celine? And for some reason the face of Beth Henry appeared in his mind, and he idly wondered what she would think.

Althea Middleton de Kuyper, he thought. He was in love with her, he told himself. And they would have children and be happy. The problem of her not wanting to live in New York would be solved when she saw what a wonderful place it was.

The more he drank, the more beautiful Althea became... the softer her features, the smoother her skin. Even now, the recollection of her bare breast in his hand sent shivers up his spine. Christ! Had he wanted her at that moment!

The more he drank, the more it seemed that getting married had been his own idea. *Of course* he wanted to share his bed and his life with her. *Of course* he'd never want any other woman. *Of course* he had wanted to marry her from the first moment he'd seen her.

He finished his dinner, but continued to drink. So much had happened, and he was tired. Finally, with the lazy flames helping to lull him, he fell asleep at the table.

Shortly before midnight the proprietor woke him by gently tugging on his arm. He helped the sleepy man to his room. For a few moments Drew's eyes were focused on the blank ceiling; then the image of Althea Middleton swam before them, and they began to close. He drifted off into sleep.

* * *

"Another way for the United States to raise money is to begin charging export duties," Ben Franklin was explaining to Peter as they drove back to Passy from Versailles, where the eleven-year-old boy had spent yet another week as the guest of King Louis XVI.

"Is it?" the boy said, not quite understanding what the old gentleman was talking about. But that didn't matter to Franklin, who liked to think aloud, and what his audience thought was incidental.

"Ah, export duties," the old gentleman said with relish. "A knavish attempt to get something for nothing."

"How so?" Peter asked, playing his role to perfection.

"Creating an export duty is an idea worthy of a seasoned pickpocket, my boy. There's only one problem with raising money this way: no one in America is exporting anything these days."

"There's nothing to tax."

"It does present something of a problem."

"You'll think of something, Grandpa," Peter said confidently, using the form of address recommended by Franklin himself.

"So tell me, Peter, what did you and the king do this time?"

"He's a very strange man," Peter said seriously. "His wife is always crabbing that he doesn't bother going to the parties she gives in his honor."

"In his honor, eh?"

"She says that to get him to come, but he doesn't bother. So she gives the parties anyway."

"Ah, Versailles, a playground where they hold an eternal dinner party for the gods! Or at least for those people who consider themselves gods."

The boy continued as if the old gentleman hadn't spoken a word. "We went hunting for three days. Then we came back to the palace and worked on a new kind of lock Louis is inventing. You don't open it with a key, but with a stream of water. So far we haven't been able to get it to work."

"I should think a water-opened lock might be possible," Franklin said, immediately donning his inventor's cap. "If you could harness enough force to turn the tumblers, it should be easy to cause the mechanism to swing in one direction or the other."

"That's what Louis says, but we couldn't get the stream to build up sufficient force."

"You always refer to His Majesty as Louis. What do you call him when you're with him?"

"Louis."

"To his *face?*"

"Yes," Peter said. "He told me to call him that."

Franklin shook his head. "The princes of the earth bow their knees, dukes and barons scrape before him, and you call him Louis."

"That's his name, isn't it?"

"Peter, I see a great future for you. You shall call kings by their first names and instruct them in the building of clocks and locks. You shall lead the majesties of the earth in the pursuit of the unknown."

"Louis has a big map of America, and a lot of it is marked unknown. I think I'd like to explore those places," Peter said.

"Yes, and perhaps you'll have the chance to do that. Ah, Peter my boy, if only I was your age again—your age with the prospect of the United States of America opening up before me. What I couldn't do with my life if I had your years to live it with!"

Peter didn't bother to reply. Grandpa Franklin and other older people were always making remarks like this. It seemed stupid to worry about situations that could never be.

They arrived at the Hôtel de Valentinois to find a happy surprise: Drew had returned from England. Franklin was delighted with the gold he brought, and even more delighted with the information about Lord North's plans for the devastation of Virginia.

"It gives me an idea," the old gentleman said. "I've been trying to get the foreign minister to send Admiral de Grasse and his fleet to America. I'll tell the minister that Washington is going to take his whole army to Virginia to fight, and with the help of the French fleet our combined forces will be enough to end this damned war."

"But will Washington go to Virginia?" Drew asked.

Franklin shrugged. "If Cornwallis is there with the whole British army and a French fleet shows up, what choice does Washington have? He's got to fight, because he'll never have a better chance of winning."

For better or worse, Drew thought, Lord North's ideas were about to bring about a major, and perhaps decisive, battle in the war.

"It might work."

"Let's get over to Versailles," Franklin said. "We'll see the minister and tell him what we have in mind. Be enthusiastic about it all. Jump up and down and shout, if you feel like it. Do anything to make him commit de Grasse's fleet next spring."

"I'll do it on one condition," Drew said.

"Condition?" Franklin said, a bit taken aback. "Are we now imposing conditions on patriotism?"

"In this case, yes," Drew replied, and the look on his face showed his determination.

"And what is this condition, if I may ask?"

"That I be allowed to go along with de Grasse."

"I see," Franklin said coolly.

"I don't *want* to leave you, sir," Drew said, putting as much appeal into his voice as possible. "But it's time for me to get into this war."

"I can't believe that going with de Grasse is more important than the work you're doing now. But if you must, you must," Franklin said resignedly. "But I have a better idea than if you merely go along with the French fleet."

"What's that?" Drew asked guardedly, suspecting a trap to burden him with yet another unwanted diplomatic task.

"Create a task force composed of our privateers. Make this a combined operation of French and American ships."

This was no trap, Drew thought—instead, a marvelous idea! "I'll go to Le Havre immediately," he said. "I'll find Alec Seixas, Dick Goelet, and Seth Cuyler, and we'll all go together."

"Leaving Old Ben with the mundane task of collecting the money you need to finance the expedition," Franklin grumbled; but Drew could see he was pleased at the prospect of the United States sending a naval force across the ocean with the French fleet. It would be the first such undertaking by the new nation, of enormous propaganda value concerning the world at large, and most useful in his efforts to keep the French coffers open to him. "None of this is an accomplished fact," he cautioned. "Now we must go to the foreign minister and get him to commit de Grasse's fleet."

"As good as done, sir," Drew said, delighted that the end of his long exile was in sight. And what an end! To sail back with a fleet of American privateers to join in a combined attack against the main British force!

Peter had been sitting quietly while his elders talked, but

he hadn't missed a word. Now that the issue seemed to be settled, he inquired of his own prospects.

"Could I go with you?" he asked Drew.

"I think you're a bit young to be going into battle."

"I don't know about that," Franklin said. "Peter seems to adapt to any condition."

"He's only eleven years old."

"Almost twelve," Peter said.

"My sister would kill me if I allowed him to be exposed to such danger," Drew said.

"I want to go home with you," Peter said, finding yet another reason to get what he was asking for.

"This isn't the right time."

Peter said nothing. He stood up and walked out of the room. The two men watched him in silence until the door was closed.

"Going off to sulk, no doubt," Drew said.

"I doubt it," Franklin said. "Peter's not the sulking sort. More likely he's gone off to plot how to get what he wants."

"There's no chance of that happening," Drew said firmly. "He's not going off to war, and that's that."

It was a brisk fall day during the last week of September, 1780. It had been a bad year.

Franz von Lossow accompanied General Washington as they traveled north from Philadelphia to West-Point-on-the-Hudson. They had stopped for lunch at a small inn on the road that wound its way along the western shore of the river, and the general had taken advantage of the respite to remove his boots and sit with his toes exposed before the fire. He had been riding since early morning. The former Hessian officer sat in a chair at his side, going over dispatches that had arrived within the past twenty-four hours.

"Here's a request from Greene for six hundred more men, and as much powder and shot as we can spare."

"We have no men to send," the general said wearily. "As for shot and powder, let him get them from the estimable gentlemen in Philadelphia. God knows, I have none to spare."

Von Lossow nodded, made a note on the paper, and was about to pass to the next dispatch when the general touched him on the arm. "No more for now. I find it tedious to be forced to keep rejecting sensible requests."

"Yes sir," the colonel said. He folded the papers and placed them back into a leather pouch. He poured more tea, and

Washington added generous splashes of rum to the two mugs. They were enjoying these fortified refreshments when a messenger arrived. He was sweaty and dirt-covered from hard riding.

"Emergency dispatch for the general," he said.

"Yes, give it here."

The messenger took out a folded paper and handed it over. Washington opened it and began to read, his eyes widening as he assimilated the text.

"Arnold!" The word issued explosively from the general's lips.

"Sir?" von Lossow said, half coming to his feet.

"He's betrayed us!"

"General Arnold?"

"Unbelievable, von Lossow, unbelievable," the general said, and then slammed his hand down on the table. *"Son of a bitch!"*

Von Lossow, more startled than before, waited. The general breathed heavily for a few moments and then explained what was happening.

"Major André was apprehended a few days ago with plans of the fortifications at West Point," the general said, jabbing a finger at the dispatch. "His captors sent word of the affair to our esteemed commander at West Point, none other than *our* Benedict Arnold. But it seems that Arnold was the man who gave the plans to André in the first place. And now the bastard has gone over to the British. Went aboard one of their warships—the *Vulture,* she's called. How appropriate."

"But why did he do it? What did he hope to gain?"

"Who knows?" the general said, shaking his head in disgust. "Arnold's always been petulant—said we weren't giving him his due in either cash or rank. I suppose he decided he'd be treated better by the British."

"I've always thought he was one of your best tactical commanders."

"He was. As long as he kept to his job, there wasn't a more trustworthy man in the army. Far better than most of these bloody idiots we have in command."

Washington got to his feet. "We'd better get to the Point as fast as possible. The defenses there control the Hudson. We *can't* let them fall into British hands."

* * *

They rode north at a brisk canter. The general spoke only once during the entire journey. "Just what I needed to complete this year," he muttered.

Von Lossow reflected that it had, indeed, hardly been a year to bring cheer to the general or the American forces.

Earlier in the year Charleston had fallen.

The Carolinas were gone.

Georgia was in British hands.

In late May there had been a mutiny at Morristown. The problem, as usual, was money. There wasn't any—except the paper currency issued by the Congress at Philadelphia, and that was almost useless. One continental was supposed to be equal to a British shilling, but it took forty or more of the former to equal one of the latter. Many traders and merchants categorically refused to accept the American money as payment.

Because of the lack of money and the shortage of supplies, Washington had been forced to cut rations at Morristown. The amount issued declined steadily until the men were receiving less than an eighth of what had been promised by Congress. The Connecticut regiments objected to this shabby treatment, and they staged a protest. They claimed they hadn't been paid for five months. Washington first dismissed this as nonsense, but later he found out it was the truth. After a lot of talking, and the presence of several regiments of Pennsylvanians to back him up, Washington managed to quiet the men from Connecticut. They went very grudgingly back to their posts, but agreed that the situation could not be blamed on General Washington. His clinching argument was to tell the men, truthfully, that he himself hadn't been paid in over a year. The New Englanders might not have been pleased, but at least they now knew their general was in the same rotten boat as they themselves.

An even greater blow to Washington's hopes had been dealt in South Carolina a little over a month before. The general was given a firsthand account of the disastrous battle of Camden by an eyewitness—Colonel Franz von Lossow.

The colonel had gone south under the command of Major General Baron Johann de Kalb, one of the finest soldiers to fight on either side during the war.

Perhaps the battle of Camden would have had a different ending had the baron stayed in command, but he was relieved by the "Hero of Saratoga," General Horatio Gates.

Gates proceeded to bumble his way through a few skirmishes and minor engagements. He took the wrong roads and outran his supplies, so his troops went hungry, and were stricken by dysentery because they had been forced to eat the only thing they could find—green corn. The general resisted all criticism and proceeded toward Camden convinced he was a military genius. After all, hadn't people been telling him that ever since Saratoga? That he might have been extremely lucky in that battle never occurred to him.

The command originally headed by de Kalb consisted of seven regiments from Maryland, one from Delaware, and the crack troops known as the Pulaski Legion, named for their founder. It was small as armies go—only fourteen hundred men—but it was made up of the best troops under Washington.

As they approached Camden, they were joined by twenty-five hundred militiamen from North Carolina and Virginia. The contrast was striking: the first group were trained battle troops; the newcomers were little more than a mob.

Colonel von Lossow was in command of the troops at the far right of the battle line. In drawing up his army, Gates had elected to place the seasoned troops to the right, the green North Carolina militia in the middle, and the equally green Virginia militia to the left.

His opponent, Lord Cornwallis, either because he had efficient spies or because he was merely lucky, placed his men in positions best suited to take advantage of the situation. His most seasoned troops were placed opposite the weak Virginia militia.

In the early morning the artillery signaled the beginning of the battle. The British advanced. The Virginia militia fought for about ten minutes, then turned and fled. The center of Gates's line fared even worse. The North Carolinians didn't last even ten minutes. They took one look at the British troops, who were advancing with bayonets fixed in place, and turned on their heels, bowling one another over in an effort to escape from the advancing blades.

General Gates was on a hill in position to see what was happening, and decided to stay with his men—the ones who were retreating. Within a few minutes he was at the head of the rabble, leading the ragtag retreat at a full gallop.

Baron de Kalb, on the other hand, was on the extreme right of the battle line with von Lossow, and neither man knew what was happening at the other positions. They dutifully took the brunt of the British attack, then began to push the enemy back. At one point de Kalb slapped von Lossow on the back and congratulated him, thinking they were winning the engagement. But then the truth emerged, as Cornwallis swung his victorious troops from the center and left into a flanking attack on the Americans. The result was a foregone conclusion. De Kalb and von Lossow held for a short while, but then Cornwallis hit them with a total assault. His infantry bludgeoned the Americans from the front while his cavalry swept around and hit them from the rear. It was a brutal, bloody battle, and the superior numbers of the British won the day. Baron de Kalb was mortally wounded. He stood with his troops, clutching his shoulder, his tunic splashed with his own blood, shouting encouragement.

"You must retreat, sir," von Lossow said as he held the arm of the weakened baron.

"I'll stay," the baron said. "You lead the men to safety."

"No, I'll stay and you—"

"You go and that's an order!" de Kalb said. "I'll stay back with fifty men to give you time. Get into the woods where the cavalry can't follow."

Von Lossow led the way through the woods and managed to save three hundred men—crack troops who would be ready to fight another day. Of the fifty men who had stayed back in the rearguard action, only twelve survived. The others, including General de Kalb, had died heroes' deaths.

The battered and tattered American army retreated all the way to Hillsboro, North Carolina, a distance of two hundred miles, where the now recovered Horatio Gates resumed command. Franz von Lossow was so disgusted that he left the army and returned to Washington's headquarters to give the general his report. The commander-in-chief grumbled and cursed, but realized there was nothing to be done about the situation.

And now the news of this latest disaster—the defection of Benedict Arnold.

Washington and his entourage arrived at the fort at West Point to find mild panic prevailing. Everyone knew Arnold had given the plans of the fortifications to the British—but what no one realized was that Major André had been apprehended with the plans before he could use them in any way.

Washington soon restored order. He inspected the thousand-link chain that stretched across the Hudson from shore to shore. The chain weighed over sixty tons, and it was strong enough to prevent any British ship from going upriver. It was a good way to keep the enemy bottled up in the south and unable to capture Albany.

The decision was made to hang Major André, and Washington sent word to the garrison at Tarrytown, where the spy was being held. "Don't give him a soldier's death in front of a firing squad," Washington ordered. "Hang him like a common thief."

The next day, at the point at Tappen, an ashen-colored Major André was taken out and hanged as a dozen drummers beat a mournful tattoo.

Colonel von Lossow argued that the British must be made to pay for their perfidy. He proposed a raid on one of their supply depots on Long Island. In the course of the engagement, where nothing more dramatic happened than the burning of three hundred tons of British hay, the colonel was slightly wounded in the arm, and a sergeant named Churchill suffered a flesh wound in his leg. Both men returned to camp under their own power, somewhat proud of their minor wounds. General Washington ordered the creation of a new decoration to be awarded to soldiers who received wounds in battle. He called it the Purple Heart because "it signified the shedding of American blood—blood as royal and regal and purple as that of any crowned head of Europe." In a small ceremony the general pinned the new medal on the tunics of von Lossow and Churchill. It was the first such ceremony to honor wounded Americans.

Benedict Arnold's wife, the former Peggy Shippen of Philadelphia, was still at West Point, and when the general tried to question her about her husband, she feigned madness.

"I know she's only pretending to be crazy," Washington protested. "But what can I do about it?"

Von Lossow offered to see if he could convince the woman to drop her masquerade and tell what she knew about her husband's reasons for going over to the British.

"I don't know anything," she said, remaining seated in the chair by the window in her room. She was a pretty woman, with a slight figure and a cupid's-bow mouth. Her eyes were red from crying, and her hair looked tousled and uncombed.

"Mrs. Arnold, the general wishes no harm to you," von Lossow said. "After all, he's a gentleman and hardly would blame a wife for the actions of her husband. All he'd like is to hear your version of General Arnold's actions."

"You talk like an Englishman."

"Actually, I'm German, but now I think of myself as an American," von Lossow said. "Please, can't you give us some clue why General Arnold went over to the British?"

She half-closed one eye and looked at him shrewdly. "And if I do tell, will it make any difference to what happens to me?"

"It will make no difference, madam. In either case General Washington will send you back to your family in Philadelphia."

"Then why should I tell you anything?"

"Because you might have a conscience, and some regrets about what General Arnold did. You are, after all, an American."

"Didn't they tell you I was crazy?"

"Yes, Mrs. Arnold, they did."

"And you don't think it's true?"

"No. What I think is you owe it to your country to tell us what you know."

She dropped her pose completely. In a dry, matter-of-fact voice she told him the truth. "Ben thought the war was lost, and that the British would eventually win. They offered him a commission in their army and a payment of six thousand pounds."

Von Lossow whistled. Six thousand pounds was a small fortune. The British must have been anxious indeed to get their hands on the plans of the West Point defenses. Even so, six thousand pounds seemed a mean and unworthy reason for a man like Arnold to defect. He said as much to the woman.

She smiled. "Ben was in debt up to here," she said, holding her hand at the height of the top of her head. "I guess it was my fault."

"Your fault?"

"He was always trying to please me with gifts. I knew he couldn't afford them, but I was too weak to say no. I suppose he needed the six thousand pounds to pay his creditors."

Von Lossow suddenly was very uncomfortable. He coughed and looked away.

"I know what you're thinking," she said bitterly. "If it hadn't been for me, Ben would have remained loyal to Washington and the Congress."

"I don't see any reason to pursue this conversation, madam," von Lossow said. "I intend to forget what has been said. For your sake we will pretend that General Arnold defected to the British out of deep-rooted conviction."

"You're trying to save my reputation? Why?"

"What honor do we gain by besmirching a woman?" von Lossow asked. Try as he might to become a man of the New World, a certain amount of upper-class Old World chivalry would always remain with him.

"Thank you, Colonel," Peggy Shippen Arnold said. "I'll behave myself now, and prepare to leave for Philadelphia."

Von Lossow told General Washington what had happened, and the commander agreed it was best to keep silent about Arnold's venal motivations. It could do nothing for the American cause to make an issue of them.

But of course, it was Peggy Arnold herself who couldn't keep her mouth shut, and within a week after her return to her home in Philadelphia, the true reason for Arnold's defection was common knowledge. Rather than suffer ostracism, Peggy appeared even more lovely and desirable. After all, if a man was willing to throw his career and perhaps his life away simply to buy presents for her, she must be quite something.

Benedict Arnold went to New York, where he became a member of General Clinton's staff. An attempt by a group of American patriots to kidnap him failed. If Arnold expected to be hailed as a hero by the British officers, he was sorely disappointed. Most of them refused to accept him, because by their code of honor, a traitor was a traitor no matter which side he betrayed. He was not invited to their dinners. He was excluded from their comradeship. On the streets he was treated as a pariah. The former American general became melancholic and given to lying abed for long periods of time. All in all, it had not been a very good bargain for him, but it was not possible to change the new course of his life. He learned, too late, that some decisions are irrevocable.

As winter moved across the land and the first wet snow fell and turned to slush, the war slowed to its usual hiatus, which would last until the following spring.

The long-suffering people of New York girded themselves for another onslaught of freezing weather, poor housing, and lean supplies of food. Their greatest hope was that the cold wouldn't be as bitter as during the past winter, when men walked across the thick ice from the Battery to Staten Island. But there was no assurance this winter wouldn't be as bad, and the people had gotten used to expecting the worst.

The supply of wood in the city was very low, and the men

who brought cartloads from the country made tremendous profits. None of these men, of course, would accept continental money in payment. Several wood dealers were murdered, and no one was sure whether their assailants had been patriots or merely disgruntled customers who objected to the usurious prices.

In the midst of all the poverty and suffering, the high-ranking British officers and representatives of the Crown continued to live on a splendid scale. They wanted to display their superiority as evidence that they were winning the war.

"An honor, Your Highness," Celine said as she curtsied before the seventeen-year-old Duke of Clarence, Prince William Henry, third son of George III.

The prince held out his hand. "More of an honor to me, Mrs. Murray. The general has told me of you," he said, nodding his head toward the commander-in-chief, who was standing at his right hand. "But his description did not do you justice."

General Henry Clinton coughed. He was learning the young prince had a mind of his own. The royal visitor was wearing long white trousers and the tailless blue jacket of a midshipman—the rank he currently held in the royal navy.

"Nothing said of Mrs. Murray does her justice," Clinton explained with a smile.

Celine laughed. "I see. The new British tactic to conquer North America is to use flattery."

The prince chuckled with the others. "I met your brother in London, Mrs. Murray. A shame he chooses to take side against us."

"We all must follow our consciences."

It was the week before Christmas, 1780, and the commander was giving this party—a command performance involving the leading people of New York—to honor the recent arrival of the young prince. Celine had thought it inappropriate to attend, but Marie Therese had insisted she keep up the pretense of being on friendly terms with the British.

"By now they *must* know our true feelings," Celine had protested.

"Yes, but being British they'll continue to play the game and pretend otherwise," Marie Therese had said. "To comprehend the British you have to understand they don't accept the world the way it is. In their minds they create the world the way they want it, and then decide that's the way things are.

If it doesn't seem to make much sense, just remember it's the reason they've been able to build an empire."

"And it's also the reason they're going to lose it," Celine said.

"You're going to the general's party," Marie Therese said flatly, ending the argument.

So Celine had arrived at the mansion at 1 Broad Way. Accompanying her was Beth Henry—not of her own free will, but because Celine had insisted on having a companion. Mary Delafield had flatly refused. She didn't want to risk meeting Patrick Blakely, she said, and the others accepted her excuse as valid. Beth, therefore, was chosen by Marie Therese and given no choice.

She curtsied as Celine introduced her to the prince, but there was no smile on her lips. Still, William Henry's face lit up when he saw this beautiful young woman of about his own age. Suddenly his American trip had taken on a most interesting dimension.

"Miss Henry," he purred with his utmost charm. "They failed to inform me I would meet ladies who could put those at the Court of St. James to shame."

Beth was not impressed by the flattery. "Perhaps you haven't been looking hard enough," she said.

Celine stifled a smile as the prince's face reddened slightly, and the general began to sputter as he tried to change the subject. The prince might have been slightly embarrassed, but he was accustomed to dealing with the caustic tongue of his own father. "Touché, Miss Henry," he said smoothly. "And now may I use my royal prerogative and ask if you would be kind enough to guide me around your fair city."

"It was once much fairer, Your Majesty," Beth said evenly. "But I'll show you around if you wish."

The prince bowed, and with some reluctance moved on to greet the next guest being presented. As he murmured his greetings to a fawning tory, his eyes followed Beth as she walked across the room.

"You're terrible," Celine said to Beth in a low voice as they approached a table laden with food. "And why did you agree to go with that royal brat? Didn't you see the way he looked at you?"

"Don't you think I can handle him?"

"Be wary of royalty," Celine said. "They're spoiled and used to getting whatever they want."

"He'll get what I wish to give," Beth said.

"Actually, it's not a bad idea to give him a guided tour of New York," Celine said, thinking aloud. "Maybe he'll be appalled by what he sees and do something about it."

A servant stopped before them with a tray of glasses filled with bubbly wine. Celine took one, but Beth refused with a curt toss of her head.

"Mrs. Murray," a voice spoke softly over her shoulder. She turned and saw Patrick Blakely. "And Miss Henry."

Celine nodded, but said nothing. She could never bring herself to be friendly with this man who had caused so much grief for Mary. Besides, he was a dangerous man, and the less said to him the better.

"I see you've met our sovereign's son," the captain said. "Incredible are the fortunes of birth, are they not? Because of his parentage the lad may one day sit on the throne of England."

"I take it you are not a believer in the divine right of kings?" Celine asked.

"Officially, yes. But unofficially I choose not to believe all the nonsense we tell ourselves to maintain order in the world."

"Interesting point of view," Celine said thoughtfully. "I presume General Clinton holds it as well?"

"What the general believes is his own business, Mrs. Murray, and this is a right granted to all of us."

"Then why do you insist on occupying a city that doesn't belong to you?" Beth asked bluntly.

The captain wasn't perturbed. "It's an old habit of man's to keep whatever he can—by force if necessary. And as far as the question of who New York belongs to...ah, I believe that is what the present hostilities are all about."

"And, of course, it's also necessary to keep the prisons filled," Beth said, not retreating an inch.

The captain shrugged. "Prisons have their place in this world. As a matter of fact, Miss Henry, only recently we released one of your own relatives."

Beth remained impassive, but Celine could not conceal her surprise. "One of Beth's relatives? Who?"

"Her name is Sarah Henry."

"Sarah Henry," Celine said, letting her breath out as she spoke the name. "So that's what became of her!"

"Sarah's been in your jail?" Beth asked.

"An unfortunate incident. The poor woman was deranged

and attacked a British soldier. It was necessary to lock her up for her own good."

"But now she's been released?"

"Yes, only yesterday. A man claiming to be a relative—a cousin of some sort—offered to take her off our hands."

"Take her off your hands?"

"The woman is not in her right mind, Mrs. Murray. The British army has no wish to turn its prisons into lunatic asylums."

Celine looked at Beth. "Which cousin could this be?"

Beth shrugged. "I don't know."

The captain listened closely, hoping to learn something new. After the man had bribed the guard to speak with Sarah Henry, Blakely had allowed her to be let out. Since then he had had her followed. So far he had not learned the true identity of the man, but that was only a matter of time. In the meanwhile Sarah Henry was on the loose and the captain was waiting for something to develop.

"Where is Sarah now?" Celine asked.

"I haven't the slightest idea," Blakely lied.

Celine turned to Beth. "We'd better look for her. God knows how she'll be able to take care of herself."

"This man who got her released—he must be taking care of her," Beth said logically.

"I wonder who he is," the captain said. "You don't suppose he's her husband rather than her cousin?"

Celine shook her head. "Her husband abandoned her. Why would he come to the prison to get her out?"

"So he's missing too?" Blakely asked, always anxious to find new facts."

"He's not missing," Beth said. "He's with General Washington."

The captain was surprised at her frankness. "Most people would try to conceal that fact."

"Most people are fools," Celine said, wishing to end this conversation before Beth said too much.

"If he's with Washington, I shall get to meet him one day," the captain said. "In one of our prisons, naturally."

The conversation was interrupted by Prince William Henry, who had approached with a naval officer he wished to introduce to the two women.

"This is Lieutenant Horatio Nelson," he said proudly. The

young officer bowed and smiled. "Lieutenant Nelson is one of our authentic naval heroes."

"How charming," Celine said with a glint in her eye. "Tell me, don't you find it boring when your feet are planted on solid ground?"

Lieutenant Nelson smiled. He was twenty-four years old and in command of the *Albemarle*, a rakish twenty-eight gun frigate now at anchor off the tip of the Battery. He was wearing a stiff uniform coat, and his powdered hair was tied in a Hessian tail of great length. There was a shyness to his smile, and it enhanced his youthful appearance. Indeed, he seemed more like eighteen than his real age.

"Hardly boring, madam, simply not as interesting as when I find them planted on a rolling deck." He looked at Beth for a long moment, then turned to the prince. "Your eyes didn't deceive you about the beauty of these ladies, Your Majesty," he said boldly, in sharp contrast to his shy appearance.

"More flattery," Celine said with a shake of her head. "Thank God we've learned to accept it with a grain of salt."

The prince laughed. "Perhaps the lieutenant will take us for a sail about the bay," he said as he looked at Beth. "Would you like that?"

"Only if we can sail past the prison hulks anchored at Wallabout Bay," Beth said. "After all, Your Majesty, I want your tour of New York to include everything."

The prince remained unruffled. "I'm sure the lieutenant will be happy to sail wherever you wish."

"My ship is yours to command, madam," Nelson said.

The party continued until the hour after midnight. Primus was waiting for the two women as they came out the front door.

"I like to froze out here," he complained, although he had been standing near a roaring bonfire lit by the retainers while they waited for their party-going masters and mistresses. He was also protected by a huge bearskin coat that reached down to his ankles.

"Cold air is good for your lungs," Celine said.

"Then you stand out here next time, while I go inside and have a drink."

"Let's get going," the practical Beth said as she snuggled under the furs in the back of the carriage.

As they drove toward Beth's house, which was still occupied

THE WORLD TURNED UPSIDE DOWN 453

by British officers but in which they had the use of a pair of rooms, one thought was on both women's minds.

"Who was the man who took Sarah Henry from prison?" Celine asked.

"I don't know."

"And where is she now?"

"Same answer."

"Something strange is going on," Celine said thoughtfully.

"Yes—but what?"

"So she's gone to Mrs. Murray's house?"

"Yes sir," Sergeant Taggert said to Captain Blakely. "That man took Crazy Sarah up there yesterday afternoon."

"Did he know he was being followed?"

"I don't think so," the sergeant said. "My man never went up to Beekman's Place itself. He just watched them and then came back and made his report."

"We still don't know the identity of the man?"

"Not yet, sir. He's still wearing a phony beard and those big floppy clothes. But don't worry, we'll know soon enough."

The captain considered the situation. Now was the time to get up to the Place to surprise the rebels before they had a chance to hide anything. There was a strong possibility that the printing press was there, and if it was they'd be sure to find it.

However, he had a problem.

General Clinton had called a staff meeting. His job was to report on the security measures being taken in the city. If Blakely failed to attend the meeting, the report would fall to Colonel Cunningham, who wouldn't know what he was talking about. The colonel would raise all sorts of hell if he missed the meeting—and now, of all times, when Blakely's name was up for promotion to major.

As a major, he would be reassigned as a full provost marshal in some other place. At last he would be free of Cunningham's stupidity and ineptness. He couldn't afford to do anything that would annoy the colonel at this time. He *had* to gain that promotion.

He decided to attend the staff meeting and send Sergeant Taggert to the Place.

"Take a detail of six men and a corporal," he said. "Go up to Beekman's Place. Find this Crazy Sarah and question her.

Find out the identity of the man. And look around for a printing press."

The sergeant nodded. "Should I expect trouble?"

The captain shrugged. "Take Hessians. People are less likely to start trouble with them around."

The sergeant smiled. He enjoyed being in charge of Hessians—men who used their bayonets first and asked questions later.

"Yes, sir, Hessians it will be."

After the sergeant departed, Blakely sat at his desk, drumming his fingers on the smooth wood as he considered the possibilities. He almost hated to see the printing press discovered. Whoever was writing these broadsides had an acid wit. Only a few weeks ago they printed a scurrilous attack on Colonel Cunningham. The provost marshal had been furious, stamping back and forth in his office, slamming the desk with his heavy fist, kicking the doors and walls.

The captain had thoroughly enjoyed his superior's discomfort. Served the bloody fool right! How a man like the colonel had risen to his present position was a mystery to the captain. Well, if things went the way they seemed to be going, he wouldn't have to worry about the situation much longer. He would be promoted to major and be done with this whole mess.

He would have preferred to go to the Place himself, but it was more important he attend the meeting and please the colonel: his own future depended on it.

He distrusted Taggert when it came to handling an assignment requiring delicacy. The sergeant was loyal enough, but preferred to use a bludgeon where a rapier might be better suited.

He sighed, gathered his reports, and headed for the door of his office. Maybe this meeting would be the last thing needed to assure his promotion.

Celine and Marie Therese sat with Sarah Henry in the kitchen of the Place. The day was bitterly cold, and the heat from the crackling stove very welcome. They sipped tea and munched on pieces of bread that Primus had toasted over the fire grate.

Sarah Henry, always too thin, had lost weight in prison, and her complexion was the color of fog. She no longer moved in frantic jerks, and could sit for long periods of time without changing facial expressions. Half the time she didn't seem to know what was going on, nor did she seem to care.

Neither Marie Therese nor Celine had much use for this addled woman, but they could hardly be so uncharitable as to turn her out.

"We'll have to see about getting you back to your house," Marie Therese said. Sarah did not respond.

Her mind was on the tea. It was much hotter than the tea she had been given in prison, and stronger, and she was thoroughly enjoying it. In a vague sort of way she thought she remembered at least one of these two women; perhaps they had something to do with her past life, but exactly who they were or what they wanted remained unclear. But she didn't worry about it. She was before a warm fire drinking hot tea, and that was sufficient.

Marie Therese glanced at Celine, who shrugged. They had purposely kept Sarah away from Mary and Beth in hopes of avoiding trouble.

"I think it best if she goes back to her own home as soon as possible," Celine said. "Who knows what will happen if she sees... our two friends."

"Someone will have to take her. And stay with her."

Celine frowned. Who could they get to do such a disagreeable job?

The back door opened, and Philemon Peabody entered. "Good morning," he said.

Both women looked at him with distaste. He was still wearing his false beard.

"Good morning," Marie Therese said softly, but Celine said nothing.

"Nice brisk day for a walk," he said, going to the stove and warming his hands. "Cold, but lovely."

"Oh, shut up!" Celine said. She turned to her mother. "I still say we ought to throw him the hell out of here."

"Now, Celine..."

"Dirty little bastard!"

"Celine! He was trying to do the family a favor by bringing Sarah here. She *is* related to Beth by marriage. We can't throw him out."

"Yes, all I was trying to do was be helpful," Peabody whined.

"When are you leaving?" Celine asked, cocking her head to one side in the classic manner of an angry de Kuyper.

"Let me rest today," he said. "I'll leave tomorrow."

"Right this minute wouldn't be soon enough," Celine said. She found it impossible to be civil with this little rat who had betrayed her father.

Peabody had shown up yesterday with Sarah. He claimed that he had learned about her being in prison from a friend; that this friend told him who Sarah was and said she had some connection with the de Kuyper family. Out of respect for all that he owed Jan, he said, he succeeded in getting Sarah out of prison. Now he had brought her here.

Celine didn't believe a word he said, but just what his motive was, she didn't know.

Peabody was a crafty man. He had counted on the de Kuypers' gratitude. He intended to snoop around the Place and find out what he could about a printing press. Then he would go back to New York and exchange this information for a pardon from Captain Blakely. He might even collect the reward. If everything worked out as he hoped, he would have made peace with Blakely and walked away with a pocketful of money.

"Good morning, Sarah," he said airily as he brought his cup of tea to the table. She looked blankly at him and went back to slurping her own tea.

Celine looked at the madwoman and shook her head. Just what we needed, she thought—a lunatic. Under the same roof with Mary and Beth. And Franz, she told herself, don't forget Franz. The colonel, too, was paying a visit and had been ordered to stay out of sight while Peabody was in the house. Who could trust the little rat?

Primus came back inside from the woodshed, where he had begun gathering more fuel for the stove. "Men in uniform riding toward the house," he announced.

"British?" Celine asked.

"What other kind do we see around here?" he asked innocently, and flashed a surreptitious look of warning to his mistress.

"I've got to hide," Peabody said quickly.

"Why?" Celine asked.

"They may know I've been working for Washington," he lied.

"You've been working for the general?" Celine asked in disbelief.

"Yes," he said. "As a spy."

He wanted to avoid any confrontation with the British until

he had the information needed to trade with Blakely. Until he got that information, he was a wanted man.

"We'd better hide him," Marie Therese said.

"All right," Celine said with reluctance. It wouldn't do to have him hide upstairs, where he might meet up with Franz. She looked at Primus. "Take the little rat down to the cellar and hide him behind the turnips."

"How about Sarah?" Marie Therese asked. "Should we hide her as well?"

Celine shook her head. "What can she tell anyone?"

"She might say who brought her here."

"Brought me here?" Sarah asked in a bewildered voice.

"I don't think we'll have to worry about her," Celine said.

Primus disappeared down the back staircase with Peabody, and Celine went upstairs to warn Franz to stay out of sight. She bumped into Mary and Beth and told them what was happening, then returned to the kitchen to rejoin her mother and Sarah. Celine hoped it was simply a British patrol out on a routine inspection, although she doubted it. There hadn't been a single patrol on this part of the island since the previous fall. The British preferred to remain in their snug barracks near the fire during the cold winter months.

The soldiers rode up to the railing in front of the house, dismounted, and tied their horses. While the Hessian corporal and his men stomped about to restore circulation in their feet and arms, Sergeant Taggert strode to the front door and pounded on it with his fist. Primus opened the door, and the sergeant went past him into the room. Celine stood in the doorway leading to the back rooms.

"May I help you?"

"Yes, ma'am," Taggert said. "I'm looking for a woman named Sarah Henry."

Celine instantly knew it would be foolish to deny that Sarah was in the house; obviously the sergeant knew of her presence. "Mrs. Henry is in the kitchen," she said. "If you'll come with me."

The sergeant nodded, and followed Celine as she went through the doorway leading to the pantries and kitchen. He did not remove his hat.

Marie Therese looked up as Celine led the visitor into the warm kitchen. Sarah didn't bother looking up, as she was occupied with a fresh piece of toasted bread. The sergeant went up to her.

"Mrs. Henry?"

Sarah regarded the man with an empty stare.

"I've got to ask you a few questions, Mrs. Henry."

"She's not well," Marie Therese said. "Is this necessary?"

"Official business, ma'am," the sergeant said, and turned again to Sarah. What was the name of the man who had gotten her released? he asked. Why had he brought her here? Where was he now?

To all these questions Sarah returned a blank stare and uttered not a word. Celine glanced with amusement toward her mother. It looked as if the Englishman could talk himself to death before he would elicit a response from the woman.

She was wrong. The sergeant accidentally stumbled onto the question that jolted Sarah from her torpor.

"Have you seen your husband?" he asked.

"My husband?"

"Yes."

"What about my husband?"

"Have you seen him?"

"Noah! You've finally found him!"

"I'm wondering if *you've* found him," the sergeant asked, a slight look of bewilderment on his face.

"I knew you'd get him," Sarah said triumphantly. "Now, where is he?"

The sergeant tried to explain that he knew nothing of Noah Henry, but he was getting nowhere. He turned to Celine and Marie Therese for help, but they looked him as blankly as Sarah had first done, and this did nothing to ease his discomfort. Then, suddenly, he had an idea. "Maybe your husband is hiding near the printing press," he said.

You could almost see a light go on in Sarah's head. "Yes, that would be just like him," she said. "Hiding someplace like that. Well, why don't you look there?"

"I don't know where that is," the sergeant said. "Perhaps you could show me and then we'll find your husband."

Sarah looked at Marie Therese. "These men are all alike," she said as if sharing a great confidence. "They protect one another. You can't trust a one of them. I've told him where Noah might be, but he won't even bother to look."

Celine had been listening to this last exchange with horror. Until this moment she hadn't the slightest notion that Sarah was aware of the existence of the press. She couldn't even remember Sarah's having been to the sheep barn. But it certainly looked as if she had. How unfortunate! And, worse news, she obviously had told the British about it, or else why would the sergeant have brought up the subject?

"I think it best if Mrs. Henry rest now," she said, stepping forward, hoping to put an end to this dangerous line of questioning. But Sergeant Taggert was on the scent of his quarry, and not to be put off.

"If you don't mind, ma'am," he said, stepping between Celine and Sarah, "I'd like to finish our conversation."

"But—"

The sergeant ignored her and turned back to Sarah. "Maybe your husband is at the printing press. Why don't we go look?"

"Yes, that would be a good idea," Sarah said, but made no move to leave the table.

"If you show me the way, I think we'll find him soon enough."

"I think it's time for your nap," Celine said, but both the sergeant and Sarah ignored her.

"Show you the way?" Sarah asked. "Yes, well, why wouldn't I show you the way? Tell me that!"

"There's no reason why you wouldn't."

Sarah stood up, her mind finally focusing on the matter at hand. "Come with me," she said as she walked toward the door.

"Don't leave the house," Taggert said to Marie Therese and Celine.

"I'm coming with you," Celine said.

"No, ma'am, you must—"

"Dammit! This is my property. I'm going with you to see what this is all about!"

The sergeant shrugged. "All right," he said.

Celine, Sarah, and Taggert left the house, after a short delay while Marie Therese insisted the women put on their coats. They were joined by the Hessian corporal and the six troopers and with Sarah in the lead, they walked down the path toward the sheep barn. Celine was frantically trying to think of something that would distract the sergeant, but could invent nothing remotely plausible. She went down the path as if she were a condemned felon on her way to the gallows.

Their passage did not go unnoticed.

Beth Henry had been at the top of the stairs, and she watched silently as the group left the house. She had then gone to the trapdoor leading to the attic and informed Franz of what was happening. He left his sanctuary, and the two of them stood at the window and watched the procession toward the sheep barn.

"I'm going down there," Franz said.

"What can you do?" Beth asked.

"I don't know, but surely more than I can do here."

"I'll go with you," she said.

Franz didn't argue. He knew that if it came to a fight, he would be glad to have Beth on his side. He had once seen her break up a fight between two large dogs. She had stepped into the middle of the snarling, biting melee and separated the animals with her bare hands. He wasn't sure he knew a man who had the courage and the ability to do that.

He took two pistols for himself and handed another to Beth. She stuck it under her belt, next to the wicked-looking knife in a deerskin sheath. They left the house by the back door and made their way down to the sheep barn, carefully keeping a high hedge between themselves and the men they were following. Primus watched from a window and scratched his head.

"Things jus' getting crazier and crazier," he mumbled to himself.

The sergeant and the others arrived at the sheep barn to find John Holt and Sisyphus in the middle of printing a new broadside attacking Prince William Henry as the corrupted son of a corrupted king who was the head of a corrupt nation. There wasn't a line printed on the paper that would influence a royal judge to accept a plea for leniency.

"There it is!" Sarah exclaimed in triumph as she pointed at the printing press.

A grim smile came over Taggert's face. He looked at Celine. "You have a good explanation for this, no doubt."

The two printers finally noticed the intruders, who had stepped through the doorway. They stopped the press, and there was a long moment of silence. The sergeant motioned for the soldiers to go to the press. The Hessians trooped across the room, stopped at the press, and looked back for further instructions.

"Shall we destroy this machinery?" the Hessian corporal asked.

"No," Taggert said. "We'll bring it back to New York." He

smiled. "Just the evidence we'll need to send a few poxed rebels to the gallows."

There was a side door to the sheep barn, and next to it a window. Franz and Beth arrived and watched through the latter, carefully keeping down, revealing only their eyes and the tops of their heads. The people in the barn were far too involved with their own drama to notice they were being observed.

"What do you plan on doing?" Celine asked the Englishman. Her throat was suddenly dry, and the words came out in a harsh, flat tone.

"What do you think?" Taggert asked with a sneer.

But Celine had no chance to reply.

Sarah Henry's mind, while not intact, was able to follow a simple thread. She had taken the sergeant to the press, and now expected to be rewarded with the presence of her husband, whom she dearly wished to berate. She looked around, didn't see him, and faced the Englishman.

"Where's Noah?"

"How do I know?" he said, finished with this crazywoman now that she had served her purpose. He started to brush past her to inspect the press.

She grabbed him by the arm. "I gave you what you wanted!" she screeched into his ear. "Now you give me Noah!"

Taggert, never a man for restraint, pushed her away. "Stay away from me, you old looney!"

"You lied!" she shouted, her lips working feverishly and a glaze lowering itself over her eyes. "I want you to arrest my husband! Arrest him, do you hear!"

"Sarah..." Celine began, but Sarah easily pushed her aside with a single sweep of her arm. Not a robust woman, she was now possessed of a formidable maniacal strength that made it beyond Celine's power to restrain her.

She grabbed the sergeant's arm, and once again he roughly thrust her away. "Stop this, or I'll throw you back in prison!"

Sarah stood with her feet apart, her hands rubbing against one another. Taggert started toward the press. He had taken two steps when the woman was on him like a wolf attacking a stray sheep.

"Liar! Liar! Liar!"

Her hands moved quickly, and before the sergeant could react, he had several long scratches and gouges from her nails on his face. He managed to get his hand up, and then howled as she sank her teeth into it.

The pain surged through his body, and he reacted with a demonic strength no less than his attacker's. He also vividly remembered that once before this madwoman had torn his face with her nails. He went berserk.

He threw her to the ground. She flailed at his legs as he raised his right boot and brought it down with a sickening thud right into the middle of her face. Sarah's nose seemed to explode, and there was blood all over her face.

The sergeant stepped back and aimed a vicious kick at Sarah's temple. He kicked a second time, a third, and finally a fourth. Then he stepped back, panting and wheezing, looking down at his bloody handiwork. The crushed features of the woman told the story.

Sarah Henry was dead.

No one else in the barn had moved. The attack and the killing had taken only a few seconds. The spectators were too stunned to do anything; and now, as everyone stood as if posed for a portrait, a slender figure stepped into the side doorway, drew back her arm, and sent a razor-sharp knife flying across the room.

The blade caught the sergeant in the throat. It entered at the left side, and, as if by magic, the bloodied point popped out on the right of his neck. His hands started to move up toward the butchered throat, but made it only halfway. He gave a startled grunt, then made a horrible gurgling sound as he fell to the floor, dead before his body landed.

All eyes were on Beth Henry.

She took the pistol from her belt. Franz stepped into view at her side. He held no weapons in his hands. He looked at Taggert and then at Celine, who was staring at Beth in horror.

The Hessian corporal was the first to react. While the other soldiers were still standing with their mouths open, he started to raise his musket.

"Achtung!"

It was the imperious voice of Franz von Lossow, *Colonel* Franz von Lossow, cousin to, and in the service of, the prince of Hesse-Cassel.

"Stand at attention!" he commanded in German. The Hessians had been subjected to a merciless discipline that made them react automatically to the orders of their officers. Their bodies went rigid as they snapped to attention, their muskets pulled close to their sides. Before they had time to think about why they were obeying the orders of this strange man, he stepped forward.

"I am Colonel Franz von Lossow. I now serve in the army of General George Washington. I invite you to join me."

The Hessians were confused. They looked at one another, and back at Franz. He spoke rapidly in German as he explained the advantages of deserting.

"If you join the American army, you will be free men. You will be allowed to stay in this country. After we win the war, you will be given land to farm. It will be yours free. You will become rich."

He walked up to them and lowered his voice to a conversational tone. "Why fight for the prince of Hesse? What has he done for you except sell you into bondage and flog your backs? Leave him and be free."

The Hessians again exchanged uneasy glances. It was the corporal who spoke first. "How can you be sure we'll win the war?"

"There is no doubt about it," Franz said. "The British can never conquer a country this vast."

A dark-haired Hessian with intelligent eyes stepped forward. "I'll join you, Colonel."

"Good man," Franz said, extending his hand for the other to shake. "What's your name?"

"Ashdour, sir. Henry Ashdour."

"Congratulations on becoming an American," Franz said, turning now to the rest of them. "Who's next?"

"How can we be sure the Americans will accept us as comrades?" the corporal asked.

"You have my word on it, as an officer and a gentleman."

The Hessians were impressed. Von Lossow came from the class of rulers whose word they had learned to accept as law. To question his word would be the same as calling him a liar, and such a thing went against the training of a lifetime. But still, they were peasants, and cautious; a prudent man did not jump into a pit without knowing what was at the bottom.

"If we agree to join Washington, will you personally take us to him?"

Von Lossow nodded. "If that is what you wish."

"I'll go," the corporal said.

Without another word, the remaining Hessians stepped forward. Franz welcomed each one with a handshake. When he was finished, he turned to Celine. "This settles one problem.

But now we have another," he said, looking at the corpse of Sergeant Taggert. "There'll be bloody hell to pay for that."

Celine forced herself to look at the two corpses. "Maybe we can bury them and hope no one discovers the bodies."

Franz shook his head. "We might get away with the woman, but not the soldier. They must know where he went today. They'll miss him and come right here looking for him."

The two printers had joined the group around the two corpses. Sisyphus understood the problem, and a shrewd look came over his face. "Why don't we blame these murders on the Hessians?"

"What do you mean?" Franz asked.

"Just what I said. Report that these Hessians attacked their sergeant and deserted. They're deserting anyway, right?"

"Brilliant," Celine said.

"I see," von Lossow said slowly. "Blame it on men who will be with Washington and safe. Good. But how do we tell the British authorities about what happened?"

"I'll tell them," Celine said. "I'll say I watched it all happen on the road outside my house."

"You'll have to put on a good act," John Holt said.

"That's *my* problem," Celine said. "In the meantime we've got to take this man's body out on the road and stage the mayhem."

Franz spoke rapidly to the Hessians in German. They nodded and picked up the corpse of Sergeant Taggert. They left the sheep barn and headed for the road.

"Now what about her?" Franz said, looking at Sarah's body.

"We'll bury her," Celine said.

"John and I will do that," Sisyphus said. He looked at Beth and shook his head. "Who would think it, to look at you!"

"Think what?" Beth said.

"Never mind, let's go back to the house," Celine said.

They returned to the kitchen of the Place and discussed what had to be done. Celine would go to the authorities, but they were certain to come back to the Place.

"The printing press has to go," Franz said.

"John and Sisyphus can take it up to the woods," Celine said.

"I know the perfect place to hide it," Beth said. "A cave."

As they were tidying up their plans, Philemon Peabody came up from the cellar. In a few minutes he knew all that had happened.

"Now I want you to clear off my property," Celine said.

"Yes, yes," Peabody said, anxious to be on his way. He now had an even better story for Captain Blakely than he had before. The murder of a British sergeant! "I'm going right away."

As the little man disappeared through the door, Celine looked at Franz and smiled. "I wonder what he'd think if we told him he'd been hiding in a cellar with a fortune in gold?"

"Kidd's treasure?"

She nodded. "A lot of it is still there."

Franz smiled. "He'd probably think of killing himself. But now, it's best you get to the city immediately and tell the British what happened."

"*Our* version of what happened," she said.

"Is there any other?" Franz asked blandly.

Patrick Blakely was furious as he rode his horse through the gates at the Place. He was more than a mile ahead of Celine, who was returning to her home in a carriage driven by Primus.

That damned lying woman, he thought, as he mentally reviewed the previous events.

Less than an hour ago Celine had entered his office and announced that Sergeant Taggert and Sarah Henry had been murdered within sight of her house by a group of Hessian soldiers. The Hessians, she informed him, had escaped up the Post Road after the unfortunate incident.

The captain was certain the story was a lie. What really happened, he thought, was that Sarah had led Taggert to the printing press, and both had been killed to insure their silence. That still didn't explain what happened to the Hessians, and the captain was determined to find out. Leaving a startled Celine in his office, he ran from the building, mounted his horse, and rode furiously to the Place.

He arrived at the main house, tied his horse to the hitching post, and strode inside. The first person he met was Mary Delafield.

"Good morning," she said, her eyes widening. "I... thought Celine went down to the city to see you."

"With a foolish story that wouldn't convince a child," he said. "What really happened here?"

"Why don't you come into the kitchen and have a cup of tea? We'll talk about it there."

"I didn't come here for tea," the captain said angrily. "I want to know what happened to Taggert."

"If you're going to be nasty I won't even talk to you," Mary said. She was wearing a high-necked dress that accentuated her pretty features, and the captain was suddenly reminded of other times and other circumstances. His attitude softened.

"All right," he agreed, and they walked into the kitchen.

Two-year-old David was seated in a high chair next to the table, being spoon-fed by a young servant girl. "Mama," he chortled happily when Mary entered the room. "Man!" he added, pointing proudly toward Blakely.

"It's a brand-new word for him," Mary said. "He uses it every chance he gets."

The captain didn't reply. He walked over to the child and looked down into his chubby, smiling face. The little boy's hair was dark, his ears lay flat against his head, and he had astonishingly full eyebrows. As full as my own, the captain found himself thinking. He held out his hand, and the little boy grabbed it.

"Man," he said again, looking pleased with himself. He pushed his bowl of porridge forward. "Want?"

"No, thank you," the captain said, a smile crossing his lips.

"Thank you," little David parroted, happy to display yet another expression in his constantly increasing vocabulary.

Mary came over and stood beside the captain. She signaled for the servant to leave them alone. They waited in silence until the girl was gone; then she turned and faced him.

"I used to be afraid of you, but now that I have David I've learned more about you."

"Yes?"

"He *is* your son, you know, as anyone with half a mind could tell by looking at the two of you. But the resemblance goes deeper than looks. David *thinks* the way you do. Even at two years of age."

Patrick Blakely looked down at his son and was touched. There was a resemblance in coloring and features, but the captain looked beyond those and saw a young man as he would be in twenty years; he saw a mirror image of himself.

"He is a beautiful child."

"I want you to leave this house," Mary said. "I want you to accept the story that the Hessians killed your sergeant and Sarah Henry, and then deserted."

"Why should I accept lies?"

"Because I ask you to," she said.

"That makes me one hell of a soldier."

"Is that all you think about? Don't you ever think about your son? He wants you to accept the story and leave."

"He knows nothing about it."

"You gave me your word that you would never do anything to harm him."

"Or you," the captain added.

"Then go back to the city. Report the story as it's been told to you. No one will question the word of the deputy provost marshal. So a few more Hessians deserted? So what?"

"A British soldier is dead, Mary. Let's not forget that."

"You can't bring him back to life."

He was silent for a moment. He looked at her with a touch of that mad whimsy that was a constant factor in his life. "Very well, I'll do as you ask. But on one condition."

"And this is?"

"That you tell me what *really* happened."

Mary mulled it over. Patrick was a strange man with strange values. He was just perverse enough not to do anything about the situation when he knew the facts. On the other hand, if she told him, she was putting several lives in jeopardy. She looked into his eyes and remembered how deep they had always seemed—dark and deep, their secrets stretching to infinity.

What she had shared with this man was unique. She was fairly certain it would never happen to her again, even with a man she truly loved. What they had shared were moments of absolute physical bliss. Their coupling at times had approached hysteria. What Patrick Blakely had given her was an awareness of her body that she hadn't dreamed could exist. But she was equally certain it had worked both ways: she had given him moments of pleasure that were better than any he had ever known.

It had been something they shared. And the fruit of it all was little David, who was seated next to them in his high chair.

She decided to trust him.

"Your sergeant came looking for a printing press," she said. "He found it and was killed. The part about the Hessians deserting is the truth."

"Who killed him?"

She hesitated. "What if I told you I did it?"

"I wouldn't believe you."

"What happened was Sarah Henry went crazy. She attacked your sergeant. He defended himself and killed her."

"Crazy Sarah, they called her," Blakely mused. "I can believe she attacked him. And knowing Taggert, I can also believe he killed her. But you still haven't told me who killed *him*."

"Beth Henry."

A look of disbelief crossed his face. "She's only a slip of a girl."

"Looks can be deceiving. Beth used a knife."

"It's hard to believe."

"It's the truth. I swear it on our son's head."

He nodded. "I believe you."

"Because I've told you the truth."

"You've placed Beth Henry's life in my hands, you know that?"

"Yes," she replied. "And mine. And David's. We're all in this together."

Blakely looked pained. "Now that I know what happened, I wish I didn't. Tell me the rest of it. Is there a printing press here? And is it the one printing the attacks on us?"

"Yes."

"And you've been here and known all along, haven't you?"

"Yes. Now look here, Patrick, I've kept my part of the bargain and told you the truth. What are you going to do about it?"

He reached out and touched his son's shoulder. "As far as I know, a detachment of Hessians killed Sergeant Taggert and Sarah Henry. Then they deserted to Washington's army. That's your story, and now it's mine."

Mary took his hand in hers and started to speak, but couldn't as she fought back the tears. She pressed his hand against her lips and kissed it. Patrick would never change his story. Beth and the others were safe.

"I ask one favor," he said. "No more printing presses here. My honor as a British officer demands at least that."

"You have my word."

He patted his son on the shoulder. The little boy smiled. "I must get back to the city to make my report. Not that anyone will grieve over Taggert. Come to think of it," he said with sardonic amusement, "I suppose I was the best friend he had in this world."

She walked him to the door, and didn't resist when he held her in his arms and kissed her on the mouth; the fire was still there. Then he was out the door, on his horse, and riding down the path to the road.

He encountered Celine in her carriage at the gate to the Place. She was coming back from his office.

"Well?" she said, surprised to find him leaving her house so soon. "You couldn't have been at the Place long. What's happened here?"

"I've always said Hessians are not to be trusted," the captain said. He spurred his horse and galloped down the road.

A puzzled Celine went to the main house, where a smiling Mary Delafield awaited her.

Philemon Peabody was waiting in Captain Blakely's office when he returned from the Place.

When the captain realized who his visitor was, he was surprised and angered. "What the hell are you doing here?"

"I think we'll have a mutually profitable day," Peabody said smoothly as he rubbed his hands together. "Yes, Captain, very profitable for both of us."

It was an interesting opening, and Blakely sat down in his chair. "Tell me why," he said.

Ten minutes later the captain left the room, walked down the hall, and entered the provost marshal's office. During the walk he thought about what Peabody had told him about the Place, the deaths of Sergeant Taggert and Sarah Henry, the location of the printing press...all of it.

Blakely didn't let on that he knew all about these things. He nodded pleasantly and made Peabody feel as if he truly valued the information. When the little man had concluded his account, the captain said he wanted to tell all this to the provost marshal immediately. Peabody beamed with happiness. He was certain his story had made a big impression on the captain. Yes indeed, this was going to be a very profitable day.

Colonel Cunningham looked up from his work as his deputy entered the office.

"Yes?"

"A British sergeant has been murdered," the captain said.

"Wonderful," the colonel said glumly, and went back to his paperwork.

"Sergeant Taggert. He was a good man."

Cunningham, surprised, looked up again. "He was with us a long time."

"From the beginning of the occupation."

"What happened?"

"He was leading a detachment of Hessians. They killed him and deserted to Washington's army."

"Damn those fucking krauts! I wish to hell we'd ship them all back to Germany."

"There's more to it, however," Blakely said, sitting down in a chair and stretching his long legs in front of him. "It seems these Hessians were paid to desert. They also got a bonus for killing Taggert."

The colonel jumped to his feet. "Jesus Christ!" he shouted and the veins stood out on his forehead. "How do you know this?"

"Because I know the spy who paid them."

"Who is he? I want to know. I want to hang the bastard and leave his carcass for the birds to eat."

"His name is Philemon Peabody."

"Put every man we have on this. I want New York turned upside down until we—"

"That's not necessary," Blakely interrupted. "I already have the man. He's sitting in my office right now."

"Good work, Blakely, good work."

"The man's guilty," Blakely said calmly. "There isn't a trace of doubt about it. And because the crime is so vile, I have a suggestion."

"What is it?"

"Let's not waste time on this scum. Let's not bother with prison. Let's not even bother with a trial. I say we take him out and hang him. Now."

"You mean *right* now?"

"Yes."

"It's a bit out of the ordinary. After all, we are British, and we do believe in justice."

"What justice should the murderer of a British sergeant receive? I say no more than he gave the sergeant. An example must be made of this man."

"You're right," the colonel said, smacking his fist into the palm of his other hand. He reached for his hat. "Bring the bastard down to the courtyard right away."

"The back courtyard with the gallows?"

"Of course. We're going to hang him."

The captain nodded. He returned to his own office as the colonel strode toward the staircase.

Philemon Peabody smiled when the captain returned. "Tell me," he said. "What did the provost marshal have to say?"

Captain Blakely returned the smile.

"We're to meet him outside. The two of us."

"When?" Peabody asked.

"Right now."

Patrick Blakely and Philemon Peabody were both smiling as they walked out into the courtyard behind the Provost.

Peabody even waved when he saw Colonel Cunningham.

Noah Henry was with Washington's army at Morristown when Franz von Lossow arrived with the seven Hessian deserters. The colonel sought him out and conveyed the news of his wife's tragic ending.

Noah was a stoical man, and he accepted Sarah's death without a meaningless show of remorse he did not feel. Sarah had made his life painful, and had brought no joy to his years. Even so, such a death degraded the human spirit, both in the dead person and the killer.

The event, of course, changed the course of his life. Sarah was no longer a burden for him to bear. He was a free man, a single man, and now he could be more open about his feelings.

"How is Mary Delafield?" he asked.

"Quite well," Franz said. "She's prettier than ever."

"I think she's the prettiest woman I've ever seen," Noah said quietly and with great feeling.

Franz glanced over to see if the man was being serious, and the look on Noah's face told the whole story to a man as worldly as he.

"How long have you been in love with Mary?" he asked.

"From the first day I met her," Noah said dreamily. Then he reddened. He really had only been thinking aloud, but the other man had caught him at it. "What I mean is . . . I've always admired her, and—"

Franz held up his hand. "Don't explain it to me. The only person who has to know is Mary."

"I helped deliver her child," Noah said. "It was a difficult birth, and I didn't really know what I was doing. But everything went well. I think of little David as my own son."

"Why don't you write to her?" Franz suggested. "The British never interfere with the mails. It's one of their oddities about fair play and all."

"What would I say to her?"

"Good God, man, you love her. Tell her that."

"I've never been much of a hand with a pen," Noah confessed. "I learned as a child, but I've never had much call to keep it up. I wonder if..."

He hesitated, and Franz knew what he was leading up to. "I'll be glad to write down what you wish to tell her," he said.

They worked for over an hour. At first Noah was reluctant to say what was on his mind, partly because he felt foolish saying it to another man, and partly because he was afraid he would offend Mary with his forwardness.

Finally Franz convinced him the only thing that mattered was that he tell Mary what he felt in his heart.

"You're not ashamed of it, are you?" he asked.

"Ashamed of being in love with Mary?" Noah was horrified. "How could a man be ashamed of that?"

"Exactly. Now get on with it."

Franz wrote the final, agreed-upon version in his elegant hand.

My dearest Mary,

I have heard the news about Sarah. I grieve for her because it is never a good thing for a person to die before their appointed time. But, as you know, our marriage was not a happy one. The only good time, in fact, was when you and David shared my house and brought light and happiness into my life.

I have tried to find a clever way to say the following, but it seems there is no clever way, or if there is, I am too simple to think of it.

I love you.

Now that we have both lost our spouses, we are free to say what is in our hearts. Mary, I would care for you and your son with as much love and devotion as is in my heart and powers. I would raise David as my own. I would teach him to be a man. I would help him claim his place in the world.

I do not claim to be worthy of you, but then I can't think of a man who is. Nor can I think of a man who would love you more than myself. With you at my side I would stand close to God and be afraid of nothing.

Franz von Lossow is writing this down for me, and thank God, because I would never have the courage to say these things to your face.

I now know what love is, and you have all of mine for the rest of my life.

You are my life.—

Noah Henry

Noah reread the finished letter. "Do you think it's good enough?" he asked.

Franz had been comparing Noah's simple phrases and words from the heart with the kind of letter he himself might write under similar circumstances. No doubt he would have thrown in a Shakespearean couplet, or something from Pindar or Ovid. How much more honest and direct was Noah's letter!

"It's quite good enough," he said.

"I've never written a letter to a woman before," Noah said.

"After this you'll probably never have to write another one," Franz said.

Alice de Witt had gone to the cemetery north of the Fresh Water Pond to pay her respects to her dead son.

She stood over the grave for a time, her breath coming out in clouds of steam, her thoughts on the little lad who never really had a taste of life. She prayed for his innocent soul and felt sure he was with God.

After a time the wind began to cut through her coat and chill her to the bone. She said a silent good-bye to the boy and started back toward the gate.

She arrived there at the same time as an army wagon driven by a British corporal. Two old grave diggers who were warming themselves by a fire looked up at the new arrival. They both scowled.

"Sorry to spoil your leisure," the corporal said. He climbed into the back of the wagon. "But here's more work for you."

Alice stopped. She was half concealed by a tree and none of the men saw her. She didn't know what made her pause, but what happened next kept her rooted to the spot.

"What have you got?" the first grave digger asked.

"Just one," the corporal said, and he grunted as he pushed a sack off the back of the wagon. It landed on the ground with a sickening thud, and Alice realized it was a body wrapped in a canvas shroud. It was an outrage to be so disrespectful of the dead, she thought.

"Must be fun digging holes in frozen ground like this," the corporal said.

"See how much he knows. That must be why they made him a corporal," the first grave digger said sarcastically.

The second grave digger laughed. "We dig all the holes in summer and fall," he said. "This time of year we only fill them up."

"There are tricks to every trade," the first grave digger assured the soldier.

The second grave digger went over to the body and pulled the top of the shroud down, revealing the shoulders and head of a man. "Jesus! Look at the face on this one!"

The first grave digger came closer, and his face mirrored his revulsion at what he saw. "What the hell did you do to him?"

"Hanged him," the corporal said. "But it was a bad drop, and his neck didn't break. So he took a long time strangling to death."

"What did they hang him for?"

"Who the hell knows? Why? Did you know him?"

The first grave digger peered more closely at the tortured face. "Never saw him before in my life."

"Probably looked a hell of a lot different before they did this to him," the second grave digger said.

"I guess you're right," the corporal said.

Alice suddenly wanted to hear no more of this conversation. She walked out from behind the tree and passed through the gate. The corporal, startled, jumped back. Then when he realized Alice was a flesh-and-blood woman, he relaxed.

"Crikey, but you bloody well took ten years off'n my life."

The two grave diggers looked at one another and cackled. One of them had almost no teeth, and those that were left looked yellow and cracked.

"This place make you a bit nervous, do it?" the first one said.

"I don't know how you can stand being here all the time," the corporal said.

"Don't pay no attention to him, missus," the second grave digger said.

Despite herself Alice looked down at the face of the dead man. Her face registered horror, and her hand flew to her mouth and she bit on the heavy glove. The dead man's face was frozen into a picture of contorted agony.

"Dear God!" she whispered.

And then she realized she knew the identity of the dead man.

"Best not be looking at it, missus," the first grave digger said in a kindly voice.

"Yes, yes, of course," Alice said. She pulled her shawl tighter about her shoulders and hurried away from the cemetery. There was no doubt in her mind who the man was: Philemon Peabody. She had seen him around the de Kuyper offices many times. Whatever had brought him to such a horrible end? she wondered as she went toward Whitehall Street to tell David Sackett about what she had seen.

The two grave diggers watched her for a moment and then turned back to the business at hand.

"Do you want to shovel the dirt in? Or do you want to tamp this time?" he asked as he went to one end of the corpse to get a carrying hold.

"I'll do the tamping," the second man said.

"You always take the easy jobs," the first one said, picking up his end of the body and looking blackly at his companion.

Several weeks after it had been sent, Noah's letter finally made its way to the Place, where Mary read it and cried. She handed it to Celine, who was looking queerly at her as she wondered what had brought on the rush of tears. The *old* Mary might have cried easily, but the *new* Mary that had come into being after the birth of David rarely cried.

"Well, he certainly sounds sincere," Celine said when she had finished the letter. "What do you think about it all?"

"Noah is a gentle and considerate man. I think I could easily fall in love with him."

"But you're not in love with him now?"

"What's 'in love with' mean? I was married to Robert, but I was never in love with him. I had a passion for—you know who, but was that love? Maybe what I feel for Noah really *is* love. It's tenderness and caring about him. He makes me feel safe."

"So, write and tell him. He obviously wants to hear from you."

"The only thing that bothers me is David. The boy's my responsibility. Why should Noah be burdened?"

Celine shook her head. "You don't understand men. He *wants* the burden of a child. It will make him feel he's really doing something to prove his love for you."

"Maybe I will write to him," Mary said. She left the kitchen, and Celine was alone until her mother came down from her bedroom. They talked about Noah's letter, and Marie Therese smiled. "Did I ever show you the letters your father wrote to me back—oh, heavens, during the war with the French?"

"No."

Marie Therese came back to the kitchen bearing a packet of letters tied with a bright-green ribbon. She selected several passages and read them to her daughter. At moments, both of them felt as if they were once again in the presence of Jan de Kuyper. The letters weren't flowery, but clear and honest as Noah's had been.

"I loved getting every letter from your father, and hated it at the same time, because it was a tangible reminder that we were apart."

"You really loved him very much, didn't you?"

"Jan was my world," Marie Therese said, looking thoughtfully at her daughter. "I only wish your life were blessed with such a love."

Celine shrugged. "I married too young and I married the wrong man."

"And ever since you've been flitting from man to man like a moth from candle to candle," Marie Therese said. "Did you ever notice that sometimes the moth gets too close to the flame and dies?"

"Are you trying to give me a message?" Celine asked. It had never been Marie Therese's way to interfere, and this line of conversation came as a surprise.

"It's something I've been wanting to say to you for a long time. I've kept quiet because, as we've discussed, I believe it's best to let people learn from their own mistakes."

"Are you trying to tell me my involvement with Franz is a mistake?"

"I've always wanted my children to have the best of life. It doesn't really matter what I think about Franz. The question is, do *you* love him? And is it a love that will last?"

"One like you had with Father, you mean?"

"I wouldn't be surprised if half the people on earth never loved anyone the way I loved Jan. I've watched you with many men, Celine, and there's always been one thing I've looked for and have never seen." Marie Therese spoke quietly and gravely, and Celine became very interested.

"Yes?"

"It's not enough to love a man, you've got to respect him as well. Otherwise you'll never worry about what concerns him. When you care enough about someone to stop being selfish, when you're willing to do what he wants, and not what you want, then you'll have it all." She smiled. "And of course the man should feel the same way about the woman he loves."

Celine applied the idea to Franz. Did she respect him? Yes, she answered honestly. Did she worry about what concerned him? Again, yes. Was she willing to give up what she wanted to do in order to accommodate him?

This was a tougher question.

Marie Therese understood the turmoil in her daughter's mind. She looked away when she spoke. "When a woman loves a man the way I loved Jan, it isn't necessary to think about the answer."

"I envy you. Your life's been so much simpler than mine."

"I made it that way," Marie Therese said. "You only get what you work for."

Celine accepted her mother's censure. She *had* been frivolous and too concerned with her own pleasures—even at the expense of her own son's love. He had been in Europe for such a long time: why hadn't she at least tried to go over to see him? Why? Because she had wanted to stay in New York. Because she was involved with a man.

She thought of Franz von Lossow and realized she *was* in love with him, and there was a good chance it was the sort of love her mother was talking about. For the first time in her life she was willing to consider putting what a man wanted above her own desires. It had never happened before. Certainly not with her husband, nor with Nathan Hale, nor the almost faceless parade of men preceding him.

"It's taken me a long time to grow up," she finally said. "It must take longer for some people than others."

Marie Therese looked at her daughter with compassion. "I can tell what Franz thinks by the way he looks at you," she said.

"And?"

"I think you're lucky. Most people don't get another chance at your stage in life."

Celine laughed. "You make me sound like an old lady. If so, what does that make you?"

"An old lady's mother," Marie Therese said, a smile growing on her lips. "The two of us are ready for rocking chairs, the way I make it sound."

Celine hugged her mother. "Not quite yet, I think. And thank you for being so honest."

"I've always been honest," Marie Therese said. "Only sometimes you never bothered to listen."

It was late in the summer, and Andrew de Kuyper was on his way back to America at last.

He was aboard the frigate *Avenger* with Alec Seixas, Dick Goelet, and Peter Murray. Seth Cuyler was aboard the *Kieft*, and these ships, with a third de Kuyper privateer, the *Peter Minuit*, made up the American contingent sailing with the fleet of twenty-four warships under the command of the French admiral de Grasse. They were presently in mid-Atlantic, heading toward the West Indies.

Peter came to be with the fleet even though Drew had sworn he would not expose his nephew to such danger. The lad had convinced Ben Franklin he was homesick and that his longing was putting him in a weakened condition. There was a mild outbreak of plague causing deaths in France, and Peter claimed it would be sure to claim someone as ill as himself. The old gentleman wasn't fooled by these dramatics, but he secretly agreed with Peter and so brought all his influence to bear on Drew. The convincing argument came from the king of France himself. He sent a note to Franklin that, in essence, said it would please His Majesty if his young American friend's wishes were accommodated. Franklin was delighted with the French fleet being sent to America and didn't think it was a good time to annoy the king. Hence young Peter went along with his uncle.

Drew was standing at the rail with Dick. On the other side of the quarterdeck, Peter was holding a sextant and having an animated discussion about it with the first mate.

Drew made a sour face as he looked at his nephew. He knew he had been duped, but also knew there was nothing he could do about it. "If that kid is sick, I'm the prince of Hesse," he complained.

"Looks healthy to me," Dick agreed.

"He needs the flat side of a stick across his rump," Drew grumbled.

"Do it and he'll find a way to get even," Dick said. "Remember, he has friends at court."

Suddenly Peter was distracted from his sextant lesson by a group of whales passing the ship. He came over and stood next to Drew and Dick to watch them.

"There must be over a dozen in that herd," Dick said as he watched the leviathans move effortlessly through the water.

"A pod, not a herd," Peter said. "That's what you call whales when they're in a group—a pod."

"Where did you learn that?" Drew asked.

"Louis gave me some books about the sea as a going-away present," Peter said. "I've been reading them every day."

"Did he give you anything else?"

Peter nodded. "Lots of stuff, including this," he said, reaching into his pocket and taking out a brilliant diamond.

Dick's eyes widened as he took the stone and held it up in the sunlight. "This must be worth a fortune," he said.

"Do you want me to mind that for you?" Drew asked.

"No," Peter said, putting the stone back in his pocket and continuing to watch the whales.

"Our ancestor Pieter was a whaling man," Drew said. "Whale oil, in fact, was the foundation of our family's fortune."

"They're such remarkable animals," Peter said. "It seems a shame to kill them."

"Their oil makes it a lot easier to read at night," Dick said. "What would we do without whale oil?"

"We'd find something else," Peter assured him.

The sail continued without incident, and the flotilla arrived in the Indies on a beautiful, clear day. Admiral de Grasse split his fleet into three groups and sent them to different islands for reprovisioning. The American ships went to the port city of Fort de France, on the island of Martinique. There were eight ships in this group, and they anchored near the quay in the center of the harbor.

Drew, Dick, and Peter went ashore and found an inn that served food. After eating the usual tasteless concoctions served aboard ship over many weeks at sea, they were anxious to taste real food again.

They were attacking a spicy fish soup when a tall, well-muscled man came over to their table. He wore a dazzling white shirt that accentuated his blackness.

"I'm looking for a man named Andrew de Kuyper," he said in a deep-bass voice. He was well over six feet tall and in his middle twenties. When he smiled, it was a pleasant sight.

"I'm Andrew de Kuyper," Drew said. "What can I do for you?"

"My name is George Gerait," the man said. "I have an uncle named Primus. I understand he works for your family."

"Gerait!" Drew said in surprise. "Good God, man, it's like you're almost part of the family. Sit down. Join us in a meal."

"I didn't know Primus had a nephew," Dick said as the black man sat down.

George Gerait ordered a mug of ale and a bowl of soup and related his history to the others. He was the son of Primus's younger brother, who, though born in New York, had spent a great part of his life at sea. He had married a Martinique woman, and their son, George, had called Fort de France home all his life.

"But you speak perfect English," Dick said. The people in Martinique spoke French, and when they ventured into English, they usually mangled the language.

"My father taught me English," George said. "He insisted that one day I would go to America—to New York, in fact. I guess that day has come. I would like to go on your ship."

"There will be fighting," Drew said.

George smiled. "One reason I want to go."

"Didn't our great-grandfathers fight together against the Indians?" Drew asked.

"So my father told me. The earliest ancestor that I know of was named Manuel. He was freed from slavery by Pieter de Kuyper and worked for him for the rest of his life."

They returned to the ship, and Alec Seixas was delighted when he saw the new man: he was as big as a house and carried a heavy trunk on his shoulder as if it was a feather.

"I can't wait to see him in a scrap," he said.

"I'll stand next to him when there's trouble," Dick said. "When you're my size, you look for all the help you can get."

There was some grumbling in the fo'c'sle when George selected a berth. Not every man was happy about the proximity of a black. But peace was maintained, because no one was particularly anxious to find out if George was as strong as he looked.

Peter and George quickly became friends. The black man obtained horses and took the boy on a tour of part of the island. It was a beautiful place, filled with flowers that were a treat for the eyes and filled the air with their perfume.

Peter, however, was less impressed by the beauty of Martinique than by the fact that the entire economy was based on slave-run plantations. "The white men sit around and do nothing while the black men do all the work," he said.

"That's the way it is in places like Georgia and the Carolinas," Drew said.

"If you sit around all day, you get lazy," Peter said. "Before long you'd forget how to work. I'll never let that happen to me."

"The whites claim the blacks are better suited than whites are to work in this climate," George said.

"Do you believe that?" Peter asked.

George smiled. "No, but it pleases the whites to think so."

After two days the ships had taken on all their stores, and they left Fort de France and sailed north to rendezvous with the rest of the fleet.

The twenty-four French ships and three Americans came together and headed north to Chesapeake Bay and the Virginia coast. Long ago, messages had been sent to General Washington, and it was expected he would bring his army south to join up with the fleet. Then the combined forces would smash the army of Cornwallis. If that happened, the war would virtually be over, because the British would no longer have a major force in America.

Four days after leaving the rendezvous point, Drew had his first taste of battle at sea. A British squadron of six ships was sighted, and de Grasse sent nine ships—including the *Avenger*—to do battle with the enemy. The Englishmen realized they were outnumbered and tried to run before the wind to escape, but two of their ships were slow and the pursuers caught up with them after a chase of twenty miles.

The *Avenger* was a particularly fast frigate, and Alec whooped with joy when he realized his would be the first ship to overtake the plodding Englishman.

The *Avenger* came up steadily on the port side of the British ship, and her batteries began to fire. The Englishmen returned the fire, but the *Avenger* had superior weaponry; soon the American ships had reduced the enemy's decks to chaos.

Drew had ordered Peter below, but the lad ignored this advice and stood behind the helmsman on the quarterdeck, where he could get a good view of all the action.

Alec decided the Englishman had been punished enough by the cannons and gave the order to close, grapple, and board.

The two ships came together, the irons were thrown that bound them together, and the men of the *Avenger* swarmed onto the enemy deck.

Drew was one of the first to board the other ship, and he rapidly got all the fighting he'd been wanting. He cut down one sailor with his cutlass and instantly found himself engaged with another one. He fought for a few minutes and then took a nasty slash on his shoulder. The blow knocked him to the deck, and the Englishman probably would have killed him had it not been for George Gerait.

The black man had crossed to the other ship and was a few feet from Drew when the latter was felled. He bellowed mightily, and threw himself at the Englishman who stood over Drew. The Englishman was decapitated by one swoop of George's cutlass. Then the big man hurled himself bodily into a group of four royal marines and killed or disabled them all within a minute.

Soon afterward the fighting stopped, the British captain having signaled surrender, and the panting combatants glared at one another.

A French ship pulled up on the other side of the Englishman, and her captain discussed the fate of the conquered enemy with his American counterpart, Alec Seixas. The decision was made to put the living Englishmen aboard their longboats and then to scuttle their ship. It was one ship that would never fight again.

As the squadron made its way back toward de Grasse's flagship, the doctor tended to the wounded, including Drew. His was only a flesh wound, but it hurt, and he found himself no longer so anxious to get into battle as he once had.

"It's a good thing we had them outnumbered," Peter said.

"Why?" Drew asked.

"The Englishmen were good fighters. They had more discipline."

"But they were only fighting for their pay," Drew said. "Our men are fighting for their freedom. It's a better reason."

Peter wasn't convinced. "Their discipline makes them fight more as a unit than our men do."

"George Gerait is a unit all by himself," Dick said.

Alec smiled. "Can you imagine a whole crew of men like him?"

* * *

The French fleet, with its American auxiliaries—a force of twenty-seven ships boasting seventeen hundred guns and carrying three thousand crack army troops—arrived at the mouth of Chesapeake Bay at the beginning of September. The Americans stood at the rail and admired the shores of their homeland. Some who, like Drew, had been away for years had tears in their eyes. Even Peter was touched, although he spent most of his time taking sightings on the land and working with the mate's instruments to figure out the fleet's exact position. By this time the lad had learned enough to be a fair navigator.

The return to their homeland seemed to relax the men, and they allowed themselves to speak of subjects they had kept to themselves.

"I received a letter from Althea Middleton," Drew said to Dick as the two of them sat near the hatch that led below to their cabins.

"A letter," Dick said in surprise. "Where? And why didn't you say anything about it before?"

"It came just before we left France. I suppose I should have told you about it, but it seemed we had other things on our minds. But Dick—Althea and I are to be married."

Dick couldn't hide his shock. "You and . . . Tell me about it."

"Her parents have agreed. As soon as possible—and, of course, the war being over—I'm to go back to England and marry her."

"You'll live there?"

"No," Drew said in annoyance. "We'll come back to New York."

"I don't know," Dick said thoughtfully. "The daughter of an English peer might think our little city a bit backward."

"It's no more backward than London. And a good deal cleaner. She'll learn to love it."

"Obviously none of the family in New York knows about it."

"Obviously."

Dick was silent for a long time, and Drew finally asked him what he was thinking.

"This may have its good side," he said with a shy smile. "Good for me," he added.

"What are you talking about?"

"With you around, Beth Henry would never look at another man. But when you show up with a wife—well, that will change her mind."

"So?"

"So, my dear cousin, there may be a chance for me to convince her I'm the man for her."

"Be my guest," Drew said. "There's never been anything between Beth and me."

"She's been in love with you, you idiot," Dick said.

"Puppy love," Drew said. "She'll grow out of it."

"Are you happy with your forthcoming marriage?" Dick asked.

"Of course. Need you ask?"

"You just don't seem to be as enthusiastic about it as you might be."

"Althea is a beautiful girl, and we'll be very happy."

"I hope so," Dick said, but there was a shadow of a doubt in his mind. The happiness his cousin claimed seemed a bit forced. But maybe he was only imagining that, he decided. Also, it was none of his business. He resolved to keep his mouth shut in the future.

The next day the fleet anchored in a small cove, and Admiral de Grasse sent his fastest schooner out to look for the British ships. In the meanwhile, the French and American ships prepared for battle. The tension mounted, as everyone knew the coming fighting might have a decisive effect on the war.

Drew was already looking beyond the battle to the time when he could return to New York.

"I can't wait to see Mother," he said to Peter. "And Celine and the others."

Peter nodded. "It will be good. I've missed Beth. She probably won't even recognize me. I've grown about a foot since I last saw her."

Drew smiled. It was true that Peter had shot up in height in the past year. He couldn't wait to see his sister's face when she saw she had an almost grown son.

"If your mother starts picking on me because I brought you along on this warship, I hope you'll explain I had nothing to do with it."

"Of course," Peter said. "It was all my own idea."

"And you were never really sick?"

"No, I made that up. It was Louis's idea."

"The king told you to lie to your uncle?"

Peter shrugged. "Louis told me a man has to tell certain

little lies if he's going to get anywhere. Many people just don't want to hear the truth."

Drew shook his head. "I guess you're right, but I still don't like it."

"I'll lie only when I have to," Peter said. "That's a promise."

"You're going to go far in this world, Peter, very far."

"I plan on doing that."

Celine was nervous as the carriage bumped and jostled its way over the narrow New Jersey road. Beth Henry sat beside her with a pistol in her hand. Primus Gerait was driving.

The reason for Celine's nervousness was the quarter keg of gold coins hidden beneath the floorboards of the carriage. It was being taken to George Washington so he could give his soldiers their back pay. Congress had not been able to send any money in over six months, and the men were on the verge of another mutiny.

Franz von Lossow, who was riding his horse a few paces behind the carriage, had come to the Place to borrow the money from the de Kuypers to help the general keep his army together at this critical juncture. The French fleet was expected in Chesapeake Bay, and it was imperative that Washington's army march the four hundred and fifty miles south to join de Grasse. The American commander-in-chief already had a force of over two thousand Continentals and five thousand French regulars. It was the Continentals who were demanding payment before they would fight another battle, and the general was desperate.

The carriage containing the solution to his problem, meanwhile, continued to bump and bounce its way across New Jersey.

"Stop worrying," Beth said. "Nothing's going to happen."

"Half the people in New York would slit our throats if they knew what was in this carriage."

"But they don't know," Beth pointed out. "Besides, I've got this," she added, holding up the pistol.

"That would do us a lot of good if a dozen men jumped out and attacked us."

"Franz is here."

"I still think he should have brought soldiers."

"He thought we'd attract less attention this way."

"Less attention and more danger," Celine said doggedly.

"You worry too much."

Celine smiled. It wasn't long ago everyone had told her she

was too flighty and didn't worry enough. The side effects of a war could be very strange, she thought.

By nightfall they approached the outer perimeter of Washington's camp, and Celine finally began to relax. Actually, the gold under the floorboards was only a part of the reason for her nervousness. *Everyone* in New York was nervous these days.

The rumor was that Washington was planning an attack on New York. The last five years had been bad enough for New Yorkers, but how much worse would things get if a major battle was fought in the city? General Clinton obviously believed the rumor; he had brought up hundreds of troops from the Carolinas and Delaware to bolster the city garrisons.

What the people didn't know was that Washington had absolutely no intention of attacking New York.

He planned on bypassing the city entirely on his way to Virginia to rendezvous with the French. He himself had started the rumor for the express purpose of confusing the English. A soldier that was tied up in the defense of New York was a soldier that couldn't be used to help Cornwallis—and that was where the war was really going to be decided.

When the carriage pulled up in front of the general's tent of unbleached linen, he came out to greet his visitors. He only hoped they were bringing what Colonel von Lossow had promised. He bowed low as he formally kissed Celine's hand, then Beth's.

"A pleasure to see you again, Mrs. Murray. Miss Henry."

"We just dropped by to pay a social visit," Celine said.

"Social visit?"

"What else would bring us here?"

"Ah..."

Celine decided it wasn't fair to bait the general. "The gold is under the floorboards," she said, pointing back toward the carriage.

Franz had already begun to take up the boards. Washington hurried to his side. "I think it's more than you need, sir," the German said.

"More than I need? Good, good, then maybe I'll have enough to avert the next crisis."

"Are you planning another?" Celine asked.

"It seems to be a way of life these days."

"I'm glad we were able to help," Celine said.

The money was turned over to the paymaster, who quickly

began passing it out to the men. The general gave the order that the army would move south in the morning. Not a single man complained.

"If I had told them we were moving before I paid them, we'd have had a riot on our hands."

Franz, Celine, and Beth joined the general for dinner. As usual, the fare was plain and not overabundant. The conversation turned to the course of the war, and Washington assured them he had no plans to attack New York. He was, he said, going to pay a call on Cornwallis in Virginia.

"It could be the final battle of the war," the general said. "At least I hope it will be."

"And what then?" Celine asked.

"We try to remember what life was like during peacetime."

Franz smiled at Celine. "And we begin our new lives."

"I'll be glad to take off this uniform," the general said. "I'm really a farmer at heart."

"Do you think the new government will let you go?" Celine said. "Surely they'd prefer to find a post for you."

The general sighed. "I suppose. I remember having a conversation years ago with your grandfather..."

"James de Kuyper?"

"Yes. We talked about raising workhorses. That's what I'd really like to do."

"Maybe you'll get lucky," Celine said.

The general couldn't help but notice the looks and smiles exchanged by Franz and Celine. "Speaking about our futures, Mrs. Murray, are you planning to steal one of my colonels from me?"

Celine nodded. "I should think that's obvious, General."

Franz blushed. "I promise to remain at your side for as long as you need me, sir."

The general smiled and turned to Beth. "And what about you, young lady? Is there a lucky young man in your life?"

"I don't think so," Beth said quietly.

The general was surprised. "I would think the young men would be falling all over themselves to get close to you."

"They are," Celine said. "She's even had Prince William Henry chasing after her."

"The prince himself?" Washington said in astonishment. "But we can't have you consorting with the enemy."

"He behaved himself," Beth said.

"The reason Beth isn't making any definite plans is that she's in love with a foolish, selfish, blind ingrate," Celine said with some fervor.

"Who's that?" the general asked, taken aback by the virulence of the woman's tone and language.

"My brother!" Celine said.

"Oh," the general said in confusion and embarrassment. He proceeded to become extremely interested in the bits of barley floating in his soup.

The next morning the entire American army of seven thousand men broke camp and began a rapid march to Virginia. Speed was of the essence, and Washington had made the decision to leave tons of supplies and equipment in New Jersey. "Either we'll win this battle and the war will be over and we won't need this equipment," he said, "or we'll lose and won't need it in any event."

Hasty good-byes were made as Franz took his place at the head of his troops. Celine, Beth, and Primus watched the long procession wend its way down from the Morristown heights; then they started back toward New York long before the last of the army passed. The extended column would take over eight hours to pass a single spot, and they hadn't the time for that.

They rode back to Manhatan, crossing the river on a small barge at Tarrytown, not far from the spot where the Americans had hanged Major André. His confederate in crime, Benedict Arnold, was presently leading a force of British regulars and loyalists that was causing havoc in Connecticut. Stories of burnings and butcherings filtered back to the city, and the name Benedict Arnold was becoming one of the most hated to emerge from the war. It was said his wife no longer wanted anything to do with him, and had informed him she would not go back to England with him after the war was over. Certainly there would be no place for him save the gallows in the new nation of the United States.

A despondent-looking Jemmy Sackett was waiting for them when they returned to the Place. "It's Jenny," he informed them. "She's going to get married."

Celine and Beth exchanged surprised glances; everyone had become accustomed to thinking of the Sackett twins as a unit.

"His name is Marcus Thompson, and he's a commission agent with an office near Coenties Slip," Jemmy said. "Jenny said it's time she settled down and made a home for herself—maybe even have kids."

"Not a bad idea," Celine said. "Could be that it's time for you to do the same."

"I've never really given it much thought," he admitted. "I've always had too many other interests. I thought the same was true of my sister."

"The war'll soon be over," Celine said. "I'm sure you'll be able to find a girl who wants to get married."

"Married? Have children and all those problems?" Jemmy said, making a sour face. "Until now my life's been simple. And anyway, who are you to talk about getting married?"

"As soon as the war is over I intend to marry Franz."

"The German?"

"He's going to stay here and be an American."

"Little old Celine is going to try marriage *again*," Jemmy said maliciously.

Celine ignored his remark and turned to Beth. "Do you have any ideas about a girl for Jemmy?"

"Seth Cuyler has a niece who isn't married," Beth said. "Her name is Jane. I saw her only the other day."

"She's a skinny little twit," Jemmy said. "With hair in long braids hanging down the back of her neck."

"When was the last time you saw her?"

"Oh, maybe four years ago. Five? I don't know."

"I thought so," Beth said. "Jane Cuyler is a very pretty young woman. And she no longer wears her hair in braids."

"She's still a twit."

"I'm going down to the city tomorrow," Beth continued. "While I'm there I'll invite Jane up here for a few days."

"I think I'll be busy," Jemmy said.

"You just became unbusy," Celine said in a no-nonsense voice. "Besides, you think Jenny deserted you, right?"

"Right. She *did* desert me."

"Well, turn the tables on her. *You* desert *her*."

This last bit of perverse logic appealed to Jemmy, and he agreed to be available if Jane Cuyler came to spend a few days at the Place.

The next evening Beth returned from the city with Jane Cuyler in tow, and Jemmy surprised everyone by appearing for dinner dressed in a burgundy coat of velvet, silk kneebreeches and waistcoat, and a soft scarf of silk; quite a contrast from his usual scruffy self. If he had been interested in meeting this girl only to annoy his sister, he forgot about it when he took one look at her.

Twenty-one-year-old Jane Cuyler was petite, with great wide eyes, and silky blond hair that met her shoulders. She had a shy smile and spoke in a soft voice, but didn't miss much that went on about her.

"It's been a long time, Jemmy," she said.

"Y-you don't look anything l-like I remember you," Jemmy said.

"*You* do," Jane said. "And I always keep hearing about what you're doing. I heard about your boat that goes under the water. How wonderful! Tell me, are you doing anything more with it?"

Jemmy Sackett became Jane Cuyler's slave. Here was the answer to his sister's defection—another partner who would share his dreams and inventions.

"Would you like to go out in the river on it?" he asked.

"Don't do it," Celine warned. "He'll drown you before the day is over."

"I've been out in that boat more than twenty times, and I haven't drowned, have I?" Jemmy said in his own defense.

"You're not a fair example, you're like a cat with nine lives," Celine said. She turned to Jane. "The first thing you've got to learn is how to say no to Jemmy."

Jane looked coyly at the flushed man. "I don't think Jemmy would ask me to do anything I wouldn't want to do."

"That's right," Jemmy said indignantly. "Celine doesn't understand we're living in a free country."

Celine and Beth exchanged knowing glances.

"Now tell me more about your boat," Jane said, linking arms with Jemmy.

They walked together into the next room, chatting, delighted with one another. Celine laughed. "And to think we almost had to break his arm to get him to meet her."

"Maybe the twins will have a double wedding," Beth said. "Wouldn't that be ironic?"

"I'll bet David would be happy to hear the news. His kids have been driving him crazy since they were three."

"They'll find new ways to drive him crazy," Beth said.

"There they are!" Drew said in a tone of hushed suspense as he spied the first British ships coming toward them through the early-morning mist. There were almost two dozen ships in the British line of battle.

"And here *we* are," Alec Seixas said, waving his arm back in the direction where the forces of Admiral de Grasse were swinging into an opposing battle line.

It was a beautiful fall day as the two fleets moved ponderously toward one another. The Atlantic Ocean sparkled as the rising sun began to dissipate the mist, and the lands surrounding the mouth of Chesapeake Bay could be seen in the distance, behind the lifting curtain of gray.

"When the fighting starts, I want you to go below," Drew said to Peter, who stood at his side on the quarterdeck.

"It's no safer below," the boy said.

"How can you say that?"

"The British will aim for our lower gunports, and their cannonballs are more dangerous down there in a confined space," Peter explained patiently.

"That's the truth," Alec agreed. "There's no safe place aboard ship once a battle starts."

Drew swore under his breath and cursed himself again for having been duped into having the boy aboard. Celine would have his head if anything happened to her son.

He looked down along the deck of the handsome frigate and could see Dick Goelet at his gunner's post near the main port battery. For a man who claimed he abhorred violence, he had turned into a fair gunner.

The British fleet was coming to the aid of General Cornwallis, who was surrounded on the Virginia coast at Yorktown. Various units of General Washington's forces were assembling and encircling the besieged British commander, and the fleet was supposed to help relieve the pressure. Admiral de Grasse had moved his own flotilla into a position between the British land and sea forces. His intention was to drive off the enemy ships, thus leaving Cornwallis to his fate.

The French fleet was split into two files. The American privateers were stationed at the front of the starboard file and would engage a line of lumbering British frigates that carried supplies and troops. The privateers were not as large as the ships they were attacking, but were swifter and more maneuverable.

Alec proposed a novel method of attack to de Grasse, and the French admiral had the imagination to see that the daring plan had an excellent chance of surprising the tradition-minded English.

Alec proposed that just as the two lines were to pass alongside in the conventional method of fighting ships, his American and French ships switch tacks and cross in front of the bow of the first British ship. This vessel would then take a severe pounding during the run. Then Alec would swing around and make the next pass in back of this ship, but in front of the second British ship.

It was a risky plan, because there was a good chance the privateer could not clear out from in front of the second ship in time and would be rammed amidships. Alec, however, maintained that his ships were too swift to allow this to happen. The admiral told him to put his idea into action.

"By the time we've passed the first ship, she'll be in a shambles," Alec said.

"They might do the same to us as we turn to make our second pass," Drew warned.

"Not if we turn quickly enough," Alec said. "It's all a matter of speed and timing."

"I hope we're up to the task," Drew said skeptically, but there was nothing he could do to change what was about to occur. The file of three American ships followed by three swift French frigates sliced through the deep-blue water, coming closer and closer to the guns that bristled along the sides of the British ships.

Farther in the distance he could see the other ships of the French fleet moving toward the British line. The numbers today were on the side of the French, both in ships and guns. Since these were the two biggest fleets in the New World, the winner would own the coasts of America.

"The British don't understand what we're doing," Alec said to Peter. "See how they keep plodding ahead as if we were going to pass on their portside."

"How soon do we begin to turn?" the boy asked.

"I want to be within a hundred yards when we start blasting away," Alec said. "So we'll start the turn when we're about two hundred yards from them."

"Stand back here against this bulkhead," Drew said to his nephew. "It's about as safe a place as there is."

"You'll be able to see everything from there," Alec assured him.

The ships closed, and Alec gave the order that told the

helmsman to swing the wheel. The *Avenger*'s crew hauled at the lines, and the frigate set out smartly on her new course. The other ships followed the maneuver with a precision that justified Alec's faith in his captains and crews.

The *Avenger* came closer and closer to the British ship, whose perplexed captain stood on his quarterdeck wondering what trickery the enemy was using against him. He didn't have long to wait.

As the *Avenger*'s bow crossed in front of the Englishman, her guns began to boom, sending solid shot flying across the water. Some hit the hull itself. Rigging and spars were also blasted, and two holes were punched at the waterline.

The *Avenger* passed the Englishman, but the attack continued as the second privateer picked up the pounding. The other ships followed suit. The last ship—the sixth, a Frenchman—barely got out of the way: the bow of the British ship missed her stern by less than five feet.

By now the leading British ship was a burning wreck. Forty to fifty rounds had crashed into her; half her crew lay dead or dying on the decks. Her bow had a gaping hole in it, and water was rushing into her holds. She listed to starboard, her foremast and mainmast broken. The deck was cluttered with rigging, spars, torn canvas, and bits of railing.

"What a mess!" Peter said in awe.

"Look at the other Englishmen," Drew said. "They'll hold their line even though they can see what we did to one of them."

Alec's assessment held true. The British kept to their formal battle plan, and the American and French frigates cut through their line, isolating a single ship and ripping it to shreds. By noontime Alec's file had scored a tremendous victory.

The remainder of Admiral de Grasse's fleet, though not meeting with such spectacular success, was clearly victorious. By mid-afternoon the British admiral decided he had had enough and broke off the engagement. The remaining British ships limped north as the victorious French fleet regrouped at the mouth of the York River.

"So much for the theory that the British are masters of the sea," Alec said.

The British fleet did not regroup and resume the attack as de Grasse had suspected it would. The British admiral sailed up to New York Bay, informed General Clinton of the disaster, stayed in the area for a short time, and then took the bulk of his ships back to England.

De Grasse and his American allies kept the British army stranded at Yorktown while Washington built up his land forces. By the beginning of October almost seventeen thousand troops surrounded Cornwallis's army of slightly more than six thousand. The siege began, and the fighting moved toward its inevitable conclusion.

On the seventeenth of October, 1781, the British surrendered.

The troops of Lord Cornwallis's, as tradition required, marched out from their battlements between lines of cheering American and French troops. The British band marched out playing "The World Turned Upside Down." It was, certainly, a most fitting piece of music. The fledgling nation of the United States of America had defeated the combined army and naval forces of the mighty British Empire.

The marquis de Lafayette summed up everyone's feelings when he wrote in a letter: "The play, sir, is over."

No one was more aware of this truth than Lord Cornwallis himself.

General Washington proved to be a chivalrous victor. He invited the conquered British general to dine with himself and a few of his officers. Drew was invited, because, after all, it had been his family's money that had prevented a possible last-minute mutiny by the troops in New Jersey.

Peter—who was invited by the commander when he learned Mrs. Murray's son was with the fleet—accompanied his uncle, and the two sat between General Washington and Colonel Alexander Hamilton. Lord Cornwallis was directly across the table from the general.

"To the end of the war," Cornwallis said as he held up his goblet.

"We've won a battle," General Washington said. "As far as I know, the war isn't over."

Lord Cornwallis shook his head in disagreement. "This defeat will mean the fall of Lord North's ministry. The people back in England are tired of the constant drain on their resources."

"Our resources haven't been doing much better," Washington complained.

THE WORLD TURNED UPSIDE DOWN

"But you're only fighting one war," Cornwallis said. "The British Empire is engaged in many. We're fighting here, in the West Indies with the French and the Dutch, and in South Africa and Sumatra. Our forces in India are besieged, and we're at war with half the nations of Europe."

The British general was smiling sadly. "The least popular of our wars is this one in America. It's a nasty war that pits cousin against cousin."

"Lord Howe said almost the same thing to me only last year when I was in London," Drew said.

Cornwallis's eyebrows lifted up. "London? And now you appear here at Yorktown with a French fleet? Mr. de Kuyper, how do you explain such odd doings?"

"Drew was with Ben Franklin in Paris," Colonel Hamilton said. "They've been having a dialogue with your government. Not, obviously, that the talks have done much good."

"They've done *no* good, because the British Parliament refuses to accept reality," Drew said tartly.

"I understand Lord North has been offering terms that you would have been only too happy to accept not too long ago," Cornwallis said, voicing the British government's standard argument.

"Five years ago we would have accepted them," Hamilton said.

"Too much has happened in those five years, sir," General Washington said. "Too much blood's been shed, too many men killed."

"If North's ministry falls, what makes you think the next PM will act differently?" Drew asked.

"What else can a new man do?" Cornwallis said, holding his hands up in a gesture of resignation. "The reason for North's fall will be this war. The new man will have a mandate to end it. The prosperity of the Empire demands peace in America."

"Ben Franklin said the same thing," Peter chimed in. "He said if the British keep fighting, they'll soon be as poor as the French."

This information surprised both generals. "But how can you say France is poor?" Cornwallis asked in disbelief.

Drew concealed a smile as he listened to his twelve-year-old nephew lecture two of the most famous generals in the world about the realities of European finance.

"Mr. Franklin told me the French have given a great deal

of their wealth to help us win this war," Peter said. "He says they've almost emptied their coffers."

"Do you know just how much money the French have given to the Americans?" Cornwallis asked, looking at Washington.

"The Congress might know, but I don't."

Drew answered the question. "I may be a bit off, but the figure I heard quoted was in excess of a hundred and thirty million dollars."

Again, both generals were astounded.

"A hundred and thirty million dollars!" Washington exclaimed. "My God! I didn't think there was that much money in the world!"

"No wonder we haven't been able to beat you," Cornwallis complained.

"Drew's figure is fairly accurate," Alexander Hamilton said.

"You never told me," Washington said accusingly.

"I didn't want to bother you with details."

"No wonder the French are in trouble," Cornwallis said, his bad eye squinting more than usual. "They've spent more on this war than both England and America combined."

"Louis doesn't care," Peter said. "He says the only thing money is good for is to spend."

"Louis?" General Washington asked.

"The king of France," Drew said dryly.

"The king of France?"

"Yes, my nephew is on a first-name basis with His Majesty."

Lord Cornwallis broke into laughter. "And here I've been wondering why a boy was at table with us. Now I learn he's the personal representative of Louis XVI!"

"What sort of man is Louis?" Washington asked, and not only out of idle curiosity. The general realized that as an independent nation the United States would have to deal with France and her king. Young Peter's intimate knowledge of the man might prove valuable.

"He's a good man," Peter said. "Only I don't think he should be king. He doesn't really care about it."

"So we ourself have heard," Washington said.

"You used 'we,'" Peter observed. "Louis uses 'we,' too. He says it's because he speaks for all of France."

Colonel Hamilton suppressed a smile and looked away from Washington, who was turning red. The commander, of late, had indeed fallen into the habit of using the imperial 'we.' It was difficult for him *not* to act this way, since many people had already begun to treat him as if he were royalty. As a matter of fact, in some Philadelphia circles there was talk of creating a new monarchy and crowning General Washington king.

The general was opposed to this. "We're getting rid of one son of a bitch," he was reported to have said, "and these fools want to make me the next one."

"I'll try to remember not to use 'we,'" the general said.

"It sounded quite natural on your lips," Cornwallis observed. "What's wrong with an American king?"

"What we're interested in establishing here is a republic of equals who work together for the common good," Washington said.

"Surely you don't believe that all men are equal."

"Perhaps not, but I believe every man has the right to be treated equally under the law," Washington said. "A right your king has failed to grant us, hence this war."

"So all men will have an equal say in your government?" Cornwallis said.

"There will be certain requirements necessary before a man will have his say," the conservative Hamilton said. "Perhaps property requirements and the like."

"The fewer 'requirements,' the better," Washington grumbled.

"If we start setting property requirements for full citizenship, we'll be establishing a class system," Drew said. "I don't think that's what the United States is all about."

"A classless society..." Cornwallis said musingly. "I wish you luck."

General Washington understood that the aristocratic Englishman didn't think such an experiment could succeed. There were in America, as a matter of fact, a good number of men who thought as Cornwallis thought. "We'll need more than luck," Washington said. "We'll need hard work and a determination to succeed."

After dinner Peter and Drew walked back to their ship, which was anchored in the York River. "Mr. Franklin believes a classless society *will* succeed in America," the boy said. "He says that's because we have enough of everything to go around."

"Which is not true of Europe, is that it?"

Peter nodded. "Mr. Franklin said that when everything in America is owned, and things become hard to get—the way it is in Europe—then we'll have the same problems as they do."

"There's so much of America," Drew said, thinking of the maps he had seen where most of the continent was marked *terra incognita*. "Go inland a hundred miles and there's nothing but wilderness. God knows how far it stretches. It could take forever to tame such a land."

"Maybe we'll never run out of space the way they have in Europe," Peter said.

"It's not a question of running out of space," Drew said, "but in keeping it from being owned by only a few people like the kings and nobles in the European countries."

The next morning General Washington met with his officers and announced his plans.

He was moving the army north, because it was time to take New York back from the English. Admiral de Grasse was to take his fleet south to the Indies to clean out whatever British ships were left in the area.

Drew would take his three privateers north. He was to keep them in a secluded spot on the northern shore of Long Island, ready to be added to Washington's forces should an attack on the city be necessary.

"I hope it doesn't come to that," he said.

"So do I," Washington agreed. "We'll try to work out a peace treaty before I do anything."

"Adding the destruction of New York to the list of war casualties doesn't make sense."

"I agree," Washington said. "Remember it was I who wouldn't order Nathan Hale to burn it a number of years ago."

Drew smiled. "That seems so long ago—almost as if it happened in another life."

"It did happen in another life," the general said. "We were British subjects then. Now we're Americans."

When Drew, Peter, and Dick Goelet walked through the front door of the Place, everyone in the house swooped down on them.

Celine almost squeezed the breath from her son. Drew was amazed to see the stream of tears that poured out of her eyes. "Oh dear, oh dear, oh dear," she said over and over again.

She went to the desk in the parlor and pulled out the letters Peter had sent to her from France. She had saved them all.

"I read each one at least a dozen times," she said. "Every time I received one, it was as if you were paying a visit."

"I'm not paying a visit now," the boy said. "I'm home for good."

Jenny Sackett was there with her fiancé, Marcus Thompson, and announced they were getting married in the spring. A little while later Jemmy showed up with Jane Cuyler and, not to be outdone by his sister, announced that he too was getting married in the spring.

"Giving up your freedom, are you?" Drew said.

"Marrying Jane isn't giving up anything," Jemmy replied.

"How about all your inventions?"

"What about them?"

"Aren't you going to settle down?"

"What does that have to do with getting married? Jane will help me in my work."

Somehow this made sense to Drew. He shook his head. He'd definitely been away too long when it seemed to him that Jemmy Sackett started to make sense.

"Look at Peter," Mary Delafield said to Beth Henry when the two women came into the room. "He's almost a man."

Beth smiled. "He's been a man for a long time."

Peter blushed when Beth kissed him on the cheek. The last time he had seen her, he'd been only a boy; a kiss was a harmless thing. But he was changing rapidly, and his perception of Beth was changing too.

Marie Therese hugged her son and her grandson, managing to fight back the tears of happiness. "The men in my life!" she said. "It's good to have you back."

"I agree," Beth said, looking straight at Drew. "This is where you belong."

Drew suddenly became uncomfortable. He was seeing Beth for the first time as others saw her; she was a beautiful woman, everything they said of her was true, and more, he thought.

Dick sensed what was going on in his cousin's mind and had seen the way Beth looked at him. It was time to do something about it.

"Drew is engaged to be married," he said to Marie Therese, but his words were meant for Beth.

"Married? To whom?" Marie Therese said.

Drew's throat suddenly felt dry. "Her name is Althea Middleton. She's the daughter of an English peer."

A stricken look crossed Beth's face, but she said nothing.

"Well, you certainly bring surprises with you," Marie Therese said. She avoided looking at Beth, because she was aware of how the girl felt about her son. "I guess congratulations are in order."

"Yes," Beth said. "I hope you'll be very happy." She turned and walked from the room. There was a long, uncomfortable silence, broken finally by Celine.

"When do we get to meet this lucky girl?"

"We're planning on a spring wedding in England. You'll be there, of course. And we'll both bring her back after that."

"I can't wait," Celine said acidly, making no pretense at disguising her displeasure. She turned to Peter. "Come upstairs. I want to show you what I've done to your room."

Later Marie Therese managed to draw her son off alone. "Beth wasn't too happy about your wedding plans," she said.

Drew shook his head. "I don't understand. There's never been anything between the two of us. Now I find everyone has been matching us up. Don't you think they should have asked me first?"

Marie Therese sighed. "Yes, but you can't always expect people to act logically."

"Well, logic or no, I'm going to marry Althea."

"If that's what you want."

"It is."

Marie Therese patted his hand. "Then I'm on your side."

The next morning Drew saddled a horse and rode to the city. After stabling his mount, he walked around the streets he knew so well. It was a depressing experience.

New York had once been a thriving place, with goods from all over the world for sale in its shops and markets. Now many of the shops were boarded up; some others were empty buildings that had been gutted in the fire. The markets still existed, but the goods were few and the prices astronomical. Many of the buildings that had been destroyed in the fire had never been rebuilt. People still lived in tents and hastily constructed shacks. There was a shabbiness to the city and its inhabitants.

The Broad Way area had fared better than the rest of the city, because that was the area populated by the English conquerors. Here, at least, the homes looked well cared for.

Yet only a block off the main thoroughfare, he could see rows of tents that people called home.

Broad Street made him morose. In former times there had

been many prosperous commercial houses here, but now they were boarded up and ignored; empty shells where rats and mice squabbled and cats came to hunt.

Stone Street. Bridge Street. Dock Street. All the same: quiet, unprosperous. These were the bones of a dying city.

"Drew!"

He turned and smiled when he saw Alice de Witt with Elly, who was now a splendid-looking nine-year-old. They kissed each other on the cheek and then gossiped for a few minutes.

"We're going over to the Swan & Bear for lunch," Alice said. "We're eating with Caleb North. Why don't you join us?"

Soon Drew was seated at a table near the small fire with Alice and Caleb. Elly was seated across the room with several girls of her own age. "Sorry about the size of the fire," Caleb said. "But the price of wood is not to be believed—another challenge to be met."

"Just staying alive these days is a challenge," Alice said; but from the way she looked at Caleb, it was obvious some aspects of her life were happy. In turn, the innkeeper was very protective and possessive with the woman.

"Thank God the war is coming to an end," Caleb said. "Now it's only a matter of time before the British clear out."

"The sooner the better," Alice said, helping herself to more tea. She poured some more for Drew and looked thoughtful. "For a spell we didn't have any tea," she said. "Somehow the world isn't such a bad place when you're able to pour yourself a nice hot cup of tea."

"Do you still work at our offices?" Drew asked.

"Yes, but there isn't all that much to do. David Sackett spends most of his time in Philadelphia with the Congress. And our business has more or less come to a standstill."

"We'll have to change all that," Drew said determinedly. "As soon as I return from England."

"England? Why are you going there?" Caleb asked.

Drew told them of his plans to marry Althea, and Alice and Caleb exchanged glances. Drew saw this, but made no comment. Here were two more people who knew about his non-existent romance with Beth, he thought sourly.

"I hope you'll be happy," Alice said. "Happier than my marriage made me."

Drew had avoided the subject of Enoch, but now that she had brought it up, he asked her about her husband.

She sighed. "He's around. Still drinks. Lives the life of a bum. I rarely see him, and then it's only by accident."

"Bloody shame, what he's done to Alice," Caleb said. "If you want the truth, I'd like to marry Alice. But how can I do that while she's got a husband?"

Alice reached out and touched Caleb's arm. "Life has a way of working things out."

Drew wandered around the docks after lunch. He was disturbed by the lack of activity. He finally wandered over to Pearl Street and went into Fraunces Tavern.

Sam Fraunces let out a whoop of delight when he saw him. "Another of the old bully boys has returned. Pretty soon it'll be like old times."

Drew accepted the large mug of ale the proprietor thrust into his hands, but he soon switched to the fiery ale-and-rum favored by dedicated drinkers. Within an hour he was joined by Seth Cuyler and Dick Goelet, and the three of them swapped stories with the other men who gathered about the fire.

By seven o'clock Drew's head was spinning: the drink; the depression he felt when he looked about his city; his family's cold acceptance of his forthcoming marriage; his own realization that he had, perhaps, been mistaken about Beth Henry— all these things made him terribly tired. Sam Fraunces offered him a bed in one of the small rooms on the second floor of the tavern.

After Drew was gone, the owner winked at Seth and Dick. "Maybe we ought to send a young lady up to entertain him."

"Good idea," Seth said. "Got anyone in mind?"

Sam whispered quietly to a newly arrived servant girl from the Indies. She was a buxom lass with a wicked gleam in her eye. She agreed to do her part to make young de Kuyper feel at home.

However, she had been gone only about fifteen minutes when she reappeared in the taproom.

"That was quick," Fraunces said.

"That was *nothing*," the girl said.

"What happened?"

"I just told you. Nothing. He's asleep."

"And you couldn't wake him up?" Dick asked.

The girl shook her head. "Men are not like that down in the islands."

Sam Fraunces laughed. "Drew's got a lot on his mind. The war, probably."

THE WORLD TURNED UPSIDE DOWN

"War is no good for pecker," the girl said sagely.

Sam Fraunces couldn't disagree with her.

The year 1781 drew to a close, and New York was still in the hands of the British.

General Clinton's headquarters at 1 Broad Way was no longer the scene of happy parties. The British remained, but they lived on the island in the middle of a sea of rebels.

Washington resisted the urgings of his officers to attack the island and drive the British out. He claimed it was only a matter of time before Ben Franklin got the British to sign a peace treaty.

Noah Henry proposed to Mary Delafield and was accepted. They were married immediately, although Noah was still in the army and living at the winter quarters at Morristown.

Drew and Marie Therese left for Europe on a privateer that was carrying several diplomats back to England to advance the peace negotiations.

With Drew gone and Franz von Lossow and Noah over at Morristown, life at the Place settled down to a quiet time of waiting. Peter no longer went off hunting with Beth; instead he became enamored of anything that had to do with ships. He read books. He made frequent trips to the docks. Ships and shipping became a burning passion.

"Your grandpa would have liked to see this," Celine said. "He loved ships, too."

"Grandpa once told me that ships were the most beautiful things in the world."

"Some men think women are more beautiful," Celine said playfully.

Peter nodded. "I suppose. But a man must be serious about his work. I think mine will have to do with ships."

"Don't be serious all the time. Have some fun, too."

"You can say that because you're a woman," Peter said very seriously. "People expect more from a man."

"That's old-fashioned," Celine protested. "Work is just as important to a woman."

Peter didn't argue with her, but she could tell from his expression that he didn't agree. Her own son was a snotty little kid, she thought.

She brought the subject up when she was alone with Beth. To her surprise, Beth agreed with Peter. "Most people don't take women seriously," she said. "That's because we don't even take ourselves seriously. We're expected to sit around and look decorative."

"How can you say that about yourself?"

"We don't really have control over our lives at times. Look at me. I'm in love with your brother. What good does it do? He makes all the decisions."

"You missed your chance when he was here," Celine said.

"But he announced he was going to marry another woman," Beth protested. "What could I do?"

"You could have figured out a way to get him into bed with you."

"That's crude!"

"It might have done some good, however. My brother's one of those men who carry on about their honor. After he'd had his way with you in bed, he might have felt he had to marry you."

"I don't want him if I have to do things like that to get him."

Celine shrugged. "My motto is get what you want any way you can get it."

"You didn't have to trick Franz to marry you. He wants to do it."

"Yes, and my dear brother would want to marry you, if you made it easy for him."

"It's too late."

"Maybe not. Life plays strange tricks on us," Celine said philosophically.

On Christmas day a heavy snowfall blanketed the city, and a severe period of cold followed. A dozen people living in ramshackle quarters were found frozen to death.

Hard upon the heels of the American victory at Yorktown, the deaths were a sobering reminder that New York was still not a free city, and that many of its people lived with scarcity and want.

In England the diplomats sat around a table and dickered over the wording of the peace treaty, while life for the average New Yorker was much the same as the year before, and the year before that.

7

Patriots, Heroes, and Lovers

1783

"WE *MUST* KEEP THE BEDROOM FIRE GOING ALL DAY long," Althea complained. "With this cold weather, it isn't enough to burn it only at night."

Drew shrugged. It was January fifth, and New York was held fast in the grip of icy winter. Althea had done nothing but complain since her new husband had brought her from England the preceding fall, and the complaints had increased as the temperature had decreased.

"All right," he agreed. "We'll find wood somewhere."

"No one ever told me the weather here was so cold," she said in an injured tone. "It *never* gets this cold back home."

"You agreed we'd try to make this our home," he reminded her.

"Yes, well, but that was before I knew how *unpleasant* New York could become. I can't *understand* why anyone would want to stay here when they could live in a *civilized* place like England."

Drew sighed. It was about the hundredth time she had made this statement in the past week. Each time, her air of astonishment made the complaint sound like a brand-new thought.

She sat down in the chair closest to the fire in the kitchen hearth. She groaned and patted her stomach, which clearly revealed her six-months pregnancy; a new de Kuyper was expected around the beginning of April—another source of irritation, because in Althea's opinion it would have been far better for the child to be born in England. Now, however, it was far too late to contemplate the rigors of a winter ocean crossing.

Drew went over to the fireplace and threw on several logs to forestall further complaints about the lack of heat. If it hadn't been for his sister, who was able to spare him a supply of wood, there would have been a great deal more unpleasantness in the house on Maiden Lane.

Soon after Drew had brought his bride to New York, he reopened the house, which had been closed up ever since King's College had moved to other quarters. During the week they had all lived together at the Place, Marie Therese had decided it would be better if she stayed there with Celine in order not to interfere with the newlyweds. "They've problems enough without a mother-in-law underfoot," she told her daughter. In the intervening months she had never stopped congratulating herself on the decision. Living in the same house with the nagging English girl would be intolerable. She pitied her son.

Well, it was Drew's own doing, she thought, and he would have to live with it—especially now, with a baby on the way. There were some decisions in life that, once made, could not be taken back.

"How come we've never been invited to Guy Carleton's house for dinner?" Althea asked, referring to the newly appointed British commander in chief of New York. "Papa said he was going to write to Guy, as they're old friends."

"It would hardly be fitting for me to have dinner at the English commander's house," Drew pointed out. "After all, I was quite an active rebel."

"Oh, for pity's sake, the war's over, everybody knows that."

"Yes, but the treaty hasn't been signed and the British still occupy New York. General Washington has had a terrible time restraining his own officers this past year. They want to attack the city and drive the British out. The general insists on waiting for the treaty, which he claims will be signed any time now. Then the British will leave peacefully."

"And take what little civilization there is here with them."

Drew didn't bother answering. He'd heard all this before, too.

Althea picked up the piece of lacework she had been passing the time with. After less than a minute she dropped the fabric and sighed loudly. "I'm bored. There isn't *anything* to do in this place. Except freeze."

Again, he didn't bother answering. Even if he had responded, it wouldn't have mattered to his wife. Her objections to New York, New Yorkers, and Americans in general never varied, and she never listened to any of his defenses or answers.

It had been a terrible mistake to marry her and bring her here, Drew realized. But she was his wife and soon would have his baby. How could any man walk out on that situation? But also, how could they go on like this? And for how long?

"Why are your people taking so long to sign the treaty?" she asked.

"I believe it's more the fault of the British than ourselves," he answered.

"Well, *whoever* is behind the delay, they're making asses of themselves," she said, dismissing all the negotiating diplomats, of whatever country, with a wave of her hand. "They ought to sign it and be done with it."

It was one of the rare instances in which he totally agreed with his wife.

The year 1782 had come and gone, and the treaty still wasn't signed, despite all that had happened during that twelve-month period.

On the fifth of March the members of the House of Commons had passed a bill authorizing the Crown to make peace with the former colonies.

On the twentieth of the same month, Lord North's government had fallen, and the prime minister was replaced by Lord Rockingham, a man who had long been a friend of the Americans.

On the fourth of April Sir Guy Carleton had replaced General Henry Clinton as commander of the British forces in New York, and he had immediately recalled to the city all troops that had been based in Connecticut and Long Island. There were now more than ten thousand British soldiers on Manhatan, and very few people doubted Washington when he said that a major battle with them would mean the destruction of New York.

April twelfth saw the beginning of the peace talks in Paris. Leading the American delegation was Benjamin Franklin. The talks continued through the spring and summer, and were still going on in September, when the prime minister, Lord Rockingham, died and was replaced by the Earl of Shelburne.

By the end of the year, the main points of the treaty had been agreed upon:

1) Britain recognized United States independence.
2) The boundaries between the United States and Canada were agreed upon and drawn up.
3) The United States was granted fishing rights off the coasts of Nova Scotia.
4) The territory known as Florida was formally ceded to Spain.
5) Debts due citizens of either the United States or Britain by citizens of the other country were deemed valid and collectible.

However, the final set of peace articles had not been signed as of this January fifth, 1783, and the hostilities had not technically ended—although everyone accepted that in fact they had.

They would have to sign the peace treaty soon, Drew reasoned, and then things could go back to normal and he might be able to convince his wife that her new home wasn't all that bad a place. At least this was his hope, but every day brought new evidence that he was living in a fool's paradise.

"Really, these *servants* you have in *this house!*" Althea said, finding a new complaint to voice to Drew. "They just don't know how to do *anything*. I'm forced to correct them all the time. It's almost like having no servants at all."

"They have to get used to your ways, Althea. Once they understand what you want, they'll be fine."

"We'll see."

Drew found an excuse to leave the room. In this he was following the example of the servants, who constantly contrived ways to stay out of whatever room enclosed their griping mistress.

So when there was a knock at the back door, there was only one person in the room to hear it. Althea made a sour face as she got out of her chair and walked to the door.

Drew was attending to some correspondence at the desk in the parlor when he heard his wife's loud shriek. He jumped up and dashed for the kitchen.

Althea had backed away from the open door and was staring in horror at the tattered-looking man standing at the threshold. He was bearded and wore a long, ill-fitting coat, and looked as if it had been a long time since any soap or water had touched his face.

"What's the matter with you?" Enoch de Witt asked Althea just as Drew entered the room. The visitor transferred his attention to him.

"Is this your wife? I've never met her. What's wrong with her?" he asked, shifting his eyes back to the woman, who was acting as if she thought he might attack her.

"Althea, what are you thinking of?" Drew said sharply. "This is Enoch de Witt. He's a cousin of mine," he added, eyeing Enoch and half empathizing with his wife in her alarm at finding such a man at her door. At least Enoch wasn't falling-down drunk and incoherent, he thought; thank God for little favors.

"Your *cousin*? Him?" Althea said scornfully.

"What can I do for you, Enoch?" Drew asked, annoyed by his wife's behavior.

"I just thought it time to pay my respects and welcome you back to New York. Wanted to meet your new wife, too, although I can see that was a bad idea," he added, stroking the end of his beard in short, nervous motions.

"Althea, where are your manners?" Drew asked. "Welcome my cousin to our house."

"I will not. He looks like a tramp. My God! What if we had guests? People who *counted*. I'd be *mortified*."

Enoch stared at her for a moment, then looked at Drew and shrugged. "Sorry I caused all this trouble, Cousin. I'll be on my way."

"Come in, Enoch, you're welcome in my house," Drew said evenly. "Perhaps you'd like a cup of hot tea to help ward off the cold?"

"Ah... tea is fine," Enoch said, and took it upon himself to shut the door behind him. "But it would be even better if you added something that gave it a bit of authority."

Drew smiled. He didn't approve of Enoch, nor of the way he lived. But you could say one thing for the man—he was consistent.

"I'm not staying in the same room with this man," Althea said, tapping her toe on the floor.

"Then you'll have to leave the room, I'm afraid," Drew said.

"Leave my *own kitchen*?"

"If you act like a brat, I'll treat you like one."

"Well!" she said, and her petite features seemed to close up. She whirled about and stalked from the room, her nose high in the air.

"Listen, Cousin, I didn't come here to cause trouble between you and your wife. I'd better go."

"You're going to stay here and have a drink, dammit!" Drew said, and grabbed a bottle of rum from the sideboard.

"Well, if you put it that way..." Enoch said, looking appreciatively at the full bottle.

Althea retreated to her bedroom, where the fireplace was consuming several new logs that had been placed on top of a thick bed of embers. She took one look at the height of the flames, went back into the hallway, and called for a servant. She waited as the black houseman looked skeptically at the fire.

"Too big a fire is dangerous, ma'am," he said.

"Just shut up and do as you're told."

He went to the woodbox and added more logs. Then he left the room, and Althea was alone, standing in front of the roaring blaze, considering her predicament.

New York was impossible.

She would have her baby, and then she would return to England. It was the only answer. There would be no debate about it with Drew, no argument, no discussion, no change of mind.

She didn't even care whether her husband went back with her. Drew had seemed wonderful in England—lively, sophisticated, worldly-wise. Here she saw him in a different light. He was one of the *rebels*—a colonial bumpkin who thought New York splendid instead of what it really was—a provincial sewer with nothing at all to recommend it.

"Bumpkin!" she said aloud.

Even the house depressed her. She looked out the window and saw a frozen street, a few scruffy people, and a row of depressing houses. How she longed for the beauty of an English garden! A *formal* garden with roses and hyacinths and carnations. The view from the Maiden Lane house contained no flowers. Never mind that it was winter and flowers would bloom here in the spring; all she knew was that she wanted flowers now, and there were none.

She patted the swelling in her belly. A boy? Yes, she hoped

it would be a boy. An *American* boy? She shuddered at the thought. Not *her* son!

She began to go through her wardrobe and pretended to select a gown to wear to this evening's ball, although she knew there weren't any balls in New York these days. But even pretending was better than nothing.

The thought of leaving this place and returning to England with her son pleased her, and she began to hum a little ditty.

George Gerait carefully placed the wedge in the split log and picked up the twenty-pound sledgehammer. Peter was watching him. "The idea is to drive the iron wedge down far enough so the log splits completely apart," George said.

Peter nodded. He watched as the black man raised the hammer over his head and brought it down with tremendous force. The log split neatly into two equal parts.

"See?"

"Good," Peter said in a flat tone. He wasn't too impressed. When a man was as heavily muscled as George, it didn't seem to be much of a feat to split a log. But he liked George, and was polite.

"Shall I do another?"

"Sure."

After the battle at Yorktown, George had come to New York and visited the house at Beekman's Place to see his uncle, Primus. It seemed his visit was turning out to be permanent, because Primus had taken one look at his nephew's mighty frame and immediately put him to work—and had kept him busy thereafter. George was an educated man and wouldn't be content with such menial work for long, but there wasn't much opportunity to try anything else until the British evacuated the city. In the meantime, George lived and worked at the Place.

As Peter was watching George work, Beth Henry returned to the house. She was wearing her deerskins. Ever since Drew had arrived from Europe with his wife, she had withdrawn more and more into herself, and had almost no diversion except hunting. Dick Goelet had tried courting her, but had been rebuffed, and none too gently. "Leave me alone," she had snapped when he had asked her to go riding.

"Catch anything?" Peter asked her now.

Beth shook her head. She looked up at the sky. "A storm is coming and the animals have taken cover."

"Franz left a little while ago," he informed her.

"He was here only one day this time."

Peter nodded. Franz and Celine's situation was frustrating both of them. She wanted to get married, and so did he, but he insisted on waiting until Washington disbanded his army— and that meant until the British were gone.

"It's difficult for your mother," Beth said. "Franz appears, then disappears."

"She's not delighted," Peter said in quiet understatement.

"It must be hard on you, too."

"I'm not the one who's in love."

"When people are in love they should be together," Beth said with conviction.

Peter had a quick mind and was maturing rapidly. A year ago he might not have observed the sadness in her voice, nor understood the cause. But now he knew.

"I'm sorry about you and Drew," he said. "I'm sure he'd be much happier with you than with that woman."

"You don't like her, I take it?"

Peter smiled. "Who does? Certainly not my mother. And my grandmother avoids her. I'm beginning to think even Drew doesn't like her anymore."

"It's sad. And now she's going to have his baby," she said.

"All these people getting married and finding happiness," Peter said thoughtfully. "All except Drew."

It was true. Noah Henry and Mary Delafield had gotten married and, clearly, were delighted with one another. Noah doted on little David as if the boy were his own flesh and blood. By tacit consent, the lad was universally known as David Henry.

Jenny Sackett was now Mrs. Marcus Thompson, and she was expecting a baby. The change in her had been startling. From tomboyhood she had changed into a dainty and fastidious woman, allowing her husband to do things for her that she was perfectly capable of doing for herself. He would pull out a chair, and she would smile and act as if she had been used to such accommodation all her life. A year ago she would have snatched the chair away from any man rash enough to try such a thing.

Jemmy was also married, and so blissfully content with Jane Cuyler that there were times he appeared to glow. He was still involved with his inventions and schemes, of course, but his wife was his partner.

"I never go down to the Maiden Lane house anymore," Beth said. "Althea makes everything so unpleasant."

"Nobody goes there if they don't have to," Peter agreed. "Even my grandmother. When she avoids something, you know it must be really rotten."

Beth chuckled. "You shouldn't say things like that."

"Why not, if it's the truth?"

Inside the house, Celine and Marie Therese were discussing the same topic.

"I swear I'll haul off and bust her in the mouth," Celine said, continuing to go through the stack of records of all the goods that had passed through the Place when it had been used as a secret storage depot by General Washington. The Congress had asked for such records because, it said, it wished to repay all the people who had been so generous during the lean years. The fact that the new government had no money made Celine wonder why she was bothering to go to all this trouble.

"Don't talk that way about your sister-in-law," Marie Therese said. "She's from a different world and has a lot of adjustments to make here."

"I'll agree with that," Celine said, nodding her head. "The real problem is that he doesn't love her."

"How can you say that?"

"Because of a few things he's said to me."

"Like what?"

"You really want to know?"

"Yes."

"Well," Celine said, taking a deep breath, and then plunging ahead. "For one thing she virtually trapped him into asking her to marry him."

"I didn't know that."

"And the poor jerk decided it was a matter of honor and he wouldn't back out. Can you believe it? Your son's destroying his life because of a point of honor. Men are such fools."

"Speaking of sons," Marie Therese said, deciding it was time to change the subject. "Peter is certainly turning out to be a young man with a good head on his shoulders."

"One of the good de Kuypers," Celine said. "More like his grandfather than me. Maybe that happens in families—there's a generation with sense, then one without, then back again to one that has it."

"Don't be unkind to yourself."

"I'm serious," Celine said. "Neither Drew nor I seem able

to do the things that will make us happy. Peter will be different, I hope."

"I do see a lot of his grandfather in Peter," Marie Therese agreed. "But I'm bound to be prejudiced. One was my husband, the other my only grandson."

"You might have another grandson soon."

"That's right. Althea is due in April."

"It'll be interesting to see what happens then."

"You mean all her talk about going back to England?"

Celine nodded. "I think she's going to do it. The question is whether or not Baby Brother is stupid enough to go back with her."

"He won't go back with her," Marie Therese said without hesitation. "I know my son, and he'll never live anywhere but New York."

"Let her go back. We've spent the past seven years trying to drive the British out, and Baby Brother is going around marrying them and breeding more."

Marie Therese tried to suppress her laugh and failed. "I never thought of it that way. And I'm sure Drew hasn't either."

"It's about time he did. And to think he once questioned the propriety of my being seen with a Hessian!"

"Franz is a good man," Marie Therese said. "I think you'll have a happy life with him."

Celine sighed. "I know. The only problem is—when is it going to begin?"

"I respect him for staying with Washington until the war is officially over. He's a man of honor."

"Honor! God save us from men of honor! All they seem to do is wreck everyone else's life."

"You'll live," Marie Therese said dryly.

"There were times when you were separated from Father," Celine said, ignoring her mother's jibe. "Didn't you ever get where you wanted to scream and climb the walls?"

"Of course, but I always knew it was only a temporary separation."

"It's the same with me. I know I'll see Franz again. But in the meantime it's hard to go on with a normal life."

"I'm very happy for you, Celine," Marie Therese said.

"Happy?"

"Because when I hear you talk about Franz this way I know you must really love him. We had this discussion once before, remember? I told you I hoped you'd find a man to love the way I loved your father."

"I remember."

"Well, my dear, I think you've found him. Your life will be complete."

Celine took her mother's hand and pressed it against her own cheek. "You know... I think so, too."

Beth returned to her room and saw a sealed letter on the desk near the door. She recognized the seal, picked up the letter, and opened it.

It was another letter from William Henry, the duke of Clarence, the third she had received since his return to England. The prince spoke of hunting grouse and fox and of the pleasures to be found in London. In the third paragraph he got around to the real point of the letter: to invite Beth once again to come to London as his guest. He would be delighted to make all the arrangements, including the use of a fine house not far from the royal residence.

Beth had no illusions about what the prince was asking her to do.

If she would come to London, he would put her up in luxury and fulfill her every desire—if she would fulfill his. Not long ago she would have been angered and torn the letter to shreds. Now? She wasn't so sure. After all, what was there to keep her in New York? The heart and soul of the place seemed to have departed with the arrival of Althea Middleton de Kuyper.

Mistress to a prince...

She thought about it for a few minutes, and then dropped the letter back onto the desk. Like the ones preceding it, this one would go unanswered.

She went to her bed and stretched out on it. She lay rigid, her eyes on the ceiling. *Hopeless* was the word that kept entering her mind. She would not cry. What good would it do? What good would anything do?

She lay still for a long time. But there came a point when she could no longer remain in control of her emotions, and she rolled over on her stomach and her tears ran into the pillow.

It was the fifteenth day of March.

The sun shone brightly, foretelling the imminent arrival of spring. An early-morning misty rain had cleansed the streets and the houses, and the air was crisp.

Patrick Blakely was taking a morning inspection walk near the west-side docks. There wasn't much activity. A few ships were tied up or anchored, but not nearly as many as in bygone days. The constant comings and goings of troops had stopped. There was a strange lassitude about the men he saw. With not much work to do, there was no great hurry to get on with it. He remembered the docks when they had been crammed to capacity with ships—loading and unloading cargoes and troops, the streets around piled high with crates, barrels, boxes, and bales.

The war was truly over, he thought; he was already drawing up plans for the withdrawal of thousands of troops from the city. Also, there were the loyalists to be considered: thousands of them had requested passage to Canada or England. These people no longer wished to live in America if it was not under the sceptre of the king of England.

He came to Little Dock Street and saw a sight that brought a smile to his lips. On a chair outside a dilapidated building a man sat with his shirt off, enjoying the sun. It was still not warm enough for such a pastime, and the captain wondered what was wrong with the fellow. Blakely looked closer and recognized him as a fixture around the docks—a tramp, another piece of human wreckage. That explained it: no doubt the man had consumed so much rum or gin that, with the help of the sun's rays, it kept him warm. The captain was about to move on when the man opened his eyes and looked up.

Enoch de Witt knew who the captain was; everyone in New York knew the deputy provost marshal. Last fall all the prisons and prison ships had been emptied, and the newly freed men told tales of the degradation that had taken place in the British penal institutions. Almost to a man they placed the blame for such conditions on Captain Blakely; he had been in charge of it all. It had been his under-officers who ran the places, his orders that had kept the prisoners half-starved and ill-treated by their brutal guards.

But this morning Enoch was feeling mellow. He had drunk a great deal the previous night and wakened with his usual hangover, but the bright sun appealed to him after the rigors of winter.

"Good morning," he said pleasantly.

The captain nodded and started to pass on, having no desire to engage in small talk with this man.

Enoch called to him. "Captain Blakely!"

"Yes?"

"Soon you'll be leaving us, Captain. I hope when you sail you have as fine a day as this."

The captain didn't know whether the man was being sincere, or mocking. In either event, he was annoyed.

"I'll still be here after you're dead and buried," he said.

"With the way I live, Captain, there's a good chance of that," Enoch agreed. "But I wouldn't bet on it."

"And after I leave, what about yourself? I suppose you'll go back to being the powerful, successful man you were?"

Enoch smiled, having caught the sarcasm in Blakely's voice. "Ah, for sure I was never that, nor will I ever be. But at least I'll be living as a free man in a free country."

"Free to starve."

"Perhaps," Enoch said, and then he became bolder. "But in the meantime you could save me from such a fate by offering me a bit of work."

It was the last thing Blakely expected. "Work? What work can you do?"

"Anything that doesn't require too much thinking or a steady hand," Enoch said. "I'm not a proud man, so anything at all will do."

The man was a tramp, and a drunk, and probably worse, the captain thought. But despite it all he had retained some spunk, and this appealed to Blakely's Irish nature. It also amused him that in one breath the man was bragging about being free, and in the next asking the man who had been his conqueror for work.

"What's your name?"

"Enoch de Witt. A noble name, sir, and far too good for me, but that's the way it is."

"Old Dutch family?"

"Way back. One of the first here. But I doubt if my ancestors would care to admit I came from their seed."

Blakely smiled. "Can you clean out a building?" he asked. "I warn you, it's as filthy as a pigsty."

"Why not?"

"The prison section of the Provost is empty," Blakely explained. "After all those years of holding prisoners, it needs a good cleaning. Do you want the job?"

"As long as you don't expect me to show up every day," Enoch said honestly.

"Start whenever you want. I'll tell the sergeant-of-the-guard to expect you."

"The pay?"

"A shilling a day."

"Make it two, Captain. Be generous to a conquered foe."

Blakely thought he detected a tinge of sarcasm. After all, who was the conquered here? But he let it pass. "Two it is, but only for the days you work."

"Ah, Captain, among my many other faults I also count honesty. Fear not, I shall take only what is due me."

Blakely nodded and walked away. He arrived back at the Provost and his footsteps echoed as he strode down the empty corridor. He was displeased by the quiet and the inactivity. He entered his office, placed his hat on the rack, and sat down in the chair behind the desk.

That drunk had been right. He would soon be leaving New York. His promotion to major would be coming through, and he would be posted somewhere else. The only thing wrong with it all was that he would be leaving New York as a member of a defeated army; leaving like a whipped dog with his tail between his legs.

He couldn't leave that way. No, he would have to do something to show his contempt for these Americans.

But what?

He sat at his desk for over an hour, wracking his brain for a plan. He dismissed idea after idea. Then he began thinking about the great fire he had caused not long after the beginning of the occupation. The effects of that little scheme were still to be seen all over the city.

But the situation this time was different: then he had wanted to do something to provoke General Howe into giving him a free hand to discipline the rebels; now he wanted to leave behind a symbol of the emptiness the rebels had won for themselves.

And then the idea came to him.

The British had occupied a number of public buildings in New York—the Provost, the commander's quarters, the military and naval headquarters, hospitals, churches, and many other buildings.

Why not destroy them?

The easiest way would be with fire. He hated to repeat himself, but fire would have to do. The public buildings would burn, and the rebels would be forced to find new places to house their government. Good. Let them start from scratch.

The captain opened a desk drawer and took out a sheet of paper. He began to draw up a list of buildings to be targeted.

The name Patrick Blakely would long be remembered in New York, he thought.

It was the first week of April.

The group in the private quarters at the back of the Swan & Bear tavern was in a festive mood. Alice de Witt had finally taken the step she had long been planning—moving in with Caleb North, ignoring that her husband was still alive and living in the city. It had never been much of a marriage, and now it was dead.

"You look wonderful," Mary Henry said to her hostess. "You should have done this a long time ago."

Alice did, indeed, look the picture of health and happiness; relaxed and content with life now that she had worked things out for herself and eleven-year-old Elly. Living in a home with a man was good for the child, and she was blossoming into a fine young lady.

"I guess we get smarter as we get older," Alice said.

"Let's face it, we both had terrible first marriages," Mary said with disarming honesty. "I've been happier since I married Noah than ever before in my life."

"I'd like to marry Caleb, but—"

Mary patted the other woman's hand. "Don't worry about being conventional. These are unconventional times we live in."

"It's kind of you to say that."

"It's the simple truth."

They were in the large keeping room that served as parlor, dining room, and kitchen at the back of the tavern. Caleb had opened a new pipe of Madeira, and his eyes widened as he took his first sip.

"Here," he said, handing the pewter cup to Noah Henry. "Take a sip of this."

Noah did as he was bid, and nodded his head. "This is the real thing. Where did you get it?"

"Last week a ship arrived from the Canaries. I made sure I got my share."

"I guess things are getting back to normal," David Sackett

said, holding up his own mug for Caleb to fill. "About time! The Articles of Peace were ratified over two months ago."

"I hear several boatloads of loyalists are due to leave the port within the next few weeks," Caleb said.

David nodded. "The British have offered free passage to anyone wishing to return to England. More than twenty thousand have taken advantage so far. I suspect the number will be a lot larger when it's all over."

"Good riddance to them all," Caleb said.

"There's still a question about their land and houses. Do they still own them? Or do they forfeit it all when they leave?"

"They forfeit, of course," Caleb said with indignation. "What right do they have to any land in a country they've abandoned?"

"Perhaps," David said, his legal mind examining the shadows. "It will be a matter brought up in the courts—and not an easy one to settle."

"When is Washington going to disband his army?" Noah asked. It bothered him that he had been released from service when he had married Mary. It was a common enough practice, but he felt he should have stayed with the more than ten thousand troops that remained in the Hudson Valley camps.

"The schedule calls for next month," David said. "That's when it will be—unless, of course, the British don't keep their word and leave."

"Don't you think they'll keep their word?" Caleb asked.

"I don't see why not," David replied. "They've lost the war and they know it. If they tried to stay, we'd beat them again, and they know that too."

"That's for sure," Caleb growled.

"But aside from those reasons," David continued, "the new prime minister is well known as an advocate of peace. Unlike Lord North, Shelburne is his own man—strong enough to stand up to the king."

Caleb took another sip of the Madeira, and a dreamy smile came to his face. "I guess we'll be getting used to wine like this again, but right now it's a treat. Drew and his wife had better hurry if they expect to taste any of it." He looked at David and added, "We invited Jemmy and Jenny too, but neither could make it. Said they had previous plans."

David looked uncomfortable. "Well, I ought to be honest with you about that. The truth is they both made excuses when they heard Althea was coming. They don't like to be around her."

"Can't say that I blame them," Caleb admitted. "But she is Drew's wife, and that makes her part of the family."

"I told my kids they were wrong," David said. "But they want nothing to do with her."

"Shame about that," Noah contributed. "I've only met Althea a few times. Pretty girl," he added, in an attempt to say something nice about her.

"Pretty isn't enough," David said.

"I didn't even bother asking Celine, because I knew she wouldn't come," Caleb said. "And Marie Therese hasn't been feeling too well and didn't want to make the trip down from Beekman's Place."

"I wonder if we can believe that?"

Caleb smiled. "Things are pretty bad when even Marie Therese starts lying."

David shook his head. "That woman has caused nothing but trouble."

"But we must try to make her feel at home," the good-natured Noah said. "For Drew's sake."

"I agree," Caleb said. "After all, people have been known to change."

"Yes, of course, that could happen," David said, but he had a skeptical look on his face.

A little while later Drew arrived with Althea. Her time was almost upon her, and her belly protruded formidably. On entering the keeping room, she announced she was dizzy and had to sit down immediately. Drew helped her to a stuffed chair, plumped up a pillow, and brought her a glass of Madeira. Althea sipped it, made a face, and placed the glass on the table at her side.

"You're carrying the newest member of the family," David said to her with a smile. He wanted her to feel at home; then maybe she might come around to being reasonable. "Do you want a boy or a girl?"

Althea sighed wearily, as if it was a great chore to talk. "A boy, naturally. They're messier than girls, but the first child should be a boy."

"It doesn't really matter, does it? As long as the child is healthy."

Althea sighed again. "Isn't there some other kind of wine?" she complained to her husband.

The men drifted into a group around the pipe of wine, their conversation sticking to the war and the city, avoiding touchy family matters.

Attempting to be friendly, Mary came to sit in a chair near the Englishwoman. "At your age you should have an easy childbirth," she said. "With someone my age, it's more difficult."

Althea looked at her with curiosity. She knew from Drew that Mary's child had not been fathered by her husband. It was typical of these provincials to breed indiscriminately, she thought. *Like animals*. "And under such trying circumstances," she said silkily.

Mary ignored the remark. "The thing to do is to get as much rest as you can. It keeps your strength up, so when the baby arrives it becomes an easy delivery."

"Middleton babies are always born easily," she said with the conviction of one who had a history of two hundred years of titled forebears.

"Except this one will bear the name of de Kuyper," Mary reminded her.

"I suppose," Althea said, and her tone indicated she was only barely tolerating such an absurd situation. Who would choose the name de Kuyper over Middleton? A fool, perhaps; certainly no one in his right mind.

"To the new father," David said amid the small circle of men around the pipe. He held up his glass. The others raised theirs, smiled at Drew, and downed the contents.

"It feels strange to think of myself as a father," Drew said. "I keep comparing myself to Jan, and I come off second best. When I was little, I thought of him as a demigod. I doubt my son will think the same of me."

"Don't believe that," David said. "Little boys always idolize their fathers."

"What if the child is a girl?"

"She'll adore you even more."

"That's a great deal of responsibility."

David shrugged. "We ask for it. We must accept it."

"There's a rumor going around that some of the British officers are against a peaceful withdrawal," Caleb said, bringing the conversation back to politics. "My customers talk about it all the time."

"Only talk," David assured him. "The treaty with Parliament calls for an orderly and peaceful withdrawal."

"I don't trust the British," Caleb said. "Look at their record. At one time or another they've broken every promise they ever made to us."

"Give it some thought," David said. "What can they do? They're hemmed in on this island, surrounded by a hostile continent. They're pretty helpless."

"If they want to make trouble, they'll find a way," Caleb insisted.

"The British follow orders," David said. "If nothing else, they're professional in that respect."

"They may follow orders," Drew said. "But it's not beyond them to bend their orders a bit."

"Don't be too unkind," David said. "They've been through a long war..."

"As have we."

"Yes, as have we, but don't forget they lost."

"If it were up to me, I'd run them out of New York on the end of a bayonet," the normally mild Noah said with some heat. When he saw the startled looks on the faces of the others, he explained. "I fought against them too many times, I guess. I don't like them. I don't trust them. And I won't be happy until every last one of them is gone."

"I hope you're not including my wife?" Drew asked, hoping to add a note of levity to the conversation.

Noah reddened. "Of course not, Drew, I don't mean her. I'm talking about British soldiers."

On the other side of the room Alice had joined Mary and Althea. She was telling the Englishwoman how much she was going to enjoy having a child, and how Elly had added such joy to her own life.

"But don't you think it's dangerous for a child to grow up here rather than in England?" Althea asked.

"I've never been to England," Alice said, "so I wouldn't know."

"Oh, but you must go for a visit. The climate is much nicer and milder. Here it's either too beastly hot or too bloody cold."

"We survive," Mary said drolly.

"Yes, but that's because you're used to it," Althea insisted. "I'm sure *I* could never have survived if I'd had to endure such weather as a child."

"Have you picked out a name for the baby?" Alice asked.

"Jane after my mother, if she's a girl. And Roger for my uncle the viscount, if he's a boy."

"That's odd," Mary said.

Althea bristled. "What's odd about those names?"

"Not the names. I'm just surprised Drew wouldn't want to name his first son after his father or grandfather."

"We haven't even discussed the matter," Althea said. "In cases like this where one of the parents has titled blood, the practice is to name the child after that side of the family."

"That may be the case in England, but it's not the way people do things here."

"*Some* people do," Althea said, clearly implying these were the better people and she was one of them. "Who cares what the *bumpkins* prefer."

The party had become stiff because of Althea's presence, and she was restless. After an hour she announced she wasn't feeling well and wanted Drew to take her home.

"Of course," he said solicitously. "We'll get you home and back into bed."

"Drew! Be careful!" she complained as he attempted to help her out of the chair. "You can be so *rough*."

"I'm sorry."

Althea looked at the other two women. "The men *here* just don't know how to treat a lady."

Alice and Mary exchanged glances. "I don't know," Mary said, looking across the room fondly at Noah. "Some of them can be gentle enough."

Althea noticed where Mary was looking, and a scornful expression came over her face. "Of course, *certain* women have reasons to be grateful to *certain* men. So, *naturally*, they have no right to complain."

"What do you mean by that?"

"You know what I mean."

"As a matter of fact, I do," Mary said evenly. "But I'd like to hear you tell me."

"I doubt if you'd understand," Althea said.

"Afraid to say what's on your mind?" Mary asked, refusing to back down.

"You wouldn't like what I'd say."

"Try me."

"Everyone *knows* Noah Henry gave his name to your son, even though he's not the father."

"Yes, everyone knows that. So what?"

"Well, if I have to explain why you're grateful to him, there's no sense in even trying."

Mary smiled. "Did you marry me out of pity, Noah?" she called across the room.

"Out of pity! God forbid!" Noah said fervently. "I married you because you're the most wonderful woman on earth."

"I wonder if anyone will ever say that about you?" Alice said to Althea. "I rather doubt it."

"Look who's got the nerve to say *anything*," Althea said nastily. "You who live with a man while your husband is still alive!"

"That marriage has been dead for years," Alice replied. "I love Caleb and he loves me. That's probably more than you have."

"Drew, it's time to leave!" Althea said.

"That's a good idea," Mary said.

"Don't talk to me, you *whore*," Althea cried. "And you're *another* whore," she added for Alice's benefit.

Drew's embarrassment was profound. "These people are my family," he said to his wife. "Apologize."

"I will not!"

"Don't be a spoiled brat."

"How dare you!"

He was about to say more when his attention was diverted by her swelling belly. He instantly felt remorse about upsetting her, and made silent excuses to himself for her behavior. "Althea... I'm sorry, I guess I'm feeling out of sorts."

"I should say you are!"

"Let's go home."

"That's *exactly* what I've been suggesting, only you've been too busy *abusing* me to pay attention," Althea said angrily.

"I'm not abusing—"

"Oh!...Oh!" Althea staggered back a step, bringing both hands to her stomach. "It hurts!"

"Maybe you'd better sit down and—"

"No, no! Just get me out of here.... These *people*," Althea said, waving her hand, implying that what she thought could not be spoken in polite society. "Oh! Oh! Another pain!"

Drew took his wife's arm to prevent her from falling. David Sackett took the other arm.

"We'd better get her home to bed," he said. "I'll go with you."

After they were gone, Mary put into words what the others

were thinking. "Drew's not going to have a peaceful moment as long as he's married to that woman."

Four days later Marie Therese entered the house on Maiden Lane, and the first thing she heard was a scream from the second floor. A haggard-looking Drew came to meet her. He was rumpled, bleary-eyed, and distraught.

"It's Althea. She's in terrible pain."

"Who's with her?"

"Alice."

Marie Therese hurried toward the stairs. "Alice is capable, but where's the doctor?"

"He was here, but he had to leave on another emergency. Caleb North's gone out to bring him back."

"From the sound of it, we'll need that doctor."

Drew followed his mother up the stairs and to the bedroom at the end of the hall. They paused as a moan of agony emanated from the room, then opened the door and went inside. Althea was on the bed, her face contorted in pain, her eyes red, and her face flushed and sweat-streaked. Alice de Witt stood at her side, bathing the fevered forehead with a cool, wet cloth.

Drew hurried to the bed and took one of Althea's hands, pressing it in his own.

She looked up. "It hurts!" she wailed, and her cry stabbed him like a knife.

"Everything will be all right. My mother is here and—"

Althea shrieked again and Marie Therese moved to the bed. She turned down the covers and gently placed her hand on Althea's stomach, eliciting another scream.

"You're hurting me!"

"Shh."

"Stop!"

"How much time between pains?" Marie Therese asked Alice.

"A few minutes now. And getting closer together."

"This is no place for you," Marie Therese said to her son. "Go downstairs and wait for the doctor."

"But..."

Marie Therese took her son by the arm and led him into the hallway.

"There's nothing you can do," she told him softly but firmly, and stepped back into the bedroom. Marie Therese closed the door, and Drew stood alone for a moment, then started slowly down the stairs. He stopped as another shriek pierced the air. He took a deep breath, then hurried down to the kitchen, where he poured himself a glass of straight rum. He swallowed it and felt the fiery liquid burning through his body. After a few seconds a pleasant warmth dulled his senses and his breathing returned to normal.

In the bedroom, Marie Therese felt the fevered brow of her daughter-in-law. She turned worriedly to Alice. "If the doctor doesn't get here in a few minutes, it will be up to us."

Alice stepped closer to the bed. "I've done it before."

"So have I," Marie Therese said. "But this looks like it'll be a difficult one."

"We'll do our best."

Marie Therese regarded Alice. Only a few days ago the girl in the bed had called her a whore, and now the woman was ready to do everything she could to help her attacker. There was a great deal of character in Alice's makeup, she decided.

"Let's prop her legs up," Alice said.

Althea screamed as Alice touched her bare leg. She tried to sit up in bed, but it was beyond her strength and she fell back, sobbing and moaning.

"Easy, child, easy," Marie Therese said soothingly.

Drew paced back and forth in the kitchen.

He forced himself not to have another drink. The easiest thing in the world would be to get drunk, he told himself, but he was part of this birth, and he was going to stay sober and see it through.

The doctor arrived a few minutes later, looking harried. Caleb held his arm and half-dragged him into the house. As they entered, another scream came from upstairs. The doctor wasted no time, taking the steps two at a time as he rushed to the bedroom.

Caleb came over and put his arm about the woeful-looking Drew. "Relax, lad, there's not a thing you can do."

"But the screams..."

"Childbirth is never easy. She'll be all right." Caleb grabbed the rum bottle and pulled out the cork. "Have a drink."

"I just had one."

Caleb shrugged and made one for himself. As he downed it, Althea screamed again.

"Give me a drink," Drew conceded.

Marie Therese hurried into the kitchen. She went to the

stove where cloths were sitting in a pot of simmering water. She used tongs to take several cloths out, and placed them in a bowl.

"What... what..." Drew managed to whisper.

"It's a difficult birth," Marie Therese said.

"Will... will it be all right?"

"With the help of God."

When his mother said that, Drew knew the truth. Marie Therese was not an alarmist: if she sought God's help, then there was trouble indeed.

"With the help of God," he repeated softly.

Marie Therese went back upstairs, and the two men sat in the kitchen, averting their eyes from one another. Over the next hour the shrieks came less and less often, and more and more feebly. Finally there was a time when Althea could no longer be heard, and Drew began to pace again.

Drew and Caleb heard the sound of footsteps coming down the stairs. The doctor walked into the kitchen. His face was white, and his hands were shaking. "Give me a drink," he demanded in a hoarse voice.

Caleb poured some rum into a glass and handed it to him. The doctor lifted the glass and emptied it in one swallow.

"How—" Drew started to ask about his wife, but couldn't bring himself to finish the question for fear of the answer.

The doctor shook his head. He spoke to the room in general. "The baby wasn't in the right position. It was all wrong. And there was something the matter with the woman—"

"Goddammit!" Drew yelled. "Tell me what happened!"

"I saved the child. There was nothing I could do for the mother."

"Jesus," Caleb breathed softly. "Sweet Jesus."

Drew was numb.

I saved the child. There was nothing I could do for the mother.

The words kept racing through his mind. Althea was dead. *Dead.*

He had stood in the center of the room when the doctor entered. Now he slumped back into the chair. He took the glass of rum offered by Caleb and swallowed it. He no longer felt the heat of the liquid as it coursed down his throat. He no longer felt anything.

"How's the child?" Caleb asked.

"Seems to be a fine, healthy girl," the doctor said. "We'll

have to watch her for a few weeks, but my first impression is that everything's all right."

Drew heard the words through the fog that had settled over him. A girl. He was the father of a girl. A healthy girl.

"Jane," he said softly.

"What was that?" the doctor asked.

"Jane. The name Althea wanted for a baby girl. That will be her name. Jane."

"A fine name," Caleb said. He looked at the doctor. "Can Drew see his daughter?"

The doctor nodded. "The women will let us know when they're ready."

"I want to see my wife," Drew said, standing up.

"There's no need to torture yourself," the doctor said.

"There is a need," Drew said between clenched teeth.

The doctor looked at Caleb, who shrugged. "All right," the doctor said, holding his hands palms up.

A few minutes later Drew entered the darkened room, where the still form of his wife lay on the bed. Marie Therese put her arms about him for a moment, then left him alone. He walked to the bed and looked down at the covered face. He slowly pulled back the blanket.

Althea looked peaceful. It was hard to imagine that the agonized screams had been coming from those reposed lips. Finally, he thought, she is free from pain. At peace with herself. And at peace with her husband.

He dropped to one knee and stared at the face. It had hardly been a good marriage, but no matter what, it had been a marriage in the eyes of God.

This was my wife.

And now she was gone. Forever. There would be no more unhappiness between them. No more tension. Or arguments and rancor. And on the other side of the coin, no more sparkle in her eyes as they made love, no more tender touchings. Despite everything else, he reminded himself, they had had their moments.

And they were all in the past.

The problem of how to live his life with Althea no longer existed. It passed away even as Althea had passed away. In a way he was relieved. And yet it was hardly the sort of relief he would have wished. It wasn't really Althea's fault that she couldn't adjust to America. It wasn't her fault that she had come here.

No, it was *his* fault.

He should have known better. If only he had been stronger; if only he'd been wise enough to have seen into the future and to have realized what might well happen...

But he had been none of these things, and now a young woman was dead. He looked at her face and his eyes misted. *Good-bye, my wife, good-bye. I'm sorry I didn't fill your days with happiness and peace and joy. I'm sorry. Sorry for everything.*

For a moment he thought he would weep, but he stopped himself. There had been enough weeping in this house; there would be no more.

He stood up and walked out of the room.

Marie Therese was waiting for him in the hallway. In her arms she held a small bundle wrapped in a pink blanket. She uncovered an end of the blanket, and for the first time Drew looked upon the face of his daughter.

"A fine girl," Marie Therese said.

"Jane."

"Her name?"

"Yes. It was the name Althea wanted."

"It was also your grandmother's name," Marie Therese said.

Drew nodded. "James's first wife. She died not long after Father was born. Even he never knew her."

"So now we'll have another Jane de Kuyper," Marie Therese said. "May she live long and happily."

"May she have a life filled with love," Alice added.

"She'll know nothing else," Drew promised. He held out his arms, and his mother gave him his daughter.

Such a small weight, he thought, such a tiny bit of humanity. And she would depend on him alone. There would be no mother to comfort her, no mother to soothe her, no mother to caress away the tears of childhood.

My daughter, Jane, he thought. And for the first time this day, he smiled. Whether it was a trick of fate or a coincidence, it seemed his daughter actually looked up at him. Could she see him? Could she see anything through those newborn eyes?

It didn't matter. It pleased him to think the first view Jane de Kuyper had of the world outside the sad chamber of her birth was the smiling face of her own father.

* * *

Over the years the de Kuypers had become as English as the English themselves; but Drew reminded them all of their Dutch heritage when he commissioned his daughter's birth certificate from a Pennsylvania Dutch artist, Johannes Spangenberg, renowned for his *Fraktur*—illumination on parchment. The *Fraktur* used Gothic-style capital letters, each of which was broken and embellished with brightly colored calligraphic strokes.

Spangenberg used a bright-blue milk-based paint to enrich Jane de Kuyper's record of arrival in the world. The parchment was a work of art. The border was decorated with a labyrinth of twisted vines, throughout which grew a paradise of flowers. The top of the parchment was decorated with tulips of gold leaf, the bottom with gold-leaf goldfinches.

This hand-painted *taufschein*, as the Dutch referred to such certificates, was edged with gold leaf and came rolled in a container of the softest doeskin.

The entire work constituted an allegory of a baby arriving in the world, living a pure life and, at the end, ascending to eternity among the splendors of heaven.

At the bottom of the parchment, in Dutch, was an admonition, which might be translated into English as:

Jane

The world is a desert
enameled with the flowers of God.

Marie Therese moved back to the house on Maiden Lane and assumed the task of caring for the child. Helping Drew provide for the infant seemed to make her younger, filling her with vigor. A wet nurse was found to provide nourishment for tiny Jane, and she flourished.

Within two days the family members came to see their latest relative. Their emotions and reactions varied.

Celine was relieved that she could once again enter the house where she had grown up without enduring a scene with her sister-in-law. She wasn't happy that Althea was dead, but neither was she spending her days in grief.

Peter looked at the infant and shrugged: another baby, and a girl at that.

Jenny Sackett Thompson held the child in her arms and

crooned softly. It wouldn't be long before she would be able to do it with an infant of her own.

Beth visited twice. The first time, Drew was at home.

"I'm sorry, Andrew," she said simply.

He nodded. He looked at her and wanted to take her in his arms, but knew it would be a horrible breach of taste so soon after the death of his wife.

She was proud and waited for him to talk, but he said nothing, only sat there looking miserable.

She became uncomfortable and left. She returned at a time when she knew Drew wasn't home, and during this visit spent a long time looking at the face of the sleeping infant. She felt strange. After all, if things had worked out differently, this might have been her own baby.

Marie Therese noticed how long Beth lingered with the infant. She crossed the room and stood next to her at the side of the crib.

"She looks like Andrew," Beth said.

"She has his eyes and mouth," Marie Therese said. "But it's a bit early to really tell."

"I wonder if I'll ever have a child," Beth said with a trace of sadness.

Marie Therese truly loved this girl as if she were her own daughter. She also knew that Beth was in love with her son; and now there might be a future for this love. But she felt it was not her place to say so.

Celine, later on, was not so restrained.

"You ought to grab the stupid clod by the ears and tell him how you feel."

"I couldn't do that," Beth said.

"Why not?"

"I'm not that nervy."

"Nervy? You can go out with a bow and arrow and kill a bear, but you're scared by that ninny of a brother of mine? Come on, Beth, your whole future is at stake. You've got to *do* something."

"It's too soon after the death of his wife. Anyway, if he wants something to happen, he has to come to me."

"More pride!" Celine said, throwing her hands into the air. "Next you'll be telling me about your honor. What a dumb situation. Here are two people who are absolutely perfect for one another, and they won't even talk to each other. All right.

If you won't do anything, Beth, then maybe I'll have to get involved."

"I'm asking you not to."

"But why, for heaven's sake?"

"Because I don't want to push him into anything. It has to be his idea. Look what happened the last time he was pushed into a marriage."

"I see your point," Celine conceded. "But there is a difference. Drew could be happy with you. If you want the truth, I'm almost glad Althea's gone. It's best all around."

If she expected Beth to be shocked at her candor, she was wrong. "I knew you felt this way."

"And you don't?"

"No. I didn't like her. But I'm not pleased that she's dead."

"You're a better person than I am, Beth Henry," Celine said. "After all, you've more to gain from her death than anyone else."

A touch of scorn crept into Beth's voice. "When I hunt, I take live animals, not carrion left behind by others."

Celine laughed. "Wouldn't Baby Brother be pleased to hear you refer to him as carrion."

Beth managed to smile. "That's not exactly what I meant."

"So what's going to happen?"

"We'll see."

"Aren't you going to do anything?"

"Hmn."

"Do you have some plan in mind?" Celine asked, suspicion beginning to grow in her mind.

Beth smiled. "As a matter of fact, I do."

"Well, well, Congress finally came through," General Washington said as he looked down into the opened chest, which was filled with money.

"Almost as much as you asked for," David Sackett said. "That's the first time *that's* happened."

Washington chuckled. David had arrived at the camp with the money only a few minutes before. Congress had provided it to pay the soldiers. David and Jemmy had brought it up from Philadelphia. And just in time, because the soldiers were grumbling again.

Their pay wasn't much, but it added up. A private was paid $6.67 a month, with $1.67 deducted for clothing. A full lieutenant made $18 a month, but $6 was deducted from this amount. A man could live well on the $166 a month paid a major general, but no man of general officer rank had received as much as a penny in the past two years.

"Beautiful day to receive money," Washington said as he looked out the window. It was the first day of June, and the land was bursting with color as the wild flowers and trees and grasses came to life. It was a balmy day, and many of the idle soldiers were walking around with their shirts off, glorying in the gentle rays of the sun.

"Any day is a beautiful day to receive money," David said.

"Especially when thousands of men with guns keep telling you that you owe it to them," the general added, thinking of the many times his army had almost mutinied because the Congress didn't have the funds to pay them.

"It's all over, General," David said. "Only a week ago, over seven thousand loyalists sailed from New York. That's just about the last of them."

"And within two weeks our army will start disbanding," Washington said. "Soon this'll all be in the past and we'll be back leading normal lives."

"What about yourself?" Jemmy asked.

"I'd like to return to Virginia and see my farm. That's where I'm happiest, and that's where I belong."

"The country's going to need you," David said. "We've only begun the task of building a nation."

Washington sighed. "I know, and I promised I'd serve if asked. My only hope is that nobody asks."

"Not much chance of that," David said. "I guess you've heard the rumor that whatever form of government we finally settle on, the Congress is going to ask you to head it."

"I've heard it."

"It's more than a rumor, sir."

"Well, let's hope they create a monarchy, because I've sworn my oath I'll never be a king. If a king's what they want, they'll have to get someone else."

David approved of this stance. "The men who want a king are in the minority. Our new government's sure to take some other form."

"Just my luck," the general said glumly. He turned to Jemmy, who was closing the money chest. "And what are you up to these days?"

"I'm working on a new kind of whippletree."

"Interesting," the general said, almost sorry he had asked. "But just why do we need a new kind of whippletree?"

"The ones we have now are too cumbersome," Jemmy said. "When a team of oxen wears one, they have to make very wide turns. What I want to create is a whippletree that allows the animals to turn in a narrow circle."

"Not a bad idea," Washington admitted. "How far along are you?"

"Finished," Jemmy said.

"It does have one little problem," David reminded his son.

"Oh yes," Jemmy said. "But we'll have that solved in no time. Jane is working on it."

"Jane?" the general said, cocking his head to one side.

"My wife," Jemmy informed him. "She's quite an inventor in her own right."

David explained the problem to the general. "Jemmy's new whippletree has to be of light enough construction to allow the oxen to make a tight turn. Because it's light, it has a tendency to break."

"Yes, we've lost a few oxen that way," Jemmy said blithely.

"You lose oxen?"

"Yes, they just wander off if no one is around."

"I see," the general said. "I wish you luck," he added, but there was no conviction in his voice. He hadn't forgotten the time Jemmy had tried to use some black substance from the earth as a fuel for stoves and almost burned down his headquarters.

"When are you coming to New York?" David asked.

"Not until the British soldiers've left," the general said. "I don't want to see them when I return to New York."

"That'll be some day of celebration!"

Washington told them of his plans to enter the city at the head of a column of his officers. It would be a fit ending to the long, drawn-out war: the triumphant general returning to the city in a victory parade.

An hour later, when David was walking about the camp, he saw a familiar face.

"Franz!"

Colonel von Lossow smiled and walked over to shake hands. His face was deeply tanned. "How are you, David?"

"Well—and you look the picture of health yourself."

"On the outside," Franz said. "On the inside I'm burning to get back to New York and marry Celine."

"I'm delighted for both of you. My only regret is that her father didn't live to see that day. He would have admired her choice."

"Soon I'll have to decide what to do with myself," Franz said, and his brow contracted into little furrows. "All my life I've been a professional soldier. There won't be too much demand for them, I think."

"We may all hope not!" David said fervently.

"So what am I going to do with myself?"

"Why don't you come into the family business? We'll be getting back to work and we'll need good men like you."

"To do what?"

"Who knows? But when you marry Celine, you'll be part of the family. You'd at least be working with your own people."

"An interesting proposition, David. I'll give it some thought."

"Why think about it? My God, we've got a lot of time to make up. There'll be plenty to do."

"If I can be of use..."

"Definitely."

"Then why not? I'll be happy to join you."

"You won't regret it."

"The other thing on my mind is that I'll have to learn to be a sort of father to Peter. I've had no experience at such a thing. It scares me."

David glanced across the parade ground. He could see his own son huddled in conversation with Alexander Hamilton. He couldn't hear what they were saying, but he had a good idea what it was about. Jemmy had an idea about creating a system of bringing fresh water down from the northern end of the island, and it was well known that Hamilton had often spoken about the atrocious and skimpy New York water supply system. No doubt the two of them were discussing the problem and a scheme was being hatched in Jemmy's fertile brain.

And yet, David thought, even Jemmy is beginning to settle down. He has a wife and will soon be a father himself. Despite his earlier erratic behavior, he was turning out to be a responsible adult.

"You don't need experience to be a father," he said to the worried-looking colonel. "Just endurance."

A month later Jemmy stopped into Fraunces Tavern for a late-afternoon ale on his way home. He saw Drew sitting with

Dick Goelet and Seth Cuyler. The latter two were relatively sober, but Drew obviously had been drinking heavily.

Jemmy pulled up a chair and joined them at their table. "What's the occasion?"

"Ask him," Dick said, jerking his thumb toward Drew.

"I don't want to talk about it," Drew said immediately, a slight slur to his speech.

Jemmy was understanding. "All right, don't talk about—"

"She can't *do* it!" Drew said. "She can't do such a thing. It's immoral, and wrong, and stupid, and un-American."

"That about covers it," Jemmy said, nodding his head sagely. Then he looked toward the other two men for an explanation.

Seth shook his head. "It's up to Drew to talk about it if he wants. It's his business, not mine."

Dick was more helpful. "Beth is moving to England."

"Beth Henry?"

"How many other Beths do you know?"

"A few," Jemmy said. "It's not that uncommon a name."

"Well, you know which Beth I mean."

"Beth Henry?" Jemmy persisted.

"Yes."

"And she's moving to England?"

"To be somebody's mistress," Drew groaned.

Jemmy's mouth dropped open. *"Our Beth?"*

Drew nodded. "My sister told me."

"Does she have anybody particular in mind?" Jemmy asked, but his sarcasm was lost on Drew.

"William Henry is his name. *Prince* William Henry, no less, the son of the king."

"Have you ever heard the like of it?" Dick asked, and it was clear he was almost as upset as his cousin.

"It's a shame, all right," Jemmy said. "But why are you taking it so hard? What does Beth mean to you?"

Drew shook his head. "You wouldn't understand. What do you know about it? What do you know about anything?"

"He knows enough not to marry the wrong woman," Seth said, and Drew looked ready to jump across the table and hit him.

A little light went on in Jemmy's head. He had heard something about Beth's love of Drew from Jenny. But when Drew had come home with an English wife, it had all seemed over.

Now, however, with Althea gone, things had changed—for the worse, so it seemed. Instead of falling in a heap at Drew's feet, Beth was running off with the son of a king. My, my, my.

"You had your chance with Beth, and you messed it up," Dick said with relish. Somehow, Beth's rejection of him was a little easier to take now that she was rejecting Drew as well.

"Shut up," Seth said. "Don't start trouble."

Drew finished his drink and pounded the mug on the table to attract the attention of the serving girl. "Let's have another here!"

"You look like you've had enough," Jemmy said.

"Becoming a whore for a son of that bastard, George III," Drew said, ignoring his cousin's admonition. "I can't believe it, I just can't believe it."

"She's a little traitor," Dick said.

"Don't you call her names," Drew warned, instantly springing to Beth's defense. "I won't have that."

"It's the truth," Dick said stubbornly.

Drew started to get out of his chair, but Seth placed a big hand on his shoulder and pushed him back down. "Let's take it easy, shall we? We'll have no fighting among cousins."

Drew regained control of himself and nodded. "But I still don't want to hear bad things about her," he warned.

"I take it you love her?" Jemmy asked.

"Yes."

"Why not tell her?"

"I can't," Drew moaned. "Not after the way I treated her. I can't even talk to her. Especially now when she's already decided what she wants to do."

"If you love her, the least you could do is talk to her," Jemmy said reasonably.

"She doesn't want to talk to me. She avoids me."

"It's true," Dick said, unable to conceal his happiness at having company in his misery over Beth.

"And you're absolutely sure she's going to England?"

"Celine told me."

The serving girl brought another mug of foaming ale laced with rum. Drew grabbed it and took several big swallows. "Why can't we trust women?" he asked.

The serving girl gave him a dirty look as she passed on to another table.

By the time Drew was through drinking, the others had to carry him home.

By the end of August Beth was beginning to wonder about the wisdom of her plan. She had expected Drew to beg her not to go to England when he heard about it. But he hadn't said a word to her; and, worse, it was obvious he was going out of his way to avoid her.

"It's not working," she said to Celine.

"It's working. My mother tells me he mopes around the house—feeling sorry for himself, drinking, acting like a crab."

"But he's not doing anything to make me change my mind."

"So, we'll have to put more pressure on him."

"How?"

"We'll find a ship that's due to leave in a month or so, and tell everyone you're sailing on it. Right now he thinks you're going to England, but he doesn't know when."

Beth nodded. "This way he'll have a definite date in mind. He'll have to do something before then."

"It's killing him to think you're going away to become someone else's mistress. He just needs a prod to get him to act."

"You talk of Andrew like he's a horse."

"Sometimes he thinks like one."

"I'm starting to feel guilty about all this," Beth admitted. "It's not very honest."

"What's honesty got to do with love?" Celine asked.

Franz entered the room. After he had been released from the army and had come back to New York, he and Celine had been married in a quiet little ceremony, just three weeks ago. Only the immediate family had been invited.

"You two doing more plotting?" he asked. Celine had told him all about the planned entrapment of Drew.

"Yes, we've got to goad my brother into action."

"You're already ruining his health," Franz said lightly, but there was a note of seriousness in his voice. "He spends far too much time at Fraunces Tavern."

"Will you help us?"

"That depends on what it is you want done."

"Find out when a ship's due to leave for England," Celine said. "Say in about a month—the end of September or the beginning of October."

"We've already booked space for some company cargo on a Dutch packet that leaves October seventh."

"Good. Now I want you to make sure Drew learns that Beth is sailing on that ship."

Franz looked at Beth. "Are you really doing it?"

"Not if things work out," Beth answered.

"They will," Celine assured her.

Franz nodded. "I'll take care of it. And I'm sure glad I don't have you two plotting against me."

"What makes you think we haven't been?" Celine asked. "After all, I did get you to marry me."

"It was the only way of making an honest woman of you."

Beth lay awake on her bed.

Enough moonlight filtered through the window to allow her to see the ceiling. At Jenny's invitation, she was staying in a spare bedroom at the Sacketts'.

It was October third. In four days she was supposed to sail for England.

Four days.

And if Andrew didn't do something before then, she *would* sail, and she *would* accept William Henry's offer to be his mistress. Why not? She was tired of wanting something she seemed doomed never to have. The idea of sharing her life with Drew was proving to be a vanity. It was time to stop wasting her life.

She placed her hand on her breast, then slowly moved it down over her belly and brought it to rest in the space between her legs. She wondered how it would feel if Drew did it. How would it feel if *any* man did it? Damn it all! She was twenty-two years old and still a virgin. Saving herself. *Saving herself for what?* Saving herself for a man who didn't want her—or, if he did want her, didn't have enough sense to know how to go about getting her. Saving herself—Christ!

Twenty-two and running her own hand down her body when there should be a man doing it. Lying here in bed and wanting, wanting, wanting. The hell with Andrew de Kuyper! It was time to get on with her life. She was going to England. She'd let the prince run his hand over her belly, let him caress her and shower her with presents. She'd make love to him and cry out in passion; make love the way she'd always dreamed she would. She and the prince. What did she need Andrew de Kuyper for?

PATRIOTS, HEROES, AND LOVERS

* * *

She was still wide awake when she heard the first shouts in the street. She sat up in bed and listened intently. Her highly developed hunter's sense of hearing allowed her to pick out one word that was being repeated over and over again.

Fire!

Fire!

She leaped from the bed, donned her buckskins in seconds, and was out the door and running down the stairs. A frightened Jenny Sackett Thompson was peering bleary-eyed from the half-opened door of her bedroom.

"What's happening?"

"Fire!" Beth shouted as she took the last three steps in a single bound and dashed across the reception hall to the front door. She was out in the street, looking around for the direction of the trouble. Only it wasn't one fire, but many.

Dear God, she thought, *not another fire!* Not another one like the great fire that had almost destroyed New York.

A man came puffing down the street, his fat legs carrying him as fast as they were able. He was carrying a bucket.

"What's burning?" Beth asked.

The man stopped and paused to catch his breath. "It's the British," he gasped. "They're burning all the public buildings."

"The British?"

The man nodded. "Damn them!"

"Where are the fires the worst?"

"By the park, I've been told. I'm on my way there now."

Beth didn't hesitate. She started running toward the triangular park at the Common.

The shouting and general commotion also brought Drew out of a deep sleep in his house on Maiden Lane. He dressed quickly and, after making sure his mother was taking care of the baby, went out into the streets.

"I'll take her to the cellar," Marie Therese said as she cradled Jane in her arms.

Drew nodded. Even if the fire became widespread, the deep cellar beneath the house was probably one of the safest places in the city.

Drew soon found out what was happening, and he headed for the Common, because there were a good number of public buildings in that area—the upper barracks, the Almshouse, the Provost, and the powder house, among others.

As he raced up Broad Way and came to the corner of Vesey Street, he could see flames shooting from the roof of the long barracks building. The Almshouse was also burning, a thick column of smoke billowing from its west end. He could see more fires beyond that, and knew they were in the vicinity of the powder house. Christ! What a noise *that* would make if it blew!

He glanced back down Broad Way, and his heart skipped a beat when he saw a red haze against the sky. Something near the fort at the tip of the island was burning—the lower barracks, or even the fort itself. He started running toward the Almshouse. Even from this distance, he could see people stumbling from the doomed building, choking and blinded by smoke, many of them needing assistance in reaching safety.

Well, he thought, at least here was another pair of hands to lend to someone who needed them.

The author of this latest plague to descend on New York was seated behind his desk in his office at the Provost. Captain Patrick Blakely was congratulating himself that everything was going according to plan. Twenty British soldiers had started the fires at exactly the same time—one o'clock in the morning; but the honor of putting this building to the torch was to be his. Piles of highly flammable material were ready and waiting. Once started, the fire would take over in minutes.

He picked up the paper that listed the proscribed buildings.

Lower barracks
Upper barracks
Fort
Almshouse
Arsenal
Powder house
City Hall
Naval headquarters
John Street theater
Presbyterian meeting house

The list went on and on, but finally came to the last entry:

The Provost

Captain Blakely smiled grimly as he drew a line through the last entry with his pen. He crumpled the sheet of paper and tossed it across the room. Several pitch-soaked torches stood by the door. A lit candle stood on the nearby table. He stood up and walked over to it. A simple matter. The candle would light the torches, and they would start the fire in the building—several fires, which would eventually become one huge fire.

Very well, you rebel scum, he thought. You may be driving us out of New York, but we'll leave the taste of ashes in your mouths. He smiled, anticipating Colonel Cunningham's surprise. As usual, the provost marshal hadn't the slightest idea what his deputy was up to.

He hadn't informed his superior because the stupid fellow would have raised a dozen reasons why the fires shouldn't be set. Cunningham had no imagination.

He picked up the candle and selected two of the heavy torches. He began to light them. The pitch caught quickly, and the air was immediately filled with an acrid smell.

As the captain was preparing to burn the building, a man sleeping below in one of the abandoned cells finally was wakened by the shouting in the streets.

Enoch de Witt blinked his eyes and put his hand to his head. He had passed out hours ago, after drinking his usual amount of rum. He hadn't bothered to go to the Almshouse, where he had a corner of a room to call his own—a room he shared with a dozen other men. It was easier to stay at the Provost. Not that anyone cared. Ever since Captain Blakely had hired him to clean the prison, he had become a well-known fixture to the soldiers who still worked in the part of the building that was divided into offices. He had become as much a part of the place as the furniture.

Now, however, the commotion was too great for even a man in his condition to ignore. He left the cell, went to the end of the corridor, and ascended the stairs. On the upper levels he crossed from the prison section to the office section. As usual at this hour, there wasn't a soul to be seen.

And then a door ahead opened and he saw a man step out into the corridor. He was holding two burning torches. It was the deputy provost marshal.

Blakely saw Enoch only a second after he had been seen.

"What the hell are you doing here?" he snapped.

"I work here, Captain. Remember?"

"Get out of the building!"

From where he stood, Enoch could see through a window,

and he realized the Almshouse was on fire. He looked with suspicion at the torches in the other man's hands.

"Setting fires, Captain? Is that what you're up to?"

"It's none of your business," Blakely said, suddenly annoyed with himself for standing there discussing the matter with the town drunk.

"Get out of here before you get hurt."

"But why are you setting fires, Captain?" Enoch persisted, shaking his head to clear it. This was important, he told himself; important to know more about it.

Blakely laughed. "I'm going to leave the rabble with a rubble."

Enoch sucked in his breath. His head seemed to clear instantly. Equally quickly, he knew his duty.

"Captain," he said quietly. "I can't let you do this."

The naval headquarters was burning fiercely as Drew arrived. He took one look and realized the blaze was hopeless. He looked past the building and saw more people being helped from the Almshouse. He decided to go there to see if he could be of any assistance.

Beth didn't see Drew, although he was less than fifty yards from her.

Her attention was devoted to the chapel of St. Paul's. A fire had been set in the vestry, and over a dozen men were struggling to contain it. Beth joined the bucket brigade.

Only a few minutes later, she realized the vestry fire was almost out and the church would be saved. She stepped out of the line and looked across the Common to where the Almshouse was burning fiercely. The dark hulk of the Provost building, off to the side of the Almshouse, caught her eye. The immense, forbidding structure didn't yet show any trace of fire. She decided her time could best be spent seeing if she could do anything to prevent the flames from spreading from the Almshouse to its neighbor.

Unlike the buildings around it, the Provost was dark and silent. There were no flames, no shouting men, no terrified people struggling to safety. Beth felt something ominous in the contrast.

She went up the stairs quickly, slowed her pace at the top, and cautiously entered the building.

* * *

Drew was outside the Almshouse when he saw the lone figure entering the Provost. At this distance he couldn't identify Beth, even though the flames from the burning Almshouse made the night almost as bright as day. Curious, he started running toward the other building. When he reached the top of the steps, he too slowed down and entered the building, his senses alert.

Captain Blakely tried to hold both torches in one hand as he reached for the pistol hanging from his belt. In a surprising display of speed, Enoch leaped forward and crashed his fist into the captain's jaw. The burning sticks fell from his hands. One torch rolled against the wall, where it smoked and sputtered. The other, still blazing brightly, rested not far from the feet of the grappling men.

The captain expected to have no trouble with his ragged opponent, but Enoch was endowed with a strength born of desperation. He clasped the captain's arm as he tried to pull out his pistol. "You'll not burn this city!" he shouted.

"Try and stop me!" Blakely said, managing to free his pistol. He pointed it at the other man.

Enoch's questing hand touched the end of the heavy torch. He grabbed it, and whirled it in a vicious arc at the same instant the captain pulled the trigger. The bullet struck Enoch in the chest just as the end of the burning torch crashed into the captain's face. He screamed as the pitch struck and burned into his flesh. The weight of the club broke his nose and split his lips. The hissing pitch splattered into the openings in Blakely's skin, searing, scorching.

Enoch was knocked back by the force of the lead slug. He hit the floor, brought one hand to his shattered chest, and began crawling toward the man who was screaming in agony and clawing at his burning face.

Enoch seized the captain's pistol, which had fallen to the floor. He dragged himself forward until he was in striking distance. The butt of the heavy pistol cracked into the side of Blakely's head—once, twice, three times, crushing the skull. It was an act of mercy. The horrible screams stopped, and Enoch slumped back to the floor, his eyes beginning to glaze over.

It was upon this scene that Beth arrived. Her face registered shock at the awful sight of the dead captain. She gasped when she saw Enoch, bleeding the last of his life onto the floor.

He looked up at her, barely alive. "I stopped him from burning New York," he said in a weak, cracking voice.

"Enoch..."

"Finally did something good," he said; and died.

Drew ran into the room, and then stopped when he saw the results of the tragedy that had been played out.

"Enoch was a hero," Beth said.

Drew stamped out the burning torches. When he was finished, he came over to Beth. "What are you doing here?"

"I came to help."

Drew looked at the mutilated face of the former deputy provost marshal. "What a way to die," he said in awe.

"He was burning the building," Beth said. "Enoch stopped him."

"Enoch stopped him," Drew repeated softly, looking down at the body of his cousin. Beth was standing beside him, their bodies inches from each other. He turned his head and looked at her, and all his pent-up hostility and anger erupted. "Why are you going to England to be a mistress to some man?"

"*The* mistress."

"*A* mistress, *the* mistress, what the hell's the difference? You're still only a mistress."

"There's nothing here for me."

"Only your whole life."

"I don't see it that way."

"Look, Beth, I've been trying to work this out in my mind, and I realize that—"

"Oh, shut up!" she said fiercely.

"I'm trying to apologize about—"

"Then do it right."

"Right?"

"Less talk."

"I don't understand what—"

She cut him off by grabbing his hand and leading him into Blakely's office. She closed the door, then flung her body against his.

"Hey—"

"Do it! Love me!" she said fiercely, in her deepest voice.

"You mean here? Now?"

"I'm not waiting one minute more."

Her hands began to explore his body, and he was helpless to stop himself from doing the same. Their movements became more sensual, demanding, hungry.

She sat down on the wooden floor, and in seconds had removed her buckskin shirt. She guided his hand to her breast. His fingers caressed it, and the nipple hardened. She shuddered, and a low gasp of passion came from her lips.

"Jesus, Beth..."

And he spoke no more as her hand reached out and found his manhood. Instinctively, she knew what to do to arouse him to fever pitch.

They took each other on the floor. There were no preliminaries, no conversation, and no fumbling. When he entered her body, he could feel her unintentioned resistance, her struggling, her bewilderment, and then her scream as he broke the virginal hymen. He knew what was happening, and the thought of it drove him to new heights of wanting.

Beth was hardly passive. The thing she had dreamed about so often was happening, and every inch of her knew it. She writhed and slithered on the boards of the Provost. She moaned and cried and bit his shoulder. She gathered him into her body and they became one.

In the middle of it all, the powder house exploded. The tremendous blast tossed debris for half a mile in all directions. Neither Beth nor Drew knew anything about it.

When it was over, they were side by side on the floor, sweat-covered, exhausted, dreamily contemplating their impassioned lovemaking. Through the window the lurid flickering of the burning Almshouse could be seen. The red glow filled the room and made the scene unreal, mad.

He finally regained the breath to speak. "It was never like this before..."

"I have nothing to compare it with, Andrew," she said with a smile, "but it was wonderful."

She propped herself up on one elbow. Her hair fell casually over her naked shoulder.

"You look like you've been raped," he said.

"I *was* raped. Not now, but all the times you *weren't* with me."

"I'm sorry. I never really knew."

"But that's the past," she said. "What about the future?"

"Now that we've discovered each other, we can't stop."

"No?"

"I want to marry you."

"Have you forgotten I'm going to England?"

"You're not going," he said flatly. "You're going to stay here and be my wife."

"I have something to say about that," she said sharply. For years she had been hoping to hear him say these words. But he had taken his time, and now she was going to prolong the moment and savor it.

"Don't you want to marry me?" he asked, perplexed by her sudden coldness.

"I haven't heard you say anything about love," she said. "It's a word that's customarily used in connection with a proposal of marriage."

"You want me to say I love you?"

"Only if you mean it."

"I love you."

"That doesn't sound too convincing."

"I love you with all my heart and soul," he said, and then his voice took on an edge. "But I'm not going to start off this marriage with you playing games with me. Now stop it."

She smiled. "Is that an order?"

There was something about her smile—something deadly—that warned him not to push his luck. He did the only sensible thing—took her in his arms. They kissed for a long time.

The lovers were brought back to reality only when they heard the sound of boots in the outside hall.

"We'd better get dressed," Drew said.

Beth nodded, and they put themselves together.

Drew shook his head. "The damned city is burning down and we're making love on a wooden floor!"

"Sinful, isn't it?"

"It seems wrong," he said.

She grabbed both his shoulders. "Listen, Andrew de Kuyper, I never want to hear another word about our lovemaking being wrong anywhere, anytime. Do you understand? I'll be your wife, and I'll be a good one, but the one thing I won't stand for is to have you question our love. It's always right and good."

He cupped her chin in the palm of his hand and smiled. "Feisty little devil, aren't you?"

"You'll learn to be glad I am."

The door burst open and a man entered. "What the hell's going on in here?"

"We were just putting out a fire," Beth said, looking into Drew's eyes.

"That's right," he agreed, squeezing her hand in his own. "One hell of a big fire."

It was noon, November 24, 1783.

Beth was at Drew's side in the crowd gathered at the Battery in front of Fort George. Marie Therese stood near by, her hand on the handle of a carriage inside which slept the infant Jane de Kuyper. Peter was next to her. At his other side were Franz and Celine, holding hands, more involved with one another than with the unfolding pageant.

The big day had come.

Sir Guy Carleton and the last of the British troops were evacuating Manhatan. They were being rowed out to the ships anchored off the southernmost tip of the island. From there they would transfer to Staten Island, where a fleet was being assembled to take them away from America for good. Some were going to Canada, some to the Indies, and some back to England—but the important thing was that they were going.

Beth held tightly to Drew's arm. Her dark eyes shone with anticipation.

"It's finally happening," she said.

"About time."

"Now we can live normal lives."

"And we'll lead them together."

"Celine once used an interesting phrase to describe the way things were at the beginning of a romance," she said.

"What's that?"

"The man-oh-man stage."

He chuckled. "Let's see if we can keep it that way for the rest of our lives."

"I'll do my part."

Franz was suddenly aware of a man staring at him from a few feet away. There was something familiar about him.

"You are..."

"Henry Ashdour, Herr Colonel. You...recruited me into the American army," the man said in German.

Franz studied the other's face, and then remembered he had been one of the Hessian soldiers up at the Place the day Sarah Henry and the British sergeant were killed.

"Good to see you again," he said in German, his eyes straying over Ashdour's civilian clothes. The man seemed to be adapting well. Franz held out his hand; they shook.

"I am staying here in America," Ashdour said, switching

to heavily accented English. "You see . . . I am learning to speak like an American."

Franz smiled. "Aren't we all," he said, also switching to English. "So what do you plan to do here to make a living?"

"I am a butcher, sir. And a good one."

"America can use men who are good at their trade."

"Yes, there is much opportunity here. I am even changing my name, so it will sound more American."

Von Lossow wasn't sure he liked that idea. After all, what was wrong with a good German name like Ashdour? But he said nothing.

"I am also writing home and suggesting that my younger brother join me. He is only a boy, but he is having a good head on his shoulders," the German said, quite proud of his use of the English idiom.

"What's his name?"

"John Jacob Ashdour. . . . Well, no, I suppose when he gets here will change it the same as myself. John Jacob Astor, he will be known as."

Franz patted the other man's shoulder. "Good luck to you and your brother."

"The same to yourself, sir."

But now everyone's attention was diverted as Sir Guy stopped to salute the British colors flying at the top of the fort's flagpole. Then he stepped into the longboat. The sailors pushed it away from the quay. The last of the British occupation forces had left the island. A great cheer went up from the crowd.

It had been seven years two months and ten days since that fateful moment when General Howe landed his army at Kip's Bay and began the occupation of Manhatan.

And now it was over.

New York was a shambles, a shadow of her former self.

The houses, for the most part, were shabby and in need of repair. Much furniture had been carried away or destroyed by the British. Gardens were torn up and neglected; the vestiges of a vegetable garden could be seen here and there.

Many stables, outbuildings, and fences were gone, having been used as firewood during the years of scarcity. The churches looked respectable from the outside, but they were hollow shells, their pews and benches having gone for firewood. They had also been used as prisons, barracks, and hospitals, and their mottled walls and stained floors reeked of the poverty, hunger, and despair to which they had borne witness.

A number of buildings lay in ashes; others were charred and blackened—mute testimony to Patrick Blakely's last-minute treachery.

The sugarhouses were dilapidated, the warehouses empty and showing signs of neglect; the wharfs and docks had been used but not maintained, and most of them were almost unserviceable.

Even the fort looked as if it had been through a long siege, though no battle had ever been fought at the site. It simply looked weary and abused, like the rest of the town and its inhabitants.

But it was all over now.

The crowd became restless as the last longboat was rowed toward the waiting ships. This was the moment they were waiting for. The plan was for General Washington to march down Broad Way at the head of his officers, and a company of musicians were gathered to play a victorious march as the general made his way to the fort. He was to halt at the flagpole and watch the colors—the new flag of thirteen stars and thirteen stripes—go up to the accompaniment of a thirteen-gun cannon salute.

It would be a momentous occasion. The stars and stripes would replace the colors that had flown at the fort for one hundred and nineteen years, with a short interruption in 1673 during the Dutch reoccupation, and again in 1776. It was the fervent prayer of the onlookers that the Union Jack would never fly there again.

"Here he comes," Drew said to Beth, pointing up Broad Way to where the first of a line of horsemen could be seen. General Washington, as usual, was astride the magnificent white animal that had been given to him several years before by the royal governor of New Jersey—a man who liked to cover all bets to insure his own future.

The general rode to the head of the park as the cheers of the crowd sounded in his ears. Jenny Sackett and Alice de Witt were with a group of women who strewed flowers on the gound before him. The day of victory had been a long time coming, and the general was weary, but this triumph was sweet indeed to him.

He dismounted and walked to the flagpole, his officers arrayed behind him. The drummers began to beat the tattoo that signaled the exchange of flags.

It was then the general realized something was amiss. He studied the top of the pole for a few moments, then scowled.

"The top halyard is fouled," he said loudly. "Someone will have to climb the pole."

"There's something else, sir," Alexander Hamilton said. He stepped up to the pole, touched it with his forefinger, and made a sour face. "This pole's been greased."

The general touched it with his own finger. "The sons of bitches!" he hissed to his aide.

"Get me a hammer and some cleats," Drew cried out, stepping forward and taking off his coat. "I can climb to the top, General."

"It's covered with grease, de Kuyper," Washington said. "And so much for the British having a sense of fair play."

A sailor jumped from his ship and brought a hammer and a handful of cleats. Drew took them and hammered two of the iron rungs into the slippery wood.

He nailed another at eye level, then, using this as a handhold, used the lower two cleats to support his feet. From this elevated position, he drove in another cleat still higher on the pole.

"It may take a few minutes," he said, "but I'll make it to the top."

"Good luck, you crazy Dutchman," Hamilton said, giving Drew a friendly pat on the shoulder.

"Just don't fall," the general cautioned. "With my luck, I'd have to catch you."

As Drew slowly crawled his way up the pole, the onlookers watched with a mixture of pride in his daring, fear that he would fall, and anger at the British, who had stooped to such a petty trick. He finally reached the top and unfouled the halyard. Grasping the British flag in his hands, he let himself slide slowly down the pole, using the cleats to brake his descent. When he reached the bottom, the crowd gave a mighty cheer. He dropped the old flag on the ground and stood on it, and Beth threw herself into his arms.

The Stars and Stripes was raised as the cannons boomed the thirteen-gun salute into the bay. The British aboard the ships glumly looked back as their former subjects took possession of their new land.

Nine days later General Washington took leave of his officers in the long upper room of Fraunces Tavern. Drew and Franz were among the invited guests.

The ceremonies were brief.

Various officers proposed toasts, and then Washington stood in the center of the room for the final toast.

"What can I say to you?" he asked. He took out a piece of paper. "I've written a little farewell. With a heart full of love and gratitude I now take my leave of you. I most devotedly wish that your latter days may be as prosperous and happy as your former ones have been gracious and honorable."

He handed the sheet of paper to Alexander Hamilton. "If anyone's interested in recording my words for posterity, let them record those," the general said. "But what I really want to tell you..."

A knowing smile came to his officers' lips.

"Is that you're the greatest bunch of reprobates, sons of bitches, and ne'er-do-wells who ever walked the face of the earth. I couldn't have won the war without you. And I'll never forget a single one of you as long as I live."

There were cheers and applause.

"Go on, you bastards!" Washington said. "Make noise!" He then proceeded to go around the room shaking hands with every man present.

"Ah, de Kuyper," he said when he came to Drew. "If I run into any more greased flagpoles, I'll know who to call upon."

"Anytime, General."

They shook hands. "And thanks for everything else you did for our cause. Ben Franklin had nothing but praise for you."

"Mr. Franklin is too kind," Drew mumbled, embarrassed by such flattery.

"And you, von Lossow," the general continued. "Congratulations on your new homeland. We're proud to have you."

"My wife said to remind you that you'll always be a welcome guest in our home."

Washington smiled. His memory conjured up a picture of Celine, and he remembered there was a time when he had entertained thoughts of a romance. "Please convey my regards to your lovely wife."

"What are your plans now, sir?" Drew asked.

"I'm fifty-one years old," Washington said. "I think it time I returned to the farm. I'm trying to convince my friends in Congress to leave me alone."

Drew shook his head. "I don't think they will. Our new nation has need of your talents."

Washington moved closer and whispered conspiratorially in Drew's ear. "The dumb bastards don't seem to realize I'm just a middle-aged, cranky old hick."

"If someone else said that about you I'd call him out," Drew said.

Washington smiled. "See, you're just as bad as the rest of them."

When the general left the tavern, a double row of men from Lafayette's old command, the Light Infantry, lined the way to the Whitehall steps, where a barge was waiting. The officers looked splendid in their blue coats, white breeches, and helmets topped with broad combs of brown fur. These were tough men, seasoned battle veterans, and yet there was hardly a dry eye among them when the general stopped at the barge, turned, and waved farewell to them. The barge pulled away from the shore, taking the general to Paulus's Hook. From there he would go to Annapolis, where he would formally resign his commission and revert to being George Washington, private citizen.

The soldiers gave three lusty cheers.

Drew was as misty-eyed as anyone else. "He'll be back."

Franz nodded. "As head of the new government."

"Which means he'll live here," Drew said. "New York'll be the capital of the new nation."

"I understand there's a lot of debate about that," Franz said. "They may pick someplace else."

"It has to be here. The rest of the country is just too provincial," Drew said with all the moral indignation and insularity of a true New Yorker.

Drew and Beth were married on Christmas Day, 1783, in the parlor of Celine's house at the old Beekman's Place.

The rector of Trinity Church performed the ceremony. Celine was the maid of honor, and Dick Goelet the best man. Noah Henry gave the bride away.

Next to the wall a tall clock, made by David Rittenhouse of Philadelphia—a wedding present from Marie Therese—ticked away the seconds. Three *Geikenspielers*, Dutch country fiddlers, stood ready to play. It may have been an English wedding, but the de Kuyper's Dutch heritage, too, was honored.

It was a short ceremony, and simple. Afterward everyone stood drinking champagne as a prelude to feasting in the dining room.

Marie Therese hugged her new daughter-in-law. "Now I can be happy," she said. "My children have found their lives."

"We both went about it in a roundabout way," Drew said wryly.

"I'm satisfied," Marie Therese said. "How can anyone argue with a happy ending?"

One by one the members of the family and their friends came up to congratulate the newlyweds... David Sackett, Jemmy, Jenny, and their spouses; Alice de Witt and Caleb North; Seth Cuyler; and Alec Seixas.

"There's a rash spreading in this family," Mary Delafield Henry said. "Marriage."

"And it's Dick's turn next," Drew said, clapping his arm about his cousin's shoulder.

"Yes, of course," Dick agreed, but everyone knew the woman he wanted had just married another man.

George Gerait, dressed in elegant French clothing he had brought from Martinique, handed Beth a bouquet of fresh tropical flowers. When asked how he had managed to get such a thing in the middle of winter, he smiled. "Let's call it one of life's great mysteries," he said. Only Peter and George himself knew that a French ship had brought the treasure of live flowers, carefully tended and kept heated, specially for this wedding. It had cost a great deal of money, but George thought the occasion amply justified the expense.

Alexander Hamilton was a guest, and he stood in a corner of the room explaining his plan of using wooden sluices to build an aqueduct for the city. Nobody was particularly interested in this except Jemmy, and soon the two of them were alone in the corner, exchanging ideas and plotting the future.

Elly de Witt handed Beth an exquisite lace handkerchief. "I made it for you myself," she said.

"Thank you."

"My mother said she knew all along that you'd marry Drew," the girl said with charming innocence.

"Everyone seemed to know it," Beth said, and then smiled. "Everyone except Andrew and me."

Alice congratulated Beth and thanked her again for the knowledge that Enoch had died a hero. "It makes it easier, somehow, knowing that."

"He's up in heaven right now," Beth said. "Approving your new life and happiness with Caleb."

"I hope so."

"It would be his way of atoning for all the trouble he caused you."

"Congratulations," Peter said to his uncle. "When all this fuss dies down, Drew, I'd like to talk to you about something."

"What?"

Peter reached into his pocket and pulled out what appeared to be a gnarled vegetable root. "This is ginseng."

Drew nodded. He had heard of the root, but knew almost nothing about it or its uses. It grew wild in many parts of the Northeastern United States. "What do you have in mind?"

"When I was in France, Louis told me this is used as a medicinal cure-all by the Chinese. They'll pay a lot of money for it."

"So?"

"What I'd like to do is fill a ship with the stuff and send it to Canton. With the war over, our family will get back into shipping and trading, won't it?"

"Yes, but we've never traded with China before. Not many people have."

"Exactly. We'll be getting in at the beginning when there's no competition. We stand to make a fortune."

Celine and Marie Therese couldn't help but overhear.

"No business talk today!" Celine said in annoyance. She looked at her son. "You can be trying at times."

Peter was unruffled. "Just because two people get married doesn't mean the whole world has to stop."

Celine winked at her mother. "It's hard to tell he's a de Kuyper, isn't it?"

Marie Therese smiled and looked at her grandson. Like Celine, she saw in him the single-minded determination that had marked his grandfather's approach to life. It was strange, she mused, how the de Kuyper family seemed to produce such a man every other generation. Jan had been a hard driver, but his father, James, had been much more easygoing. And James's father, Jacob Adam, had been, by all reports, a veritable shark in the waters of shipping and trading.

Her own son, Drew?

One of the easygoing de Kuypers. He would be surpassed by Peter, it seemed, but there was no sorrow in the thought.

Of the two lives, Drew's would probably be the more pleasant, especially now that he had a wife like Beth.

Her reverie was interrupted by Celine. "It's time to eat," she called out. "Would everyone please go into the dining room?"

Drew held Beth's hand and watched as their guests filed out of the room on their way to the feast. Finally there was no one left but the two newlyweds and Primus Gerait. The old black man looked at them expectantly.

"You go ahead, Primus," Drew said. "We want a moment alone."

Primus nodded. "You two take it easy," he chuckled. "You got the rest of your lives to be alone."

He left the room and closed the door. Drew took his bride in his arms.

"Now, Mrs. de Kuyper, is everything to your liking?"

She tilted her head back, and he was again struck by her extraordinary beauty. It was enough to make a strong man weak. He kissed her gently on the lips. "And to think we almost never came to this."

"We would have wasted our lives," she said.

"But we came to our senses in time."

"On a wooden floor in the Provost building," she said with a smile.

"People who haven't tried it don't know what they're missing."

"One other thing happened on that day."

"Yes?"

"I'm going to have a baby," she said softly.

Drew's eyes filled with love. "You're pleased?" she asked.

They joined arms and walked toward the door.

"Our son will hold New York in the palm of his hand," he said proudly.

**A Tale of Lovers and Dreamers,
Scoundrels and Rogues, Long Ago,
on an Island Called Manhattan...**

FROM DISTANT SHORES
The Novel of New York 1613-1667
BRUCE NICOLAYSEN

**Book I in a Five-Book Series
that throbs with all the passion,
danger and excitement of a mighty land...**

The deKuypers were courageous Dutch settlers who came from distant shores to carve a place for themselves in the settlement called New Amsterdam. There was Pieter, explorer, builder and whaler; Christiana, his bride, brave because she had to be; Young Pieter and Anne, their eldest children; and Jacob Adam, the bastard son who would usher in a ruthless new breed of empire builders on the long island...

AVON
75424 ... $2.50

Available wherever paperbacks are sold, or directly from the publisher. Include 50¢ per copy for postage and handling; allow 6-8 weeks for delivery. Avon Books, Mail Order Dept., 224 West 57th St., N.Y., N.Y. 10019.

From DisShores 8-81